The Complete P

BOOKS BY MI

SHADOW OPS: THE SECRET EXPLOITS OF PRISCILLA ROLETTI
Vol. 1 Flashbacks
Vol. 2 Shadow Chasers
Vol. 3 The Unseen
Vol. 4 Revelations
Vol. 5 Retribution
Priscilla Roletti Omnibus

Rosecroft Chronicles
The Master and the Apprentice
Valeria
Tales of the Order of the Samurai
Rosecroft Chronicles Vol. 2*
Rosecroft Chronicles Vol. 3*
The Dark Stalkers*
Charlene*
The Dragons Wars

Angelina Marin and the Eye of Amun-Ra
Angelina Marin and the lost city of Atlantis*

Redd*

The Ties that Bind*

Time Immemorial

Mercenaries Gambit

Denotes Forthcoming

The Priscilla Roletti Series

The Complete Exploits of Priscilla Roletti

Mike DeClemente

The Complete Priscilla Roletti Series

Vol. 1 Flashbacks was originally published in 2010
Vol. 2 Shadow Chasers was originally published in 2009
Vol. 3 The Unseen was originally published in 2009 and under the title of 'My Mom the Secret Agent, the Secret Exploits of Priscilla Roletti in 2007
Vol. 4 Revelations was originally published in 2011
Vol. 5 Retribution was originally published in 2012

Cover Art Vanessa Solis
Instagram vsolisart
Title and Chapter Font Galdino Otten
www.galdinootten.com

ISBN: 9781073459216

I can't believe it's been over ten years since I started with the first book. You know, these books were originally based off a dream I had. It was me as a kid, calling my mom at work, who just so happened to be in a one person submersible in the middle of a mission. That dream wasn't too far from reality. When I was a boy I used to call my mom at work. The payphone was reserved for all employee in-coming phone calls. They would answer "Hello, second floor?" And I would be like "Is Priscilla there?" So yes, Priscilla Roletti is very loosely based off my mom. Mostly in name, as for the other stuff, I'll keep that to myself and allow your imagination to run wild with what was real and what was not. Because that's half the fun in reading fiction, wondering what indeed was real. When I started this series It was originally titled, 'My Mom the Secret Agent.' It was catchy and I used it for a while but then I thought about it, and figured people might think it was a parody or a comedy which it is not. Another thing was the third book was actually written first and was the starting point. My idea was to start there, and then Shadow Chasers followed by Flashbacks. I wanted to promote a mystery about who Priscilla was, almost like a Star Wars feel. But this isn't Star Wars and I'm far from George Lucas. So, with some tweaks I was able to release it with Flashbacks being the first book and then moving on. So that's pretty much the main back story of Ms. Roletti and how she was created. Of course, there are many more homages and references to some of my favorite movies as a kid. But make no mistake without 007 there would be no agent Roletti and I hope people see in these books how much I love and respect the work of Ian Fleming. So, without further ado, allow me to thank you, for taking the time to read this, and hopefully you enjoy these books as much as I did writing them! Until the next time.

May the Fates be kind to you all!

Mike DeClemente

For the single, married great moms.
the Road Warriors, the nursing and support staff.
The advancements of science and of course
the 'real' Priscilla Roletti.
Thank you, love you mom

Vol. 1 Flashbacks

Prologue
The Blonde and the Sniper

Alger, Algeria.

The barrel of Arthur Zipp's high-powered sniper rifle was perched on a small, collapsible tripod. He was as still as a statue. It appeared as if he wasn't even breathing, taking in just enough air to sustain himself; it took years of training to master this. If you blinked, you wouldn't see him, as he was camouflaged to his surroundings atop the sand-colored roof.

Underneath his sand-colored tarp, sweat peppered his forehead as he waited for his intended target to make his final appearance before the elated masses, chanting for their re-elected president to make his acceptance speech—a President he helped place in power in what seemed like a lifetime ago.

Peering through his scope, Arthur readied himself, licking his thin lips, his thick gray mustache sweaty. It was one of the most uncomfortable things, the sweat tickling his upper lip. But he dared not to wipe it—for just moving a centimeter could throw off his aim and give off his position to the sharp eyes that would, no doubt, be watching for someone such as himself.

Zipp kept his sights locked on the balcony, waiting for his target to walk out at any second. While he waited, his mind drifted off to the events that led him here.

Arthur Zipp was a soldier of fortune or, in another term, a Mercenary. He was a former Army sniper who did three tours in Vietnam and in that timeframe, became the most successful sniper in the history of the U.S. military amassing more kills than any other sniper before him.

After serving his country proudly, Zipp fell off the grid. He knew all too well that he'd never fall into the life he had before the war. So, he lent out his talents to the highest bidder. During his almost 20 years of Merc life, he helped topple regimes and despot dictators who were a cancer to their countries. He even worked freelance for the U.S. government from time to time.

But things changed for him though, when he met the woman he'd later call his wife. At her request, he left behind the life, settled down and had a kid. For the first time in his life after the war, Zipp was happy and complete; he lived and breathed his wife and daughter.

But all that came to a tragic end. Unfortunately, he had made a lot of enemies, people who had long memories and who would stop at nothing to exact revenge if given the opportunity. Zipp had made the rookie mistake of trying to put his past behind him, pretending it never happened. Because when you leave too many loose ends untied, they will eventually trip you up—that's a fact in this profession.

Zipp came home to something only his worst nightmare could produce: his home looked as though an army had raided it. It was in shambles. The first thing he did was search the house for his beloved wife and young daughter.

He never found his child in the house, but he found his wife—lying in her own blood, dead. He felt the last bit of warmth fade away as he cradled her limp body in his arms. Pinned to her body was a letter of demands all impossible. The kidnappers were led by an exiled despot dictator. They demanded Zipp assassinate the President and the cabinet members that he helped place in power.

And so, like any man willing to do whatever he had to, to rescue his little girl, Zipp went and did just that. Before going on his mad quest, he sought out the help of someone he had hoped would help him. But he was turned down. Alone, and with only himself to rely on, Zipp used the resources available to him.

The final obstacle keeping him from his daughter was right before him. The cheers from the crowd down below snapped him out of his daydreaming. He refocused now and saw a flurry of activity. Within seconds, the President came forward, smiling and waving to the crowd that so adored him. Zipp hoped that, after his actions today, the country wouldn't fall back into the pit of chaos it once was. He kept telling himself that this was a means to an end, a life for a life.

He lined his target square in his cross-hairs as he steadied himself. Taking one last breath, he exhaled it slowly as he squeezed the trigger. His rifle had a silencer on it so that he could take out as many members of the President's cabinet as he could.

The high-powered bullet pierced through the air, connecting with his first target. Zipp, from years of experience, smoothly moved to the next target and squeezed off another round. In less than 12 seconds, he had fired off four, precisely-aimed headshots. But then, just as he was about to go for the fifth target, Zipp noticed that none of his intended kills had gone down. In fact, they appeared just as they had before—and with the President well into his speech.

During the rush of killing, Zipp had failed to notice these key things. He gritted his teeth in frustration, not knowing what had happened. Then a surge of emotions ran through him. He realized he had been set up! All the while, the predator was the prey. The only option was to flee.

Not caring about being seen at this point, Zipp jumped up with the speed and agility you wouldn't think he possessed, being that he was over sixty years old. He made a run for it. But before he even took two steps, a surge of pain engulfed him. His kneecap was shattered. As he fell, another silenced bullet nailed him in the shoulder, sending him sprawling on the rooftop.

Almost totally incapacitated now, Zipp lay on his back. It didn't take long for him to regain his bearings and push aside the extreme pain he was in. He rolled over and tried to crawl to his escape, but it was a futile attempt. It would only be a matter of time before soldiers came for him.

Zipp wasn't sure how much time elapsed, but he heard someone approach from behind in an unhurried manner. He was stopped from crawling any further by a foot being planted firmly on his back. He was rolled over, with the tip of a steel toed boot and found himself looking up at a blonde American woman. She was dressed in all black military style clothes, with the butt of her sniper rifle perched upon her hip. She wore a smirk of arrogance that he wished he could wipe off.

"Arthur Zipp, Priscilla Roletti. I'm pleased to make your acquaintance. Major John Derlin sends his regards."

He looked up at her, squinting in the blinding afternoon sun. He tried in vain to stifle the blood flow coming from his shoulder. Priscilla carefully placed her sniper rifle to the side and went to one knee, taking a closer look. None of his wounds were life-threatening.

"You've caused me quite the trouble these last few weeks. You haven't made things easy for me, you naughty boy," she said, shaking a finger, scolding him like a child. Finding a newfound burst of energy, Zipp tried to claw at her booted foot.

"You bitch! You killed her, didn't you? You killed her! Now I'll never see my little girl again. I'll kill ya!"

Priscilla regarded him closely. She was truly amazed at this man. He looked like an old man, balding, with gray hair. You'd never believe he was a pro sniper. He wore glasses as thick as bottle caps.

"No, Zipp, you see, aside from being asked to bring you in before you did something stupid, I also rescued your kid. That proved easier than tracking you down. But we knew you'd be here eventually. You can thank Derlin for that when you see him."

John Derlin was the Chief Executive of Shadow Ops, a secret, covert organization linked to the CIA. He was once Zipp's good friend during the war. It was he who Zipp had gone to for help with this. Derlin was more than happy to help his old friend, but not in the way Zipp had hoped. Zipp had wanted him to aid him in the assassinations. Derlin obviously refused. But thanks to Zipp's desperation, Derlin was given a heads-up. He made the arrangements to warn the local government of the situation, which allowed them to deal with it with their help.

"Your daughter, Sammy, has been in our custody for almost two weeks now," she told Zipp. Hearing Priscilla mention Sammy's name made the corner of his lip twitch. To further confirm her story, she reached into her pocket and handed him a picture. It was of Sammy and Priscilla, with Sammy holding up a sign. On the sign she had written, in crayon, "Daddy come home. I miss you." As he looked at the photo, his eyes welled up. A single tear fell slowly down his cheek.

Shouldering her rifle, Priscilla helped him up, throwing his arm over her neck. "You can thank Derlin personally when you see him. He's here and is looking forward to having a long talk with you. And, by the way, just for peace of mind, I wouldn't worry about those who made you do this. They've been taken care of." If he wasn't in so much pain, he'd have smiled.

As they slowly made their way towards the middle of the roof, Zipp asked her a question.

"How in the hell did you play me back there? Were they holograms or something?" She nodded, confirming his suspicions. The projectors had been positioned days ago on the balcony, out of sight from anyone. It was a clever ruse.

A small chopper slowly came into view, descending on them. Just before it touched down, the wind picked up, sending dust all over. They squinted their eyes. Priscilla cuffed her eyes with her hand as the sliding door opened.

Stepping out with a smile was John Derlin. He was a man of average height. His hair was light brown with graying sides, and he had a thin mustache. He wore a black eye patch since losing his eye in the war. Clenched between his teeth was his trademark pipe. He helped them aboard the chopper, and took off just as quickly as it had arrived, leaving behind the sounds of cheering people.

Chapter 1
A Bad Deal

Tehran, Iran.

Two men hurriedly made their way down a dark, musty hall. They had a third man between them, with a black blindfold tied tightly over his eyes. His hands were bound behind him. They came to an abrupt stop and pulled the bound man back forcefully. Then a loud bang was heard. One of the men spoke in Arabic. The blind folded man heard a rusty metal door being opened. He was then forcibly pushed inside and planted firmly on a chair.

Through the black cloth covering his eyes, he saw a faint light, but all he could really see were shadows. The blindfold was then cut away and a familiar face stared at him, grinning. He didn't need his eyes to adjust to know who it was.

"Vladimir, so nice to see you again," the Iranian president said in heavily accented English. "So, I'm curious. Were you ever going to make good on your debts? Because if so, you surely didn't show us this since you forced us to track you down. This is not good for business!" The Iranian scolded, shaking a finger at him.

Vladimir looked at him. The Russian was middle aged, with a receding hairline of close-cropped hair. He had a scar on the left side of his face, with the left eye whited out.

He showed no sign of the fear that was making his heart pound in his chest. Here was a man who was used to war and death; this was how he led his life. And as many others like him, he gambled and lost. He knew what the stakes were and he dreaded it.

The Iranian took a sip of his water, placing it gently back on the table.

"So, what would you like me to do? How would you like to handle this? Because I can't have you walk out of here without repercussions for your actions. And I don't want to just kill you, considering you've done great service for my country over the years. So killing you would be a waste."

Vladimir nodded. Leaning forward, rubbing his wrists, he took a deep breath before he spoke.

"I have nothing to offer you, my friend. I have no available funds. As you know, I was shut down."

The little man nodded.

"It's hard out there now. The Americans are coming after everyone—me, you and the others," he said, pointing to each of them. "But it still does not leave you without the responsibility of making good. These are the risks we all take. I know this, and you should very well know this, of all people." Vladimir nodded. "But alas!" The little man said, raising a finger. "Perhaps you can make good on the debt you owe." Taking a sip of water again, he relaxed further into his chair and then continued. "I understand you have a few former soldier friends in America, correct?" Vladimir nodded, pretty impressed that they knew this. The Iranians evidently checked him out better than he thought they could.

"And how would that interest you?" Vladimir asked, sitting back, crossing his arms over his chest. The little man smiled.

"As I said, the Americans are becoming more and more of a threat, and I cannot have them interfering in our affairs again. They destroyed our nuclear weapon facilities some years ago. The time has come for retribution. And besides, we have the Jews to contend with. And they are what makes them stronger," he said.

He then thought more about his next words before he spoke again. "As it turns out, through superior Iranian technology, we were able to not only find but retrieve two nuclear weapons." Vladimir was pretty shocked at this one, but he kept his face neutral.

"Now, since you were tasked at getting us the weapons and failed, you owe us. I understand, as you stated, you have no funds. This is ok. But you will repay us," the little Iranian said, pointing a finger at him. "You will take on the mission of planting the weapons in the heart of New York City." Vladimir almost fell over in his chair. The Iranian was truly as nuts as everyone had said.

The Iranian smiled, reading him clearly. "Yes, this is a suicide mission. And I'm sorry to ask this of you. But it's either this or we hang you by your toes, lash you and put you on display for all to see. For all to know that this is what happens when they evoke my wrath. I assure you, dying like that is not the way you'd like to."

Vladimir nodded. He broke out into a cold sweat. His heart raced even faster. His back was truly against the wall. He hated having zero options. He had no choice but to agree.

Chapter 2
A Day in the life of a Secret Agent

"Son of a bitch," Priscilla muttered under her breath, as the zombie dog on the screen in front of her mauled her. The countdown appeared on her side of the screen, prompting her to pump more quarters into the machine.

Priscilla and her kids were at the local Dave and Buster's, which had all your entertainment needs. There was a full bar, pool hall, a large family dining area, and a huge arcade where they were now. There was even a bowling alley in another part of the building.

Feeling bad about having been gone for so long, Priscilla wanted to make it up to her son and daughter. So, she decided a night out would be great. Her daughter, of course wanted to invite some of her friends along, something that Priscilla didn't mind at all.

She looked down at her son, who was wild-eyed with a two-handed grip on the orange gun, hoping to advance more than his mother. She watched him intently, smiling to herself. He was such a smart little boy, able to get a grasp of things quickly. All kids were like that nowadays, she thought, but one day she'll beat him in these games he loved playing so much. Priscilla was never really fond of playing games; she only did so because it made him happy. She figured that if she really put her mind to it, she'd beat the little shit. But the last thing she wanted was to be in competition with a five-year-old.

"Ah, mommy, you died again!" Her son Jonathon said, not looking at her. It didn't take long after Priscilla's demise for him to follow. They had been playing this game for almost a half an hour. As they played, it seemed that he was getting better and she was getting worse, she chalked it up to her being overtired.

"Mommy, you have any more quarters?" Priscilla looked down to her son, nodding. "Can we play the racing game over there?" He asked, pointing.

"Sure. You had enough of beating me in this game?" She asked. He giggled, grabbing her arm, and pulled her to the stock car racing game that could pit up to eight players against each other. She got her ass handed to her by her son in every game they played. Meanwhile, Patricia was off with her friends doing their own thing, acting cool and pretending to be grownups.

After losing in the racing game, Jonathon pulled her to some of the token spewing games. They both played the basketball games where the hoops slid back and forth, making it harder to get the ball in. In this game, she did actually try to beat him—only for the fact that it made him happy to get lots of tokens. He was hardly making contact with the hoop. It was a cute sight to see him trying so hard to get it in.

Even though Priscilla was exhausted from her globe-trotting, and wished they could go now. She played almost every single game here with him. Because the last thing she wanted to do was rush them. Her kids deserved this. If at eleven, they were not ready, she'd try to coax them into leaving by offering to go for ice cream.

As if her silent wish came true, her daughter came up to her from behind, tapping her on the shoulder while she was taking her last shot. A shot, she missed, thanks to her.

"See? Look what you did. I was actually doing well for a change," she said, as she turned to her daughter with a smile. Her son was laughing at her.

"Sorry, Mom. Can we go get ice cream now? Kristen has to go home soon. Her mom called her and asked what time she was coming home and I said you'd call her."

"Ok, when we get to the car. You ready, little man?" Her son looked up to her.

"Wait, I have to cash in my tokens," he said as he waved them at her.

"Next time. Here, give them to me," she said.

"But Mommy…" he started, but then stopped. She raised her eyebrow at the start of his whining something she hated. He knew enough that when she gave him that look, it meant: don't even continue a fight he wasn't going to win. He reluctantly handed her the tickets. She stuffed them in her purse. She then took hold of his hand and started to leave, with the small army of teenyboppers leading the way. In all, there were a total of six girls with them.

The group made their way to the minivan. As they got in, they were calling seats with loud, high-pitched laughing and screaming. They were goofing around the whole time as they made their way to the ice cream shop. They all ordered their ice cream to go.

By eleven-thirty, all of the kids were dropped off into the waiting arms of their parents. Once home themselves, the kids went inside, knowing what they had to do. It was showers and right to bed. They ate their ice cream as they waited for each other to finish up showering.

Priscilla went upstairs, throwing down the covers to their beds. She came back downstairs to the laundry room and started a load of whites. By half-past midnight, they were ready for bed. She kissed them both goodnight, hugging them tightly.

The house was finally quiet—music to her ears. Priscilla double-checked the doors, making sure they were locked. Going to her bedroom, she'd shower in the morning. She wanted to hit her head to the pillow so badly. Since she picked them up, the kids ran her ragged. It was nonstop. Before the night out, they had to go to a few stores. Her daughter needed something for school and she promised her son something for getting an A+ on his spelling test. The trip to the toy store was a long one while he picked out something.

All in all, even though the day was long, she had a great time. She loved every minute of it. Putting smiles on their faces was something she always tried her hardest to do. Priscilla always thought it was funny, her being this doting mom, sitting at the table doing homework, going to the arcade, acting the part of a naive mom not in the loop, letting herself be at ease.

But if you were the unlucky person to be in Priscilla's way while working, no one close to her would believe how she could truly be. How she managed to do both and remain sane, God only knew. She always wondered where she would be right now if not for her kids. In her youth, when she first became an agent, she was somewhat reckless, not a care in the world. What for? Just as long as the job was done, right? And if she was killed, they'd send someone else to pick up where she left off. That was the way it was.

But, how quickly things changed for her. Now she had a reason to come home every day; she had a reason to live. Something that she didn't care about a long time ago. Now she hoped she could retire from field duty in one piece, watch her kids grow up into something, maybe even be a grandma one day.

She got undressed, putting on a silk nightgown, and threw herself into the open arms of her bed. It didn't take long for her to fall asleep, with a slight smile on her face.

Chapter 3
It's Sunday

The morning melody of birds chirping at the first sight of the sunrise would've been therapeutic. The few times she could, Priscilla definitely took advantage of sleeping late, something that was a rarity, with having two kids.

But instead of birds chirping or the warm rays of the sun waking her up, she was woken up by a texting notification. She tried to block it out, to no avail. The phone would repeat the alerts every two minutes. She would go back to sleep, only to be awoken again by that goddamn beeping. She was tempted to throw the phone across the bedroom. Adding to her misery, was the blaring TV. She rolled over and looked at the night table, eyes wide open now.

"Fuck it," she said, under her breath. Even half-asleep, she knew which phone was beeping away. It was the company phone. As she finally sat up, throwing her legs over the bed, touching the carpeted floor, she slipped into her slippers. Getting up, she grabbed her phone, and made her way into the living room. The living room was of course a mess, as usual. On the coffee table there was an empty bowl and a Nintendo DS. The TV was not being watched either and it was on as loud as could be. She lowered the TV as she read the text.

"Priscilla, please report at 13:00, thanks, John."

Fuck, what the hell is up now, she thought in between yawns. She just got back! Throwing the phone on the kitchen counter, she made coffee. As the coffee brewed, sending the fine aroma through the house, she made her way upstairs, to her son's room.

"Uh, excuse me? Why is the TV on and no one's watching it? And why is there an empty bowl on my coffee table?" She asked, crossing her arms over her chest as she spoke. Her son was playing a video game. He looked to her quick, and then looked back to the TV.

She walked over, smacking him in the back of the head to better grab his attention. He paused the game, making a face while rubbing the spot she had smacked. It wasn't a hard slap either, he was such a drama queen. She had hardly touched him.

"Did you hear me?" She asked.

"Yeah," he said, looking down at the floor, knowing he did something his mother always told him not to do and that was, eating in the living room.

"The last time I checked, there was no maid in this house. Go clean up the mess," she said, pointing to the doorway. He got up and she followed him out. She looked around, shaking her head. One of the things she wanted to do was clean this pigsty up. Toys were strewn all over, something that annoyed her to no end. But it would have to wait. She watched him go down the stairs.

"Shut the TV off, since you're not watching it!" She yelled down. She waited at the top of the stairs before going into Patricia's room. The TV was quickly turned off. Priscilla then knocked on her other hell-child's door. Knocking twice, she entered to find her daughter on the phone.

"Uh, good morning, young lady." She looked to her mother, placing the phone on her thigh.

"Hey, Mom."

"Clean this room up, please. You're just as bad as your brother. Bring down all your laundry too. Also, what are your plans for today, Miss Busybody?"

Patricia flashed a quick smile, shrugging her shoulders and replied,

"I'm not too sure yet. Why?"

"Because I have to go into the city today, so if you have no plans, you'll be going to Uncle Pat's house, if he can watch you."

She nodded.

"Ok, I'll let you know, Mom."

"Ok, well, I need to know, like, now!"

"Alright, Mom!" She yelled back, gesturing her mother to leave.

"Damn kids," Priscilla said under her breath. Not a care in the world, other than what the next plan or get-together is. She shook her head, wishing her life was that simple. She made her way downstairs. Her son was already back upstairs, picking up right where he had left off. It was good to be a kid, that was for sure. Not a worry in the world.

After getting the house in order and moving the kids along, they made their way to Uncle Pat's house. She stopped in for a few, just to say hi. She told him that on her way back, she'd stop off and get something from the food store and they'd all have dinner tonight. Her having suggested that brightened him up a bit. She could tell he missed her and she missed him as well.

Truth be told, Pat was the closest thing to a father figure and best friend Priscilla would ever have. He was the only one that knew what she really did for a living. She went to him quite often, when the weight of the world would be too much. And, like always, he had some way of showing her the bigger picture. Priscilla put him right up there with John. And on top of all that, she could never thank him enough for the times she was called to duty at a moment's notice and had no one else to turn to, to watch her kids. She often wondered what she would do without Pat.

Priscilla then finally made her way to headquarters. She hustled upstairs to where John Derlin's office was located. She headed down the long, carpeted walkway. As always, this floor was ripe with activity, people coming and going at a rapid pace. The blaring of phones was always a constant sound in the office.

Before she knocked, she overheard conversation, but couldn't make it out. She did try to strain a bit to hear what was being said, before the muffled,

"Come in."

She saw John sitting at his desk, which was strewn with various papers. To her right was a man seated. He was about mid-30s or so, suit and tie, dressed like a typical Fed. Their suits always looked like they were bought off the rack.

"Priscilla, I'm sorry to have called you back so soon." She looked to John after she quickly eyed the stranger in the office.

Throwing an open hand to the man sitting, Derlin said, "Meet Agent Monroe of the FBI." Monroe got up from his seat, putting out a hand. She grabbed it firmly, smiling. "Pleased to meet you, Mr. Monroe," she said.

"Likewise, Ms. Roletti," he said with a smile. She sat in the only other chair in the office, which was next to the FBI man. She crossed her legs and folded her hands in front of her. And waited for either of them to speak first.

John turned to Agent Monroe.

"Now, Monroe, you may proceed." At that cue, he sat straight, clearing his throat and got right into it.

"Ms. Roletti, you ever hear of the Hottt Boxxx?" She thought about this for a moment.

"Yeah, one of the hottest nightspots in the city," she replied. "I hear ads on the radio for it every weekend."

The agent nodded.

"Do you, by chance, know who owns the place?"

She shook her head no. Monroe smirked before telling her. Already she didn't like him. "It's owned by a Pietro Mastrandrea. You heard of him?"

The way he asked, it was as though she should know the answer. She did, however.

"Yeah, I've heard the name tossed around before. He's an up and coming figure of the New York mob, correct?"

Monroe nodded in approval.

"Yes, he's very popular with the underworld and well liked. There's even rumors on the street, he's slated to head the family in a few years. We've been after him for some time, but the bastard's always slipping away from our grasp like sand through a closed fist." She noticed a bit of frustration in his words from the mere mention of this man's name. "We can't even touch him."

She looked to John, then to the agent. She interrupted him just as he was going to continue.

"So? What? Is this an assassination job?"

He disappointingly shook his head.

"No, unfortunately that's not why I'm here." Monroe took a deep breath and then continued. "The other night some of our agents reported something that needed further investigation. We ran their pictures through all our resources and they came back just last night. One of them we couldn't get anything on. But the other, I'm sure you've heard of before."

He handed her a folder that had been tucked in the chair. She took it from him, opened it up, looked over the pictures. She did recognize one of the men, while the other was a burly bearded older man who she did not.

"Vladimir Petrov. A Russian arms dealer. Used to be huge on the black market until about a year ago. Word was he cheated the Iranians, and now he's on the run." She handed Monroe back the photos, leaning forward crossing her fingers. "So, a known wanted arms dealer just happens to walk into a club, which happens to be owned by an up and coming mob Capo. I don't believe in coincidences, especially one like this."

Monroe nodded, and then ran his fingers through his hair, looking slightly annoyed.

"Me either, just what we need: mafia soldiers walking around with enough firepower to take on the police force."

Priscilla raised an eyebrow at the comment.

"What makes you think it's an arms deal? From what you're saying, this guy is one step ahead of you. I highly doubt he'd be that cocky to do something like this. He has to know his place is being watched."

The agent looked at her.

"You don't know this bastard like I do, he's arrogant."

"Arrogance doesn't mean stupid either," she said. She could tell Monroe didn't like to be challenged on this. The look in his eyes said it all. Who was this woman to tell me about someone she'd never even laid eyes on before? He didn't have to say it aloud for Priscilla to know what he was thinking.

"Trust me, if we didn't have to go through all the red tape, we would have rousted the place ourselves. But that bastard Pietro would have turned the tables with his bloodsucking lawyers."

She nodded. It must be frustrating indeed to know that, no matter how much you know someone is no good, you still had to walk that fine line of the law—something she'd never had to do. Being an Op for so long, she'd never be able to join a regular police force or the FBI and deal with that crap.

"When was the last time you went out, Priscilla?" Derlin asked. She knew where this was going already and was not happy about it.

"Well, John, it's been a while, unless you want to count Dave and Buster's as a night on the town. Why?" She asked, trying to be as sarcastic as possible. He smiled at her for her efforts.

"I would like you to go down to that club tonight and check it out. If possible, talk to this Pietro. See what he knows." She nodded, figuring as much.

Monroe came back quickly, trying to get in what he had to say as fast as he could to get his point across. "Priscilla, just one thing, be very careful. This man, he is the devil himself. Two years ago, we planted a female agent, hoping to try to coax him into giving up valuable information that might incriminate himself." He took a deep breath before finishing. It seemed he was getting stressed out just thinking about this.

"This agent fell in love with this man. She ruined the whole operation, turning on us, telling him everything. He literally twisted her mind." Monroe's face turned red, reliving that moment, she smiled.

"You needn't worry about that. I don't turn that easy. Trust me, many have tried, all have failed, and will continue to do so. "

"Don't get too cocky. You've never come across someone like him before. Just keep this in mind. He is a smooth talker and his extreme good looks don't make it any easier."

She nodded. She thought the worry was funny. But she didn't tell the agent that no man could make her giddy—period. If he knew her, he'd know she was beyond all that. If he did try to smooth-talk her, he'd be in for a rude awakening.

"Well, I think that's it. Unless you have anymore to add, Monroe?" John asked. He seemed a bit rushed now, checking his watch.

"No, John, I'm done here. I'll come back tomorrow to follow up on what she finds out. Thank you. Good day to you both." He walked out, closing the door behind him. Priscilla looked back to John.

"Wow, you'd think that guy was going to cry or something, huh?"

John nodded.

"Yeah, Pietro has been a thorn in their side for years now. The Feds call him the new Teflon Capo. Oh, I'll have a picture of Pietro sent to your phone by tonight."

She started to make her exit when John continued talking.

"So, what do you think?"

She looked at him, thinking about the question.

"Don't know. Even though this Pietro is a crook, mob bosses never turned to guys like Vladimir. You really think Pietro's buying some high-powered weapons?"

"Maybe. The word out there is that Vladimir is on the run. The Iranians want his head for a double-cross of uranium he promised them. So maybe he's looking for a quick sale in some stock he has."

She thought on that angle. It made sense.

"Yeah, maybe, but something's not right. It's too easy, like they're flaunting it."

John considered that, raising his eyebrows.

"Yes, I agree." He looked at his watch again. "Oh, damn, I'm late. Got a conference call with the Joint Chiefs today." He got up quickly, gathering papers up. Walking around his desk, Priscilla got up, opening the door for him. Making their way out before splitting up, he said to her,

"Good luck, be careful." She nodded.

"I will."

She watched him go off down the hall, disappearing from sight. She walked back down the walkway and headed to the elevator.

Chapter 4
Italian Dinner

She pretty much cruised home, calling ahead to let Pat know that she was on her way to the food store. As it turned out, a short time after Priscilla had dropped the kids off, Pat had already gone to the store. Dinner was more than on its way of being started. Priscilla was not at all surprised. Pat was never one to wait to the last minute when it came to dinner. He was Italian, and Italians know what they're having for dinner by noon.

So she used the extra time to rush home, pack the overnight bags for the kids, and try to find something to wear for the night out on the town. It took her longer to find something because Priscilla hadn't gone out in a dog's age. All her dresses were stuffed in the back of the closet. She wished she had more notice; she'd have gone to Macy's and bought something. It would have made it a whole lot easier. Finally satisfied with what she found, she raced to Pat's.

The remainder of the evening was filled with laughs and conversation. Eating at Pat's house was always something of an experience. Pat himself hardly talked because he was too busy stuffing his face. His uncouth table manners were somewhat gross, but the kids found this funny. The only words that did come out of his mouth were "More drink" to whoever was by the soda bottle.

While trying to ignore his eating noises, Priscilla talked to his mother. For a woman of her age (close to 90), his mother was one of the feistiest women you could ever meet. She had a mouth like a truck driver. She wouldn't think twice to tell you to go fuck yourself if you got on her bad side.

As for Pat's father, God rest his soul, he had died a few years back. It was somewhat of a shock to everyone. The loss of Pat's father hurt Priscilla more than she thought it would have. Like his son, he was one of the most kind-hearted men you could find.

After the hearty meal, Priscilla helped Kathleen, Pat's ever-faithful wife, clean the mess everyone left behind. Once the dishes were cleaned, dessert was promptly served with coffee.

While the kids played, Priscilla went into the TV room where Pat was watching a documentary on World War II on The History Channel. As he gobbled down his cake, Priscilla sat down in the other recliner, sipping her piping-hot tea. Her mind was in another place at the moment. With an ever-keen eye, Pat saw this and lowered the TV's volume. Priscilla didn't even notice. Pat watched her for a moment before saying something.

"What's the matter? You ok?" He asked.

She looked up to her friend, nodding her head as though to convince herself more than him. Knowing her all too well, Pat swiveled the chair towards her and leaned over. "You may fool others, but you don't fool me. I see right through you. Tell me, what's the matter?"

She turned to him with the look of a child, shrugging her shoulders.

"Do you feel you're neglecting your kids again?" He asked bluntly. This was a topic that had been brought up a few times already. It was one of the many issues that Priscilla deals with on a day-to-day basis. It's the fact that sometimes, for days or weeks at a time, she leaves her kids with their uncle while she's off globetrotting after maniacs.

At his remark, she looked down at her feet again, not saying a word. This just confirmed what Pat thought. He took a deep breath.

"How many times do we have to go through this? You're not neglecting them at all. I mean, look at them. They're happy."

She followed his pointing finger, and watched Jonathon playing GI-Joe's with his son, while her daughter was, downstairs with Pat's daughter. Looking back to him, she nodded, agreeing with him.

"I know Pat. It's just I…I never saw this coming. At times I wish that I'd never found them. I just wish I had cut and run, like anyone else would have done in my place."

Pat scowled at her. "Don't talk stupid now. Now stop that. You sound like a goddamned moron when you talk like that."

One thing about Pat was, he didn't hold back and always had a way to convey his thoughts no matter how brutal it was. He was one of the few people able to talk to Priscilla like that, without having his teeth knocked out.

In all honesty, she knew he was right. But, at times, she had trouble convincing herself of that. She never would have thought in a million years that she'd be caring for kids, not with her upbringing.

"I know, I know, Pat. But I just want to be there for them more. And they're getting older now. Patricia is getting older now. It's going to be hard lying to them. They're smart kids, they'll start asking questions. I just don't want them to hate me. I don't want them to think I'm dumping them off here or wherever. To be honest, that's my worst fear."

Pat waved a hand of dismissal.

"What are you talking about? They're with family. Don't think for one second that your kids will grow up thinking that. You provide for them. They have everything they could ever want and more. Come on, Priscilla, you know I hate when you talk this nonsense."

"I know, Pat, I'm sorry. It just gets to me sometimes."

"I know. But for all you've been through, this is garbage. It's not like you're going out acting like a whore. Look, all I'm saying is, stop worrying about whether you're a good mom or not. You are. There's no question about that at all," he said, in one long breath before taking in a new one.

She nodded. When she talked to him about these matters, he had a way of putting her back on course again. She really wouldn't know what she'd do without him. She'd have gone and committed suicide, if she didn't have him to talk to about her double life. She just needed to unload all her burdens sometimes. And, like always, like the father she never had or knew, Pat was there to listen and give advice. It was as though he healed her with the words that came out of his mouth.

He turned back to her, smiling.

"You know, I think about how we met," he said, trying to lighten the moment. "Who would've thought someone like you shopped at flea markets, huh?" She nodded in agreement.

"Who would have thought that is right," she replied. She was very lucky the day she met him at that flea market. She used to buy from him and, over the years, their bond became unbreakable.

Priscilla glanced back at her son, smiling to herself. She never thought she could love two people as much as she did her kids. She turned back to Pat, changing the subject.

"About tonight. I don't know what's going on yet. The kids may have to stay with you for a few days. I'll be home tomorrow, so don't worry about getting them after school. I'll cook dinner and bring them back with a few days' worth of clothes, ok?"

Again he waved a hand in dismissal, a trademark move of his. Nodding his head, he replied.

"No problem. Do what you gotta do." And that was the end of the conversation.

Chapter 5
Preparing for a night out on the town

Checking the clock, she didn't realize how late it was. She rushed about, saying her goodbyes to Kathleen and Louise and everyone else. Then she embraced her kids tightly, not wanting to let go, as though she'd never see them again.

She was finally off, racing to the city. When she arrived, she made her way through the employee-parking garage. It was on the east side of the black skyscraper. She parked and then made her way to the shower area.

The personal shower areas were located on the floor below where John's office was. She ran into some people she knew along the way. The workforce was thinning out. With it being the end of the day, people were closing down computers, locking desk drawers and doing last-minute things before heading home to their loved ones. By the time she had finished getting dressed and doing her hair and make-up, she was pretty much the last person on the floor.

After hours, the building had a skeleton crew. It consisted of mission support staff and guards. She was surprised she didn't see John. He was always one of the last to leave.

She was just about to put the finishing touches of make-up on, when a hard slap on her ass startled her. She almost put the touch of lipstick on her cheek. She didn't even have to guess who that was. She saw his grinning face in the mirror. In his hand was the ever-present V8 drink.

"Wow! I've never seen you look this good. I knew one day you'd come back and try to seduce me," Pete teased.

She rolled her eyes to the remark. Pete was Shadow Ops' engineer /mechanic/gadget maker extraordinaire. He was the first in the tech department and tormentor of many. There wasn't a person in the place he didn't mess with. She never saw him screw with John, but she would not be surprised if he did either. If you were around Pete, you were a target to his constant banter, sexual innuendos and outright insults. Anyone here for a while was long used to it and no one thought of filing sexual harassment against him. Who were they going to tell? On the record, they didn't exist, and secondly no one took anything he said seriously.

"Only in your dreams, my friend," she replied. "I have an assignment tonight, not that it's any of your business, by the way. And why are you still here? The wife finally smarten up and kick you out?"

"Ha-ha, that's pretty funny. Think of that all by yourself? No. She knows she has a good thing." He said, puffing his chest out. "But really, I was staying late tonight, trying to finish up the new fuel system for the company cars. It's a bitch, too, but I think another day or two and I might get it."

He took a swig of V8, and then went on. "If I can make this work, maybe by two years' time, all Ops will never have to worry about fuel."

Pete, for all his nonsense, was a great man. And, believe it or not, with all his sexual comments, he was a very happily married man with kids, too. He was just the kid that never grew up, stuck in the body of a fifty-something man. Put very simply, he was harmless once you figured him out.

After Pete finally grew bored of pestering her, she was able to put on the finishing touches on her make-up. Priscilla then bolted out of the office and made her way to the lion's den.

Chapter 6
The Hottt Boxxx

The club was packed, for a Sunday night. She wasn't surprised, though. It was one of the most popular places in the city, the line to get in was long. To get in faster, you either had to know someone or have a nice bribe handy for a bouncer's waiting hand. It didn't hurt either if you were a hot piece of ass. They led you right in, no questions asked, not even a cover charge. The more women, the more men, the more money. It was a simple and effective moneymaker.

Priscilla was already in the place for two hours. She was nursing the drink she had ordered, a vodka with a lime twist. She never really liked the club scene too much. Too many bimbos and too many muscle heads with something to prove if they were rubbed the wrong way.

And the most annoying thing was being hit on. This was the last place Priscilla wanted to be hit on. In places like this, the only thing a guy was looking for was a 'piece' and that's it. And, of course, she was hit on at least five times, with all the same corny lines.

"Hey honey, buy you a drink?"

"Hey, do I know you?"

"Hey, my name is…."

She grew tired of it very quickly. All were brushed off for their efforts, with the same cold, hard look that pretty much said to get the fuck away. There was one guy that was way too persistent, when he got a little too close. She threatened to shoot him in the face if he touched her again. She even took out her gun just so he knew she meant business. Stuttering, with an apology mixed in there, he quickly went on his way.

She wore a fitted red dress, with a loose-fitting skirt that stopped at the knees. It was just enough not to impede her movements if she had to move fast. Her hair was pushed back. She wore more than what she would normally wear in the make-up department.

Besides trying to keep the lions at bay, she was staking the place out. She had all the exits memorized and the bouncers sized up. They were just the run of the mill street toughs, nothing she couldn't handle if it came to that.

It was close to one in the morning when he finally showed up. He came from the upper tier of the place, coming down the glass steps flanked by two bouncers. He greeted patrons as he walked, eyeing the women who walked by him, undressing them in his mind. She turned in her seat to get a better look at him. All she saw was his profile, as if he sensed he was being watched. He turned in her direction, flashing a smile.

Right then, Priscilla almost felt drool coming from her mouth. The guy was freaking gorgeous! He was tall, dark and hot! Handsome was an understatement. He had slicked-back black hair, brown eyes, with lightly tanned skin and a cleft. She felt a tingly sensation somewhere she hadn't felt in years. She swallowed hard on a dry throat, reaching for her drink to quench her thirst. But vodka was not a smart thing to drink right about now. The closer he got, the more nervous she became.

What the hell is going on? She thought. Was she drugged? Maybe she was. She could have been spotted by someone with a keen eye. Her drink could have been spiked while her attention was diverted to the men trying to pick her up, in hopes of later having their way with her. If that was the case, she was gonna blow outta here. She even went as far as to reach in her purse, grabbing a pen that was actually not a pen. It was a device that, when the tip of it touched anything like food or water, the small bar in the shell casing would glow green, stating "OK." But a red light would indicate that something was indeed in the drink other than what should be. But the light was green. She breathed a sigh of relief.

By the time she did this, he was already on top of her. He flashed her a smile that would make any woman swoon. He slowly looked her up and down. She never took her eyes off him. She tried to convince herself she was getting a better read of him, but who was she kidding?

"You know, I saw you look my way. Have we met before, sweetheart?" He asked, pointing in the direction from which he just came. All the while, he never took his lust-filled eyes off her.

She shook her head and cleared her throat before speaking.

"No, babe, I don't think so. I'd have remembered someone like you. You come here often?" She asked, playing the role well, taking a sip of her very warm drink. Her mouth was very dry.

He laughed slightly at her query.

"I'm always here, this is my place. I guess it's safe to say you've never been here before, huh?"

"Nope. I haven't been out, period. I was married, divorced. Now I'm making up for lost time."

He arched an eyebrow to that false statement. She could see the thoughts racing through his head. His eyes gave it all away. They continued to talk for quite some time, more yelling than anything, with the loud dance music playing in the background.

Priscilla hated to admit it; but she was really enjoying his company. She somewhat wished that the circumstances were different. Two hours passed, when she looked at the time, even she found it hard to believe.

Another thing that surprised her was that he never made a move. It was something she was disappointed by. But was that because of the mission or because of herself? Even she didn't know for sure. Everything in her body was turned upside down. She figured she might have one chance to get him alone though. If she acted as though she was going to leave. And, just like she figured, he asked her to come up to the office. She was more than willing to accept.

He led the way. His office was located in the back of the club, just through the kitchen area and down a semi darkened hall.

They entered the very swank office. It had white carpet that looked as soft as cotton. Two chairs faced his large brown desk, which was loaded with various papers. He gestured her to one of the seats. She sat as he walked behind his desk. There was a cabinet that housed all kinds of liquor.

As he poured two drinks with his back towards her, he spoke. His tone suddenly changed.

"Ok, so what's your game?"

She blinked twice from the question, it totally caught her off guard.

"My game?" She said, trying to play along.

"Yeah, your game. Because I don't care how good-looking someone is or how good their line of shit is, it's not this easy."

"That's interesting. So let me ask this then: If you knew that, then why bring me up here?" It was pointless for her to try to deny anything. Doing so would only insult his intelligence.

He turned around, looking her right in the eye. He placed a drink towards her, and then sat down, sipping his own.

"Because, in my world, you just don't walk away from a potential threat, you feel them out."

"And do you think I pose a threat?" She asked, with a bit of sarcasm.

He leaned back, looking at the ceiling as though it would reveal the answer to him. Then, finally he answered.

"To myself, I don't know yet. But I can tell you this. You're definitely not someone to fuck with. But if I thought otherwise, I could have you killed just like that," he said, snapping his fingers to drive home the point.

Priscilla smiled. She thought the last line was pretty funny.

"Very good read. I'm impressed."

"Like I said before, I gotta stay one step ahead of everyone, even the ones that are my supposed friends."

She nodded, leaning a bit closer now.

"But the last part about you having me killed just like that," she said, mimicking his earlier gesture. "I'd love to see that. I can assure you this: Even if you were to succeed, you wouldn't live to gloat about it sweetheart." She leaned back in her chair.

He raised an eyebrow to the veiled challenge, smirking slightly. The tension was thick in the room, but not a bad kind. Priscilla didn't understand this type of tension, it was weird. Then Pietro leaned forward over his desk.

"Well, we established that much then. Let's get down to why you are here."

She eyed him, nodding. Before she could even take command of the conversation, he took it right from her. "So, who are you?

Who do you work for? And, most importantly, what do you want?" He asked, flashing a quick smile.

He got right down to it, surprising her a bit. This was a man used to telling others what to do. He was used to people fearing him. Getting this from a woman was something he wasn't expecting at all, but yet, he never wavered. She was impressed.

"My name is Priscilla. You don't need to know who I work for. Just know I'm not with the FBI."

He nodded. He looked to be thinking a bit.

"So, what?" She got right to it.

"Two nights ago, two men came to your club. Both Russian. One of them we know as Vladimir. He has a scar on the left side of his face. His left eye is whitened out, cloudy. Ring a bell?" He nodded.

"Yeah, it rings a bell," he said with a smirk.

"Good, tell me all about it." She said, giving him a smirk back and nodding her head.

"Ok, word for word, I don't remember everything. But the Russian, he told me his name was Stefan. Anyway, he came to me about a proposal. He wanted to buy my club, right on the spot. He even had the cash with him."

"Really? How much was he offering?"

"Five mill. I told him, look, I can't just sell you my club just like that. We gotta go to lawyers and shit," he said. As he told her the story, he reached into a small wooden box. Priscilla was watching him very carefully, but all he did was pull out a cigarette, lighting it.

"Obviously I refused."

She raised an eyebrow in surprise. She was skeptical.

"Why?" She asked. "That's a lot of money. Untraceable, tax-free. A nice, quick, easy sale under the table."

"Why? Simple. I'm not stupid," he said. "Number one, I got feds watching this place 24/7. They'll find out. And two, this place is legit. I'm slowly getting out of this life I've been in. Took me a long time to do so, and besides, why would they wanna offer me that kind of money? That definitely arouses my curiosity."

She nodded in agreement. What was so important about this place? She thought to herself.

"Let me ask you one more question before I wrap this up. What type of reason could you think of for someone to just happen to walk in here and want to buy a place that wasn't for sale?" She asked.

He shrugged his shoulders with a small grin.

"Hey, he was a foreigner. They don't know how fucked up this country can be at times. They think if they throw some money around, they can do whatever. But it did get the wheels turning." He snuffed out his cigarette. "Why are you asking about these guys?" He asked her.

"I'm sorry, but that's classified for now."

"Classified for now, huh?" He said mockingly. He smiled at her. She studied him, looking right into his brown eyes. He was not lying. He didn't have anything to lose by lying. He had all the confidence in the world from the look on his face. He knew he could do anything he wanted and pretty much get away with it. Money was truly the root of all evil.

"So, Sweetheart, now that I was a good boy and gave you what you wanted, what say you and I pick up where we left off before? I truly hope that the really great conversation wasn't all bullshit."

An ice-melting smile crept up on his face as he said this. Priscilla felt a warm feeling surge through her body. She had to admit, even she was tempted ever-so-slightly for this mafia thug. He was charming, smart and handsome, a far cry from the movie stereotypes. Priscilla knew this was her cue to leave right now, before she got into trouble. Not being with a man in a sexual way for so long was catching up to her.

"I don't think so, Mr. Mastrandrea. I think it's time to take my leave," she said, getting up.

"That's a pity." And he looked genuinely upset by that. "Perhaps maybe under better circumstances?" She thought about that. And that was a big, big maybe. Even if she wanted to, when would she find the time? She hardly had time for herself, the kids, add a man to the mix and forget it. But she didn't say all of that to him.

"Trust me, I'm more complicated than you think. Come on stud lead the way." She smiled, as she got up. He returned the smile as he stood and came around the desk. He hurried up to the door before her, opening it and letting her go first.

Probably wants to check out my ass, she thought. She was going to let him go first as she thought of this, but decided to let him play the gentleman role. Let him look at what he can't have, she mused to herself.

They talked as they made their way to the front of the club. It was almost five in the morning. Now the crowd was thinning out. The music was not as loud as before.

"Well, I have to thank you for a very good evening. I didn't think it would go this smoothly," she said to his back as they walked.

"Hey, they can say whatever they want about me. The Feds, fuck'em! You ask anyone who's close to me, they'll tell you different. What I do is only business," he responded over his shoulder. They finally got outside to the front of the club. In spite of the late hour, the sidewalk was still crowded.

"Listen, I'll have my driver take you anywhere you want, sound good?"

His back was facing the street. He had no fear, or so he thought. Just as she was going to turn down his offer, she caught the reflection in the distance. It was quick, coming from the roof of a building across the street. She didn't even think twice. With a force that took him by surprise, she tackled him. He followed her eyes to where she was looking.

Where they stood just a second before, a bullet came hurtling into the sidewalk, sending concrete fragments into the air. The shot was silent, but the people who saw the sidewalk being hit screamed. Some ducked, some ran. The bouncers standing there pulled out their guns, forming a circle around Pietro and Priscilla.

"Wait here!" She yelled to him with her gun in hand. She pushed two guards away as she ran across the street. She threw off her high-heeled shoes when she got to the door that she thought would lead her to the roof. It was padlocked, a single bullet fixed that. She shouldered the door, taking the stairs two at a time, coming to yet another padlocked door which she made quick work of.

She was on the roof, eyes wide, searching for moving shadows. She cleared the area, finally making her way to the ledge where the would-be sniper was. She only found the bullet casing. It belonged to a high-caliber rifle, one only professionals use. She ripped off a small piece of her skirt and picked it up clenching it tightly in her fist.

Chapter 7
An Uneasy Alliance

On the other side of the city was a place where the law hardly existed, a place where anything went, even during the daylight hours. The residents lived in fear; they couldn't walk to the corner store for a gallon of milk without worrying about being shot by a stray bullet. And at this ungodly hour, the only ones on the street were junkies, whores, pimps and dealers—the dregs of society. One never came to this side of town just for a stroll.

A shiny blue Lincoln Continental pulled up to a rundown stripper joint. But everyone knew it was more a drug house, a place where dirty deeds were talked about and planned. The driver parked and hustled out, opening the door for the passenger. A lanky, fairly tall man stepped out. He was dressed casually, in a simple sweater and trousers. But in a place like this, he was overdressed.

His thoughts conveyed that as he looked upon the place. Borislav walked in, unmolested. The place was dark, save for the dim pink lights on the ceiling. The women dancing on the stage were a far cry from the women you'd find in the more respectable clubs near Midtown. Haggard, drunk-looking men stared with eyes full of desire at women they'd never get, their mouths agape. They were so entranced; they could have been pickpocketed and not even notice.

Borislav didn't give a second glance to any of this as he made his way. He was thinking, why in the world would Vladimir choose a place like this? In the back, off in the corner, sat Vladimir, who paid no heed to his surroundings. The men flanking him looked as unsavory as the clientele here. They were still dressed in their sea-faring clothes. They made no effort to hide the pistols that were tucked in their trousers.

There was a vacant chair. Borislav walked over towards it, and placed a hand on top of it. The man with the white-clouded eye saw him coming, but did not acknowledge him right away. He was still watching the women dance. It wasn't until Borislav sat and pulled the chair closer that Vladimir finally turned and nodded at him. Borislav returned the gesture, glancing quickly at the men near him and to his own who were just a few inches to his right.

He was about to speak when Vladimir beat him to it.

"I've already heard, my friend, but I assure you, everything is going as I thought it would," Vladimir said in Russian. He took a cigarette from the pack that was lying on the table half-opened, placing one into a holder and lighting it.

Borislav gave him a skeptical look.

"Really? Why would you go there when you didn't have to in the first place? Flaunting yourself, the Americans know who you are." He was getting flustered. Vladimir waved a hand, dismissing his concerns.

"Do not lecture me about what I do. You're not the one with a noose around your neck. I don't have all the time in the world. I must complete this in two days. I was having trouble locating this tunnel you spoke of, but only after I talked with Pietro did I receive word that the hidden tunnel was found. So, it turned out to be a waste of time. And you were right. It goes straight from the harbor all the way to his club. Americans can be very clever, can't they? How did you know it was there?"

Borislav hesitated as if wondering if he should tell him, but then decided to.

"Someone I knew told me about it. It was used back in the prohibition days to smuggle booze in."

"And you are sure Pietro doesn't know about this?"

"No, the access point was sealed behind a wall sometime ago. I originally wanted to buy that club for the tunnel alone. I could have used it to smuggle my drugs into the city." Borislav replied reassuring Vladimir.

Vladimir chuckled at that notion.

"Drugs. This is why the Americans are weak and decadent. All they care about is getting high. This country deserves to burn."

"Whatever, just as long as your end of the deal is seen through. I did my part in helping you dock, and I paid off the customs agents so they didn't board your boat."

Vladimir, snuffing out his smoke, leaned in closer.

"Yes, you did, and I thank you. I was lucky that you have people working for you in the harbor. Right now, as we speak, preparations are underway. I'll have the warheads there in less than 24 hours. Another few hours after that to set up and arm the bombs."

Vladimir looked at Borislav intently before speaking again. "Are you afraid I'd leave you to burn, my friend? You needn't worry. And must I remind you, yet again, that I have more at stake than you? If I don't pull this off, I'll never be able to set foot in any civilized country."

Borislav nodded. He knew Vladimir was right. The trouble his former friend got himself into was something no one wanted.

"Oh yes, before you go, did you set up the 'distractions' in the places I told you to? Remember, they must go off at precise intervals." Borislav nodded.

"I did as you told me. All is ready to go on my end."

Vladimir flashed a quick smile.

"Go, my friend. And I thank you. I'll send for you once all is complete. The meeting place is the lighthouse." Borislav nodded, and left without another word.

Vladimir watched him go. He was fortunate enough to have him here in the States. If not for him, this little endeavor would have been hard to accomplish. And he'd be strung up on display, beaten in some village. That thought made him squirm. Perhaps next time he'd think twice about who he double-crosses. That is if he survives at all.

Chapter 8
Temper, Temper

By the time Priscilla left the club, it made no sense to trek all the way back home, so she made her way back to the office. She had extra clothes and showered there, then took a fast power nap. The one good thing was, she didn't have to worry about the kids; they were in school and hopefully she'd be back before they got home.

By 11:00 Priscilla was back in John's office going over everything that had happened last night. Both men listened intently, not breaking in while she talked. Once she did finish up, John leaned back in his chair musing over what she said. The FBI agent flashed a stupid smile at her and shared his thoughts.

"And do you believe him, Ms. Roletti?" This was more like a dig than a question.

She looked at him, cutting her eyes slightly. She didn't like the way he said it either.

"Yes, I do, as a matter of fact. He gave me no reason to think otherwise."

Monroe chuckled. It was loud enough that John looked over with a hard glare.

"What do you find so funny, Mr. Monroe?" He asked him. The question Derlin posed to him caught him off guard a bit.

He cleared his throat, and then said his peace.

"I knew sending a woman in there was a mistake. Look at her," throwing a hand towards her. Priscilla looked at John, then to the agent.

"He seduced her. I'll bet my paycheck on it, Derlin. I told you last night, Ms. Roletti, this man is not to be taken lightly. He can manipulate you as easy as an artist molds clay," he said pointing to her.

She leaned off her chair, getting closer to the man. Very suddenly he stopped pointing.

“Whoa, wait a minute.” She said. “You fucking kidding me? You think I was seduced?!”

“Yes I do!” He said, raising his voice a bit. She laughed.

“Think whatever you want, pal. Just remember one thing, you came to us. So if you don’t like what I had to say. Go back there yourself.”

“Excuse me?” He retorted.

“Yeah, you heard me,” Priscilla replied. “And if you say something stupid like that again, that I was seduced, you’ll be picking up your teeth from the carpet!”

“Oh, yeah? Why don’t you come and try it! I know all about how you guys handle things. From what I hear, some of you are no better than the people you put down!” Priscilla glared at the man; she was more than willing to meet his challenge. She started to get up from her chair.

“That’s enough, both of you!” John scolded, raising his voice and that was something he very rarely did. And when he did raise his voice, the room would go quiet, like now. Priscilla could count on one hand the times John raised his voice, and that was in her earlier days when she was rough around the edges. She was most likely responsible for some of the gray hairs on his head. Both stopped and looked at him, waiting for him to continue.

“The both of you are acting like damn kids. Now Monroe, as far as what you may think, Priscilla is not easily swayed. If that’s her thought on the matter, then it is with no one’s influence but her own.”

“And you, Blondie,” he looked at her with a more intense look than he had given Monroe. “If I’ve told you once, I’ve told you a hundred times, cool the temper.” She hated it when he called her by her code name. He did it very rarely and only when he was upset with her. It was like when a parent calls their kid by their full name, they knew they were in deep trouble. He looked at both of them, making sure he still had their undivided attention. Neither one looked at each other.

“Now, Priscilla continue.” Both regained themselves, sparing a quick glance to one another.

“Now, as I was going to say, I think Pietro may prove useful in this. I have a bad feeling about this, though. Why would an arms dealer offer to buy his club?” She took a deep breath and continued, "and then try to off him?" No one gave their thoughts on that one. "If you want my opinion, I think something's going down. There's something about his place that Vladimir wants and he wants Pietro dead or otherwise."

Derlin and Monroe nodded in agreement.

"We gotta track down Vladimir," she said, turning to Monroe. "What big Russian bosses, here in the city, you think may know something?" Monroe, leaned forward.

"A guy named Borislav, former Afghan soldier. Tricky bastard, too. He's always on the move. We've tried to locate him several times. We've even tried to cut deals with some of the Russians we've nailed, but they refuse to talk."

"I'll bet anything Pietro knows where to find this guy," Priscilla said. "Perhaps Borislav knows something. It's a shot in the dark, but that's all we have to go with now." Monroe chuckled under his breath.

"And you think you can make someone like Borislav talk to you?" He asked. She nodded.

"Oh, he'll talk to me. Trust me on that one." Priscilla then turned to Derlin, ignoring the Fed. "I'll go back to the club tonight. I'm sure Pietro will be more than happy to help. He'll do it just so he can say he helped the government and hold it over us for later." Derlin leaned back in his chair, mulling this over.

"Alright, go with him. Find out what you can, and keep me posted on it. This may be a complete waste of time, so don't stay with him any longer than you have to."

"Yes, sir, of course. Oh, and one more thing," she said, with a smirk looking at Monroe. "I'll need you to stop whatever surveillance you are doing on him till further notice."

Upon hearing that, Monroe's face turned red.

"What?! How dare you tell me what to do! You have no authority to tell me that!"

John rolled his eye, shaking his head slightly. After this, he'd need an aspirin.

"Yeah, I do," she said. "As far as I'm concerned, this is now a Shadow Ops assignment and I don't need your boys getting in my way."

Monroe was flustered now. Not knowing what to say, he looked to John for some kind of support but didn't get any.

"I'll have to agree with her," John said. "The less people involved, the better at this stage. Or if you want to take this further, Agent Monroe, I can make a call to your director and see what he says?" Just after he said those words, Monroe cooled down, nodding his head in defeat.

"Good. Make sure your people are packed up and gone by the time she gets to his club tonight. Now that we've agreed, Monroe, I need to talk to Priscilla for a moment. I'll keep you in the loop, so don't worry."

Monroe looked to John, then to Priscilla. He nodded to Derlin; got up and shot one more piercing look at Priscilla as he walked out the office.

When the door closed, John gave Priscilla 'the look.' It was the fatherly look she was all too used to at this point.

"Priscilla. Would you mind telling me why you felt the need to not only antagonize the man, but threaten him?"

While he waited for her to reply, he lit his freshly packed pipe. She cleared her throat, looking out the window behind him. When John acted like this, it made her feel uneasy. Made her feel that she somehow disappointed the man that put one-hundred percent of his trust in her something he didn't have in everyone that worked under him.

"Well…the guy was a jerk. He said I was seduced. He made me look like I was incompetent. It pisses me off when people talk to me like I'm a kid or something."

John took a deep inhale of his pipe, letting the smoke out slowly.

"And why should you care what he thinks? Did you for a second think that I was going to sit here and agree with him?"

"No, not at all-" she started to say, but he cut her off before she could even finish.

"Good, I'm glad you have that much confidence in me still. The point I'm trying to make is this. You've come a long way from the time I recruited you. But you still have this angry-at-the-world attitude. It's something that's going to get the better of you in the long run and I don't want to see that happen. I may not be able to keep you in check when you're out in the field, but dammit, I'll do my darndest while you're here in my building. We clear?! I don't need you to embarrass me in front of people like that. It's not the first time either. I'm not asking as a friend, I'm telling you as your superior, don't do it again. We clear?"

Priscilla had her head slightly down, looking at the floor. She could feel her face flushed with embarrassment while he spoke. She didn't even look at him when she answered him.

"Yes, sir. Will that be all?"

"Yes, go on. I don't want to keep you any longer than you need to be. Keep me informed if you come across anything." She nodded, then got up and started to walk to the door. Just before she opened it, he called to her.

"By the way, nice job last night. Good luck...be careful."

"Thank you, sir," was all she said as she closed the door behind her.

She stood in front of the door, trying to regain her composure. Aside from Pat, John was the only person to be able to talk to her like that and not get their lights punched out. When she did give John a reason to reprimand her, she felt like she let him down and she hated doing that to him, of all people.

When she first started out as an Op, she had a temper and an attitude like nobody's business and John was the only one to keep her in check. But not always, some of her actions caused John a bit of trouble in the past on more than one occasion. Like the time the Secretary of State was kidnapped by pirates. The Secretary of State wanted her head for the way she treated him. In her defense, he was a douche bag and had to be put in check.

"Priscilla? Hey, Priscilla, you awake?" It took a moment for her to respond, she was so deep in her thoughts to realize that John's secretary was talking to her. She was fairly new to the company. She and Priscilla became fast friends. Priscilla liked the fact that she was, in a way, innocent.

"Oh, sorry Jenny, I was kinda in my own little world," she said. Jenny placed a warm hand on her shoulder, smiling.

"It's ok, I know how it is. I heard John yell before. I hate it when he goes on the war path." Priscilla nodded, perking up, a smile spreading across her face. Jenny did that to people in the office. That was why she was one of the popular ones here.

"So, what's going on with you? Haven't talked to you in a while. How's the boyfriend?" Priscilla asked her, changing the subject. They both started to walk back to her desk.

"Good, thanks. Can you believe it's been almost a year!"

"Yeah, I remember you telling me about him when you two first met. When you get to be my age, the time goes faster." They both laughed.

"Oh stop, you make yourself out to be some old lady!" Priscilla nodded.

"Yeah, well, have one of my bad days and then tell me what you think." They both laughed.

"So, how bad is it?" She asked Priscilla.

"What?"

"The assignment," Jenny clarified, as she sat down, fixing some paperwork on her desk.

"Oh, you know, same shit. I'll probably be shot at and who knows what before this is over. The only good thing is, I'll be local at least. Listen, Jenny, I hate doing this, but I gotta go. I have a ton of stuff to do before the kids get home."

"Oh, yeah, sure, no problem. I'll call you in a few days," Jenny told her.

"Ok, great." Priscilla walked off, feeling slightly better than she did before. Jenny had a way of doing that to people.

Priscilla picked up her pace getting to the elevator. On her way down, she was in deep thought. She kept thinking about John. She felt ashamed, hurt even, when she let her mentor down like that. His words upstairs hit home, too, stinging her. She was a very angry person at times, and she had good reason to be. Her life before Shadow Ops was not pretty in the least. And reflecting on his words, the distant memories of the past that she wished could be erased started to engulf her.

Chapter 9
Flashbacks of Motherly Love

The woman you know as Priscilla Roletti: Agent Blondie of Shadow Ops. The doting mother who attends Open School night, goes to concerts and has had a house full of children for sleepovers. If any of her friends or family knew that this woman could go from being a kind and caring mother to a cold-blooded killer that could take the life of another at the snap of a finger, they'd never believe it.

Her life was never as good as it is now. In fact, her past was a nightmare. She should have been one of those many statistics, either becoming a junky or an alcoholic, an abused wife to some drunk or worse, a streetwalker. But she overcame the odds to get to where she is now. It's something that few people can accomplish, but nevertheless something that can be done if one puts their mind to it and doesn't feel sorry for themselves. You just have to stay the course, keep focused no matter how hard life kicks you. And when life and bad circumstances does kick, you kick back even harder. Because if you have the talent and the drive, anything is possible no matter where you come from.

On July 7, 1967, Priscilla Ann Roletti was born in East New York. She was the fifth of six siblings born to Elsie Roletti who, for the most part, was a mother who took care of her kids only because she had to. Most of her children were unplanned. And while, there was no proof, there were whispers in the family that she had sold some children on the black market. In those days, in the ghettos, all you had to do was go around the corner. And your local butcher may not only be cutting beef for you.

Elsie was an abusive, horrible woman to her kids. It was mostly verbal, but she never shied away from physical abuse, either, especially with Priscilla for some reason. She'd get the brunt of it. It was as though her mother hated her and treated her as the black sheep of the family.

Priscilla could vividly remember one day when her mother beat her over the back with the belt buckle. She couldn't sit, back straight in a chair for a week. They were very poor, growing up in a one-bedroom apartment. The conditions were far from anything you'd want to raise your child in.

In those days, to pass the time, it was either read, study or stay outside. She always chose the latter for the fact that she was less likely to get a beating for no reason. She loved being out all day, playing stickball, seeing her friends after school. She was an average student at best. She had a good grasp on life at a young age. She was a smart kid; it was just that school never really held her attention, even as a little girl she was tough. But that didn't stop kids from trying to pick on her or her siblings.

Due to the fact that her mother was the neighborhood whore. She and her siblings didn't know their father or, the correct way of saying it would be their fathers, since they all had a different one. There were many knocks on the door late at night or even during the day. Her mother, chose the easiest and oldest profession to support her children. It made for a horrible scene when an angry wife pounded on the door.

Thankfully though, time moved fast. When she grew into her teens, that was when things took a turn for the worse. The abuse from her mother only increased, which led her to stay out more and more. The less she had to be home, the better. In her teens, she found quite a lot of trouble hanging with the wrong crowd.

Priscilla even ran away a few times. One time, in particular, she remembered. Her mother found out through word of mouth where she had been staying. Priscilla was at the house of a much older boy who was known for trouble in the neighborhood. Like the phony she was, Elsie would portray herself as this upset mother wondering why her daughter gave her so much trouble. The act would end once behind closed doors. That night, and like many others before, she often wondered, Why me? What did I do to deserve this? She was just a kid; she hadn't even started her life yet.

Things quieted down for a while, but that didn't last very long; peace never lasted in that household. When she turned sixteen, it started to fall further downhill. She totally dropped out of high school. She wasn't learning anything there that she couldn't teach herself. She was growing frustrated with things at home.

The main reason she dropped out was to get a job so she could save enough money to get the hell out of there. But that fell short when her mother got wind of that.

"Oh? You want to leave? Not happy here? You think by dropping out of high school you'll make something of yourself? Well, be my guest!"

She remembered her mother saying those words to her in the most sarcastic, vile way. Her mother just threw her out into the street. She'll always remember that day. For the first time, Priscilla was scared. No matter how often she ran away and wanted to be out of that house, she knew she'd end up back at some point. But now that her mother had kicked her out, she was done. She begged and pleaded, telling her mother that she was sorry and she'd go back to school the very next day. But that didn't help. Her mother had had enough of her.

Elsie threw her down the stairs by her hair. She would have been hurt more than she was had Priscilla not caught a hold of the railing. Tears fell from her eyes, uncontrollably, like a burst water pipe. Her mother went back inside, returning with an arm full of her clothes, throwing them at her. They landed on the dirty street.

She stood on the stoop; staring at the closed door. She didn't remember for how long, it felt like hours. The people who witnessed it went back to what they were doing, not offering her any type of help. The unspoken rule of the streets back then was to mind your own.

She gathered her clothes as best she could, going to the corner store and asking the old guy, whose name she could never remember. It was Harry, that's it. He was a kind-hearted old man. He knew the family, she came from. When she walked into his store, she asked him for a bag for her belongings. He gave her a pitiful look. She could tell he was searching for something meaningful to say. But nothing came to mind, as he handed her a dusty plastic trash bag.

"Thank you…" Priscilla said with a lowered head.

She quickly ran to the front of her house and picked up whatever she couldn't carry before. Priscilla fearfully glanced at the front door, every time she picked up something and stuffed it in the bag. She kept imagining it would fly open at any second. She could feel the eyes of the devil on her, all the while as she gathered her stuff off the street. Once done, she ran back to thank the old man once again. To her surprise, when she came back, he had a little bag for her.

"Here, I know you're in for some hard times, kid. Take this." At first she was not going to take it, but he insisted. Along with the bag of food, he gave her a twenty-dollar bill, which back then, was like giving someone a fifty today. She thanked the man many times, promising to repay him someday for his kindness. He waved it off, just telling her to do something with her life.

For the first time in her life, she was totally alone. With nowhere to go, no one to turn to. For the vast majority of people out there who were thrown into this type of situation, there was an awful lot of temptation. The easy way out, being a girl of sixteen and mature enough looking, was to fall into a known prostitution rings. But that was never going to happen. She heard stories of runaways going that route, the easy way, and the pathetic way she thought. She was never going to be disrespected like that; she'd eat out of garbage cans if it ever came to it. One thing she learned at a young age was that whatever doesn't kill you only makes you stronger. It was going to be rough from here on out, she knew that. But she had the most important thing: her street smarts.

As she walked into the unknown, she kept telling herself that it could be worse and that things from here on out can only get better, if she wanted them to. She hoped so anyway. Even with a positive outlook on the situation, she still felt a slight feeling of pessimism. Whenever it crept up, she pushed it out of her mind just as quickly. There were always better days ahead, it was just sometimes getting to them took a little longer for some.

Chapter 10
Flashbacks of the good, the bad, and the downright evil

In the following days, she slept where she could. She tried to find the safest places, with people close by. She didn't want to be seen by cops since they would most likely take her in, and then send her back home, or worse, to a boys and girls home. That was something she didn't want; she was on her own and that was the way it was going to be.

Alleyways were a nice place to stay for the night, but you had to sleep with one eye open. Needless to say, in the coming weeks she became sleep-deprived. In the second week of her homelessness, she discovered a nice park on the other side of the neighborhood where the rising crime had not yet found its way. But that was soon going to change; she could see it as every day passed more and more riffraff came along, staking their claim. This park, she found, was not yet overrun by the creeps that would stalk the night. She felt safer here, but still had to keep one eye opened though. Only a week into this and she was growing tired, weary. She knew she could only last for so long and she was not going back home. She thought about going back too, but that's what her mother wanted a sick way of teaching her daughter a lesson of how the grass isn't greener on the other side. But if she did that, then in Priscilla's eyes, her mother won and she'd rather starve to death than have her win. She'd suffer just to spite that bitch.

Being alone gave her time to reflect on her life, as short as it had been. She could not believe all the heartache she had endured thus far. Like all little girls growing up, all she wanted was to get a good job, maybe get married, have a kid and live a meaningful life. Was that too much to ask for? She felt it was, being where she was now. She often wondered why some people had to suffer like her, when others were just handed things on a silver platter?

She figured that this was the way that life could be at times, but she hated it. In her travels, she met various people in the same situation as herself. She kept them all at arms length, though these were desperate people like her. And even though she'd never look to better herself off of someone else's misfortunes. She couldn't be sure about other people in her situation, no matter how nice they seemed.

Nevertheless, it was nice to have someone to talk to every now and then. Through some of her newfound friends she found some of the soup kitchens. Through word of mouth, she found out about a shelter not far from where she was now. She was in a rather bad part of Brooklyn, just on the outskirts of New York City.

During her travels, she found a place to call home for the time being. The homeless shelter was mostly male occupants. She wanted to just walk in and not be noticed, but she felt like all the eyes of the place were bearing down on her. It was as though they were all wondering what her story was, who she was, and god only knew what else.

She kept her head high and never met the gaze of her onlookers. The shower area was as dirty as a sewer, but feeling the water hit her unshowered body made her overlook that. The shelter was staffed by volunteers. They kept a close eye on her, as they did with the other few women and young adults.

Over the next few weeks of staying there, she befriended pretty much anyone that was decent. She stayed in the shelter for quite some time and, surprisingly, was left alone by the creeps that were there. She could thank the volunteers, as well as some of the other homeless men who kinda felt like they needed to look after her. Some of them turned out to be Vietnam veterans who came home to a country that had turned their backs on them, brave men who sacrificed themselves in a hell hole of a country risking life and limb.

She had heard horrible stories. One man came home to find out his wife had left him, taking everything. Another was beaten only hours after he came home by anti-war protesters, while others were looked upon as baby killers, being spit on. And because of this, almost all of them could not find work. No one wanted to hire these so-called baby killers or whatever other names they were given.

It saddened her and made her angry to know that this is how these men were treated. It was just not right. And after hearing the tales, she knew that her life wasn't as bad as she thought. She was lucky in a way; these men not only had physical and emotional scars, but a shadow loomed over their heads that would follow them for years to come.

The weeks passed by rather quickly. She needed to find work because, for as nice as the shelter turned out to be, it was not going to be her permanent home either. By sheer luck, she got a job nearby, making deliveries for a local deli. The pay sucked, but it filled her pockets with much-needed cash. It helped fill her stomach as well. The shelter food was rather terrible. And ever since being alone, she had not eaten right. She had lost quite a bit of weight during her ordeal.

Three months had passed from the time she was kicked out of her home. Her birthday came and went. Before she knew it, the summer weather was subsiding for the fast-approaching fall. She was seventeen now. Everything was slowly, looking up for the most part. She wasn't going to be leaving the shelter anytime soon, which was somewhat of a disappointment to her. She wanted out of there in the worst way, but it was impossible with the money she was making.

As November came around, Priscilla wasn't any closer to her goal. While working at the deli, she befriended a lot of the neighborhood regulars that came in. They'd always come in at the same time and always ordered the same thing. There was Sam, the painter, who always looked like he never showered from the day before. He always had more paint in his hair every time she saw him. She often wondered if he got any paint on the actual thing he was supposed to be painting.

Then there were the regular cops that came in. Every time she saw them, her stomach turned. She had always thought they'd find out her story and take her back home. But after a while, that fear was gone. They were pretty cool.

Then there were Brad and Will, two brothers who were always together. She had never asked them what they did, but from the looks of them, she assumed they worked in some type of construction. They were rugged-looking, with flannels and boots. They always seemed cheerful too. Out of all the regulars, they talked to her the most. They were always willing to listen to her. Even though she knew a lot of people now, no one ever had the time to stay and chat; it was always the quick "Hey, how's it going?"

"Good thanks, and you?" Type of small talk. But these two, they took an interest in her.

At the time, she didn't think anything was wrong with it and they never gave her any reason for her to think otherwise. They were always respectful towards her. Brad was the more talkative and outgoing of the two while his brother, either nodded in agreement with what was said or threw his two cents in when he disagreed. He was a little weird, but harmless in her eyes.

Her boss at the deli took notice of this also and took her aside. She thought she was in trouble, but he gave her some smart, sound advice that she should have listened to.

"Just be careful around those two," he had said. She asked why. He couldn't give her a sound reason in her eyes. He told her, "Just a feeling, that's all. Just looking out for you, kid." She thought about his words, not fully understanding. She understood his concern, but why? With those two, they seemed harmless enough.

That very same night, it was her late night. She got paid and was thinking of taking in a movie. As she walked down the street, she heard her name being called out. She turned around to see Brad and Will walking briskly towards her.

"Hey, Prissy! Where you off to?" Brad said, shuffling her hair. She looked to Will, saying hello. The man gave a quick wave, and then went back to biting his fingernail.

"Hey guys, I'm thinking about taking in a movie. Why, what are you guys up to tonight?" She asked. He shrugged his shoulders.

"The same. We were thinking of going to see Indiana Jones, the new one that came out." That was one of the movies she wanted to see also.

"If that's where you're heading, wanna tag along?" She thought about that for a few seconds and would have said yes in a heartbeat. But the words the deli owner told her rang in her head now more than ever.

But, really, what harm would it be? Maybe the guy felt they were too old for her to hang out with and talk to, but what was wrong with that? After all, like some people in the last few months, the deli owner looked after her, so she understood where he was coming from.

But she was tired of always being alone. She tossed away the concerns and went along with the brothers.

The movie, to say the least, added to her already-adventurous soul. She first realized her taste for adventure from other movies, but this movie Indiana Jones and The Temple of Doom was awesome! She never saw the first one, but she heard great things about it. The adventure was so intoxicating, she wished she could be like Dr. Jones, going on these death-defying treasure hunts for "fortune and glory" as the woman named Willie Scott told him, in a mocking tone.

To her disappointment, the movie was over way too soon. They made their way out onto the street. As the crowd dissipated, Brad and Will walked with her back to the shelter.

"Prissy, you wanna come hang out with us for a little while?" Brad asked, walking on her left while Will flanked her on her right. She turned to look at him and that's when she felt her stomach tighten. With a tension of warning, she looked over to Will. She caught him eyeing her up and down with a sheepish grin on his goofy-looking face.

Then she looked back to Brad, walking slightly faster.

"Nah, Brad, I gotta be at work early tomorrow and I'm kinda tired."

Brad shook his head. He threw his hand out, grabbing Priscilla. She felt her arms numb up immediately. He pulled her close, licking her cheek. She could hear Will giggling at that while he, kept a close eye out.

"See, Prissy," he said, saying the nickname he gave her with a sexual undertone. "You are gonna come with us. We've been watching you. We know you. And, to be honest, I hardly think anyone is gonna miss some homeless slut. Ain't that right, Will?" His brother nodded.

"Sure, sure. No one is gonna miss her. Brad, let's take her now. Let's go man!"

Brad looked back to Priscilla. He leaned in closer, taking in a deep breath. She wanted to scream out, but lost her voice right then and there. She was panic-stricken with thoughts of what they were going to do to her. She imagined things she'd never thought of on her own and they scared the shit out of her.

"I've always wanted young pussy, it's so smooth, even newborn." Brad said. And with those disturbing words, the world went black, and she feared nothing no more.

Chapter 11
Flashbacks of the First Kill

Priscilla awoke sometime later, in a dark, damp room. The shadows jumped and danced in her imagination. It didn't take her long to figure out what had happened. She tried to bring her arms from behind her, but they were tied with something. It felt like twine. She tried to scratch at it, but her hands kept getting numb before she could do anything that would somehow loosen it.

Her eyes started to water. She felt the tears. She wanted to cry out in a vain hope that someone would hear her, but thought better about it, for fear of their reprisal. Her heart was beating so fast that she couldn't keep up with it. She thought she was going to drop dead right then, but she wasn't that lucky. She knew before that would happen, she'd suffer. She came to the conclusion that perhaps she was born to suffer. Maybe she was a real fuck in her past life, if one believed in that stuff.

But then a voice kept coming up, telling her to stop feeling sorry for herself and try to get the hell out of this. She nodded to the voice in her head as though they were in the very same room with her. She tried loosening the twine again, but her hands got numb.

Then, as she waited to feel her hands again, the door swung open. She couldn't tell who it was. When he grabbed her, she knew it was Brad. He was the bigger of the two. He picked her up like a rag doll, throwing her onto the bed. She begged and pleaded with him to stop. The tears flowed from her eyes like a river. As he tore off her pants, he took out a knife. He cut off her panties, throwing the knife to the side. He then pushed her legs apart.

"Relax, Prissy, just relax," he said, with the smell of stale booze coming out with the words. "It'll all be over soon. Trust me on that one."

He then proceeded to violate her in ways she'd never thought of. As she tried to resist, she was given a punch to the head for her efforts, with threats of death. All she could do was lay there. She mustered up one last ounce of strength to resist, but then was sent back to the world of darkness.

She awoke yet again, with a start that she soon put in check. She was quickly realizing that what she went through was no nightmare. She tried to open her crust-filled eyes. They itched. She was able to rub them, her hands were still bound, but were in front of her now. She was still in the bedroom and she wasn't alone.

Her body ached all over, as though she had been run over by a freight train. Most of the pain came from the waist down, her legs and her vaginal area. She moved ever so slowly to her left to see who was next to her. She could only make out the silhouette. Then she realized it was Will. He was laying down on his back in a deep sleep, snoring loudly. As her eyes adjusted to the darkness, she saw his pants off. She wanted to cry aloud again, but quickly put her emotions in check. She feared waking him.

But the silent tears came. They had violated her, raped her, made her into this sub-human. She wanted to throw up right then and there. She turned to her right. The door was open and the area out there was pitch black. She strained her ears to hear anything coming from outside, but she was sure there was no one else in the place but her and Will.

Brad must have left, she thought. Her mind raced now. She inched closer to the edge of the bed. She started to throw her feet to the floor slowly. They both touched without a sound, as her left foot touched something cold, sending a chill through her body. She eased herself off the bed and to the floor to pick it up. She almost cut herself, not realizing it was the knife Brad had used before.

Holding the knife as best she could, she cut the twine that restricted her wrists. After a few strokes, she was finally free. Then she looked around the room for her clothes, which was not easy. There was shit everywhere. Then her heart stopped beating at the sound of Will moving. She froze in fear as she watched him slowly get up, and put his hand where she was just moments ago.

Even half asleep, he realized she was missing. At that moment something popped in her. Feelings and emotions raced through her like never before, but not of fear, dread or despair. The only thoughts crossing her mind were murderous. In those few seconds she realized, if she didn't do something, she'd be back right where she was and found dead somewhere.

As Will reached over to put the lamp on, Priscilla ran to his side of the bed, positioned the knife overhead in both hands, and thrust it down into his chest with all the strength she could call upon. Will fell back from the unexpected attack. He jolted and tried to cry out. She didn't give him any time to recover. She thrust the blade again and again, until he went limp.

She stood there, hunched over him with the knife dripping blood. She was poised to thrust the blade into him again just in case he moved. But he wasn't moving ever again.

By the time she was done with her blind rage, the entire bed was blood-soaked. Her face and upper body were, too. Will had bloody holes all over his chest. Priscilla looked upon the body, transfixed. She never saw a dead person before, not like this, and not something that was done by her hand, no less. Tears once again flowed down her cheeks, leaving streaks in her bloodstained face.

She sobbed, not knowing why. She was borderline hysterical. Panic was starting to take hold of her. She just killed a human being in cold blood. She took a life. While she was wrestling with that notion, the other part in her said that if she hadn't, she'd be the dead one.

"You defended yourself." An inner voice told her. She nodded, as though the voice told her this from across the room. Minutes passed. She was coming down slowly from her adrenaline-filled rage. Paranoia was setting in. With every noise she heard, she envisioned Brad rushing in and smashing her face in. With that thought alone, in a panic, she was finally able to move her feet.

She quickly went to the bathroom, washed her face clean of the blood and looked at herself in the mirror, making sure she got all of it. Priscilla rushed back into the bedroom, not having to worry about keeping quiet. She grabbed whatever clothes she saw that belonged to her. Putting them on, she quickly pushed her bloodstained hair out of her eyes, then looked over to the body of Will. She felt her pants pockets and realized that whatever money she had was gone. At first she was hesitant, but time was running short. She needed to be long-gone before Brad came back.

So she looked for Will's pants on the floor. She thanked whatever god there was that she didn't have to search his pants while he wore them. She wouldn't be able to with the thought he'd somehow come back to life and grab her. In the first pocket, she checked, she found a $50 bill. Good enough, she thought as she threw the pants to the side. She walked out without so much as giving the place another look.

Once outside, she never ran so fast in her life. Her heart felt like it was going to burst from her chest. All the while, she kept throwing her eyes in all directions, thinking Brad would pop out of nowhere and grab her. She ran for what seemed like forever, never stopping. Jumping on the first subway, she came across.

That night, she made her way to Central Park. She wanted to get as far away as possible from what just happened so.

And so here she was, laying down on a bench, huddled, trying to keep as much warmth in her as possible. It was chilly that night. She wasn't sure what she was going to do at this point, but she needed to get some rest. She had come down from the panic-stricken high and was exhausted. At first she didn't think she'd fall asleep. She laid down, looking to the sky, wishing she had something under her head. She took a deep breath to calm herself. She tried to think of other things besides the last few hours. She wasn't even sure how long they had kept her.

"ENOUGH!" She screamed to herself. "Stop thinking about what happened and relax!" She took another deep breath and let her mind wander to other places. She thought of her life up until now. What has she truly accomplished? Not a goddamn thing, that's what. The only thing she is now is a murderer.

"NO, you're not! Stop thinking about that! You did the right thing. You did what anyone would have done!" That same inner voice told her. She agreed, but it still didn't feel right no matter what the circumstances are. But, on the other hand, the more she thought of what led her to her actions, the more she started to think that it was the right thing to do. And she'd do it again, if need be!

"No!" She whispered, with a shiver. At this point, her thoughts weren't making any sense. They were one big contradiction. She closed her eyes and took a deep, calming breath. Another deep breath and her mind went blank. She fell fast asleep.

The next morning she awoke to the sound of blaring horns and voices. The quiet street from last night was ripe with activity. She shot up quickly, almost forgetting where she was. People walked by her, glancing, with looks that echoed that she was a little worse for wear. She quickly got up and made her way towards Times Square, rubbing out the sleep from her eyes.

All the while, the paranoia started to itch at the back of her mind. She kept thinking that cops would appear out of nowhere and arrest her. Or worse, that Brad would somehow find her. She felt a little better once she was off the open street, making her way to a coffee shop.

She was starving by the time she got there. A cup of coffee and something warm to eat was just the things she needed. When she ordered her food, the waitress complimented her on her hair and asked how she got the red coloring to fade in and out like that. She felt her face flush red.

“Oh, uh, I went to this club last night and they sprayed this stuff on people.” Was all she could come up with. Before her food came, Priscilla quickly went to the bathroom and stuck her head under the faucet as best she could. She tried to get every speck of blood out of her hair.

Looking back in the mirror, she saw a person she didn’t recognize. Sure, it was her, but it was as though she had aged 20 years. She looked terrible. By the time she came back to her table, the food was there. Wolfing it down as though she had never eaten before, she didn’t stay any longer than she needed and paid for the meal.

Once back outside, she looked to the left and right. She needed to make some decisions and there weren’t many on the table either. She wasn’t going back home, not like this. That would only make matters worse. The only way she was going back home was when she made something of herself. She stood on the corner waiting to cross, when her eyes fell onto a sign on the next block over. It was a rather large sign, with a red background and yellow letters. For some odd reason, this particular sign stuck out to her. She stood in front of that sign for some time, re-reading what it said countless times over.

"This was it!" That little voice inside, said to her. "This is your way to start over and begin a new life." The ever-familiar picture of the bulldog painted just below the words.

USMC Recruiting office, with an arrow pointing right to the door of which it was in front. The Marines. She toyed with the idea about two years ago, but didn't really put too much thought into it. She was too young then. But now… how bad could it be? It couldn't be any worse than what she'd been through. She'd be taken care of, housed and educated, then when her time was done in the military, she could take what she learned into the world or even stay and make a career out of it. She heard they paid pretty good, too, if you did that. She knew it wasn't going to be a walk in the park either. She wasn't afraid of that in the least. She felt she could handle the boot camp. She had no choice, it was this or the streets. So, failure was not an option.

She walked in, going into the unknown. Little did she know that she'd come out a changed woman in more ways than she'd expected. Upon entering, she spotted some chairs along the wall. The walls were adorned with posters citing all of the advantages of joining up with the most elite fighting force in the world. In front of her, she saw five makeshift desks with the recruiters behind them, helping would-be volunteers. High above them was a banner that read "The few, the proud, the Marines"

Just reading that slogan alone would make someone want to join. There was one recruiter who wasn't helping anyone. She walked over to the desk. It didn't take long for him to realize that she was there. He looked to her, flashing her a smile. She returned one back. Before he could say a word, she sat down in the chair facing his desk, about to start her journey into the unknown. A journey that she hoped would be for the better…no, she didn't hope. She knew it was.

"Good morning sir, I'm here to sign up."

Chapter 12
Flashbacks of the First Meeting

Thirteen weeks later.

The seventeen-year-old blonde that walked into the recruiting center looking like a train wreck, was transformed from a skinny little nothing to a filled-in, head-turning woman. This was thanks, in part, to the rigorous training that started almost the minute she was brought to the Marine Corps Recruit Depot/military installation located on Paris Island.

The base was seven miles from Beaufort, SC. The closest major city was Charleston. And, even if she had the energy to go to any town or city, she wasn't allowed to leave for the entire thirteen weeks. They cut you off from the outside world. You lived and breathed the Marine Corps only.

Priscilla's battalion was the Fourth Recruit Training Battalion, the only women's battalion on the island. Every recruit was put into the most stressful of situations, both by the courses and the drill instructors who trained them. They were always yelling over your shoulder, in your face and in the most extreme circumstances. Some recruits would be pulled, kicked, shoved, and even smacked around if they were not on par with what their unit commander wanted from them.

Initial training of the enlisted included a wide variety subjects, which varied from weapons, Marine Corps Martial Arts training, personal hygiene and cleanliness and sexually transmitted diseases to formation drilling and Marine Corps history. That was just the beginning. Physical fitness was the most strongly emphasized thing they drilled into you. You would either excel or be made to at least pass the minimum standard of fitness in order to graduate. This included the three-mile run, pull-ups and crunches. They are all tested as part of the PFT (Physical Fitness Test).

Recruits also must meet the minimum combat-orientated detail, swimming qualifications, qualify in rifle marksmanship with the

M16A2 service rifle, and then excel at a 54-hour simulated combat exercise known as The Crucible.

To say those thirteen-weeks were hell was a pure understatement. Each and every night, Priscilla hit her bunk half-dead, muscles strained to the point that she thought they'd tear through her skin. She really was second-guessing herself. She had known it was going to be tough, but not this tough.

But the weeks passed, filled with the constant repetitious schedules, the training, the humiliation of being yelled at and forced to do simple tasks over and over again. Leadership was hoping that all this would instill teamwork. She had to hold her tongue the first few weeks. She knew that nothing the drill Sergeant said or did was personal to her or to her fellow recruits. It was just the way of life in the Corps, until one earned the right to call themselves a Marine.

By the third week, the thoughts of giving up were expunged from her, first because, as hard as it was for her body and mind to keep up, she was not going to go through the added humiliation of not being able to see this through to the end. Those that could not pass were placed in a Physical Conditioning Platoon where they were basically treated like an idiot and looked down upon by their peers. She did not want to be included in that class.

Second, and this was the main reason, it was not in her nature to give up. The more they pushed her, the more she gave them. The last thing she wanted was to go home a failure and that was not going to happen. Not after all the shit she went through leading up to this.

With the thirteen-weeks behind her, graduation was next week, something she was ecstatic about. She couldn't wait to tell her mother and siblings. Her mother would have told her that she'd never make it through the training.

"What the fuck's the matter with you?! You can't do that!" Her mother would have told her. Priscilla could hear those words ringing in her ears as if her mother was right next to her. She couldn't wait to go home in her uniform and see the look on her mother's face.

Even with all the training behind her, she really had only just begun. After graduation, she needed to choose what military occupation specialty to do. On top of that, there was a rigorous infantry-training course. She was so deep into her thoughts that it took her a while to register that her instructor was standing before her. Priscilla jumped up saluting.

"Nice of you to finally acknowledge I was here. At ease." She said. Priscilla did so, putting her hands behind her back. "You have a visitor. Second floor, in the complex meeting room."

"Yes, Ma'am!" She said, and then sprinted towards the exit of the barracks. As she made her way, she wondered who it could be? She hadn't talked to anyone since she left. It would've been impossible for someone to know where she was. Maybe her mother tracked her down somehow; she had a way of doing things. Priscilla threw that thought to the side. That would be the day hell freezes over. But it was always a nice thought though.

As she walked through the door of the main complex, she quickly feared that the police were here. Perhaps they linked her to the murder of Will? But no, that thought was quickly put aside. That would implicate Brad also. The one thing she hoped was that she'd forget what had happened that day. But, like the plague, it never left the back of her mind. And the day would come when she'd find Brad. She never really put much thought into what she'd do if that day ever came, but the feeling she felt was so intense, it sometimes scared her. But first thing's first, she thought. First, make something of yourself, and then worry about the garbage last.

Making her way to the second floor, heading down one hallway and then turning right, she came to a white door with a gold plate that read, 'General Purpose Room.' The polish on the plate was so clear she could see herself as clearly as if in a mirror. She looked both ways, making sure no one was around. She strained to listen, wondering who might be in there waiting for her. She still couldn't figure out who wanted to see her. She didn't hesitate any longer. She knocked twice, a muffled man's voice responded. As she entered, she thought it must've been an officer. She closed the door behind her, and then came to attention.

"Private First Class Roletti reporting, sir!" While her words hung in the air, she thought for a second, she heard a chuckle under his breath.

"At ease, there's no need for that with me. Have a seat, please." He replied. She did so. When she entered the room, she didn't get a good look at the man that summoned her. It was always common for the saluting soldier to stand at attention, looking straight ahead. Already feeling the relaxed atmosphere, she observed the man who wanted to see her. He was middle-aged, with creeping grays at the temples, light brown hair, with a thin mustache. To top it all off, he wore a black eye patch covering his right eye. Clenched in his hand was a pipe, with freshly-packed tobacco. He never once looked up at her. He kept looking over a file. She stole a quick glance and spotted her name. That didn't make her feel any better. Who the hell was this guy? She asked herself. He obviously wasn't military, with his casual clothes. Which were simple dark pants, shoes and a dark blue turtleneck. After the seconds crawled by, he finally looked up at her. He then lit his pipe, the sweet-smelling smoke quickly spread through the small room.

"Uh, sir. There's a strict no-smoking policy on base." She warned. Either he didn't hear her or didn't care. She didn't know which one, as he inhaled deeply, letting it out slowly through his nostrils.

"I'm sorry, Private, what was that?" He asked in an almost-serious tone. She swallowed hard at the inquiry. She felt a little jittery.

"Uh, no smoking, sir. There's no smoking anywhere on the base…" she tapered off. The look on his face as she said those words made her feel very uneasy. There was an uncomfortable silence for a few seconds, as though he was pondering something. Then he cracked a smile.

"Indeed there is." He said, taking another pull from the pipe. "Now, let's see, your name is Priscilla Roletti, Private First Class. It says here, you have remarkable firearms handling, good hand-to-hand combat skills. That's excellent."

She watched him reading her file intently, growing more and more uneasy. Who the hell was this guy? She was just about ready to ask that question when he spoke to her directly.

"You never graduated high school?" He asked.

"No, sir. I finished my education here. Got my GED."

He nodded approvingly, returning back to her file. He didn't get too far with his reading.

"Sir, would you mind telling me what this is all about?"

From the look on his face, the question didn't catch him off-guard. He closed the file, and then emptied the pipe residue into the waste paper basket. As he spoke, he refilled it anew.

"I'm sorry, I didn't even introduce myself. I'm John Derlin." He smiled and extended his hand to her. Priscilla was reluctant to take it. But did so.

"Nice to meet you, sir. So what is this all about?"

"Recruitment, Private. And your name came up as a possible candidate." If she thought asking him would clear the air, then she was wrong. She was more confused than before.

"I'm sorry, sir. Recruit? For what?" John smiled as he leaned forward and looked her dead in the eye.

"Helping to make the world a better place." She raised an eyebrow, really confused. "I head a branch of the CIA, known as Shadow Ops. I saw your file, and was impressed."

"Like spies?" John nodded.

"Something like that, and more."

"Sir, I'm sorry you have the wrong person. I'm no spy, aren't you guys like smart? I'm…I'm just…I joined because, this was a free ride. Everything paid for by the Government. Free schooling, I'm sure-"

"What we're looking for are smart, resilient people who can overcome insurmountable odds. Like yourself." He said cutting her off. She sighed and did a little chuckle before continuing.

"Sir, no offense. You don't know a fucking thing about me. You looking into my file doesn't mean a damn thing. In fact, it means jack shit, sir." She added the 'sir' part just to be nice. Truth be told, she was at the end of her patience. Whatever this guy was selling she wasn't interested in it. She was wise to the game. For all she knew he could be some Pentagon lackey trying to recruit her for some experiment. Blow smoke up her ass, build her up a bit. She knew they used to do that all the time. Testing drugs on recruits to enhance their combat abilities, only to leave them whacked out from the side effects.

Derlin smiled. She was filled with spirit he had to give her that. And although he was enjoying this little verbal sparring. His time was limited. Derlin then closed her file and pushed it away. He leaned back and crossed his arms over his chest.

"As you wish Private…Your full name is Priscilla Ann Roletti, born in East New York. To say you came from a loving home would be like me saying I didn't lose my eye. Your mother, if you'll excuse the term, was a streetwalker. You were thrown out at sixteen, lived on the streets for a while, and then a shelter. From there, you joined the Marines. If that's not something to be proud of, coming from where you came from, then I don't know what is." He stopped for a moment, and then snapped his fingers remembering something. A smile crept up on his face.

"Oh, and how could I forget this! In between the time of you joining the Marines, I believe you were forcibly taken against your will by two men you thought were your friends. And as a result of that action, one of them was brutally murdered stabbed if I'm not mistaken…by you."

Priscilla jumped up from the chair, knocking it to the side. Her whole world was about to be turned upside down again. She ran for the door, ready to throw it open and get the hell out of there. But something dawned on her. She stopped and looked back at him and realized Derlin was sitting down. As though nothing had just happened. He was about to light his pipe up again.

"Were we going somewhere, Ms. Roletti?" He asked. She stepped away from the door. She was waiting for the MPs to come take her away.

"I'm awfully sorry about that, really I am." He lit his pipe and inhaled deeply, letting it out as he spoke. "But we weren't getting anywhere. Now please sit down. I know what you're thinking. Don't worry. Nothing is going to happen. Anything said in here stays in here, ok?"

She slowly nodded. And then picked up the chair and sat slowly back down. Her heart was finally slowing down.

"You did what you needed to do, end of story. In my opinion, he got what he deserved. Now… back to you. You possess exactly what I want: someone that can come out of something like that virtually unscathed. Who is able to readjust and make something of themselves."

Priscilla tried to swallow. She had to close her eyes to do so.

"How… how…did you find out?" Was all she managed to say. Derlin smiled.

"We closely vet the people we look at. From top to bottom. It didn't take a genius to figure it out, Ms. Roletti. When I pulled your name for interviewing, and crossed referenced every thing. I realized your entire Recruitment application was a lie." He was right about that one. She had lied through her teeth to get into the Marines. "We cross-referenced all events that would lead someone like you to join the military. It took us some time, but we figured it out. Your prints were in the room, along with the knife and your DNA. But, being you had no prior history of unlawful behavior, the police had nothing to go with."

He took another deep breath. "I wasn't going to mention it. It's something I'm sure you want to forget. But we weren't getting anywhere. I just wanted you to have a better idea of who I am and what I represent."

She nodded, feeling somewhat better. She couldn't believe that this man knew all this about her.

"Now," he said, sitting up straighter, smiling. "Do you remember what we were talking about?" He snapped his fingers and pointed at her remembering. "Ah right, you were just about to tell me what you had planned after your graduation." She was speechless, at first. It took her a few seconds to register what he asked her. Sitting up straighter, trying to regain some of her composure from being scared out of her mind. She cleared her throat, and then answered,

"Well…enrolling into nursing school was an idea." John leaned back and gazed at her.

"Very good, that's excellent. Goodness knows more nurses are needed." She thought for a second that he was mocking her. "But, maybe, if you were inclined to do so, you can go this route. Like I stated before, I'm here recruiting. I'm looking for people with unique talents other than combat skills. The most important trait I look for in someone is a strong will, someone who can take whatever life throws at them but still stay on the course at hand. You, by far, have everything I'd say that meets that criteria. Now, if you were to accept this, you may leave here as soon as tonight. You'll get full credit for your time here. You'll graduate with full honors." He stopped for a moment to let it all sink in. Her mouth was agape. This seemed to be going way too fast for her. She hated the unknown and hated being fast-talked into something that was so vague. But she couldn't help not to be curious.

"It sounds mysterious, sir. Interesting. But how long will I be gone for?"

"You'll be gone between one to two years. The only downside to it is all contact from the outside world will be cut off. No phone calls, no mail, not anything. So, if you have anyone back home that you may want to talk to, you better start thinking of something to say for your absence. That is, if you choose to come, of course."

She stared into his eye as he spoke. This was totally coming out of left field. For as vague as it was, it sounded adventurous. His words played on her like a harp; the melody was enticing. In the blink of an eye, she thought of a possible future, with kids, maybe marriage living a meaningful but meaningless life. But then there was another side to her. She always wanted to help the helpless. With herself being a victim, she knew firsthand what that felt like. She wanted the power to hurt others before they could hurt anyone else. If she didn't take this offer, she might never forget about the "What if" factor years down the road.

"Ms. Roletti? Hello?" John had to call her twice more after that to get her out of her daydream. She shook her head, her face flushed with embarrassment. But the feeling quickly faded as she looked him dead in the eye.

"Sir, you sold me. I can't believe I'm doing this, but what the hell, right? You only live once." He smiled. He seemed a little surprised at her answer. Without a word more, he got up, grabbing her file. She followed suit. "I'll make the arrangements. If I can arrange for departure tonight, you'll head out. Be ready just in case."

"Yes, sir." She said. He walked ahead of her, opening the door and gesturing her to proceed forward.

Some might think of her as stupid for doing what she just did, volunteering for something she really had no idea what she was getting into. But really, what was she going to do? Finish up here and go where? Back home to what? Her mother and her family? She'd wind up living a life she may regret. Sure, as a child, she wanted to live the white-picket-fence dream like every other woman in the world.

But things happened that put a bad taste in her mouth with the whole marriage thing. She'd never be tied down, and she didn't want a "normal" life anymore. She wanted to do things that no one could do or wanted to do. She didn't know what they were yet, of course. It was just her burning desire to be different. But, in any event, she had a feeling her life would be far from normal from this day on.

At almost, half past 20:30 that evening, John Derlin came for her. Even though she was leaving, she couldn't believe it. How could this man, whoever he was, have the kind of pull to arrange this?

They were driven to the nearby airfield. To her surprise, there awaiting them was the Commanding Officer. He stood erect like the straightest tree when he saw them. The CO saluted Derlin, who nodded back. Then the soldier looked at Priscilla, handing her a rather large yellow manila folder. He congratulated her on graduating from the Corps and saluted her. She returned the gesture. John looked at her, then to the CO.

Then, without a word he walked to the plane. She was two steps behind him. As she walked with her duffel bag over her shoulder, she looked to the sky quickly. It was one of the lightest nights she could remember in a long time. They walked towards a small jet, she wasn't familiar with it. It was painted black with no identifying marks or symbols on it. It was windowless except for the cockpit.

Derlin stopped at the stairs leading up and motioned for her to go first. She took the stairs two at a time, stepping in. John came right up behind her, pressing a button the door slid closed. To her right was the cockpit. He gestured her to go left. Pulling back a curtain, she saw about ten other passengers, men and women looking no older than her. Some were sleeping, some reading, some chatting. As she walked down the aisle, heads looked up at her, seeing the new arrival. She took a seat in the back next to a young man with a crew cut. Stowing her bag above, she sat down.

Not too soon after, the jet was already moving, she looked down the aisle, checking things out. She felt trapped. There were only two doors, the one she came in from and the one right next to her. She figured it was the bathroom. She sat back a bit, trying to calm herself. She always hated the inevitable takeoff, but was getting better with it the more she flew. She looked to her companion, he looked at her at the same time. He smiled, throwing out a rather large hand. Her hand almost disappeared in his grip.

"I'm Raymond. How are ya? One of the chosen, huh?" He said with a slight chuckle. She nodded, smiling back.

"I'm Priscilla. Nice to meet you, but Chosen for what though?" The big man nodded, fingering through a magazine.

"To live the life of a super-spy." He said with a tinge of amusement. "The Patch sure talks a good game. He should've been a car salesman." If she wasn't nervous about the takeoff that was fast approaching, she would have laughed. Ray was right. Derlin did talk a good game. She was just about to say something when she felt her heart skip a beat from the force of the plane increasing speed. Then, soon after that pinging feeling in the stomach came from the liftoff, her knuckles turned white as she held onto the seat handles. Ray looked at her and smiled.

"You ok lady? You look as white as a ghost." He chuckled. His deep voice wasn't soothing at all. She nodded,

"Yeah, I'm fine. I'm still not used to the takeoff, but I'm getting better with it. I usually hide it better. Do you happen to know where we're headed?" He shrugged his shoulders.

"Not too sure. Flight time should be about five to six hours from what I hear." She nodded. There was no point in asking anything further. She'd find out soon enough for herself. In the meantime, five or six hours was enough time to gather her thoughts and rest her eyes. So, she'd be able to face the unknown future with focused eyes and a clear mind.

Chapter 13
Mom by day, Secret Agent by night

Priscilla was sitting in her minivan, parked in the driveway for almost twenty minutes. Her eyes were transfixed on nothing but seeing everything in her mind. Coming back to her senses, she shook off the memories like the plague that they were. It was the past, nothing more. That was who she used to be: a helpless naïve girl who didn't know any better. Now she was a strong, smart woman who would have no qualms about putting down anyone that tried to hurt her or her loved ones. She shuddered at those memories. It embarrassed her to think of those bad times. You'd never believe that was her, knowing the woman today. She told herself to snap out of it.

She reached into her purse and grabbed her cell phone. She called Pat to confirm what she thought from the beginning, that this was going to take a few days, if not more, to complete. She didn't get into what was going on over the phone, telling him she'll fill him in on it later. He offered to pick up the kids. But Priscilla told him it wasn't necessary; she'd have plenty of time to do what she needed to before tonight. And besides, this was one of the few times she could actually work and be with the kids.

She quickly gathered her things and walked into the house. Once Priscilla settled, she sat down in the comfy reclining chair in the living room, closing her eyes for a moment. But there was no rest for the weary. She had some minor things to do before the kids got home, and she had to be at the bus stop for Jonathon by 3:15p.m. With a sigh, she got up and proceeded with her chores. There was a ton of laundry to do and dinner to cook.

By the time she was done with her other little odds and ends, it was five after three. She didn't even realize the time. She hurried out the door, hastily walking to the bus stop where two other parents were waiting already. She knew them for as long as Jonathon was in school, nice people too. Thankfully the bus came quickly, she just wasn't in the talkative mood right now.

As soon as the bus stopped and the doors opened the kid's came running out. Her son was last, jumping off the last step and making a monster noise. Running to Priscilla, he hugged her tightly.

"There's my little man!" She exclaimed. "How was school? You have homework?"

"Yeah," he said, with less enthusiasm. What kid liked homework? She took his hand into hers as they walked back to the house.

Once home, Priscilla pointed right to the dining room table.

"Ok, get to the table," she said. He knew the rules. Homework first, before anything else. He lugged his book bag on the dining room table and unzipped it. He pulled out his homework folder and got right to work. Jonathon was a smart kid. He rarely needed help. But she liked to sit by and watch him and go over what he did. As soon as they finished up, Jonathon ran up stairs. And while she was preparing dinner, the side door opened and Patricia came in, red-faced from the breeze that could be heard kicking up as the day came to a close.

"Hey honey, how was school?" Priscilla asked. Patricia gave her mother a quick kiss on the cheek.

"Good," she said, throwing her bag down.

"If you have homework, get it done, please," Priscilla reminded her.

"Yes, Mom," she said while rolling her eyes behind her mother's back.

"So, what's up? Anything new going on?"

"Oh, you know, the usual stuff, Mom. Kyle's dating Michele now, after dumping Carmen. Now she's upset, so she's spreading rumors about her that she's a whore." Priscilla shook her head, listening to the teenage nonsense that goes on.

"Well, just make sure you don't get involved."

"I'm not. It's so stupid," Patricia said as she pounded her way up the stairs, opening her bedroom door and slamming it. Priscilla rolled her eyes.

"Goddamn, those stairs are gonna cave in one day." She said under her breath. Then, seconds later, footsteps pounded the stairs coming back down.

"Easy on the stairs!" Priscilla yelled.

"Oh, sorry. What's for dinner, Mom?"

"Pasta and sauce."

Her daughter rolled her eyes at that and made a face. Priscilla ignored her.

"Oh, and call your brother in here. I need to talk to you both for a moment," Priscilla said as she reached into the refrigerator.

By the time she was done adding olive oil to the water, they both were in the kitchen. She turned to them, wiping her hands on the dishtowel.

"Pack a bag with a few nights worth of clothes. Both of you are going back to Uncle Pat's." They both looked at each other. But before they could say a word, she followed up, "I have to go out of town."

"Where are you going?" Patricia asked.

"I'm going up to Connecticut for a medical reform seminar," Priscilla lied, saying it rather quickly. But Patricia, being relentless at times in her questions, asked again.

"No, Mom, I mean tonight? Are you going somewhere tonight?"

For a brief second, Priscilla stopped what she was doing, then continued. She didn't see that question coming for some odd reason. She cursed herself for not thinking better about what to say. She had her mind on more important matters from tonight to making sure her kids were taken care of.

Without thinking, she just blurted out the first thing she thought of just to pacify their nosiness.

"I'm going on a date tonight." She soon realized that maybe she should have put a little more thought into it. They both looked at each other, trying to hold back the laughter that was soon to come.

"You have a what?! Come on, really Mom, seriously. You're kidding, right?" Patricia said, trying to keep a straight face. Both her kids were staring at her with sheepish grins. Priscilla turned around and placed both her hands on her hips.

"Am I not allowed to go on a date?" They couldn't hold it in any longer. They burst out in laughter. Priscilla could feel her face getting flush with embarrassment. And as the children had a nice laugh at her expense, Priscilla went back to what she was doing, trying not to show a smile herself.

"So who's the lucky guy, Mom?" Patricia asked, finally getting her laughter in check.

"Oh, uh, just someone I met while I was working last night."

"What's his name?" She asked, pressing more. Priscilla raised an eyebrow to the question. She wasn't totally secretive with her kids, with the exception of what she really did for a living. But if she said a name, she knew what would come next.

"Never mind what his name is. Just go wash your hands. Dinner's gonna be ready soon." As Priscilla prepared for dinner, she caught both the kids look at each other out of the corner of her eye. She knew what was next, and in sync they started.

"Mommy and whoever, sitting in a tree, k-i-s-s-i-n-g. First comes love, then comes marriage and then comes Mommy in the baby carriage, sucking on her thumb, pooing in her pants…"

Hearing that song, Priscilla's face turned beat-red, from embarrassment.

"I'll give you pooing in your pants! When I smack the both of you! Now go!" In a delayed reaction, they both ran, laughing all the way to the bathroom.

With dinner done, the clean up was somewhat of a chore. The kids, of course, hated doing it and would try to get out of it. But, for the most part, they did as they were told. As Priscilla finished up the dishes, she looked up at the clock.

"Oh shit." She said. She was running late. She hurried herself along. The kids were taking their time, but she finally got them both to their uncle's place. She didn't walk them in.

"Ok, you two. No nonsense tonight. Better go to bed early, school night, remember?" She said, helping them out of the minivan and grabbing their bags. They gave her that, 'who, us?' look. She never bought it either. Time was short. She kissed and hugged them both goodbye and watched them run inside. Her son looked back quickly to blow her a kiss. She returned the gesture. She saw Pat by the door, waving.

"I'll see you later!" She yelled out and sped off.

She arrived back at the nightclub close to ten o'clock. The place was packed. It was as if the place never closed from the night before. The city that never sleeps is right, she thought, as she made her way through the crowd. She headed to the stairs that led up to Pietro's office. Two heavyset guards stood there, arms crossed over their wide chests. Before she could even say a word, they stood aside, allowing her to pass.

She memorized the way to his office and knocked on the closed door. She heard the muffled "Yeah?" She entered the room. Pietro was at his desk going over paperwork. It took him a few seconds to acknowledge her. When he did so, he cracked a smile.

"Ah, there's my girl. How was your day? Or am I allowed to ask that, with you being a secret agent and all? I don't wanna pry. I was afraid I'd never see you again, you didn't call me."

Starting already, she thought. She knew this was going to be a long night. The last thing she needed was to be partnered up with a smart-ass. She'd humor him for now.

"My day was fine, thank you for asking. I would have been here sooner, but I do have a life outside of all this." She said as she sat down in the same seat as the night before.

"Good, I'm glad to hear you managed that, at least. Would you like a drink?" She waved her hand, dismissing the offer. She wanted to get right down to it.

"I hope you don't have any plans tonight, sweetheart," she told him. "Because I need you to help me find someone by the name of Borislav. You know him?" She could tell right away from the face he made when she mentioned Borislav's name. He knew him all right.

"Yeah, I know him. We had some problems in the past and the resolution didn't turn out in his favor."

"Well, I need to find him. And the Feds don't know where to look. Perhaps you do." Even though it sounded like a question, it wasn't.

"Yeah, I do. I make it a habit of knowing these things," he said.

"Good. Whenever you're ready then."

It took him a moment to realize she wasn't kidding. He put the papers he was working on to the side and got up. He locked his desk drawers and stepped to the side. Walking over to a wooden cabinet with a numbered keypad, he punched in the code. He opened the door, revealing a small but impressive arsenal of weapons all handguns. He was just about to reach inside when he looked at her.

"I hope, being that I'm helping you, that this is off the record, of course?" He asked, turning his attention back to what he was doing.

"Of course, and now that you mentioned off-the-record, let me just make one thing perfectly clear: That whatever I tell you from this point on, or what you see from this point on, must never be told to anyone, period. Not to your thugs, your buddies, no one. And don't even think of trying to blackmail the government to get them off your back either. The organization I'm with are not the Feds. We don't need a warrant for anything and we will kill you. I'll personally see to that if you betray this trust." She warned.

Her words hadn't even settled yet, when Pietro moved in a motion so fast she was caught off guard by it. On reflex, she started to reach for her gun. He turned to her, slamming down the empty gun on the desk and leaned over to her. His eyes were red with anger.

"Ok! Number one, you're gonna stop with the threats here and now! Woman, secret agent, what the fuck ever, you threaten me again and we're gonna swing it out. Got me?! No one's ever threatened me more than once without having to nurse a busted jaw. I don't like this anymore than you do, so let's just get along until we're done, like civilized people, ok?"

She just sat there stoned-faced, looking him in the eye. He knew she was not intimidated by him in the least, but she had to respect him. He wasn't any more afraid of or intimidated by her either.

"Fair enough. We have a mutual understanding then. I'm glad we're on the same page," she said. He nodded, grabbing the gun from the desk and went back to the gun cabinet. Once he grabbed what he needed, he shut the cabinet. He was dressed in all black, slacks and collared shirt. He jammed a clip in the glock 9mm and loaded a round in the chamber and holstered it. He turned to her as he put on his black blazer and buttoned it.

"How do I look?" He said, flashing a smile that she was finding harder and harder to resist. She made a mental note to herself to work on that, but she was failing and miserably, too.

"Alright," was all she would allow herself to say. What she really wanted to say was, fucking hot! The more she was in his presence, the more alluring she found him.

"Am I driving?" He asked, coming from around the desk, stepping a little too close to her.

"No, I'm driving. I have my car out front."

"Good enough," he said, putting his hands together and allowing her to take the lead. Once in the club, he took the lead, noticing that the crowd was thick. Like a wading river, the crowd made way for him. There was more than enough room for her to walk alongside him.

"So, where to?" She asked, in a slightly raised voice. He shrugged his shoulders.

"I'll tell you when we get outta here."

They said not a word more. Someone brushed up against Priscilla, hard enough for her to turn to them and give them the evil eye. The man in question looked like he was going to take on the unspoken challenge, but seeing who she was with, he thought better of it and quickly went about his own affairs. Just as she made her way outside, she looked to her side, not finding Pietro. She turned quickly, searching for him. How could I have lost him? He had been right next to me, she thought.

It didn't take long for her to spot him. She wasn't surprised either to see who he was with: a scantily-clad woman who looked like she should have been on a street corner calling down cars. She had long black hair, and a very short, tight dress on.

Priscilla crossed her arms over her chest and with a look that could kill. It couldn't be any more obvious that she wanted him. All that was missing was drool coming from her mouth. If she got any closer to him, she may as well start humping his leg.

Pietro finally caught Priscilla's icy stare and so did the woman, following Pietro's gaze.

"The fuck you looking at bitch?!" Priscilla said, loud enough to attract the attention of some club goers standing outside. Before it could escalate into anything, Pietro quickly ended the conversation, with a quick kiss on the cheek, he sent her on her way. The woman didn't even look towards Priscilla, she just disappeared into the club. Pietro walked over to her, smiling.

"I'm sorry for interrupting you, but we do have something that might be a little more important than you trying to set up a potential piece of ass," she told him. Before he could reply, she turned away, quickly walking to a black Dodge Charger.

"Hey, what's this? No Aston Martin?" She ignored the comment, giving him a side glance of frustration. "Do I detect a slight hint of jealousy?" He teased. She could feel her face getting flushed. She was far from jealous, that was for sure or that's what she was trying to tell herself.

"Oh, get over yourself. What the hell does that skank have that I don't? Nothing!" She said, getting in and slamming her door. Pietro thought about that for a second before getting in and continuing the debate.

"Well, nothing of quality, but at least she would give me some play, unlike someone I know." To that comment, she tore out onto the street, cutting off a taxi.

"Did I touch a nerve?" He asked. She didn't reply. She kept her eyes on the road. She could still feel his eyes on her for a moment longer. She was about to say something, but she noticed he was checking things out in the car. He reached into his jacket pocket and pulled out a pack of cigarettes.

"Mind if I smoke?" He asked.

"Be my guest, it's a free country," she replied tartly.

"I just wanted to make sure. I didn't want you hitting the passenger ejector seat or some shit like that." She glanced at him with a raised eyebrow and a slight grin.

"Keep it up with the wise comments and I just might do it." She said. He smiled back, lighting up his cigarette. He offered her one, but she turned him down.

"So, where to?" She inquired.

"Brighton Beach. You know of it?"

"Uh, yeah. I grew up in Brooklyn. East New York to be exact." He seemed surprised at that.

"No shit, me too. What a small world. Whereabouts?"

She ignored the question. She didn't need to start with the memories again.

"Where are we going?" She asked again.

He took the hint, at least for now, she mused to herself.

"The place we're going to is a Russian tea house, an after-hours joint." She nodded, smiling a bit. A thought just came back to her.

"What's so funny?" He asked.

"I just remembered. I'm dying to know. The guy that came to us with this, his name's Monroe. You heard of him?" Pietro flashed a smile, laughing.

"Ah, Special Agent Monroe, head of the organized crime task force. He speaks very highly of me, I'm sure, huh?"

"Oh yeah, very highly. He'd love for you to fall down a flight of stairs and break your neck. So, it's true? The reason he hates you so much? You seduced an undercover agent?"

"Yeah, it's true. An undercover agent who turned out to be his fiancé, of all things," he said. It looked as though he was going back to that moment. "What a shame, too. She wasn't a good-looking bitch." Despite herself, she couldn't help but laugh with him.

They were just coming up to Central Park. As he kept talking, it was the first time in a while she passed this particular section of the park. In fact, it was an area that she subconsciously avoided. Of all the times to pass this particular part, she thought. She tried her hardest to keep the floodgates closed, but a new wave of memories came back again and there wasn't anything she could do about it.

Chapter 14
Flashbacks of Day 1

Once new recruits arrived at the training facility they were immediately processed. Photos were taken, along with blood samples and fingerprints. Once that was done, the recruits were brought to their dorms to drop their baggage off. The dorm rooms housed two recruits per room. There was no separation of men and women.

They were then brought to a rather large assembly hall. On the stage was a podium. Waiting at the podium for all the recruits to settle down from their chatter was John Derlin. He stood waiting, with his hands clasped behind his back. Like a tidal wave, the chatter died down and all eyes were on him. Derlin leaned forward to the podium, clearing his throat. He took out his pipe and lit it. Taking a large puff and letting it out slowly, he eyed the recruits. This stare made some people stir in their seats.

"I welcome you all. I know that the circumstances of the recruiting are questionable, but warranted, as you'll find out in the months to come," he said, walking from the podium. "Now, I know the first question on everyone's mind. What is this? And here is your answer. All of you have been chosen, some of you personally by me, to be a part of an organization that was put into initiation by President Regan shortly after he took office. We are called Shadow Ops. What we do is very simple. We act, with no questions. We see a threat, we take it out." He said, smacking his fist into his hand for emphasis. It made one or two recruits jump in their seats.

"There are things that go on in the world that no one ever finds out about, and we make sure no one will either. You will be trained in weapons and technology. Each and every one of you will know how to pilot planes, from a single engine to a supersonic bomber." He stopped pacing and stared at the recruits for a moment before speaking again. "Another thing is, many of you may not be suited for field work. And there is nothing wrong with that. If it's not fieldwork you're suited best for, then there are other jobs that will be available to you. So if you feel this is not something for you, walk out now. You will not be looked down upon. Someone will greet you outside and take care of you from there."

He waited a moment longer. Priscilla craned her neck, checking to see if anyone was going to walk out. Not surprisingly, no one did. Derlin grinned in satisfaction. "Very well. Go, relax, walk the grounds. Get familiar with everything, because at 05:00 hours your training starts. Dismissed." And he walked away before anyone could get up.

When Derlin was out of sight, people started to get up, stretch and make their way out. Priscilla branched off from the small group she was with and started to take in the place. She walked outside the double glass doors. When they had arrived in the pre-dawn hours, she couldn't really be sure where she was. Now, with the sun out, she had a better idea.

They were surrounded by desert. Nevada or Arizona came to mind, from what she could tell. The complex was gated. The entrance leading out had two guards flanking each side. She thought about approaching them, but thought better of it. She didn't want to start asking questions that she wasn't supposed to know the answers to.

Walking back inside, she went to her right. It seemed the place was a large, circular building. From her exploring, she had discovered that this place was more self-contained than it looked. She came upon a coffee shop. Through the glass, she saw a few recruits chatting at the tables. She walked inside and ordered a cup of coffee, hoping it was good. To her surprise, it was.

She walked back out and continued to check out the area. There was even a newspaper shop with everything you could want, from smokes to newspapers from all the major cities across the U.S. You didn't need money, being you were stuck here. She never envisioned a secret training facility to be so posh. But, in truth, she didn't know what one looked like anyway. All she knew of anything like this was from movies she had watched. Coming full circle, back to the front again, she ran right into Derlin.

He was standing there, talking to three recruits. He had just finished up with them when she approached him.

"Priscilla. How do you like the layout of this part of the complex?"

She nodded her approval.

"It's really nice, I'm a bit surprised Mr. Derlin. I expected something a lot more different. I feel like I'm on vacation." John chuckled.

"Well, you won't think that after a few weeks of training, I can assure you." Priscilla nodded and felt a tinge of nervousness creep up her spine. Was she going to make it through this? She had better, she told herself, because there's nothing else out there for her now. She was beyond the point of no return. She voiced her concerns to Derlin about that.

"I hope I don't make you regret choosing me, sir." John smiled, placing a hand on her shoulder.

"Come, let's take a walk. Now, I have no doubt in the least that you'll make me proud, Priscilla. I have a feeling about you."

That was great, she thought, as though she wasn't nervous enough already.

"Thank you, sir."

"Please, John will be fine, Priscilla," he told her.

"Ok...John." She awkwardly said. "So, are all places like this? You know, these secret government training facilities?" John nodded to the question.

"For the most part now, yes. But in the beginning, we looked for people who were the derelicts of society, people who had absolutely no place out there. We thought we could change them around by giving them a purpose. On top of that, we placed them in a more structured environment. Some places were underground; they were a far cry from this." He gestured around them.

"In the end, that proved to be the wrong method. Caging up someone like an animal will lead to disaster, especially the people we used to pick. So we came up with this type of setting. You're cut off from the outside world, but you're not at the same time. Recruits are able to go wherever they want to inside the city, if you want to call it that. This is just one area. There are four other parts, living quarters, a training facility, which is the biggest and there's another rec building with a movie theater, bar and grill."

Priscilla was impressed. He continued. "This was one of the first to be built. When Shadow Ops is not training, CIA, NSA and others come here. We're in the process of building two more facilities. One on the east coast and the other in the northern United States."

John mostly talked the rest of the time, showing her around, introducing her to various people, mostly instructors and some of the help they happened to run into. By the time they reached her dorm, he walked her through a good portion of the facility.

"And here we are." He said, stepping aside from the dorm entrance. "I hope you find yourself comfortable here," he said while packing his pipe.

"Yeah, wow, I still can't believe this place. I guess it's good to know my government dollars are put to some good use." Either John didn't find the humor in the quip or just didn't show it, because he didn't laugh. That didn't make Priscilla uncomfortable in the least. She was just trying to read the man better.

"Go settle in, eat, then get a good night's sleep." He then relit his pipe. "This will be the last time you see me in quite a while. But I'll be watching you closely. I know you'll do fine." She nodded and wondered why this man had so much faith in her. He hardly knew her. She was about to walk into the dorm when the question she asked herself came out of her mouth unexpectedly.

"Sir, why do I feel like, Uh, I don't know, that you're favoring me or something? Something tells me you don't give personal tours of this place on a regular basis." John smiled.

"You're very right, indeed, I don't. Let's just say, I've been around a long time. I know the special ones. And most of all, the trustworthy ones." She was floored by that statement. But happy that someone like him, felt he could trust her. She wasn't going to let him down.

"Thank you." John nodded, and left. She watched him, as he disappeared down the hall. Before going into her room Priscilla reflected, for a moment. It was so much to take in, it could be overwhelming. But she was going to do this. She wanted this, she needed it. And once this was done, she would start her life anew. Her future was looking brighter than she had ever thought. And the possibilities were endless. She was excited by that notion. For the first time in her life, she was looking down the tunnel of a future, fully in her hands to control.

Chapter 15
Flashbacks of her agent training

Training to become a Shadow Ops Agent wasn't that much different than her stint in the Marines. The only major difference was there was zero room for failure. If you failed, you were sent home. They only wanted the best. There were two different classes, one was for regular field ops. The other was for people who were to be codenamed Watchmen. Super smart recruits that when they completed their training, would know every language, observe every custom. Their job, unless otherwise instructed, was to observe and report nothing more. They were considered highly valuable to the organization to be risked. The Watchmen classes were of only five people.

Priscilla's only consisted of twenty recruits. For their first weeks of training the group was taken to a large windowless room with headsets that were suspended from the ceiling. They looked like oversized helmets that only covered half the face, leaving the lower part exposed. It was called flash training. And just like it sounds, you were taught by images, and instructions that were meant to be memorized in a short time. You don't sit down while you're doing this, you stand the whole time. The instructor said at the time, that the standing builds stamina.

This part of the training was broken down into two steps. You spent four hours a day being flash taught, then the next 4 hours using the skills you should have retained in real time. The next phase of training was weapons handling. Which consisted of the breakdown and reassembly of said weapons used and target practice. In the advanced training they were thrown into scenarios with holographic targets. It was pretty much any situation that could be compiled, from hostage shielding to straight out gun battles. They were also taught the key fundamentals of sniper training, from observation to concealment.

The next part was martial arts. They were trained in Shinsai

Goshin Kai. It was a combination of two distinct fighting styles, which were Filipino Kali and Jeet Kune Do.

As the weeks went on, the training was more brutal. The 05:00 run sucked to no end. The lead Instructor Conner, who was a prick, didn't care if there was a sand storm, you were out there in the desert running. Throughout all of this, so far true to his word, Priscilla never saw Derlin. No one mentioned his name or spoke of him. But she knew he was watching them all somehow. You don't run something like this without the ability of being everywhere at once.

At some point they moved back to the flash processing. This time they were all taught the basic handling of planes. The layout of every possible craft from single to two engines, fighter jets, helicopters and supersonic jets. Once that was completed, the simulator was next, which as the names states simulated actual flying in any of the crafts. These lessons went fast. It wasn't Priscilla's favorite, but she did her best. Once those main parts were completed the rest of the training was pretty much anything and everything. From academic schooling for various languages, to bomb making to disarming, to survival training in hostile environments.

The time of their training quickly came to an end, and by then they had parachuted from planes, were taught advanced first aid, advanced evasive and defensive driving and the layout of the company car which had a ton of modifications from missiles to machine guns. This was the most important also, because they had to learn the layout without even looking at what they were touching. The last thing they wanted was someone shooting a missile at an unintended target.

With all of that finally behind her, the day came when everyone found out whether they made it or not. Before you were to learn your fate, you were given the run down. And made to sign a nondisclosure. Stating that any mention of such a place was forbidden and if you were to say something. The United States Government had the right to sue you for everything you were worth. And no one wanted any part in that.

On the day of departure they all waited in the auditorium. Before Derlin saw each of them individually, he spoke to them.

"You've all worked hard in the last year. You should be proud of yourselves. Now before I see each of you individually, I have something to say. You are all trained weapons. You're the best. And the law does not hold for you. We operate outside the law, but that doesn't mean breaking it whenever you choose to. Don't let the power you've received go to your head because you still have to answer to me. And if I have to, I'll put you down. I've done it before and I won't think twice about it again. So consider this your one and only warning. I don't need to be anymore specific than that. You should be able to know what and what not to do. Pick and choose your battles. That is all." Then one by one they were called to see him. Priscilla's roommate Amanda was one of the first to see him. During her time here, they got pretty tight. She was a pleasure to bunk with.

Amanda was going to be in the west coast branch, that was a bummer for them both since they were hoping to work together. They embraced and Amanda was off getting ready to depart. That was the last time Priscilla saw her for quite sometime. Priscilla was one of the last to be called. She made her way to a little makeshift office. Not only was Derlin there, but Conner also. He nodded to her as she walked in and sat down.

"Come on in Priscilla. Have a seat. This won't take long. Ok, now I'm assigning you to New York City, that's our main HQ and you'll be reporting to me.

Now, have you thought of a code name?"

"Code name, sir?" She sounded a bit confused.

"Yeah, code name. Have you thought of one?"

"Um, not really." And that was the truth, she didn't think of one, she didn't think she had to.

"Well, now is a good time to think of one and we don't have all day." She stole a glance at Conner, who looked amused. She was waiting for him to put his two cents in. She thought this was stupid. Why the hell a code-name? Then the first name that came to mind was blurted out.

"Blondie?"

"Blondie?" John said with an amusing gaze. "Are you sure? You can't change it." She wasn't sure, but what other name was she going to use. She couldn't sit here all day thinking about it, she nodded.

“Ok then, Agent Blondie it is.” He looked to Conner. “You have anything to say Conner?” John asked, signing off on something. Conner shrugged his shoulders.

“I don’t have anything to add Derlin. All I want to say is good luck to you out there Priscilla,” Conner said, addressing her by her first name for the first time. She smiled. He threw out his hand and she took it, shaking it firmly.

“Thanks Conner” John looked up.

“Well, you better get moving. The transport is set to leave soon. I’ll see you there in ten minutes.” She nodded, got up, and left.

Chapter 16
Flashbacks of the Return of Priscilla Roletti

Priscilla was back home, in New York and it never felt so good to see the sights and sounds again. Everything felt new and yet the same. Instead of the city life she wanted to see how Long Island was. She had enough of the city life, and Long Island was totally new to her. It was exciting, new places, and new faces. She rented a hotel and looked for apartments setting up appointments for some potential places. It didn't take long though for her to find a nice cozy place in Merrick. The renter was an elderly woman by the name of Mrs. Weinstein. After taking a walk through of the second floor apartment that was a spacious one-bed room with a living room/dining room kitchen, Priscilla instantly fell in love with it. It didn't hurt that Mrs. Weinstein was a sweetheart either. After she agreed to take the place, the kind woman insisted she stay for dinner and tea. At first Priscilla was going to turn her down, but she thought better of it. It had been some time since she had a good home cooked meal. After dinner, she was glad she did stay. The food was delicious. Mrs. Weinstein made a pot roast with mashed potatoes and vegetables. Priscilla was never really one for seconds, but took more at the urging of her host. Over tea, Priscilla discovered that Mrs. W, as she insisted Priscilla call her, was widowed for two years now with two children who had moved away quite some time ago. She was a grandmother of six. She beamed with joy as she talked about them. Priscilla was having such a wonderful time, she lost track of the time and realized it was almost ten o'clock and she'd had gotten there just a little bit after four. She felt bad for calling the night to an end. But had to, she had so much to do. With the free time she had, which would be longer than she expected. It took almost six months before Priscilla was called to her first mission. She made good use of her down time. She bought furniture and other necessary household items, and was finding herself in Mrs. W's company a lot. She pretty much had dinner with her every night. It got to the point that Priscilla started to make the dinner, while she took a break, something that didn't go over well. Mrs. W for a woman of her age, didn't like to sit still. Priscilla hoped that at that age, she'd be the same way.

One evening after they both ate a hearty dinner, Priscilla and Mrs. W sat on her porch, drinking their tea. It was a cool summer night. The cool breeze was welcome from the hot summer they were dealing with thus far. Breaking that silence was a pretty bad argument coming from the house across the street. There was screaming, banging and glass being shattered. She looked over to Mrs. W who didn't even move. She looked to Priscilla with a weary smile.

"What the hell was that?" She asked. Mrs. W shrugged her shoulders, looking back to the house.

"That's a once a week thing, over there. You'll see that the police are frequently called a lot." Priscilla looked back to the house, then to her.

"What's their story?" Again the old woman shrugged her shoulders.

"I'm not too sure dear, it's one of those things I guess- that's none of our business." The old woman replied sadly, pretty much ending the conversation. Priscilla looked back and moments later a patrol car came pulling up in front of the house. The old woman didn't need to elaborate anymore. Domestic violence was probably one of the worst crimes out there for the fact that people knew about it and did nothing to do anything for the victim until it was too late. She felt her face get flushed. Her mind told her to get up off that chair while her gut told her to stay put and not get involved. She gritted her teeth as her mind harked back to what Derlin said about not abusing one's powers. She looked back to Mrs. W. She didn't look down upon her for not wanting to get involved, what was she gonna do? She probably feared if she did get involved, she'd be on the receiving end of the husband's wrath. To Priscilla, though that didn't mean a damn thing. She didn't fear someone like that, and as hard as it was she restrained herself and turned a blind eye.

Little more than a week later, it was late in the evening and with her third cup of coffee. Priscilla was curled up on the couch reading, with her window open. She was never a big reader, but with all the down time on her hands, she tried to make good use of it. She was starting to doze off, when she was startled by yelling and screaming. Closing the book, she looked out the window and saw that the woman from the house across the street was being forced back inside. In the stillness of the night she heard the crackle of a smack. She turned away, biting her lip, running her fingers through her hair, and wishing she had just gone to bed earlier. Sitting there for a few seconds longer, her mind was wandering to that woman who may very well be in danger. She could even be getting killed right then and there. If that were the case, which she didn't think would happen, then she'd never be able to get over the fact that she could have done something. What she just saw ignited thoughts of her own past. When she was taken against her will. She could remember it as though it was yesterday how she wished beyond anything that someone would have helped her.

But no such savior came and she was forced to take her first life. Gritting her teeth, she got up going to the bedroom and grabbed her gun, chambering a round and stuffing it in her waist, she quietly went downstairs. She walked across the street. Priscilla looked up and down the street; she hoped no cops were called. She was in no mood to deal with them, with their probing questions and arrogance she so loathed. She knocked on the frosted glass door three times. It didn't take long for a man to answer wearing a tank top that didn't belong on him and holding a beer bottle. He took a gulp as he swung the door open.

"Yeah? What the fuck do you want? Got a problem?" He said loudly.

She didn't reply and in a flash she took out her gun and hit him in the forehead. She forced her way in the house, pushing the stunned and drunken man into the couch. Priscilla then closed and locked the door. The wife was sitting on the opposite couch got up and screamed.

"Shut up! Pull yourself together!" Priscilla ordered as she grabbed the man by the hair and pistol-whipped him again. She then dragged him into the bedroom, closing and locking the door. By then the man was on his feet and tried to defend himself, but was pushed back against the wall. Priscilla then slammed his head so hard into the sheet-rocked wall, it left a dent. If the man wasn't sober before, he sure was now as Priscilla squatted down and forced her gun in his mouth.

"Here's how we're gonna do this." She said with murderous intent. "That's your wife right?" He tried to nod as best he could, with the gun in his mouth, confirming her question his eyes were watering. He was fighting back tears of fear, she loved it when the so called strong ones were brought down like this. "Ok, she's coming to my place to spend the night. If you so much as make an ounce of trouble, I'll kill you, and there's not a person that can stop me. If you call the cops, I'll kill you right in front of them and get away with it, got it?!" Again he nodded. "I sure hope I can talk some sense into her, because if she wants you out, you better fucking leave because if not I'll kill you. Understand?" He nodded again. She grabbed a chunk of his hair, pulling it tightly. "I'm so glad we're on the same page." She said, slamming his head into the wall again and walked out. The woman was waiting there looking dumbfounded. Priscilla tucked the gun into her waist, opened the door, and led the woman outside.

Deb, which was the woman's name, sat at the kitchen table while Priscilla went about to boil some water for tea. Priscilla stole a fast glance at her. Deb was still visibly shaken by what just happened and rightfully so. Being in something like that for so long, with no way out and no one either willing to help or knowing about it to help, can play with your head. She glanced back to Deb, noticing she was fingering through a textbook.

"It's for the nursing class I'm taking." Priscilla said, trying to lighten the mood up a bit. She turned a page or two more and closed the book looking at Priscilla.

"You're studying nursing?" She asked skeptically, Priscilla nodded. It was something she had taken up to pass the time.

"Is that bad?" She shot back sounding slightly defensive, Deb shook her head.

"Not at all…I just kinda thought that maybe you were a cop or something." Priscilla shook her head.

"No, I'm not a cop…in fact, I hate cops." Deb chuckled at that,

"Really, what do you do?" The question hung in the air as Priscilla took the screaming kettle off the stove and made the teas bringing both to the table and then grabbing milk and sugar. The piping hot tea felt good going down.

"So why do you stay?" Priscilla asked bluntly, ignoring Deb's question. Deb stared at the table while contemplating, she shrugged her shoulders.

"I don't know to be honest with you…I guess maybe I'm afraid to leave …I'm so confused." Taking another sip of her tea, Priscilla put the cup down, and looked the woman in the eye as she spoke.

"That's all bullshit, let me tell you something. How would you like to be taken against your will from someone you thought was a friend? I was raped, beaten and abused." Deb looked at her unblinking. The look on her face said what she was thinking.

"What happened? Obviously you got out of it and overcame it. How did you do that?" Priscilla cleared her throat and said simply.

"I killed one of them as he slept." Deb had nothing to say, as she took in what she just heard, Priscilla walked into the living room and came back with a pack of cigarettes.

"Want one?" Deb took one nervously tapping the cigarette she said again.

"You study nursing huh?" Priscilla nodded. "What do you do for work?"

"Honey, you don't want to know what I do. Trust me on that."

The woman nodded, going back to her tea.

"So what's your story then?"

"What's with the twenty-questions man? There's nothing special about me ok? I came from a hard life and don't take anyone's shit, ok?"

"Ok, I'm sorry didn't mean to pry. It's just I've seen you around I waved to you a few times. I just didn't expect you to be like 'this.' That's all, just a little shocked." Priscilla nodded, taking a deep breath.

"I'm sorry, didn't mean to snap at ya. You had a rough night. I'm just not used to people trying to probe me about my past."

"Sorry to hear that."

"Don't be, I'm not. It made me into who I am today. So what are you gonna do about him?"

"I don't know, this is nothing new. He gets drunk and then in the morning he's back to his usual self, apologizing like crazy."

"Don't go making damn excuses for people like him, I don't want to hear that line of shit." Priscilla cut her off quickly, then thought perhaps she should take it easy on her. Deb looked as though she was going to cry again. She walked over rubbing her shoulder.

"I'm sorry, I'm just a little tired." Deb nodded as she took a drag of the cigarette; Priscilla went to the bedroom and came back with a pillow and a blanket.

"You can stay here tonight, if you like. The couch is comfy enough, ok?" Deb looked at her and smiled.

"Thanks." Priscilla smiled back, placing them on the couch.

"We'll talk more on this if you want tomorrow ok?"

"Ok, thanks."

"Good night." She said, trying to stifle a yawn. She made her way to the bedroom. Getting undressed, she curled up, trying to sleep, but that was hard now the events of the evening set off her own memories of her own horror. Brad… that was a matter she knew she had to address sooner or later. But Priscilla would put it off for as long as she could. She gritted her teeth, a dirty habit she was getting into. It helped to control her anger, but was slowly ruining her teeth. It was the lesser of two evils, she had to do something to stifle her anger, otherwise she'd be kicking the crap out of everyone that got under her skin.

With the coming of the new month, to Priscilla's delight, Deb left her abusive husband and moved back home with her family in Washington State. They stayed in touch for a little while, but as time went on, both grew busy with their own personal lives. It wasn't too long after that Priscilla was finally called up for her first assignment.

Chapter 17
Flashbacks of putting to rest a scumbag from her past

She remembered being nervous as anything. The target was an engineer/ technician who worked for a company that exclusively developed experimental aircraft for the U.S Government. It was learned that he was funneling data to an unknown source. The data in question were blueprints of a new combat aircraft, the X-GL interstellar combat fighter. To save themselves the humiliation and the media blitz that was sure to follow, a death warrant was issued.

The man knew nothing of his exposure in any way. That made for an easy target and less likely to make him run for it. A false sense of security was something that could be used to one's advantage. The killing was done at his home, Priscilla stalked the man for a few days, all the while compiling information of who he knew in the area and the like, just in case she failed in her first attempt. Part of the mission was to retrieve the data and find out his contact or contacts and eliminate them also. She also had to make the hit look like a random robbery.

On the third night she made her move. It was just past 8.p.m. She circled the house looking for the best way to enter and found a side door. She picked the lock, and entered. She walked through the posh home in silence. As she made her way to his study the door was half ajar. With a lightning fast kick, the door flung open. Her arms extended as she rushed in. The man almost fell back in his chair from the surprise of the intruder. She looked at him for all of five seconds before she pulled the trigger. From the impact of the bullet to his forehead, he fell back, overturning the chair. She walked over to him, placing two more muffled rounds in his chest. She held the gaze of his death face for an untold amount of time. For a second she thought she saw the face of Brad, her constant tormenter.

She shook it off. Her mouth was dry, she took a mental note that the Brad issue, as she called it, was going to have to be taken care of sooner rather than later. For a moment she thought she heard something. She told herself it was just the house settling, but still to be on the safe side, she cleared the house before she went to work stripping the PC of all the files regarding the X-GL. She searched the office from top to bottom, tearing it apart. She took everything she thought might be important. She was about to leave when she caught notice of a palm pilot that was sitting on his desk. She almost overlooked it. It was a good thing she didn't, there was a message. Evidently her dead friend had an appointment at ten tonight, she looked at her watch. It would be close in getting there, but she had to try. With her work done here, she destroyed the PC and left, taking a long overcoat and a hat.

She was almost late getting there. His contact was already there waiting with a suitcase. He greeted her, and she returned the greeting with a bullet in the face and two more in the chest. She checked the dead spy and took everything she thought of value. The suitcase contained more payoff money that Priscilla was all the more happy to keep for herself.

Ten hours later she was back in New York, debriefed, and was sent home. As time passed revenge was starting to creep up on her like a returning rash. She thought of Brad. It was because of him she'd never wanted to be with a man in a sexual way. He had ruined that for her. She'd never admit it out loud, but from that day forward the thought of being sexual with a man turned her stomach into knots. She would never trust anyone again.

Derlin was one of the few she found she could ever trust. During the fall, she had some down time, after a recent mission, she was on in China that took longer than expected. By that time her obsession for finding Brad consumed her. She dove into police files looking for anyone that matched his description. Hours upon hours were spent clicking away. At times her eyes would burn in protest, but she ignored that and pressed on until she got a match. She found Brad.

She was surprised she didn't find him sooner since he had a rap sheet longer than her arm. By now he'd be in his fifties, or so she estimated. And as it turned out, karma caught up to him. He was diagnosed with Parkinson's disease and now he was residing in an assisted living/ nursing home in upstate NY. According to the medical files, he still knew who he was and what was going on around him. He was just in a comatose like state. She was disappointed in that. She wanted to meet him when he was fully able to defend himself against her. She wanted to show him just how much of a low life he was. That he was nothing against someone that could fight back.

Nevertheless, that wasn't going to stop Priscilla from doing what she needed to do. That following morning, with little sleep, she went up there. The drive was only about an hour. She'd never been more focused on anything before, even the scenery was non-existent and she loved taking that in as she drove. Once she pulled into the place she sat in the car for a half an hour, staking the place out. She left her purse in the car and only took her ID, which was fake. She walked the longest walk in her life as a wave of emotions washed over her. It was the fact of confronting the man that stole a piece of her that she'd never get back. Embarrassment and humility of being so defenseless and naive at the time crept up on her. She threw those feelings aside because, there was no turning back. This was the demon that needed to be put to rest before it ate her from the inside out like a cancer.

Upon entering, she took notice of all the exits and sized everyone up who could be a potential threat. For the most part, women worked here. There were a few men whom she didn't see as any threat. She walked the halls. They were busy with activity and they didn't give her a second glance. She said hello to those that did so to her. As she approached the front desk, she noticed only one nurse.

"Hello, good morning," Priscilla said, hoping she didn't look as nervous as she felt.

"Morning, how may I help you?" The nurse said politely, but from the look on her face, wishing she wasn't bothered at that particular moment.

"I'm looking for Brad Vickers?" The nurse gave Priscilla a surprised look.

"And you are?"

"I'm his cousin."

"Right, I see, I'm just asking because Brad has never received a visitor since he got here." Priscilla nodded.

"Well a lot of our family is gone. My mom passed away a few months back. I'm just trying to reconnect with anyone that's still around.

"I'm sorry to hear that." The nurse said, interrupting her.

"Thanks." The nurse flashed a fake smile and then turned in her chair. She got up and pointed down the hall behind her.

"Go down this hall and make the left. It's 105."

"Thanks." She said and walked not too quickly. She felt a tinge of sweat creep up on her brow. As she approached, the door was opened. She glanced in each direction down the corridor. No one was in sight. She then quietly walked in and closed the door. She slowly made her way; to the man whom she hated for so long. Sitting there lifeless, worn from years of living on the streets abusing his body, he never even looked up at the sound of her footsteps.

She stood there staring at him. Her hands were balled up as she tried to suppress the urge of just breaking his neck. She wanted him to know who she was and her purpose. She wanted him to feel the same fear she did, knowing that there was not a damn thing he could do to stop her.

"Brad? Wake up Brad." She said softly, not wanting to scare him. She wanted him calm. She wanted the fear to creep up slowly. It proved for better results from her experience.

"Hello, Brad. You remember me, don't you? It's Priscilla Roletti. Or perhaps maybe you know me by the nickname you gave me, Prissy." The decrepit man looked up at her once she mentioned her name. Even though his body was lifeless, his eyes had a spark of life. That said, he knew exactly what was going on around him. Priscilla nodded, smirking.

"Yeah, of course you remember me you piece of shit." She looked around the room, which had nothing other than a TV, the chair he sat in and a rather uncomfortable looking bed. The room was as lifeless as he was. She looked back to him laughing softly.

"This is a fitting place for someone like you, huh?" She didn't expect the question to be answered. She leaned in closer to her former tormenter.

"Remember how I butchered Will? I'm sure even in this state you're in now, you remember don't you?" And with those final words, an ice pick slid from her sleeve into her awaiting hand. She grabbed him by the hair, jerking his head back, and repeatedly thrust the pick into his throat splattering blood everywhere. Then for good measure, she slammed the ice pick into his heart. She backed away, out of breath, looking down at the man. She felt a weight lift from her. She finally put to rest the last of her demons. Priscilla regretted he didn't suffer more. Maybe he did, but was so far gone that it didn't show. She stood there, staring at him. The revenge that engulfed her for so long was gone. She regained her focus, when the door swung open and two nurses entered looking down at the floor and then to Priscilla who was covered in blood. For a second she thought about fighting her way out, but these people were innocent. She had no problem taking a life. But not like this…she calmly sat on the edge of the bed and awaited whatever fate was in store for her.

Chapter 18
Flashbacks of Redemption

By the time she was booked and processed, almost ten hours had passed. As per protocol, all she gave was her name and a number they could call. They threw her in the local jail, which turned out to be a mistake on their part. Seeing a blonde haired, blue eyed woman who didn't look at all threatening, a few of the hardened jail birds thought an easy target was in their midst.

But after three broken noses, a few knocked out teeth and a concussion, they realized they were mistaken. The cops rethought the idea of keeping her there and put her in a small private holding cell. She sat on her bunk, knees to her chest, face hidden when the cell door finally opened. She was taken to the interrogation room with no windows, a table and two chairs. Sitting there, she expected an overweight miserable cop, but when the door opened, her heart skipped a beat as John Derlin strolled in.

It looked as though he was awakened from bed. His hair was not neat and perfect as it always was. Turning back to the cop who let him in, he gestured him to shut the door. Priscilla sat straighter. She was slumped over. She was dead tired as she hardly slept or ate, but all that was washed away seeing Derlin. She couldn't gauge what was on his mind. The man was unreadable. Derlin picked up the other chair and brought it closer to her, taking out his pipe he sat and lit it. She got the signal that he was waiting for her to speak. She cleared her throat and didn't want to look at him. She felt ashamed, embarrassed, and most of all, she let him down. She wanted to cry like the helpless little girl she once was, but held back. She wasn't helpless, and she wasn't a little girl she had to face the consequences of her actions head on.

"Sir…I'm… I'm sorry. I didn't mean…" She quickly stopped, didn't mean? You meant it all, she told herself. You have no regrets about your actions. It's just the fact that you got caught. As she sat there trying to gather her words, she felt a warm single tear slide down her face. Derlin leaned back, and took a deep breath.

"You know, for the first time in I don't know how long, I was home sleeping when I got the call." He chuckled. "Needless to say, I wasn't surprised it had to be you. Perhaps it'll be best for me to do all the talking." He said, and then took a large puff of his pipe. "I can see it in your face, you feel like you let me down don't you? Because I know you're not afraid of me killing you right here and now, right?" She nodded.

She remembered Derlin's speech all too well to all the newly sanctioned Ops. If need be, you'll be put down, and he was right. She wasn't afraid of that in the least. If that was the case, then so be it. She understood that the government couldn't have their Ops going around settling old scores. The thing that killed her the most was the fact that Derlin saw something in her that she didn't. He trusted her, depended on her, and gave her a chance at doing something. She hated betraying someone like him. Derlin leaned forward, clasping his hands together.

"Agent Roletti look at me." He said sternly and she did so, as she wiped her cheek.

"We didn't spend millions in taxpayer dollars to train you, only to kill you for something as trivial as this. I knew the urge for vengeance was there, it was noted on your psychiatric test. Something isolated like this can be overlooked in my eyes. This man took what was left of your innocence something...something that you'll never get back. We've all been down this road at one time or another, some act on it, some don't. It's what makes us human beings." She nodded, taking in his words

"So, what now?" She asked weakly. If she wasn't going to be killed, then what? Put behind a desk filing paperwork until she retired.

"What now?" He repeated and got up and stepped back from the table looking at his watch. "Well, I don't know about you, but I'm famished. I'm sure you haven't eaten anything either… so why don't we get a warm meal in you and a nice cup of coffee and call it a day?" She was too tired to smile, but she was relieved. She slowly got up and led the way out. From that day on, the loyalty to him would run deep and never waiver no matter what happened in the future.

Chapter 19
Teatime with a Russian

As the last image faded away, Priscilla heard Pietro calling her name. He sounded like an echo. She didn't know why, all of a sudden, she was thinking about her past. She couldn't remember the last time she thought about it. Maybe it was John yelling at her the other day that sparked it. No, she quickly told herself. That wasn't it either. Maybe she was reflecting on her life. It has been a long time, and as much as she hated to think it. She was getting older and with old age brought reflection.

She shrugged it off, and then turned to Pietro, who called her name again and this time Priscilla heard it crystal clear, now focusing on him. She hadn't realized that he left and went to get a cup of coffee for them. Which sounded real good about now, all she needed was a cigarette and it would be perfect. In the coffee tray there were some sugar packets and a stirrer.

"You ok?" He asked as he reached for a cigarette and lit it.

"Yeah, why?" Priscilla said, then sipping the hot coffee.

"Well, not long after we were driving you kinda zoned out on me. You looked like you were deep in thought, so I left you alone. You didn't even respond when I asked if you wanted coffee. I figured in your line of work you did, though." She sheepishly smiled at him, nodding and she took another sip.

"Mind if I bum a smoke from you?" Without a comment he held the pack open for her, she grabbed one. He lit it for her. She took a big drag, slowly blowing it out. At once she felt slightly relieved. She looked at her watch. They've been parked down a side street for some time watching the Russian tea parlor. There was no sign of anyone they were looking for. Only patrons coming and going. She sat up a bit opening her window more; the cool night air always did wonders to clear the cobwebs. She quickly wondered about the kids. She knew they were tucked away sleeping, dreaming of things far more innocent than she could ever have at their age. After her trip back in time, she wanted nothing more than to lie down next to them, and hold them close to her. They were at times her rock, in this insane world. The silence in the car was somewhat uncomfortable as they sat there. She stole a quick glance at Pietro. What was she going to talk about? How could they have anything in common? They were worlds apart on many levels. He was a crook, while she was a government agent. It doesn't get any further than that. Then, as if he must have been bothered by the silence as well, he broke the uneasiness.

"Do you guys have like code names? You know, like in the movies?" He said. It sounded slightly awkward too, even from him and that was hard to believe. She hesitated to answer. But then did so in a matter of fact tone, hoping he'd drop the subject.

"Yeah."

"What is it?" She rolled her eyes. Why did he have to ask that? She said to herself. From the first day she picked the name, she hated it. But it was the first thing that came to mind when she was asked; she figured she'd be given one from Derlin.

"Blondie." She finally said, to appease him. He chuckled a bit.

"Really? And that's the only thing they could come up with? Blondie? Pretty weak ass name. What other code names are there, Tweedledee, and Tweedledum?" She could feel her face getting flushed from the mocking.

"Look pal, I'm trained to kill people, I didn't care at the time. I just blurted it out. What would you have preferred I pick 007?"

"You know agent Blondie," He said in the most cringing way possible that sent chills of embarrassment up her spine. "It would have sounded a hell of a lot better than that."

"Whatever." The awkward silence again.

"So what was your life like growing up?"

"Huh?" The question totally caught her off guard. "Me?" She said, knowing the reply was a silly thing to say.

"Yeah, you, unless there's someone one else in the car I don't know about." For one thing she was glad they were sitting in a dark car. It hid the fact that her face was turning red.

"Why do you care? Didn't you get enough laughs at my expense tonight?"

"I don't care, and no I'm not going to laugh at you. Just making conversation." She'd hoped by not answering or looking at him, he'd get the hint. But no, he didn't. She could still feel his eyes on her and it was making her uneasy. She glanced quickly at him.

"Well?"

"Well, what? My life is not any different from anyone else's out there."

"Come on, I've never met a secret agent before." He said in a mocking tone, yet again, something she was getting used to.

"Come on. I'm curious to know what makes someone do what you do." She took a deep breath. Damn nosy people. She hated it when someone pressed her like this.

"Ok… my Mom was a street walker, abusive would have been the understatement of the year. I was kicked out of my home at sixteen, lived on the street for a little while, then joined the Marines… I have no idea who my Dad is and to be honest with you, don't care." She said it all in one breath hoping that it would be enough to put the shock and awe in him and shut him up on the topic. She should have known it wouldn't work. Especially on him, everyone wants to give counsel nowadays.

"Really? Wow, sorry to hear that, you really don't mean that, do you?"

"Mean what? It's the truth. You wanted to know, so now you know. Satisfied?" She flashed a quick smile.

"No, I mean about your Dad?" That caught her off guard.

"Yeah, I do mean it, even if I wanted to search for him it wouldn't be easy even with the resources at my disposal. But why bother? He didn't stick around, that tells me he didn't care, so why should I seek him out, he should seek me out."

"Maybe he tried to, being who you are might make that more difficult." She was growing tired, of his, always having an answer ways. Couldn't he just shut up, and talk about something else?

"No...no, it wouldn't. He could've tracked my mom down. She wouldn't be that hard to find. Other than East New York, the only other place she'd lived is Rockaway." There was silence for a minute or two. She thought that finally shut him up on the topic and they could move onto something else.

"Typical woman answers for everything… I would have looked for my Dad, just for the fact to ask him why? But I thank god that he didn't leave us, it broke my heart when he died. I was only a teenager and we were so dirt poor. It was only my mom and my sister and myself. We had no time to mourn. I didn't know much of anything but the streets. I was good in school yeah, but what good was that going to do for me when I had to provide for my mom and sister? One thing led to the other and here I am today.

I'll tell ya now, if I had a chance to do it over, I would have. This is no life for anyone. I don't care how glamorous, it looks. I see these young punks out there, these wannabe gangsters. I wanna smack'em in the mouth, you know? It broke my mother's heart. She knew what I was getting into, she tried to stop me but I didn't listen. I thought at the time I was doing the right thing for my family. I know my mother died broken hearted, and my wife, God rest her soul. I… I know she died broken hearted too. Knowing what a scumbag she was married to. If only I had smartened up then and showed her more how much I loved her…every day I see her in my kids." He reached into his wallet and took out a picture of them, showing it to her. She used the light from her cell phone to see it.

"Beautiful children, what's their names?" She felt the words almost choking her as she said them.

"Anthony and Isabella. I do all that I can for them and one day I'm gonna get outta this and be the father they deserve…do you have kids?"

Yet another question that caught her off guard. She never really talked personal with someone like him. Maybe that was why it bothered her so much. She felt so comfortable, it was like she knew him already. She swallowed hard before answering.

"Yes, two. Jonathon and Patricia."

"Nice names. The wonders of birth. I was glad I could be there seeing it. It was the happiest days of my life." She couldn't add anything to that because she didn't know what that felt like. But she often wondered, since finding her kids.

"I wouldn't know. I couldn't have kids." She didn't look at him when she said this and he didn't ask further, he understood. She asked about his wife, bringing the conversation back to him. The last thing she wanted was to become a mess herself in the middle of a stakeout. She kept her eyes on him as he spoke. He never looked at her, as he reminisced about his beloved wife that died of ovarian cancer. It seemed like he was afraid to look at her for fear that he may cry, and it sounded like he was on the verge of doing so. If anything in Priscilla's life caught her off guard, this was one of those moments on that short list. She could not believe that someone like him was on the verge of breaking down. Needless to say she was totally shocked and had nothing to say when he was done.

"So, in a way, you and I are pretty much the same, Priscilla... both of us thrust into something that maybe neither one of us wanted to do, but got so knee deep in it there was no turning back." His last words dwelled in her mind. She never really thought of her life like that. He finally looked at her, his eyes looked heavy as if all the years of heartache came tumbling down in that short moment. She had an overwhelming feeling to embrace him, to do something. Whether it would be to lay his head on her shoulder or gently rub his shoulder. But she caught herself in the flood of emotions. He cracked a smile. She returned the gesture, not saying a word. Whatever built up emotions he may have had from the years, all came tumbling down on her.

"Yeah... it does seem we come from the same place, but in two different worlds" He nodded.

"Thanks." He said. She looked a bit surprised; in her opinion, she didn't really do anything to deserve his thanks.

"For?"

"For listening, I've had that in me for a long time. Being in the world, I'm in, I could never show weakness like that, they'd eat me alive." She nodded again.

"No problem. My pleasure ...and don't worry, on this one my lips are sealed or you can send me to sleep with the fishes." She tried to lighten the moment a bit. It worked. He chuckled. For another hour, the car was silent, leaving her to her own thoughts. She'd dated men before, talked to them, but never had a connection like this. Sure, it was only the second day she knew him, but still. It was something she never felt before in her entire life and it scared her. The voice in her head wondered if he felt the same way about her. When she looked at him, she saw her equal. Someone just like her. Pushing those thoughts out of her mind for now, she'd have plenty of time to think about all this later....much later.

Priscilla went back to her coffee that was just warm enough to drink when a black Cadillac drove past them. Pietro and Priscilla watched it go past slow and steady until it came to a stop in front of the teahouse. Three medium sized men got out first, wearing casual clothes. Each one was looking in different directions for anything out of the ordinary, with their hands inside their jackets. Once they were satisfied, the passenger door was opened and a lanky, fairly tall man stepped out wearing a designer sweater and slacks. He stood still for a moment, glancing to his sides. He then walked forward and the door opened for him.

"Is that our guy?" Pietro nodded.

"Yup, you ready? These guys don't play. A lot of them are ex-KGB and military." She gave him the, are you kidding me look.

"Trust me they won't be a problem, but thanks for your concern. I find it flattering."

"Don't mention it. I'd hate to see a pretty woman such as yourself lose those pearly whites." They both got out, closing the doors quietly. Pietro waited for her and they walked together side by side all the while giving her the run down as if she needed it. She knew the Russian mafia's reputation of being cold blooded. The word was, when they took a hit out on you, it extended to your whole family. Priscilla found that to be quite pathetic. It was one thing to kill someone, but to go ahead and kill one's wife and kids, that was barbaric. What these guys needed was to be brought down a notch and she was more than willing to go toe to toe with them. While he kept talking to her, she had realized she almost forgot to give him something.

"Wait...I almost forgot. Take this." She fished in her pocket, pulling out two very small earpieces. They were practically un-noticeable once placed in the ear.

"What's this?" He asked, taking the earpiece and turning it around in his fingers.

"It's a language decoder. It's programmed with over thirty languages. It instantaneously interprets the closest languages within earshot." She explained while she inserted her own earpiece. He looked at her with a not so convincing look.

"Well, at least that little voice in my head will be real this time." He said with a quick laugh, as he inserted his own. Priscilla didn't find it funny, as she continued on her way.

"Uh, it was a joke, I really don't hear voices."

"If that was a joke, then you're slipping sweetheart. Getting a little nervous?"

"Fuck no…but I was wondering. With you being a super spy shouldn't you know every language out there?" She should have kept her mouth shut.

"Honey, you think this is James Bond? No one's that perfect and besides, my Russian is a little spotty. I want to be able to hear everything they say. I hate it when people speak in their own language. It pisses me off …like they're getting one over on you and besides, knowing could be a matter of life and death." They were inching closer, crossing the street. They had one block to go.

"Listen, let me do the talking, ok? From what I've seen you're not the negotiating type." She made a face, feigning insult.

"I can be when needed." Pietro didn't respond, but he highly doubted it.

As they walked in, no one looked in their direction right away. Pietro stood with an arrogance that Priscilla would have found amusing under different circumstances. Unfortunately for Pietro, he was right. She wasn't going to play the negotiating game tonight. Priscilla had other plans. She threw her eyes around. Aside from regular patrons there was a bartender, two men who were seated with Borislav and two more sitting close to the door. Once the door closed behind them, the two closest men looked in their direction and were about to get up, when Priscilla took out two Beretta's and shot them both in the head. One fell on the table, overturning it.

Borislav and the two men at the table, almost jumped from fright by what they heard. Priscilla walked forward with her arms extended, another man ran from the back with his gun drawn. She shot him down before he could even get a shot off. As she walked closer towards Borislav, one of the men at his table went for his gun. She pumped two rounds into him for his effort. Borislav and the last man had their hands up. She looked around the place quickly. The bartender had his hands raised high. The patrons scurried under their tables.

"Everyone stay where you are, and don't fucking move!" She said, loudly and sternly. She repeated the same command in Russian just to make sure she was understood by everyone. Priscilla then glanced at Pietro, whose jaw was dropped. He couldn't believe what just happened. He totally lost his cool demeanor.

He ran a hand through his hair. It was shaking.

"You just gonna stand there?" Her somewhat nasty tone snapped him out of his disbelief, as he slowly walked to the table and sat with Borislav and the last remaining thug. If it weren't for the fact that she needed to be sharp, she'd have laughed. The smart ass was at a loss for words now. Priscilla stood behind the last remaining thug. From this position, she was able to watch everything, the front door, the back and the bar area. Pietro quickly glanced at her, then to Borislav who was so filled with fright he stared at the table.

"Borislav, listen, bro…. we… I." Pietro quickly corrected himself, throwing Priscilla a look. "I... just wanted... to come and talk to you about some things." Pietro really made sure he emphasized the words 'I' and 'wanted to talk.'

Now she was really losing her patience.

"Forget it…Yo Russki look at me." And he did so. "Two nights ago, two men walked into Pietro's place, wanting to buy it under the table. One of which is an arms dealer named Vladimir. Fairly tall, crew cut, slightly balding with a whitened out eye and a scar. Ring any bells?" He shook his head no rather too quick for her liking. The cocking of the hammer caught his attention rather quickly.

"Now comrade," she said in the most cynical way. "I'm not playing fucking games. You're gonna tell me what I want to know, got it?"

As he contemplated this, his eyes were darting around. It was as though he was waiting for his savior. Without taking her eyes off him, Priscilla shot the man behind the bar in the head. A shotgun dropped next to his body.

"Now, I'm looking for an arms dealer. I have reason to believe that he's here for other reasons than wanting to buy a club. I want to know if you've been in touch with him and if so, where he is…and I want to know now."

She said, cocking the hammer again on her gun. Borislav swallowed on a dry throat. He had no other choices left to him.

"If I tell you, will you promise me protection?" She nodded and that seemed to relax him a bit.

"Only if you have something to tell, now stop fucking stalling and get on with it!"

"Ok." He clasped his hands in front of him, "I'm not sure where or when but he's planning to set off something in the city. My involvement was to help him get around in the city, that's all." Priscilla flashed a smile of impatience. She hated being jerked around. He knew where and when she was positive about it, and she didn't have time for this.

"So, what you're telling me is that he said he's setting off something. He asked you to help in some way. But yet you don't know with what, right?" He nodded, confirming. "And you guys served together in the Afghan wars?" He nodded.

"Yes, correct. He saved my life quite a few times."

"Right…" She said as she shot the last man at the table. Pietro and Borislav jumped from the gunshot. Blood and brain matter splattered the wall and Borislav. He screamed out.

"Okay! Okay! On my son's life! He's got warhead!" Priscilla wasn't sure she heard that right. A warhead…the thought there might be a nuclear device in the city rattled her to the core. Now the stakes were really high, and all bets were off.

"Why the interest in the club?" She pressed, clenching her jaw. Borislav stalled for a moment.

"I…I…don't know…he never said. Please, I'm supposed to meet him tonight, at the lighthouse in Seagate. To take me out of the city. Go meet him! Stop him! And now you protect me, yes!" He was outright lying to her, he knew more than that. And yet he expected her to just be taken in by his bullshit. Had she had more time, Priscilla could've gotten the information out of him. But time was short, and so was his.

She shot him three times, and then walked away. She looked at all the people still hiding underneath their tables.

"Ok, everyone leave." She said in Russian. She didn't need to raise her voice, in a delayed reaction they all got up, gathering their stuff and left with no one so much as glancing in her direction. Pietro broke the uneasy silence.

"You... You...killed them all?" She looked at him, nodding, stuffing her guns behind her back.

"Yeah." Pietro nodded. He couldn't believe that this woman just shot and killed six men in cold blood.

"Stay here for a second." She told him as she took out her cell phone and walked outside.

The phone rang quite a long time before Derlin picked up.

Priscilla gave him the run down on everything that had transpired. He listened intently as she talked, the only thing she heard was his inhaling of pipe smoke, no doubt. Priscilla paced back and forth in front of the tea parlor as she spoke.

"I'm heading for that lighthouse. They won't be expecting this, we can take them all."

"Maybe…Blondie, be careful. If what he said is true, then that's gotta be the missing warheads I was informed about just a short time ago. I'll see what I can do on my end. I'll get in touch with the Coast Guard."

"Copy." She ended the call. She took a deep breath as she walked back in. Pietro turned to the door as she opened it.

"What's up?"

"We gotta book, I'll explain in the car." She responded noticing Pietro looked a bit agitated. She didn't really care either.

Luckily for them the lighthouse could be accessed from Brooklyn and didn't require them to use a boat. That was good for Priscilla, because her and boats don't mix. She unfortunately found that out during her basic training in the Marines. They didn't even make it to open water, when she got seasick and threw up on the deck. Thankfully a Dramamine quickly fixed her sea sickness. But unfortunately, she didn't have any on her now.

As they made there way, Priscilla stole a glance at Pietro. He smoked three cigarettes in a half an hour time span. Priscilla had to open her window, and he was muttering something as he rubbed his temples.

"What's the matter with you?" She asked. He looked at her, almost wide eyed.

"You're kidding, right?"

"No." She said flatly.

"I can't believe you did that"

"Did what?"

"Did what?! Did what!? Gee, I don't know, maybe killing a Russian mob boss with me in the same room. I thought I was gonna do the talking? You know what's gonna happen? All eyes are gonna turn to me. By tomorrow morning, word will get around."

He said sitting up straighter now, his face turning red. Priscilla just looked at him, angry herself. If she wasn't driving she'd have punched him in the jaw.

"Are you fucking kidding me? You're worried about some douche, meanwhile there might be a nuclear device somewhere in the city? There's a lot more going on, than your petty bullshit right now!" Pietro, lowered his head and rubbed the side of his temples with his thumb and middle finger.

"You're right…" He then picked up his head and looked at her. There was nothing but sincerity in those brown eyes. "I'm sorry." Priscilla held his gaze for a moment longer before putting her eyes back on the road. She believed him, she understood that he was scared. How could he not be? She'd be lying if she said she wasn't. She was frightened to no end. The thought of a bomb going off in Manhattan froze her heart. She couldn't imagine it. With the fate of millions in the balance, she pressed down hard on the pedal.

Chapter 20
Into the sea

It wasn't long after they arrived at Seagate, a small private gated community. There was a guard at the booth and as they approached, he came out to see what they wanted. Once Priscilla flashed him a fake police badge, he questioned them no more and allowed them entry.

The lighthouse was on the other side past the darkened homes. It was enclosed by a metal gate that had seen better days. They pulled up as close as they could, with the headlights off. Priscilla scanned the area. It was awfully quiet. They got out and walked briskly towards the locked gate. She took out her lock pick and made fast work of it. Proceeding through a small ankle high patch of grass. They made their way to the reef and stopped just at the base of the old white lighthouse. She pointed spotting a rusted spiral staircase.

"Come on!" She whispered as they made there way. They took the stairs, stopping at intervals to listen, and then continued on.

"I don't like this one bit." Pietro whispered, when they were half way up; Priscilla raised a hand to quiet him. She thought for a second she heard movement. Her mind was playing tricks on her. She scanned the calm seawater for oncoming boats, but saw not a single one. Once at the top, they stood stock-still guns at the ready. Priscilla peeked around the open doorway. She saw nothing, and slowly inched in followed by Pietro. Even on this cool night, both of their faces were peppered with the sweat of anticipation of some kind of attack. They both relaxed after a few moments,

"Looks like we're the first ones to the party." Priscilla said, tucking her gun behind her back. Pietro nodded, relaxing as well, and lowering his weapon.

"So, what now? We just wait?" Priscilla glanced at him and nodded, as she approached the giant window looking out on the inlet. She stood there taking in the scene. It was tranquil with the clear sky and bright moon reflecting off the calm water. Priscilla cast her eyes further out and caught a glimpse of a rapidly moving shadow over the water. Her stomach turned upside down, as she grabbed Pietro by the collar.

"Out now!...Now!" She screamed. Frantic, Pietro turned back towards the door, almost tripping down the first step. With a steady hand, Priscilla prevented this. In her mind the seconds were ticking down. There was only one way…she hoisted herself up on the steel railing. Pietro mimicked her and they pushed off, hoping they propelled themselves enough to miss the jagged rocks below. Not seconds later, the mini-missile slammed into the lighthouse the explosion lit the night sky for miles sending flames shooting into the heavens.

With a grin of satisfaction, Vladimir watched the video feed from the missile go dead. It was a shame he couldn't watch as the lighthouse crumbled into the sea. He turned to the Captain of the Freighter, smiling and nodding. It was not mere chance that this happened. Vladimir had men watching the tea house for sometime, because he didn't entirely trust Borislav. The lookout had informed Vladimir of the events that were transpiring. He could have killed her while in front of the teahouse. But then Pietro could have escaped, and who knew what Borislav revealed before his untimely demise. This was an ideal moment to kill the two people that may be on to his plan. With that problem gone, there was no longer a chance for error now. He turned back to the Captain speaking in Russian. Vladimir then reached into his pocket and pulled out a cell phone. The conversation didn't last long. But he was satisfied by what he heard from the smug look he wore on his face. Maybe he'd be able to pull this off and survive. It was a long shot, but anything was possible. But time was of the essence, and he had very little of it. Because come tomorrow morning, the city known as Manhattan will be nothing more than a wasteland of despair and death.

Waterlogged, disgusted, and with enough salty sea water to last her a lifetime. Priscilla and Pietro leaned against the Charger staying out of the way of the NYPD and Coast Guard, as blue, red and white lights lit up the night sky. They had barely escaped with their lives. The blast was so close to her, she felt the flames licking her neck, before she hit the cold water. Priscilla was beyond annoyed at everything that had transpired since she was assigned to this. Teaming up with a criminal, that she thought she was starting to have some type of crush on like a high schooler. On top of the fact that they were almost blown to hell. And now the threat of a nuke somewhere in the city. As the police and Coast Guard investigated the scene, Priscilla was smoking her second cigarette. She felt a headache coming on, and it was going to be a nasty one.

She lowered her head and closed her eyes. She wished she could just snap her fingers and be home with her kids right now. She missed them so much. Just as Priscilla picked up her head, and took a drag, she caught sight of a little girl in the arms of her father.

She was leaning her head on his shoulders with a scared look. Witnessing that scene, her thoughts suddenly wandered more on the past. A past that truly changed her life and her way of thinking. More memories flooded her, but this time they were nothing but good ones. Memories that in the end, would leave a smile on her face even with the threat of nuclear destruction.

Chapter 21
Flashbacks of a miracle

Now at twenty-seven years old, Priscilla was one of the best agents to ever come up through the ranks since Shadow Ops was founded. John had complete trust in her. He knew that when she was on a job, she followed it through to the end and made sure there were no loose ends.

That was why she was chosen for the next mission. A mission that would change her life, in a way she never thought possible.

When agents were sent out, they were on their own. Missions had no time frames. But regardless, all agents in the field were required to report in. It was left to the discretion of the agent, on how many times he or she could do so. And if for some reason after a week there was no contact you were listed as overdue. They would then give you another week to report in. By then a mission handler was already trying to contact you. And when all efforts of contact failed. The company would send in another agent to investigate what became of them. And if necessary and or possible, pick up where the agent left off and finish the mission. This was standard procedure.

After some time, Priscilla managed to track down the missing agent, to a complex on a very isolated piece of property in Southern Texas. From his last contact, he stated he was close to busting up a large international Human Trafficking ring.

What she found was a massacre. From her initial observation, whatever was going down didn't end well for anyone. The gun battle was messy.

She stood in the middle of the massacre, trying to picture the battle in her head. She looked at the walls and the floor, taking note of all the missed shots. She eyed the bodies on the floor. There were quite a few. She checked them for signs of life, but everyone was dead. Including her fellow Agent, with a gunshot to the head at point blank range. Someone survived, that was obvious. But they were long gone. Probably over the border by now.

She took a deep breath, not even knowing what to do. And as she went to reach for her cell phone someone approached her from behind. Priscilla in a blur, drew her gun and spun into firing position hammer cocked ready to shoot.

"What the fuck!?" Her mouth was agape, she took a double take not believing it. A little girl was stumbling towards her. She was dirty, dressed in rags and malnourished. She had blood on her face. She was in shock. Priscilla eased back and approached the child. "Easy, take it easy…you're alright now." The little girl looked at her, with wide eyes, and trembling lips. Priscilla was on one knee, looking her over. There were no apparent injuries that she could see. The little girl tried to speak, but no words were coming out, she was so frightened. She convulsed and spasmed dropping into Priscilla's arms. She fainted. Priscilla stood and with the child in her arms, looked for a safe spot. There was a table that she cleared away. Checking her over quick revealed she was indeed ok physically. Priscilla sighed, as she observed the child who was no less than five years old. Such a damn shame. It broke her heart seeing this.

With the situation more complicated than she realized. Priscilla went and checked the rest of the property. Outside of the main housing area, was another area that housed the 'live stock.' Priscilla didn't even worry about any threats. There weren't any, and if her suspicions were correct whoever was running this was cutting their losses. Once she entered the dilapidated house. And checked each and every room, she almost cried by the senseless violence.

The children were executed in cold blood, in their small rooms with no toys, and some without even a bed or something for them to sleep on. She'd never seen anything like this before. She couldn't even look at it anymore. She turned to leave, when she heard something from another room. Priscilla stopped. Sweat peppered her forehead, she knew the sound and it scared her to no end. An unknown instinct propelled her into that room. She stopped just at the threshold and gasped. Her eyes immediately fell to a worn bassinet, with two bullet holes.

"Oh my god!" She exclaimed not prepared to see a mortally wounded baby, as she rushed to it. And to her shock and dismay, there was indeed a baby boy starting to stir. She couldn't help but smile.

"Lucky little shit." She reached in and picked up the baby very carefully. She hadn't had much experience with children, let alone baby's.

"No...no...shhh." She tried rocking back and forth, it helped somewhat. But the child was hungry. Priscilla made her way out, and back into the main complex. Normally she would process the scene take whatever material pertaining to the case she could find. And either call in the locals or firebomb the place. But being there wasn't anything here of particular value on a National Security level. She scrubbed the second part and called in the locals. Priority one was their well being. She'd call John later, and explain the details to him. He'd understand and, no doubt, do the same thing if in her position.

Chapter 22
Flashbacks of the beginnings of a new life

"And that's pretty much it. I've already dispatched two Ops, with the information found we'll catch up to them. I brought Interpol in on this as well." John sighed as he caught Priscilla up to speed on the investigation. For a brief moment she was gonna ask who he sent. But then didn't. She wanted to put this behind her. He sighed again, as he lit his pipe. Priscilla heard the striking of the match even on the phone. It was a sound she was very familiar with after all this time of talking to John.

"Now...how about you? You okay? And the children?" Priscilla nodded, getting up from one of the uncomfortable seats in the hospital.

"I'm okay...tired as anything. Fucking scumbags! How can anyone do these things John? It was...horrible." She walked past a couple in the waiting room, as she said these things. Catching the attention of them and a few others as she left. They gave each other looks, and then went back to what they were doing.

"That's the world we live in Priscilla. Nothing you can do about that. That's why I signed off on this. I detest these people as much as you. I wanted them in the ground instead of a jail cell." She nodded as she walked down the hall and made a right into the lobby and out the doors. The warm Texas breeze felt good.

"Hey bud?" She walked over to a cowboy who just lit up a cigarette. "Mind if I bum one?" He smiled at her,

"Of course not lil' lady."

"Hold on John." She put the phone down, taking the cigarette. He was kind enough to light it as well. "Thanks." She inhaled deeply as she walked away.

"I'm back..."

"And the children?" He asked again, as she took another drag.

"Fine, they're severely malnourished, dehydrated. But otherwise ok. The baby, won't remember a thing. The little girl, we're not sure. She's still out."

"Understood. Okay Priscilla, you tend to things there. Keep me posted, and please get some rest, okay?" She nodded even though he couldn't see her.

"Yes, sir." And ended the call. Priscilla savored that cigarette, taking slow, deep drags as she looked to the night sky. Her jaw was clenched.

"Mother fuckers..." she said under her breath had she not had this dropped on her lap. She'd be out there now hunting those lowlifes down. Human traffickers were the lowest scum out there. Kidnapping, tricking and fooling teenagers into servitude on the promises of false hopes. Only to sell them to the highest bidder, which was usually overseas. That was why Shadow Ops was asked to handle this. The disappearances of children across the country were happening at an alarming rate too much for the locals to handle. And the powers that be wanted to send a message. That to continue with this type of behavior would result in your death. She had just flicked her cigarette into the street and started to make her way back when a nurse rushed outside.

"Ms. Roletti!" Priscilla ran towards the woman, feeling frightened at that moment.

"Everything okay?!" The nurse out of breath shook her head.

"She's awake and hysterical screaming for her mother!" Priscilla stopped in her tracks.

"Whoa, wait a minute. Nurse I'm not her mother I-"

"Ms. Roletti, whether or not you are, is irrelevant. You were the last person that she saw before blacking out. We don't know what her psychological state is. She may just as well assume you are. Now come on!" The nurse gripped Priscilla's hand and pulled her along. She had never been so scared before now, and she didn't know why.

As they approached the room Priscilla could hear the faint sobs of the girl. Priscilla not realizing it picked up her pace and entered. There were two other nurses in there trying there best to calm her down. The little girls face was red. As soon as she saw Priscilla, she smiled and stood on her bed.

"Mommy!" Priscilla's face nearly dropped, as she went into the embrace of the child. She had no choice. Everyone was watching the scene thinking of it as such a nice moment. All the while Priscilla was cringing on the inside. This was not her. She wasn't a mother, she wasn't loving. She was an assassin for United States government. And now she was roped into this out of obligation. She couldn't just leave these kids alone either. She had to make sure they were taken care of and put into the hands of loving people. Namely, their parents, if they were even alive. And if not them, then Social Services would be the next obvious choice. Because she couldn't be tied down like this. Just because she rescued these kids didn't mean she had to take them home either.

In the comforting embrace of Priscilla, she quieted down and stopped fidgeting. Before long the little girl was slacked in her arms asleep. The nurses by now had left them alone. With her arms getting numb, she eased the child back into bed and covered her up. And as she turned the Doctor was just coming in. He stopped, and gestured for her to come outside.

"Ms. Roletti, she was awake? That's excellent. How was she?" Priscilla shrugged her shoulders as they walked down the hall.

"Fine, I suppose. Aside from the fact she thinks I'm her mother."

"Really? It was just as I suspected." She turned to face him fully now. Ready for his further explanation. "From the neural patterns, in her brain scan and MRI I concluded from the horrific events and the shock she has acute amnesia." Priscilla blinked her eyes twice. This was getting better by the minute.

"Amnesia? Will she ever remember anything Doctor?" The old man shrugged, as they walked on.

"Hard to say. Amnesia can be cured through therapy yes. But that's in adults. Your case is slightly different. Her brain is young and still developing. The probability of her remembering anything is very small. She may not remember the events let alone who she is. And from what you just said, she now thinks you are her mother." She nodded again.

"Okay..."

"What are your plans now Ms. Roletti?" She glanced at him.

"My plans? I'm hoping to hand them off to child servi-" The Doctor stopped her, gripping her forearm tighter than one would expect from someone that looked like him.

"Ms. Roletti, I don't think you really understand. This is all the child knows now. Effectively making you her mother. In her current state, if you were to dump her off. The shock of that may turn her into a vegetative state. The mind is the most fragile thing of our bodies Ms. Roletti. More so than anyone thinks. It is my professional opinion that you care for this child until such a time comes where you can either give her to child services or when and even if she remembers anything." If she had a pair of balls, it would have felt like she was kicked in them just now. She didn't know what to say now. A kids life...her state of mind was literally in her hands. Basically, she was stuck with her.

"And the infant?" The Doctor released her arm waving a hand of dismissal.

"Perfectly fine! Healthy as can be! Just dehydrated. I'd also suggest not separating them, in the possibility they may be brother and sister." Another kick in the nuts had she had any. She didn't know a fucking thing about a toddler and now a baby! This was getting really fucking better and better by the minute. Priscilla nodded, looking away from the Doctor. The argument was over, she lost. And she was with not one, but two kids. And the irony here was she couldn't have any. Thanks to those scumbags that raped and beat her.

"Whatever you say Doc." Was all she could say.

"Welcome to motherhood." The old man said, with a smile as he left her to her thoughts.

Chapter 23
Flashbacks of a Reluctant Mother

When you're single with no kids, one doesn't get the full scope of being a parent. It doesn't count if your boyfriend/girlfriend has kids. Your kids are your kids period. And with that, you get to enjoy all of the trials and tribulations of raising a child. And two months into it, Priscilla was about to shoot herself. Yes, it was rewarding, and nice to be able to nurture a young child. Watching them grow up into a wonderful human being. It was all nice indeed. But not, when it's thrown on top of you in a single day.

She was back in New York. When Priscilla told Mrs. W about the bundles of joy. She was excited at the notion that her house would be once again filled with the sounds of running children. Yeah, great for her...Priscilla thought to herself when Mrs. W had told her that. She was grateful, however, that Mrs. W lent a hand. It would've been impossible for her to do what she had to do, which was find out who these kids belonged to. At least with that part of the job, she didn't have to leave the house.

Also, aside from her time not being used up between 'motherhood' and searching for their parents. Priscilla had to go out and buy a ton of stuff. Toys, dolls, coloring books and that was the easy stuff. He needed a crib, high chair and you can't forget about diapers. In two months she spent hundreds on them. And now sitting at the kitchen table with her laptop Priscilla searched while the baby slept and the little girl played with her dolls. She was right in the living room only a head turn away. The little girl never left Priscilla's sight.

"Look!" She raised the doll just now to show her 'mother' the style in which she did the doll's hair. Priscilla looked at her and smiled.

"Very nice...sweetie." It was so hard to talk like this. 'Sweetie' 'baby' these words weren't in Priscilla Roletti's vocabulary. Once the child went back to doing the doll's hair again Priscilla carried on with her search.

It was discovered in the last two month the kids were not related. Which she assumed anyway. She had their blood drawn and hair samples used to check. And then with that information she searched. Data bases came up dry, with no leads. The internet at the time wasn't as evolved as it was now. It was hard to search for someone via DNA if they didn't have the others on file. Her eyes were growing heavy, as she glanced at her watch. She was about to call it quits when there was a knock at her door. Priscilla was startled by this. Her first impulse was to reach for her gun.

She hated unannounced company. She got up and then walked towards the door. She was surprised she didn't hear anyone coming up the stairs. She must've been deep in her own world to miss that. Priscilla passed the child on the floor and smiled. The kid smiled back, oblivious to anything at all. By the time she got to the door, there was another soft knock. She looked out the peephole and saw Derlin.

"John?" She said as soon as she opened the door. Derlin was in a light trench coat, and no tie. This was as casual as she's seen him since he recruited her. "What are you…come in come in!" Derlin, stepped through. As Priscilla closed and locked the door, he turned and admired the place.

"Nice little place." He said with a smile.

"Thanks, and getting smaller. Look." She gestured at the crib, the high chair and toys all over. Romper room in Roletti's house.

"I remember those days. Every new parent starts out like that. Small place and lots of toys." He laughed. Priscilla just nodded with an uncomfortable smile.

"So, what's up? Not that I don't mind you here. But you're not here just for tea I take it?" John was about to answer when the little girl got up and came over to them showing off her new dolly to the new man.

"Hi! Look!" Derlin seeing her beamed, he shuffled off his coat and then bent down and scooped her up.

"And hello to you too, there beautiful!" The girl giggled when Derlin playfully touched her cheek. "And what do we have here!" She showed him the doll. Derlin made a face of excitement. Priscilla never saw this side of him before and it was both surprising and heartwarming.

"That's a pretty doll. Did mommy buy you that?" The little girl nodded, looking at Priscilla. Derlin laughed along with her. Every time that word 'mommy' was directed at her, she felt her face flush. Derlin then looked at Priscilla as he was tickling the child on the neck.

"Yes, tea would be nice." She nodded as she made her way to the stove. She couldn't wait to find out what brought him here at this hour.

Once the little girl had her fill of Derlin, she went right back to her dolls and coloring books. She loved to color. With two piping hot teas they sat at the dining room table. Derlin regarded her for a moment as he stirred his tea.

"Priscilla...how's things? Motherhood treating you ok?" She couldn't help but chuckle. John was being a smart ass. Something he's not all the time. People at the office must be getting quite the chuckle at her expense in finding out about this.

"As good as can be expected I suppose." She sighed.

"How's the searching on your end?" He asked and then sipped some tea.

"I got nothing, although I'll admit I haven't been researching as much as I should be."

"Of course, you have a lot on your plate now. Which is why I took the liberty of having a few other Ops do the foot work. And they found something." Her eyes widened.

"What?" Derlin took a moment to respond, as he slid his tea away and reached for his trench coat. He grabbed a large manila folder from the inside pocket. He handed it to Priscilla to open. She did so going over the pages before her as Derlin spoke and took up his tea.

"The boy's birth name was Richard Fin. Son of Marty and Tina Fin. Both of which are in prison now serving ten years for drug possession."

"Drug possession." She repeated disgusted.

"We believe they sold the baby when he was born. They were homeless, living in crack houses." Silence, long echoing silence. She clenched her jaw tight. If she could hit someone now she would. Fucking scumbags, the very same shit that her mother did, was still going on even now.

"Son of a bitch." If she had a pack of cigarettes she'd have lit one.

"And the girl?" John sighed.

"On her nothing. But we're still searching." She nodded, and looked over to the child with no name. She was still playing with her dolls. Derlin sat back and carefully regarded Priscilla as she took this all in.

"Priscilla?" It took her a moment to respond. She was still looking at this sweet innocent child. A child that did nothing to anyone. And yet was thrown into hell. The world fucking sucked.

"Yeah…" She said in words that got caught in her throat. Derlin leaned in closer.

"Priscilla, may I speak to you, not your boss, but as a friend for a moment." She sat back, running her fingers through her hair.

"Of course John." She finally turned to regard him.

"I understand this has been rough on you, and quite frankly overwhelming. But have you considered-"

"Keeping them?" She finished his sentence. He leaned away, nodding.

"Yes. Look at that little girl." Priscilla did so. "She's a very content little girl. To up heave her now or at anytime could be disastrous to not only her but yourself." She looked at him with a raised eyebrow.

"I don't think so… yeah, they're nice, but John… I can't do this alone, I'm not a mother!" She exclaimed smacking the back of her hand into her open palm. "John, this isn't me!"

"And how do you know?"

"Because…" Derlin just gave her a look.

"Because? Because isn't an answer Pricilla. You look at me right now in the eye and tell me you didn't once think of keeping them? I dare you too, and if you do, I'll call you a damn liar." Priscilla lowered her head, then lifted it, taking in a deep breath as if to say something but then lowered it again and sighed.

"Fine…fine you win. I've thought about it, okay, happy now?" Derlin nodded, sipping more tea. "I…I.. I'm just scared, that's all. Even though I say otherwise… it's been nice having them. To take care of them. I just want to give them a good home that's all." Derlin smiled, as he placed a hand on her shoulder.

"Priscilla we're all scared. And I have no doubt you will be a great mom. You deserve this, and they deserve you. I mean, look at this house? There is nothing here to indicate you are not going above and beyond taking care of them." She nodded.

"Yeah…" Derlin then reached back into his trench coat and retrieved yet another manila folder this one thinner.

"I've also started the process for you…" She looked at it, not understanding.

"What's this?" She opened it and gasped. Inside were two birth certificates. Blank of both names and birthdates.

"All you need to do, is fill in the names and birthdates and I'll handle the rest, and we can make it official." Holding these made her cry just then. She'd never ever think of crying in front of Derlin but she couldn't help it. It just flowed out. Derlin got up and embraced her, wrapping his arms around her. The unnamed little girl got up from playing with her dolls, with a concerned look on her face.

"Hey, momma?" Priscilla eased out of Derlin's embrace and looked down upon the child with teary eyes.

"I'm okay! Everything is gonna be okay baby!" Priscilla then scooped her up and kissed her. Allowing all of her emotions and feelings that she tried so hard to suppress come out. It was long overdue. She didn't have to be afraid to love and cherish these children. This was the day she would start a new life, with new beginnings. She would heal old wounds and mend broken bridges. God, it felt so good to finally be at peace.

Chapter 24
The horrifying reality

She was pulled from the past by her vibrating phone in her pocket. Priscilla slowly raised her head, the red, white and blue lights were still lighting up the night sky and stinging her eyes. She reached into her pocket, putting the phone to her ear, as she used her free hand to block the lights.

"Priscilla! Thank god you're all right!"

"It was a close one John." She sighed as she walked away from the flashing lights and commotion. "Our one opportunity, just got blown to hell." She tried to stifle a yawn, but couldn't do so. It was after 04:00.

"I'm gonna wrap things up here and-"

"Let the locals handle it Priscilla. F.B.I., and DOH are on there way. I need you here now." Priscilla bit her lower lip in frustration. A long night was gonna be an even longer fucking day she thought.

"Copy, see you soon." She ended the call.

Putting the phone back in her pocket, Priscilla turned and walked back to the Charger. Pietro was now in the passenger seat with the door open. His head was leaned against the headrest, his eyes were closed. But he wasn't sleeping. She stopped in her tracks for a moment. She forgot to ask Derlin about him…what should she do with him? He may prove useful in this yet. She rubbed her chin, thinking on this. On a normal day she couldn't just waltz into HQ, with anyone least of all him. But today wasn't a normal day, and she wasn't in the mood to make another phone call. She'll deal with the consequences of that later…if there is even a later.

"Don't fall asleep yet. The nights far from over." Pietro, cracked open an eye and smiled.

"Why am I not surprised." Priscilla closed the door for him, and then went over to a group of detectives. She spoke to them quickly. When the Police had arrived, she had identified herself as a government agent, and told them everything she knew at the time. Hopefully with more eyes and ears out there they may find Vladimir.

"I'll be in touch, boys. Thanks!" And then she hustled back to the car and sped off.

Once they arrived back at HQ, they didn't even refresh themselves. They immediately went to see John. Derlin was in one of the briefing rooms, with a slew of paper work on the table and behind him was a giant map of Manhattan, and a giant view screen.

Derlin at the sight of the pair was relieved. Embracing Priscilla and then throwing out a hand towards Pietro.

"Mr. Mastrandrea," Pietro took Derlin's hand.

"Hey." Pietro was clearly overwhelmed by all of this. And now with hardly any sleep it was most likely fucking with his head. Once the introductions were over, Derlin gestured for them to walk over to the view screen.

"There's not much time…so this will be fast." He paced back and forth, hand to his head as though trying to rub out a bad headache. He walked to the view screen that took up almost the entire wall. A picture of what looked like a sunken sub was up there.

"This sub, the USS Mantis sank in June 1968. Its location is southwest of the Azores. It was too deep to risk retrieval so the Navy left it there. It had two nuclear tipped missiles on board. During a routine check of the site, it was discovered they were missing! I was only informed of this hours ago." He lit his pipe, and then looked at the both of them.

"Do you know what today is?" John didn't wait for either of them to answer. "Today happens to be the United Nations General Assembly Council. All the world leaders are here, except for the Iranians and the Syrians. Now if-"

"Sir, just in. Three bombings…. Downtown, Wall Street!" An office worker rushed in yelling. John's face went from pale to transparent. But to his credit Derlin recovered quickly, waving away the office worker and then looked back at them.

"Son of a bitch is trying to divert our resources. He planned this all beautifully, or he just happened to have a great deal of luck and I think time is running out and fast."

The screen changed from a sunken sub to the aerial view of Times Square animating the potential blast.

"Now....from the data that I compiled, maximum effect would be-"

"Pietro's club." Both John and Pietro looked at her as she approached the view screen. She then turned to regard them both. "Everyone seems to be forgetting, this started with him." Priscilla gestured at Pietro. "Why? There's something we're missing." Her eyes then widened.

"John, can you magnify this?" John nodded, picking up the remote from the table and with a few clicks it was on the screen. The aerial view of the club morphed into a three-dimensional blueprint outlining the club and the sewer systems below it. Priscilla analyzed it intently, trying to make the connection.

"The sewers!" Derlin exclaimed never thinking of that.

"What's that right there?" Priscilla pointed out, "That's some type of access into the sewer, isn't it?" Every one's eyes fell on that point of interest.

"Did you know about this? According to this there's an access point that leads to the sewer from your club." She asked Pietro, who walked closer to the map squinting.

"I've never seen that before. I know where you're talking about. That's a storeroom, solid concrete." Priscilla looked back to the map biting her lower lip,

"Priscilla, these might be the old prohibition tunnels bootleggers used to smuggle liquor into the city." Derlin said, stepping next to her as Pietro watched on.

"Look at this!" Derlin pointed and traced his finger along a long straight stretch of tunnel that led from the club and into the harbor. Priscilla couldn't believe her eyes. Something so simple, yet overlooked.

"Son of a bitch! Is there anyone at your place now?" Priscilla spun around asking that question.

"There's no one there now, not till later this evening."

"John we're going down there!" She made her way for the door.

"Get Peter...he'll be able to dismantle the nukes. I'll alert the police, and the Coast Guard."

"I'll be in touch! Pietro!" At the calling of his name, he jumped glancing back and forth between them and then ran to catch up with Priscilla.

"NO…Fuck you! And fuck you…and fuck Derlin…" Peter said, pointing a ratchet at her, Pietro and the ceiling. "I'm not going out there. I'm not a field agent!"

Priscilla knew she'd get this response. Peter was not trained as a field agent; he was the gadget guy, nothing more. In all his years, he'd never been asked to go out there and stick his neck out like this. In a way, she didn't blame him, but at the same time, he should see the big picture of what's at stake here. She just stood there, arms crossed over her chest, waiting until he was done going off. But time was not on their side either.

"I don't care what you like or don't like. You're coming with us, end of story. There's no time for debate!" He waved a dismissing hand at her, as he turned his back on them, hoping to quiet her, but it didn't.

"Listen fuck head…I'll shoot you right now and drag your ass with us, your choice, there may be resistance and I can't dismantle a bomb while-"

"Okay! Give me five minutes I'll grab what I need."

"You have two!" He gave her the finger as he walked away.

Chapter 25
Into the Sewers

In less than five minutes they were on their way to the Hottt Boxxx. They raced in and out of traffic pulling up to the club in record time.

"Well…are you two lovebirds gonna stare at one another or are we gonna find this bomb. I wanna be back in time for lunch." She glared at the mechanic and then started to open her door when the Hottt Boxxx exploded. Pedestrians close enough to the explosion were thrown back in a wave of screams.

Pietro managed to close his door in time before that side of the car was pelted with fiery debris.

Once they felt the last of the heavy debris had fallen they all got out. Pietro looked as though he wanted to scream. He turned to Priscilla, who had nothing to say. She glanced around, thankfully, it looked like no one was badly injured. These side streets near Midtown while yes, were busy during the day. It didn't compare to the night life, had this happened then, the aftermath would have been far worse.

Nevertheless, she ran over and helped those that needed assistance, and checked on people with cuts and bruises. Pietro did so as well once he snapped out of his stupor.

As they did that, Peter walked ahead of them, Geiger counter in hand, scanning the area. He got as close to the flaming building as he dared to. The crowds starting to form were on their cellphones no doubt calling 911. On a normal day, commuting through Midtown was hell, today…it was going to be a bitch.

"Whoa! Looks like you were right…the readings are off the chart." At those words, Priscilla glanced at him.

"You okay?" She asked a young lady, the woman nodded, thanking Priscilla. She then turned away, and approached Peter. Pietro was right at her side.

She swallowed on a suddenly dry throat, running her fingers through her hair in frustration.

"This fucking guy sure knows how to cover his tracks doesn't he?" She said to no one in particular. She was frustrated beyond belief. She jogged to the street corner; she didn't know what to do now. She was about to turn and walk back to the car when her eyes spotted a manhole cover on the side street, she pointed to it.

"You think this will lead us to the source?" Peter, stood next to her shrugging his shoulders.

"Perhaps, but it's a gamble without a map. We could get lost, don't forget there's over one hundred years worth of tunnels down there all crisscrossing each other. Some may be blocked off. The best way would be going in from the point of entry they used." She nodded, looking back to the club. The fire was no way near subsiding, not to mention that tons of rubble blocked their path. She bit her lower lip, the choices were few. She'd have to gamble on this one.

"It's a chance we'll have to take. You have something to demo walls with?" She said looking over her shoulder as she made her way to the manhole cover.

"Yes of course I do, retard. You think I'm like you? I always come prepared."

Priscilla ignored the insult, as she went to one knee and dug into her pocket. Her pen laser torch was gone.

"Fuck...I lost my torch." Peter shook his head.

"Idiot! Here!" He reached into his pocket and handed her his. The pen laser torch was a piece of field equipment that every Op was required to carry and she lost hers, and of course she had to do so with Peter. "Wait till I tell Derlin his 'All Star' misplaced her laser torch!" He mocked. Of course he wasn't going to tell Derlin. Peter was an antagonist, that loved to screw with people.

She ignored him once again as she twisted the cap. A yellow beam shot forward, immediately cutting through the steel cover. While doing this, Pietro walked over to her, watching closely. Peter stood over her, arms crossed, tapping his foot. The urge to point the laser at his tapping boot was awfully strong. Once she cut the cover in sections, it took three forceful stomps to break it apart. She was already climbing down the slimy steel ladder before the pieces crashed below.

Once inside, the putrid smells engulfed her. She closed her eyes, suppressing the urge to gag. She touched down in calf deep water; Pietro and Peter were right behind her.

"Take point." She told Peter, with the Geiger counter in one hand. He grabbed a mini-flash light from his pocket that lit the way. She looked all around them, the bricked walls had a hundred years of mold and sewage. Rats scurried along the sides with some taking an interest in the new arrivals with a quick sniff in their direction. The stories of the cat-sized rats flooded her mind. She hoped it was nothing more than bullshit.

"You know…I'd love to see one of those cat-sized rats man. I'd like to take one back to the lab" Peter said only cementing her fears.

"Hey bro, I saw one from far away…there're bigger than a cat." This from Pietro, she was about to tell them both to shut up, when Peter called out and pointed.

"Over here!" He shined the light on the wall. "I'm getting a strong signal." Priscilla touched the wall. It was solid. Taking a closer look, it was a different shade of color from the surrounding area.

"This must've been sealed, sometime back." She said, Peter nodded.

"Hold the light, keep it on the wall." He said, handing it to her. He fumbled in his pocket, taking out another laser torch. As Peter cut through the wall Priscilla and Pietro, regarded one another in the yellow hue of the laser. He flashed her a smile.

"This is the wildest first date I've ever had, shoot outs, trekking through sewers, this is stuff you tell the grandkids." She nodded.

"If you think this is fun. Maybe on our next one we-"

"Ok, done!" Peter cut away a section of the wall big enough for them to get through once they pushed the section he cut through and into the other tunnel.

Priscilla was the first to enter. She looked forward and then left and right. Peter was next scanning the area.

"This way." Peter said, walking forward. "If I'm right, we're right underneath your club, or pretty close to it. The readings are going off the chart. There has to be a tunnel close by, so keep your eyes open."

Peter was in the middle, slowly scanning the area. The clicking of the Geiger counter sounded loud in the vast tunnel, too loud for her liking. If anyone was expecting them, they could be heard from far off. Priscilla counted their paces. They walked 20 yards thus far. Her eyes were everywhere. She hated being so exposed. She expected them to be fired upon, at any minute.

"Here! Over here!" Peter called out as he felt the wall, "This has got to be it!" He said "Okay, watch your eyes!" Seconds later, another yellow beam shot forward lighting the tunnel in a yellow hue as it made fast work of the wall. All three of them pushed the cut section forward to the other side.

This time they waited a few seconds. The only thing that could be heard was running water. Priscilla was at the edge of the hole straining her ears. At first, she thought she was hearing things, but she heard voices echoing, Russian speaking voices. She looked at Peter.

"Stay here till I yell for you." She told him, then she looked at Pietro

"You ready?" He nodded, taking out his gun. Priscilla eyeballed what she could of the new tunnel from her position. There was a small crevice not far from the opening. Hopefully she'd be able to make it. She didn't hesitate, she ran through the opening and was welcomed with gunfire that barely missed her. She ran for cover, planting her back as far as she could. She peeked out. There were two men, while a third was still working on the bomb. She dared not fire, it would be poetic justice for her to be the one to set off the nuke from a stray bullet. She had no choice but to wait. She glimpsed back to Pietro, who was all too eager to join her. She gestured him to stay put. She stole a look, and the two men fired almost hitting her face. She ducked back, spitting dust.

"Damn!" She stood there helpless. She was literally stuck between a rock and a hard place. She was readying herself to peek out again when she felt her phone vibrating. She then looked in the direction where Peter was, he held his own cell phone to his ear, as he gestured for Priscilla to answer hers.

"Yo stupid, listen!" Even under circumstances like these he let the insults fly.

"Pete! You idiot! The signal from the cell phone might set off the nuke!"

"Don't worry about that, if they were going to detonate it remotely, we'd be dead already. With all the radio and cellular waves just above us. But never mind that! Don't worry about your bullets hitting the warhead! Even if you manage to penetrate it, it's conventional nuke, it won't go off unless armed, which it isn't...not yet, so get moving!"

"Yeah, that's easy for you to say!" She yelled in between gunfire getting too close for her liking. She threw the phone back in her pocket and called out to Pietro. She gestured for him to throw her his gun, he did so without hesitation. She caught it, taking a deep breath.

She leaned her head back, gripping both guns tightly, she readied herself. It was now or never. She came out from her cover firing wildly at her attackers who were not expecting such a brazen move. She managed to hit one, while the other fled out of sight. As she ran closer, she took aim and fired on the man who was attempting to arm the warhead, killing him. With no regard for danger, she followed the third man that escaped.

Pietro and Peter were running to catch up. When she turned the bend there were two more tunnels to her left and right, and a vast tunnel on a straight path. At the end of the tunnel was a bright light. The third gunman fled in that direction on a sled-like transport. With no chance of getting him she turned her attention to the man she wounded, putting him out of his misery with a round to the head. She ran to the nuke, which was now armed.

"Shit!" She turned to Peter, who came right up next to her. "Time you earn your keep mechanic." They had five minutes before life in the city burned.

Chapter 26
Nuke disarming 101

The sled-runner reached the end of the vast tunnel in a matter of seconds. The gunman climbed the funnel as quickly as he could, coming out the other end, he was helped aboard by some crew members. The freighter had a number of modifications-one, was a funnel system, enabling an airtight seal to any underwater surface. It was a valuable tool for someone like Vladimir, being able to store and hide his weapons when he needed. The gunman wasted no time, telling Vladimir what had happened. He knew he was cutting it too short.

The man informed him that instead of setting the timer to the original one-hour before detonation, it was set to go off in five minutes. Vladimir yelled out instructions to the crew. The original plan was to reseal the opening, but with time too short and the chance of them disarming the nuke too high, flooding the tunnel would put an end to that threat.

As the funnel was retracted, Vladimir watched via underwater camera as the water rushed in. He smiled to himself, taking a look at his watch. He had hope that they could make it. At worst they'd be exposed to radiation, something that could be rectified. Yes, on this day, the city known for its bright lights and wonders would be extinguished and Vladimir would be able to breathe a sigh of relief.

"Oh shit! Shit! You better hurry up!" Priscilla yelled, as she saw the rushing wall of water coming for them. She ran back to Peter, watching him intently over his shoulder. She felt so helpless with the fate of millions hanging in the balance. She turned back and forth from Peter's flying hands to his intense look as he worked on the device. She walked away again. Listening intently, they were about to be washed away. Her life was flashing before her eyes. Every event that happened was as clear as day....they were mostly of the kids, thinking how she'd let them down.

Hopefully they wouldn't be affected by the fallout. But she sure as hell wanted to avoid that. She ran back to Peter.

"Come on, god dammit!"

"Shut up! You think this is so fucking easy! Then be my guest." She looked at the wiring that was sprawled out. There were five wires in all, red, blue, green, yellow, and white. She glimpsed at the numbers counting down there was 0:20 seconds to go…. she looked back to Peter who didn't know what to do; he was talking to himself. The water was coming, the sound of it was echoing through the sewer. She looked back to Peter, 0:07 seconds…with the time ticking down, there was really nothing to lose at this point. She was about to shove him to the side and rip the wires out.

"I did it! Disarmed!" He yelled, throwing his arms up in victory! It didn't take him long to register the sound coming to his ears.

"Is that what I think it is?" His question went unanswered as she saw the countdown to their doom shut off. But before she could breathe a sigh of relief, they were engulfed by the rapids. Priscilla managed to grab hold of the nuke and climb on top of it. Pietro and Peter were holding onto it as well and she helped them up. The water was rising and with that the nuke started to float away taking them with it. They slammed into a brick wall as they picked up speed, bouncing off. They slammed into the other side, smashing a hole. Priscilla saw that and pointed.

"Let's go!" She grabbed Pete's hand and in turn he grabbed Pietro's as they jumped.

The undertow took them through to the other side. The current was powerful as they were thrashed along barely missing the walls. Perhaps this wasn't the best idea, but it was all they had. Just as they were about to be slammed into a wall, they came to a sudden jerking stop. Priscilla screamed out, as she grabbed a ladder rung. Pulling them close to her, they grabbed the ladder as well and made their climb to freedom.

Priscilla led the way climbing slowly, spitting out the sewage mixed with seawater. She had all to do from puking right then and there. She felt like she swallowed a stomach full. She reached into her pocket and took out the pen laser torch and proceeded to cut away at the manhole cover's bolts that locked it in place. As she did this, she stole a glance down. With the yellow hue of the torch they looked just as terrible as she did.

Finally done with her cutting, she tried to lift the steel cover to no avail. She called down for one of them to give her a hand.

With some effort, they were free. The smell of hot dogs and city smog never felt so good at that moment as she climbed out. She turned, helping Pietro and Peter. The street they came up on was flooded out. But she didn't care she was exhausted, she fell to her knees trying her hardest to suppress the urge of puking. She looked up and saw people standing around looking at them while traffic was at a complete standstill. She looked over to her partners. Pietro was on his rear looking like he hadn't slept in a week, and even though he looked grimy, he still managed to retain his uncanny good looks. Peter was standing with his hands on his hips, looking around with that stupid smile.

"Not too bad for a day's worth of work I gotta say. I'm pretty proud of myself." Priscilla had nothing to say, she just gave him that evil eye that he didn't catch because he was mouthing off to the crowd.

"What the hell are they looking at? What? You never seen someone crawling out of a sewer before?" She wished someone, would punch him in the head. But unfortunately for her, no such luck. She took a deep breath; and closed her eyes for a moment, but then heard a cell phone ringing which was Peter's.

"Yeah, John!…Yeah, she's right here." He turned to her, throwing her the phone, "It's for you stupid." She glared at him as she caught it and placed the phone to her ear.

"Yeah..." her voice was hoarse.

"Priscilla, Vladimir is blasting his way through the harbor, making for the open sea. NYPD and the Coast Guard are-"

"So let the Coast Guard take him." She started to say as she got back to her feet.

"Blondie, I've been keeping the President up to speed with this situation, and he wants Vladimir. He has too much Intel. We can't afford him to be tied up in the judicial system. And we certainly don't need the ACLU or anyone else protecting his civil rights! I don't care how you do it, just get on that ship." The call ended, Priscilla wanted to crush the phone in her hands. But before succumbing to that she threw it back to Pete, who still wore that stupid shit eating grin that she could not stand right about now. She turned to Pietro, who was looking at her. He looked just like she felt, like shit.

"Well…what happened?" He asked, "Can I go home now?" She nodded.

"Yeah, you can… me, I gotta intercept that ship and unless I can teleport, that's not happening." She looked at Pete who was typing away on his cell. She shook her head, then walked away, knowing there were no solutions to her problem.

"Hey stupid!" She turned to Peter, ready to threaten him with bodily harm if he called her that one more time. "Catch!" He threw her the very cell phone he was just typing on. She caught it, not really knowing what was so important about it. The GPS app was opened with a blinking red dot.

"Yeah, and how is this gonna help?" Peter rolled his eyes.

"Stupid ass, look closer." She did so. "That map you're seeing is where you are. That red dot is your ticket for catching that boat. It's something I've been working on. Head west to the piers, and your ride will be there." She didn't even reply; she ran past Pietro, and he followed her.

"Bon voyage assholes!" Peter yelled out with his hand to his mouth. "As for me, I think I'll get a beer and a slice of pizza." He sniffed under his armpits. He stunk of sewer water and sea. But he didn't care, Peter never took anything serious and he was glad because then no one would sit next to him and he'd get served quickly. A win, win for him. He thought, chuckling away not really feeling sorry for the person that has to serve him.

Chapter 27
Having a Thunder-ball

At the first car she saw idling, Priscilla ran to the driver's side opening the door. She pulled out the driver who was not very happy, and of course he resisted. But water soaked, not only twice in the last two days, on top of being drenched in sewage, Priscilla wasn't in any mood to be resisted.

"National security sir!" She said as she twisted his arm to the point of breaking it. Pietro jumped in the passenger side and she sped off before he could even close the door. With the pedal to the metal she raced through the deadlocked traffic, jumping sidewalks while leaning on the horn to alert the pedestrians of a maniac coming. Luckily, they were only a few blocks from the nearest pier, jumping the curb she parked the car blocking half the street.

They both ran to the dock. She kept one eye on the cell display, the other on the water, not seeing a damn thing. Then her ears caught the sound of a boat engine. She followed the sound and just at the end of the pier, a black speedboat was just sitting there with the motor idling. As they ran towards the boat, her eyes went to the sky. Of all the times she thought, dammit! There was a storm coming in and fast. The blue sky gave way to the ashen clouds as thunder echoed in the distance slowly getting louder. Her stomach turned with the thought of having to get on that goddamn boat. Pietro rushed past her, jumping in and heading for the controls. He turned around, seeing she was still standing there.

"Well? You just gonna stand there?!" She made a face, wishing right now lightning would strike her. She moaned as she jumped down. Pietro pushed the throttle forward so hard she had to grab hold of the seat as the boat took off. She looked to the sky, again. The heavens opened up as though the end of the world was upon them. The sky quickly turned from the ashen gray to the blackest abyss. Priscilla cursed her luck. Now of all times, a bitch of a storm to hit, even near the piers the water was rocky as they made their way towards the speeding freighter which had a hydrofoil modification. They had a good lead.

The seas only got worse. She already felt her stomach doing somersaults. Lightning lit the heavens followed by the thunderclaps. She often thought it was funny that she was this super spy that would get seasick. How the hell could she jump from a plane at 30,000 feet and feel nothing but a surge of adrenaline, and yet put her on a boat, and she turned as green as lima beans.

A massive wave rocked the boat. She swallowed hard, then unexpectedly another wave, and that was a wrap. She upchucked on the deck before she could make it over the side. Pete was not going to be happy with that clean up, she thought. And thinking about his reaction actually made her gag a chuckle out. Pietro turned around, calling her. She looked up and turned to him. She couldn't hear what he said, but she waved him on. He watched her for a few seconds more, then turned back around. Judging from the look on his face, she must have looked like hell. Get yourself together, she told herself. And she did so. She tried her hardest to shake off the seasickness, as she stood back up, balancing herself. The good thing was she didn't have to puke again, her stomach just felt like it was trampled on, something that she could deal with.

She slowly made her way next to Pietro. They were gaining, from her estimate they were 200 yards away. She looked ahead of the freighter and caught a quick flash of light other than lightning. She grabbed a pair of binoculars from the side, and bit her lip. Bearing down on the freighter were three Coast Guard cutters.

"Shit!" She said aloud, to herself, Pietro managed to hear her. She pointed in the direction he nodded. With the freighter getting closer she readied to board going down below. She came back up within a minute, brandishing a magnetic grappling gun. She watched intently, trying to keep focused on the task at hand; she could feel the effects of seasickness creeping up on her again. She swallowed hard. It felt as though she had something caught in the middle of her throat. Then out of nowhere, a wave rocked the boat. Priscilla lost her footing, flying backwards and slamming dangerously close to the edge, almost dropping the magnetic gun over the side. Pietro called out to her.

She could hardly hear him between the thunder and gusting winds. Rubbing her backside, she got up slowly. Thankfully the pain took her mind off her spinning stomach. He turned to her.

"You ok?!" He asked. She gave him a thumbs up. He nodded, throwing his chin to the left. They were almost side-by-side with the freighter.

"Can you get closer?!" She yelled,

"Any closer and we'll be torn apart!" Priscilla, secured her handgun as best she could. "You ready?!" He yelled with one eye open, trying to keep the stinging seawater from his eyes. "I'm as close as I can get!"

"Ok!" She yelled back. She went to the back of the boat, hoisting up the magnetic grappling gun. Taking careful aim, she fired, her eyes followed the magnetic tip, losing it. She waited for the line to go taut, when she was suddenly pulled over the side thrashing about in the rough seas. If not for the wrist strap, she would have lost her grip. She had no hope of righting herself.

This wasn't a smart move. She was going to be torn apart. With an effort, she double clicked the trigger and the line propelled her upwards, slamming into the side of the freighter. A striking pain went through her body, but she made it.

Reaching for the rail, she hoisted herself up almost slipping on the steel deck. She took a moment to settle herself. Pulling out her gun, she walked as fast as she could towards the bridge. Walking down the narrow walkway, she turned to the sea watching Pietro going in the opposite direction.

She felt an overwhelming desire to wave, but did not. She continued on the path, keeping an eye out for any hostels. Moments later she came upon a rusted metal door. She pushed it open with a whine of protest and quickly walked down a narrow passageway turning right, then left. She felt like a rat, trapped in a never-ending maze, while trying to remain on her feet from the constant swaying. Then out of nowhere two pirates came running around a bend. Judging by their faces, they had not expected to see her. Before they could even react, she opened fire, killing both. She stood still going down on one knee, incase more were right behind these two.

But she didn't have much time to spare. So, she moved on, picking up the pace. She hoped the rest of the pirates would be busy at the moment in the middle of a storm with the Coast Guard bearing down their necks. After more winding twists and turns, she came to a lounge area with secured tables and benches, and a full view on both sides of the rough seas, which didn't help her seasickness. She spotted a door straight ahead. She ran towards it only to be tripped.

She fell forward with the momentum, dropping her gun; instinctively her hands took the impact of the fall. As she rolled to her feet into a crouch, she spun around to see the burly, bearded captain coming at her with a rather large knife in his hand. He thrust it at her chest, she dodged to one side, while countering with a kick to his knee which he saw coming and jumped back. In the seconds she had to recover, she unsteadily flipped backward and squared off.

The Captain, was already coming at her with quick strikes that she dodged and batted away. The captain had no skill whatsoever, but he was tough and unorthodox, and that made someone more dangerous than knowing how to fight at times. He lunged for her again, faster now. She almost underestimated his speed because he looked old and beat up from a life on the high seas. It almost cost her. One strike came too close to her throat. She backed away trying to get space between them. He came at her again with a combination of strikes faster than before, she tried to grab his arm. The slippery raincoat made that difficult. On the last strike she caught it, and twisted his wrist enough to drop the knife.

Wincing in pain, his other hand caught her square in the face, breaking her nose. The pain was intense. Her eyes started to water, she let go of his arm. She could feel the warmth of the blood on her face. He did not let up for a second. She managed to clear her eyes at the moment he was attacking again. She ducked under the punch, countering with an uppercut, knocking his head back. She clamped both hands around his head, driving his face into her knee. Before she could do anything else, he grabbed her by her thigh and picked her up with enough force to send her flying back into a wall. It took her a few seconds to clear her head.

As her vision cleared, she saw the knife he dropped just inches from her. She reached for it, clutching it in her hand, and was back on her feet in an instant. The captain had yet another knife and was swinging it at her. Priscilla backed away from the slashes. She readied herself for an opening that would come and it did. She came around with a roundhouse kick aimed for his head, but he ducked. She didn't stop her momentum and came around in a circle for a follow up kick, aimed for the ribs. But the old salty captain once again surprised her, taking the blow as though it was nothing. Clamping her leg to his side and using her momentum, he flung her across the dining room. She slammed into the glass window cracking it, and fell on the table.

She rolled over and dropped on the bench almost falling to the floor. She was barely conscious when he pulled her up from the seat and slammed her down on the table. His knife cut through the air aimed at her face. At that split second, she caught his wrist locked in a battle of strength, she tried kneeing him and kicking to no avail. Her blows were just glancing. The tip of the knife was getting closer, his eyes blazed with victory. Her arms were faltering. He was too strong, his weight was too much.

Then the boat jolted, sending them flying in separate directions. Priscilla fell to her butt; the captain was already back on his feet coming for her. Getting a second wind, she sprang to her feet. She needed to end this now! As he came for her, she met him head on ducking under a slash. She countered with a hard punch to the stomach, which had little effect, but enough to stun him. Before he could counter with another strike, she managed to grab his wrist and hold it long enough while she struck him dead in the nose, palm out, thrusting the cartilage into his brain, he fell instantly, face first to the deck dead.

She didn't even catch her breath. She wiped her face of blood and sweat with no time to spare and picked up the knife continuing onward.

Priscilla burst through the threshold onto the bridge. Vladimir was wildly steering the freighter from the incoming boats. Surprisingly, he was alone. She wasted no time as she made her way towards him. He just happened to turn his head as she approached; he grabbed the gun on the console and blindly fired. His aim was nowhere near her.

Priscilla dropped and rolled in one smooth motion coming to her feet, she threw the knife. The blade found its mark-impaling hilt deep into his forearm. Vladimir screamed out, as Priscilla closed the gap, batting away the gun in his other hand. She then finished him with a crushing blow to the temple, knocking him out cold. She looked up and now joining the Coast Guard was a Navy destroyer.

She had seconds before they blew them out of the water. She tugged him closer to her, pushing him out of the side door, not caring in the least of hurting him further and hoisted him overboard. She followed his unconscious body into the sea, she hated so much. She had just managed to grab him too, before he sank to the depths, pulling him away as fast as she could paddle. All the while trying to avoid swallowing any more seawater, she had enough of that to last her a lifetime.

She glimpsed back at the now out of control freighter being fired upon. In one succession of cannon fire, the ship burst into flames, slowing it down to a crawl. She paddled on, growing tired, looking to land and seeing it ever so far. She looked back, wishing that the Coast Guard could see her. Then in the distance, she heard the familiar sound of the speedboat.

That gave her newfound energy. She looked about, trying to see where it was coming from. She called out, but her voice was hoarse. She finally spotted the idling speedboat with Pietro getting a line ready. She'd never been so happy to see anyone just then. She would have smiled, if not for more water entering her mouth. He helped both of them aboard, settling them. As Pietro sped away, Priscilla stole a look at the freighter now sinking to the depths.

As she sat back water logged, and in massive pain from her broken nose. It dawned on her that she didn't even thank Pietro. She thought he'd have gone back to shore, but here he was rescuing her. For a split second she felt bad for how she treated him in the beginning. Of all the people she could trust with her life, she'd never have thought it. But it was nice to be wrong sometimes.

Chapter 28
Washing away the filth

Down in the bowels of Shadow Ops HQ, after her Decontamination shower. Priscilla sat in the small doctor's office, while the doctor on duty, set her nose back in place. She teared every time he adjusted it. She tried to hold back as best she could, but couldn't help it and to make matters worse. Peter was standing there the whole time laughing and making fun of the whole ordeal while he dried himself off from his Decontamination shower.

"You know I think that might be an improvement, your nose was always crooked! Hey doc maybe you should put it, a little bit to the left." He walked over to do it himself, but a firm smack on the hand from the doctor stopped him. While being worked on and trying to block out Peter. She was trying to think of something to say to the kids. They were not stupid and would be bombarding her with questions.

A car accident would be the simplest thing to say. It left no room for further explanation. And then, the last dilemma was Pietro. She was glad he left after his Decontamination shower. It gave her an easy out. She walked into this clear headed, now walking out, her feelings were torn. She was experiencing a whole slew of emotions going on in her body and mind. And she didn't like it at all. Yes, it felt good, but different. She never felt this way about a man, at her age this was all new. She never fell in love or loved someone other than a friend, and her kids. She started to get a headache thinking about all of it. It was too much right now and needed to be attended to later with a clearer mind.

Because she knew one thing and that was Pietro wasn't going to just up and disappear. After finally cleaning up and being debriefed by John, she left the office heading home. She didn't pick the kids up. She needed to be alone. She was tired and beat to hell, she wouldn't be able to give the kids her undivided attention. Not to mention her patience was rather thin at the moment and the last thing she wanted to do was take it out on them. Pretty much once she stepped into her home, she found her way to the bed, not bothering to get undressed. She threw herself into its embrace and fell fast asleep.

Epilogue
Monthly Visit

The following morning came and she was refreshed. Although still in pain it wasn't something she couldn't deal with. She didn't wake up on her own either. The chiming of her doorbell pulled her from her sleep. She figured it was the neighbor. He was nice enough to grab her mail when she was out of town. She cursed his timing; she could have used a few more hours. Wiping the sleep away from her eyes, she opened the door greeting whoever it was with a bandaged nose and a yawn. She was immediately taken out of her half-asleep stupor seeing that it wasn't the neighbor. But a flower delivery. The man had a large bouquet of red, yellow and white roses, to say she was surprised was the understatement of the year.

"Uh.... I think you have the wrong house mister." The man looked at the invoice quickly shaking his head.

"Sorry, this is the address, 44 Roc Lane."

He said flatly, not showing any reaction to her appearance. "I'll take it you're Priscilla Roletti?" She nodded. "If you wouldn't mind signing, please." She did so, taking the flowers.

"Who sent these?" She said as the man turned to leave.

"Don't know, ma'am. There's a card attached, have a great day." He said rudely and left. She didn't blame him, she'd have responded with the same answer. She closed the door, inhaling the fresh scent of the beautiful roses. She hated flowers they reminded her of wakes. She then immediately ripped open the card wondering who in the world would send her such a gorgeous arrangement.

"Priscilla, we didn't get a chance to say goodbye, so I thought it was best to send you some roses. I hope you like them. I didn't get the chance to say thank you for saving my life. It's something I'll never forget. In the short time I've known you, it felt like forever. I've never met a woman like you before, and I'm sure I never will. You're one of a kind! In my eyes you're the perfect woman. With that, at the bottom of this letter is my number. Please do not hesitate to call for anything, and if not, I wish the best to you and your family. I only wish we met under better circumstances and we were in different places in our lives.

Pietro."

She reread the letter five times... She was dumbfounded. She didn't know what to say, or think for that matter. Her heart was racing, thinking of what the possibilities could be... It took all of her will power not to call him right then and there. Plus, she wondered how the hell, he found out where she lived? She'd think long and hard on all this later…much, much later...right now she was running late.

Before taking care of a very important errand. Priscilla wanted to quickly stop by Pats' to see the kids. As soon as she walked in the door, the kids ran to her with open arms hugging and kissing her. Asking what happened, where did it happen, and if the guy who hit their mom was arrested. Kids, she often wondered where they picked this stuff up from. It was amusing at times. Once she felt the kids were content, she told them to go and play while she talked to their uncle. She could tell from the look on his face that he wanted a moment alone. Pat already had the morning's paper and thrust it in her hands. The headline read.

'Terrorists foiled in attempted NYC attack!'

She didn't read further. She had no interest in the spin that was given to the public. Pat beamed like a proud dad.

"I'm gonna frame this! I swear to God." He said smiling. He hugged her tightly, "I want you to sign it before I do of course." He said when he pulled away. She wanted to stay and fill him in on everything. She most definitely needed to, especially pertaining to Pietro. But she had to go. She didn't even tell the kids she was leaving, she wouldn't be gone for long.

It was raining…. that slow constant drizzle. It always rained for some odd reason when she came here. It was like an unseen sadness coming from the heavens. There were many people here today as well. Walking the narrow walkways of grass with tombstones on either side of the lost but never forgotten loved ones. One particular person walked alone deep into the cemetery. She walked past a grieving widow in the row to her left. She paid no mind to her and kept walking with her head down. She finally made her way to the second to last tombstone. She stopped, lowered her head, and said a silent prayer. She then placed a single orchid on the stone. The rain was coming down a little harder now. She paid little mind to it though, she was lost in thought, staring at the name inscribed.

Anthony Joseph Roletti
Born 1939
Died 1992

Like Priscilla told Pietro, she never met her father, which was the truth. But what she did lie about was the fact that soon after she was in Shadow Ops she did seek out her father. She wanted to know why? Why he abandoned her to the care of a cruel woman? Why he chose not to watch his daughter grow-up, into a fine young woman? Priscilla hoped that maybe she could find a piece of herself that she was long missing.

But she was too late… by the time she found the man she'd call dad, he had died. As it turned out, her father never left her. He had intended to come back when he became someone his daughter could look up to. He came around, almost two years after she was born, and her mother lied to him saying that she lost the child. She found out these facts by going to see his wife. Priscilla's father married the following year to a good woman, a far cry from her mother. The woman told her that Priscilla's father was heart stricken with grief that not only did he leave you, but then finding out you had died in childbirth. It was something that stayed with him until he died. The woman was nice enough to give Priscilla a picture of him. Thinking of these things, Priscilla wanted to cry. She wanted to cry until her eyes went dry. But unfortunately, she could do nothing; all she could do was learn from it.

She never confronted her mother with this either. What was the point? It was yet another sin she found herself to forgive her mother for. She was almost in her eighties and no doubt, guilt was tearing at her for all the things she had done. Hence her complete turn around when Priscilla came back into her life and was the grandmother of the year, or so she liked to think she was. No, she'd let the guilt eat at her. She figured starting a fight over it would benefit her mother more anyway. She thrived on controversy and confrontation.

An hour passed by and Priscilla never moved from the spot she was in. She was sopping wet, but it was time to go. She'd be back in a month, and sooner or later she'd see him when it was her time. She stepped closer to the stone, kissing the top, resting her lips there for a few seconds. She then finally pushed off, reluctantly walking back to her minivan and going home.

Vol. 2 Shadow Chasers

Chapter 1
Hitting the Road

San Francisco, California.

The night was clear and crisp; the breeze coming in from the San Francisco Bay was a relief from the unseasonably humid day. It was almost midnight; the weather for Sunday was supposed to be a little cooler than the day before. At this hour many were in bed sleeping, while others were out partying and drinking to their heart's desires. Boats littered the Bay, anchored in for the night, some with lights on, some with lights off. There were even parties on the larger boats, with people dancing the night away. In one of the many buildings overlooking the Bay, there was a single light on that stood out in the skyline.

That lonely office was on the top floor, and inside that office was Carmine Christie, he was an out of shape man in his mid-sixties with a full head of gray hair. He shuffled off his tailored suit jacket, and threw it across his chair. He was pacing back and forth behind his large black desk. His footsteps were barely audible across the dark gray carpet.

On the other side of the office sitting, and facing him on the white couch, was his brand new and very beautiful secretary who only started a week and a half ago. She had been working late nights like these almost ever since she started there. She was casual in her white collared shirt and black loose fitting silk skirt that stopped right at the middle of her knees. Her black-rimmed eyeglasses were perched atop her short blonde hair. She had her legs crossed, with a laptop leaning on her thigh. She was typing an email that he was dictating to her. For the last week, he has been tying up loose ends, and taking care of business before relinquishing control of his company to his partner.

Carmine was going away, never to be seen again. He knew he'd be leaving, but didn't know when until two nights ago. It came very suddenly; that was the reason for the late nights. He stopped by the window looking out on the Bay, probably wishing he were on one of those boats. He stopped talking as he looked out, and his secretary stopped typing while she waited for him to continue. The sounds of footsteps fell faintly behind the closed door; inside neither one heard the footfalls approaching along the thickly carpeted hallway. If they did, they'd assume it was the custodial staff hurrying about, trying to finish their work early so they could spend the rest of their shift relaxing.

But they would soon learn it wasn't, when three men suddenly burst their way into the office, with guns drawn, they were dressed in black suits and ties.

The last one in backhanded the secretary hard across the face. Her glasses flew off, hitting the floor, she tasted blood as she fell over stunned. The laptop she was using almost fell to the floor, but she had enough sense to grip it tighter. The man that smacked her stood with his back to her, not worrying about the helpless woman being a threat.

The other two men stood facing her boss now. Carmine had his hands raised high and you could see the sweat beading from his forehead. There was fear in his eyes as all three men were pointing their handguns at him. The man closest to Carmine spoke.

"Well…well Carmine, it was a long shot you being here still," the man said, looking to the other two men behind him. "So much for the freelancers, huh boys?" He said through grinning teeth. His partners agreed with him. The man that spoke looked back to Carmine, with his smile fading.

"Please! Please! I will give you anything please! I just wanna be left alone! I'll quadruple whatever you're being paid I swear!" Carmine was frantic now. He would make a deal with Satan himself to get out of this one.

"Oh yeah? Well, what we're being paid is an awful lot." It looked as though the man was thinking about it. "Nah, we don't negotiate with targets, besides I wouldn't want to cross this guy. Now if you have anything pertaining to our client on that computer I want copies and then delete it."

Under the watchful eyes of the three men, Carmine went and did what he was told to do. They seemed to have forgotten about the lowly secretary sprawled out with her eyes closed. She waited until she felt the men were totally focused on Carmine.

She opened one eye slowly, then the other. She sat up, firmly holding the laptop on her lap, and removed the screen that was attached to the base. She did this while keeping her eyes on the three men. Not even Carmine could see what she was doing. His nervous eyes focused on his computer monitor.

Underneath the base was a cleverly concealed button. Pressing it, she pulled the bottom piece sideways, which revealed a holdout automatic weapon that was hidden within. Her sapphire-blue eyes were filled with anger as she raised her weapon with the controlled precision of a pro; she fired, taking out the man closest to her with a clean headshot. The other two turned around the instant they heard the gunfire, seeing their comrade fall.

Carmine ducked underneath his desk like a scared kid. Before the second man closest to her could fire his weapon, he was shot twice in the chest and dropped. She kept her finger on the trigger firing in the direction of the third intruder, punching holes in the thick glass window that might have shattered if the weapon had not jammed just then.

The third man was nowhere to be seen. She tossed the useless automatic to the floor, and got up, walking towards the desk when the third man sprung up from behind it, arm straight in a firing position. She darted forward and to the side before he could react. Closing the gap quickly, she grabbed his wrist and elbow, twisting them into positions they couldn't go naturally. The cracking of bones filled the air as the gun dropped to the floor, the man winced in pain. She pulled his now broken arm behind him, and kicked him in the knee. Twisting his head almost backwards, he fell forward with a thump. She picked up the dead man's gun and kicked the door closed. Discovering the lock was busted; she pulled the couch over quickly. It was a loveseat and easy to move. After she blocked the door shut, she turned to the desk.

"Carmine get up…we're leaving." She said in a matter of fact tone, as if none of the events had happened. He got up slowly, his hands were shaking. He stood before her looking around with an obvious fear in his eyes.

"Who… Who are you?" He blurted out.

"I wouldn't worry about who I am right now, shut up, and do as I say, got it?" He just nodded.

"Good. Now gather whatever you need and hurry up!"

"Yes…yes right away." As Carmine, made various copies of data, he couldn't help glimpsing at this beautiful deadly woman. She tore away her black skirt revealing not her undergarments, but the top half of black slacks with a .22 caliber pistol concealed at her waist. The leggings fell down over her firm legs to her ankles, covering the black high-heeled boots she wore. The material of the slacks was so light you couldn't even notice that she had anything like that on underneath her skirt. As he was working, she walked to the bodies and knelt down, checking them.

She took the pistols from the dead men and checked their pockets for ID. They had none. She checked the cell phone of the man who she thought was the leader of the trio, scrolling through the menu. There were no saved numbers and no calls made or received. Tossing it to the side, she stuffed the two guns in her waist. She then walked to the large window overlooking the city; it was so peaceful, so quiet.

"I'm guessing you're my contact, right?" Carmine asked, intruding into her thoughts. She turned around, and studied him with piercing cold eyes.

"Yes Carmine, my name is Priscilla. I will be your guardian angel for the next few days."

"Thank God, you were here. I didn't know how long I could stall them." He grabbed a brown leather suitcase from underneath his desk, it was packed with the essentials he'd be needing for his abrupt departure. Deodorant, a change of clothes and a few other personal hygiene items.

He turned to her and she looked at him, never blinking. Keeping her eyes right on his, she wanted to make her point clear.

"Now listen to me and listen good. You need to do exactly as I say. Interfere in any way and I'll kill you myself…understand?"

"Yes, you'll get no trouble out of me."

"Good. Let's go." They made their way over the bodies. As they stepped on the blood-soaked carpet, Carmine looked down and quickly looked away in horror. He was going to gag. She pushed the loveseat aside and swung the door open. She looked down the hall, ready to jump back into the office if she had to. From here, it looked to be clear. She took point and they walked quickly to the elevator without incident.

When they got down to the white-tiled lobby, the black marbled desk where the night guard should've been was vacant. She walked over and saw the guard laying face down in a puddle of blood. Before her was a glass wall leading out to the street. In the center was a revolving door and two side doors flanking it. She wasn't sure if there were more men out there lying in wait. She took out her cell phone, flipping it open she tapped on some keys and closed it, stuffing it back in her pocket.

"What are we waiting for?" He asked nervously.

"Our ride." They heard a car in the distance. "Move!" Grabbing him by the arm, she pulled him into one of the halls that connected to the main lobby. Right where they had just been standing, a light shone on the white wall. A black Dodge Charger smashed its way into the building, sending glass and debris everywhere. The vehicle parked where the circular desk used to be. It was angled sideways; the driver's door was facing the wall where they had just been standing.

She walked out from their cover, looked around, and then quickly walked to the door. Opening it, she gestured for him to get in. He moved as fast as his out-of-shape legs could carry him. Holding the suitcase in both arms to his chest, he moved over to the passenger seat. Just then, gunfire hit the window where his head had been. He ducked down. The window was still there protecting him as the bullets harmlessly ricocheted off. She quickly followed him in. The bullets were now flying relentlessly as she slammed her door closed.

"Buckle up, Carmine!" She spun the back tires, creating a cloud of smoke, the car bolted out of the lobby. Two men firing their automatic weapons stood in front of her trying to stop the speeding car. She careened straight for them. One man got out of the way in time; the other was not so lucky. She ran right over him and they both felt his body underneath the wheels as they sped off into the night.

Carmine twisted his shaking body around. He watched the building that housed his company fade into the distance. He saw more figures running towards a car in front of the shattered lobby.

As his eyes were on the car that was about to give chase, he didn't take notice as to what Priscilla was doing.

She engaged her weapons system that were concealed in the middle console. The LCD touchscreen that was installed in the dashboard, served as the HUD (heads up display) for her rear defenses. A green cross hair centered itself on the car behind them. Seconds later, Carmine heard something that sounded like bottle rockets being fired off. He could not see what it was, but he saw two trails of smoke rocketing towards the car from the rear of their car.

The explosion of the other car lit up the night sky for the moment. The vibrations shattered the rest of the glass entranceway to his office building. He turned around not saying anything. He didn't even bother to ask what that was or where it came from. He looked at the woman whom he thought was his new secretary, eyeing her up and down. She had a look of stone as she drove. She was a pro, taking corners at high speeds, without even flinching.

"What are you looking at?" She asked suddenly.

"Nothing… I-" He was going to continue saying something, but was cut off.

"Good, keep it that way and we'll have no problems." He stared straight ahead, watching her weave in and out of lanes going even faster. He was scared.

"I think we're safe now, don't you?"

"Shut up!" She snapped, looking at him quickly with menace as she drove. Keeping her eyes on the road, she took out her cell phone, and sent a text message. For the past week and a half she had been there, playing secretary to her boss, she had to endure his nastiness. He spoke to people as if they were below him. He was just like many other white-collar bosses, a total scumbag. It took all her will power not to smack him upside his head when he spoke to her like that for fear of blowing her cover.

But now she wouldn't hold back if he stepped out of line. His eyes shifted back to the road, watching where they were going and watching the signs. They were coming up to a sign that read 'Airport.'

"Wait! You're not going to the airport are you?"

She didn't answer him. "We're not flying out of here, are we? Please tell me we're not!" He said this with a hint of annoyance laced with an underlying fear. "I'm not a healthy man. I have medical ailments that restrict me from flying! And I...I…oh my God! I have no medication either!"

"Relax Carmine, relax. Don't have a breakdown on me already. I'm well aware of your health issues." She leaned over opening the glove box in front of him, revealing five bottles in single file. He picked one up, squinting as he read the label, then placed it back inside with a look of worry in his eyes.

"I also know about your issue with flying, so don't worry, I wouldn't want anything to happen to you, now would I?" She said ever so sarcastically. She paused, and then continued. "Just sit back and relax. Try not to aggravate me too much on the trip ok?" He said not a word more, his face said it all. The fear he had turned to frustration over the helplessness of the situation. She was going to enjoy putting him through this. The high and mighty man next to her was now a nobody.

As they crossed over the Bay Bridge, Priscilla couldn't help but take in the view. How nice it would have been to come here and just be on vacation. From her time in San Francisco, it seemed to be a nice enough place to visit. Right at the end of the bridge, was their exit. The I-80, was the main artery that went across the country East and West. It was now a straight path to the finish line. Hopefully it would be an easy straight path, but she knew it wouldn't be. With this job, the word easy was nonexistent.

Chapter 2
John Derlin

It was 2 a.m. Eastern time and sitting at his desk was John Derlin, Chief Executive Director of Shadow Ops. Shadow Ops, was a mere rumor among the other agencies of the government, it was founded to handle the most delicate 'dirty' assignments. They operate under their own set of guidelines; they have been known to bend the rules to the breaking point in the name of justice.

Although they work outside the law, they are not above the law; Derlin believed, along with Ronald Reagan, that swift and decisive action was needed to handle matters of great importance. He was reading the text message he had just received from Priscilla.

"Homeward bound." That was all it read and that was all he needed to know. He got up from his chair, looking out to the city. Seeing the cars from this height made them look like little specks of light going back and forth. He lit a match, and inserted it into the pipe clenched between his teeth. The lighting shadowed his face and reflected his image on the window.

"And so, it begins." He said softly, as he blew out the smoke in a slow exhale. This was going to be a nail biter, the Intel on what to expect was minimal.

The man they were protecting, Carmine Christie, was a slippery little bastard indeed. He had valuable information, and would only give it up if he was promised that he could be brought in and protected. In the very beginning, when he came forward, he was asked to show proof of what he had to warrant such demands; and he did, presenting only enough to whet their appetites. As it turned out, the information he provided was legit. When he was convinced he was safe, he would divulge the rest of the data.

According to him, he had this information in New York City and only he could ascertain it. For almost six months, he established contacts and brokered deals that promised to bring him in under protective custody. But the catch was, how to do it. The best way was to fly, but that was a no-go. Carmine had issues with his health, and an outright fear of flying. Plus, there was the known factor of potential hostiles.

Therefore, driving was the only way. The oversight committee hated collateral damage; something that was most likely to happen. Even an organization such as Shadow Ops couldn't cover that up.

If the wrong people wanted something badly enough, they would go through extreme measures to get it. Reports surfaced from informants close to the 'underworld' that a contract was out on Carmine, and a very large one. It didn't matter that no one knew who put the hit out, but every 'pro' in the business would be all over it. It would be only a matter of time before they tracked down Carmine.

Chapter 3
The Gathering

That very same night, in the middle of nowhere, far off the main road in the vast Nevada desert, there was a gathering of the most wretched scum and villainy you could possibly imagine. The night was already dark and eerie, and the individuals congregating there made it worse. Their vehicles were parked in a circle and all the occupants were in the middle talking. There were eight souls in all.

The Tomma sisters, Lisa and Kim, were almost identical twin sisters who grew up in an upper-class environment. Yet, for some odd reason they decided to embark on a journey into the world of professional killers. These two were thrill-seekers that wanted the real life-or-death experience of the chase.

The Applegate brothers, who were not blood-related at all, were a bunch of derelict country boys who didn't have a great record of accomplishment in this business. Sure, they were a tough bunch, but they were considered fuck-ups who always got close at times, but never close enough.

There were two other rogues' also. They were all called here for the same purpose. In the distance, headlights were piercing through the darkness, heading towards them, the bright beams of light caught their attention, putting a halt to their conversations.

The outline of the vehicle looked to be a new model Hummer. As the vehicle came closer, its lights were shut off. It stopped in the open gap of the vehicles. They all waited for their host to get out. A figure made its way out of the passenger side, walking towards the front of the vehicle; he stood there looking at the ensemble.

He wore a trench coat with a fedora that was tilted down, covering his face. Even though it was dark, he could still make out some of the faces of the other people standing before him. He peered at the vast turnout, sizing them up; he was pleased that his call had received so many takers.

"Thank you all for coming. I must say I'm quite impressed with the response that I have received." He spoke with a German accent.

"Well, what you're offering is quite impressive." The burly voice said, interrupting his would-be boss. The voice came from the man standing off to the side. He was a six-foot plus mountain of muscle. His head was shaved bald and he had a sleeve of tattoos on both arms. The T-shirt he was wearing looked to be a bit small for him as if it was straining to cover his mammoth torso.

He was an Aryan skinhead known as Shultz, and someone who dared you to fuck with him. He was so full of hate and anger that it was said even his own brotherhood of Aryan skinheads looked upon him with distaste for the way he carried himself and turned their backs on him not wanting anything to do with him. He then decided to use his talents elsewhere, by being a hired thug. Bruising, beating or even killing for a price.

"Yes, it is, my friend." Said the Shadow, looking to the mountain of a man. He then continued to address the rest of them.

"Now here it is in full everyone." He was about to continue when he took notice to something. He did not see two very familiar faces. "Wait, there are two missing. I guess my offer did not entice them enough. Oh well what a shame."

Just as the words came from the Shadow, in the distance, they all heard the sound of a speeding motorcycle racing towards them. Like the other pros here, no one knew this was going to be a meeting with other hired guns, except the Shadow, and the Shadow knew who was coming. The Ninja motorcycle pulled right up into the middle of the circle, kicking up sand and dirt. They coughed and cursed from the display of disrespect that was just shown to them all.

As the dust cleared, the two on the bike removed their helmets revealing the familiar faces known to them all. It was the infamous Trish and Omar. They shut off their bike, and got off.

"Sorry about that, we were a little tied up. I hope we didn't miss anything yet." Omar said this with fake sincerity. The truth of the matter was they were not tied up, but one of their many long lines of hapless women were. Their sexual lust, mixed with their psychotic minds, was something of a nightmare for whoever happened to be picked. Most of the time it was fueled by drug binges. Over the years, there have been many rape/murder cases that have baffled authorities by their hands.

"No, not at all my friends, welcome, I was just saying to the others that maybe you thought my offer was not to your liking."

"Not at all. For $100 million, we'd do anything."

"Yeah! We know ya freaks!" Trish and Omar looked over to where the comment came from. It was from the lips of the skinhead that was staring at them with contempt.

"Why'd you call these fucking spics for?" The Aryan looked to the Shadow asking the question, pointing his thumb towards them.

"What! You talking about us? Then look at us mother fucker!" This came from Trish, who was a curvy thick woman with long jet-black hair. She wore black spandex pants with a white tank top and black combat boots up to her knees. She may not look like much at first glance, but if you were to be on her hit list, you'd know the meaning of the word pain. With her temper, she would never back down from a fight.

"Yeah! I'm talking about you, what the fuck you gonna do about it, huh?" Shultz said, taking a step closer to the pair. Omar stood there taking it all in as he ran a finger over his thin mustache. He was the more civilized of the two and no one would ever see him dressed in the way his sister was. He always wore a three-piece suit. However, don't let his charm fool you. He was just as crazy as his sister. Maybe more so with his crazed sexual addiction. He was never the vocal type like his sister, he was more of an actions speak louder than words type.

"What am I gonna do?" She stepped closer to Shultz saying the words, as Omar followed her.

"I'm gonna bury you!"

"Yeah! I would love to see it freak! Why don't you go fuck your skinny ass brother! Oh wait, you do that already!" A loud bellow of laughter filled the air, but it only came from the skinhead. The others either didn't find the comment funny or didn't dare to invoke Trish or Omar's anger onto them as well.

"Fuck off!" She said with the deepest contempt for the skinhead. The tension was so thick you could cut it with a knife. The other pros looked on waiting, maybe even hoping that these three would take each other out, lessening the competition.

"Come on now, can't you guys just let the man say what he has to say? The more you fight the more distance our quarry gets." The words came out of nowhere. All three involved in the standoff looked in the direction of where the words came from. Walking up was the Albino, his skin and hair were as white as a skull with eyes that looked like gold nuggets in his sockets.

"Hey! Whitey! Mind your own fucking business, ok! If ya want a piece too, come on! Come on bring it! Both of ya!" Trish yelled out, with a fire in her eyes. The Albino tilted his cowboy hat up a little. Smirking at Trish, he started to walk over to take the challenge, but was stopped by the bear like hand of the skinhead.

"Hey! They're mine! I'll take a lot of pleasure in gutting their hides." A smile crept up on his face with those words as he looked over to Trish.

"Oh yeah Fucko! Come on! Do it! Let's go now!"

The four were just looking for a reason to pounce on each other when a resounding boom echoed through the vast desert. The gathering all looked in the direction of the gunshot as they went for their weapons. It came from the Shadow that had a smoking Lugar pistol in his hand.

"If you four want to kill each other, fine! But let me say what I have to say and be off, do I make myself clear?" The words hung in the air for a moment and the four nodded, stepping back.

"Good. Now, as I was saying, what I have to offer is simple. Your target is a man who I am willing to pay a hefty fee, alive if possible…if not, that is fine also, but the fee will be reduced. In return you are to ask no questions. I'm sure he knows we're after him and has taken precautions, as I would have if I were in his shoes. They will most likely be driving from San Francisco to New York City. That is all the information I have at this time. That's all you have to work with."

The Shadow turned to the Hummer, gesturing to the driver. Getting out, the driver walked towards the front of the Hummer. In his hand were five USB data sticks'. He placed them on the hood.

"All the information you need will be on the data stick, for whoever completes the mission, there is also contact information to get in touch for payment. Also, there's a bank number on all the flash drives, it's your down payment of $100,000." He looked at the group. They were all in heavy thought, most likely thinking of ways to catch their "mark" and throw a monkey wrench in their competitor's wheels as well.

"Now if there are no further questions…" He waited a moment, looking to each and every one. "Happy hunting." He stepped back as they all rushed to the hood of the Hummer grabbing a data stick. All the while, Trish, Omar, and the other two were sizing each other up. They finally broke their standoff when Omar grabbed the data. Trish stood where she was, pointing to the skinhead.

"Mark my words scumbag!" She said the words slowly, trying very hard to control herself. "I'm gonna bury you before this is over!" All the skinhead did was flash a smile, disregarding what she said with a hand of dismissal and walked off to his truck. The desert filled with the sounds of vehicles starting up, tearing up the still desert sand into a dust cloud. Inside the Hummer, the Shadow watched with a smile on his face.

Chapter 4
The Open Road

Priscilla had the pedal floored doing an average of 100mph. The car had a cloaking device that made it invisible to the radar detectors and other high tech devices the police force used in speed traps. During the night, I-80 wasn't as deserted as she would have thought. She shared the highway mostly with tractor-trailers and the occasional car, with sporadic lights thrown about that illuminated the highway. This part of I-80 was surrounded by a vast desert, save for the occasional truck stop here or there it was completely desolate.

With the sun creeping over the horizon in front of them, she put on a pair of black sunglasses and looked over to her companion. During the course of their drive, he got heavy-eyed, so he reclined his seat and nodded off. She had little to say to him. She wondered how he managed to get himself into the trouble he was in. Whatever it was, he realized he was in way over his head, and wanted a free ticket out.

This mission was unexpected to say the least. John called her on a Friday morning telling her to be ready to go by that night. She would be departing for California. She had to scramble the rest of the day; she had kids to take care of and on such short notice, it was hard to find someone to care for them.

She asked her friend Pat to watch them. Of course, he was more than willing to do so. She knew he would always say yes, but she hated to inconvenience anyone with spur of the moment things. So, with her childcare situation taken care of, she was off. John briefed her en route, telling her only the man's name, his home address, and place of business. That information was sent along with his picture to her cell phone.

He also said he was working out some arrangements with the man, and to stand by and wait for his call on when the time to move would be. All the identification for her cover would be in her car already in California and waiting for her in the airport parking garage. She asked what she was supposed to do when she was in place. All John told her was that when the time came, she was to see him safely to Manhattan and to be prepared for hostiles along the way. She was told that there most definitely would be a contract on his head, and a high one at that. As far as the takers on the contract went, she was sure the three men from last night were just the tip of the iceberg, but for now so far so good.

She happened to take notice of a caravan that drove by with three kids in the back; one of the kids looked her way, and waved.

The boy couldn't have been more than six or seven. She returned the gesture. She was reminded of her kids and now she wondered how they were doing. She had not called them in a few days. She wasn't worried, but it felt good to hear their voices at times like this, when she felt surrounded by the chaos the world had to offer. The sun was shining on Carmine's sleeping face. A few minutes later he opened his eyes to the blaring sunlight. He blinked rapidly as he tried to block it out with a raised hand. Sitting up, he yawned and looked at his bodyguard.

"Where are we?" He asked, groggily.

"We're almost out of Nevada, believe it or not, just coming up to a town called Elko."

"Never even heard of it," he said dryly, slowly waking up.

The highway was slowly coming alive with traffic. With the morning hours, various cars and trucks were cruising by, people going to work, going on vacation, or going to wherever their destination was to be. During the night, she didn't really see the landscape well, but now, for as far as the eyes could see, it was all desert, vast and unending.

"Are we going to stop soon? I gotta take a piss. Maybe a place where they serve breakfast too would be great. I'll treat if you like." His usual demands were now requests like a kid asking his mother for something. She was glad that he was learning his place with her, but this was going to be fucking annoying every goddamn morning stopping to eat. She could go for a decent amount of time not eating a good meal.

While in San Francisco, she prepared for this inevitable road trip. In the backseat, she had a black duffle bag that had a few protein bars, and bottles of water. All she wanted to do was get him from point A to point B. She wondered if he knew the kind of people that would be coming for him eventually. Come to think about it, she was wondering too. She reached in the backseat; grabbed a protein bar and threw it on his lap.

"Eat that for now. I wanna get a good distance away and then we'll stop. And hold it in, you're a big boy. I'm sure you won't wet your pants." She could see it in his eyes, he was cursing her, but he knew better than to say it to her face. She would not think twice about giving him a black eye. She had to protect him, not be nice to him. He tore into the wrapper with his teeth, taking a bite he chewed slowly. He gagged on the foul tasting bar, with his face turning red, he rolled the window down and threw it out.

"What the hell is that? Are you trying to kill me?" He said, wiping his mouth on his sleeve, his face looked contorted with the bad taste he experienced. She blindly reached in the back for a bottle of water; handing it to him, Priscilla smiled.

"Didn't like my protein bars, huh? Oh well, fine. We'll stop at the first roadside rest area, we see, ok?" He nodded. The diner they came up upon was a small mom and pop place. The food was good, but Priscilla couldn't stand the overly friendly waitress, she found her to be annoying. Carmine didn't seem to care. He ate his two scrambled eggs and hash browns without a word being spoken. Finishing, he pushed his plate to the side, taking up his coffee.

"You know, if we have time when we get closer to New York, I know of some great places to eat." He said, looking at her over the rim of his cup as he took a sip.

"Yeah, that's nice." Her tone implying she could care less. That's why you're out of shape too, you fat ass! She wanted to really say that, but held her tongue since he was behaving himself now.

"Oh, come on! Stop being a bitch, will you? Are you mad at me for something?" She looked to him with a raised eyebrow; she was going to say something, but thought better of it shaking her head.

"No, not really, just keeping you in check."

"Hmm, there was a 'not really' in there, what was it? Tell me?"

She put her coffee cup down, giving him that look of you asked for it.

"Well, for starters, the way you not only talked to me, but to the people who worked under you. You have no idea how badly I wanted to smash your face in the other day." He looked at her puzzled; he was trying to remember what she was talking about. Then with a snap of his fingers, he remembered what she might have been referring to.

"Ah, yes when you brought me the wrong documents, well honey, that's how it is in corporate, things have to be done, and there is no time for screw ups. I'll be honest with you; I had left a memo for my partner to fire you. I didn't think at the time you were a very good secretary, but if it's any consolation, you'd make a better bodyguard." She squinted her eyes at him while he was grinning at her.

"Gee, thanks." She said dryly. She held her face even, but it was funny though. She wasn't that great, the one thing she hated while working for him was the sitting in one area all day, it drove her nuts. Taking phone calls, typing up letters, proofreading. That whole week felt like an eternity now that she thought about it. The waitress came over with a pot of coffee, checking to see if they wanted a refill. She asked for the check. Finishing up, they were on their way, back on what seemed like the never-ending road.

The sun was slowly setting behind them. They were making great time so far, about 25 miles from Salt Lake City. I-80 was starting to fill up a bit the closer they got to the city. Carmine read his paper most of the way. They made small talk here and there. She wanted to ask what his deal was, but then if it was her business to know John would have told her. She'd most likely want to kick him out the car if he told her, so it was better to leave well enough alone.

With no sign of trouble, she was starting to think that maybe this would be a cut and dry run, a first in this line of work. It was something she'd take any day. Perhaps whoever is after him might not have realized their way of travel, and if they did, they would be long out of reach by now.

Well, she hoped anyway. With the increase of other vehicles on the highway, she took notice of a Ford International box truck rolling by; she watched it as it went. She looked up and saw a man in the passenger seat. He was looking down at her, smiling. He wore shades. She looked away, not even acknowledging him. He must have thought her to be a bitch, and that was fine by her, but for some odd reason she felt him still staring at her. She looked back up and she was right, he was. Only this time he waved, she returned the gesture, hoping to satisfy his ego.

Stupid ass, what did he think? I was gonna pull over and flag him down for his number? She thought to herself. The truck signaled to change lanes. Now in front of her the truck decreased speed. What did you change lanes for goddammit? God, how she hated some drivers. Carmine was not paying attention. He kept reading the paper. It was yesterday's, but it was something to keep him occupied at least. As he read the article about a house fire that took place the day before in a small suburb. The rear door suddenly rolled up. Priscilla watched it happen in slow motion, not believing what the hell was about to happen.

"Holy shit!" Before Carmine could ask what was the matter, he saw it for himself. A heavy machine gun was poised and opened fire.

Chapter 5
The Applegate Brothers

Marcus was driving, ever since they spotted the black car they were trying to figure out a way to pull it over without destroying it. They figured a few warning shots would do the trick. By now, the damned car would be destroyed along with the passengers. He slid the back viewport, yelling in.

"What the hell are you doing?!"

Clive came over, it sounded like he was rummaging through something as he replied,

"James put a few rounds in the car, but nothing happened."

"What do you mean nothing happened? Them is god damn 20mm rounds, should have tore that car apart!" Marcus said, sounding dumbfounded over the roar of the machine gun fire.

"Yeah, well it didn't. It's taking the rounds with hardly a dent to the car, so we're gonna have to resort to a more drastic measure!" Marcus watched the road, his eyes were wide, as he sideswiped cars, he passed trying to keep ahead of the Charger.

"What in the hell does he mean by more drastic measure?" He said aloud more to himself than to his passenger.

The high-powered bullets came at the windshield so fast that she couldn't see what was in front of her; the bullets were leaving white marks from the impacts. The man behind the mini Gatling gun had shoulder straps on that were latched to the inside roof of the box truck, keeping him secure from falling out with the erratic movements the driver was making to keep the Charger behind them. The gun itself was mounted to the floor on a tripod. She swerved out of the way quickly running other cars off the road. Wild bullets were hitting the cars and trucks, sending them off the road smoking from the damage they received.

There was too much traffic. Every time she ran someone off the road another car was there to take its place. She was trapped, the box truck obstructed her every move. Other cars on the road either sped up or pulled back trying to get out of the way of the flying bullets. Seeing that she was trying to maneuver around him, the driver of the box truck kept blocking her. As he did this, he too was running cars off the road. The rain of gunfire was still coming, when another man appeared from the back of the truck. In his hand was a lit stick of dynamite. He threw it at the roof of the car. It blew up on impact sending the black car swerving, which almost hit a minivan that was trying to escape the assault. She looked in her rearview mirror and saw no oncoming cars directly behind her.

"Hold on!" She yelled as she slammed on her brakes. She skidded to a halt, as smoke billowed from the tires that nearly engulfed the car. She locked her elbows, to keep from going forward with the momentum.

Carmine flew forward, flipping his paper in the air, and hit his head on the dashboard. The driver of the box truck kept going; evidently not expecting that. She righted the car and sped back up, giving chase. She reached to the middle console sliding back the cover. The HUD came up on the windshield; green cross hairs lined up the box truck. Numbers were counting down the time to when she would be in range of her target. Then the 'target locked' appeared just below the cross hairs. The front headlights had already slid back into the vehicle revealing two rockets that came hurtling out, trailing lines of smoke in their wake. The two in the truck gazed in horror at the unexpected attack.

On impact, the truck exploded, sending large chunks of debris all over the road.

"Hold on!" She yelled to him again, as they rocketed through the remnants of the truck that lay on the highway. They were going almost 150mph now, weaving in and out of lanes that other cars occupied. Leaving behind the destruction that was now helping them make their getaway.

Chapter 6
Don't get Cocky

"Not a bad bit of driving huh, Carmine?" Priscilla said with a hint of cockiness. As they continued on their way, he didn't even bother to look or respond to her comment. He kept his eyes on the road. For a second, she thought he was going to have a nervous breakdown back there. While she was trying to save their skin, he broke out in that cold sweat. Now with it all clear, he sat back up a little, wiping his brow on the sleeve of his suit jacket. He loosened his tie, with trembling hands.

He looked to his right and left, seeing cars go by in a blur. He gasped as he looked into the mirror. Hearing it, she looked at him and saw the look on his face as he turned to her.

"I think we're in trouble," was all he said. She looked at him for a second longer, then into her rearview mirror.

"Oh damn."

Chapter 7
Trish and Omar

"Well? Did you pick up anything yet?" Trish asked her brother with a bit of an attitude. Omar was in the back of their black Sprinter. Mounted on the wall was an array of screens. He sat in a chair, bolted to the floor, scanning radio waves and cell phone frequencies for any tidbits of information that might lead them to their target. One of the small screens was a GPS, as he called out directions to her, they checked every pit stop they passed, quickly doing a visual inside as well as the parking lot, then going on to the next. He was flipping switches listening intently for anything. It cost them quite a bit of money, but the equipment they had was top of the line and could descramble any type of encrypted frequency no matter how advanced.

They learned from experience, this was almost always a surefire thing. No matter who you were, you always needed to talk to someone and they were sure their quarry was no exception.

Once locked, the CPU would send the coordinates to the GPS and, bingo. She watched her brother every few seconds while keeping her eyes on the road. She was starting to think this whole thing was a wild goose chase. Trying to locate a single car was hard enough, but having competition was going to make it tougher. That fucking German didn't say anything about that in his message, telling them about this job of a lifetime. If he had, she might have said no. It's bad enough your quarry is a threat, but to have more than one person to watch out for was never a good thing, no matter how experienced you were.

For the better part of the morning, they were driving along on route I-80, then decided to hit the various other routes. They went south of I-80 first, which turned up nothing, now they were heading back to I-80.

"Omar!" She said, yelling louder, glaring at him in the rearview mirror. In all honesty, she wasn't really pissed off that he hasn't answered her yet, she was used to it by now. He never answered her the first time. She knew it was something he did on purpose to piss her off; he loved to push her buttons. No, she was still pissed off at that Aryan skinhead son of a bitch. At the first opportunity, they were going to take him out. One less skinhead in the world would surely be better.

“No Trish, I’m not picking up anything. If I was don’t you think I would have told you?” He said, interrupting her thoughts about the Aryan. She knew he would but her patience was growing thinner by the minute and thinking about the skinhead didn’t help matters. She just hated the whole Neo-Nazi thing. White trash motherfuckers thinking they’re high and mighty, and to call her a spic, that just pissed her off even more. For that she’ll make sure he dies a slow and painful death.

“Ah sis, I have something, about twenty minutes ago, there was some kind of fire involving a box truck. According to the police scanner, there was a black Dodge Charger involved. It left the scene and the police are in pursuit right now as we speak.”

“Box truck, that was the Applegate brothers right?” He nodded. “Dead already.” She said aloud more to herself, without stopping, Trish viciously turned the Sprinter around, she cut off an oncoming car that had barely swerved out of the way, they sped off in the opposite direction to the sound of a pissed off driver.

Trish and Omar got to the scene within 20 minutes only to be stopped by a traffic jam. Ahead of them were the smoking remains of their competition. She couldn’t see the wreckage well, but she could see the billowing black smoke reaching for the sky. She slammed the steering wheel in frustration, cursing, there was nothing they could do at this point. If they double back it would cost time, too much time, and plowing through this would not be smart. They had to keep their cool for now. Something Trish was not so good at.

Chapter 8
The Albino

The dark blue Toyota pickup that was parked in the lot; was nothing special, just another Toyota only this one was an older model with wear and tear. The driver opened the door and a black cowboy boot stepped to the ground, kicking up a bit of dust from the graveled parking lot. The driver looked around. Other than the pit stop, there was nothing but the highway, and the vast desert that surrounded it, a no man's land. The parking area consisted mostly of tractor-trailers along with some cars here and there.

The person in question was the Albino. He drove around the lot before getting out, checking for the Dodge Charger. From what he heard, the bounty was in a black one. They could have ditched it; but it never hurt to make sure. They could be right inside and if not he'd just move on. Besides, with all the searching he'd done so far he wanted a cup of coffee. He could smell the rich aroma protruding from the place as the wind carried it towards him. This pit stop consisted of various enterprises ranging from Dunkin Donuts to a Nathan's and newsstands. There were also small stores that provided everything that the would-be traveler needed while on the road.

As he walked closer he took notice of the sun setting, there was always something peaceful about it. He walked slowly without any purpose in his step. He wore black pants with a black collared shirt and a black leather vest. Atop his head was a black cowboy hat. No one took notice to him at all; at truck stops people saw every type of person imaginable. At this hour, the place was crowded. It was dinnertime and many truckers were pulling in for their coveted home-cooked meal which was dearly missed while living on the road day in and day out. The place even had a buffet.

He was tempted, but from personal experience, these types of buffets were not ones you'd write home about. Making his way to the Dunkin Donuts counter, he ordered his small coffee, paying the clerk with exact change. He walked away, sipping the hot liquid, while peering over the rim with his golden eyes that had this creepy look to them, as if the mere sight of them would evoke death itself. He walked to a vacant table by the wall with the windows to his right. He sat hunched over a bit, but kept a wary eye out. He took in each and every face. He had memorized the picture of this Carmine fellow.

As he took in his surroundings, he could not help but hear laughter next to him. He turned his head slightly, seeing three averaged sized men. They were truckers with flannel collared shirts and caps. They were scruffy faced from not being able to shave for a few days, and they looked at him with wide grins; they tipped their hats up a bit.

"Can I help you boys?" His voice was grainy like sandpaper rubbing in his throat. Their smiles faded after being addressed, and stared at with his golden eyes. As one of them swallowed, you could see his Adam's apple bounce up and down from the fear that was now laid into him and the rest.

"N...no, sir." The one on the right said, trying to keep his fear in check.

The Albino nodded.

"Good." He said, going back to his coffee. Even after the concealed threat he made to the trio, he still felt the six eyes on him. Sometime later, the three men started to talk amongst themselves. He got up and walked to the exit, heading back to his truck. One of the men saw him leaving and waited for him to walk out of the building before he even spoke as if he had superhuman hearing.

"Man, you see that boy? He looked like he could melt ice with them there eyes." The man on the far left said, the man in the middle nodded,

"He sure did, yeah; you both just froze up though, buncha pussies, we should go out there and smack him around a bit." He continued feeling brave now that the Albino had left.

"Tough talk now, huh? So go outside, then, you could, handle him couldn't ya? Besides, it would be fun, he's an albino; he couldn't see a barn in front of him." The two other men laughed, the third smiling, one of the men looked at his watch.

"Oh shit, boys, it's getting late. I gotta get this haul in by tomorrow." The other two nodded in agreement. They were here for quite some time. “If that stupid albino is out there still I’ll show you both how tough I am.” He said as they got up, throwing their cups in the trash can nearby, and making their way outside to the hazy landscape. These three knew each other from being on the road, meeting up here from time to time. Their rigs were parked about fifty feet from the dwelling they just walked out of. They didn’t go out of their way to look for the albino. They just eyed the area as they walked.

Getting closer to their rigs, one of them heard an extra pair of footsteps walking behind them. He glanced over his shoulder, and saw the Albino walking towards them. The man tapped his friend on the arm. When the two stopped and turned, the third, followed suit wondering why the other two had stopped. One of them had that worried look on his face. The man in the middle was about to say something when in a flash, the Albino pulled out two silver Colt .45s concealed in his black leather vest; pumping one round each into their foreheads.

It was too loud inside the place for the fatal attack to be heard.

Holstering his weapons, he walked over to the fallen three looking them over. He took a quick look around, and then he reached inside his vest, pulling out a flask. It had intricate designs engraved on it. Screaming skulls to be exact. Opening it; he proceeded to pour the liquid onto their faces. He emptied only about half of the liquid before he screwed the top back on, tucking it back where it came from. Within minutes smoke rose, sending a small stream skyward.

When the smoke cleared their dead faces turned as white as their killer’s was; including their hair, into that bone white color. He smirked at his calling card; something he did to all his victims.

The Albino was a man of few words. He hated wasting his time on nobodies like these three, but one thing he despised, was being made of a fool. He knew what they were thinking, staring at him for the way he looked. He never fit in with the rest of the people in there. It was something he was used to since he was a child, but as a man, he would not tolerate it.

He walked on, leaving the bodies where they were. As he made his way to his truck, his eyes caught something in the distance; it was a pillar of black smoke. He hastened his pace, being in the trade as long as he was; he knew that this was related to him. That old gut feeling never steered you wrong.

Chapter 9
Obstacles

Barreling down on I-80 the black Dodge Charger led the way with police cruisers in hot pursuit. They used every trick in the book to stop her, from the pit maneuver, to boxing her in. When they attempted to box her in, she rammed the lead cruiser off the road, propelling it into a ditch. This was hard for her. Shadow Ops had free reign over anyone that got in the way of an objective, but when it came to other law enforcement in the U.S. just trying doing their job, deadly force was strictly denied. Anything else was acceptable just as long as they lived, so launching a missile or two was out of the question. John himself would arrest her.

Priscilla's eyes constantly moved back and forth from the windshield to the rearview. She was kicking herself in the ass for thinking this would be a straight up dry run. She wished she had never thought it.

"Well? What are you going to do?" Carmine said in a panic, breaking her out of her thoughts. She looked to him with squinted eyes. He was right though, what were they going to do? She couldn't exactly fire off missiles at them. It would only be a matter of time before they set up a roadblock; her car was equipped to pick up police frequencies. She had it tuned in ever since the police began to give chase.

"Did you hear what they just said?" Carmine said in a somewhat frantic tone, as if she were deaf. She heard it, loud and clear, a few miles ahead spike strips were in place.

"Carmine, do me a favor and shut the fuck up!" She spat out, not looking at him; fucking backseat drivers were the worst. In no time, she came within sight of the spike strips. She couldn't drive off the road; police cars were blocking her way boxing her in, keeping her on course.

She pressed the pedal down, rocketing towards the spikes; she hit them, the popping of the tires was ear shattering. It was like going over a speed bump. At this speed, the car jerked and fishtailed spinning around in three complete circles before coming to a stop facing the incoming squad cars. The tires were made from a Kevlar like material, making them super tough, but not resistant to flats. When normal tires went over spike strips, they would rip right off the rims. Hers just popped and deflated. While they were stopped the cops came running to her car with guns drawn and screaming for them to get out. She then pressed a button, reinflating the tires. On the inside of the rim was a special sensor that would automatically release a cement-like liquid that was kept underneath the car.

The cement would flow from a tube that was connected right into the rim, plugging the tires up; a small air compressor attached to the underside of the car would refill the tires. The cops watched this in awe, but quickly snapped out of it trying to open her door. One cop opened fire with a shotgun. In less than a minute her tires were fully inflated. She pressed down on the pedal, spinning out and taking off in the opposite direction. The cops scrambled back to their cars to give chase.

"Wow! I must say you have some good gadgets in this car." Carmine said with a tone of amazement.

"Shut up!" They were back on course once again, but with nowhere to hide from the pursuing police it would only be a matter of time before they got her, she couldn't keep this up the whole way. Helicopters were now involved in the pursuit, a police chopper and what looked like a news chopper were watching their every move. Analyzing the situation she had no answers and no solutions. Then out of nowhere, massive explosions caught her attention from above, she looked to the sky in horror as the fiery skeletal remains of two helicopters came crashing down around them.

Chapter 10
The Tomma Sisters

As they approached from the South, they could see the two helicopters ahead. The Tomma sisters, Lisa and Kim, approached unseen. Lisa jumped into the back and strapped in as her sister flew their own helicopter. It was a single engine chopper with a few customizations added for good measure. It had light armor, bulletproof glass, and even a rocket boost. Lisa placed an Avcomm headset on to better communicate with her sister over the blaring helicopter blades.

"Kim? Do you read me?"

"Loud and clear."

"Get me in closer!" Her sister did just that; Lisa reached over to the side, grabbing a custom-made rapid firing grenade launcher. Slamming in a 20 round revolver drum she leaned over, sliding the door open, which let in the rushing wind. With a sharp jerk of the control stick, Kim put her directly in line with the two choppers and the road. She aimed, taking her time, waiting for the right moment; she fired three rounds in quick succession. Two for the police chopper and one for the news chopper. Both exploded into flames as they plummeted towards the landscape.

One crashed right on top of the police cruisers, engulfing them in flames. Another explosion soon followed the impact, lighting up the semi dusk sky. The fiery wreckage blocked the rest of the cars while the other chopper hit the desert landscape, sending the area up in flames upon impact. Lisa flashed her pearly whites at the sight of her handy work. She then leveled the weapon again firing random shots at the cop cars that made it past. As the barrage of death came from above, the cops in pursuit of the black Charger halted. Cruisers swerved to avoid being hit, while others backed up colliding into their fellow officers trying to escape. Satisfied that they would not be in the way, Lisa turned her attention to the Charger.

"Oh my God, look out!" Carmine screamed out in a panic, pointing a shaking finger at the windshield. Priscilla jerked the car hard not knowing where the fiery wreck of the chopper would fall; she only hoped to avoid it. If not for his seat belt, Carmine would be on her lap. Soon after that narrow escape, grenades were fired at them, hitting only a few feet from where she was; they kept coming, one after another. Ahead she saw a side road, route 15, which headed north, and according to the GPS it was a mountainous highway. She took the turn sharp jerking the car. She could feel Carmine press up against her from the momentum.

"More of your friends, huh?" She was taking the winding road at breakneck speed. This highway only had two lanes. Every now and then, she narrowly avoided oncoming traffic and all the while, she was being barraged with death from above.

"Well, what now!? I hope this car has some more gadgets!" Carmine exclaimed. She ignored him, holding back the urge to smack him upside his head. Now was not the time to pay attention to him or his stupid wiseass comments. Carmine was holding on for dear life as chunks of pavement pelted the car. She looked at her GPS for some kind of direction, but it offered none; the mountain was blocking the signal.

The higher into the mountain they went, the darker it got as the last remnants of the sun were blocked out. The chopper had a spotlight on the black Charger, but even as bright as it was, it was hard to get a fix on the car since it blended in so well with the dark.

"Hold the fucking chopper still, Kim!"

"I'm doing the best I can; if you don't like it you come and fucking fly!" Kim added, "The wind up here is kicking us around something fierce." Lisa didn't reply; she went back to the job at hand. She knew her sister was trying her best. She was a damn good pilot, but with the wind knocking them around, she was trying to avoid crashing into the mountain. On top of that, it was dark; even with the spotlight following the Chargers every move, it was still hard to get a good shot off.

Dodging and weaving, Priscilla narrowly avoided the wild shots; she knew her luck was not going to hold up eventually they would connect. Goddamn mechanic puts all these gadgets in but nothing to defend from an air attack, her hands held the wheel tightly turning her knuckles white.

Carmine sat there just watching the events unfold before him helpless to do anything about it, as his life was now in the hands of a woman he hardly knew and just as equally didn't like him.

Shultz was speeding through the traffic by way of the desert on the side of the highway kicking up a sandstorm. Passing by the traffic in a blur, he smiled to himself. He too had a police scanner. According to what the pigs were saying, the black Charger left them behind with a chopper in hot pursuit. He wondered who it might be, he was hoping it was the two who started talking shit earlier, he wanted to rip them apart, and he hoped that the opportunity would come up for him to do so.

"Fucking spics!" He yelled out in a rage. If it was them, he would show them not to fuck with this "white trash mother fucker" as that bitch had put it. He came closer to the wreckage that was once the Applegate brothers. Cops were all over the place directing traffic while trying to figure out what happened.

He smiled at the opportunity to waste some pigs now. He hated cops just as much as he hated everyone else for that matter. With his oversized boot, he slammed the pedal to the floor. The state troopers never saw him coming. By now, the sun had set into the horizon, leaving darkness upon the land. Shultz didn't put his headlights on as he headed for the three unlucky souls that happened to be standing with their backs turned. Between the running engines of the cars and trucks caught in traffic, and being close to the inferno in the middle of the road, they never saw or heard the roaring diesel engine of the black Ford F-650 extreme pickup truck. Hopefully they didn't feel a thing as he barreled down into them, throwing the cops in the air like rag dolls. The black Ford then burst through the line of police cars, sending sparks flying.

Going through the wreckage, his truck was singed. He turned around in his seat, grinning, showing his yellow-greenish stained teeth. He then came to more wreckage. Something that used to be a chopper was sitting right in the middle of the highway. He hoped to maybe run over some more cops, but word got to them that he was coming. The road was empty save for the burned up cop cars that were still smoking. Shultz weaved side- to- side, avoiding them; the cops, now seeing this new threat, scrambled to give chase.

He approached the turn that led to the mountain pass, taking it a little too fast, one-half of the pickup came up off the ground a few inches.

As he started up the mountain, he readied himself. On the seat next to him was a rigged control box with two wires and an air hose heading straight to the bed of the pickup. He flipped two switches and two small lights upon the box lit red.

He looked in his rearview mirror with excitement as two Vulcan Gatling guns started to rise on hydraulically operated, electrically fired mounts out of the bed. These guns could hang over the bed of the truck or they could be raised up to ten feet above the cab and turn 160 degrees. Protruding from the sides of each gun were the ammo belts filled with 30mm rounds. He pressed his truck to the max, sweat broke out on his baldhead with the anticipation. But then red and blue lights caught his view, cops were now giving chase, Shultz cursed in frustration as he toggled the switch on his control box, the Vulcan's swung around unleashing their hell fire, utterly destroying the lead cars in mere seconds and blocking the path.

"Put your window down and lean back!" Priscilla yelled. Carmine did as he was told, and put the window down. But had some trouble hitting the lever for his seat, due to his shaking hand. With the interior light on, Priscilla blindly reached into the back, grabbing an MP-5 submachine gun. She extended her arm over Carmine trying to keep an eye on the road while taking aim in the darkness. She could barely make out the chopper, but the spotlight gave her a good idea. She held the trigger down, sending a barrage of gunfire at it. Bullets ricocheted in all directions. Her attackers closed their side door quickly as she emptied the clip. As she lowered her arm to reload, she only took her eyes off the road for a moment.

When she looked back up, she was veering off into the other lane with an oncoming car heading straight for them. She swerved hard to the right, trying not to fall off the mountain cliff. The grenade fire started anew, pelting the car with indirect hits. She extended her arm once again, preparing to fire, when a grenade grazed the back windshield cracking it. She looked to the back quickly surveying the damage. Turning back to the chopper, she took aim once again, but something caught her eye in the rearview mirror. Headlights were coming up on her fast. She might not have thought anything of it, it could've been an unlucky bystander. But the spotlight had a wide range engulfing her and the pickup truck. She saw the silhouette of a Vulcan Gatling gun. It was yet another assassin trying to claim the prize she had next to her. She took her attention off the chopper, throwing the gun into the backseat. She went to her control console and armed her rear defenses. The HUD came online. She was lining up the target when she heard the monstrous roar of the Vulcan's come to life. She was expecting to be torn apart just then, but to her surprise, nothing happened. She looked to the sky and saw the chopper, being pelted with the 30mm rounds.

"Kim? Check out that pickup, you see it?" Lisa was momentarily focused on the black pickup. At first, she thought it was a passerby trying to get away from the carnage, but when she got a better view of it in the light and saw what kind of pickup it was and what it had in the bed, she knew otherwise. Then she remembered that it was the Aryan skinhead. She swallowed hard, her grenade launcher was empty. She unlocked the large revolver drum; threw it to the side and replaced it with a loaded one. Kim saw the pickup, she was falling back some to get more in line with it.

"Lisa take out the skinhead!" Lisa nodded to the back of her sister's head. She took aim, but before she could press the trigger, she saw death coming for them, all she could do was quickly throw the side door closed, duck, and hope not to be hit.

Shultz saw the chopper lining him up. The spotlight was on him like a bullseye. The bright light blinded him for a moment, but he ignored the black spots across his field of view. He wondered who it was for a moment, but really, he didn't care. Whoever it was, they were in his way and had to be removed. Now was the best time since they had stopped shooting. He eyeballed the chopper, trying to line up the Vulcan's as best he could. He saw the chopper almost directly to his side. He had no fancy targeting system, or computer to guide him as he lined it up.

When he first bought these two Vulcan's all he did for hours on end was practice aiming them from inside the truck. By now, he was pretty good at judging the trajectory of where the bullets would go. He knew at any moment grenades would be coming for him. He fired, pressing the button on the control box. With 30mm rounds coming at you at 6,000 rounds a minute, one either had to be blind or a really shitty shot to miss.

Priscilla couldn't see the chopper, but she saw the bullets connecting in the dark. It looked like firecrackers going off against it. Hot bits of shrapnel flew in all directions. Even though armored, the chopper didn't stand a chance. It was torn to pieces. The pilot tried to bring it down close to the road, but to no avail. The chopper was heading into the mountain and then veered sharply, flying over them by only a few feet. The spotlight was shot out, but the fire from the Vulcan's lit up the night sky like hell itself. She slammed down the pedal racing through the tunnel that was coming up. She never looked back. All she wanted to do was get as far away as she could from that, as fast as possible, because she knew they'd be next if they didn't move their asses.

As she rocketed through the tunnel, she heard a crash from behind echo through the tunnel, followed by a resounding boom. She hoped maybe that the chopper took the pickup with it.

Chapter 11
The Skinhead

Shultz kept an eye on the chopper and on the car. He saw the car speed off, the red taillights getting further away, disappearing from sight. I'll catch up, he thought, while putting his full attention to the chopper now being made into Swiss cheese. The mounted Vulcan's followed the helpless and out of control chopper. That pilot is damn good, Shultz said to himself. Like a dying winged beast, the chopper came crashing down in the middle of the road, just missing Shultz. He had to veer sharply to the right to avoid being crushed; it burst into a fiery ball of flames that lit up the night sky. Shultz never looked back, as he focused on the important matter ahead. He rocketed down the highway, pushing the oversized pickup truck to its limits, entering the tunnel.

Priscilla had the pedal to the floor. She wasn't sure how far the highway went through the mountain. She did wish it ended already though. She looked over to Carmine, who was still lying down.

"You can get up." Her words were like ice, cold enough to chill a person. He sat up, looking around. There was really nothing to see. There were no streetlights, only her headlights guided her. It was as dark as the deepest pits of hell. He strained to look out his window, but all he saw was darkness. Carmine shivered a bit from the frosty mountain air that was seeping in from the back window now cracked.

She looked at him and even she had to admit she was a bit chilled. She turned the heat on high. The hot air did the job of warming the car up.

Priscilla eased back a little, slowing the Charger, she was confident that they were at least safe for now…but those thoughts were quickly thrown out the window when out of nowhere two bright headlights flashed on them from behind.

In a mindless reaction, she looked into the rearview mirror; she regretted it, the lights blinded her for a moment followed by the black spots before her eyes. She swerved, but not enough for her to lose control of the car and send them falling to their death below.

It should be impossible for a bulky Ford pickup diesel to catch up to a supercharged Dodge Charger but Shultz did and the only reason he did was because his truck had a nitrous speed boost. He had shut his lights down until he was right on them, hoping to catch them off guard; he figured he did by the way the car swerved. Shultz had the mini control box on his lap; he was toggling the small lever with his giant fingers, trying to line up the shot as best he could. After a couple of seconds, he got tired of trying to aim at the weaving car and he just fired. The Vulcan's had enough ammo to waste and Shultz was not a polished man at all. He was more like a bull in a china shop. The Vulcan's came to life lighting up the darkness and illuminating his face in a demonic visage.

"Holy shit!" Priscilla was hoping that the wreckage of the chopper had either fallen right on him or blocked the tunnel. No such luck it would seem. She looked in the rearview and she saw the skinhead getting ready to fire on her at any moment. She brought up her HUD and her defensive weapons came online. She was lining up the pickup when she saw the Gatling's start to rotate. Her eyes widened and she ducked down in her seat, the thunderous bellow of the Vulcan's came to life bombarding the car. The car's armor was damn good, yes, but the 30mm rounds were no doubt doing a number on it. She could tell from the sounds the bullets made on impact.

She tried swerving to avoid the shots, but still couldn't get away. The road was too narrow, and with no lights other than her own, she would not have enough time to react, if something came up unexpectedly, she would wind up crashing into the mountain or falling off the cliff. Hunched down, and barely seeing over the steering wheel, she poured on more speed. As the gunfire bombarded her, she toggled the switches, the green cross hairs on the LCD were lining up the pickup and within seconds, he was marked. She had him now. She hit the button releasing two missiles, but nothing happened. A slight pinging noise caught her attention, Carmine's too; there was a readout on the screen.

"Bay door jam." She couldn't believe it.

"What happened?"

"Rear missile doors are jammed, most likely melted from the bullets." She looked over to Carmine. He looked surprisingly calm, even though he looked sweaty. Probably getting use to all the near death encounters today. The snapping of her fingers brought him out of his daydream; he looked to her seeing a fire in her blue eyes.

"Sit back, and buckle up!" He did so without saying a word. The gunfire was relentless. Priscilla sat back up holding the wheel tight getting ready.

Shultz could not believe the pounding he was giving the car. Even he was impressed. The car was like a tank, and even with that extra armor, he noticed he was causing a lot of damage to it. Deep in his thoughts, he was all but guaranteed victory. It would only be a matter of time before they had no choice but to give it up. Then, unexpectedly, the Charger braked, then with screeching and smoke, the car spun around and the front was now facing him. He stopped firing for a moment, more amazed than anything else, and seconds later; he saw what was coming for him. His eyes widened in shock and disbelief. There were two small missiles headed straight for him.

"Oh fuck!"

Priscilla counted backwards while going full speed. The maneuver was not the smartest one, but had to be done to get this bastard off their ass. It was going to take split second timing on her part or they will be taking a swan dive. She braked hard, cutting the wheel even harder to the left. With the momentum Carmine leaned into her even with the seat belt on. He held onto the door handle as the car spun in a quick smooth motion, tires screeching and smoke billowing from them. She was a bit too close to the guardrail. Her back end grinded on the steel, creating a shower of sparks. Her front was now lined up with the truck for two seconds at most. She let loose two missiles that hurtled towards the skinhead, and then she made a complete circle back around the way they were previously heading.

Shultz saw them coming and had seconds to do something about it. The only thing he could do was hold down the firing button and pray. The unaimed barrage of bullets caught one missile. The other was hit as well, but because it was so close; the impact of the blast propelled the truck up and over flipping it on its side, sending it crashing to the pavement. The momentum was so great that the truck slid a few feet on the pavement before coming to a slow stop.

The Charger was gone within seconds. The night was quiet again; all one could hear was the cool mountain air whipping around. Breaking that quietness was the smashing of glass as Shultz crawled out of the driver's side window barely fitting. With some effort, he finally managed to dislodge himself from his would-be tomb. His head was throbbing; it smacked the side of the metal doorframe as his truck flipped over. He took a few seconds to gather himself, and then surveyed the damage. Both Vulcan's were damaged beyond repair. They were useless, and his passenger side tire was almost falling off the rim. Other than that, the truck itself looked fine. He looked in the direction where the Charger headed; he spat on the concrete in disgust. He was no pro in this new endeavor, that was for sure.

Standing there, he was thinking how in the hell was he going to get back on the road again. Now all he needed was the cops to show up, then he'd really be fucked.

Chapter 12
Mark Lewis

Darkness fell upon the land, and replacing the warm golden sunlight, were rays of high-powered lights set-up on the side of the road and above from helicopters, both police and news. Traffic was backed up for as far as the eye could see. Just an hour ago, police finally opened up one lane to allow travelers to go about their business. The wreckage of the box truck was now a black twisted mess, still smoking from the fire that had engulfed it earlier. Ambulances, and police cars were all over the place.

One cop stood and waved on the single file of cars, while the rest of them checked over the wreckage for evidence and questioned the witnesses as to what had happened. Three men were surveying the remains. Two were sheriffs talking amongst themselves while the other was a few feet away with a flashlight probing around the blackened wreckage. The man was in a black suit with a red tie, close-cropped hair and he was clean-shaven. He looked at all this with a tinge of disgust.

"Damn terrorists." He said aloud, not really saying it to anyone but himself. The world we live in was a wild and crazy one. The man came from his thoughts as he noticed from the corner of his eye a cop running towards the two sheriffs.

"Sir, we just got a report that there's some type of huge wreckage blocking the tunnel on the mountain pass." The older of the two sheriffs' thought on this for a moment, while rubbing his lightly stubbled chin.

"Must be the same folks that did this. Send over two cars and see what's going on. Go with him Joe." Sheriff Joe and the Deputy ran off, nodding to the order. "Be careful!" The older sheriff yelled, not knowing if either man heard or not. The suited man walked over to the remaining sheriff.

"What was that?" The cop glanced at the suited man that asked the question.

"Oh, something just happened on the old mountain pass, over on route 15." The suited man turned back to the wreckage gesturing at it, as he spoke, he turned back to the cop.

"Most likely the same people." The cop nodded in agreement, and then looked at the suited man as he spoke, while adjusting his cowboy hat with the gold star badge pinned to it.

"So, they only sent one of you?" The suited man nodded.

"Yes, the FBI is vastly undermanned nowadays. My superiors didn't think it was necessary to send a slew of agents for something like this, not when no one really knows what the hell happened here." Special Agent Mark Lewis stood among the battlefield that was the I-80. He was stationed at the Las Vegas office of the FBI. When the call came in, details were sketchy at best. All they knew was there was some type of altercation on I-80. When he arrived, that was an understatement. Not only was there the wreckage before him, but there were countless shell casings from some type of Gatling gun. Many bystanders were wounded, over 20 damaged vehicles, not counting the destroyed police cruisers from the grenade firing, and the two choppers that went down. There were also a slew of eyewitnesses to the events that transpired. Lewis had only been here for two hours and he heard more than one story, but all of them were pretty much the same.

A box truck was shooting at a black Dodge Charger that seemed to be like a tank taking little to no damage. One witness said that two small missiles shot out of the Charger's front headlights destroying the box truck. Another said, someone used a rocket launcher, but no matter what the stories were, they all pointed to the same thing.

One eyewitness said the driver of the Charger was a woman with blonde hair; that wasn't anything concrete either. No one could get his or her story straight; besides, anyone could wear a wig and pose as a woman. Lewis looked back to the wreckage; he knew the answers were in there. He just had that feeling, Lewis then looked at his watch. The more time they wasted, the more time the ones responsible had to disappear.

"Sheriff?" Lewis turned to the brigade of reporters trying to get a better angle of what was going on. The old-time sheriff jumped at his tone. He was a simple lawman, about ready to retire. And now with a month to go, he was playing lap dog to some hot shot Fed. "Get those goddamn reporters outta here!" Lewis spat.

"Yes, sir." He shook his head. Lewis hated the press, damn nosy bastards, always wanting to know everything. While the old sheriff played ringmaster, Lewis pulled out his flashlight and probed the mess. He hated the locals almost as much as they hated the Feds. If this was New York or someplace more civilized, this scene would have been collected already and done with. How they even solved anything in this part of the country was beyond him. He looked over to the sheriff now going over statements, taking in the spotlight as if he would become a big star. He thought of going over there and putting a stop to that, but figured he'd leave him alone and let the moron make an ass out of himself.

Getting back to his task, Lewis walked towards where he guessed the front would be. The cab was wide open, revealing two charred corpses. You'll need dental records for these guys, he thought.

He stepped closer, getting a better look inside the cab, probing some more. He was about to move on, when his eyes caught something, something that should have been totally destroyed. A somewhat conserved blackened laptop that looked to be intact for the most part. Inserted in the USB port was a data stick. This might be able to shed some light on what happened, he mused to himself, placing the small flashlight in his mouth. He fished for a pair of rubber gloves in his suit jacket pocket. He reached into the cab, trying not to disturb anything else while he grabbed the laptop. He had to move the charred black hand of the user. As he moved the hand, a bone protruded out of the burnt flesh with a wet sound that sent a chill up his spine. Finally, he grabbed the laptop, folding it; he placed it under his arm. He was careful not to fall as he made his way out of the wreckage.

Lewis was a man of action. He felt the longer you wait, the further the perps got. He walked to his own car, which was a Crown Victoria, and placed the laptop on the hood. Just for the hell of it, he tried to power it up, but nothing happened, he figured as much. Going to the backseat, he grabbed his own laptop. Taking the data stick out of the blackened laptop, he inserted it into his own.

He kept an eye on the proceedings going on about him; making sure things were getting done, as the information was being uploaded. Once the download was completed, he focused all of his attention to the data scrolling before his eyes.

What was on the data stick was quite interesting indeed. Something that was right up his alley. A smile crept up, what were the chances of him being assigned to this? It was too good to be true. He got slightly excited from what he was reading. His palms were getting sweaty at the thoughts going through his head. Being special agent Mark Lewis for the FBI was his official job. He considered himself to be a straight up agent that would do everything in his power to get the job done.

However, during his ten-year career as an agent, he dealt information to local mobsters. He'd divulge on anything that would line his pockets. From the whereabouts of certain government witnesses, to ongoing investigations, he proved to be a valuable asset for his mob bosses. But unfortunately for Lewis, he got sloppy, he grew arrogant to the fact that he'd one day be discovered. At the time he didn't think they'd ever catch on, he thought he had covered his tracks thoroughly, but they did. From what he had heard through a few loyal coworkers, the FBI only suspected something involving him. If they had known for certain, the last thing they would have done was send him out into the field.

But nevertheless, he had to make a move. Lewis was no fool. He knew it would be only a matter of time before the FBI connected the dots. It was inevitable that they'd come for him when he least expected it, and that was something he was not going to allow. He was not going to be in the middle of some media frenzy, not to mention the fact that the mobsters he worked for would no doubt put a contract out on his head, not wanting to take the chance that he'd belly up and turn witness against them.

That thought scared him, he's seen the way they dealt with people. He'll never forget one informant's fate that he helped locate. They made an example out of him, warning those who would think of turning snitch; cops found him in the trunk of a car filled with rattlesnakes. Thinking about that now, he shivered in fright. But now with this new turn of events, he might just be able to prevent all of that from happening. With $100 million he would be set for life sipping margaritas on a sandy beach, knowing that he was able to escape the legendary FBI and say "fuck you!"

He looked over to that fool of a sheriff still taking in the spotlight. Peering back at his screen Lewis took in all the details regarding this potential ticket to a new life. Was this Carmine to be alive upon delivery? Dead was always easier in his mind. He checked the contact information. As to the person or persons who wanted this man, it did not say. He could care less, all he cared about now was getting the bounty before the other assassins did and he had the advantage, he had a whole police force at his disposal. He closed down his laptop thinking of how to ensnare this elusive prey. But the real question was who was protecting him? There could be a number of freelancers out there doing it, even a government agent of some kind, but it didn't matter who it was. They would be dead, he would see to that. He looked back to the crowd.

Throwing the laptop into the backseat of his Ford Crown Victoria, he started to walk towards that moron of a sheriff that just finished soaking up his fifteen minutes of fame. A plan was forming on how to go about all this. It should be simple enough to hopefully wrap up everything in less than 24 hours. The sheriff, walking with two other deputies, saw Lewis coming towards them. The three waited for him to approach.

"Now that you're done spilling your guts to the world, do you think we can come up with a way to catch these perps?" Lewis said, placing both hands to his waist. The sheriff looked embarrassed. If it wasn't dark, one would have noticed his face flush at the insult.

"Yeah, what do you have in mind?" The Sheriff said, trying to regain some composure.

"Get me a map of the area and gather every available officer." The Sheriff nodded, walking off. Moments later, Lewis had the map. In all, about twenty officers were around him. With the map laid out on the hood of a police cruiser, and his flashlight in hand, Lewis went over it.

"Ok everyone, now listen up!" Yelling loud enough to be heard, "We know that a black Dodge Charger was involved with today's events. From the scene, it most likely suffered heavy damage, so be on the look out for that. Remember, there are two people in that car, a man and a woman, and according to witnesses the man is older, late fifties to early sixties." He stopped for a moment, looking at each and every one of them, letting it all sink in before continuing.

"Now, I just got off the phone with my superiors, so listen closely. The man with this woman is to be taken alive, unharmed. As for the woman, well, consider her armed and dangerous. Now if any of you do happen to spot them, detain them. You are to contact me immediately. The man, whose name is Carmine Christie, is to be taken by me."

"Uh, excuse me, sir?" Lewis looked in the direction of where the voice came from. It was a young deputy looking as though he was still in his teens. "What did this individual do? I mean, is he dangerous? And what about the other feller driving the black pickup? Is he involved in this somehow too?"

"As to what this Carmine is wanted for that's classified, the threat factor from him is minimal." The young man nodded, "As for the man in the pickup, I'm not too sure of him yet. Most likely just some nut, with dangerous toys. Who knows, the world is a crazy place son, but if I were a betting man, I'd also say he too is involved in this somehow." He waited for any more questions; not hearing anyone else, he continued.

"As to where they are going, all directions point east, but from their little detour, they are now headed North and will most likely head back towards the East when they have a chance. Check everywhere! Every back road and main road, every goddamn pit stop, and hotel along I-80 and anything North and South of that! Work around the clock! These people must be found and remember as your fellow deputy just pointed out," He pointed to the man as he was finishing the sentence, "We might not be the only ones tracking them, keep that in mind." He looked at every single face.

"Everyone get that?" They all nodded, some saying yes, while some said nothing at all. "Good! Let's go, let's go, move!" With a somewhat delayed reaction, they all moved. It had to be done quickly. Lewis was taking an awful gamble with this. He hadn't heard from his superiors; but they'd call, that was for sure. They always checked on the status of an investigation. But this was his game now. All it would take is one phone call from one of these locals to the FBI. If one of them felt he was not being on the up and up, he would be finished. However, he believed that they weren't smart enough to do that. Why would he not be on the up and up with them? They had no reason to doubt him; nonetheless, he really put himself out there now.

He knew the rewards far outweighed the risks he would be taking; then again, he had nothing to lose. He watched as they got in their cruisers, speeding off. The highway was no way near being cleared yet. By morning, it would be done, hopefully. Normalcy would be back on this side of the road. Lewis then got into his own car and sped off. The last possible sighting of the Charger was on route 15. He figured he would quickly check there, see what was on the scene and then go on from there.

The mountainside highway was just as bad as the main road. Just as he made his way up the mountain pass, he came upon several police cruisers that were strewn all over the narrow two-way road which was closed off. Further up, was a helicopter wreckage, which he didn't even bother to inspect, it was a steaming pile of metal. As he drove by, a deputy on the scene informed him of what they found so far, which was one body burned beyond recognition.

The Ford Pickup down the road, he did check finding nothing of interest. This confirmed what he surmised before, that there are other parties in the chase; this was something that was going to be trouble down the road if he didn't get a handle on the situation quickly.

The driver, whoever it was, scraped off the registration and inspection stickers; the license plates were missing as well. Every piece of information that could help in finding the culprit was gone. Lewis was standing near the back of the overturned pickup, checking over the Vulcan's.

Nice piece of hardware he thought, as flashing yellow lights caught his attention. They belonged to a tow truck getting ready to right the pickup and tow it away. A slight chill crept up on him; it was damn windy up here. He stepped out of the way, as the tow truck driver fastened harnesses to the side of the Ford pickup securing them. Lewis walked past the other police, looking to the vastness of the highway before him, thinking, wondering where they could be at this very moment.

Chapter 13
No End in Sight

On what seemed like a never-ending highway, they drove for another four hours in the eerie darkness. She had not realized this road went so far up North. Just after she managed to take care of their pursuer, Priscilla was waiting for another surprise to come up on them. She was jumpy but she tried her best not to show what she was feeling to her passenger. As time went by, she became more and more relaxed. Carmine sat in his seat sleeping like a baby. They were still driving North on route 15 with the GPS still not working well. There was too much interference this far up North. They didn't speak for the four-hour drive; something she was glad about, since she didn't really have too much to say to him.

Finally coming to the end of the mountainous highway, they came to a small town that had streetlamps scattered about, as she passed local stores, restaurants and bars. There was no sign indicating the town or the road they were on; at this point, she really didn't care. All she wanted to do was lay low and find a place to crash for the night. Hopefully by morning the heat would cool down, and besides, she was driving almost twelve hours before all this happened. So some well-needed rest was something she could go for now. She also wanted to survey the damage and see if she could possibly fix the bay doors for the rear missiles. She hoped the damage wasn't too extensive, otherwise she doubted it.

The town looked almost deserted. The local bars they passed had one or two cars parked in the lot. All she wanted was a hotel, but she didn't find one. It was better off anyway, she told herself. Common sense told her that was not a good move right now. They'd be trapped if they were still being tracked. At this point, the first place she felt comfortable with would do.

A nice little hiding spot to park in for a while, just to close her eyes for a few hours. About a mile later, she came up to a strip of stores. The whole parking area was pitch black. A streetlamp was twenty feet ahead of the strip of stores itself. It gave off some illumination, but not much. Slowing down, she pulled into the parking lot. In the darkness, she could faintly make out the signs. There was a stationery store, a deli, a souvenir store and one or two other stores she didn't care to read the signs of.

She came to the end of the strip and on her side; she spotted a narrow one-way road leading to the back. She shut off her lights, taking the path slowly. The pathway ran along the back and she could faintly see loading docks for deliveries.

It was big enough back there to turn around and face the way she had just come from. Doing so quickly, she shut the engine off and took in the quietness of the night. Hearing the sounds coming from the wooded area that was in the back of the store was therapeutic enough for her to lose herself.

She was glad Carmine was passed out; she wasn't in the mood for him objecting to sleeping in the car. But after what just happened, she figured he might not want to leave the car anymore, at least until they got to New York. Annoying fuck and useless too, she thought looking over at him. All she could see in the blackness was his outline being lit by the moon. She saw him stirring while trying to get comfortable and then she leaned back herself. She reached for the GPS, which was finally working. She recalibrated it hoping that maybe she would have some sense of where they were and according to what it said, they were just North of Helena, Montana. If she wasn't so tired, she'd have been more shocked by that. Not only did they just have a day from hell, but now, they were all the way up North totally off the main track. This might be a good thing under the circumstances, but being detoured was something she'd rather not deal with. If it wasn't for the cops getting involved she would have had no problem shooting it out with her pursuers earlier in the day.

Priscilla scrolled down the screen, trying to figure out the best possible route to take. As it turned out, they really weren't out of the way. They were on route 90 now, so if she headed East, then South she'd be back on course. At least that was a good thing from all this. She shut down the GPS, and placed it back in the console. Looking at the screen made her eyes even heavier than they were before. Now in total darkness, she laid her head back. She placed her gun on her lap, ready at a moments notice; it didn't take her long to fall asleep.

Chapter 14
The Plan

Later that night, about fifty miles from the incident that took place earlier on I-80; far off from the main road in the desert and far enough not to be seen from passing cars, a black Sprinter was parked, it was getting pelted by the blistering sand laced winds. It was so harsh and windy that the van was swaying from side to side. The windows were tinted, but if one looked closely, you could see a faint light inside. It was a quiet night out here in the desert, with the exception of the wind whistling its eerie tune that would send chills through someone that didn't have nerves of steel.

"So…what's our next move?" Omar asked his sister who was in the driver's seat, leaning against the door with her legs extended to the passenger seat. Her window was cracked open slightly while she smoked a cigarette. Even with the window cracked open she could feel the wind coming through sending a chill throughout the van. Nevertheless, the wind didn't bother her; she was too heated from the day's events to be chilled from the breeze. Omar was in the back, sitting with a map as he asked the question looking for her opinion.

"Well?" He looked to his sister now. She was deep in thought, eyes staring into another world as she took a drag from her cigarette, letting the smoke out slowly from her nostrils.

"Well, being that we lost them, I'm not too sure, I'm beginning to think this whole fucking job is a waste of time. I mean trying to find a single car on the move. And to top it off we have to watch our own asses." Omar straightened up while looking at her.

"It's not like we haven't tracked people before and I'd hate to inform you of this, but in this business we always have to watch our backs. Only this time we know who we have to watch out for, so what's different now?" He added the last sentence with a bit of sarcasm as he crossed his arms over his chest, waiting for her reply. She looked at him, straightening herself up, planting her booted feet hard to the floor.

"What's different now? Nothing, I just don't like the fact that we're in competition with the others, especially that skinhead." He shrugged his shoulders, clearly not concerned about what she said. In a mocking tone he replied,

"My dear sister, you're not scared of that skinhead are you?" He got what he was looking for. She squinted her eyes at him. She was so easy to get to.

"I'm not afraid of anyone! I'm just saying what I think that's all!"

"Ok fine, now listen. While you've been in another world, daydreaming, here's what I think our next move should be. I've been mapping out a projected trajectory of our targets." Getting up, he walked to the passenger seat. Sitting down, he laid the map before her, Trish leaned over, looking at it. With a pen, he showed her what he was planning, her eyes followed.

"Ok, now, according to reports, they went up route 15, North of here. The most logical way to go since they are heading for New York is to take this all the way up to I-90 which is in Montana." He stopped, giving her a moment to process this, then continued. "Now, I think they are most likely going to go east from there on I-90, going through South Dakota, Minnesota, and finally into Wisconsin, then head South for a bit, and back East. The road they'll be on will change back into I-80." She looked over the marks he'd made, pointing to other routes other than the ones he showed her.

"That's not the only way. There are other routes leading to where they want to go as well." He shook his head in protest.

"Yeah, I know, but they are more detours than anything else. This is the only way to go if you want to move quickly." She sat up, looking into the blackness of their surroundings. Omar looked at his gold Rolex watch.

"If we move now, we can gain some ground. Most likely they'll lay low for the night, which will give us added time." She nodded in agreement.

"So, we'll head them off, get ahead and wait." He shrugged.

"Yeah, seems good enough. Depending on the time, we can either head them off or be right behind them in two days with no stops."

"I'll drive first." She righted herself, sticking the keys in the ignition and holding her fingers there for a moment, staring out into the blackness. Omar looked at her, he was about to say something. She looked to be in deep thought, far away from here.

"You know something, Omar? We'll try to get this guy, but if we don't, I say kill everyone involved. Follow whoever does get him to the rendezvous, kill them, and kill the German too. Take the money, and fuck'em all! But remember," she said the last part with emphasis, "I don't care where we are, or what we're doing, at the first opportunity, I want that fucking skinhead!"

He nodded at her words with a sinister smile, as he swung his legs forward, propping them up on the dashboard as he reclined the seat. She put out the interior light. The starting of the powerful engine broke through the howl of the wind as they drove off.

Chapter 15
New Day

Priscilla awoke with a start, leveling her gun. Once she realized it was only a bad dream, she took a deep breath trying to relax. Her heart was racing; she could hear the beating in her ears. She touched her forehead and found it had a slight stickiness to it from her sweating during the night. She really didn't sleep well, most of the night; she was plagued by nightmares that she couldn't remember.

She tried to stifle a yawn and failed, looking up to the sky; the sun was bright, the golden rays pierced her half-closed eyes; stinging them. She put up a hand, shielding them and then looked at her watch. It was half past six; none of the shops were open yet, which was a good thing for them. The less anyone saw of them, the better. She then turned to wake Carmine, only to find him gone.

"Shit!" Priscilla jerked up and threw the door open and jumped out scanning the area, he fucking ran! She thought, but then she heard the cracking of branches to the side of her. She leveled her gun towards the direction of the sound only to see her passenger emerging from the woods, zipping up his pants. He looked up, not really shocked to see her; he gave her a smile.

"Good morning, sorry if I scared you, but I had to go bad, and I didn't want to wake you, you looked so peaceful sleeping."

"Thanks for your concern, but next time tell me, ok?" She tucked her weapon away, turning from him as he nodded. Now with the light she walked around the car surveying the damage from last night, which wasn't too bad. They'd get by. A few bullets penetrated the armor, and there were scattered white marks almost covering the entire back of the car. She squatted examining the taillights, and just as she figured the bay doors were melted to the car's frame, she thought she might be able to fix them. She got up, went to the driver's side; kneeling she disabled the weapon systems.

There was a small switch underneath the dash near the emergency brake, she pressed it. She then went to the rear of the car again.

She propped herself up on the trunk, feeling for a release button on her boot. Pressing it, the heel of her boot came off. Sliding out of the heel compartment was a small laser torch. It was one of the mandatory pieces of field equipment an agent must have at all times. Replacing the heel and locking it back in place; she slid off the trunk and looked to Carmine, who was standing by the front of the car, taking in the area as if he had not a care in the world.

"Yo!" She yelled out. He looked towards her. "Hit the trunk release, please." Without a word, he did so, popping it open. She leaned in, fishing for the small toolbox. Every company car had a basic tool set, ratchets, crossbar, and a screwdriver set just to name a few. She grabbed the thinnest screwdriver and went to work. The laser torch casing was about the size of a pen. To activate it you twisted the back in a clockwise motion. The more you twisted it the wider the beam got. The torch itself had a life span of about two hours give or take. She torched the outline of where the headlights would open up to release a missile; it took only a few minutes for each one. While cutting with one hand, she was prying open the hatch with the screwdriver in the other.

Sparks were dashing in her face as she did this. Finally done, she tucked the laser torch in her pocket going into the backseat she grabbed a bottle of water from her bag. She used the entire bottle to cool the still hot taillights, steam flew up in her face, choking her.

Priscilla waved a hand in front of her face as she walked and sat on the hood of the car. Carmine came along side of her, standing next to her with his arms crossed.

"So, what now? Do you even know where we are?"

She nodded, not looking at him as she spoke.

"We're just inside Montana." He didn't look surprised to hear that, his face was neutral.

"Wow, we really went out of the way, huh?" She nodded. Priscilla was deep in thought now, thinking not of their way home, but of who the assassins were. She really didn't care, she was just curious that was all. Anyone in her way would meet the same fate as the ones in the box truck.

"So, do you have a route?" He asked, breaking her out of her thoughts. She looked at him, nodding. Only after a day of traveling, Carmine looked tired and haggard, with slight fuzz growing on his face. This trip clearly would take its toll on him with further delays.

"We're right on route 90. If we take this East, right before Billings, we'll head South, then back East again. It's a little longer than what we were going to do, but hopefully we'll get by unnoticed."

"Yeah, hopefully." He added with a bit of sarcasm. She couldn't help but to agree. It would only be a matter of time before someone would track them down again.

"Hey, whatever you think, you have my full trust." He said with a fake smile. She looked at him tempted to smack that smile off his face, but thought better of it. She got back up to check the lights; she looked at them first, then touched them. Playing with the doors a bit, she moved them up and down, making sure they were unhinged in their movement. She'd do a systems check to make sure the missiles were okay.

"Carmine, come here, watch these hatches, I wanna make sure they still work." He walked over, and she went to the driver's side sitting in the car, pressing the switch and watching him in the rearview mirror. She heard them opening and closing before he yelled.

"Ok, good," with a thumbs up. Leaning down, she reactivated the weapon systems, the CPU did a quick systems check, reassuring her everything was ok. Closing her door, she started the car. Carmine didn't need to be told to get in.

She peeled out kicking up dirt, heading towards the path they came in from hours earlier. The town that was dead the night before was rife with activity now. They had just left in time too, a small delivery van drove down the path they had just exited from. They hit route 90, going east, as they drove she noticed people looking their way. The car was drawing way too much attention. Something had to be done to at least cover up what had happened.

Moments later, they came to a gas station/car wash. She pulled in; it wasn't too busy, just a regular day. They pulled up to the entrance of the car wash. Rolling down her window, she paid the attendant. He regarded the car; the look on his faced betrayed what he was thinking.

Seeing such a nice car, that looked like it went through a war zone. Hopefully word hasn't gotten here yet about a Dodge Charger being involved in a highway battle. She doubted it. Places this far off were always late in getting the news from other parts of the country. The locals didn't care what happened outside their town, just as long as it stayed out of their town. Finally, on the other side, they were bombarded by five men wiping the car down. When they finished, she rolled down the window and as one of the men walked over, she handed him a fifty, something he was not used to by the look on his face as he ran off to the next car following hers. Before leaving Priscilla pulled right up to the convenience store.

"You want anything?"

"No, I'm good thanks. Oh wait, maybe a paper if they have one." Carmine said with a smile. Minutes later, they were finally off, leaving this quiet town behind them, getting one-step closer to home.

"Did you take your pills?" Carmine looked up to her from his paper. All they had in the station was the local town paper. Something Carmine didn't really care for, but at this point, it was something to occupy himself with, reading about what made news in this part of the country.

"Oh, I forgot, I'm glad you reminded me." He said, sounding not really concerned that he forgot, he reached into the back, grabbing a bottle of water. Priscilla shook her head; like a fucking kid.

"What are they for anyway? I only checked quickly to see if they were in there when I first picked up the car." He didn't answer her right away; he just swallowed the last pill, gulping down some water.

"They're for my heart condition. I was one-step away from a transplant, until the doctors told me to try these. Without my medication, even if I miss it once, well, you know." He was calm as he said this too, knowing that at any moment his heart could stop without the lifesaving meds. This was something she might not be so nonchalant about like him if she knew she had something like that.

"That's why I can't fly. My heart races too much. I never really liked to fly to be honest with you," he said and went back to his paper, finding the spot where he left off. With silence now between them, it gave her time to think, and there was no better way than listening to some tunes. She hoped Carmine didn't object, not that she would care anyway. She found a local mixed station. She eased right in, pouring on more speed getting closer to home.

Chapter 16
Can't keep a good Skinhead Down

Shultz was back on the road, heading the way he last saw the Charger go the night before, north on 15. The bright rays of the new day were stinging his tired and bloodshot eyes. The previous night took a lot out of the Aryan; he looked over to his passenger, who was staring into the open road with the mask of death. Last night with no options to go on, Shultz stripped his vehicle of anything the cops could find to ID him and then started walking. He must've walked maybe ten miles before the headlights of an oncoming vehicle came into view.

There was no place to hide. It was open, just the mountain to his left and nothing but a free fall to his right. He figured he'd make his last stand here and now. No way were the cops going to take him again. He had been in the clink before; something that he wasn't afraid of, he just hated dealing with all the spics and niggers, their shitty music drove him nuts.

On top of that, the fat oversized hacks barked orders at you all day thinking they were tough with everyone locked up behind bars or handcuffed. He'd love to run into one of them now. He reached for his revolver touching it; he was ready to draw. But coming up fast was an old looking, beat up pickup truck. The driver slowed down some as he came closer to the stranded skinhead.

"Hey there son, you be needing a lift somewhere?" The old man asked him with a wad of chew in his lower lip; spitting out a clump to the pavement. Shultz looked at him, and then looked back and forth down the road. He nodded.

"Yeah, my truck stalled, back over about fifteen miles or so down the road. I was just heading into town to see if I can get a tow or something." It was dark out on this desolate road, the old man could hardly see him, and nodded,

"Why don't you get on in here? I'll give you a ride back to town. You'll be walking for a good long time, son." Shultz nodded, walking to the truck. He passed the bed, throwing his license plates inside, and then got in the passenger side. Before the old man could turn around and talk some more, Shultz's bear like hands, reached for him; twisting the old mans neck around. The sound of cracking bone echoed through the stillness of the night. Now four hours later he was just heading into town; the roads for the most part were empty except for a car or two here and there.

He recognized where he was. He had passed through here a long time ago. This town was called Boulder Hill, a quiet town of church going folks that lived life day by day. Just as the south is ripe with activity of groups such as the KKK and his fellow Aryan brotherhood, up here in the northern parts of the country like Montana, there were plenty of anti-government militants.

He saw a gas station just up the road. He pulled in. Before getting out, Shultz pulled the stiff body of the old man down closer to the floor. He got out and bought a map of the area. Looking it over he found out where he needed to go next, about twenty miles or so to the east. Shultz really didn't want to stray from the job but with no supplies, this was the only way. The old man that he was going to see, sleazed him out to no end, but with great apprehension, he drove on.

As he got closer to his next destination, he became more nervous. Shultz knew there was a chance at any time he could be nailed with this stolen truck. It won't take long for this man's family to call him in as a missing person. About half an hour later, he came to a dirt road that was hidden from the main road. If you didn't know where to look, you'd miss it. He almost did, jerking hard on the steering wheel. With the grinding of gears, he threw the old truck into four-wheel drive heading up the steep hill.

Ten minutes later, he came to a clearing surrounded by a thick forest. In the dead center was a sugar shack of a house. It looked to be abandoned for some time, but he knew better. Not because of the smoking chimney, but because he knew the man who lived here would never leave his quiet little home that secluded him from the outside world. He stopped just 20 feet from the house, shutting down the engine. Getting out, he looked around quickly, then started to walk. All around the house was a junkyard of trash. There were two broken down cars with a beat up looking Blazer that looked like it'd still run.

He wouldn't bet on it though. He walked up on the porch; the old wood creaked under his massive frame. For a moment, he thought he'd fall clear through. He knocked on the beat up door, but no answer, so he rapped harder. His knocks echoed throughout the vast woods around him. He waited a moment, listening to see if he stirred anyone inside. Just when he was about to knock a third time an old sounding but unafraid voice was heard faintly from within.

"Get the fuck off my property! You have five seconds before I pump the door full of lead!" Shultz jumped back and to the side of the door, but being the house was so run down looking he didn't think he'd be safe there either.

"Yo! You old coot it's me, Shultz!" The old man didn't reply, he walked quietly to the door and opened it, with a shotgun ready to fire.

"Shultz huh? Well, come forward now!" He did so, blocking the doorway with his frame. The man that sounded old was far from it; he looked to be in his late fifties, he had tats of Aryan symbols and brown hair. He was a medium build but solid from living the hard life as he did. He gave Shultz a half toothless smile. Shultz returned the gesture.

"Well, I ain't seen you in how long boy?" They embraced. "What the hell happened to you? You look like dog shit." Shultz shrugged his shoulders.

"Long night Bern, long night." Bern looked him over.

"Yeah, well come on in and tell me all about it."

Bern's house was just as bad inside if not worse than the outside. If someone came here not expecting what to see, they might have thrown up with the stench of what smelled like rotting food mixed with mildew. The couch was in what was supposed to be the living room. When he sat down on it, Shultz thought for a second he broke it. Shultz told Bern about the last few nights and what was going on. Bern was an anti-government militant from the old days. He, like the rest of them, were still waiting for the big uprising to take back their country, he also rolled with the Aryans from time to time. Shultz knew him from a few years back.

"Wow, sounds like some story there boy. You're up against some tough folks, huh?" Bern said, as he gulped down the rest of his beer, which was the only safe thing to drink in this house of filth.

"Yeah," Shultz said, leaning in closer to the old man, his face grim.

"Listen, I need to dump this body." Bern thought about this for a moment, nodding yes.

"You gonna be needing some fire power too? I'm guessing." Shultz's eyes widened to the sound of that, he nodded to the old coot.

"Yeah, something big too." Bern laughed at that, slapping his knee.

"Well, son, you've come to the right man. Come on, let's go downstairs and see what I can dig up for ya." They both got up, Bern leading the way through the disgusting confines of the house, headed downstairs to the basement. Bern used to be a weapons dealer in the old days. Not only did he supply the anti-government movements up here, but he also supplied the Aryans and the KKK. From what Shultz knew of him, he made some money doing it too. Why on earth he lived like this was something he could not comprehend. Walking down the creaking steps, it was pitch black. The old man told him to wait there until he got the light on. It took him a minute until he finally found the overhead light string; pulling it.

Once illuminated Shultz walked further in, almost hitting his head on a beam. As tired as he was, his eyes widened at the sight of the small arsenal. On the wall were automatic rifles and sub-machine guns neatly arranged from sizes small to large. He walked closer; the old man moved out of the way, letting him pick whatever he wanted.

"No, no I need something big Bern. I told ya about the car. The damn thing is like a fucking tank." The old man frowned.

"Hmm, I think I got just the thing for you," he said, rubbing his chin. Moments later, after making an awful racket of moving stuff and throwing things to the floor, he came back holding an M80

Zolja disposable rocket launcher. It was small enough to sling over your shoulder and when ready to use, just pull the pins, and extend the tube. Shultz grabbed it, his eyes lighting up like the brightest stars in the night sky.

"Nice Bern! This will do! You got any extra rounds for my piece?" Shultz showed him his silver revolver. The old man went to a drawer at his workstation, throwing him a box. One thing about this crazy old coot, he lived like an animal, but he had the best shit around. They made their way back upstairs and outside. Bern helped get the body out of the truck. They carried it off to the back of the house, dropping it. Bern said he'd bury it later. Going back to his 'new' pickup Shultz grabbed his plates, taking off the old ones and replacing them with his.

"You heading off?" Bern asked, Shultz nodded.

"Soon, I wanna catch a few z's then go. I won't be a bother to you. I'm gonna sleep in the truck anyhow, and go from there." Bern nodded, secretly glad about that. Even in his hay day, he was always a recluse. He loved talking to people but hated to have them around for long periods of time. He was getting worse in his old age.

"Good, the faster you leave, the better my boy. Don't get me wrong, I enjoyed our talk and all, I don't get many visitors up here, but it's been quiet and I'm too old for the shit that we used to do. Don't need any heat from you, but I can't turn down a fellow white brother of the cause." Shultz nodded, looking out to the dirt road that he came up from, he turned back to Bern throwing out a hand, Bern grabbed it,

"Thanks again Bern, I'll pay you back when I can." The old man waved a hand in dismissal.

"No need to son. I'd rather someone get some use out of this stuff. Now being out of the weapons gig, it'll just sit down there and I'd dare not get back into that again, damn Feds are everywhere nowadays." He paused a moment continuing, "Besides, if what you're doing might get rid of some them there niggers, spics, and whatever else, then I'm happy to help. I hate the way times are nowadays, I do miss the old days though when the white man ruled…It seems now the goddamn niggers and whatever else is taking over." The old man said this, as he reflected back to the old days. Shultz nodded at him agreeing.

"You be careful out there, white power!" The old man said.

"White power!" Shultz replied. They both said this putting their fists to their chests in a roman like salute. Shultz watched the old man hobble back inside, closing the door behind him. He turned to the pickup, climbing in; and sprawled out on the seat. If he had wanted to push the issue, he could have stayed inside the house, but didn't only for the fact that he might have a bug crawl up his ass. He shivered thinking about it. It wasn't long till his eyelids got heavy and he fell asleep to the sounds of the forest around him.

Chapter 17
Goldeneyes

As the sun rose high in the crystal-clear blue sky above the peaceful town of Boulder Hill, the ominous blue Toyota pickup truck pulled in at around ten in the morning. Unbeknownst to the Albino, he had just missed his prize by mere hours. Turning onto route 90, heading east, he drove at his own leisurely pace; taking in the sights-which weren't many at all. He didn't bother stopping at any of the stores or restaurants he passed. He knew from years of experience that they wouldn't be there. They were on the run, desperately trying to outrun their shadows. He knew they'd come this way though. It wasn't hard to figure out.

After the events that took place yesterday on I-80, like so many others, he too was stuck for quite some time in the traffic jam that was the result of the foolishness of his former competitors the Applegate brothers. He had a police scanner and was listening in the whole time on what was going on. It said the Charger went up route 15, something that the Albino knew even before they did. It was the only way to go if one wanted to lose someone. With the dangerous winds and mountains blocking your way, no one sane would dare fly a chopper up there. And, unless you were a skilled driver, one would not take the road at high speeds like his prey did. This was very intriguing to him; it gave him some excitement knowing that his opponent was formidable.

Being in the game for as long as he was, it was hard to find someone out there to keep your interest. When he finally did get to the mountain pass he not only saw what he assumed to be an unknown assassin's downed chopper, but that Aryan's truck was being towed also. As he made his way up the mountain, he shook his head at the thought of him. The Albino never saw him until the night before, but from talking to him for a short time his impression was that he was a complete and total moron.

Whatever happened to him, he deserved. Plus, that was one less likely thug to deal with down the road. Even the Tomma sisters were no big threat to him. The ones he would have to keep an eye on were the crazed duo Trish and Omar. Those two were going to be trouble, he knew that. Nonetheless, just like so many in the past, he'd take them out.

It was almost noon now. A cool breeze kicked in from the north, rattling the trees into one another. The rustling of the trees awoke Shultz. Groggy and weary, he looked around. Rubbing his shaved head, he yawned like a grizzly bear. He got out and stretched a bit, then took a fast piss and was back on the road. He thought about saying goodbye to the old man, but he figured he'd leave well enough alone. The crazy old bastard might start shooting this time if he knocked again. When he started the engine, he was surprised. For a beat up, old looking pickup, it sounded great and ran fairly well too. The old man he killed must have kept up on the maintenance.

Heading back down the dirt road, he thought of what to do next. With all the lost time, he'd be hard pressed to catch up, but he'd try at least to do so. Coming to the opening that led to the main road, he inched out a bit. There was a nasty blind spot on the left. He saw his opening and was about to gun it when out of nowhere a blue pickup came into view moving at a good speed.

If he'd not seen it in time he would have smashed right into it, something he didn't need right about now. As he watched the pickup go; he thought for a minute that it looked oddly familiar. He scratched his head. Then it came to him.

"Could that be the Albino?" He said under his breath. He now had this newfound opportunity of getting rid of another competitor. He checked again for oncoming cars; flooring it, he hoped to catch up to see if it was really the Albino and not his tired eyes playing tricks on him. Shultz readied himself. If he could take this guy out, then he'd only have to worry about the freaks Trish and Omar and the Tomma sisters. As he came closer to the pickup, what he thought was confirmed. How could you miss that milky white hair, and matching skin color?

He sped up, clutching his silver revolver, getting ready to make fast work of this freak of nature. Just as he was about to speed alongside him, he thought of something better, why not follow him? After all, Shultz wasn't a real pro. He didn't know the first thing about tracking people like his competition. They could get into the heads of their quarry; think like them, and use their gut instincts, something he wasn't good at. Shultz slowed down, falling back. He ducked down into his seat a little. He looked around the cab, finding an old oil stained cap. Shultz was going to let the Albino do all the work; he had a good feeling that this guy was going to catch up to them. Now all he had to do was be patient.

Chapter 18
Phoning Home

Aside from their detour that took them somewhat out of the way. The last 24 hours, has been smooth sailing since the confrontation in Utah, Priscilla even let up on Carmine a little bit. They made small talk, mostly just to pass the time away. She realized he was ok to talk too, but still a pompous ass.

They swapped stories about their past, mostly the humorous ones anyway, she never gave anything away either. She'd outright lie like when he asked her where she lived, or if she had kids or not. She replied no without even thinking. Even though it sounded like small talk, she was very calculated as to how she answered him.

To her, he was some two-bit informant. She'd be damned to tell him anything on a personal level. She'd never see him again, and on top of that, if he were found one day; by the people after him, he might drop a dime on her to save his own skin. Sure, they were having a swell time now, but she wasn't going to be swapping numbers anytime soon; he was a job and nothing more.

About an hour later, the conversation died down. There was really nothing more to say. She had the radio on low while he had his eyes closed, but he wasn't sleeping. It was a little after eight in the evening.

In the silence of the night as they were driving, a faint sound caught her ear. It wasn't the "company" cell phone it was her personal phone. She raised an eyebrow. She reached into the middle console blindly feeling for it. Who the hell is texting me? She thought as she fingered through the menu.

"If you have a chance can you call the house?" It was a text from Pat. That was the last person she wanted to see come up, her stomach tightened. Her kids were with him. Pat was the only one of her personal friends to know what she did for a living. He knew when she was on a mission to only call her if it was a dire emergency. What was the matter?

She wasn't scared yet, but she wondered, she had to call back, if she didn't it would eat away at her until she found out and she didn't want it clouding her judgment. Personal calls were something she did not do while on assignment. To her knowledge, no agent did in the middle of a mission, for any reason. She took a deep breath and thought about calling now, but with Carmine next to her? She didn't want him to know any more than he knew already. What if her pursuers were scanning the airwaves? In this day and age, the last thing she wanted was her enemies to know about her personal life. There were no doubts, both past and present enemies that would act on that information just to retaliate against her. Carmine pulled her from her thoughts.

"Everything ok? You look like you've seen a ghost." He asked. She slowly nodded, wishing the look on her face didn't say otherwise.

"I'm fine; we just have to make an unscheduled pit stop real quick."

About fifteen minutes later, they were coming up to a truck stop. Just past the parking area, were a few restaurants. A Wendy's, Burger King and Dunkin Donuts. Right outside of the Dunkin Donuts was a row of payphones all unoccupied. Hardly anyone used a payphone nowadays. She pulled in a little too quickly making the sharp right turn off the main road. She drove through the lot twice, scanning the surroundings for anything out of the ordinary. When she was satisfied with what she saw, she made her way to the payphones, backing up.

"Wait here, if anything honk the horn." She said, not adding any more than he needed to know. He nodded; he looked a little puzzled, but didn't ask why they were stopping. She was surprised; she figured he'd press her to know what she was doing. She pulled out her gun, and got out of the car. Before, taking a step Priscilla shoved her pistol in her waist.

As she made her way, with her 'company' cell phone in hand, she locked Carmine inside. To her relief there was no line inside the Dunkin. She ordered two coffees just to make sure she got the change she needed to make the call. Coming back out, she placed the steaming hot coffees that were in the tray on top of the phone. She then dialed the number, inserting the desired change that the automated voice asked for. Any human being who had kids would do the same thing; she had to make the call. If, God forbid something happened, it's not like she could up and go there right now, but it was more of the need to know than anything else.

As the phone rang, she kept her back to the wall, watching the cars that came in. She stared them down, making sure there were no threats. The phone rang for quite some time before Pat picked up.

"Pat? Everything ok?" She kept her voice even.

"Oh Priscilla. Yeah, yeah everything is fine. I'm awfully sorry, but your son is really sick. He started showing signs of it today. He has a high fever and a bad cough you know. He was crying, and all he wanted to do was talk to you. I said that you might be busy, but then I gave in. I did it, figuring it would appease him, I didn't think you'd have your phone on you anyway." That gut wrenching feeling went away as quickly as it came on.

"No stop, I'm never too busy for my kids. Is he there? Put him on quick Pat, I'm in a hurry." Pat took the phone from his ear. With the sound of faint footsteps and the turning of a doorknob, her son's voice came on the phone. He sounded terrible; his voice was hoarse.

"Mommy? When are you coming home?" He said in between sniffles. This was the time when she hated what she did; not being there during a time like this tore her heart out.

"Oh, mommy's coming home soon honey, Uncle Pat told me you're sick. I'll be home as soon as I can to take care of you ok?"

"Ok…I miss you, I love you."

"I love and miss you too, baby boy. Tell your sister I love her too ok? Now get some sleep or otherwise you won't get better, I love you a lot."

"Love you a lot too, mommy." Pat was back on the phone.

"Pat, I have to roll. Do what you have to do; you have all the info on their doctors if he gets worse." She felt like she was rambling, and stumbling on her words. Pat knew that when it came to her kids she was a nervous wreck. He finally interrupted her.

"Priscilla, take a breath, calm down. I have everything under control; you're getting yourself all worked up, over nothing here. Go… go. Please be safe will ya." She stopped for a moment, gathering her thoughts. He was right, she was rambling.

"Ok, sorry… Thanks, bye" She said quickly, ending the call. She held the phone for a few seconds. She then called the local information center, asking for the nearest hotel phone number. The operator put her through; she made a reservation that she wasn't going to keep. She didn't want anyone getting the number she just called, on the outside chance she was being watched, if they tried to trace the last number they'd think they were going to the hotel for the night. It was always better to be overly cautious. She stood there for a moment, thinking, and calming herself, she closed her eyes. Goddamn her luck; never there when her kids needed her.

She was broken out of her thoughts by the shine of a headlight in the distance. She reached for her pistol, but it was nothing, only a couple of kids pulling up. Picking up the tray of coffees, she pressed the button on the cell phone. Unlocking the driver's side door and getting in quickly, she placed the tray of coffees onto Carmine's lap. Without a word, she raced back onto the main road. Carmine quizzically looked at her. Priscilla could feel his eyes on her as she drove.

"What?" She defensively asked, glancing at him, she knew it was coming.

"Who was that you had to call so badly? Boyfriend?" The way he said it was not in a mocking tone at all but there was something hidden in the way he said it; like she shouldn't have done what she just did. She didn't answer him. She hoped that he would get the hint, shut up, and drink his coffee.

"Well?"

Just to appease him, she answered.

"If you really must know, I was talking to my son. My kids are told to only call me if it's in the most extreme circumstances, so I thought there was something wrong, that's all."

He chuckled; it was almost an involuntary reaction. She gave him a side-glance that could have killed.

"You have kids? You said no before, there was no reason to lie. If you thought for a second I'd do something, believe me, I'm not the violent type, trust me on that." He chuckled again. "Wow, I never would have thought that. Is this something of a regular thing you do while on a job of this magnitude? Stop and check on your kids?" She could feel her face getting flushed. One thing she never did learn was to control her temper when she was pushed to her limit. She came to an abrupt stop, almost sending the coffee's flying into the windshield.

"Yo hold on! First, you don't tell me what the fuck to do, got it?" She said, pointing a finger right in his face.

"I did what any parent would do. Yeah, I'm in the middle of an important assignment, but I still have a life outside of protecting your sorry ass! So, if I want to call my kids all fucking night, at the top of every fucking hour, I'll do so, and you'll shut the fuck up about it!" She looked like she was ready to explode; her face was flushed with anger. Carmine raised both palms out in defeat with a small grin.

"Ok, ok, I just asked, that's all. Sorry, I should have guessed you were the overprotective type."

She didn't answer him or look at him. She took off into the night. She wanted to get this over with as soon as possible before she was the one that killed him.

Chapter 19
A Night on the Town

About an hour later, they broke into the Eastern Time zone. Upon hitting that Priscilla was excited; she was almost, home free. She figured it would be another two days, maybe three before they arrived in New York. They were just coming to an exit marked Lake View City. Carmine saw this, and pointed to the sign looking a little excited.

"Ah Lake View, I've been there before, really nice place. The restaurants by Lake Michigan are really fabulous," he said. Priscilla nodded, not really caring. She had not been there before and wasn't planning to go anytime soon either. She was still pissed off at him with his big commenting mouth that she would love to smack. It was almost half past nine. A yawn snuck up on her with Carmine taking notice he snapped his fingers.

"I have a great idea, why don't we go for dinner? Maybe get a nice hotel for the night, you know? I mean we've been sleeping in this car since we started."

"No way, Carmine. I can last a bit longer. If we stop now we'll lose time. Besides, you never know who might pop up if we stay somewhere for too long." He dismissed what she said with a wave of his hand.

"Oh, come on! Stop it already, we lost them, we're home free now. If you're still pissed at me about before, I'm sorry ok?" He went into his jacket pocket, pulling out his wallet and waving it. Priscilla glanced at him,

"Come on, what do you say? Don't worry; the company doesn't have to treat. You're on my tab tonight. We'll stop off get some dinner clothes. Think of it like a date." At those words, she looked at him with a raised eyebrow.

"Now don't be getting any funny ideas my friend."

"No, no I'm not. I'm just trying to sway you a little."

"Oh yeah? Well, you're not doing such a great job."

"Come on, Priscilla. I'm in desperate need of a shower." He said, smelling his armpits, trying to make a point. "I'm sure you could go for one yourself, along with a really good meal and a warm place to sleep for the night."

As the exit quickly came up, she considered his words. He was right, it had been too long without a shower and a warm bed to sleep in; and come to think of it, some hot food didn't sound too bad either. At the last possible moment, she turned off I-80. Seeing this, Carmine perked up a bit; telling her where to go. Maybe he was right, but she knew better than to assume you lost anyone, unless you put a bullet in them yourself. She figured what were the chances of anyone finding them here. If anything, they were in more danger on the open road. By now whoever was after her friend, must have figured out they were heading somewhere towards the east coast.

It took 20 minutes to roll into the brightly lit, fully active city by the great lake.

From what she'd seen so far this was the ideal place to take a vacation or maybe even a honeymoon. It reminded her a little bit of New Orleans. Carmine was rattling off places he was familiar with as she followed his pointing finger, nodding, half listening to him while keeping an eye out for trouble.

"Two blocks ahead is a women's store. I think you'll like what they have. Please pick out whatever you want and spare no expense," he said with a straight face. The shopping took almost two hours. They finally made their way to the hotel that looked to be out of place here. It was a classy hotel; which was marble and gold-plated on the inside. An intricate chandelier could be seen in the main lobby.

Bellhops were ready and eager to take whatever bags you had, showing you to your room. Their room for the night was a decked out suite on the top floor. It had wall-to-wall blood red carpet, white furniture, a 50-inch TV, and one king sized bed. The living room even had a Jacuzzi in it. Priscilla took a fast shower and put on her dinner clothes. She'd picked out something very simple with a little bit of elegance; a dark blue, strapless dress that fell below the knee, and a nice pair of closed toe heels. Carmine also picked out a similar colored Italian made suit with a white collared shirt and a skin colored tie.

When Priscilla made her way out of the bathroom fully dressed in her new attire, Carmine could not help but smile.

"Wow, you clean up nicely." She kept herself from smiling at the comment.

"Thanks, you are the charmer; I'll give you that, but again, I'll warn you, this is just dinner. Don't think this is going to turn into a James Bond scene where we wind up fucking, because it ain't gonna happen." He crossed his arms.

"My dear woman, I'm not looking for that. Like any man, I enjoy the company of a woman, but believe me, seeing how you operate I wouldn't even think of touching you even if you came on to me. I have a good feeling that the sex would be far too rough for a man like me." He said without sarcasm.

"Good thing then, for both of us." She said flashing a smile to him. He returned it in kind; grabbing his wallet and cash. Before he saw it, he heard the familiar sound of a gun being locked and loaded. He smiled, watching her slip it in her purse.

"Even dressed up, there's no changing you, huh?" He chuckled.

"Nope." Carmine just shook his head and then led the way, opening the door for her and allowing her to exit first.

They didn't take the car; Priscilla feared it would arouse suspicion. Being somewhat beaten up as it was, and if their Chasers were around, it would be an easy target to spot. Before going to the hotel, they parked it for the night in a lot a block away. She also deactivated the weapons systems; you'd be hard pressed to find anything as far as the car's extra accessories, unless you really looked. But why take any chances? Making there way outside, they walked over and got into one of the many cabs that were parked right in front of the lobby.

One thing she had to give Carmine; the guy knew how to live. When they pulled up, the restaurant looked like a palace. You could see inside the entire place, it was a sparkling glass building. Once they sat down, she ordered Italian while Carmine had the sirloin and a bottle of red wine. Sitting in here, she felt like a movie star as she looked around. Everyone had money and showed it off too, from Rolex's, to minks, to rather large diamonds that sparkled in the overhead lights.

She could also tell that half the people in here were just a bunch of stuck-up rich dicks, people she really didn't like too much. People she would run into from time to time while on assignments. Being here, she wished for a moment that the man sitting across from her was someone else. If this were a perfect world, he would be here with her now. But certain circumstances denied her of that, and that was a whole other story of its own. Carmine happened to take notice of her daydreaming.

"Everything ok Ms. Roletti?" It took a few seconds for her to realize that he was talking to her. Coming out of her daze, she replied,

"Yes…yes fine, just daydreaming a bit, nothing important."

"Really? Well, if it was nothing important, you'd not think of it." Her cheeks reddened; she was embarrassed.

"So now that we're not being shot at would you mind telling me what you did, because you certainly pissed off the wrong people." She was changing the subject. He smiled since it was so obvious.

"Well, let's just say for now that I stole a lot of money and keep it at that. I'll tell you, I promise, but I just want to enjoy the evening here without thinking of what's out there for me, ok? By the way, I like this nice woman I see here tonight; keep it up and you'll get a nice tip for your services." He said, winking at her and tapping the left breast of his suit jacket. She nodded in agreement. He was right about the first part; that was why she agreed to do this in the first place, change the pace, but the last part; a tip? What was he talking about? She didn't put too much thought into it.

They continued to eat while looking out over the Great Lake. She looked at Carmine; he was surprisingly good company in a more relaxed atmosphere.

He was quite the schmoozer too. She wondered how many women fell for this type of treatment. Even though with all this niceness she was receiving, she still didn't care for him much. She only put on the nice act just to lighten the mood a bit; she couldn't be a bitch every waking moment.

By the time they finished their meal, it was close to one in the morning by the time they made it back to the hotel, settling in for the night it was just after one thirty. Priscilla had the cabby drive by the place three times just to make sure there wasn't anything out of the ordinary waiting for them. Carmine loosened his tie and took his suit jacket off. He turned to look for Priscilla, who had already ducked into the bathroom. Moments later, she reappeared in the same clothes she'd had on before; white collared shirt, with those form fitting black slacks. Carmine looked her up and down, grinning.

"I kind of figured the dress was killing you." He said, chuckling.

"You're a real comedian tonight, huh? Take the bedroom and I'll take the couch, enjoy the bed tonight. We're not stopping like this anymore for the remainder of the trip." He looked over his shoulder as he walked to the bedroom.

"Yeah, I kind of figured as much." Turning in the doorway, and facing her now, he said with the utmost sincerity, "Good night Ms. Roletti, it was really a pleasure." Not waiting for her reply, he closed the doors. Finally alone, Priscilla went to the couch, sat down and sighed to herself thanking whatever God there is that the night went quickly. She didn't feel comfortable being his 'dinner date'. She got up and walked to the window overlooking the city below. It was so quiet from up here. Her thoughts wandered to her kids then. She wanted to call Pat and check on her son, she should be there to take care of them, not someone else.

She hoped her kids would not resent her for not being there when they needed her. She had no doubt they knew she loved them more than life itself and would do anything for them. To a kid though, the most important thing is not what you can buy them or give them, but to be there when they need you. She pushed aside the thoughts to avoid feeling depressed. It was late and she was tired. In the living room, there were two couches and a small single chair. Picking up one end of the chair, she dragged it across the carpeted floor. She put it in the corner for a good view of the door, and out of sight from the balcony. She sat, putting her feet up on the coffee table; leaning her head back, it wasn't long before she fell into a light sleep.

"Wake up sleeping beauty, it's time to roll." Carmine looked up with half opened eyes. He turned to the window, as the curtains were drawn open. The sun was not even up yet. All you could see were the faint rays rising over the horizon. Throwing his head back in the pillow with a muffled voice, he said,

"What time is it? It's not even light out yet."

"It's five-thirty, come on, move your ass! I want to be on the road by six, come on!" She threw the covers off him, and turning the light on, she saw the unpleasant sight of him with nothing on but his underwear.

"Come on, get dressed. You have five minutes, move!" For a moment, she had a quick flashback of her days in the Marines. She turned and left, closing the doors. They didn't really have anything to carry except for the dress he bought her and his extra clothes. She used the large shopping bag, and stuffed the items inside. Carmine made his way into the living room, not fully awake yet. Yawning, he went to the bathroom, and came out a few minutes later.

"What the hell took you?"

"I had to brush my teeth. I guess secret agents don't brush their teeth?" She rolled her eyes to the comment; she was tiring from his constant wisecracks. Once they made their way to the lobby, Carmine walked to the front desk, giving the keys back to the clerk. He then made his way towards Priscilla; she was waiting by the revolving door.

"Wait here, don't move, and watch for me."

"Ok."

"Give me the bag." She took it off him, walking outside into the pre-morning chill. She forgot her coat, something she was cursing herself for as she walked down the block in hurried steps, more for the fact that her skin had goose bumps.

Five minutes later, she approached the parking garage attendant, she handed him the slip and paid. As soon as that was done, he ran off retrieving the Charger. She stood outside, keeping an eye out. The streets were quiet and dark; streetlamps were slowly turning off now. She looked to the east seeing the sun just coming up. Faint orange rays filtered through the opened crevices in the city landscape to start a new day. A new day that got her closer to her objective. She broke out of her thoughts thanks to the headlights engulfing her from behind.

As the Charger came towards her, she stepped aside. The attendant parked and got out. Priscilla handed him a fifty. Seeing the bill, he gave her a large grin of appreciation saying thanks. She hit the trunk release, and placed the bag of clothes inside. She walked over to the driver's side, the attendant held the door for her.

"Nice car miss, but what the hell happened? Damn shame." He was referring to the white marks left by the deflected bullets.

"Hailstorm." She replied with a straight face as she got in and drove off without another word. The attendant shrugged at the comment, going back into his booth. Pulling up to the hotel front she honked twice. She then reached underneath, reactivating the weapons systems. Carmine quickly came out, got in, and they sped off into the morning.

Chapter 20
Desperate

Mark Lewis was getting rather impatient. With midday fast approaching, the progress of his investigation was going nowhere. For two days, there were no sightings of this infamous Dodge Charger. The goddamn car didn't just disappear, that was impossible. It had to be somewhere, even if they ditched or burned it, it would have to be somewhere, and dealing with these locals was getting on his last nerve. They would be lucky to wipe their own ass, let alone find anything out in these god-awful sticks.

Lewis was about 20 miles from the Pennsylvania border. From the highway battle Lewis had very little to go on. This whole investigation was progressing on hunches more than anything else. They knew the car was heading east, but where exactly? That was the question. Even the data Lewis found in the blown-up box-truck didn't reveal anything like that. He poured over it for hours thinking maybe he missed something, which he did from the fast look he gave it before; he failed to notice bank numbers. Curious, he checked into it and found the untraceable account that held $100,000.

He surmised it was some type of down payment. Which was a relief because if all else failed, he could cut and run if he needed to. But for right now, he'd still try to go for the larger sum. However, to go about that he needed to be one-step ahead of her.

Lewis had checkpoints set up not only on I-80 but also on the side streets and back roads. Manpower was very limited, so he had to work with what he had. Overall, he had a good radius for the ground that needed to be covered. They even tried to check each and every rest stop, hotel and rat hole they could think of and yet nothing. Where did she go? Lewis wanted to scream aloud in frustration.

This goddamn bitch didn't just up and disappear. While the locals were doing that, Lewis stalked I-80 hoping that maybe he would spot them himself. Even Lewis, a man that always knew it was never over until it was over, was having his doubts. He also wondered who this woman was. She had to be some type of assassin or bodyguard, yet another obstacle to contend with. The longer this dragged out, the more the odds increased against him. The FBI could be sending someone to arrest him now for all he knew, and that was a thought that didn't sit well with him at all.

Chapter 21
The Grim Reaper and the Hound Dog

It had been two days since the highway incident and there was no sign of the Charger anywhere. No news reports, no sightings, nothing. For the time being, calm returned to the land. Now driving along during the peak of midday where the sun was shining its brightest; the nameless killer only known as the Albino stalked on, traveling from Boulder Hill, Montana to his current location. He just crossed into Pennsylvania.

How he made it this far without, food or even an hour's worth of rest was beyond anyone's understanding, but he did it. This was what he did. He was like the storm cloud that never stopped blanketing the land in darkness. To the few that knew him on a personal level, it was futile to run. Your only chance was to take a stand and hope that it would be over quickly, or just kill yourself.

On one job in particular, he drove the poor unfortunate soul over the cliff of insanity.

By the time the Albino caught up to him, the man opted to slit his own wrists rather than stare into the eyes of this white-faced demon.

It was disappointing to the Albino that; the mark took the coward's way out. He loved to put that fear into their hearts. He loved the sight of their wide-eyed looks of terror.

He reveled in the fact, that he had complete control over people in such a way. As he became known throughout the assassin community for his ruthlessness and cunning ways. More ran in fear when word got to them that the skull-faced killer was coming. Rumors spread quickly that anyone who so much as stared into those golden eyes would have their own face turn white like his.

When he first heard that one he couldn't help but laugh, even in this modern age we live in, people still fell for ghost stories and the like. What they were referring to was with each victim, he laid to rest, he would proceed to leave them with the same visage as his own, that skull death mask, like he did on the three trucker's days ago. No one knew for sure how this tireless tracker did his job so effectively. Again, there were rumors and speculation. But the truth was this, it was a matter of simple number crunching, common sense and intestinal fortitude; something that you can't be trained or taught. He knew how to read people, whether by seeing a picture, or being told about them. He had this knack of getting inside someone's head, and knowing what they'll do even before they would. It was a very hit and miss way of doing it, and he had his failures, but overall it served him well over the years.

Now driving on route I-80, he was using that same talent. He concluded that this woman, being the pro he thought she was, would not stop, not yet anyway. If only he had known how wrong he was on that one. No this grim reaper had the feeling they'd stop closer to their destination. During his trip, the Albino only stopped to refuel.

No matter how good you are, you had to stop and rest at some point. Now in Pennsylvania he figured this would be the time they'd stop, letting their guard down. He figured she probably thought they made it, coming this far and not facing any further threats. Even if she was like him and could go for long periods without food or rest, he was sure her companion couldn't. The man she was protecting would be their undoing in the end.

As the Albino made his way into Pennsylvania, deep in his own twisted thoughts, he failed to notice he was being tracked himself. Since he spotted the white-faced killer back in Montana, Shultz, the Aryan stayed on him like a hound dog. During the day Shultz would stay as far back as he could, letting cars get in front of him, just so long as he didn't lose sight of the Albino. At night, Shultz kept his headlights off, continuing in this never-ending drive. In the middle of the night on route I-80, one would think, even in the dead of night, the main artery across the country would be somewhat packed with cars and trucks, but it was the complete opposite. Every now and then, a semi would pass, but that was it.

At midday on the second day of following the Albino, Shultz was all but beat. As he kept up his tag along, Shultz kept thinking about how the hell this guy just kept going the way he did. He had to be as tired as he was right about now. The only damn thing he stopped for was gas. He did not even stop to check roadside rest areas or hotels they'd passed. After the Albino finished up at the gas stations they hit along the way, Shultz would pull up just as the Albino would make his way back on the highway. He'd get gas along with a rather large cup of coffee, and a few red bulls for good measure. If Shultz kept his eyes closed for longer than a blink, he'd fall out while behind the wheel.

The skinhead hated to admit this, but he was thinking that maybe he was far out of his league. It was like this guy was a goddamn robot or something.

The hazy afternoon sun was burning Shultz's sleep-deprived eyes. If this son of a bitch doesn't stop soon, Shultz was going to just throw his hands up and say, 'Fuck it.' This whole chase cost him too much as it was. Then, out of nowhere, the blue pickup made a sharp right off the highway.

The Aryan, seeing this, sped up now trying to see where he was going. Right off the highway there was a diner, surrounded by what looked like a cornfield, with a large parking lot that was almost filled. Shultz drove on by it, catching a glimpse of the Albino parking. Shultz then sped up more, passing the diner, going up the road for a half a mile, then cutting across to the other side of the highway and coming back around to the diner. After about five minutes, Shultz pulled off the same exit, heading towards the parking lot, trying to find a spot in a corner somewhere. All the while, he kept an eye out, since this could be a set-up.

Maybe that white devil saw me, he thought. He came to the end of the parking lot, close to the field. When he finally parked, he sat up in his seat trying to get the kinks out of his neck from all the driving.

All he wanted to do was put his head on the steering wheel just for a moment. The Aryan took a quick glance of the lot, but there was nothing there, why would this stupid Albino stop here? Then his eyes fell on the black Dodge Charger, with the white-pitted marks most likely left by him from the other day. Seeing this, Shultz's tiredness was gone in an instant.

New found energy was building up in him, energy that was fueled by greed and the lust for revenge. Shultz reached down to the floor of the passenger side, grabbing the disposable rocket launcher. Getting out, he went into the field just far enough to keep an eye on the diner. He released the pins, sliding the tube to its six-foot length. Now all he had to do was wait. He was close now and victory was for the taking. When they came out, they'd have the surprise of their life. Hopefully, the distraction would give him time to kill the woman, the Albino and grab the old man before anyone was the wiser. Shultz smiled, for the first time in his life he used that walnut he called a brain.

Chapter 22
Let's do Lunch

It wasn't until the early afternoon when she felt the hunger pains. She'd not eaten anything in almost two days. Food sounded really good right about now, she was starving. She looked over to see Carmine curled up like a baby in a crib. He'd be happy to stop for a bite, she knew that for sure, but being so close to home, it would be only another five hours or so. They were just coming up to Sharon, Pennsylvania and to delay this hell of a road trip was something she did not want to do. All this driving was starting to take a toll on her though. She reached into the back with a free hand, feeling inside her bag to find nothing. No more water or protein bars.

"Shit." She whispered as she looked over to her passenger. She started to tap him on the back. "Hey sleeping beauty, wake up." Not getting any type of reaction, she started to poke him in the ribs a few times. Each poke had more force behind it than the last. Finally, he stirred a bit, talking in his sleep. Rolling her eyes, she smacked him in the head. He jumped up.

"What? What?" He asked, lazy eyed, turning to her. "We're here?" He said half asleep.

"No, we're stopping for food, thought you'd like to know." He perked up rather quickly hearing this. Just after the exit for Sharon, Pennsylvania, there was a diner right off the highway surrounded by what looked like corn or wheat fields. They pulled into the busy diner, and parked in a spot that would be out of sight, but easy enough to make a fast getaway if need be. Both got out in the mid afternoon stretching their backs. Priscilla kept a wary eye open for anything while Carmine was oblivious as always. He looked like he had not a care in the world, even though they had three attempts on his life already.

She gestured him to lead the way up the concrete steps into a small foyer with double doors leading into the diner. It was a run of the mill diner that you would find anywhere else. Straight ahead were the counters where you'd find the old men sitting. The smell of eggs brought on a hunger she didn't realize she had until then. A pleasant young woman with two menus approached them with a warm smile.

"Good afternoon, just the two of you?" She had a light southern accent. They both nodded, returning her smile, she led them to a booth close to the counter. Priscilla sat facing the door to keep an eye on who was coming and going. They both sat in silence while they looked at their menus.

Carmine fished into his jacket for his reading glasses while the busboy came over placing two waters on the table. Soon after, the waiter came over with a notepad in hand, eager to take their order. They both ordered coffee. Carmine had scrambled eggs with fries and bacon. Priscilla had the same only with home fries instead. Taking their menus, the waiter hurried off, coming back in a flash with their coffees and milk. She only added milk to hers. While Carmine was preparing his she looked at him waiting for him to notice. It didn't take long. He looked back at her over the rim of his cup as he sipped the piping hot liquid.

"What?" He put his cup down, adding more sugar.

"You know what. Don't give me that shit. You said once we had a moment, you'd tell me what your story was. So we have our moment, now talk." He smirked, he knew her well enough to know that she wasn't going to let him slide now. Carmine took a deep breath surrendering to her demand.

"I worked all my life living the best I could, never really caring for anyone, or anything. The corporation I worked for suddenly went belly up." He stopped, taking a sip of coffee. "I looked for work right away, and found a very lucrative private accounting job. And I mean very lucrative I was being paid five times the average rate."

"Ok, I don't need to hear every minor detail." She said, cutting him off with a tone of impatience matching the look on her face. She didn't care to hear his whole life story.

"Anyway, I was working one evening checking files, when I came across something, by pure luck. I found hidden funds, not just a couple of thousand. I'm talking millions being funneled to overseas banks, mostly Middle Eastern, and it was set up brilliantly. Even I was impressed. I thought I had seen every type of money funneling scheme, but this was perfect.

So anyway, I looked deeper into it. I found some records; the man that I was employed by was funding a worldwide terror network right here in the U.S. He was also sending money to Al-Qaeda, Hamas and other organizations of terror. I found more documents with code names. Then I uncovered something in all my digging that showed just how good this was really set up. This guy funded the U.S. embassy bombing in Greece last year, you remember that right?"

She nodded, how could you not, over a hundred people died in the blast, the Feds said it was Al Qaeda. Even her own organization thought the bombing was by their hand.

"After I realized what I had just discovered, I got scared but then." He raised a finger. "I thought about it a little. During that time, I was going through my own shit. I was diagnosed with my heart condition, like I said I was one-step away from a transplant. I had nothing to lose, and everything to gain. Therefore, I proceeded to copy everything a little at a time. When I finally had everything I needed, I not only left without a word, but I proceeded to give myself a little retirement bonus." He said with a smile.

"How much?" She asked

"Oh, about a half a billion dollars"

Priscilla almost choked on her coffee at how nonchalantly he said that figure. Her eyes went wide and she repeated the figure again just to be sure. He nodded and continued. "I haven't said a word, to anyone since then.

The man in question is no fool. I traveled the country having a grand old time, but unfortunately all good things have to come to an end. So, I went to San Francisco and opened my firm. I thought for sure he'd never find me, but I underestimated him. When he found me, the threats started to mount, day in and day out, it wasn't the money he wanted back it was the documents. He told me he would not harm me. If I gave back all the data, he said he'd leave me be, but I'm no fool either. I knew that once those documents were handed to him I'd be a dead man walking. I refused, and when the first attempt on my life came that was when

I called someone who in turn got me in touch with your boss." She leaned back in her seat, eyeing him with an evil look.

"What? You don't believe me?"

"No, I do, but why didn't you come forward sooner? I mean what you did was a selfish thing. God only knows how many lives were taken up till now, and could've been saved by what you know." She felt her face turning red with anger. He shrugged at her words without a care in the world.

"Let me tell you something, in this world you have to look after yourself and to hell with anyone else, remember that! It wasn't my problem at the time; it was my ticket to good fortune." He raised his voice somewhat starting to point, but then thought better of it as he saw her eyes look to the almost extended finger. By then she had heard enough. Trying to keep her voice low, she cut him off as he spoke.

"So now it's your problem, huh, because the heat was too much for you? Now, the great Carmine can tell all he knows, because he's a fucking pussy?" Even with her words, it still looked like he really didn't care. He had the 'what can I tell you' look. During this trip, she actually started to feel sorry for him. Aside from being an asshole at times she took a liking to him, a little bit. He was funny and charming when he wanted to be. Now she looked him over with disgust. She wanted to break his face.

Once again, the power of greed has led to the deaths of innocent people. A tale that will always repeat itself from now until the end of time. She leaned back folding her arms across her chest. She was aggravated with him, even disappointed a little, but not surprised. Just then the waiter came with their food. He asked them if they wanted a refill on their coffees and both said yes. He left and came back with the pot of coffee, refilling both to the rim, Carmine then started to eat.

"So, who is this guy?" Priscilla asked, he looked at her wide-eyed. He chuckled a bit too loud, catching the attention of a couple sitting across from them.

"Ha! Like I'm gonna tell you Ms. Roletti, if that's even your real name. That's my guarantee that you will take me to your boss."

"Oh, come on, you think I would leave you here if you told me?"

"To be honest with you no, you're a bitch, yes, but I don't think you'd leave me flat, you seem to be the type that when you start something you see it through." He stopped just after the backhanded compliment, taking another gulp of coffee.

"Ok, instead of a name tell me something else." She said pressing more. Reluctantly, he placed his cup back on the dish,

"Ok, one of the many things I discovered was that he was funding human experimentation, ways to make the ultimate soldier, freaky stuff, like right out of a sci-fi movie. Happy now?" He said, going back to his food. There was no need to press him further, Priscilla sat back finishing her food.

There were no more words to be spoken. They continued to eat in silence, with the exception of chatter, and the striking of silverware hitting the plates from the patrons around them. Priscilla thought about what Carmine had said. Shadow Ops knew of a player behind the scenes for some time. No informants out there could ascertain the identities of said person or persons until now.

She wondered who this particular person was. Coming up with more questions than answers to this new twist, she placed her mind on what the kids might be doing at this moment.

She was hoping that her son was feeling better. As soon as she got back to New York, she'd call. The sound of the door chimes, pulled her from those thoughts. She looked up to see the new patron walking in, and her stomach closed up, tightening like a knot. She never knew exactly who was chasing them. But when she saw the Albino walk in, she just knew from the sight of him that he was indeed trouble. He had an aura of menace that billowed from him.

He looked creepy; those eyes alone could instill fear in you. He walked to the counter, ignoring the hostess talking to him. He was scanning the diner's many patrons, some also looked up to the new customer, but quickly went back to their meals and conversation. He found what he was looking for. At the same time, he and Priscilla's eyes met, the feeling in her gut was confirmed with the locking of her blue eyes to his golden ones.

"Sir? May I seat you?" The hostess asked for the third time, he looked over to her finally,

"I'm sorry ma'am, I was meeting some folks here and I just found them." He said as he tipped his hat to her and walked towards their booth. The hostess, satisfied with the answer went back to the front counter. Before he could get a clear view of them, Priscilla already had her gun on her lap.

As he approached, he looked like the grim reaper with black jeans, a collared shirt, black vest, and a black cowboy hat. They never took their eyes off each other; it was as if time froze. She wished she could be invisible right now. He stopped, standing over their table like a shadow.

"Well, good day to you both." He said, tipping his hat a bit. Carmine looked up turning almost as white as the Albino himself. "May I sit down?" He wasn't asking permission, though; it was more like 'I'm sitting down thank you.' He sat right next to Carmine. He had his gloved hands on the table where Priscilla could see them; her hands were on the table too. He looked at her then to Carmine,

"Well, it would seem I won the prize." He said with a smirk,

"You didn't win anything yet asshole!" She spat out in a low tone looking him dead in his golden eyes. He laughed softly.

"Really? Little lady, do you think you can stop me? I take what I want, it's as simple as that."

"Oh yeah? Well, you're welcome to try cowboy." He stared at her.

"Listen little lady, I'm trying here to be civil, I'm willing to let you walk outta here alive. I'm not one to walk away from a fight, but being there are others out there I really don't have the time to deal with you. Then we have these fine folks here." He gestured about with one gloved hand. "I don't need witnesses. I can't go on killin' the entire place, and besides, ridding the world of a beautiful lady such as yourself would be a shame."

"Spare me please!" She quickly shot back at him, the tension was starting to build, and Carmine sat there with a look that said he wanted to be somewhere else.

"The others would just shoot you on sight if they saw you now, two of the animals after you are Trish and Omar. You heard of them right?"

She nodded. Anyone in the intelligence community knew about them. They were some of the most bloodthirsty assassins out there, and psychotic was an understatement. He reached over for a French fry from Carmine's plate. Shoving it in his mouth, it looked like he just swallowed it whole, there was no chewing.

"Now, I'll ask one more time. You want this done the clean way or the messy way? Either one suits me just fine." She glared at him, she did not like how this was going. She was stuck; she couldn't start a shoot out in here. There were too many men, women, and children. That was all she needed to do was hit a bystander. This scum couldn't care less. She was just about to say something when the doors opened again. She kept her eyes on him since she was going to say something. Her mouth started to move, but a loud scream caught her attention, as well as the Albino's, and the rest of the diner's.

"YOU!"

Chapter 23
Two's a company, Three's a crowd

Priscilla, the Albino and Carmine stayed in the booth. The other patrons all sat as still as statues, with looks of fear. Limping closer to them was Kim, battered, bruised and bloodied. The hostess rushed to her aide, but was thrown to the floor for her effort.

"YOU!" She screamed again at the trio as she leveled the grenade launcher at the booth they were sitting in, finger on the trigger. All three in the booth looked at her.

"You two stand the fuck up! Now, Slowly!" Priscilla and the Albino looked at each other.

"NOW!" Kim said, spitting her words. Both complied with the request, the Albino stood up first, hands raised. Priscilla followed, taking the gun off her lap, and placing it on the table. Kim limped closer; she looked like she was about to fall over. Her one-piece jumpsuit was in tatters and her left eye was closed up. She really looked like the walking dead. How she survived and made it this far was anyone's guess. You must be kidding me, Priscilla thought to herself.

The Albino's attention was totally focused on the new threat. The situation went from bad to fucked. Kim was looking for bloodshed now. All she needed was a reason to shoot. Licking his lips nervously, the Albino spoke softly.

"Well, Miss Kim, I'm glad to see you're ok. Listen, why don't we all go outside and talk this over. You're scaring all the people here, and besides, if you shoot that off, you might kill yourself too. You don't want that, do you?" By the look on her face, she was not going to be sweet-talked by him or anyone. The other patrons looked on in horror. Some were praying, while others held their loved ones tightly, looking on waiting and hoping the outcome would be a good one.

Behind Kim, on the other end of the diner people were on their cell phones, calling the cops. She was just about to say something when the bellow of sirens could be heard pulling up to the diner. She turned her head for a moment, taking her attention off the two in front of her. That split second was all Priscilla and the Albino needed. Both reached for their guns, someone screamed, bringing Kim's attention back to the two. Just as she looked back, her body was riddled with bullets, dropping her to the floor. She was dead before she hit the ground. After the barrage of bullets was sent, both turned, pointing their guns at each other now. Back to square one. He smiled at her; his aim was firm, as was hers.

"Well, looks like we're back here again." He said, reading her thoughts.

"You know, we think alike, why don't we hook up, we'd make a good team. I'll split the money with you," he said. She was just about to reply when someone else rushed in kicking the door open.

"FREEZE! Drop your weapons and lay face down now!" Just as the words came from the state trooper's mouth, both the Albino and Priscilla turned their guns on the trooper. Now back to negative square one, another stand off, the Albino's full attention was on the new threat. The troopers face dropped seeing this.

"Now…now… everyone, let's just calm down ok." The trooper said in a soothing voice with his palm raised forward. Seeing there was no other way out of this, Priscilla in a blinding motion reached behind her back, grabbing the .22 caliber from her waist, putting it inches from the Albino's skull. Just then, the officer was going to cry out a warning, when two shots went off simultaneously. When the smoke cleared, the Albino was on the floor dead and the cop was grunting in pain from a well-aimed bullet to the kneecap. Priscilla stood ready in case any more unexpected surprises came through the door.

"Carmine! Come out from there, let's go!" As he crawled out from under the table, Priscilla grabbed him by the arm pulling him up and forward. Approaching the front door, the cop was on the floor holding his wound rocking back and forth in pain. Blood was seeping through his fingers. She looked around quickly, scanning the diner. Everyone was hidden in his or her seats or underneath the table. The only sounds that filled the air were coming from the cop grunting, she kneeled down quick to look at the wound.

"Sit still goddamn it!" She spat out as she moved his hands away. "Put your hands back over it and press hard, you'll be alright," She said with very little care in her voice. Grabbing Carmine by the arm, they left the diner.

"Move your ass! This place will be crawling with cops!" As she pulled him along, she halted by the door, peering outside to make sure it was good to go out there. All she saw was the cruiser that belonged to the cop in the diner. She glanced once more behind her taking notice to the people staring at her. She looked down to the cop still wincing in pain with the hostess crouched by his side. She too was staring at them in silence. Priscilla had no words of comfort to say. What could she say? Sorry? Not likely. She was never sorry for doing her job and never would be. She turned back to the door, swinging it open, she stepped out slowly at first; the wind was cool and brisk.

The sun was tucked behind some clouds for the moment. She took another step forward, eyeing the area. There wasn't anything to see really, only the cars from the patrons inside who would no doubt scramble out of here once they made their exit. Looking back to Carmine, who was tucked by the doorway, she gestured for him to come. She broke out in a slow walk with her gun in hand. Carmine was right behind her. They both made their way to the Charger when it exploded into a ball of fire, propelling them both to the ground from the shockwave.

She lost consciousness, for how long she didn't know. It took her a while to regain her bearings. Her vision was blurred, dirt and gravel covered her. Staying still, she moved her head about trying to see what just happened. Twenty feet from her was their ride, a shell of a car now engulfed in flames. She wanted to cry. Not out of fear, but out of frustration and anger. Placing both palms to the ground, Priscilla slowly started to get up. Her gun was inches from her, she stretched out her arm, her fingers barely touched it when it was kicked away. She looked up at the skinhead, whose massive frame blocked the sun. She squinted at him. Over his shoulder was the limp form of Carmine, who was awake but dazed. He leaned in closer to her smiling.

"Well, it would seem I was right to follow that stupid albino. Now, thanks to you, I don't have to go through the trouble of killing him." He laughed.

"You're a good looking' bitch, maybe we could hook up once I claim my prize." Fucking men, they all thought the same. Was there ever a time when they didn't think of getting into a woman's pants? Not likely, she thought.

"Dream on white trash!" The comment took him by surprise; he frowned and shook his head in disappointment.

"And tough too. I like it, but you're right. It is wishful thinking on my part." With those words, he reached into his pants, and took out a silver revolver cocking the hammer back. Priscilla saw the cylinder rotate. In the distance the sound of a speeding vehicle emerged, Shultz turned his attention to the direction of the new arrivals, forgetting about the helpless blonde, he brought his gun to bear on the black Sprinter that just pulled up.

It was more luck than anything else that Trish and Omar happened to be in the area and picked up the scan of the 911 calls from the diner. It was a long shot that it could have something to do with them, but it was worth a look into. They had to pass the area anyway, and pulling up, she was glad they did so. High in the sky, was a tower of black smoke coming from the burning car. As she came to the scene, her eyes immediately fell onto the Aryan. Trish sped up, she knew she'd attract the attention of the skinhead, but now was not the time to play games.

Just as she pulled up, Shultz turned in their direction; aiming his weapon at them. Trish and Omar got out with their guns drawn, in yet another stand off the Aryan smiled.

"Well, look who it is. The fucking freaks." Ignoring the comment, Omar spoke up first.

"Why don't you put the old man down, scumbag?" Shultz of course did no such thing, but this banter gave Priscilla time to make her move. As this was going on, she lay as still as she could as she fished in her pocket. She felt the two cell phones inside. She grabbed the company phone, she had the menus memorized along with the button sequences to activate what she wanted.

What she was doing was setting the self-destruct mode of the now burning car. Even though it exploded into a heaping pile of scrap, the self-destruct was still intact.

She programmed it to go off in one minute, which was ticking down. She leaned over, the Aryan's back was turned to her, Trish and Omar were not even looking at her. They were focused on their new foe. Priscilla readied herself. She turned hard and quick, kicking the tree trunks that were Shultz's legs out from under him. She sent him falling backwards towards her. Rolling out of the way she readied a telegraphed kick to his head the moment he fell to his back, it stunned him. As he went down, Carmine fell to the ground. The move caught Trish and Omar by surprise, but it didn't take them long to focus their attention on her. Within seconds, she was on her feet. Grabbing her gun and hoisting Carmine up with a strain, they ran for it through the smoke her burning car provided.

Trish and Omar fired wild shots, missing. They started to give chase, but were thrown back from the second explosion she timed. With the confusion, she created, they made their way running hard through the parked cars and into the field. She held onto Carmine, pulling him by his arm.

He was tiring her out. She looked back at him, he was sweating and his face was red. Moments later, they broke out of the field and into the parking lot of a mall. They stood there for a moment, looking at the large complex. They were not sure how they managed to get to the mall, but they did. Continuing onward, Priscilla was practically dragging Carmine by the arm. He was slowing her down badly. The old man was out of shape. On top of everything else, with bloodthirsty assassins on their ass, the mall was ripe with activity. Goddammit, she thought as they walked closer. She was running out of options now. She had to find a place for Carmine, where he could lay low while she took care of these bastards.

One of the things she hated was running. Sure, it was something that was done a lot in this line of work, but only if the odds were stacked against you. Now with no car there was no place to go. It was time to end this, odds in her favor or not. There were only three, one as dumb as an ox, Trish and Omar. She knew Trish and Omar's reputation. Everyone did by word of mouth. She handled worse and she would handle them just the same as anyone else.

"Almost there, hang in there!" She said, not looking at him. When they broke into the parking lot, she tried to straighten up.

Priscilla slowed her pace with his. She was eyeing the area cautiously. She looked over to him; his face was as red as a beet. He loosened his tie a bit, and unbuttoned the top of his shirt.

"Where… where are we going?" He said in between gasps for air.

"We are not going anywhere, my friend. You are going to a nice shady spot to hide while I take care of some business." He didn't answer her.

The glass doors slid open as they approached, hitting them with a rush of cool air that felt good against their faces. The place was laid out like any other mall in America, with storefronts covering every space. She kept him close to her, holding him as if they were a couple. They kept a nonchalant pace.

"Men's store… men's store." She said under her breath as they walked around a bend, going deeper inside. She needed to change his appearance, hide him among the crowd, and take out their chasers. Then hopefully finish up this mission without any more obstacles.

Chapter 24
On the Hunt

Shultz pulled up to the large parking area, driving very slowly through the lot, eyeing every face he saw. His quarry was nowhere to be seen. The veins in his massive arms were bulging from the stress; the fact that this bitch still eluded him pissed him off to no end. How could some broad be so tough? In a way, he had to thank her. If it wasn't for the explosion from her car, he might have been killed in a shootout with those freaks. That distraction was all he needed to get in his truck and speed off while Trish and Omar recovered.

Having no luck in the lot, Shultz pulled into a parking spot and jumped out rather quick for a man of his size. He shoved his silver revolver into his pants, throwing his shirt over it, he lumbered towards the mall. He wasn't even sure they'd be here, but leave no stone unturned was something that is momma told him as a kid. As he made his way closer to the mall, the people he passed glanced at him as they walked further away. Being he was so big and having a swastika tattooed right on his forearm, looks were something he was used to. At first, he hated it and would threaten people for staring at him, but then over time he rather liked it. They feared him, he thought, and he wanted people to fear him, he wanted them to know who their superior was.

Chapter 25
Late to the Party

Mark Lewis once again arrived too late. When he received the call, he was a good thirty minutes away. He was getting more and more frustrated with this. All that was left of what had happened was the burning wreck of the Charger, inside the diner was an albino with a .22 caliber bullet stuck in the back of his head. Lewis was surprised he wasn't dead, and then there was the broken and battered corpse of an unidentified woman.

Another assassin, he mused. He'd get the ID on her soon, along with the albino's. If he survives his injuries, Lewis will get him to talk. The troopers scrambled around taking statements from the patrons. The hostess and other patrons all had the same story. The parties involved consisted of a blonde, the man she was protecting, and the two assassins. Lewis stood in the front of the diner, away from the crowd, deep in thought. Things were starting to look up now.

Two assassins were caught. All that was left was the woman and the man. The bounty was now minus transportation, at least for the time being. Once he arrived at the diner, he sent some troopers to scurry about the area with the hope of finding them. He looked back to the burning Charger. He wanted to have a closer look at the car, there had to be something in there. As of yet, there was no fire truck on the scene to put out the flames, something that was increasingly annoying to him right now. Time was running out. He looked at his watch; he walked over to the deputy and tapped him on the shoulder as he spoke to a witness.

"Where the hell is the fire truck deputy? This heap has been blazing for almost a half an hour now."

"I'm sorry, sir, but they are on their way, it's a volunteer fire department and they're two towns away from here." Lewis turned, saying nothing more to the cop, what could he possibly say? Fucking backwards ass hicks, the whole fucking place could burn down and they'd have their fingers up their asses, watching it. He took a deep breath to calm himself, getting frustrated was not going to do him any good now.

Chapter 26
The Mall

They made there way into the main area of the mall; looking for a suitable spot to stash Carmine. As they walked out of Macy's, Priscilla turned to regard him, it wasn't perfect, but it would have to do. She bought him a black blazer and a fedora, a brown one. As they walked, she spotted the perfect place for him.

"See that KB Toys over there?" He nodded, following her pointed finger.

"Go and stay there until I come get you. If you're not in the store itself, then stay within the area, got it? Take my cell phone." She handed him her company phone and she kept her personal one.

"Blend in." She said.

"What do you mean blend in?" He said with a look of worry. She almost smacked her forehead at the question.

"Blend in dammit! I don't have time to teach you spy 101. Blend in, go and pester a clerk, ask questions, whatever, pretend you're a grandfather shopping for your grandson, now go quick!"

He walked off, sliding right into the crowd. After watching him disappear into the store across from her on the other side of the mall, she breathed a slight sigh of relief. Not having to watch out for him would make this easier now. She turned to the matter at hand. Her gun was tucked into her waist; her collared shirt concealing it.

She had two extra clips and the .22caliber still sitting in her waist just in case she needed more firepower. She walked through the crowds at a quick pace, passing slow, as molasses people who were in another world, talking to their companions or on their cell phones. That was something she hated when she shopped herself, loud-mouthed people talking about their business so everyone could hear them. Priscilla often thought they did this to sound important, but it only made them look like an ass. She walked slower, watching the floor below her as well as the upper floor where she was. She was looking for a spot where she could stand and watch.

She figured the best place would be the front entrance where they came in. Anyone else who was chasing them would probably come in that way as well. Like every other mall across the country, it had more than 20 access points and she couldn't check each and every one. She figured if she couldn't confront them now then at least the mall itself would be a place to lay low for a bit until the heat blew over.

This was not a smart move, coming here, because there were too many bystanders, kids especially. But, there was no other way. She hoped that if something did happen it could be contained in a far off place.

She leaned over the railing a little, watching the throng of shoppers. Her hand was on her gun ready to draw at a moments notice. It didn't take long for one of her pursuers to catch up. The skinhead obviously didn't try to conceal himself. His presence reeked of cockiness and stupidity, something that would lead to his downfall very quickly in this line of work.

She got a good look at him too. Big motherfucker, she thought. The guy was literally a mountain of muscle. His head was turning back and forth, checking faces. She had a good idea that the Aryan, Trish and Omar were not good friends. If given the opportunity, Priscilla had, no doubt, he'd take them out as well, perhaps that was something she could exploit if she had to. Priscilla watched his every move as she made her way to the escalator, going down.

She was now on the first floor walking towards the skinhead. His back was facing her. With Carmine safe, and not having to worry about him, she focused. As she made her way closer, she picked up the pace even more, while trying not to bump into anyone.

The closer she got to the Aryan, the angrier she became. Her temper flared like a phoenix coming out of a fire. She hadn't been this heated in a long time, and that was dangerous, it was when you made mistakes. She couldn't help it, seeing this disgrace to her race. She was a few feet from him now, she approached quicker, she had her hand close to her gun.

At this point she didn't care about making a scene in here, she was going to take him out. Once close enough, she'd pump three fast shots into his side and walk away like nothing happened, following the panic that would definitely ensue from the gunshots.

The Aryan suddenly stopped turning his head back and forth, she was glad too. Trying to keep up with him and not bump into anyone was irritating her and slowing her down. She could see the bulge in his waist a gun most likely. It blended in well, but to a trained eye like hers, it stuck out. She was twenty feet from him when he spun around fast on his heel. Their eyes locked. He at first had a look of surprise, which quickly faded to distain.

Shultz was getting pissed. He kept thinking this was a waste of time. While he was fucking off in here, the bitch could be long gone. She could have stolen a car for all he knew. He had walked the whole downstairs of the two-floor mall, finding nothing. And he wasn't in the mood to go into each and every store looking for them either. He figured he'd make one more pass down here, then head upstairs and maybe find a place to perch for a while. If nothing, he'd move on.

He turned quickly on his heel to lock eyes with the woman he was just thinking about. Was she behind me the whole time? He thought. Shultz was no pro, he wasn't trained to play these games of hide and seek. He was used to the more direct approach, and now with her standing in front of him, you couldn't get more direct than this.

She stared him down, sizing him up. Hand to hand was out of the question. She was no match for him even with her skills, his strength would prevail. She walked towards him; and he just stood there waiting for her. She tore her eyes from his, and glanced at his hands every couple of seconds just in case he was stupid enough to draw his weapon. She would definitely be the faster to draw, but that was something she would rather not do in here. But today, she was hoping he would try it.

She was now six feet from him. She stopped; they were both standing in the center circle of the mall. The passersby's didn't really take notice to the standoff that was going down in front of them. Some looked, but turned back to what they were doing. She figured if someone saw what was going on and knew this was potential trouble, they would call the cops, this was something that could possibly be in her favor. But then again, maybe not.

“So you’re braver than I thought, huh? To confront me? I’m impressed,” he said.

“Yeah… Now let’s see what you got, when you’re face to face with someone, and not pushing their face into the dirt,” she said, trying to keep her cool, but it was failing. Looking at him made her blood boil, fucking white trash.

“So come on!” He said, in a mocking tone, gesturing her to come at him. She was more than happy to oblige him. She stepped closer, she’d have her hands full, but she’d manage. All it took was one mistake on his part, and this would be over faster than it began. While both combatants were getting ready to have at each other like gladiators in an arena, a small crowd gathered watching on. If either Priscilla or Shultz noticed, they didn’t care at this point. She was about to lunge for him; she wanted to rip his eyes out.

But a loud whistle filled the mall, breaking the tension between them. Priscilla and Shultz looked in the direction of where they thought it came from. Neither was surprised at who it was. They looked at each other, making sure either one didn’t try to make a move against one another. Then they looked back to the new players that just came into the arena. The whistle blowers were none other than Trish and Omar.

Trish and Omar spotted them at the same time. The urge to blow them both away right then and there was overwhelming, but their main target was missing, so they needed her alive for now. Omar’s mouth was slightly agape as he stared at the blonde. Trish noticed this, reaching to shut it for him. He jerked his head away from her hand.

“Dear sister, you’re not jealous are you?” He said, in a wise ass tone.

“No, not at all brother, but you could be a little less obvious about it.” He grinned.

"She's a hot little number, nice ass for a white chick too, don't you think?" He licked his lower lip, fantasizing about what he would do to her.

"Yeah, she is, just keep your dick in your pants for now."

"Yeah, whatever, you take things too seriously." He put two fingers in his mouth and blew an ear-piercing whistle that caught their attention along with a few shoppers.

Trish and Omar were like night and day. He wore a three-piece suit, all black with white pinstripes and she wore a purple tank top with black spandex pants and black combat boots almost touching the knees. Priscilla felt a chill crawl up her spine, with the way Omar was staring at her. There was a monster deep within, his sister had a face of stone with hateful eyes that could kill.

They stopped, standing right next to the Aryan, about ten feet to his right. They all stared at each other for a moment. Priscilla had no idea of what to do; she could take out one, maybe two, but three? She wasn't that fast. One would certainly get the drop on her or maybe if she were lucky they would just go for each other before going for her but she couldn't take the chance. She'd have to stall them and make a move when the opportunity came up.

Shultz backed away from the duo, his lip curled at the sight of them. He loathed them more than the bitch here that gave him all this trouble to begin with. His hand was only inches from his gun. He was very tempted to go for it, but even he knew it might not be the smartest thing to do, there were too many guns to avoid with no cover to hide behind.

No one said a word; the silence was driving Priscilla mad. Then, as if Trish read her very thoughts, she spoke.

"You caused us a lot of trouble bitch. But we'll give you a chance to walk away with your life, we'll even let the skinhead walk, just tell us where Carmine is." Shultz looked sharply at Trish, Priscilla grinned.

"Yeah, right, think again." Priscilla said in an even tone.

"Walk away? Fuck you spic! I don't walk from no one!" Shultz added as Trish glared at him.

"Oh yeah! Well, if you're so bad, then make a move motherfucker, come on! You Neo-Nazis talk a good game, but you ain't got shit!" Trish spat back at Shultz whose eyes were getting red with anger.

Shoppers all around them took notice to the stand off before them. The ones passing them would go around, and others just stood there watching the events unfold before them. Some were on cell phones while others hurriedly ran away, most likely getting mall security. She needed to make a move and now, but then one of her fears came to pass. Two mall guards came from nowhere, one black and one white. This was not going to be pretty. They both stopped near the skinhead eyeing him closely.

"Excuse me? Is everything ok here?" Those words came from the black security guard as he looked at each of them. Shultz turned to him with a look of disgust. Then the 'word' came out, the 'word' that was not going to calm this down at all.

"Yeah, nigger, everything is fine. Now why don't you go and pick a cotton field and get the fuck outta here!" The man frowned at the words being directed at him, but he did not waver in the least. He stood his ground. Priscilla didn't say a word, she watched very closely. Her hand was itching to grab the gun and take her chance.

"Excuse me, sir!" The man took a step closer to the thug skinhead, his partner stepped up with him as well.

"Ma'am? Can you tell me what's going on here?" This came from the same guard that Schulz just insulted, trying to remain even tempered. Priscilla didn't realize at first, he was talking to her.

"Everything is fine, just a personal matter." She knew it was a bad line, but what else was she going to say?

"Yeah, right, I'm sorry; I'm gonna have to ask you all to leave before I call the police." That came from the other guard. Just as the words were spoken from his mouth, the other guard made a move to grab the Aryan on the shoulder.

"Oh, fuck this! Enough talk! You're all gonna die!" The words caught them all by surprise as Trish pulled two handguns out from behind her, leveling them in a blur. At the same time, Shultz reached for his gun, pointing it at the guard. Just as Shultz pulled the trigger, the other guard was faster and sidestepped into the line of fire even before the shot rang out. The crowd of onlookers screamed in terror, bursting into a panic, distracting everyone.

The bullet hit the guard in the shoulder as he rushed to protect his comrade. Shultz then turned his weapon to Trish with no clear shots to take. By the time Shultz fired, the mall was now in a frenzy. People scurried in all directions. The panic was uncontrollable.

In the mass confusion, Priscilla lost sight of Trish, Omar and Shultz. She had her weapon leveled and ready for anything, but instead of her finding them, Shultz found her. His bear like hand wrapped around her neck from behind. She dropped her gun from the shock, and in a vain attempt she tried to pry his iron grip. He threw her away like a rag doll, before she hit the floor; she turned her body in midair, letting her side take the brunt of the impact. Before Priscilla could recover, she was hoisted from the front, being choked out. She felt her throat closing. He had her up, extending both arms as straight as he could, she was starting to black out when she thrust her knee into his throat.

Instantly he let go, gagging. She fell on her feet a bit unsteadily. The giant was on one knee, holding his own neck now. Priscilla ran to him, coming up on his side, and gave him a double-fisted blow to the temple. She was going for it again when he swept her off her feet with his massive forearm. His face was red. He was still gasping for air, but that didn't stop him. He lunged at her; she scampered back, giving herself some space. At the last possible moment, she unleashed a quick and forceful kick in the face of the juggernaut of a man.

That gave her no more than six seconds to regain her posture; she was back on her feet in a snap. Still on his feet, but staggering back a bit, the skinhead threw a wild punch that she easily dodged, countering with a quick jab to his throat once again. She quickly kicked the side of his knee, toppling him down to her size.

With a grunt of pain, she finally collapsed the brute with a double-fisted blow to the back of his head. He fell face first to the floor. She was going in to finish him off, but the Aryan was the least of her worries. She had something else more important to take care of and that was Carmine. She ran back up to the second floor, pushing and squeezing her way through the mass of people.

Trish and Omar split up in the stampede of shoppers all heading for the same exits. It looked like a cattle rustling of human beings. They kept in touch via Bluetooth earpiece.

"Omar, we'll meet by the van in fifteen minutes if we don't spot them, copy?" Trish yelled over the screams, she could just barely hear his reply.

Priscilla was on the second floor, and having no luck in finding Carmine. With all these faces, it was hard to spot just one person. She went back to the place she saw him go into before, but there was no sign of him. She was heading for the nearest exit; maybe he was in the middle of a crowd trying to get the hell out. As she made her way, she felt a vibration in her pocket. Suddenly, she remembered she gave him one of the cell phones. She answered as she continued searching.

"I'm heading for the second-floor east side exit." He said, as loud as he could into the phone. She didn't reply, she just ran in that direction, shoving people out of her way. Priscilla finally caught up with Carmine, grabbing him by the shoulder, she startled him. Priscilla led the way, pulling him faster than his legs could keep up, leading them to freedom.

Schulz lost sight of her, he spotted the blonde heading for the second floor, but then lost track of her. He stopped running, and looked around, but it was like looking for a needle in a haystack with all the other blonde-haired women in here. He headed outside. He shoved and punched people in his way, saying racial slurs as he went. His massive frame plowed through the double glass doors, almost taking them off their hinges.

Trish was outside; she cuffed her hand over her brow, searching for her target, sweeping back and forth with no luck. She moved forward, running, and stopping a few times. She was about to call Omar and ask where he was when she finally spotted them. She called Omar and said,

"Omar, I'm down in the east side parking lot. The target is not more than 30 feet from me, get your ass over here!"

"Copy that sis, on my way." He sounded a bit out of breath answering her.

Omar sprinted like a marathon runner, his long legs propelling him faster and faster. He never lost stride as he weaved in and out of the parked cars. He came into view of his target. As he ran, he reached inside his suit jacket. He pulled out, one of the six knives he kept tucked away. He poured on the speed, getting closer. Omar could hit the center of a bulls-eye nine out of ten times, now almost within ten feet he let the blade fly.

Shultz was outside with his silver revolver in hand. He ran and stopped repeatedly, searching for his targets. Shockingly, he found them, amongst the mass of people who were racing to their cars and peeling out of the lot. Shultz had to dodge an oncoming car or two as he kept his eyes on Priscilla and Carmine. He picked up speed, but with some stragglers in his way and the size of him, he was not going to catch up. He wished the crowd would thin out more.

He wasn't able to get a clear shot, he could care less about hitting a bystander, but that would cost him precious time he didn't have. Also, if he missed, it would give off his position to the blonde, leaving him open for return fire. He continued to run, getting tired and out of breath with every step he took. All that muscle was a heavy burden when in a rush. On top of that, his knee was throbbing from the fight before.

Then to his surprise in all the confusion, he found his opening. He had a clear shot of the woman. He stopped, took aim, pulling back the hammer, he squeezed the trigger, but instead of the sound of a firing bullet, a scream of pain was heard from him instead.

A blade that came out of nowhere was now impaled through his hands, blood spewed on the pavement. He fell to his knees, his revolver hit the pavement as well. He was about to slam the tip of the blade into the concrete forcing it out, when a shadow covered his body. He looked up and was greeted by a metal pipe right square in the mouth. He fell over on his back; Trish was standing over Shultz pummeling him with the now bloody pipe, cursing him. She was so enraged that she was spitting as she spoke, with every blow.

“Call me a spic!! You white trash mother fucker prick bastard!” She screamed. The beating stopped, when Omar joined her; standing by her side with three more blades in hand, that matched the one still impaled in Shultz’s hands.

Trish was breathing hard, her face was flushed, and sweat covered her brow. Looking down at the now battered skinhead, she spat on him.

“Hey, what the hell! What did you do to that man?” Both Trish and Omar turned around at the comment. It was a medium sized man, just a ‘nobody’, sticking his nose into something that did not pertain to him. As he walked closer, Trish took out her gun, shooting the man in the chest without saying a word. Turning to her brother, she tucked the gun in her waist.

“Quick, grab his arm!” They both took an arm, hoisting the dead weight of Shultz off the ground. Their faces turned red from the strain. When she called Omar before to have him delay the target, she fetched the van bringing it closer, to save time on their getaway. They managed, with some effort, to throw Shultz’s unconscious body inside, slamming the doors closed. They raced off, falling in line with the other cars making their escape.

Chapter 27
Fitting the Pieces

Three hours later, things had finally quieted down at the diner. The parking lot was vacant, except for the destroyed Dodge Charger, and some police cruisers. The owner of the diner closed up for the rest of the day while the police finished their investigation that still yielded no answers.

Everything was quiet, until the mall incident happened. Lewis was not going to play the game any further of picking up the pieces; he'd leave it to the so-called state troopers. He had other things to do now.

Finally, with the car cooled down enough, he inspected it from front to rear, finding only burnt remnants of a toolbox in the trunk, an MP-5 submachine gun and a suitcase most likely belonging to Carmine, which may have held valuable information. The car held nothing of value. With that, he started to walk back to his car. Might as well go check out the mall and see what happened there, he thought to himself.

It wasn't much of a lead, but it was all he had to go on, he was just about to head off, when he heard something fall to the ground in the vicinity of the Charger. Turning back, he saw that the front headlight fell off, hitting the ground and breaking upon impact. He gave it very little thought until something out of the ordinary caught his eye, something that didn't belong.

As he walked back to the Charger, Lewis glanced over to the state trooper, who was leaning against his cruiser as he waited for the flatbed tow truck to arrive. He knelt down, peering inside the now uncovered headlight. Taking out a small flashlight, he looked closer as to what was inside.

He couldn't believe his eyes, he saw a small missile. At first, he almost jumped back but thought better of it. The missile, wasn't a threat any longer. He quickly went to the driver's side door, opening it with an annoying squeak. He squatted and leaned in taking a closer look at the dashboard, probing it with his fingers looking for something, anything. Then he found it. Prying off a piece of dashboard he found the LCD screen, but it was burnt-out and useless. He then checked the middle console, and found the melted buttons and switches that would have controlled the weapon systems. He crouched there thinking. Could this mysterious woman be a government agent? Very few, freelancers could afford hardware like this. If she was, then what agency he wondered?

Lewis strained, thinking hard, he closed his eyes. The answer was buried in the dark corner of his memory. Then it came to him, could it be the mysterious Shadow Ops? The name was mentioned to him more than once in the past. They were like ghosts, whispers in the wind. No one knew for sure if they even existed, they were only rumors, water cooler talk. It was said they had this type of hardware, and were highly trained. These rumors seemed to be more of a reality now.

Another rumor he recalled hearing a long time ago was that their main HQ was in New York City. Again, when he heard this he never really cared at the time. There was no reason to. Lewis never cared for the conspiracy bullshit, he only believed in facts. But now thinking about what he could dredge up from memory, it made complete sense. They were about 5 hours away from New York City. He quickly stood, leaving the door ajar and picked up his pace.

"Trooper?"

"Yes, sir?"

"I'm going back out on the road, tell the deputy that I'll be in touch." The trooper nodded at Lewis' back as Lewis quickly turned and got into his car. If they were heading to New York City, the best way would be to head them off. Before leaving, Lewis reached into the backseat, grabbing his laptop. He went to Google and did a search of the area for airports or anything that had a plane nearby. As luck would have it, there was a small airfield about fifty miles east of here. Writing down the directions, he threw the laptop in the back and sped off.

He'd have a pilot fly him to New York, then use the NYPD as he did these dopes. He looked at his watch; he'd make it just after the evening. He had to hurry though; he had received two phone calls from the home office wanting to know what was going on out there. With very little information, even he could only stall them off for so long before they sent other agents to help with the investigation. If that happened, then he'd be screwed. At this point, he'd do anything, to free himself of a fate that meant certain ruin.

Chapter 28
See you in Hell

The moon was bright tonight. It had been nearly six hours since the mall incident. The breeze in the open country was cool, a sure sign that fall was in full swing.

They drove for a number of miles. At some point during the drive Shultz awoke to pain so great, he thought that his body was going to explode. His head throbbed, he felt disoriented; all he saw was a vast blackness as deep as space itself. He couldn't even remember how he got here in the first place. The more he thought, the more the pinging in his head flared up, and that would start a chain reaction of nausea to the point where he almost vomited.

He heard voices coming from somewhere, they sounded a million miles away, but yet so close. His face was numb and sticky, he felt something, restrict the movement of his massive forearm. With just that small effort of touching his face, he tired. He tried again to tug at whatever it was to no avail.

He was not going to try to force it anymore. In his current condition, he'd be lucky to get up, let alone break free of anything. If he were in better shape that would have been a different story.

Pondering more on what the hell happened to him, he tried to gather the memories from his twisted mind. Suddenly, out of nowhere, they went from a semi-smooth road to what felt like an earthquake. His body was bouncing around like a jumping bean, his head was hitting a metal surface, which increased the pinging in his skull. He tightly closed his eyes as if that would help make the pain stop. Then the vibration came to a sudden halt and the restraints that bound him pulled tight, digging into his wrists as his body was propelled forward with the momentum. The vehicle stopped. He then heard two doors open and shut.

It was quiet and still. The silence was the worst part, after the darkness, which his eyes were still having trouble adjusting to. He put his attention back to his restraints, trying to feel his way around to see what was restraining him. He felt the cold unforgiving steel chains and kept trying to pull at them with no results. He was drained. Whoever had done this to him would regret it, that was for sure.

He kept thinking in the stillness, trying to piece together the events that led him here. The memories were coming to him in flashbacks.

All he could remember was that he suddenly passed out while trying to take a shot at the blonde. He curled his hands into tight fists of frustration and felt slits on his palms. Wondering what that was, he felt his hands; feeling for what the wound might have been. They felt like knife wounds, and then it came back to him in a flood. He threw a blade in my hands. Omar, one-half of that freak show. He remembered seeing him for all of five seconds before he was whacked pretty hard most likely by his bitch of a sister.

He wasn't sure how much time passed, but he figured it was at least a good hour since they left him in their van. Then in the stillness of the night he heard light footsteps coming toward him, they were faint at first but they grew louder with each step. There was no conversation between them, Shultz wiggled a bit to the driver's side of the van, trying to gain some advantage. Maybe he could get a footing on the wall and use that with his strength to pull at least one arm free. He tugged as hard as he could, putting every ounce of strength into it. The chains were thin but strong and he was still so weak. He could feel some of his strength returning from the adrenaline rush pumping in his veins, brought on by the fear of what might become of him.

With the footsteps closing in on him, he tried once more, groaning softly. The steps sounded like an echo in his head. He was tugging for all he was worth. But now his palms were slipping from the blood on his reopened wounds mixed with sweat, making it harder to grip his bonds. The phrase 'I'm fucked' came to mind just as the side door slid open. Trish and Omar, with their backs to the bright moon were shadowed, hiding their features from their prisoner.

"Oh look sis, our passenger is wide awake now and trying to free himself. Can't leave you alone for a minute can we?" Omar said in a mocking tone, waving a finger.

"Yeah, you're right; let me fix that right away." Only seconds after the words came out, Omar moved out of the way for Trish to take up the whole space now. She had something in her hands. Shultz couldn't see it, but he felt it. Trish, with the same metal pipe that she used on him before, swung down with all the force she could muster. She hit him; once, twice, three times on each knee. On the fourth time, she heard the cracking of bones.

The calm night sky rang out with screams of wild pain. The veins in his neck might have popped if she kept hitting him. A tear streamed down Shultz's face as he clamped his eyes shut. He was breathing hard now, trying not to focus on this new, unforgiving pain.

"Is…is that… the best… you… can do spic!" He said in a mocking tone of his own, between gasps of air, he spat hitting her on the chest. Trish was more than happy to show him she could do better. She brought the pipe up again. This time it would be that ugly mug she smashed, but Omar's outstretched hand stopped the pipe in mid flight, smacking hard into his palm, it hurt but he ignored the sharp pain.

"Tsk tsk, sis, you really must control that temper, now. After all we just did it would be a waste for our friend to not enjoy what we have planned for him, wouldn't you say so?" She looked at her brother, then to the skinhead.

"Yeah, it would be," was all she said, pulling the pipe away from his hand and throwing it into the back of the van. It hit the floor with a noise that echoed throughout the open area they were in. Trish backed away so Omar could unlock Shultz's restraints. With his arms free, even if he wanted to grab the man by his neck, he couldn't do it. The pain going through his body was too overwhelming.

Omar pulled the massive body of the now defenseless Shultz to the edge of the van. Trish came over helping once she could grab his arm.

"Ready?" Omar asked,

"Ready."

They both pulled Shultz, not caring when his legs fell to the ground. He winced from the sharp pain as they dragged him off. He couldn't see where he was being dragged, they had him facing the van that was now growing smaller with every step. He could see he was in the middle of nowhere on some type of farmland. From the looks of it, it hasn't been used for quite some time. They stopped suddenly, dropping him on something stiff, his head hitting the surface. The pain started back up again, Trish stood over him looking down. Shultz looked right back at her; even in his condition, he was fearless.

"Hey! What the fuck you looking at bitch!" He said, trying to goad her some more. At this point, they were going to do whatever they were going to do, so he might as well piss them off. He looked for Omar but he was nowhere to be found.

"What am I looking at? I'm looking at one of the biggest meat sacks I've ever seen." She replied, not falling for the taunt this time.

He was just about to say something when Omar returned with his suit jacket off, the sleeves of his collared shirt rolled up.

"I'll dig, and you nail." He said as he thrust the shovel into the ground, digging a medium-sized hole. Trish went over to the wooden box that they found in the old broken down barn. Shultz couldn't see it because he was flat on his back. She bent over, taking out an old looking hammer with some rusty nails. Walking over to the Aryan's arms, she spread them apart. Shultz had a pretty good idea of what she was going to do.

He didn't bother to crane his neck for a better view, he just waited for it. He felt the cold steel lightly press against his wrist, and then came the impact of the hammer to the nail.

The pain was sharp. He concentrated on holding his face still. The less reaction he gave these bastards the better. When all was said and done Trish hammered five nails in each hand and wrist, throwing the hammer aside, she used rope and tied it around his arms tight. She doubted the nails would hold him in place. She then reached over for the other half of the unused rope, tying it to a section of the wood that was protruding where Shultz's head was lying and then walked the rest of it over his body towards her brother who was leaning on the shovel waiting.

"You're a tough fucker huh?" That came from Trish taunting Shultz as she handed the rope to her brother. Trish walked back to where she was, bending over, and at the same time, Omar pulled as he dug his feet into the hard ground. Trish hoisted up as hard as she could. At first, they weren't sure if they'd be able to lift him, but Trish and Omar never gave up, trying harder, and with a little more effort they managed to pull the skinhead up.

The cross that Shultz was nailed to fell into the hole Omar had dug only moments ago. Now, Shultz was vertical and high up in the air, looking down on his soon to be killers. He then looked over to his impaled arms then back to them. Trish was standing near his dangling feet, holding the make shift cross from tipping over as Omar replaced the dirt back in the hole, packing it tightly.

"You done?" He nodded as the last pile of dirt was being stomped. The night was chilly but he worked up a sweat rubbing his white rolled up sleeve on his wet brow.

"Damn, I just bought this shirt," he said, spotting a dirt smudge here and there. Trish didn't answer him; she didn't know why he would wear a white shirt to begin with. She did at times too, yeah, but never bitched about it getting dirty either. Sometimes she wondered if her brother was half a fag. They stood at Shultz's feet now, stepping back a bit. Omar took out a cigarette, and placed it to his thin lips. The flame illuminated his face, as he puffed away. By their feet Shultz could see the red gas can, but still he never wavered, never begged for his life. That was something he knew would give them pleasure.

"So? What the fuck you gonna do now, huh spics?" Omar and Trish looked at him, and then she spoke first.

"Well, you dumb fuck, use what you have as a brain and think." Omar picked up the gas can and unscrewed the top, hoisting it to his waist. He had the cigarette in his mouth; he leaned to his sister who took the cigarette, holding it for him. He then proceeded to splash the Aryan with the gasoline, emptying the can.

The chilled air now sent a shiver through him. Omar threw the can at his feet. He wiped his hands on his pants and took back his cigarette that his sister was just taking a drag from. The windy night filled with a maniacal laughter coming not from Trish or Omar but from the skinhead. The veins in his head could be seen, he was laughing so hard.

Trish was getting pissed. She expected this pussy to start begging for his life and now he was laughing at them?

"What the fuck is so funny?" She spat, if she had a knife in her hand, she'd rip out his heart to hear him scream, this was how crazed and psychotic Trish and Omar were. They actually took the time from the chase to do this. They found the abandoned old barn out in the middle of nowhere, and then they built the cross from the wood they found on the property. This was what they loved the most before the kill. They enjoyed the fear that they would instill into their victims. They loved seeing the fright build up, but this prick denied them of that, laughing at them instead.

"The cross is the light… if you knew anything that I believed in you would know that the burning cross is the light." Shultz swallowed hard then continued. "The light will burn, and when my brothers hear about this… it will not be over…we will finish this in… hell!" He said through toothless gaps.

"We look forward to it!" Omar said as he flicked his burning cigarette at Shultz's gasoline soaked body. Immediately, Shultz erupted into flames. He started to scream, but his screams turned to laughter that echoed through the open field.

"That's for whoever you did that to you fucking white trash mother fucker!" Trish spat out taking one-step closer to the inferno, she doubted he heard her. His laughter was getting louder; soon the entire cross was engulfed in flames thanks to the breeze, feeding the fire, making it stronger. Shultz's laughter died out slowly, until there was only the sound of cracking wood; they saw his now darkened and charred body through the flames. They stood there for a moment longer watching their enemy burn. The stench of burning flesh was hideous. Then picking up their belongings they nonchalantly walked back to their van. The starting of the engine broke the silence of the night yet again; Omar drove this time. Trish reached up putting on the overhead light and looked over the map.

"So, where to now?" She asked him. He glanced at her, placing a finger on the map.

"Really? You think we can make it there before them?" She said, sounding somewhat surprised. It was a bold move, but there was no other way to go, it was do or die time now.

He nodded yes. They drove off into the night, leaving behind the flaming cross that could be seen from miles away. As the fire ensued, the cross-started to crack under the pressure of the weight, until it finally toppled over sending a slew of cinders into the night sky.

Chapter 29
Lost

It was a cold night. The sky was clear and the moon was out, brightly illuminating the lands below. At least no rain, Priscilla thought, as she sat with her knees to her chest, arms wrapped around them, trying to keep in as much body heat as she could. Carmine was lying down next to her fast asleep snoring. She thought back to the events that happened only 6 hours ago, as they sat in a cornfield about 20 miles from where they almost lost their lives. The circumstances of how she got here pissed her the fuck off. The car being blown up, then the whole mall thing, now this, she looked at Carmine with a slight sneer, fucking dick.

If she didn't have to worry about him she would have stood her ground. Now here she was this secret agent, hiding in a goddamn cornfield like a criminal. She dug her hand into her pocket, pulling out the company cell phone, and looked at it. Stealing a car was out of the question because the owner would surely call it in.

It wouldn't take the law that long to piece it together, public transport was a no go as well; she was not going to jeopardize anyone else. The way she saw it at this point, she had two options. One of them, she'd rather not use, but would have to if she had no other choice, more for personal reasons. The other option was to simply call John, and hope that they could be picked up, but even that she knew was going to be a no go. Once you were out in the field, you were on your own, period. Shadow Ops didn't have agents just lying around waiting for assignments. Many were like her, with a home life, family. By the time any agent made it out here, they could be dead and to make matters worse, she'd have to make the call from a payphone.

Knowing that Trish and Omar were involved now, she knew from past reports that they had the ability to pick up cell phone conversations even if they were encrypted; she leaned over poking her companion in the back.

"Sleeping Beauty, wake up," she said in a low but forceful tone. He muttered something in his sleep. She got up, dusting herself off, having no more patience left with Carmine, she kicked him in the small of his back, not hard, just enough to grab his attention.

"Wake the fuck up!" She yelled a little louder, that worked. When I try to be nice, it never works, she thought.

"W…w…what! Come on, give me a break, huh?"

"Yeah, I'd like to give you a break, let me tell ya!" She replied, placing both hands to her hips. He sat up; she extended a hand helping him to his feet. He was grunting as she pulled his out of shape body up, he ran his fingers through his uncombed hair.

"So, where are we going?" He asked sleepy eyed, with a yawn following right after.

"We are going to make a phone call."

"Huh? You have your cell, right?" She looked away, rolling her eyes; she was in no mood to explain anything to him. All he needed to know was to move when she told him to. They walked without another word. They made their way closer to the road for a better view, it was desolate. She didn't hear a single car pass by all this time. They trekked onward through the cornfield; its uneven footing was a sprained ankle waiting to happen. They tried to make as little noise as possible. The night had this eerie quietness to it, like out of a horror movie just before the hockey mask killer would strike. She didn't hurry her companion, even though the slow walking was starting to get to her.

They came to a streetlamp that could be seen high above the field. Sitting next to the streetlamp was a small rest stop. It was a shack of a place, made out of wood older than her mother. They could smell the bathrooms from where they were. Right at the edge of their cover, Priscilla stood still, watching and listening. The sounds of nature around them were playing tricks on her ears. She waited 20 minutes before going out to the payphone she spotted. She turned to Carmine, who was sitting down; she went to one knee getting close to his ear.

"Listen, I'll be right back, don't move." He nodded and she nodded back. She crept up, took her gun out, cocked the hammer back, and then waited, counting to three. She took off out of the field in long fast strides kicking up dirt. All the while throwing her eyes in many directions watching out for any sign of movement other than her own.

In 20 seconds she made it to the payphone, she put her back to the wall of the shack, watching for anything unexpected, before picking up the phone. She calmed her breathing, taking in deep breaths; she stood still for a minute more listening for anything. Even as she picked up the phone, she watched everywhere, she didn't have to look at the phone to dial.

She had the keypad memorized. What she dialed was an 800 number; the number would direct you to a voice recognition security feature. As you gave your ID number, the computer on the other end scanned the number as well as the vocal patterns. Once identified, the call would be placed, then the computer would go through the pre-programmed numbers until someone answered. She was hoping John would be there, the man ran the whole show. He gave the final word on everything, and she wasn't the only Op out there. It rang once, and then the familiar voice came on.

"John, it's Priscilla." She could hear his breathing.

"Priscilla, what the devil is going on out there?!, I've been getting reports from all over, the car blowing up, some incident in the mall. I even had the Secretary of Defense breathing down my neck, asking me if I knew what was going on, is everything ok? Where's Carmine?" She took a deep breath before replying.

"I have him, and everything is fine, for now anyway. It turns out your boy is hotter than you thought."

"Yes, it would seem so, where are you?"

"I'm in Pennsylvania, maybe 5 hours away. Listen, we're in need of immediate evac. There's a lot of heat bearing down our necks right now." There was silence on the other end; she knew what the answer would be before he said it.

"Not sure if that's possible right now, I have no available field agents." She closed her eyes, disappointed and pissed off.

"You have your phone right?"

"Yes,"

"Ok listen, do whatever you have to do, I'll see what I can do for you. I'll contact you. John out." She held the phone in her hand even though he hung up.

"Fuck! Goddammit," she slammed the receiver down, she was deep in thought. Now she had one option, one she really didn't want to go with but had no choice, she took a deep breath.

The option was not a bad one at all, at least not in her eyes. She knew one-hundred percent without a doubt that the man she was going to, would do anything for her, no questions asked. It was a situation that was very complicated to say the least. And if not careful, she could find herself intertwined in a web of wild emotions. She started walking back to the field, thinking how they would get to New Jersey. As she was making her way back to Carmine, she heard something. For a second she thought her ears were playing tricks, she stood still, her ears were not playing tricks, and the sound was that of a train, she could faintly hear the air horn.

"Carmine! Come on! Hurry! I think we have a ride!" She said yelling as loud as she could, not caring about giving off her position if someone was indeed nearby. He emerged from the field, huffing and puffing, he tried to talk.

"Where?..."

"Just shut up and come on!" She exclaimed, as she ran towards him, grabbing a hold of his arm. As they ran closer it was clearer, she could hear the metal wheels grinding over the tracks. Sweat covered her forehead even in the cool night air, she looked to Carmine.

"Come on!" They broke out of the field. Finally seeing the tracks, they stopped just short of the gravel that lay beside them. She looked to her left not seeing anything then to her right, her luck was good tonight. She thought they'd have to run after the train. That was not going to happen with her out of shape, red faced friend. The train was coming straight for them, and it wasn't at top speed either. It was one of those older freight trains, following behind it were three open-end cars covered with large white tarps.

"Come on!" Pulling him before he hunched over, they ran to meet the oncoming train. As they came up to the second to last open-ended car, she reached out for anything that would help pull them up. There was a metal handle by the back. Grabbing it, she pulled herself up. While doing so, she was holding tight onto

Carmine, who was being dragged by the train. She strained with his weight. Her grip was loosening, but surprising her with a determined look on his face and a burst of energy, Carmine kicked off the ground, and slammed into her. She was caught off guard, almost falling off herself and taking him with her. She steadied him on the small footing at the base close to the wheels. Climbing up, she reached down, grabbing him by the hand and pulled him up with both hands, straining her back to the point of almost giving out on her. To her advantage he helped by pulling himself up. He was on his knees, breathing hard.

She fell to her knees, exhausted from all the day's events. The cool wind felt good hitting her sweat-covered face. She pushed one of the many boxes off to the side, making just enough room for them to lie down without fear of falling.

Finally catching her breath, she looked to her side. There was a large crate next to her; she fished out her company cell phone. The light from the device illuminated it enough so she could find some type of writing. Maybe something that would tell her where they were going. She found a town name and zip code stamped on the crate, she typed it in, checking the GPS she got the trajectory of the train route. According to what it said, the train was heading close to where they needed to go. After that it was about an hour more of travel time. As she put the phone back in her pocket, she turned on her side, tucking her arm under her head. She emptied her mind as she watched the terrain scroll by like a slide show.

Chapter 30
Going Clubbing

The train ride brought them to a depot just outside of Secaucus, NJ. As the train came to a sudden stop, Priscilla awoke with a jolt. During their ride, she fell into a very light sleep. Leaning up on her elbows, she eyed the area quickly. Then turning to Carmine, she elbowed him awake. They had to hurry before this shipment was unloaded.

They made their way from the train yard to the streets; they were desolate at this time. Some neighborhoods by train yards were ripe with crime, drug addicts, pimps, streetwalkers, and god knows what else.

She was hoping her luck would hold out just a little bit longer, she didn't want to run into anyone that could impede her way. She was in no mood to deal with wanna be gangsters, her gun would be doing the talking if she did. But as it happened, her luck did hold out. Walking at a brisk pace under the streetlights, Carmine kept to her stride. She looked over to him, he was breathing rather hard. Placing a hand on his shoulder, she asked,

"You ok? You don't look so good." He dismissed her concern with a wave of his hand.

"I'm ok, just need to hopefully sit down soon," he replied in between breaths. She didn't believe him. He has not had his meds for almost a day. This was not good for his heart ailment. His heart was definitely pumping harder than it was used to with all this running. That was all she needed, for him to have a heart attack right now in the middle of this slum hole they were in. She'd leave him right where he dropped. They kept walking with no sign of a cab; the only cars that were on the street were parked. Coming to the corner there was a payphone. She walked over hoping that maybe a number to a cab company might be scrawled on it somewhere. No luck though, she had a few quarters in her pocket, and inserted them into the payphone. She dialed information asking the operator for the local cab stand number. As the woman gave her the number, Priscilla was dialing it on her cell phone.

Within fifteen minutes a cab came. The driver, an overweight man wearing sweatpants with a T-shirt looked them over with a wary eye. He didn't let them in until she gave him the fare beforehand, just in case she were to pull a fast one. She didn't blame him, the guy must've thought they were junkies just coming back from buying their high for the night. They got in, driving off. She told him where to go, the trip took less than ten minutes, and not a word was said as they made their way to their destination. Upon arrival, she instructed the driver to let them out a block away. Thanking him, they both got out and she watched the cab speed off, down the side street.

Abrams City was west of Weehawken, NJ. It was a small little place filled with an upper middle class community, and a hot nightlife. Priscilla thought it was funny, here they were in a lively more lit up area and just one town over was a crime-ridden one. Eyeing their surroundings, Priscilla put her full attention to the place in question and that place in question was called Deja'Vu. One of the hottest places in the tri-state area.

The bright neon lights flashed on and off illuminating the faces of people outside smoking cigarettes. It was almost one in the morning and the party looked to be only getting started with more people coming in than leaving. In New Jersey, bars were supposed to be closed by two in the morning. She wasn't surprised though, knowing who owned the place. She looked to Carmine standing by her side looking somewhat better than before, he took notice to her concerned look, flashing a quick smile.

"Let's go, and stay close to me, this place can get a little rough." He nodded as they both walked side-by-side crossing the street; she took her time approaching the place. As they walked, she fixed herself up a bit pushing back her hair, and straightening her collared shirt as best as she could.

She must have looked a mess, she thought. Carmine did the same thing when he saw her doing this, fixing his tie, and buttoning his suit jacket. Arriving in front, they entered into the lobby area. Off to the side was a booth. There was a woman inside behind a thick glass window, she eyed them suspiciously. As

Priscilla and Carmine approached, the woman wondered what the hell they were doing there. The look on the woman's face gave away what she was thinking.

"Hi, is there a cover tonight?" Priscilla asked,

"Yeah, twenty bucks, but you two can't go in, you don't meet the dress code lookn' the way you do," the woman replied in a very snotty tone. Priscilla fished in her pocket anyway, disregarding what the woman said. Grabbing a fifty, she slipped it underneath the glass; the woman didn't take it.

"Listen crackhead! I said no entry for you, got a hearing problem? I'm so sick of you junkies comin' around here!" The woman said loud enough to attract the attention of a nearby bouncer. The brutish looking man with a large scruffy beard looked like a biker. He walked to Priscilla's side, eyeing her and Carmine, then looking at the woman that was giving them a hard time.

"Rose, these two giving you trouble?" He said looking back to Priscilla. The woman nodded.

"Yeah, they want in, but they don't meet the dress code." Nodding to Rose, he looked back to Priscilla and Carmine.

"Ok, you heard the lady, go on get outta here!" The bouncer said, crossing his arms over his massive chest. Priscilla turned and looked at him dead in his eyes.

"No. You're going to let me in, and that's it." The bouncer was not swayed in the least, in fact, he thought it was somewhat amusing that a woman such as her would challenge him, men twice her size thought better of it. He went to grab her by the arm, she saw it coming before he even made the move, sidestepping, she grabbed the back of his head and with his momentum slammed his face into the glass booth cracking it. Rose jumped and yelped, while the brutish bouncer fell to the ground, out cold and bleeding from the forehead, the people that watched this did not dare to get involved.

Turning back to Rose, Priscilla gave her the fifty, she tried to give before. A ten was promptly slid back to her; she stuffed it in her pocket. While that was going on, Carmine stood there frozen. When Priscilla turned to go inside, she had to pull him out of his fear-induced trance.

Chapter 31
Pietro Mastrandrea

The club was pumping that night; scantly clad women tore up the dance floor to the beat of the music, while the eyes of desire looked upon them sending hormones through the roof. Carmine, with Priscilla in tow, made their way deeper inside; the strobe lights reflecting off the disco ball bothered Priscilla's eyes at first. The place had a dim looking atmosphere, but light enough to see who was standing next to you. Trying to squeeze their way through the crowds they were careful not to bump into anyone, if they could help it. This place was known to get a little rough, and she had no time to waste knocking someone's head in. She wished they didn't have to come here at all, but this was the only way to get a car on such short notice.

Continuing on their way, her stomach tightened with that nervous feeling of butterflies, she felt like a little schoolgirl. At the back of the club, she spotted an upper level that led to where she guessed his office would be. Two more large looking bouncers guarded the stairs. Just as they were about to break free of the partygoers, her luck took a turn for the worse. It happened, something she was hoping to avoid. Carmine, bumped into someone.

All she saw now was a pissed off man with a large red wet stain on his teal and white collared shirt. The man was looking right at Carmine. Carmine must have thought all he did was bump into the man and was about to turn and offer his apology, but it wouldn't have mattered if it was his fault or not, either way, there was going to be trouble.

"Yo! Mother fucker!" The man said, throwing his now empty glass to the floor, shattering it into a million pieces. Carmine didn't hear him over the loud music, some of the beats were rather deafening. He was just about to utter the words "Sorry" when he was grabbed by his suit jacket, and pulled closer to the now enraged man. His friends gathered around to watch. The nearby partygoers, stopped what they were doing, wondering what would unfold next. Some of them wanted to see this old man get a beat down.

"Now how the fuck am I gonna get this stain out? Besides that, I look like an ass with this blotch on my shirt!" Carmine was sweating; he was trying to get his words out. He was frantically looking, hoping to find his guardian angel. He then looked back to the man that was at any second going to pummel him into next week.

"Yo! He's with me," Priscilla said, raising her voice so she could be heard over the blaring music. She placed her hand on his shoulder, to further grab his attention just in case he didn't hear her. He looked over to the blonde.

"What? Who the fuck are you, bitch?" Trying hard not to lose her cool, she ignored the comment, she then replied as nicely as she could,

"Listen, I'll tell you what, let me buy you and your friends a round and we'll call it even, how about that?" She said this with a false smile, hoping he'd go for it. She knew he wouldn't, but you couldn't kill her for trying. He let go of Carmine and turned to her smiling his pearly whites.

"Baby, it'll take more than a round of drinks to clear this up. But you can start by suckin' my dick."

He and his friends laughed at that one, they now turned their full attention towards her, forgetting about Carmine, which was good. She flashed a thin smile at him and gestured in a very flirtatious way for him to come closer. He was all the more pleased to hear what she had to say. When he leaned his ear in, Priscilla, grabbed him by the back of the neck and slammed his forehead into the bar, sending the drinks flying. She then uppercut him square in the chin, knocking him to the floor.

His friends still had the look of shock on their faces by what they'd just witnessed. They could not believe what this good-looking blonde just did. The man on the right was the first one to step up. He came at her, fists ready to strike. Keeping her eyes on him she blindly reached for the bar, finding a bottle that she used to crack over his head. With blood pouring out, he fell next to his friend. The other three were in motion, before the next man could pull what she thought was a gun, she punched him in the throat, then followed up with a hard punch to the chest, knocking the wind out of him.

He was fairly skinny and went down fast.

By then the crowd had cleared them a path. Screams from the women close by were muffled by the still blaring music. She didn't want to fire off any rounds in here for two reasons. One, it would cause a wave of stampeding, people running for their lives, and two, someone was bound to call the cops and she'd had enough run ins with cops already. But she had no choice to go for her weapon. She wasn't going to reach the other two in time.

She reached behind her back, when bouncer's bum rushed the men from behind, grabbing and taking them down hard. There were three bouncers, one was a fat man and the other two were built like brick houses. The owner of the nightclub was close behind, the only man that was known to make this cold-blooded killer weak in the knees, Pietro Mastrandrea. He walked over to her side, looking down at the men with a smile.

"I see you haven't stopped causing trouble, huh?" He said in a voice that could hypnotize any woman. By now the music had stopped, the background was a sea of muffled conversation, she looked at him with a smile.

"Hey trouble always finds me, you should know that," she said slightly out of breath.

"Yeah, I know it all too well, just give me a second, and I'll be right with you." He walked over to the DJ, gesturing for the mic, as he cleared his throat.

"Hello ladies and gentlemen, I'm truly sorry for this disturbance just now." He waited for a moment, scanning the crowd, then went on, "I'd like to offer my sincere apologies, drinks are on the house for the remainder of the evening." The place let out a roar of approval, as people rushed the bar. Pietro handed the mic back to the DJ. By then the bouncers had the five men gathered up, and Priscilla found Carmine, hiding behind the bar. How he managed to find his way there was beyond her. She grabbed him, practically pulling him over the bar by his shirt. The bouncers led the way, walking the five men as best they could. Pietro gestured her to follow.

They made their way, going through double doors guarded by two beastly looking bouncers, down a narrow hallway that led out to the back alley. She stayed behind though; she didn't need to be there to hear what was said. She watched him, doing what he does best, putting the fear into the hearts of people who do him wrong. She stared at him with eyes of desire. He was over six feet tall and medium built. Just enough to make a woman drool over his dark skinned body. He had thick black neatly combed hair, like James Dean. Even Priscilla had to admit it, he was gorgeous.

Pietro could have any woman he wanted. All he had to do was smile and it was over, the same could be said for Priscilla but she had the will power to resist his charm otherwise she might have been one of the many conquests as well.

They met sometime ago. To say their relationship was complicated was an understatement. When they first met, there was an instant attraction both physically and mentally, for the both of them. It just felt right, and incredibly natural. Pietro used to be an up and coming mob figure in New York. For the short time they worked together, a few days to be exact, they got to know each other pretty well. Yes, he used to be a gangster, and still had ties to that world, but he wasn't like the ones she ran into before. He was different somehow, he wasn't meant to do this, and only got involved because it was the easiest way to earn a living at the time.

From then on, they spoke to each other on occasion, maybe once a month, if that, but never saw each other. He would intrude her thoughts from time to time. Like when she was with Carmine at the restaurant, she wished she were with Pietro instead of her obnoxious companion, she'd been dealing with for the last few days.

Nevertheless, for obvious reasons she could not take this lust or whatever you wanted to call it further.

She snapped out of her thoughts when she saw him approach.

"Let's go to my office and have a drink, I wanna hear why I'm so lucky to have you in my club, beating up people."

"Lead the way," she said, smiling, and gesturing him forward. They made their way upstairs to the lavish office with red carpets, and two couches. His desk had papers on it along with a few stacks of money. It seemed he was counting it when he was disturbed. He had Carmine wait outside. She was going to refuse at first, but decided she needed a break from him and nothing was going to happen to him in here. She sat down on one of the two chairs facing his desk.

She explained the situation to him as he poured them drinks from a bottle taken from a vast assortment of liquors he kept on ice. He then made his way behind his desk, handing her the half filled glass.

She stopped for a moment to take a sip. Her eyes turned red and she coughed a bit from the foul-tasting liquor. He chuckled at the sight; she was no drinker. Placing the glass on his desk, she finished the story.

"So that pretty much sums it up. I have a Neo-Nazi Aryan skinhead; along with a crazy incest brother and sister hit team on my ass. My only hope is that they kill each other first… oh yeah, I also put a bullet in the head of an albino." She finished; he smiled, slowly shaking his head.

"Well, that's an amazing story Priscilla. I'm glad that you at least cleared the air on who that was you were palling around with in here. You scared me for a moment, had me thinking you liked older men. Now at least I might have a chance still," he said, followed by that gorgeous smile of his. She couldn't help not to smile back, she didn't get it sometimes. Yes, she was a pretty woman, but nothing to go crazy for. There were a million better looking women, but yet she was always hit on. Like in the bar before and now by Pietro, she couldn't figure it out. Maybe it was some type of aura she gave off that turned men on.

"Well Pietro, you just might have one, if you clean up your act, and from what I've been hearing, you're doing a good job thus far, but I'm not promising you anything." And she meant it. Getting down to the reason she came here in the first place she leaned in closer.

"But let's talk about that later. Now what I'm going to need from you is a car. Something fast and inconspicuous, do you think that could be arranged?" He sat back in his chair thinking a moment.

"Yeah, I think something could be arranged," he said with both hands clamped together.

"How long?" She asked.

"Hmm, a few hours." She nodded in approval.

"Perfect, thanks," she felt relieved, they had a ride now. "Oh, you think I could freshen up? Please tell me you have a bathroom with a shower."

"Come on Priscilla you know me, of course I do, shall I join you?" He said slipping that right in there, very slick she thought, she laughed.

"Nice try babe, but no."

"Hell, one day you might say yes,"

"You know what, I just might…" she replied with a wink.

The hot bath was so invigorating. In the cabinets, there was a large assortment of soaps and body washes that a woman loved. As she climbed into the hot bubbling water, she closed her eyes and leaned her head on a rolled up bath towel. It was there she lost herself and nodded off.

An untold amount of time went by, when Priscilla awoke neck deep in the now cool water, she was groggy. She looked to the wall for the time, but there was no clock hanging anywhere. She looked at her hands, her fingers were pruned. She figured she slept for two hours, maybe more.

She got out of the tub with minimal splashing, and slipped into a bathrobe that was hanging on the door. Priscilla quickly combed her hair and walked into the bedroom, going to the chair where she laid her clothes, but did not find them. All of her other belongings were there, including her gun, she looked around, and spotted her clothes on the edge of the queen size bed. They were neatly folded. They had that recently cleaned smell to them. She was just about to get dressed when Pietro walked in. She felt her face starting to blush. He must've seen it too. He smiled at her closing the door,

"Wow, I'm just in time," he said. Priscilla held back a comment not trusting herself. Oh, my fucking God! She thought, even as strong as she was, she felt her desires starting to take control. Oh, just come here and fuck me! She was half saying to herself while her conscience told her otherwise.

Easy! Control those hormones. This is something you can't get involved in! She kept saying to herself, but how could you not want to? The man standing before her was too gorgeous to take your eyes off of. You could get lost in those brown eyes forever.

Blocking all those thoughts, she gathered up her clothes and went back to the bathroom, locking the door.

"I'll get dressed and that's it," she whispered to herself, not sounding at all convincing. She doubted being dressed would kill her sexual desire.

The desire would always be there when he was around. Thankfully, she learned to control herself. Sure, she'd let go in the past, but not here, not now. She was in the middle of a mission for God's sake. What is this, James Bond? In no time, she was dressed. She fixed herself up and walked back out. She found him at the mini bar pouring himself a drink, he turned around at the opening of the door.

"Wow mmmm, looking good honey, I had the clothes cleaned. Those pants are light but feel strong."

"Yeah, something from the company." She replied, thanking god that the conversation changed to something more friendly. He took a sip of his drink while staring at her.

"When did you want to get going?"

"As soon as possible. I've already put you in enough danger. I stayed too long for my own good."

She was telling the truth. Pietro may have influence over normal people, but the ones chasing her are far from normal. They didn't fear former mob linked guys or anyone else for that matter. He wouldn't stand a chance against the likes of Trish and Omar or any of the assassins she faced.

"Ok, I understand, I have a car for you downstairs out back, whenever you're ready." He said with a hint of disappointment.

"Thanks Pietro, I really appreciate it." He waved away her thanks.

"I know you do. That's why I did it, sweetheart." She smiled, feeling her face getting warm from the kind comment.

Before her already shaky will power shattered and she wound up doing something she might regret, Priscilla gathered her stuff, and made for the door.

Once in the hallway, Pietro led her to Carmine. He was in a room just down the hall from her. She collected him, then Pietro led them through the winding hallways, outside to the back lot. It felt good being outside, Priscilla looked to the east, the warm rays of the morning sun rejuvenated her.

"And here's your ride." His frame blocked her field of view for a moment. He moved to the side unveiling her new ride. It was a red Ferrari, an older model, but a Ferrari nonetheless. To be more precise it was a Ferrari 288 GTO.

"I said fast and inconspicuous," Priscilla looked at him smiling, as she crossed her arms over her chest. He shrugged his shoulders.

"Well, you said you needed a car, and this was a quickie. It's mine, someone owed me some money, and they didn't have it so it was either they gave me the car for payment or their kneecaps and the money they owed me. He chose to give me the car." He said this with no humor in his voice, but Priscilla couldn't help but smile.

"I think it's great Mr. Pietro, I thank you." Carmine said, putting his two cents into something he didn't need to. Priscilla and Pietro both looked at each other, then to him with a look of shut the fuck up.

"Would you get in the car," she said, pointing to the passenger door. Like a scolded child, he went and did what he was told, while Priscilla walked over to Pietro. He had the keys in his hand, and he placed them into her open palm. She looked him dead in his eyes, something that was hard to do without wanting to kiss him.

"Thanks Pietro really, thank you so much, you came through for me." She said, taking a step closer.

"No, don't worry about it, it's my pleasure just remember you owe me now." They both laughed. He then added, "I know you don't have that far to go, but do you want some back up to escort you the rest of the way? A little added muscle never hurt." She gave him a look of amusement with a raised eyebrow.

"Yeah, right, that would go over real well, me pulling up flanked with a couple of bull bouncers. Thanks, but I think I can manage." He meant well, though. Silence followed, as they looked at each other, that awkwardness was starting to creep up. It was time to leave. Her mind went blank, she couldn't get the word "good-bye" out, then something that she had no control over at that very moment happened. She pressed her lips hard to his, holding them there for a moment. Pietro was totally caught off guard. By the time he realized what she had done, she pulled away, gently biting his lower lip as she did. She stepped back from him, his face was blank as he stared at her, she took two more steps backwards never taking her eyes off him, she then turned and got into the car, starting up the engine. One of Pietro's men opened the gate that led from the alley to the street and just like that, she was gone. Pietro was still standing there totally entranced by what just happened. It took one of his men to tap him on the shoulder for him to come out from the daydream he was in.

"You know, for someone who works for the government, you have some questionable friends." Carmine said, in a disapproving tone. She looked at him,

"No one asked you for approval," she snapped back.

"It's also something a little more I see, hmm interesting." He rubbed his hand over his scruffy chin. During this trip, he learned how to press her buttons. She also learned not to answer him, but being hot headed at times, it was hard for her. She was thinking of maybe giving him a good rap in the mouth once this was over. Silence ensued through the car as they sped off. She thought about what just happened. She let go for that split second; Pietro really wasn't a bad guy. He was the best guy she had ever met, she'd never say this to anyone or out loud but she loved him. And hoped one day she could tell him.

Chapter 32
Jacobs

New York City. It was half past eight in the morning, as John Derlin sat in his office. He turned at the sound of his door opening; a young man walked in and closed the door. He had a boyish look to him with long slicked combed back hair. He wore a two-piece suit, teal tie, and a black collared shirt. His name was Jacobs; and he was new to Shadow Ops. He'd only been a field agent for little over a year. He was still a rookie. He was a fine young man and he'd make a fine agent one day. John just hoped that his maturity would kick in soon.

"You wanted to see me, John?"

"Yes." Before John could continue, Jacobs placed a file on his desk.

"My report, sir-"

"We'll discuss that later son." John didn't mean to cut the young man off, but time wasn't on their side. "Right now, I need you back out there. Priscilla Roletti, Agent Blondie. She's in a bind, possibly without transportation, or maybe even in a stolen car. I need you to find her and bring her in; I'll text you her number, try to contact her. We can't even track her, her GPS is off. I'm hoping, she'll show up any minute, but I can't assume anything."

"I'm on it, boss." Jacobs said, he oozed with over confidence at this easy assignment. John hated when the newbie's acted like this.

"Jacobs?" The young man turned around before he opened the door,

"Be very careful, she's up against some tough people, ok? Not just your run of the mill thugs," his warning fell on deaf ears it would seem. Jacobs smiled at Derlin,

"Hey, I can handle anything, I'll have her back before lunch." And he was gone. John leaned back in his chair, frustrated now. One problem with the new batch of recruits was arrogance, and cockiness, they thought they knew it all. Some even thought they were invincible, if only they knew how wrong they were, because the fact was that no matter how many years you did this, there was always someone out there better than you.

Chapter 33
So close yet so far

Half past eight and it was just like any other day during the New York/ New Jersey rush hour. The trucks and cars were jockeying for position, in constant stop and go traffic. It seemed everyone was in a hurry, but was going nowhere. Why there was traffic to begin with was anyone's guess. You could blame it on an accident; maybe people were half-asleep, shallow women worrying about their appearance putting on makeup or someone not paying attention while they talked on the cell phone. Whatever the reasons were, it was bad.

This is what Priscilla thought sitting in her red Ferrari, and it was fucking annoying her to no end! She looked over to her passenger who had his eyes closed, he was breathing heavily. Carmine had his window open because he wanted some fresh air. He didn't look that great either. Not having his heart medication for the last 24 hours was starting to take a toll on him. She put a hand to his forehead, he broke out in a cold sweat. She was not highly educated in medicine, but from the look of him, he might be in the early stages of cardiac arrest. Fortunately, they still had time, she hoped anyway.

"You ok?" She asked. It took him a few seconds to respond, as he sat up a little straighter looking at her nodding.

"Yeah, I'm ok, I haven't been feeling good for the last day now, I didn't want to bring it up, and give you more to worry about. I tried to hide it as best I could, but for some reason, since we left your friend's place, it got a little worse," he then looked forward again.

"What's wrong?" She asked, hoping to keep him coherent and alert, his eyes looked heavy.

"Having a hard time breathing and my body just feels weird, I can't explain it," she nodded.

"Just hang in there, ok? Put your window up, I'll put the air conditioner on." Where they were didn't have the cleanest air for anyone to breathe, with all the fumes from the cars and diesel trucks you might as well wear a mask. He did what she asked, rolling up his window. She blasted the A/C to its max, turning the vents on him. She then looked ahead; they were almost home free as they inched their way to the island of toll booths, the entrance of the tunnel came within sight. Seeing it, she let out a sigh of relief.

She caught movement by the booths other than the hands of the tellers popping out to return change to the drivers. Her gun was in easy reach, but it turned out to be a transit cop walking the island. There was always a few of them hanging around, watching with the eyes of a hawk for anything out of place.

Pulling up further Priscilla was third from the booth now, she reached into her pocket grabbing a bill, a twenty, she stuffed the rest back in. Oh, how she missed the E-Z pass that all the company cars had. She would have been halfway through the tunnel. Now second from the booth, she sat up straighter with anticipation, her palms were sweating. She looked back to Carmine; he seemed a little better with the ice-cold air bombarding him.

"Hang in there kid, we're almost there." No answer, all he did was nod; he had his head back and his eyes closed. She wasn't looking for an answer either, she was just trying to relieve him a bit knowing that he'd be taken care of soon.

Finally! They were next. At the booth, Priscilla handed the bill to the teller. The skinny woman smiled at her. She returned the gesture, then looked straight ahead. Just when the teller was about to return the change to Priscilla's opened hand, the passenger side window of their Ferrari imploded. She barely managed to cover her head from the shower of glass. Some small pieces pricked her arm but not enough to break the skin. She turned to see what the hell caused that, Carmine managed to shield himself from the glass also. As she looked back, the door was flung open.

Priscilla unbuckled herself and leaned over, grabbing Carmine before he fell out of the seat, but then Omar came into view, as he tried to force the door open further in the confined space of the toll booth. He pulled out a gun as he leaned into the car, leveling it at her.

Priscilla grabbed his wrist; a wild shot rang out going through the windshield as she punched him right in the jaw. He fell back, slamming into the other booth. Then, throwing it in first gear she peeled off. The passenger door closed itself from the momentum. The teller had ducked at the sound of the discharged weapon. She then stood up, gun in hand, looking dumbfounded as she saw the red car bolt off. Omar got up off the ground, wiping his mouth on his sleeve looking in the direction of where the red car sped off. The teller immediately saw he was not one of her colleagues and raised her gun.

Seeing the teller's movement in the corner of his eye, Omar, who was faster on the draw, shot her in the face. He then turned back to the fleeing car breaking out into a run.

"Trish, where the fuck are you?" Omar yelled into his earpiece. His sister was already on the move. She ran across the road with an automatic machine gun in hand, sending a spray of bullets into the speeding Ferrari. All the while, she was trying to avoid fleeing cars escaping the mayhem. Firing wildly, she managed to hit the Ferrari putting a crooked line of holes in the door, before the car disappeared into the tunnel. She turned back around looking for her brother, doing so she saw a car coming straight for her. Opening up more gunfire, she sprayed the windshield shattering it. Blood splattered the inside of the vehicle, as the dead driver slumped over, he crashed just on the outside of the tunnel.

Port Authority cops, came running out of their station house, with their guns locked and loaded. Trish, spotting the door fly open, sent a barrage of bullets their way. They didn't even have a chance to defend themselves as they were viciously gunned down. The traffic had stopped; travelers and tellers were hunkered down taking cover. Time was short, Trish and Omar had the opportunity and failed, now all they could do, was even the score for the time they invested into this. Omar caught sight of a vacated Honda motorcycle with the engine still running. The rider was off in the opposite direction, Omar ran towards the bike, pulling off his black, clipped on tie that went with the tacky uniform of the Port Authority cop that was lying dead in a ditch nearby. Hopping on the bike, he revved the engine and popped a wheelie as he took off. Trish heard the bike coming. She leveled the machine gun taking aim, and then quickly lowered it, seeing the familiar figure upon it. He stopped right next to her and she quickly straddled the back as Omar took off.

Chapter 34
To the Rescue

Jacobs, in the company black Dodge Charger, raced towards the Lincoln tunnel. He kept an eye on the road as he reached into his jacket, for his cell phone. As he dialed Priscilla's number, Jacobs took a deep breath of annoyance, he wondered what the hell kind of Op she was, that she needs to be picked up?

Jacobs didn't say anything to John, but he thought this was a waste of time for a man of his talents. He had to play chauffeur for a seasoned Op. The call he made didn't go through, it went right to voice mail. He tried again getting the same response. Throwing his phone on the passenger seat, he put on more speed, weaving in and out of the side streets. He passed double-parked cars and other obstructions that made driving here a nightmare; finally, he came to the corner of 10th Avenue and 34th street.

He could see the sign marked for the Lincoln tunnel, but for some reason, there was more congestion than normal. He drove on inching his way to the entrance. Just as he came within sight of the ramp leading into the tunnel, he saw a whole lot of activity going on. Police roadblocks were set up right at the entrance. To his right there was a side street, he turned onto it. He listened to the police frequency thanks to the scanner that all company cars had built into their regular looking radio. The chatter was fast paced, going on about an incident happening right now inside the tunnel that all started with a shootout on the other side. Subjects involved were unknown. What kind of a coincidence could this be, he mused, could Priscilla be involved in this somehow?

The call to her phone didn't go through, that could mean a lot of things. One in particular, was that she could be in that tunnel now. It would be hard to get a signal in any tunnel, even with a company phone. He pulled over, quickly dialing the number again, and like before, he got the voice mail.

"Damn." Well, it wouldn't hurt to stay close by and see what's up. With those thoughts, Jacobs drove on turning at the corner. He went back down the block coming around and double-parked, on

38th street right at the corner of 9th Avenue. He would have a perfect view of what was transpiring. Getting out he stood nearby watching the events unfold along with other people now standing by watching with him.

Mark Lewis finally arrived in New York City, it took longer than he wanted. The airfield he went to in Pennsylvania had only one chopper and it was out at the time, so he waited for the pilot to come back. Little did he know that it would take almost six hours for the chopper to finally return. Lewis, to say the least, was not happy at this point; he tried to control himself from not lambasting the pilot too much.

From what the pilot told him, he was on a search and rescue detail. A group of hikers had gone off in the early morning hours and had been declared overdue. As it turned out everyone in the group made it back safely. Lewis explained the situation and with great reluctance, the pilot agreed; refueling quickly.

Upon arriving, Lewis had the pilot land at the first helipad they spotted, which turned out to be on top of a hospital and wasn't far from police plaza, which was a plus. Not even thanking the pilot, Lewis rushed off making his way to the streets and hailing a cab.

When he finally arrived at the police plaza he threw his weight around, flashing his ID, grabbing their attention. Mark Lewis went over the whole story in detail of the past day's events. He told them everything that has transpired until now, of course leaving out a few small minor details that the NYPD didn't need to know. Such as the posse of bounty hunters involved and his findings that this woman was a government agent. And the fact that the whole reason for this chase was because this man she was protecting must've been some type of informant.

The events he made up were simple and to the point. A sting operation he was in charge of, was tracking the movements of anti-government terrorists. The woman in question had eluded them. He also stated she was on a suicide run, set to deliver a bomb of some kind in the heart of the city. The story was elaborate, yes, but it got the job done.

There were quite a lot of sick people out there, and of course when someone mentioned the word terrorist in New York City especially to a cop, one would expect no less of a reaction. At first he thought the captain wasn't going to buy into it, he threatened to call the FBI to confirm this, if that had happened then it was over for Lewis right then and there, but his luck held out, a call came in over the police ban. One of the street cops nearby turned up his radio.

According to the dispatch, there was a shootout that had just occurred at the Lincoln tunnel. With that, there was no further reason to talk. They all moved, the captain, turned and barked orders at everyone within earshot. He called in any officer that was in the area. SWAT teams were mobilized. Within five minutes of receiving the dispatch, they were on their way to the tunnel. By the time Lewis and company got there, the area was ripe with activity.

Cops, SWAT, and EMS, were getting into positions, roadblocks were up, onlookers, and pedestrians were told to keep away from the scene by a cop with a bullhorn. As Lewis pulled up, he was quite impressed on how fast the NYPD mobilized on such short notice. Lewis and the captain got out of the police cruiser.

"So how do you want to proceed? This is still a federal matter," the captain asked, with a disdained tone, not hiding at all how he felt. NYPD hated the feds, especially one like Lewis, who had this cockiness about him. The FBI guy turned to him, and then looked back to the tunnel, as he pointed,

"Well, captain, the only thing to do is wait, tell your men that the shoot to kill order for the woman is highly advised."

"What about the hostage?" The captain reminded him; this crooked agent of the law didn't even bat an eye.

"As far as I'm concerned the hostage is expendable, one life is worth thousands. I will take full responsibility for this from here on out." The captain was about to say something further, but didn't. The look on his face said he didn't agree and with great reluctance he nodded. Leaving Lewis alone with his thoughts, the captain ran off. Lewis watched him go over to his men and relay his orders. This was it, he had her, she was dead! At this point he'd sacrifice the bounty he had the $100,000 that was more than enough to disappear.

At the beginning of this chase, Lewis treated it like any other assignment, but the discovery of the bounty changed that. It was his ticket to a new life. It should have been cut and dry, but with the constant failures not only on his part, but also on the part of the hicks he had to deal with; it was slowly getting to him. It was the straw that broke the camels back. His discovery that this woman was a Shadow Ops agent sent him over the edge, now he was obsessed, with the notion of putting a bullet in this woman's head for all the grief she caused him.

He also hated the idea of these so-called elite agents doing whatever they wanted to do and never having to answer for it. Maybe this would bring them down off their pedestal. Coming out of his thoughts, he could now hear rapid gunfire echoing from the tunnel followed by screams.

"Get ready! They should be coming out at any moment!" He yelled, looking to his left and right, as the cops tightened their perimeter around the tunnel. A cop yelled something as he pointed to the tunnel, then someone appeared. A man with his hands raised high, followed by a woman doing the same. All of a sudden, there were five people following behind them with more following after that. The people making their way from the tunnel were yelling and screaming for the cops not to fire upon them. Cops off to the side went to their aid rushing them out of the way. A cop stepped forward with a bullhorn. It was set at the highest decibel telling the remaining motorists to stay in their cars and do not exit otherwise they'd be at risk. The anticipation was getting intense.

Lewis looked around quickly, checking the positions of the other cops and making sure all the areas were covered. Then something caught his eye, it was a car and not just any car, a black Dodge Charger of all things. It was sitting double-parked at the corner of the next block. He turned away shaking his head, dismissing it at first. He was tired and worn from all of this, getting panicky and paranoid. It's just a coincidence, he tried to tell himself, but being in this line of work, good or bad there was no such thing as coincidence, not by a long shot.

Sure, there are probably many Dodge Chargers all over the city, but a black one sitting there now? He looked back towards the car again. The driver was standing there looking his way, just like the other people in the area that stopped whatever it was they were doing to gawk. He looked back to the cops. Their guns were pointed at the tunnel opening waiting for anything threatening to come through. The cocking of the hammers were done almost in unison. Lewis turned back to the man, who was watching the events unfold rubbing his chin in contemplation.

Lewis then looked back to the cops. They weren't even paying attention to him, not even the cop five feet to his right standing behind his cruiser. With nothing to lose at this point, he walked away, heading for the car and driver at a brisk pace, careful not to arouse anything in the man he was approaching. All the while Lewis looked back to the tunnel. He didn't want to miss anything either. He came closer to the man that looked more like a kid; he couldn't be more than twenty-five years old. He was wearing a nice looking suit, and his hair was neatly combed back. He was a very handsome young man.

Lewis thought that maybe he was going crazy as he approached him. This kid didn't look the part of a government agent, more like a stockbroker. As he came closer, the man didn't even acknowledge Lewis. It was like Lewis wasn't even there. The young man's eyes were on the scene behind the FBI agent. Lewis reached into his jacket pocket, pulling out his thin wallet that contained his FBI credentials.

"Excuse me?" The young man looked at him finally, he nodded to him, and Lewis flashed a quick smile.

"I'm special agent Mark Lewis, FBI, I spotted your car. It resembles the one that got blown to pieces the other day. I thought to myself seeing you here with the same car is no coincidence. If you need anything from me, please say the word, I wanna get her the hell outta here fast before these trigger happy fools do something we'll all regret."

Even with that explanation, the young man didn't say a word. He gave Lewis a scrutinizing look. Time was running short, he was so close now. If this man was indeed a Shadow Ops agent then possible good fortune could still be his if this 'kid' played into his hands. Seeing that this was going nowhere Lewis tried again, this time changing tactics, with as much emotion he could bring out getting in closer where only the young man could hear him, Lewis didn't want to attract the attention of people nearby.

"For God's sake man! We don't have time for this! I know you're a Shadow Ops agent! One of your own is heading out of that tunnel, as I am sure you are well aware of. I have been in contact with her this whole time. We hooked up two states ago, and I'm trying to get her the hell outta here! I told her to meet me on 39th and 9th avenue, now please, will you help me! She's been through hell!" He said, raising his voice as he spoke. He felt his face getting flushed, the image of the police captain popped into Lewis's mind for a moment.

Staring the young man in the eyes, he waited for his reaction.

"Get in!" Lewis nodded, with a delay after the words hit him, a look of surprise almost showed on his face. He didn't think for a second that it was going to work.

"Thank you!" Lewis said, rushing around to the passenger side getting in. Lewis didn't even have the door closed yet as they peeled off.

"Jacobs." Lewis looked to the young man, as if he didn't hear what he said.

"Huh?" Jacobs looked back to him.

"My name is Jacobs." He put out a hand; Lewis grabbed it, shaking it firmly. "Sorry about that, we have strict guidelines when dealing with anyone other than our own." Lewis nodded, then looked straight ahead, they pulled around as quickly as the morning rush hour would let them, coming to where Lewis instructed him. Jacobs double-parked and Lewis prepared to get out.

"Where are you going?" He asked the FBI man.

"I'm going to watch for her, she knows where to go, I've talked to her twice already, and I just want to make sure she sees me. I told her I'd be waiting on the corner, keeping a lookout," he said as he pointed to the corner. Jacobs followed his finger, scanning the area. Lewis then stepped out walking towards the front of the car. He spotted an oncoming car and waited for it to pass. He fished out his gun keeping it close to his thigh, Jacobs watched him getting ready to cross.

"Wait!" He said as he opened his car door, "I'll cover the other corner, better to have two sets of eyes than one." Lewis nodded in agreement. As Jacobs walked past him, Lewis looked around quickly; there was no one in the vicinity, only a few people a block ahead of them, and they weren't paying attention to anything around them. In this city, unless you sang in your underwear in Times Square, no one would give you a first glance.

He then leveled it at his walking target firing one round into the base of the skull of the unsuspecting agent. Upon impact, a small mist of blood peppered the back of Jacobs' head as he fell face first on the pavement with the sound of his skull cracking. A small pool of blood flowed from the wound. Tucking his gun away, Lewis quickly looked around; again making sure no one saw him. He wasn't worried about the sound. There was gunfire going off in the distance.

The side street, they were on was vacant right now, thanks to the commotion happening at the tunnel, but that could change at any moment. Walking to the body of the dead agent, he carefully kneeled down, watching for anyone that might see him. He dug into the dead man's pockets, finding the keys to the car. Since they were close to the car still, Lewis pulled the man towards it by his ankles, leaving a small trail of blood. Doing this left him winded.

He then rolled the dead agent underneath the vehicle out of sight. Lewis got in his new car, looking it over. It was pretty much like any other car at a quick glance from an untrained eye not knowing what to look for. Once this was over with, he'd check the car out in full. This baby alone could fetch millions on the black market, knowing what this car was equipped with. He started the engine revving it. Now all he had to do was stay in the area. He had a police radio with him, keeping him informed of what was going on.

He'd drive close by and wait. Hoping that maybe she would get through somehow, he knew she would. Even he had to admit from what he'd seen so far, she was damn good, and with any luck the ones giving chase would attract the attention of the cops allowing the woman to escape right into Lewis' waiting arms of protection.

Chapter 35
War Zone

The fire engine red Ferrari wasn't looking too hot now. When she entered the tunnel, she quickly weaved in and out of the two one-way lanes. It was a slow process, something she needed to speed up. She had to make room, creeping in where she could; she forced her way in at slow speeds grinding the bright red paint off onto other cars and trucks she sideswiped along the way. The pissed off people she hit came out of their cars waving their fists and cursing. Then to make matters worse, the traffic suddenly came to a standstill.

This was far from normal, even for city traffic. She hoped it wasn't the police setting up roadblocks in regards to the shootout. She figured she had some time before the cops mobilized. But, by the way things were looking, she had to assume the worse. She was going to have to make the rest of the way on foot. This was something she didn't really want to do right about now, especially with her immobilized companion next to her slowly slipping away. She looked over to Carmine; who looked dead if you glanced at him. His eyes were closed, his chest going up and down were the only signs of life. One good thing about the bumping and grinding off the other cars was, he opened his eyes with every impact, preventing him from falling into unconsciousness. She was pulled from her thoughts at the sound of gunfire, she ducked down. Some of the wild bullets found their mark; she could feel the vibration of each impact, penetrating the body of the sports car. She was hoping that a lucky shot wouldn't find its way into her. Keeping her head down while trying to watch the road ahead, she put on more speed, slamming violently into a Camry. The force propelled her forward, if not for the seat belt digging into her neck, she would have gone right through the windshield.

She peered over the steering wheel rubbing her throat, not daring to expose herself to flying bullets. She caught a glimpse of the car she hit. It was now sideways blocking her. She noticed there wasn't a driver behind the wheel. The car next to her, was also vacant of a driver. Throwing it back into high gear and peeling out, she rammed the car trying to push it, to no avail though. Smoke was billowing from the back tires tearing into the pavement. More shots rang out; a wild shot hit her windshield bursting shards of glass onto the hood. She looked into the passenger mirror and spotted one of those Japanese motorcycles gaining on her. The rider was weaving back and forth between vehicles with ease, squeezing through the small confines.

She kept on trying to push the car in front of her, she was desperate now. Grinding her teeth with the anticipation of breaking free she pressed the pedal all the way down to the floor. The engine whined in protest, she was waiting for the motor to seize up, due to the strain. Then she felt it, she was slowly squeezing through. She could feel the car in front giving a bit. She was almost there, just a little bit more.

Suddenly she shot through the small opening, tearing off the side view mirrors. Uncontrollably she headed straight into another car. Bracing for impact, she slammed into the backside of a pickup truck with an ear-deafening boom. The Ferrari was totaled. Smoke was climbing up from the hood with a hissing sound. Priscilla's head was on the steering wheel, it took her a moment to clear it. There was no time to sit around; she quickly regained her bearings even though she was still foggy eyed. Her body had aches and pains, racing all over. She unbuckled herself, Carmine, who was somewhat awake now, turned to her, with his mouth agape taking in deep breaths of air.

"Come on! Wake up, snap out of it!" She said with that look of determination that she hoped would rub off on Carmine, giving him some extra strength to move on. As she pulled him by his collar, the bullets were coming for them. Wild shots were hitting the tunnel walls. Throwing open her door, she crept her way onto the pavement kneeling down beside the car.

She reached in for Carmine, pulling him out with a strain, she tugged him over the gear stick, jabbing him in the leg. She tugged with a final muscle retching effort. He must have pushed off at the same time, with the intent to help her, but he did the opposite. She was not expecting the extra momentum as he fell on top of her. If

Priscilla didn't tilt her head up at the last second she would have cracked her skull on the pavement.

If she was going to be killed today that was something she could accept because it was part of the job, but she'd be damned if she'd suffer the humiliation of being killed while this fat fuck was on top of her like a beached whale. Straining her already tense arms, she pushed his overweight body to the side. She got up on one knee getting a secure hold on him and hoisted him to his feet. Her face turned red with the strain. Dead weight was the worst thing to work with. She leaned him against the car, clamping both her hands on his chubby cheeks and looked him straight in the eye.

"Listen! You have to snap out of it! Come on!" He nodded weakly to her. She threw his arm around her neck, finally moving on. She tried to walk with him, but it was more like dragging him along. She felt like at any moment she would topple over with the weight of him on her neck and back. Bullets rang out once again, shattering a door window right in front of her; it forced them to hit the ground for cover. She turned back around on one knee, pulling the gun from her waist. She pointed to where the shots came from, or where she thought they came from. Her stalkers were using the mass of the automobiles as cover so she couldn't see anything. Firing off random shots of her own now she was hoping to lure them out and maybe get lucky. But if anything, it would buy them both some time to get more distance between them.

Priscilla wanted to finish those two freaks off in the worst way, but not with Carmine in the condition he was in. Damn her luck, she thought getting back up. With one hand, she pulled Carmine by the arm, dragging his limp body across the street, like a child would do with their doll. All the while, she kept an eye out for their attackers. She hoped that just maybe she could hit one of them.

Trish and Omar were hard pressed to gain on their fleeing targets with the mass of vehicles obstructing their path. The more they proceeded the harder it was to find a way forward. At any type of movement that caught Trish's eye, she fired off rounds in that direction. But the blonde was too quick, even with a wounded companion in tow.

Trish figured she got him somehow; she ejected the magazine from her rifle letting it drop to the pavement as they rode on. She slammed her last one in. Trish continued the barrage whenever she thought she saw them. She even took shots at people getting out of their cars running for their lives. Trish was in a blood lust of rage not caring who was in her line of fire. All she wanted was to kill as many people as she could at this point.

Priscilla slowly continued on her way, dragging her helpless friend on the pavement. She strained her back from being hunched over for so long. Every now and then, she would check for a clear shot at their pursuers. To make matters worse, instead of the people staying wherever they were, they started to make a run for it.

Priscilla was not going to be responsible for a stray bullet from her hitting the fleeing drivers now starting to bombard her. Then to her horror, she caught sight of people being hit at random, as they ran. A rage filled her, seeing this made her wish at this moment she didn't have to get this guy out of here,

"Fucking psychos!" She yelled. She caught sight of them for a quick moment, she tried to draw their attention to her, as she fired off some rounds. They were constantly on the move, it was hard to get a clear shot at them.

She turned forward, the bend was coming up, they were almost out of the tunnel. She turned back checking to see where Trish and Omar were. She spotted them again for a quick moment, but her reaction was too slow. Tiring of the slow progress they were making, she threw her gun away. She used both hands to pick up Carmine by the waist and threw an arm over her neck. She trekked on, as fast as her legs could go. Her muscles tensed with the extra weight, but she pressed on. The only good thing about the people, was that she could blend in more and disappear. It was fucked up to think yes, and she didn't feel that great about doing it either, but that was part of what she did. Sometimes you had to do what you had to do to get the job done. Besides, she wasn't responsible for these animal's actions. As they trudged on, Priscilla finally saw the faint light up ahead along with the police checkpoints.

Swerving in and out of lanes in the Lincoln tunnel that was now a parking lot, Trish lost sight of their targets.

"Fuck! I can't see them! Do you?" She asked Omar over the sound of their engine. Omar shook his head as he rode on; they too were heading for the bend now. As they turned the bend, they also saw the police standing by awaiting the ones responsible to come out. Omar stopped, for a second their faces had a look of worry or maybe even concern, but those looks quickly faded. Giving way to the psychotic thoughts that raced through their minds, they both looked at each other. In a silenced agreement on what to do, they nodded in unison.

"You ready!" He yelled over the blaring engine of the bike as he revved it up. They knew it was over and they had lost. Now their first priority was to escape, and there was no turning back. It was kill or be killed. They had nothing to lose; they would not be taken alive. He revved the engine, the bike jolted ahead. Trish dropped the automatic rifle; and reached around for the shouldered rapid firing grenade launcher.

"Ready!" She finally responded back. He nodded, the back tire spun in place, building up smoke that engulfed them. They took off like a rocket. Before them was an obstruction of cars. Not bothering to avoid them, Omar went head on pulling back on the handlebars, propelling them up and over, to the other side. The tunnel exit came into view. The stock of the launcher was tucked tight against Trish's shoulder. There was a laser sight on it, but there was no time for aiming, just point and shoot. The cops by their cars were waiting for a clear shot, but as the speeding motorcycle came into view, they didn't know what to expect.

Some cops managed to fire off their weapons missing the duo by mere inches, but Trish's aim was on target, letting loose a grenade, at the first car she saw. It exploded into a ball of flames; the cops near it were incinerated. She fired off two more grenades; flames shot to the heavens as two more cars were hit. Hell was on earth this day. Cops continued fleeing, taking cover from this unexpected turn of events.

They protected their own that were wounded, as well as getting bystanders out of harm's way. Just as they broke out of the tunnel, Omar pushed the bike to its top speed, heading for an upturned car. Using it as a ramp, they both rocketed into the air. Omar almost lost control of the bike as he landed. The only thing that kept them on their wheels was the shifting of their weight at the right time upon impact. Speeding off up 39th street, Trish twisted around letting loose one more round. The grenade flew into a parked car propelling it up and back down to the street. The now flaming car blocked the way they came. She looked upon her handy work with a smile. She dropped the grenade launcher as they sped away. They would not be found, in this city when one had the will and the know-how, you could disappear and blend in. This was something the police did not expect and by the time they regrouped, Trish and Omar would be long gone.

Chapter 36
Into the nest of a Viper

Priscilla made it past the police blockade. She fell into the mad rush of people stampeding for their lives, yelling and screaming as they ran. How she managed not to be knocked over with her half dead sidekick was beyond her. The people that were further away from the destruction, were coming over, helping whoever they could. Some of the would-be rescuers saw Priscilla and offered a helping hand, which she refused.

"He'll be all right, all the excitement was a little too much for him." From the looks on their faces, they didn't believe her.

As they limped their way from the scene, she took in the death and destruction all around her. It saddened her, so many lives lost. But the one good thing that came from this, was that in this country, especially in New York. You could hate whoever you wanted for whatever reason. But, in a time of crisis, the people all came together to help one another no matter what they thought of the person next to them, everyone was your brother. 9-11 was a testament to that.

She looked to Carmine, he was in bad shape. If she didn't move her ass, he was finished. His lips were turning purple, his eyes were red and almost bulging. From the looks of him, he was starting to go into cardiac arrest. She was not in any better shape either, she was exhausted.

With his arm draped across her neck almost taking on his full weight, they finally made it to the corner of the next block.

She leaned Carmine against the metal light post for a moment, taking his weight off her. She was scanning for a cab. In New York they were a dime a dozen. She spotted one instantly. When she was about to hail it over, a black Dodge Charger pulled right up in front of her. The passenger door flung open, she bent down looking at the driver's friendly face with a look of haste.

"Quick get in!" Taking her eyes off him, she quickly looked at the car. It was definitely a Shadow Ops car, she knew that right away. She nodded quickly opening the back door. She grabbed Carmine, flinging his arm back over her neck. She winced with pain having the dead weight added to her once again. As gently as she could, she placed him in the backseat. She tried to sit him up, but that was not happening. Before she could even buckle him in, he fell over with his eyes rolling white. She was going to try again, but took notice of people staring at them. She left him the way he was and slammed the door shut. Climbing in she slammed her door closed as well and buckled herself in.

As they made their way; she breathed a sigh of relief. Finally, home free, she closed her eyes for a few seconds liking the feeling of being driven for a change. She was exhausted; all she wanted to do was sleep for a week. She took in a deep breath, trying to calm herself. She sat up and looked over to her savior. He had a rugged look to him, dressed in a black suit with a red tie against a white collared shirt. She took in his features; his hair was short and spiked. He was square jawed. She didn't recognize him, but that didn't mean anything. There were agents that she never met before. He glanced at her, feeling her eyes on him, he flashed her a smile.

"Hell of a ride, huh?" Priscilla chuckled as she looked away.

"Yeah... you could say so," she rubbed her face and then pushed some uncombed hair back, looking at him again.

"Thanks....uh."

"Mark Lewis."

"Thanks Mark."

He didn't want to give her his real name, but with things moving so fast, Lewis didn't think of one beforehand. He didn't want to sit there trying to come up with a fake name now, that would certainly arouse suspicion. It would've been a stupid move on his part to use the dead agent's name. She might have known him, but it really didn't matter though, because she was going to die.

No more words were spoken; it was quiet except for the heavy breathing of their passenger in the backseat. Priscilla turned around as much as the seat belt would allow her. Reaching over she opened one of his eyes; she looked over to Lewis righting herself in her seat.

"We better hurry," he nodded and the car went faster. Priscilla sat there watching the street signs go by, then something came to mind. They were driving down 42nd street, heading east, which was the right direction to go, but this was not the way to go though. They hit a red light, traffic today was horrible as always in the goddamn city, and what just happened was not helping either.

They were at 42nd and 8th avenue, almost by the Theater District. Now to anyone else, taking 42nd would be a direct way across the city. But the one thing they drilled in your head was to never take 42nd to HQ. It was for the sake of being followed. For some reason they were not following procedures and being an agent as Lewis was, he should have known that.

She sat up straighter thinking crazy thoughts like the man next to her was another hired killer, but her mind kept saying No! No! No! She tried to convince herself it was ok. She told herself she was being paranoid, but that gut feeling said something different. She looked to him not giving anything away. He was pouring on more speed weaving in and out of traffic and blowing lights barely missing pedestrians. She opened her mouth to speak; he glanced at her noticing she was about to say something. She thought better of it, No, I'm being paranoid, she told herself again. She looked back to the street; then seconds later under her breath she said.

"Fuck it." She cleared her throat before raising her voice to speak. "You know…Lewis." She let the words hang in the air a bit, then continued, "This is not the way we go, we should be hitting the side streets back to base." She said this not as a question, but in a matter of fact tone. She held her eyes on him for a moment, he glanced at her.

"Yeah, I know, I wasn't thinking...uh.. I was going to turn off, but the damn traffic is killer today. I'm going to turn off at the first chance I get." She kept her eyes on him for a second longer. She didn't think he was lying, or to be more exact, she was too tired not to believe him. He looked a bit nervous though. She noticed the perspiration on his forehead. She turned away, trying to ignore her uneasiness. She figured taking in the sights a little would calm her. For as much as she hated the city at times, she did like the eye candy it offered. The vast buildings reaching for the heavens were always awe inspiring no matter how many times you looked to them.

The people here were always interesting to watch; you never knew what you might see. The people of the city of New York were unique to say the least. They were just coming to the corner of 7th avenue a block before Times Square when she caught sight of a rather odd looking dog, being walked by it's even odder looking owner. The woman wore the tackiest clothes she'd ever seen, with makeup that looked like it was plastered on.

The breed of dog the woman was walking, was a type Priscilla had never seen before, only in New York she thought. Priscilla was just about to turn back around in her seat when in the reflection of her window, she saw a gun being leveled at her. Her eyes widened thinking she was seeing things but when she spun around and saw that they weren't. She reacted, grabbing his wrist with one hand while trying to pry the weapon loose with the other. In the struggle, Lewis hit the accelerator blowing through the intersection and lost control of the car. He sideswiped a limo next to them bouncing off into another car. All the while, their speed increased, she had the advantage though or so she thought.

For a guy his size Lewis was strong, he pulled his hand away from her grip slamming her face with the gun. He kept looking back and forth to her and the road trying to keep the car from crashing, Priscilla came back, punching him square in the face, drawing blood. She went in for another shot, but he moved out the way at the last second. Her fist slammed into the window almost breaking her knuckles.

She cried out in pain, Lewis didn't let up, he smashed her face twice into the dashboard knocking her for a loop, her eyes rolled back into her head. Not wasting a second, he cocked the hammer, squeezing the trigger. As he did so, the car was smashed from the front propelling both of them forward, only to be stopped by their restraints. The gun went flying, Lewis lost sight of where it went. He looked up; he slammed into a Toyota, totally wrecking the back of the small car.

He pressed the accelerator to the floor, pushing the car out of the way while sideswiping another car to continue on. If he wasn't trying to kill this bitch he would have been amazed at how this car almost took no damage. Taking his attention off his would be victim gave Priscilla the chance to recover.

She sprung up; and connected with an elbow to the side of his head. Then grabbing a handful of hair, she rammed his head repeatedly into the unbreakable door window. In her mind, she was hoping to break the fucking thing open like a walnut in a nutcracker. They continued to struggle, while the Charger bounced off cars and trucks like a pinball. They did anything they could to get one up on the other. It was going to be a matter of time before they killed each other or someone else during the struggle. While fighting, one of their hands hit the recline lever propelling Mark's seat backwards.

Priscilla, wasting no time took advantage, she was relentless as she pummeled him with fast and furious blows to the face. Her face turning red with rage, she overpowered him; she locked her hands around his throat choking the life out of him. His face turned purple, veins were bulging from his temples. With his eyes going bloodshot, he coughed, trying to take in a gulp of air. He was throwing his hands up trying to hit her. He started to black out. She kept on squeezing, lost in the moment. Then, with a jolt, and endless rolling over, darkness overtook her.

Chapter 37
Uptown, Upside Down

Everything was spinning, when she opened her eyes. Her head hurt so bad it felt like someone thrust a spike through her skull. Turning her head hurt, the spinning was slowing down, but her eyes were unfocused. She closed them tightly, as she put her hands to her eyes and rubbed them, hoping that it would clear them faster. As she touched her eyes, she felt something wet on the side of her head. The seat belt was digging into her skin. She put her hands to her head and felt her hair standing straight up, and then it dawned on her, the car had flipped over. She heard sounds, faint voices from the outside.

She heard Lewis moan, he was starting to come around. Priscilla braced her arm against the ceiling and with her free hand she unbuckled herself. She fell with a thump; as best she could, she maneuvered around, twisting and turning to get her feet lined up with her window. From this angle, she could see her shatterproof window cracked from the crash. With as much force as she could muster in the small confines, she kicked the window, the first time was to no avail, she kicked it again and again, until finally kicking it free. The window was still intact as it fell to the ground. Priscilla then wiggled herself out feet first. Her left leg was killing her, her head felt like it was going to burst at any moment.

Climbing to her feet, she felt like she was going to fall, but kept her balance. She surveyed the area.

The direction they came from was littered in destruction, mostly of smashed cars and drivers that were shaken up getting out, and trying to figure out what happened. Thankfully, no pedestrians were struck down, as far as she saw.

She turned, seeing small crowds gather, approaching slowly with looks of concern and awe. Some were on cell phones, but no one approached her directly. The moaning of Lewis, pulled her from her thoughts, she realized she had no time to stay here and lollygag. She crouched down reaching through the window, she just came out of. Feeling for the button to unlock the door, she heard the click.

She then straightened up and opened the door, which was stuck. She used two hands and pulled hard, almost falling back from the door suddenly opening, with a creak of metal being bent in protest. Going back inside the car she reached around to unbuckle Lewis, who fell to the ceiling, he was somewhat awake now. This was something Priscilla was going to fix. She slammed his head into the steering wheel twice. She cursed as she did so spitting the words out with venom. She grabbed a handful of clothes, pulling him out with no care at all for what injuries he might have had. She dragged him to the sidewalk, then went back and grabbed the gun that she happened to see near the still body of Carmine. She glimpsed at him, knowing his condition right away.

Grabbing the gun Priscilla walked back to her supposed fellow agent. He was now alert and eyeing her. He had a gash on the side on his face. She could see blood pouring from his sleeve. He had a compound fracture in his forearm. The bone was protruding through his suit jacket.

She approached with the gun pointed directly at him; he smiled at her, but grimaced with pain from his wound. He looked around seeing two people approach them. He looked back to her trying to smirk, but he was in too much pain. Priscilla limped closer, standing over him. Her aim was a bit shaky, he was about to say something, his lips started to move, but there was nothing she wanted to hear. Just as she fired, he raised his hand, the bullet went through it hitting him. Blood oozed from the wound, like lava from a cooling volcano. He was twitching in pain.

She shot him in the neck even though she was aiming for his head. She was going to fire again, but waited a moment, staring at him. His hand went to his throat in a useless attempt to stop the gushing blood; the crimson liquid was seeping through his fingers to the street. Gurgles were coming up as he tried to speak. He was suffering from his wounds, she could have ended it…. but didn't. Let the son of a bitch drown on his own blood she thought. She knew he'd be dead by the time the police came. She then turned to the car again. She wanted to make sure what she saw before was confirmed.

Kneeling, she placed her hand onto Carmine's neck. He was dead, a broken neck. All of this for fucking nothing, son of a bitch! She had very little time to spare; for she knew at any moment the police would be here. She wanted to make sure he didn't have anything of value on him. Priscilla reached into his back pocket and grabbed his wallet, then his inside jacket pocket, finding a data stick. She stuffed both the wallet and data stick in her pocket. She reached into the front, feeling for the middle console where the weapon controls would be. Concealed under a plastic cover was the self-destruct button, flipping it, she pressed it.

She had thirty seconds, turning around she saw someone kneeling over the now dead agent. The man had gone into his jacket pocket and pulled out a thin wallet. She walked as quickly as she could with a limp. The man looked up as he heard her footsteps, before the man could get a word out, she grabbed the bystander by his collar pulling the fool to safety. He tried to protest, but a quick pistol to the forehead stopped that. Dropping him, far enough, Priscilla grabbed the wallet from his hand and walked on, past the eyes watching her in the distance, she kept her head down not looking at anyone. She heard the sirens of the incoming police. As she made her way to the next block, the car exploded, all eyes were off her then. Another block over she saw a cab sitting idle at a traffic light.

He just pulled up; all he saw was the explosion. He was sitting there rolling his window down for a better look of what just happened. He took his eyes off the scene when he heard his back door open; looking in the rearview mirror, he saw a blonde climb in the backseat.

"Lexington and 40th," she said with no haste underlying her words.

She dug into her pocket grabbing the first bill she felt, it was a fifty. Her last bill to be exact, she tossed it on the seat.

"Keep the change." He looked at the note then back to her. He nodded and took off going in the opposite direction. Priscilla said not a word more, she slumped deeper in her seat, resting her head and closing her eyes. 40th street was two blocks away from HQ, she could limp the rest of the way there.

Chapter 38
Time well wasted

"Police are baffled this morning as they are trying to sift through the carnage that was left in the wake of a high speed chase through the city. With property damage estimated to be in the millions, there were countless injuries along with the murder of an FBI agent. According to officials, the high-speed chase is believed to be part of the rash of violence that hit the country over the week. Authorities believe it to be the same person or persons responsible, but they are not confirming or denying anything just yet, we'll update you with more details as they unfold, Bernie."

In times of stress and frustration, Priscilla took comfort in the toxic cigarette smoke she was inhaling now. It was odd for something so deadly to be so soothing. She sat in John's office with her elbows perched on both knees; John was at his desk also puffing away on his pipe. John watched while Priscilla listened. She didn't need to watch what was going on because she lived the whole thing only two hours ago. When she finally did get back here, she immediately went downstairs to the basement seeking medical treatment. The company doctor on duty looked at her right away. She had a slight concussion, a sprained ankle, multiple cuts contusions and bruises, she'd live. When she finally got upstairs, John had some food brought into his office. It was a good thing too, because if she didn't put something in her stomach she was going to faint. The room was silent with the exception of the TV, she blocked out what was being said by the news anchors, she didn't care about it anymore.

All Priscilla cared about now was getting home, getting cleaned up, and taking care of her sick son. But of course she needed to be debriefed first. Hearing the creak of his chair as he leaned forward to shut off the TV, she looked to John who wore a look of frustration. He turned to her folding both hands in front of him; she put out her butt and placed the ashtray back on his desk, waiting for him to speak.

"Priscilla, the only thing I can say is I'm sorry for all this." He put a hand to his forehead as if trying to rub away a headache that was about to come on. "This whole thing came down so fast; it should have been planned better. The Intel should have been checked more thoroughly." She kept her eyes on him, she wasn't mad at him, how could she be? She leaned back in her chair.

"John, no one's at fault here, it was just one of those things that wasn't meant to be, Jacobs though, what a fucking shame," he nodded in agreement. Jacobs would have made a good agent. It's always a pity when someone loses a life that was so young and promising. This whole mission was a wild roller coaster ride from the get go.

Trish and Omar, an Aryan skinhead, an albino hit man and a rogue FBI agent, it doesn't get any wilder than that.

"So what now?" She asked. He shrugged his shoulders to the question.

"The only thing we can do right now is check the city thoroughly. According to Carmine, the data he had hidden is here. If I had to guess, it would most likely be in a safety deposit box. We'll check every bank, hopefully if it's what he says it is, we'll have the identification of one of the main backers of terrorism in this country, and abroad."

"If it's even there, he was a slippery little bastard, this whole thing didn't sit right with me. I have a feeling we were being played, somehow this is gonna come back to haunt us." She added. John nodded in agreement, he started to get up.

"Well… I think we're done here, you are relieved. If I need any further details, I'll call you." She followed his lead, and without a word more she left, closing the door behind her. As always, the office was ripe with activity. She caught glances as she made her way to the elevator. She walked past Derlin's secretary Jenny, who stopped what she was doing and flashed her a smile, with worried eyes. Priscilla, returned the smile, limping away.

Chapter 39
Loose Ends

That night, across the Hudson River in Dell City, New Jersey, three thugs were out walking the streets looking for a score, or a hapless victim. They talked amongst themselves laughing loudly. As they passed a darkened alleyway, one of the three happened to look, noticing a reflection of light off a windshield. He gestured the other two to stop.

They walked back to where their friend was. Looking to the streets quickly, they walked down the alleyway. They came upon a Sprinter, with very dark windows. The trio checked it out from all sides. Trying the door handles, which were locked. One of the three stood by the driver's side door, cuffing his hands around his eyes for a better look inside; all three were not more than twenty years old if not younger.

The hoodlum looked around and found a piece of concrete. The other two stood by the entrance of the alleyway keeping a lookout. They nodded to him, stepping back, the kid, threw the ball-sized piece of concrete at the window expecting it to shatter. He was caught off guard when it sprung back almost hitting him in the face. Undaunted, he tried again, winding up.

This time the concrete shattered from the impact, leaving nothing but dust on the glass. Frustrated, he looked around, spotting a can of garbage. Rummaging through it, he found a small copper pipe that he swung at the window with all his might. His face turned red with anger, with every swing, he grunted louder. One of the lookouts put a hand up whistling, signaling him to stop.

In the stillness they heard footsteps approaching, coming into view from around the corner were two bums draped in old tattered looking rags with hoods over their heads. It was a rather chilly night. Their faces were darkened and all you saw was their breath. Slowly the bums made their way, turning down the alley, ignoring the trio they passed. The hoodlums looked at each other then to the bums, as they made their way deeper in the alley almost passing the Sprinter.

"Yo! What you got? Anything good?"

One of them said. These bums might have a nice rock on them; alleyways were a prime place to get high without prying eyes, or the bad luck of a cop on patrol happening to spot you. The bums stopped, turning around to the trio. One of the punks had a switchblade in his hand. Just as one of the thugs started to walk towards the bums, gunfire erupted out from underneath the bum's rags. The shots could be heard blocks away. The three thugs lay lifeless in a river of their own blood. Shaking off the rags, Trish and Omar stood there with the smoking guns in their hands.

Omar went to the van unlocking the doors, while Trish walked over to the trio. Seeing one still alive, two more shots rang out. She spit on the corpse walking away, not one word was said to each other as they climbed into the van situating themselves. Starting it, the looks on their faces said it all, hate and contempt. They barely escaped with their lives and all for nothing. This whole job, was a big waste of time and money. The blonde bitch, made them look like fools. They didn't know who she was, but they knew their paths would cross again; and when they did, she would die in the most agonizing way they could think of..... it was just a matter of time.

Epilogue
Reflections

Three months later.

Christmas day, at one point she hated this time of the year, she hated the whole decorating, the trees, the crowds and everything else, but that all changed when the kids came into her life. Now coming over her house, you'd never believe it if she told you she was the biggest Scrooge going at one point in her life. Her house was adorned with Christmas lights along with, Santa Claus, a snowman, and reindeer on the front lawn.

Above her fireplace, were three stockings with their names on them. She had a Christmas tree that was huge with an angel topping it off just barely touching the ceiling. There was not a free spot on the tree. To say she was becoming soft was an understatement.

With her kids fast asleep, the presents were out, the milk and cookies left for 'Santa' were already eaten. She sipped her tea, staring into the dancing flames of her fireplace; she was transfixed in heavy thought. Christmas was going to be really good this year, well, for the kids anyway. During that mission from hell, at least one good thing came her way. When she checked Carmine, grabbing his wallet and the data stick, she handed John the wallet, but forgot to give him the data stick. She didn't realize it until after she got home that evening.

She downloaded the data; thinking it might have something important pertaining to the mission. But to her amazement, it didn't. What was on there were bank numbers, one long Swiss bank account number, to be exact. She knew it right away. One of the first things she did after becoming an Op was open a Swiss bank account. Her friend Pat was the only one with the account number just in case she met an untimely death. To her disbelief, the account held $200,000. She had no idea why he carried this with him during their trip. Maybe he was planning to run at some point, maybe a bribe, or whatever, but she remembered something he had said to her over dinner.

"You better be nice, otherwise you might not get a tip for your services!" At the time, she figured he was being a smart ass; she didn't take the comment seriously. He was a jerk, but it seemed he had some loyalty to people who did the right thing by him after all.

Priscilla pushed back in her recliner closing her eyes. Her thoughts drifted deeper. Ever since seeing Pietro again, she could not get him out of her mind. Maybe it was the time of the year and being alone on Christmas. This was something no one wanted. She thought about calling him that night, she wondered what he was doing. She was close to picking up the phone, but stopped herself. She didn't want to start something that she might regret.

She'd never say it to anyone but the truth was she yearned for companionship. She wouldn't have her kids forever and before she knew it, they would be starting lives of their own. She saw everything in this man, she could ever want. That was just her luck though. She was used to it by now, she always said if things are meant to be then they'll be, but until then all she could do was dream and wonder.

Vol. 3 The Unseen

Prologue
A night of sand and surf

At night, even the clearest sea water looked as dark as the night sky, as creatures of all shapes and sizes scurried about. One such fish, with blue and yellow stripes, was at the bottom of the ocean floor poking around. When all of a sudden, a cleverly concealed fish looking like the seabed below, came to life, and snatched the fish into its gaping maw.

Before the hunter could enjoy its meal though, something moved past it, startling it. It was a black mini-sub, propelled by silent water jets.

As the black sub continued along, the bright light of the moon could be seen through the calm, clear surface. The sub slowly came to a stop, resting on the seabed. The occupant released the airlocks. Bubbles filled the area, rapidly popping before they hit the surface. The occupant swam out and up, stopping just two feet from penetrating the flat calm sea. Powerful legs kept her in place as she took count of the patrol boats above. There were four in all.

The figure held a gun like device, carefully taking aim at each of the hulls. She fired plastic explosives that cut through the water at a high velocity attaching themselves to the hulls. Once she was finished, she dropped the device and swam to the dock. Her covered head penetrated the water, with large goggles strapped to her head. Staying there for a moment longer, the figure could hear conversations coming from the boats. The dark shadow pulled herself out of the water slowly without so much as a splash, then quickly went for the shadows. Once there, she crouched motionless like a tiger ready to pounce. The dock area was clear, and the beach looked clear of anyone as well.

She stood up slowly. The wetsuit she wore fit her perfectly. She ran for the beach not making a sound. As she ran, the only illumination hitting the beach was from the moon.

Further down the beach stood trees. She quickly made her way towards them, hiding in their shadows, all the while keeping a wary eye out for a sudden surprise that might lie in wait of unwanted trespassers.

Crouching down again, she activated her goggles' HUD (Heads up-display) a computer-generated map of the mansion, that sat on the mountaintop came up, she looked over the map carefully, memorizing where she needed to go and how to get there. She then tapped her goggles again to see in night vision. Wrapped around her waist was a pouch that she tightened so it would not bounce around on her hip. Concealed behind the pouch was a holstered Beretta. She grabbed a silencer tucked in her wetsuit, screwed it on and went on her way.

The sandy road that led to the mansion had wooded areas on both sides made up of palm trees and thick bushes. She made her way towards the target, still cautious as she trekked through the woods, avoiding any type of booby traps, trip wires, or motion sensors.

Once she reached the walled perimeter of the mansion, the Shadow climbed a tree for a better view. She crouched still and silently observed the area for threats. Now, with a better view of the property, she again tapped the side of her goggles scanning the area with infrared. There were a few sentries scattered about strolling along with automatic weapons slung over their shoulders.

There was a checkpoint at the main gate leading into the property, manned by two guards. She reached inside her shouldered bag, grabbing two items. Climbing down, she crawled to the front of the gate, making no sound, slowing her breath for fear of being heard in the stillness of the night.

The two guards were less than six feet from her now. One was in the booth, the other pacing back and forth behind the closed gate. She placed two C-4 cubes near the gate itself, flipping their switches. She then proceeded to make her way back further along the wall. When she was far enough, she got back up on her feet and started to hasten her speed.

When she was about thirty feet from the front gate, she stopped, looking once again at the wall and the surrounding area.

The wall itself looked very unclimbable; the surface was too smooth, it was made of a plaster-like material.

There was a nearby tree she climbed, pulling herself up onto a strong looking limb that was close enough to the wall, she walked on it, testing it as she went along. She stopped around the middle checking the surrounding area where she planned to go. Satisfied, she bounced in place a few times, hoping the tree limb would serve its purpose, and then finally she took to the wind. Using her strong legs, she pushed off, clearing the wall and flipping gracefully, she touched down into a crouch on the soft green grass that covered the area. With her sidearm ready, she sprinted closer to the house going from shadow to shadow.

The courtyard had neatly cut bushes and trees that held the shadows well. The bushes were thick enough to hide within. She came to a hedge, staying concealed inside it for a few seconds then moving on, she heard voices, but they were too far off in the distance to bother her. She ran and slid into a group of bushes in one smooth motion, hiding underneath. Tapping again at her goggles, the HUD showed her the three-dimensional map; the most likely least guarded entry point would be the servants' quarters.

The mansion appeared to be very nice; it had elegance to it. There were two large marble columns in the front, and at a quick count, five on the side of the house. The place was completely white with beige shingles. The square footage was huge according to the three-dimensional map.

She looked to her left, where the front of the mansion was located and saw a fountain pool with two naked women carved of stone holding water jugs over their heads back-to-back. Beyond the fountain was a stone walkway that led to the marble steps of the main entrance. The servants' quarters were to the right of the walkway. She could see the way from where she was. Staying concealed for a few seconds longer, she cautiously made her way. She came up to the servants' quarters and proceeded down the three steps to the door.

As she approached, she reached inside her bag and pulled out her lock pick that worked on ninety-eight percent of the world's locks, inserting it slowly into the keyhole. She made fast work of unlocking it, slowly opening the door and slipping in, she was ready for the unexpected as she proceeded further into the kitchen.

Pots and pans hung on a rack over the large silver-prepping table. Everything was neatly stocked and labeled.

As she approached the brick oven, she spotted a conventional oven on the far side of the kitchen. Before going to it, she went down the hall where she saw a dumbwaiter on her right and a laundry room further down with two closed doors, most likely the servants' rooms. Once the area was secure, she went over to the oven, holstering her weapon. She examined the stove further, pulling it from the wall slowly, she was careful not to grind the tiled floor.

Once it was far enough out, she then reached behind it, and pulled the gas line out, the smell of gas immediately struck her. Then, reaching into her bag, she pulled out a block of C-4. Sticking it to the back of the stove, she flipped the switch on. She then made her way to the dumbwaiter quietly opening the doors and looking inside.

She eyeballed the space; she thought she would probably fit. Hitting the button to go up, she quickly hopped in, and closed the doors slowly continuing on her way. As it reached its destination, the dumbwaiter came to a stop with a loud thump. Afraid she made too much noise; she held her breath to listen if anybody had heard it. When she was finally convinced nobody had, she opened the door and crawled out. According to the map, her target's office was around the corner, first door on the left.

She flattened her back to the wall as she slowly crept to her right, and peeked around the corner down the red-carpeted hallway. She spotted the white double doors with gold handles. Just as she was about to head down there, they opened. Two scantily clad women came walking out going the opposite direction, giggling and talking. She waited a few moments and then started to turn the corner, but suddenly stopped when she heard more voices coming from the other hallway behind her. It was two male voices talking in Spanish.

"Damn," she whispered, as she readied herself. She held the Beretta tight in her gloved hands waiting for the right moment. She counted their paces and when she felt they were close enough, she turned the corner and fired two silent rounds into their foreheads. It was so fast, they didn't even have the time to realize their lives came to an end.

They hit the floor with a thud. The assassin waited a few moments, turning her head left and right making sure no one was coming from the sudden noises that were made.

She holstered her weapon, and thought about hiding the bodies in the dumbwaiter. But that would take up too much time, which she didn't have. So, she boobytrapped the bodies, with a C-4 cube, flipping the switch she tucked it inside one of the dead guards pants.

With that done, she hastened her pace, and without hesitation, she went to the double doors. It would only be a matter of time before the dead guards would be noticed missing.

The doors were locked. She quickly picked the lock and cracked the doors open just enough to see her target at his large oak desk engrossed in something on a computer.

She opened the doors a bit more and went inside. She could not tell if it was an office or a bedroom. It was probably both with its white wall-to-wall carpeting, an unmade bed, two couches, a coffee table, a big screen TV and an unused fireplace. He had statues of naked women in seductive poses, one large painting of himself above the fireplace and a few other expensive pieces of art.

With time running short, she simply walked to the desk. The man looked up, his eyes widened at the intruder. Before he could even stand up, he was shot in the face, blood splattered the wall behind him as he fell back. The female intruder stood over the body and placed two more rounds in his chest.

She holstered her weapon and threw her bag on his desk. Reaching inside she pulled out two more cubes of C-4 with detonators and a data stick. She inserted it into the PC tower, an option popped up on the screen. She hit 'yes' and the data stick started to download the entire hard drive while at the same time burning out the computer. She went back to the double doors she came in locking them, and placed a C-4 cube on the metal hinge flipping the switch. A tiny red light came on indicating it was armed. That C-4 had motion sensors, so when the door opened even an inch it would blow the hell out of the poor souls opening it.

Now, there were two ways out of here, the double doors she came through and the double glass doors leading outside to the balcony that wrapped around to the front of the house. She placed the other C-4 cube on the metal hinge of the door leading outside, but didn't arm it. She looked at the computer screen; the download was half way done. It was at that moment, the very thing she feared would happen. There was a knock at the door.

"Shit!" It felt like time was slowing to a crawl just then.

The knocks got louder and harder when no one answered. Angry voices could be heard outside; she looked at the C-4, waiting for it to go off from the vibration. Finally, to her delight, a notification popped up. 'Download Complete.' She took the data stick out, placing it inside her wetsuit and soon after, the tower started to smoke. She walked to the double glass doors leading out to the cool night breeze; reaching inside her wetsuit again, she pulled out a cell phone, which like the data stick was waterproof.

She went to a menu screen and armed not only the C-4 she just planted at the glass doors, but also the ones she set up inside the servants' quarters. Everything was just awaiting the touch of a single button. As she ran the length of the balcony, she peered over the scrolling landscape. Just then she heard the first explosion. That was her cue to set off the other C-4 she placed with the dead guards in the hallway. She felt the vibrations from the blast as she made her way to the front of the house. She was going to leave the same way she came, but obstructing her exit was a gathering of guards in two Jeeps with an automatic rifle mounted on each one.

She tried to keep up with the officer in charge, who was barking orders in Spanish, but this guy was talking a mile a minute. With her phone in hand, she looked to the servants' quarters, and detonated the explosives. That area went up in a ball of fire, bringing down that side of the manor. The guards' faces lit up as they got into their Jeeps and sped off to the scene.

Thanks to her little distraction only three guards were left behind to watch the front. She knew she could handle them with no problem. As she started to climb over the balcony, she was suddenly grabbed from behind on the shoulder. In a fluid motion, the shadowy figure turned around while at the same time, she grabbed his hand and broke two fingers. Twisting his arm, she spun and connected with a swift kick to the guard's chest. Before any more guards showed up, she jumped down to the roof below, and ran across to where the three guards were, their backs were towards her as they kept watch.

She was almost at the edge of the roof when gunfire buzzed past her from behind. Just as the three guards looked up and saw her drop down into a tight crouch. She systematically shot them in the head before they could even register their fate.

Even before the bodies dropped and settled, she bolted towards the gate, followed by gunfire still coming from the balcony. The guards at the front gate had increased from two to four. From a distance, they saw her running toward them. They ran to meet her, firing off random shots. She also managed to attract the attention of a few other guards and one of the other Jeeps.

With her cell phone in hand, she detonated the C-4 that she had planted by the gate, taking out the guards before they were out of range. Running like a bat out of hell, she hit the dirt road slipping into the wooded area for cover. The Jeep crashed through the twisted gates seconds later, swinging them in the other direction. They shined a light in the woods where she was running, taking random shots at whatever they saw moving.

She slowed her pace as she saw the beach ahead. She stopped right before the clearing, she didn't have time to sit here, but she didn't want to just run out into a trap either.

She could make it, but it would be close. The patrol boats were now alive with activity; each one wielding two spotlights, fast chatter could be heard from them. During the commotion, someone must have radioed the boats and alerted them of a security breach. She heard the Jeep getting closer, it was now or never. She took in a deep breath and ran; using all the strength that her muscles could give, but the sand hindered her.

Almost there, she thought, practically out of breath. The Jeep came around the twisting road, fishtailing. The bullets came close, whistling past her ears. The gunners on the bow of the boats spotted her and opened fire.

When she was on the dock, she took off jumping. As she dove in the water, a bullet came out of nowhere and grazed her thigh. Once in, she swam for the sub that was waiting and climbed in, not bothering to reseal the air lock. She powered it up, and sped off for the open sea. As she made her escape, she inserted a rebreather, installed into the dashboard. The assassin then detonated the last of the explosives lighting up the night sky in a cascade of hell and fire. She could feel the shockwaves, as she looked up at the exploding hulls, and the lifeless bodies that were sinking among the debris to their final resting place.

Chapter 1
Priscilla Roletti

She followed the homing beacon seven miles out. Once she arrived at the extraction point, she blew the tanks and surfaced like a sea creature, coming up alongside a rundown fishing boat that looked as if it could sink at any moment. She looked up at the friendly face, a man with a white beard, ratty clothes and a captain's hat. His face had grown old from the wear and tear of life at sea.

"Ahoy...everything go ok? The old man asked. "That was some explosion I just saw. Looked like the hand of the devil reaching for the night sky, it was a sight to be had let me tell ya."

"Lucky you, can you give me a hand?" She asked, not looking for small talk at the moment.

"Aye, miss, grab hold!" He reached over the side and extended his large calloused hand that clamped around hers like a vise. The Captain pulled her on the deck with very little effort.

"Thanks." She then turned around and opened her phone, inputting a combination of numbers, she set the self-destruct sequence for the mini-sub that sent it back to the bottom of the sea. The CPU inside would find the deepest point before self-destructing. She turned back to the salty sailor, who was staring at her. It almost seemed as if he was checking her out. He then flashed an embarrassed grin. He pointed to her wounded leg that was bleeding.

"Looks like you were hit. I got a first aid kit downstairs with a change of clothes for ya. Should be about a four to six hour trip back to the States, so rest up. There's some food for ya as well, and if you need anything, the name's Earl." As he finished, she noticed he was missing a few teeth, but nonetheless, he was kind.

"Thank you, Earl." She said, trying to sound a little more friendlier. He tipped his hat to her, then went to the ladder, climbing to the flybridge. The boat didn't look like it could go past 20 knots. But when the engines roared to life, they sounded like they belonged to a speedboat; instead of this old beat up fishing vessel. The boat then suddenly took off with the front rising. This bulky, slow-looking ship was actually a Hydrofoil. She almost lost her footing at the unexpected burst of speed.

Finally, on their way, she sat down on something that looked like a cooler, but it was a little too dark to tell. She then finally freed herself and took off her goggles and slid back the headpiece of the wetsuit to reveal shoulder-length, thick, blonde hair and blue eyes that sparkled like sapphires.

Priscilla Roletti stared up at the clear night sky. She closed her eyes, enjoying the sensation of the wind hitting her face. She was trying to focus on anything else but the choppy seas, but that was proving difficult as the boat was rocked by yet another wave; she was not feeling so hot now. She went down below, to find the food on the table. The sight of it made her feel worse. She cursed herself for not remembering to take the Dramamine, which didn't even work all the time. Near the table was a cot; she sat at the edge taking in a deep breath. By now the stinging of her wound subsided, she glanced at it. The bullet only grazed her; the blood had already clotted. What made the seasickness worse was the boat had the smell of saltwater and fish. She slowly laid down and stretched out, stuffing her face in the pillow, trying to block the rancid stench of the boat. At least the pillow didn't reek of saltwater. She rolled over and closed her eyes, hopefully when she woke up they would be in port.

Chapter 2
A friend in need

"Good morning. We start with a late breaking story out of Northern Columbia. Government officials say that reputed drug lord, Julio Rivera, was gunned down in a late night attack. Officials are saying it was the work of rival organizations, fighting over what was left of Pablo Escobar's empire after his death more than ten years ago. Officials said Rivera was one of the most wanted men in Columbia and was in constant hiding. Officials also say-"

The TV was shut off. Priscilla didn't need to hear the rest of it as she waited in John Derlin's office, Chief Executive Director of Shadow Ops. It was just her luck, she had to arrive just when he was in a meeting. The last thing she wanted to do was wait, she was tired and wanted to go home already, but her day was far from over.

She had to catch up on so much stuff and take care of the kids. She looked at her watch, she's been here for over twenty minutes. She took a deep breath and stood from one of the two chairs in front of Derlin's desk. She needed to stretch her legs, they were stiff. Even though Priscilla's been in here countless times before, she couldn't help but admire the history adorned on his walls. There were awards and citations, pictures when he was in Vietnam, and a signed photo of Ronald Reagan. This long, successful career started out like hers and many others who were in Shadow Ops. He served two tours in Vietnam. At the beginning of his third tour, he lost his eye. Never retiring, he stayed and worked his way up, until finally being tapped as Chief Executive Director of Shadow Ops by Ronald Regan himself.

She walked over to the window, viewing the city from up here was amazing. It suddenly made her remember the time she took the kids on one of those helicopter tours, that was incredible. The door opening pulled her from her thoughts as she turned around.

"Good morning, Priscilla. Welcome back." Derlin said, as he entered and closed the door behind him, with his ever-present pipe clenched between his teeth. “I’m sorry for keeping you waiting this long. Busy morning.” Priscilla nodded, understanding, she knew Derlin’s job wasn’t easy.

He was always on the go, traveling from New York to Washington at least twice or more a week. She came from behind his desk and sat back in one of the two chairs.

“I heard over the wire that your mission was successful.” He continued as he took off his suit jacket, throwing it over his chair. Once he sat, he lit his pipe inhaling deeply.

“Thanks John, my report is on your desk and here is the data stick.” She reached into the breast pocket of her black collared shirt, placing it on his desk. He took in another long pull of his pipe, the sweet smelling smoke filled the room.

“Unless you have anything to add, I think we’re done here. We’ll take a close look at the data stick before we hand it over to the DEA.”

The assassination of the drug lord was a request from the Columbian government. Derlin, also thought that if possible, she should gather whatever Intel she could find in regards to Rivera’s drug operations. The DEA would certainly make good use of it. Priscilla rose from her chair. She was happy to finally be leaving.

“Have a great weekend, doing anything?” He asked, looking up at her.

“I hope nothing…but I won’t count on that. Patricia probably made a whole slew of plans already. She’s gonna have me running everywhere, not to mention I have my own crap to catch up on.” John smiled, leaning back in his chair.

“You can’t keep the kids in the house these days. My wife gives me the run down on everything, while bitching that I’m never home and she threatens to divorce me,” he said, rolling his eye. “But, I’ve yet to see any paperwork waiting for me when I do come home.” He smiled, but it was a fake smile. Even though he tried to make light of it, it bothered Derlin.

Priscilla felt bad for him, she didn’t know how to reply. It must’ve sucked to live like that, worried that your wife would have divorce papers waiting for you. She tried to think of something to say to lighten the moment, but nothing came to mind.

"I'm sorry John…it must be hard." Priscilla, couldn't relate she never dealt with that before and don't think she could either hence why she rarely, if ever dated. To deal with someone else's shit and then have to deal with work and kids, she'd go crazy. John just shrugged his shoulders, with a helpless look.

"It is what it is, Priscilla. She knew the life I led before walking down that aisle. I was very upfront about it…I guess some people just don't know how they are going to feel, until they experience it themselves."

"Things will be okay, John." She smiled, trying to put on a happy face for him. He did the same.

"Have a good rest of the week, Priscilla." She nodded, as he logged on to his laptop.

"Thanks." She said, taking a few extra moments to regard her friend and boss. It was an awkward moment and she was glad he didn't feel her eyes on him. She'd have turned red with embarrassment. She just felt bad for him and wished she could do more than give him a useless 'sorry.' But there was nothing she could do, except be there, when he needed a shoulder to lean on.

With nothing further to add, Priscilla took her leave. As she closed the door to Derlin's office, she saw John's secretary Jenny at her desk. She wasn't there before. Priscilla hadn't spoken to her in a bit and the young innocent looking woman always had a way to brighten people's mood and after talking to Derlin, she needed a little mood change.

"Hey there! Good morning. How are you feeling?" Jenny looked up as she hung up the phone.

"Oh, hey stranger!" Jenny said with a smile. "I heard you were coming in this morning, I'm doing good. I have my days, you know, I can't wait for this baby to come already. My back has been killing me." She said, rubbing her belly, she was due sometime next month.

"The last month can be rough… I hope you picked out the color of the room already."

"Yeah, we did. I just got off the phone with Eric; he just finished painting as a matter of fact. Hopefully, it's only on the walls though." They both chuckled picturing that chaotic scene.

"I hope you didn't forget my shower next weekend." Priscilla, didn't forget and as a matter of fact, she already took care of getting Jenny her gifts.

"You think I'd forget? You should see what we picked up for you. Patricia and I went overboard a little, that kid loves to shop."

"Priscilla…I told you not to go crazy…"

"Never mind, you know how much I love to shop. Besides, it's always fun shopping for a newborn." She gave Jenny a warm smile, and then looked at her watch.

"I'll see you later, kiddo. I gotta roll, I'll give you a buzz."

"Ok." Jenny said with a friendly smile, she was a good kid. Priscilla took a liking to her ever since she started five years ago. She thought back to those days, as she made her way to the elevators. It felt like yesterday, when the young, fresh faced kid came walking through those doors. Looking overwhelmed by the world she walked into, many usually do when first hired. Before Jenny, John had two temps that quit.

She didn't have to wait long to catch an elevator down to the lower level, which housed the tech department. Running the show down here was Peter. At fifty-five years old, he had salt and pepper hair that just went past his shoulders, and a neatly trimmed beard. He was a devoted father and husband, but was nuttier than a fruitcake. He totally missed his calling, Peter should have been a standup comic. He never took anything seriously, always being the ball breaker. He had a way of messing with people, getting under everyone's skin that worked here was something that he enjoyed the most. The people that didn't know him, took him seriously in what he said. But when you got to know him, you would either laugh off his nonsense or just get back at him in the immature game he played.

Anyone who came to see him was at risk. He was the kid that just didn't grow up. How his wife puts up with him is anyone's guess. It was funny sometimes, listening to the shit that came out of his mouth. He came aboard when John started Shadow Ops. At the time, John was trying to get a research and development division, up and running. They were in desperate need of someone mechanically inclined and had no one.

John had known Pete for some years and asked him to come aboard. Peter was one of those guys that never kissed ass and because of that he languished in obscurity at his former position. He was a mechanic, and one of the best engineers out there. He kept all the company vehicles in perfect running order and fixed employees' cars on occasion if asked to… if he liked you, that is. When he did take his job seriously, Pete was really good at what he did.

The elevator doors opened to a concrete hallway that looked more like an underground bunker. She walked straight ahead entering the main workshop which was busy. This was the tinkering area, all the brains in here worked on developing prototypes and designs for future field equipment. As she walked further inside, no one looked up at her. These guys, when working, were in a world of their own. She came to an open bay area, which was the section that transported vehicles to the other floors. A portion of the floor, she was standing by was a large hydraulic lift, that went up and down. Above her was the storage area with another work area for the vehicles, and down below was the main parking garage.

"Did I ever tell you, that you have the sexiest ass of all the women here." Priscilla wasn't startled or insulted. She simply turned to where the comment came from. And there was Peter with that goofy smile, and as always he had on the same damn clothes every time she saw him. Mechanic pants, brown boots, black T-shirt, and of course, his white work coat that had more grease stains than you could count. He was wiping his greasy hands on a rag that he threw to the side.

"What's happening, sexy?"

"Just got back, and yes, you've told me quite a few times. In fact, so much that I could file sexual harassment on you." Peter laughed hard at that one.

"Yeah, okay, that's a good one stupid. Come on." He gestured for her to follow him. "So while you were away on 'vacation' I took care of that shit box of a minivan you drive.

I tuned it up for ya and changed your oil. Oh, by the way, when the fuck was the last time you changed it? It looked like goddamn tar draining out!" She rolled her eyes.

"I don't remember…" she said, not really in the mood for a lecture on proper auto care.

"You'll remember when you seize your engine stupid!" She flipped him the middle finger, as they headed into his office. He went behind his desk and on the wall were some keys. He grabbed hers and tossed them. Catching them, she turned to leave.

"Thanks, Pete. I really appreciate it. I'll get you a case of Rolling Rock for the trouble." She said over her shoulder.

"Oh hey, no problem, but listen, I have a better one. Just have sex with me, and we'll call it even."

"Goodbye Peter," she said in a tone that was obviously indicating the conversation was over as she walked away. She could hear Peter giggling to himself. She couldn't help but smile at his antics. Who couldn't? He was just a harmless nut. The world surely needed more of those nowadays.

Chapter 3
Family

The drive to Rockaway Beach wasn't as annoying as it usually was, thanks to the fact that rush hour was over. The sea breeze felt good after coming from the muggy city. People were taking advantage of the nice weather. The boardwalk had a few bicycle riders along with walkers and joggers. There was a playground and a basketball court there as well, and those were being used like always. She pulled into the complex and parked right in front of the apartment building. There was only a twenty-minute parking limit in the front and since she was not planning to stay that long, it was the perfect excuse to leave in a hurry.

The twelve floor apartments were located right on the beach, literally a stones throw away. Ideally, this was the perfect place to live, you had a killer view of the city, the subway was right down the block, the boardwalk. In a few years, this area was poised to become the next Dumbo or Williamsburg or at least that's what the developers hoped with all the construction going on. They were throwing up gated communities every year. It was nice, but not for her. Besides, this was a little too close for comfort to her mother and the rest of her family. They all lived within five blocks of each other. That was all she needed, she loved them yes, but not enough to join the flock.

The building she was going into now was one of the older ones, that was newly renovated and restored. It was updated with freshly painted hallways, new flooring, a rec room and gym. She was quite impressed, even the elevator, she got in was new. The only thing she hated was the colors they used for the hallways it was a tacky green. Once she got off at the desired floor, she waited a moment. She always had to mentally prepare herself to deal with her 'loving' mother. Even as an adult, the woman was like a shadow that could kill even the best of good vibes. With a deep sigh, she finally made her way, walking past some of the other tenants' doors that were decorated with wreaths, posters or flags. She stopped at 10B, which was decorated with a nice autumn wreath. She did a fast knock and then used her key. Priscilla's mother who was eighty, had very bad knees, ravaged by arthritis that stiffened them so bad they were nearly straight and almost unbendable. But the old broad still had her wits about her, and a tongue that never lost its cutting edge, which she had no trouble using when she was in a nasty mood. She loved picking fights and bad mouthing people.

The two-bedroom apartment, could have been spacious but her mother loved large furniture. There were two oversized couches, a larger than needed dining room table, and a knick knack cabinet filled to the brim. Not to mention every inch of the walls covered with photos of her grandkids, Priscilla's kids. Grandmother of the decade. When Priscilla entered, her mother was sitting in her chair, watching TV while her brother Bob was sitting on the couch next to her.

"Oh, hello. Look who's here." She said with a touch of sarcasm as she looked over to see who was coming in since all her children had keys to the apartment.

"Hi mom, hey Bob," Priscilla said with a false smile, Bob did his usual head bop 'hello', as he kept channel surfing.

Priscilla had a total of five siblings. Her brother John was a wealthy jerk and a real cocky bastard. He thought his shit didn't stink, and because of that they never got along. Bobby, like John, was a favorite one, who could do no wrong in her mother's eyes. Her sister Terry, who lived in the building next door, was a recluse unless there was shopping or traveling involved. Then there was Lorraine who had one grown daughter. Lorraine was divorced for many years and was Priscilla's partner in crime during their shopping sprees. Finally, there was Linda, she was married with no kids and whacked out on anti-depressants. Priscilla would no doubt be as well with a husband like him. Rumor was, he had a 'girlfriend' who he never met online sending her all sorts of jewelry and money. He was a total sucker falling for that catfish scheme.

As for her brother Bobby, he's a result of what happens when a mother shelters her son. He never moved out and never got married. The man never even went out at all unless it was to work or the basketball court. They all thought he got his first piece of ass in his mid-forties. When it came to Priscilla, all of her siblings were oblivious to what she did for a living.

"It's nice of you to come and see your mother. I would have thought you'd call ahead so the kids could come down to meet you," her mother said, in her usual sarcastic way.

"I know mom." Priscilla said, wishing now that she did just that. "I haven't seen you in a while and I'm sorry, it's been busy at work. How are you feeling? Need anything?"

"Oh, now you ask me! I'm lucky I have Bobby here with me, to depend on you…" she started to say then stopped. Her mother was more interested in listening to the news broadcast. Priscilla suddenly felt a pair of arms reach around her. Patricia came up behind her and hugged her. She was the typical thirteen year old, going on twenty-five. She was going to be a real cutie when she got older, with her long, brown hair past her shoulders, which had a few highlights.

"Hey honey…what's up?"

"Nothing, I cooked some chicken nuggets a little while ago, but I'm still hungry."

"Did your brother eat anything?" Priscilla asked.

"Nope."

"Go get him. I want to get going, I have stuff to do at home. And, we'll probably go out for dinner tonight." Patricia started to walk away, then turned and walked backward.

"Mom, we have to talk about this weekend-" she started to say, but Priscilla cut her off quickly.

"Ok, we will." She said with a hint of annoyance. Priscilla now turned to her mother who was still sitting there.

"Thanks mom for watching them. You sure you don't need anything?"

"No, no, I'm fine," she said that with a wave of her stiff fingers, the arthritis was in her hands as well. If only it affected that tongue of hers, Priscilla thought from time to time.

"You sure?" Her mother had diabetes, so insulin was needed along with other medical supplies. Priscilla didn't mind helping her mom since being on Medicare didn't pay for everything. She shook her head without looking up, with her arms crossed over her chest. Priscilla went into her bag and pulled out some money.

"Here…"

"What?" Her mother said, looking up towards her. "No, I don't want it!" Her mother loved her grandkids, but would throw things in your face if she was fighting with you like 'you dumped your kids here, they ate all my food, I'm on a fixed income.' She would pick on everyone, besides of course Bobby and John. It was something Priscilla and her sisters were all used to, but they were all tired of it. She was worse when Priscilla was younger.

That was the main reason she entered the military to begin with. Her life growing up was not a good one. It took a lot for Priscilla to start talking to her mother again. She didn't bother with her for almost ten years. She had very few memories that would bring a smile to her face. This is why she tried to be the best mother possible to her kids today.

She placed the money on the arm of her chair anyway. She was about to ask her mother something when Priscilla heard yelling from the other room. They were fighting, so she proceeded to walk to the bedroom.

"What's going on?" Patricia looked at her mother,

"He doesn't want to leave. He's playing his stupid game."

"Jonathon Christopher, put that controller down now or do I have to come over there?" Priscilla said sternly. Jonathon looked at his mother with that look that he always had when he got in trouble. He shut the game off, got up and stuck his tongue at his sister as he walked to his mother and hugged her. He was ten, with short, blonde hair and blue eyes. Priscilla embraced him, kissing him on the head. Then told them both to clean up the games and controllers they were using, under her watchful eye.

"Where are your bags?" She asked after they finished, she followed them out of their uncle's room

"Right here" Patricia said. Their bags were on the couch with whatever gifts their uncle bought them as he always did when they came over and stayed for a few days. That was one of the few things she could say she liked about her brother. He treated her kids like gold.

"Go give grandma and uncle Bobby a kiss goodbye and don't forget to thank uncle Bob." After the kids said their goodbyes, Priscilla walked over as well, kissing her mother.

"Bye mom, love you. Bye Bob," she added, as she walked passed him and to the door for her freedom.

Chapter 4
A kids life

The drive home was fast and thank god, Patricia talked a mile a minute about what she wanted to do this weekend with her friends. Priscilla tried her best to show her interest, she really did, but was so tired today. She was so relieved when they pulled into the driveway; the kids grabbed their bags and made their way to the front door. Priscilla lagged behind as she fished for the house keys from her purse.

"Do me a favor before both of you disappear, unpack your bags, put your clothes away and bring down all of your dirty laundry please." Priscilla knew once they got involved in their own thing, it would be a chore in and of itself to get them to do anything. The kids ran up to their rooms and quickly came back down with their dirty laundry, dumping it on the washing machine. While they did that, she went next door to her neighbor to grab her mail. She asked him to grab it for her while she was away.

Sometime later, while sitting at the dining room table and opening the last letter, her stomach was growling. By that time the kids were ready to eat, she was starved. And instead of going out they ordered to the relief of Priscilla.

That weekend, Patricia went to a sleepover with a few of the girls at a nearby girlfriend's house. Jonathon went to some friends' houses and went to the local park. It was a mostly relaxing weekend.

The new week was a catch-up week and there were a few things to be done. For starters, there were two more weeks until school started, and the back to school shopping had to be done. She had gotten the letter from the schools stating what the kids would need for the year. So, supplies, and of course, new clothes were a necessity. She would have done it sooner, but she got tied up with work.

Being school was right around the corner, her daughter, tried to make the most of the last days of the summer. She was all over the place. She was hardly home. Patricia was at a water park one day, a friend's house another and at the mall.

Jonathon mostly played in front of the house, the backyard or was in his room playing video games with friends. Priscilla's house, at times, was like Grand Central Station with Jonathon's friends running in and out. Even though all the noise could be annoying at times, she preferred it that way. Jonathon and his friends were too young to be roaming the streets. She let them go to the park sometimes, but never felt at ease about it. She liked being able to have a close eye on them all. She didn't like the idea of her daughter being out every chance she could get, either. But Patricia was older.

Priscilla remembered all too well at Patricia's age, being home was a drag. She couldn't hold her back all the time. Patricia knew what was right and wrong, and the cell phone was always on her, so that eased some of Priscilla's concerns. Patricia sometimes got embarrassed that her mother had to call and talk to the parents, to verify what her daughter was actually doing. She was a good kid, but would try, as she had done in the past, to outsmart Priscilla.

Before she knew it, the weekend was here. During the week, Priscilla tried to get all the errands done because on Saturday, she had Jenny's baby shower. Then she wanted Sunday to be a relaxing day with no schedules to keep. Priscilla and her daughter went to the shower that afternoon while Jonathon went to a friend's house. The shower was held at a fancy Italian restaurant, where the food was plentiful. Drinks were being served while the mom-to-be opened her gifts.

Priscilla recognized some people from the 'office,' mostly from upstairs where Jenny worked, Priscilla knew a few of them personally. Even John's wife was there, she noticed. They all talked and laughed the afternoon away into the evening. It was about half past nine and Priscilla had just started to leave when her cell phone rang, the 'business' one. It rang while she was in the van with Patricia. At first, Priscilla wasn't going to answer it, but then not answering it would make her daughter more curious. Sometimes Priscilla felt like the child, it was funny and yet annoying.

"Hello?"

"Priscilla, John here. I hope I'm not bothering you. I know you had Jenny's shower today."

"No, no don't be silly. I'm just leaving now, what's up?"

"I need to see you, preferably first thing in the morning."

"Sure," she paused for a second, thinking quickly of what was going on. Her daughter was looking at her, listening in of course. She was so nosy at times.

"Not too sure about first thing. I'll be there as soon as I get the kids settled in to where they are going for the day."

"Ok, great, see you tomorrow then....have a good night."

"Night John." She said, ending the call.

"Mom, who was that?" Patricia asked like she always did when she would get a call.

"Oh, just someone from work. I have to go into the city tomorrow morning," She said as if it was no big deal. And she hoped it was just that, no big deal. But from Derlin's tone she highly doubted that.

Chapter 5
Movie night

Priscilla and the kids were watching a movie. She made popcorn that filled the house with the smell of a movie theater. As the kids were watching the movie, she was zoning out. She was too tired to think about what may lie ahead tomorrow. From the way she looked at it, there was no point in worrying. She remembered how antsy she used to get the first couple of times when she was called in. Priscilla always tried to think of every possible problem…she always turned out to be wrong anyway.

By the middle of the movie, Jonathon was already fast asleep. Patricia helped her take him upstairs. His bedroom was filled with toys like G.I. Joe and Star Wars figures. This kid was a slacker when it came to cleaning his room. Sometimes, Priscilla had to get in there like a gangbuster and do it for him, which did not bode so well with him at all. She tucked him in, kissed his forehead and walked Patricia to her room, kissing her Goodnight.

After the kids were in their rooms, Priscilla sat in bed trying to read, she tried to fall asleep but for some reason she couldn't. Reading wasn't helping her either; she was staring at the pages. Her mind was wandering too much, thinking about her life leading up to now. She was thinking of where she might be in ten years and hopefully her kids would grow up to be something. Contribute something good to this crazy world we live in. She wanted to do for her kids what her mom didn't do. She didn't want to make the mistakes that she saw her own mother do. Her childhood wasn't easy by any means, and as for the future, she knew the kids would be well taken care of should she meet her untimely demise. That would be seen to it by her dear friend and father figure, Patrick. And as far as money, Priscilla had put enough aside for both of them.

She never would have envisioned herself to be who she was today. She had no regrets about anything she had done, but she often wondered what it would be like if she had chosen a different path in life. It was too late to change that now this far into the game. The only two things she knew how to do in life were being a mom, and a Shadow Ops agent…that was it.

She didn't think she could work a normal job…ever. Once you're used to something, it's hard to change after so many years. Tired of thinking, Priscilla turned on the TV. There was a movie on that she hadn't seen in a while and she started to watch it. It wasn't until the movie was almost over that sleep finally came calling for her.

Chapter 6
Changing times ahead

Her Sunday morning was already starting out badly. First, she woke up late and then she had to make arrangements for the kids, for where they were going.

It was finally decided that Patricia was going to a girlfriend's house for the day and Jonathon was going to her friend Pat's house. Pat was the only one who knew about Priscilla's 'job' and understood when these things came up. The man was the most trustworthy person she knew and was the closest thing to a father figure they had. He had two kids near her son's age; there would be plenty to do over there. They had video games and the block where they lived on ran amok with kids all damn day.

By the time, she made it into the city it was almost noon. She was in Derlin's office waiting for him. That man was always on the move. About ten minutes passed when he finally popped his head in.

"Priscilla, please come with me." By the time she got up and out of his office, John was already down the hall. "Sorry for calling you on such short notice." He said, just as she caught up with him. Turning right led them to the conference room. John opened one of the two double doors and had her enter first. He closed the doors behind him and locked them.

"Please sit, coffee?" He asked pleasantly.

She nodded. He walked to the coffee pot that smelled freshly brewed, returning with two piping hot cups. He then grabbed the milk and sugar and sat down with his cup while she poured her milk.

Since it was her first cup, it went down really smooth. John lit the pipe that somehow, without her noticing, was clenched in between his teeth, taking in the smoke before he began and blew it out.

Derlin picked up a remote from the table, and with a few clicks the lights went out and a thin screen slid down from the ceiling with the first image of the presentation already on the screen. It was the schematics for a large circular metal device, with what looked like a twelve by twelve window. There were a lot of side notes scribbled with lines pointing to various areas. It was long enough to store a human being in it.

"This is an incubation cylinder, first reported stolen eight years ago in France. It was treated as a local crime. It didn't even make the nightly news. This same device was found, abandoned four months later. Stripped of anything valuable. Local cops figured it was stripped of its copper and sold."

A quick button press and another slide replaced it. "Here's another one, as you can see this one is, more refined. It's all glass, with various hoses. There's a touch screen read out, fully automated, cutting edge. Another word for these devices in layman's terms is, cloning cylinders." Priscilla, stopped just short of sipping her coffee, not sure she heard him correctly.

"Cloning?" He nodded and then turned the lights back on. He then slid her a file. She opened it and then scanned over the contents. It was a list of chemicals and other mechanical components.

"That list was taken off the data you took from Julio's computer and on that list is something called Amniotic fluid." Priscilla knew what that was, that was basically a water like cocoon that protected the fetus.

"What does all of this mean John? That Julio was running a cloning operation?" She couldn't believe that for a minute. And if that were true, her mind ran amok with crazy scenarios.

"No...but he's been using his vast empire to smuggle this stuff into the country over the last ten years for someone."

"Ten years? For who? John, that's crazy." Derlin nodded,

"We don't know. Our best guess is that these shipments are coming in from Europe."

"But who..." And then it dawned on her. Carmine, that slippery bastard, he supposedly had information of a Shadowy figure that the intelligence Community had yet to identify. "Carmine..." John looked at her, not understanding. "Carmine Christie, he told me at the diner. That's the guy he was gonna identify, he was doing crazy things, like right out of a sci-fi movie." She laughed, leaning forward, thinking back to that cluster fuck of a mission. It was a total waste of everyone's time. To this day they never found where he hid the information. "I wasn't sure what to believe coming from his mouth."

"Nobody did Priscilla. But if this is even remotely connected-"

"We gotta find out, and fast." She said, pretty much cutting him off. Derlin nodded. "Do you know where these shipments have been going?" She then added.

"Yes, Pennsylvania to a hospital not far from Mt. Pocono. A recently built hospital." He added that last part with a hint of suspicion.

"Let me guess, ten years ago?" Derlin nodded.

"This is the best lead we've had Priscilla. I need you to get down there and see what's going on immediately. I don't want to bring in anyone else, on a state or federal level. Whoever this Person is, I personally believe he has some high level people in his pocket. I can't risk the chance of blowing this operation. Until you find something, this has to be kept in a small circle understand?" She understood perfectly and agreed. "I've already authorized everything you'll need, your ID and paperwork are already done. You are expected to report for work Monday night at the hospital. You're a traveling nurse, recently divorced looking to start over, and see the country until you find a place to call home. I'm sorry for throwing this on your lap, but with your past experience in this matter plus your knowledge in the nursing field you were the best candidate." Priscilla got up, and collected the file.

"Then I better get moving. I got kids to situate. I'll see you later." John nodded.

"Hey." He called after her before she was able to open the door. She turned to regard him. "Be careful, on this one." He looked genuinely concerned. She smiled, looking away for a moment and then looked back at him.

"Always am. I'll be in touch."

Chapter 7
Super mom

So much for a relaxing Sunday, she thought. Now with a schedule to keep, she needed to get some things done and get the house in order. But first and foremost, she needed to make plans for the kids for the next couple of days. Even though she was used to it, it was a damn pain in the ass to find a sitter on such short notice.

She had a few people in mind; hopefully one of them would be available. She could have easily brought them to her mothers or Pats. But if she brought them to her mothers, then they wouldn't be able to go to school, if she wasn't back in time when school started. Pat's was ideal, but she hated dumping them off.

So, if she could, she'd keep them home. It was important that her kids have a childhood. When she told the kids they were upset, because they thought they were about to be shuttled back to Grandma's. But when she told them they were going to stay home, they cheered up a bit. Especially Patricia, who was reassured she could still have her big slumber party. Jonathon was upset that he couldn't go with her; he was still a little bit of a mama's boy. As to her reason for leaving, she kept it simple. Telling them, she had a conference to attend in California, a spur of the moment thing.

As for a sitter, Priscilla managed to get the neighbor across the street's daughter to come over. She was a college kid, and it worked perfectly because if Priscilla didn't make it back in time before the kids went back to school then the sitter could get them to school and back. She'd also ask Pat to stop by everyday and check in on them.

All of her arrangements were made surprisingly smooth and the remainder of the day went like any other Sunday. Patricia was on the phone, Jonathon was playing video games, and Priscilla was still getting the house in order. By the time Priscilla hit the sheets, she was exhausted.

She woke up at six in the morning, showered and was ready to go by the time the kids woke up. The doorbell rang at 8AM right on time, Priscilla thought as she went to answer the door. Susan, from across the street, was a happy go lucky kid with brown hair tied in a ponytail. She had on jeans and a T-shirt, and her duffel bag was clenched in both hands.

"Hello, good morning, Ms. Roletti." She said with a smile.

"Hey Susan, don't be shy, come on in. I was just about to get the kids' breakfast ready. Here, let me take that." She grabbed her bag and put it in her bedroom, and then she came back out and led Susan to the kitchen. Jonathon and Patricia were already at the kitchen table half asleep.

"Of course you know my little angels…and I say that lightly." Priscilla joked, rubbing the top of her son's head as she walked by him.

"Hey Susan," Patricia said with a wave, after a yawn snuck up on her. Jonathon simply waved. He was shy around the ladies.

"I want you both to be on your best behavior," Priscilla gave them both stern looks as she placed bowls in front of them. She grabbed the milk and placed it on the table. She caught sight of the time, she needed to get moving.

"I have to go." She said suddenly, and then kissed and hugged them, "Be good for Susan. I love you. I'll call you later. Susan, would you mind coming outside with me for a moment?"

Priscilla grabbed her bags as they walked to the minivan, she gave Susan the rundown of what was going on, especially the play dates set up for her son as well as for her daughter. They were allowed to go out, but Susan had to find out what they were doing, what time they were coming back, and who was going and so forth. She told her there was money in her top dresser drawer, if she needed anything for the kids or herself.

Susan seemed to be capable of handling them for at least the week. She had a feeling that she was going to let them get away with murder, but what was she going to do? She threw the two bags in the backseat and got in.

"If you have any questions on where anything is, ask Patricia. Their uncle will stop by every day to check in on them, oh, and one more thing, as I'm sure you know, school starts next week, so just in case I'm not back, all the information, for the buses and the like are on the desk in my office." She sat in the minivan trying to remember anything she forgot to cover, but there was nothing that came to mind,

"I will take care of everything, Ms. Roletti, don't worry." Susan said with a smile. Priscilla wasn't entirely assured, not that she didn't trust Susan to do a good job, but as a parent, unless you were there, you always worried. But nevertheless, Priscilla smiled.

"Thanks, I'll call you." And she was off.

Chapter 8
Peter Held and the Charger

Once she arrived at HQ, Priscilla immediately went to Pete's shop. She hated trying to find Peter every time she came down here. She tapped a tech on the shoulder who was leaning over and working on something. He turned to her with eyes magnified five-times larger than the normal size. He had on some type of micro-scoping glasses. She almost laughed in the man's face, but asked where Pete was instead. He pointed over to the large bay area with tools in his hands. She looked in the direction following where he pointed, then looked back to say thanks, but he was already back to whatever he was doing.

She headed off in the direction, as she walked, she saw something covered in a tarp. She could tell it was a Dodge Charger from the outline. She was about to go and have a look underneath when she was smacked hard on her ass; she didn't even have to guess who it was. She turned around and saw Peter, standing behind her with that goofy smile on his face, and the ever-present V-8 in one hand.

"Didn't your mother teach you not to touch other people's shit?" She squinted, trying to hold back a smile.

"You know I could file a sexual harassment charge against you for that." He rolled his eyes and laughed as he took a gulp of his V-8.

"Yeah, whatever." He said taking another swig of his V-8, and wiped his mouth on his sleeve. He waved her over closer to the covered Charger.

"I heard you're going to Pennsylvania, I think you might like what I got for you. Peter threw back the tarp revealing a dark blue Dodge Charger. It had a nice polished look to it.

"Now, this is a prototype. First, and only one, I'm giving it to you so you can field-test it. You probably won't be using any of the new features, but I'll show you them anyway." He waved her over as he opened the driver's side door pointing inside.

"Now, the setup is the same as the other Chargers, but I've added some new stuff. The CPU is totally new, very advanced stuff, I'll tell you about that in a minute. You can now video call and I've installed a larger LCD touchscreen in the dashboard." Priscilla was used to his never ending spiel, after all these years of dealing with him, she came to the conclusion that he just loved hearing himself talk.

"Remember that, new fuel system I was working on?" She nodded, Priscilla remembered. But Peter never told her what it was exactly.

"It was based off of cold fusion technology. I really wanted to get it in the cars. But it's just not there yet, hopefully in a few years." Peter sounded a bit disappointed; she knew he put a lot of time into that project.

"Anyway… let's move on! Here's the really cool stuff!" He perked up and took a gulp of V-8 then continued.

"This Charger has much better armor, the best. It's able to withstand an RPG, it can even withstand a well aimed tank round." Peter then sat in the car and waved her over getting more excited, she leaned in as he pointed to the LCD touchscreen.

"Now, here is the last feature, I'd like you to use. This Charger is equipped with a new state of the art CPU able to automatically drive the vehicle on its own; it's a lot more advanced than the system we use now, as you'll see when you use it. Via the LCD screen, you can access the program and set it to where you want to go. The Charger will do the rest. It's a fairly simple program to use, so I doubt you'll have trouble." She watched him as he went through the menus. Priscilla couldn't help but be a little impressed.

"Wow, very impressive, mechanic," she said with a hint of sarcasm.

"Yeah, well, it better stay that way too! One fucking scratch or dent, and I'll kill ya! I swear to God. …Oh…damn I almost forgot. Right below the ignition is a thumb pad. That's new also, if you lose your keys or whatever, place your thumb there and five seconds later it'll start. The driver's side window has the same security feature. Just place your hand on it and the door will unlock. Try to use those features a little also. I wanna make sure they work perfectly." Once again, she couldn't help to be impressed.

"Well…I think that's it. Now get the hell outta here." He always had to be a dick. And she was going to compliment him too.

"You know something? I'm not sure if I'm the first one to tell you this, but you're not as dumb as you look," She said, as she got in. She tried out the thumb pad, the Charger roared to life. She liked that little modification, as she revved the engine. Standing back, Peter, with a remote control in his hand, pressed a button, sending the hydraulic lift down to the main parking area. Once it stopped and was secured, she revved the engine again, loving how the raw power of this car sounded and felt. Throwing the Charger in gear she peeled out, leaving a cloud of smoke behind.

Chapter 9
Welcome to Pennsylvania

The drive to Pennsylvania was quiet and relaxing. The sky was clear and the breeze was cool, not like the humid, hot air in New York. She wouldn't mind one day, maybe moving out to an area like this. At least once her kids were finished with school. She didn't want them to start over, again. They were set with their friends and their way of life. It wouldn't be fair to them.

She had just passed the Delaware Water Gap. Going along route I-80, her destination was Tannersville on route 611. She had never been there before. She knew friends who had stayed in the area from time to time, and a friend of hers owned a vacation home there. The area, according to what she remembered her friend saying, was very busy for a place like this. The main road 611, which was right off I-80, was littered with restaurants, bar-n-grills and the Crossings premium outlets. Along with the Candle Factory, Cheesecake Factory, and even a wholesale store for fireworks and a Target.

She came to the exit, getting off; she then viewed where she was on the GPS. The hospital was west of here on route 940 N, only about twenty minutes from her current location, and she had plenty of time before her shift started. It was only half past one in the afternoon, and her shift started at eleven that night. According to the GPS, there were two places close by, a skiing resort, and a motel down the road a little closer to the hospital. She chose the motel, pulling up on the gravel driveway. It was a nice little place, 'very cozy' would be the best words to describe it.

The whole complex was painted brown with black doors, and gold numbers on each door. Hopefully, this place would be livable during her stay here. The place appeared to be kept up which was a positive sign. The grass looked as if it had been recently cut. She made her way into the office; there was a pleasant-looking man sitting at the front desk, watching something on TV. He flashed her a friendly smile as she approached.

"Well, good day. What can I do for you?"

"Hi, I'll need a room."

"Sure, let me get the paperwork for ya." He got up from his chair, pausing the movie he was glued to. He came back with the paperwork and a pen in one hand and a cup with some tea in the other. She filled it out, handing him her ID and a credit card.

"Well, thank you kindly, Ms. Murphy. And, if you need anything, please do not hesitate to ask."

"Thank you," she said with a smile and left the office. As she drove along to her room, she noticed a few cars and trucks from various states. She pulled up to the front door of her room, only grabbing what she needed right now, and left the rest of her stuff in the car. She walked into a cozy, clean room. Locking the door behind her, she quickly closed the shades and checked to make sure the windows were locked; she could not wait to hit the shower.

The room was painted white with a peach-colored carpet that looked to have seen better days. The bed looked and felt clean and was neatly made, the bathroom was more than adequate.

It's not the Ritz, but it'll do. She could have very well gone to a more upscale place and lived it up. But Priscilla was not a materialistic woman at all. Oh, she loved nice things and treated herself all the time because she could and chose to. She never depended on anyone to do anything for her, especially when it came to buying herself things and supporting the kids. A few of the agents in the field, knowing the company funded all resources for the mission, had been known to go overboard, at times. Renting the most expensive places and dining on the best foods. She remembered John almost fainting when one agent had run up a bill in the thousands, and the cover didn't call for it. John, she was sure, had a hell of a time explaining that one to the committee.

She let the shower water run before she jumped in, the hot water felt soothing as it trickled down her spine, curving down to her behind. She lost herself in the relaxing hot shower. After her long shower, she went back to the car grabbing her bags. Once she settled herself in, she took a drive around town to familiarize herself with some of the landmarks. She toured the area for a few hours, grabbed a bite to eat, then came back to the room to at least get a few hours of sleep for the long night ahead.

At ten p.m., she got ready, putting on her light pink scrubs with white sneakers. She added a little makeup and combed her hair back. She made sure not to forget her Beretta that she strapped to her back. She grabbed her paperwork, on her way out closed and locked the door, ready to start her first night at work.

Chapter 10
Day one

When she finally arrived, she parked in the large lot and waited a few moments before going in, taking in all the details of the hospital and the area. This hospital was two floors and made of brick with a white roof. She watched some of the staff walk by, Priscilla took a deep breath. She hated these undercover assignments, even though over the years she did plenty of them it always felt awkward at first. Taking another deep breath, she got out and made her way to the employee entrance. There was a keypad for an entry code, not having one she rang the buzzer. She was buzzed in and walked down the small hallway. The floors were freshly waxed. You could see the reflection of lights overhead. She walked to the desk, with a cranky looking security guard.

"Can I help you?" He said with authority, but sounding like a miserable prick. She looked in her purse for the paperwork.

"Yes…yes you can. I'm new and supposed to start tonight. I'm Diane Murphy." She handed the guard her ID and papers. As he called the front office to verify her paperwork, Priscilla strolled around looking at the place while waiting. She walked to the bulletin board, checking out the posts from the employees. One said, looking for an apartment, another was selling their one-year-old BMW.

"Miss?" She was lost in her thoughts for the moment, the guard had to call her twice.

"Yes…sorry. That post for the BMW kind of caught my eye." She said with a little bit of fake embarrassment, adding a grin for added measure. The guard either was one of those types that were just plain miserable or maybe having a bad day.

"Here, take your papers. The hall behind me will lead you to the main entrance. Look for Dr. Manning, he is expecting you." The guard said, gesturing behind him.

"Thanks," she said, passing his desk, and entered through double doors. After two wrong turns, she finally found her way.

She passed some patients' rooms, hearing the TVs and radios from within, and some small talk amongst the patients. Along the way, she was greeted by friendly faces. When she made her way to the front desk, she saw a nurse sitting behind it, doing some paperwork. She hoped the nurse there was more pleasant than that prick guard she just left. The woman had long, red curly hair tied up in a ponytail, with a pretty face. She looked up and spotted Priscilla approaching.

"Hello Hun, can I help ya?" She asked, followed by a friendly smile.

"Hi, I'm looking for Dr. Manning. I'm Diane Murphy, I'm supposed to start tonight."

"Oh, yes, yes, right. One sec Hun, and I'll page him for you." She did so, and then turned her attention back to Priscilla. "Well, let me be the first to welcome you. I'm Kelly, nice to meet you." Kelly threw out her hand, after she hung up the phone.

"Thanks, same here," Priscilla said, shaking her hand. "It looks like a nice place to work in."

"Yeah, it is, for the most part everyone is pleasant to work with. But you still have one or two dicks floating around."

"Yeah, it seems so, like that guard near the employee entrance; he seemed a little, I don't know…"

"Like he needs to get laid maybe?" Kelly finished Priscilla's thought.

"I couldn't have said it better myself." They both laughed.

"Where you from, Hun?"

"New York City. Born-and-raised there, but after I got divorced, I went and did the traveling thing, you know? I wanted to start over, it was a rocky marriage and I needed a break."

"I'm sorry to hear that," Kelly said, with sincerity.

"Don't be. The best damn thing I did."

"Well, I'm glad it worked out for you then. I'll tell you now; it's no big city, that's for sure. The best way I can describe it is, it's an up-and-coming place." Kelly was about to ask Priscilla something, when she spotted Dr. Manning. "Oh Dr. Manning." The young doctor stopped at the calling of his name and stepped right next to Priscilla.

"Dr. Manning, this is the new girl…I'm sorry Hun, what was your name again?"

"Diane Murphy." Priscilla said, turning to Dr. Manning.

"Oh yes, right, right. Sorry I kept you waiting, I was in the middle of something when I heard the page. Pleased to meet you, Ms. Murphy." They shook hands.

"Likewise, doctor.

"Come on, let me show you the layout quick."

"Sounds great." Priscilla said falling into step with the young doctor. She turned back to Kelly.

"See you later, Kelly, thanks again."

"Anytime, Hun, good luck tonight." She yelled as they walked away. As Dr. Manning gave her the rushed tour, she analyzed him closely. He had brown hair, cut and combed neatly with some grays creeping up near the ears and big, brown eyes. Wearing a collared shirt with a tie and slacks, and of course, the white doctor's coat, he seemed harmless.

They walked through the ER, ICU, short term, and long-term wings as well as the children's wings. Seeing sick children always bothered her, it broke her heart when a young life was extinguished sooner than he/she should have been.

As they continued walking to the adult terminal wing, he asked questions about her background and the places she had worked. It was just idle conversation; nothing that made her feel like it was interrogation. The tour finally came to an end about an hour later where they had met up. As Dr. Manning continued to talk, she looked past him and spotted a man coming toward them with his hands behind his back. As he came up along side Dr. Manning the man placed his scrawny hand on his shoulder. His beady brown eyes were deep and knowing, with slicked back black hair that looked as if he had used a whole can of grease. Hanging from his neck were reading glasses. He looked like someone that could be very difficult to deal with. Feeling the touch on his shoulder, Manning turned around.

"Uh, let me introduce you to Dr. Hans Goring," Doctor Manning said, sounding as if he would rather not, but tried to cover it as best as he could.

"Dr. Goring, this is Diane Murphy." Hans stared at her a moment. It did not take long for the tension to build, as he looked at Priscilla and back at Manning.

"Who is this Dr. Manning?" Hans said, in his German accent as if he had not heard Manning, as he looked Priscilla over again. Sounding a little more uncomfortable, Manning continued.

"This is the new nurse, Diane Murphy, on the overnight Dr. Goring."

"Ah, yes…yes...I had forgotten. I signed off on her papers just this morning," he said, suddenly remembering. "So, Fräulein, how do you like my hospital?" Hans was a little friendlier once he realized who she was.

"Very nice, Dr. Goring. The people seem great as well. I'm looking forward to working with them."

"Ah, good. I'm glad you like," he said, looking at his watch. "If you'll excuse me, I have another matter to attend to." With his hands behind his back, he nodded to the both of them and left. Priscilla watched him as he walked away. She'd be sure to steer clear of him. There was no doubt he could be a prick.

She was about to turn away, when someone rudely brushed by her. But when she looked, to confront the rude person there wasn't anyone there. She held her gaze for a moment longer, and yet saw no one. She shrugged it off as she turned back to Dr. Manning. Who was talking to another nurse about a patient. After the nurse walked away, Dr. Manning came back to her.

"Dr. Manning…" she started to say when he threw up his hand.

"Please call me Tom. By the way, sorry for putting you on the spot just now. Hans is not exactly a favorite around here." He said, looking down at the floor as if waiting for Priscilla to scold him. She could tell the presence of Hans upset him a little.

"Hey, no sweat, Tom. You meet one creep, you've met them all." She said with a shrug of her shoulders.

"I have a few patients to attend to, but…for tonight, just do some rounds. Pick a department and check with the nurse on duty for what needs to be done. Get a feel of the place. The head of nursing went home for the day. She'll assign you to your permanent duties tomorrow night."

"Ok, sounds good."

"See ya later then." She watched him walk off and then she headed to the short-term, wing she figured that was a good place to start.

Other than getting people meds, helping change a bed or two, or just trying to comfort some patients, it was a pretty boring night. Rather than poke around tonight, she decided to get a better feel of some of the other staff members. She wanted to find out some of their stories and routines. She decided that tomorrow night; she'd do a little investigating of the place. As the night went on, she kept up on her duties. By two in the morning, there was nothing to do but hang around and wait to be called on. At least she had Kelly to talk to. Turns out, she also worked the night shift. They got along pretty well so far.

During Priscilla's break, she got a chance to talk with more of her co-workers. They seemed to be nice and upbeat for the most part. They liked to goof a lot about their significant others, venting about what stupid things they did, or whatever else annoyed them. Others talked about their children. Priscilla, even though having kids of her own, was not one of those parents who constantly talked about them, and how great or smart they were. Sure, she was proud of them, but she wasn't going to sound like she worshipped them either.

The last half of the shift flew by, and before she knew it, her first day was over. At seven o'clock in the morning, Priscilla and the rest of the night shift went to their lockers and gathered their belongings. Some hung around talking to the workers relieving them, but Priscilla punched out and left the way she came in the night before. Kelly was standing outside by the door smoking a cigarette. Kelly offered her one, but Priscilla declined.

"Don't you know those things can kill ya?" Kelly nodded, taking a long drag.

"Yeah, and so can fucking, eating, and drinking and I ain't stopping those." Priscilla laughed at that one. As they walked to their cars chit chatting before saying Goodnight.

Once back at her room she emailed a few names to have checked out, Priscilla really didn't do anything that would further her assignment.

After sending the email, she shut down the laptop and stretched out laying her head onto the comfortable pillow. She realized how tired she was as her eyes grew heavy, staring at the ceiling. Before long, she was fast asleep.

Chapter 11
Day two

Priscilla punched in just on the nose, avoiding being late. Undercover or not, she hated being late regardless if this was bull shit. She saw Dr. Manning for all of five minutes, he seemed rushed, mentally he was elsewhere. As per instructions left from the nursing director, Priscilla's permanent station was in the short-term wing. Even after two days here, there was nothing out of the ordinary. This was for all intents and purposes a fully functioning hospital. If there was some secret cloning facility here, then it was off grounds and the shipments were just sent here and then taken off site. Or maybe the basement. It sounded far-fetched yes, but worth a look.

But all of that was forgotten with her duties and before she knew it her shift was over and it was time to leave.

"Hey Diane!" Kelly had just punched out, she grabbed her things and caught up with Priscilla. "You're off Friday or Saturday?" Priscilla, bit her lower lip, trying to remember. She didn't memorize her schedule. But she was pretty sure she was off Friday.

"Friday, what's up?"

"Couple of girls and I are going out. We haven't done it in a while. With everyone so busy with their own shit. It's hard to sync schedules. You wanna come?"

Priscilla considered that. It wasn't like she'd be doing anything else in her spare time. May as well make the best of it while she was stuck here.

"Sure." Kelly smiled.

"Great, It's a cool place, called Smokey Bear's Steak House. Best damn steak you'll get in this one horse town." Priscilla laughed; she had no doubt about that one. "Okay Hun, I'll see you tonight, have a good day!"

"Thanks!" And Priscilla was off, making her way to her car, another night down with who the hell knew how many more were ahead of her…she hated these shit assignments

Chapter 12
Frustrations

"I've searched the place, from top to bottom. Every wing, every log. And zilch. There's not a goddamn thing there John." Priscilla was getting ready for the night out with the girls, when she decided to touch base with John. She wasn't exaggerating. In her five days working there, she searched every possible place and there was really nothing there.

"Maybe, it's old Intel. Anything on Hans or Manning?" She asked, adding eyeliner with a steady hand.

"Perhaps...and yes, both are clean." Priscilla wasn't surprised about that, that could mean a few things. They covered their asses well, or they just really remained off the grid. Derlin paused for a moment. Priscilla could see him now, leaning back in his chair, looking up at the ceiling in contemplation, with his newly packed pipe gripped in his hand.

"This is a very small hospital John. If there were something there, I'd have seen it. Maybe, the stuff was delivered here at some point. Maybe they changed the drop point. And besides, if there is some secret cloning operation, it's off site. There's a lot of forest around here." Again Derlin was in silent debate. She just heard the match struck as he started to puff away at his pipe. He sighed.

"That's a possibility as well, and I've already reached out to Norad to see if we can get a satellite over there. Just waiting for a word back. In the mean time you hang tight. Go have fun tonight goodness knows you deserve it. And by next Friday you'll be outta there. I'm sorry this turned out to be nothing more than a wild goose chase. But we had to be sure." She nodded as she looked at herself in the mirror.

"Of course. Let me go John, I wanna finish up."

"Alright, you have a good time tonight, okay."

"Thanks." And the call ended, it was her turn to sigh. If Kelly's friends were just as loose as she was then there would be no doubt about that. But that wasn't what bothered her. It was the fact she was here, and wasting her time.

She sighed again putting the last touches on her face. She straightened up and took a good look at herself. She hated makeup, and tried not to get into the habit of using it. But she had to try to at least fit in. The sacrifices we make. With that she hit the light and left as ready as she'll ever be for the girls night out.

Chapter 13
Drinks and Bullshit

"Let's go bitches! One, two, three down!" And at the same time they all downed their shots. Priscilla's eyes nearly watered the first time. Now on her third they were becoming all too easy to throw back. Oh well, what the fuck. This mission was a waste of time anyway, may as well kick back.

Smoky Bear's Steak House was a dark, family orientated place with flat screens playing the games. And of course, their table had to be the 'one.' They were the loudest, throwing back shots. Laughing at scandalous stories of themselves and of others. As well as talking plenty of shit about some of the people from the hospital. The group consisted of Kelly and Priscilla and three others.

Becky, who was the shortest one of the group and yet the loudest, and the one that drank the most. Rebecca, who was the tallest of the women. She had a set of legs that even impressed Priscilla as well as her body. You could tell she took great care of herself. And then there was the goofy one of the group, Colleen. She was the heaviest of the group, but cute. And she had a sleeve of tattoos on her right arm. These three together could turn a wake into a party. Priscilla was glad she decided to go. It was a fun time. Nothing about work or the hospital came up. And she never brought anything up either.

She just wanted a night without thinking of that place. It was rewarding yes, but depressing at the same time. With the sick, dying and elderly. And the children, it was so sad seeing them in the conditions they were in. Helpless mothers and fathers with no power to do anything for them. She was glad John was going to pull her out next week, if she had to stay here another week or even a month she'd be on antidepressants or a drunk if she hung out with these three all the time.

"So Diane, what made you come to this one horse town?" Becky asked.

"Certainly wasn't the dick I can tell you that." That comment came from Rebecca, as she took a sip of her wine. "Otherwise, I wouldn't be fucking a married man."

"Becc, shhhh! Shut up!"

"What? It's the truth. The guys around here are limp dicks. It's only the married ones that aren't." Becky rolled her eyes and looked back to Priscilla, whose face was red from laughing so hard.

"Sorry, Diane, you'll have to excuse Rebecca, she's a little pissed cause she hasn't had any dick lately." Rebecca answered with a middle finger that pulled laughs from the group.

"I…know what you mean." And she did. Priscilla was after all, human herself. "No, it wasn't for the dick. Just to set the record straight everybody." That got a few chuckles from them. "I just wanted to check the scene out that's all. I just moved from California, and I'm from New York originally so I wanted to be closer to home. So I figured Pennsylvania was a good in-between. Chill for a year and then see where I'm at mentally."

"Go to Texas, I'd love to have a cowboy mount me." Again Rebecca caught wide-eyed looks and laughs. "I'd have gone, but then I'd be missing my bitches."

"Word Bitches!" Colleen raised her glass and they all toasted to that. Priscilla was able to turn the conversation back towards them. Which was good, because no matter how many times you do these undercover missions, it was always hard to think of this shit straight from the fly. All and all, the night went incredibly fast, and by the time they called it a night it was just after three in the morning. Luckily Colleen was the sober one of the group and drove her friends home. Kelly had brought her own car and was able to drive. Priscilla was tired and slightly buzzed, but she'll be okay.

"Okay, guys safe home." Priscilla said her goodbyes, and made her way towards her car. It was windy tonight. She stifled a yawn as she made her way, fishing her keys out. Once she was at the door, she was about to unlock it and get in, but then heard someone walking behind her on the gravel parking lot. She turned to greet them, just to see who they were. But saw no one.

She glanced around under the starlit sky. She felt a sweat starting to sprout upon her brow even though it was chilly. She was buzzed, her mind was messing with her she thought. A hot shower and a long sleep, will cure that. Just as she turned back around, her face was smashed into the unbreakable glass of the door. Priscilla was knocked out cold. She fell to the ground like a sack of meat. Silence ensued once again, until a single voice from thin air spoke. It was a harsh commanding tone.

"Pick her up." Coming from the wooded area just by Priscilla's car was a shadow of a man, he was tall and monstrous. He lumbered towards the unconscious form of Priscilla and without even a hint of strain he lifted her up over his shoulder. "Put her in the van." The voice said, and the giant with nothing more than a word turned and lumbered away. Priscilla's keys were picked up along with her purse. Her unknown assailant got in her car, turned it on and revved it, peeling out of the lot and into the darkness.

Chapter 14
The hangover from hell

Priscilla woke up, gasping for breath. She was in complete darkness, tied to a chair. Her head was pounding; it felt like someone nailed a spike into the top of her skull. The right side of her face was throbbing. The pain and discomfort she could deal with. It was the darkness that was playing on her mind. Her breath echoed, her heart was beating so rapidly it sounded like it was anywhere else but inside her chest. She felt panic grip her; she was on the verge of losing it as she tested the restraints holding her hands behind her. It was no use; they were so tight her hands were going numb.

"Don't struggle my dear. You will not loosen yourself I assure you." She was startled by the voice in the room. She held her breath, and tried to regain her focus. She couldn't panic, not now. She tried her hardest to regain her thoughts and push aside the cascaded memories. The last thing she remembered was standing by the car. And now here she was. She closed her eyes. Calm...calm down, she thought.

"Now, Diane Murphy if that is even your name." The educated English tone had a sandpapery feel to it, harsh, but yet artistic sounding. "You will tell me, who you are. And where you come from?" Priscilla swallowed on a dry mouth. She calmed her breathing finally, which was good. Now she just needed to focus. Her head was throbbing something fierce and only getting worse.

"My...na...me...is Diane Murphy, from California. I...I-" but before she could even get the rest out she was hit hard on the side of her face. Her headache just got worse. Whoever punched her, used something because the power behind the blow nearly knocked her out. And this was coming from a woman that could take a punch with the best of them. The voice in the darkness growled.

"Don't insult my intelligence. Now I'll ask again, who are you and whom do you represent? I assure you once you tell me the truth. Your suffering will cease."

"My name is...Di-" Her head was forcefully snapped back by her hair. "Traveling nurses don't fumble about hospitals looking for things! Traveling nurses don't have phone calls with a man named 'John' informing him that 'You searched the entire place and found nothing!'" She was released and then punched again so hard she felt a tooth loosen from the blow. She spat out blood. The horrible realization of what she was just told sent chills through her spine. How the fuck was she seen!? She made damn well sure no one was around. There were no cameras! And how the hell did this person ease drop on the conversation she had with John! In retrospect, she was glad that was the only name she dropped. The feral tone was now calm again. She could hear him take a deep breath.

"Now...I shall ask again why-"

"Go fuck yourself!" Silence. It felt as though the world had stopped. She was waiting for the inevitable retort of some kind. What she got was far worse than she imagined. The beating was brutal. Punches felt like bricks, smashing into her face. After the fourth blow she blacked out.

"Stop!" A German accented voice commanded. An overhead light was illuminated on the unconscious form of Priscilla Roletti. Hans Goring stepped out from the darkness and into the lone bright light. The German looked her over taking her pulse. She was alive. He casually pushed her head to the side. She was badly bruised. A black eye, swollen eyebrow, and a bloody lip. "Temper, temper, Claude. You kill her too soon and we may never find out who she is." The darkness around him replied.

"Don't scold me German! You are not my superior!" Hans had no fear of the man from the darkness.

"I may not be, this is true. But 'He' is. And until 'He' says otherwise, he wants us to find out who and where this woman comes from." Hans never looked back as he spoke checking over Priscilla. Hans then stood.

"She'll be alright. At least physically, let's hope your little temper tantrum didn't do any permanent damage." The voice in the darkness said nothing. "Your methods did not work so I will try mine." Hans then looked up. "D-1?" Lumbering from the shadows was the hulk of a man, the very same one that had picked up

Priscilla from the parking lot. In the light, he was monstrous, bald, and with the eyes of a corpse. If one looked closely, they'd see lobotomy incisions on his cranium. The gargantuan stopped just mere inches from Hans, he had now untied Priscilla's wrists.

"D-1, take her to room B-24." D-1 never said a word or reply, he never nodded. He just simply looked down at Priscilla and hoisted her up over his shoulder and walked her out of a now opened door. Hans watched on, proud of his creation. It took years of his life to create the first super human. And for the most part he was successful. The voice in the dark snickered at the lumbering figure.

"Your dog, obeys well." Hans smiled, casting his eyes in the direction of the tone.

"Better an obedient dog than a rabid one." He turned to fully look into the darkness with a raised eyebrow and a snide grin. "Wouldn't you say so?" The man in the dark said nothing, but Hans knew he was stewing. That mad man, had he been able to, he'd have cracked Hans' skull opened by now.

"Keep mocking me German, and we'll see how well that mouth moves when it's broken." Hans stood stock-still and never wavered from the threat, even as the man brushed passed him.

Hans never looked back. Alone now, he couldn't wait to have this partnership come to an end. Both Claude and their Benefactor were mad men. But he stayed out of fear for Claude. Until Claude got what he desired he was the most dangerous man on the planet. And Hans was no fool. He would wait, bide his time and move only when it was safe and smart to do so. And hopefully that time was soon. All that remained was this woman. Whoever she was. Hans then whirled around and made his way to room B-24.

Chapter 15
Shocking

The putrid scent of smelling salts pulled Priscilla from her unconscious state. She jerked up, feeling a stinging sensation in her wrists and ankles. She was held down by the restraints. The surface she was on was cold and stiff. She was blinded by a surgical light. It was so hot that she could feel the heat radiating from it. Her eyes were tearing and stinging from it. She thrashed her head left and right in a vain attempt to somehow escape the discomfort of a hot face and stinging eyes. With each breath she took her face slowly started to explode in a cascade of pain that made her sick. The headache she had before was only worse.

"Get this fucking light outta my face!" She yelled, thrashing her head right and left again. She again tried to get up, but was rewarded with a stiff pain in her wrists. "Get this-" before she could even finish, the light was abruptly turned off, and she was being tilted vertically.

The black spots before her eyes dissipated as she came to a stop. The room she was in had a very sterile smell to it, and it was freaking freezing. A chill suddenly shot through her body. With her eyes clearer now, Priscilla had a better look of where she was. It was some kind of examine room.

"Ah! Excellent! You're awake and fully alert this is good!" Hans strolled over in his white lab coat and eyeglasses perched on the bridge of his nose. He examined her, taking out a penlight from his coat and split each eyelid open, flashing the light in her eyes.

"You can take a beating Ms. Murphy I'll grant you that." He said carefully looking into her retinas. "No signs of trauma. Hopefully next time, someone will reframe themselves." Hans said, replacing the penlight in his pocket.

"There won't be a next time German." Coming into her line of sight was a man dressed in a dark suit with a teal tie now standing a little too close for her liking. Her eyes widened, she even tried to pull back. He was disturbing looking. He wore a hairless mask that looked like skin hanging off his face. She couldn't even see his eyes through the eye sockets.

If the eyes were the gateway to the soul, then his was a one-way ticket to hell. "Find out what we need German. And be quick about it!" Hans ignored the orders, now standing in front of a metal cart. She couldn't see what he was doing; his back blocked her line of sight. Priscilla then glanced around the room, and her eyes fell on the gargantuan man, standing like a piece of wood. He looked zombified, with a shaven head and lobotomized incisions. His frame carried muscle in the most unnatural way. She nervously chuckled, lowering her head. She was disgusted at this whole goddamn mess. What she thought was a lame mission is now turning out to be her last. Getting caught like this...never happened to her. And she was scared, because these weren't some run of the mill terrorists or mobsters. These were sick people obviously doing some pretty crazy stuff here. And it looked like they'd take great pleasure in her suffering.

"I see the hospital angle..." again she did a nervous chuckle. Lifting her head and gesturing at the monstrosity D-1. "Unlimited Guinea pigs...small town. With a lot of money, you can do whatever you want. Pay off the relatives, for bull shit malpractice." Again, she chuckled. It was easy to piece together. She was sent here to see about illegal cloning, so with that and now seeing D-1. They were obviously doing more.

"You're perceptive." Hans finally turned around; the masked man just stood there watching her. He was growing more and more agitated.

"What is taking so long?!" The masked man yelled in a frightening tone that even scared Priscilla but seemed to have no effect on Hans as he rolled a stool over and sat, pulling the metal cart closer.

"Now." Hans said the word 'Now' in a tone the clearly indicated he did not want to be interrupted again. "Without further interruption." He glanced at the masked man, saying it as well to make sure he got his point across loud and clear. Hans then turned back to Priscilla. He wrapped a rubber tie around her arm. After a few taps on the area, her vein rose to the surface. Hans then held a needle for her to plainly see. "I'd prefer to get what we need the clean way, saves us time and you a great deal on pain my dear." He squirted some liquid out before he stuck her with it. Even before he injected it into her, she knew what it was.

It was sodium pentothal, otherwise known as truth serum. And this was fast acting; she could feel the effects hitting her already. She was grateful her headache was going away, or at least she was so stoned she didn't feel it anymore. Hans waited a few moments and then again taking the penlight he flashed it before her dilated retinas. With a head nod, he was satisfied with what he saw, and then started speaking.

"Now Ms. Murphy...if that is who you really are. Why don't we start off with the basic question as to who you really are?" Priscilla giggled like a kid, stoned on pot. While training to become an agent, you were given sodium pentothal to familiarize yourself with the effects and how to deal with them. It was very hard to do so, especially with the amount given to her.

"Fuuuck Youuuu scumbaggg." The words came out slurred as she rolled her eyes in the back of her head. Hans was amused, but the masked man wasn't. He backhanded her so hard saliva hit the metal wall. Before she could even register the fact she was hit, she was hit again.

"You will talk!"

"Nein! You fool!" Hans jumped up and shielded her from another assault at the hands of Claude. "She won't talk if you give her a broken jaw!" The masked man backed away, breathing heavily.

"We don't have time for this Hans! We don't know whom she is, where she comes from! For all we know she may have been able to alert whom she represents!"

"I wouldn't concern yourself about that, my friend. The Benefactor doesn't seem to be worried. So, neither should you." The masked man then drew closer to Hans. He was shaking with anger.

"You are not my friend German! And I don't care what our Benefactor wants. We should move ahead with the timetable we have three clones ready to be deployed!" Hans shook his head, and then turned to regard his angry partner.

"You keep behaving this way. And no matter what antidote you were promised it'll be too late. Your 'infliction' will have eaten at your mind. Control yourself!" The masked man, just stood there as though trying to process what was just said to him.

"Use the more direct method Hans." Claude suggested, with a controlled tone this time. The German regarded Claude and all though the look he gave him said nothing of what was going on in his mind. Hans pitied this man and what befell on him. Granted, it was self-doing in the name of science.

But nevertheless, only a fool experiments upon himself. There are plenty of willing and unwilling for that. Hans then nodded, and then looked back to the woman, who was looking at them with a dazed look. Claude may be right. With the amount of sodium pentothal she should have sung like a bird.

"Very well." Hans then turned and stood, bringing the cart closer. Aside from an extra syringe and a vile of sodium pentothal. There was a metal box with knobs, and wires connected to it. Hans then sat back down on the stool and rolled over, lifting her shirt. Reaching back on the cart he took two electrodes, and stuck them on her breasts. He then took another set and placed them on the side of her left and right abdomen.

Hans then got up and grabbed a leather collar with electrodes. He strapped it around her neck, and connected a wire to it. The metal box was turned on via a black switch, it buzzed to life. Before sitting again Hans, forced Priscilla's mouth opened, placing a black box inside. It was to prevent her from swallowing her tongue. He then sat back on the stool, his hand hovered over a red button. He sighed, glancing at her. He had no qualms about doing this; it was just the mere fact that he felt this wasn't going to work. This woman was beyond their control in that regards.

"Fräulein… this is your last chance-" Claude reached over his shoulder growling and hit the button. Priscilla jerked and stiffened, lifting herself off the table. Her eyes rolled over white as electrical volts surged through her body.

Hans shut off the power.

"Yes, you wish to talk?" Priscilla shook her head, gasping for breath. They couldn't understand her, but her mannerisms told them she wasn't going to say anything. Hans smiled, and then started it again, the voltage increased this time. Priscilla fought against the impending darkness. If she blacked out she'd never wake up. The voltage stopped. Priscilla's head hung low.

"Now?" He was about to hit it again, but stopped. "She blacked out." He sighed and just as that happened his phone started to ring. Hans glanced at it.

"It's 'Him'." Hans didn't answer it right there. He allowed it to go to voice mail. The masked man didn't say anything. Hans then got up; it wasn't wise to keep the Benefactor waiting. "I don't think we should try again. We are wasting our time." Claude nodded,

"Yes. Let's inform 'Him' and then we can rid ourselves of her." Hans nodded,

"Let's unbind her." Hans proceeded to take off the electrodes and collar. Claude had just unlocked her ankles and now was working on her wrists. Just as he unlocked the left wrist Priscilla sprung to life.

She pushed Hans out of the way, and immediately took a swing for the masked man connecting hard. She felt a surge of vindication feeling her fist connect to his jaw. She wanted nothing more than to break his head wide open and she was. She hauled off and connected again with a fierce right sending the suited man into the wall.

She came in again to finish him off. Claude recovered quicker than she'd anticipated and came at her head on. His strength was incredible! She was like a child struggling with an adult. He was overpowering her. In their struggle she managed to rip away his mask. He immediately released her.

She stared wide eyed, and backed away, she expected a horrible scene of disfigurement. She held her breath, as the suited man turned to regard her. She gasped in horror, there was nothing there! But there was no mistaking the chuckle coming from the empty collar.

"Think you've seen it all?! Welcome to the future!" And before she could even defend herself. The headless man grabbed her by the throat and hoisted her off her feet, sending her into the abyss.

Chapter 16
The great escape

Priscilla jumped up and screamed, taking a wild swing into the darkness around her. With panic, gripping her heart, she fumbled about in the dark with arms in front of her checking every inch of her confines. She had to make sure she was indeed alone. She bumped into the cold walls, rubbing her hands along them. And then frantically pacing up and down, she exhausted herself. But she was indeed alone.

If she could even believe that anymore. She moaned and sobbed, and not from the still present skull cracking headache. She was scared, and truly alone. In the darkness of her confines she stumbled into the wall and slid down like a child. Her arms were wrapped around her body for self-protection, and it was freezing in here. She sobbed, resting her forehead on her knees. What the hell did she see before? Was it the effects of the sodium pentothal playing on her mind? She kept wishing that was the case. But she knew otherwise. The electric torture was enough to burn the effects from her body. She knew what she saw was real; she was just in complete denial about it. What the hell did she really stumble onto here? Cloning? Human experiments? And now some guy who was invisible? She didn't want to believe it. She wished, hoped it wasn't real…but she knew it was. She had to come to terms with the undeniable truth. Things just got taken to the next level, unlike anything seen. And she needed to get out of here, at any cost, and for her to do that she needed to focus.

Priscilla with newfound resolve wiped away her tears, and immediately regretted doing that. Her entire face hurt. Her left eye, she could feel it was swollen and tender. That 'Invisible' guy totally wrecked her. She shuddered thinking about that again. Invisible… she didn't even want to think it, let alone say it out loud to herself and to anyone else. What was she going to tell John? If she was having a hard time believing it and she saw it, then what the hell was he gonna think? She almost laughed at that, but that was something she'd worry about later. Now she had to get the hell outta here. The only question was how? She was in complete darkness, she had nothing.

No phone, no gun, not even…her eyes widened. For the first time, she was giddy with hope. She took off her sneaker and reached inside sliding a small section up towards the toe. She couldn't see it, but she felt it! Her pen laser torch! Touching the cold steel cylinder sent a chill through her body. With no time to spare, she held it between her teeth as she replaced her sneaker and got to her feet. She wasn't at 100% both physically and mentally and getting up as fast as she did, she caught a dizzy spell and had to lean against the wall.

Her headache intensified for that moment with the blood rushing through her head from the suddenness of her movements. Squinting and taking deep breaths until the headache subsided again, she pushed off the wall feeling around the entire expanse. It was all solid steel and plaster. She couldn't even find the door. No doubt it could only be opened from the outside. This was probably a holding cell for whatever poor soul that they experimented on. The walls would most likely be too thick to cut through as well. That notion didn't make her feel any better. As she completed the perimeter check, she felt something from above.

The source of her chill, she couldn't see it, but she managed to find it. It was a ventilation cover. Straining her ear, she could hear the cool air as well now. Directly below it, the cool air felt good. Of course it had to be just out of her reach. Priscilla had to stand on her tippy toes to feel around it to get some idea if in fact she could even use it to escape. Doing something so simple as standing on her tippy toes was strenuous and exhausting. She was holding her breath, feeling around the cover with her sweaty and clammy hands.

With a moan of both pain and frustration she fell back to her feet, breathing heavily, putting a shaky hand to her forehead. It was going to be a tight fit, but she may be able to do it. Priscilla took a moment to catch her breath and regain her focus. A minute was all she could spare, for all she knew they would come right through the unfound door right now and overpower her. That notion made her burst into a sweat of fear. To see that man, with no head, sent a panic through her again. She closed her eyes.

"Stop…" She whispered to herself through clenched teeth. She needed to get outta here, if not for anything else but for her kids. They would not be left without a mother… not again. Those thoughts alone, made her ignore the pain, and fear. Holding the laser torch in her teeth vertically, she went on her tippy toes again. With the pen torch in her mouth, she used her right hand to twist the casing releasing the yellow beam, which illuminated the room a little. With her left hand, she used that as a guide and to steady herself as she took the pen torch very carefully from her mouth and proceeded to cut away at the cover.

Sparks jumped about hitting her face; she had to squint to shield her eyes. She was almost blindly cutting at the cover with her hand as a guide. She envisioned cutting through her hand, for some reason, which only made her even more careful, slowing her down, to her annoyance. With the anticipation of freedom within reach, she was getting queasy; she felt a knot in her stomach getting stronger and stronger. Her face was wet with perspiration, of the heat coming off the laser and hot metal.

She was almost done; her toes were getting numb and were wavering a bit. Finally, feeling the cover come loose, Priscilla cut through the last corner, and turned off the torch just as the cauterized cover fell to her feet. She backed away, losing her footing her toes hurt from being on her tippy toes so long.

The small expanse smelled of ozone and metal. She wasn't sure if this place was sound proof and wasn't going to find out. She could see the square outline; the metal had a slight orange hue to it. With no time to waste, she stuck the pen torch in her back pocket. She'd take the risk of burning her hands. She took off her blouse and wrapped it around her palms.

She then jumped, trying to grab the edges. She missed the first time. The second time she managed to grab it, but couldn't hold on. It was hard to get a hold with the blouse in her hands. The headache was hitting her hard again with the increased blood flow. But she did not waiver in the least. She needed…and was going to get the hell out of here now.

She took a deep breath, ignoring every pain in her body and jumped. She managed to hold on this time as she slowly hoisted herself up. Her arms strained, she gritted her teeth, the blouse, although protecting her hands, was slowly giving way to the heat.

She could feel the burn at her fingers and palms. But she wasn't going to let go. If she did, then she wasn't going to jump up again.

Priscilla groaned, finally pulling herself up and wiggled herself inside. It was a tight fit, but manageable. She didn't even take the time to catch her breath, she crawled her way forward never looking back. That was the easy part. Now the hard part, getting outta here.

She crawled her way, trying her best not to make noise. She was successful for the most part passing so far, no vents. She was in complete darkness still. She was at least grateful there was the cool breeze. She couldn't imagine being in here with no air. She'd have suffocated. She wasn't sure how much time had passed before she came to another vent that illuminated the section in a green hue.

Priscilla tried her best to see through the grate to no avail. She licked her lower lip, not knowing what to do. She had limited time, and she couldn't use the pen torch indefinitely. Its power only lasted maybe an hour with continuous usage.

"Fuck it." She had no other options. She cut her way through. Worse case scenario if this was a dead end she'd climb back in and keep going. The only bad thing was she was leaving a trail for them to follow her. Cutting away at the vent was faster this time, being she wasn't standing on her tippy toes and was in a reasonably comfortable position to cut it much faster this time.

Once that was done, she tried to slide the cover into the shaft but lost her grip, with her hand wrapped with her blouse still. It clanged all too loudly to the floor below. Priscilla waited, holding her breath. A minute passed. Then two, she heard no movements below. Priscilla then shuffled through and slowly lowered herself down. Again, using the blouse to protect her hands, she found a footing and let go. She almost fell, from landing on unsteady feet. She didn't even have time to recover her breath as she laid her eyes on a sight she wasn't prepared for.

"Oh my god..." her mouth was agape.

Priscilla was awestruck by the sight she beheld. Today's science fiction was right before her very eyes. The green hue came from light, within the glass cloning cylinders filled with a green liquid. There were ten in all, lined around the room. She took a step towards them, scared to even do so.

There were wires and hoses protruding from the tops of them to LCD touch screens in front of each cylinder. She approached further all the while her body, cold from the temperature drop in here, and the outright fear of seeing this. She was scared to even look at what was within these glass tubes. But she had too, if for the only reason to convince herself this was real. Each one had a clone in various stages of development. There was one that had a set of arms, but its legs had not yet fully grown. Another looked to be only the size of a child. All of the clones had wires injected into their skulls and visors over their eyes. There were tubes in their forearms and one in their stomach.

All she could do was stare, as she walked passed each one. The last one she came to was the most developed. If it were clothed, he could pass for a man. She stopped before this one and really stared hard. It looked like someone. It was hard to tell at first because it still had wires injected into his skull and the visor over his eyes like the others.

She looked at it from the side and gasped in horror, taking a step back.

"No…." Priscilla whispered to herself. She could not believe her eyes, before her was a fully-grown clone of the President of the United States! Her imagination ran wild. This wasn't just some cloning, human experimentation operation. This was a full-blown, attempt to take over the government. She had seen enough; Priscilla slipped her blackened blouse back on and hopped up through the opening she made a few moments ago.

The metal was warm, but not enough to burn her skin. With a struggle she managed to pull herself up and inside. She was about to get the hell outta there when it dawned on her. She couldn't leave without taking the room out. Poking back out of the opening to her chest, Priscilla looked around and saw metal oxygen canisters on one side of the room. She took aim with the pen torch and twisted the body.

The yellow beam shot forth penetrating the canister, it exploded cracking a cloning cylinder. She ducked back in for cover, and then peeked out again. She fired off another blast into the cylinders. Cutting straight through them in half. The green liquid spewed out flooding the floor. The clones snapped from their wires, as they fell to the floor. The room was in flames now, another explosion rocked the room, destroying the rest of the cylinders.

Priscilla stayed just for a few moments longer just to make sure they were indeed destroyed. The fire sprinklers overhead started to shower the room. But the damage was done. And she was on her way, hopefully to freedom.

Chapter 17
Rage

"Bunch of bloody fools! This, needless checking in with 'Him.'" Hans was walking side by side with Claude following behind them was the gargantuan D-1 with his lumbering walk. "And your pet." Claude gestured behind, at the hulking creation of Hans. "What Good is he!? Just standing there! If it weren't for me, she'd have overpowered you and escaped!" Hans again said nothing. When Claude was on the very cusp of his anger fits it was best not to antagonize him any further. Hans couldn't wait to be rid of this crazed man.

He hoped the Benefactor had what he promised to Claude because there would be no place anyone could hide from a man that was invisible if he crossed him. Or worse yet, what would he do to Hans in his blind rage for such a betrayal by the hands of their Benefactor? He shuddered to think of it.

Claude was getting more unstable as the days went on. It would be only a matter of time before he was beyond the point of reasoning and taken by permanent madness. Again, Hans pitied the man that would not only invent the greatest find of the century. The potion for invincibility, men wrote books on it, armies of the world dreamt of such a power since the dawn of warfare. And now here it was in the flesh. If only Claude had waited. He never dreamed that the side effects would be madness.

The facility they were in was small, it did not take them long to get back to the cell they threw her in. There was a card key reader, Hans used his. Sliding it through the red light turned green with a little beep. As soon as the door slid open, Claude smelled ozone. He growled like a rabid dog as he entered, the led lights inside the ceiling came on. Hans Immediately went over to the ceiling and looked up at the cut away vent.

"How? She had nothing on her?" He bent down and picked up the cover. It was cold now. "She must be government, has to be, just as the Benefactor surmised. We bett-" an explosion cut through his words, sending Hans stumbling back. Fire alarms blared through the complex.

"That came from the lab!" Claude yelled, as he turned and ran out, Hans didn't even register that yet. The mere thought of the lab being destroyed, never occurred to him. There was no one else here, aside from Claude and himself. Surely this woman...

"Come D-1!"

The lab was located on the north side of the complex. Not a very far walk. By the time they got there smoke had engulfed the hallway so bad that Claude and a Hans were choking. D-1 did not seem to be affected by this. Once at the door, Claude swiped his card.

"Stand back!" He yelled as the metal door slid open. A backdraft of flames shot forth, catching Claude on his forearm. He screamed as he smacked his arm. If there was an ounce of damage to his skin it would show. Dead skin cells did not retain the ability to remain invisible. The overhead sprinklers finally activated showering the room as more smoke engulfed them, from the sudden cold water meeting the fire and hot surfaces.

The wait to get inside was painstaking as the steam and smoke dissipated thanks in part to the vents funneling the smoke out. Once the air cleared and it was safe Claude rushed in first, Hans was right behind him. Standing in ankle deep water both men just looked. Hans' expression was easy to read. It was one of dismay. Claude's on the other hand was not. The rubber mask he wore showed no emotion. But Hans could envision the face beneath it.

The Benefactor was a man that did not take failure lightly. He would hold them both responsible.

"No...." Claude stepped forward, taking in the scene. Clone embryos, and specimens in various stages of development were scattered all over the floor. Thousands of hours worth of work ruined…and his chance of having his life back now gone. The promised cure to his invisibility would surely be denied now. All because of her. Claude fell to his knees, and shook with rage as he laid his face into his open palms and wept.

Hans then turned to D-1.

"D-1?" The gargantuan looked down at his master, with white dead eyes ready for the command. "Find her. Destroy her." With no word of acknowledgment D-1 turned and left to fulfill the command of his master.

Barely breathing and with eyes stinging from the smoke caused by the explosion. Priscilla finally emerged from the ventilation system. Covered in soot, she stumbled out. Thankfully, the vent she found was ground level. Once she was free of her metal confines, she took a few moments to catch her breath. She had no idea where she was or how big this place was. Thankfully wherever she was there was no smoke. The fire alarms stopped, which added to her relief. Her head was still pounding.

The hallway she was in was semi lit, the emergency lights were activated. She glanced down both sides. And with nothing to lose she took the left and jogged. She should be careful where she was going, being that there was an Invisible man out there. But she highly doubted that at the moment. The fire she caused definitely kept them occupied. And there was no other guard presence, which was good for her. She was hopeful that maybe she could escape from this hellhole.

Once she reached the end of the hall, she turned left and came to a parking garage! Her heart skipped a beat seeing this. It was small, with a van and another car parked to her immediate right. And just up ahead was a roll down metal gate. She had her laser torch in hand, freedom was beyond that gate. She broke out into a cold sweat as she ran for it. Then, in the corner of her eye, she spotted something she couldn't believe.

The Dodge Charger was sitting right there. She came to a skidding halt not believing her eyes. She'd seen some pretty crazy stuff in the last few hours. But it was there, as true as could be. She bolted for it, when all of a sudden there was an explosion just feet from her. Plaster debris pelted her as she covered her head and neck with her arm. Before the dust settled, she heard the lumbering feet coming towards her. Priscilla knew what that was, and ran for the car not a second too soon.

A crushing attack would have obliterated her head. D-1 for such a slow creature picked up its pace and chased Priscilla. She dared not look back, if this monster grabbed her she was done for. As soon as she was within reach she planted her hand on the driver's side window. A green beam went up and down scanning it.

"Come on!" She yelled as D-1 was within seconds of grabbing her. Once the door unlocked she climbed in and slammed the door shut. The Charger was propelled sideways from D-1's impact. The creature never moaned or grunted. It slowly stood erect and faced the window and with a force unlike anything she'd ever seen he punched the window cracking it. Priscilla had seen enough, she pressed her thumb on the black circle, it lit up green once she was verified. Hearing the Charger's engine was music to her ears. Before D-1 could strike again, she floored the pedal shooting forward. But in an act of amazing strength the giant, latched onto her bumper! Priscilla looked in her rear view and couldn't even believe it! He was holding her in place, and lifting the back end up.

"Let's see you handle this mother fucker!" She brought the weapons systems online. She didn't even wait for a targeting HUD (Heads up-display) she armed the rear mini-missiles and fired both at point blank range. The explosion sent her flying forward, before she crashed into the adjacent wall Priscilla turned sharply spinning once before coming to a skidding halt.

She didn't even look to see what became of that abomination. She threw it in gear skidding backwards and lining up the front of the car with the metal gate. The windshield HUD (Heads up-display), appeared, the front headlights slid back, mini-missiles were armed and ready. A green cross hair appeared on her windshield HUD display.

She fired, blowing the metal door clean off, hot metal flew like javelins in all directions piercing the other vehicles. She gunned it, the Charger burst through into the darkness. She had a hard time seeing where she was going even with the headlights. She was all over the dirt road, sideswiping trees, bouncing off them like a pinball.

She finally broke out of the forest and onto a road. She turned sharply to the right and felt the back left tire come off the ground. She didn't know what road, she was on, but it was a narrow two-way street, she took the twists and turns fast. About three miles later, she shot out onto a main two-way road, turning sharply right, not even looking for any oncoming traffic.

Priscilla abruptly came to a screeching stop off to the side of the road. She leaned her head on the steering wheel and started to cry. The realization of what transpired just hit her like a punch to the gut.

She was hysterical, she just couldn't stop crying. For the first time, as an agent Priscilla felt afraid and overwhelmed. And she had no idea what to do.

Chapter 18
Cleaning up the mess

Hans stood and watched the complex burn under the tarp of silhouetted trees. It was a sight to behold, as cinders reached for the sky above. In hindsight, he was glad the complex was small, and only Claude and himself used it. It made purging it easier for one person.

"I don't know where he went. I tried my best, but there was-" Hans was interrupted again by the mysterious Benefactor. The voice on the other end was synthesized to sound more American, but Hans was no fool. He knew a European dialect when he heard it even disguised. "But he's mad! He's beyond reason now, saying he was going to find her!" Hans was frantic now. Soon after he recovered from his shock Claude did indeed go mad, he stripped down and was gone. It was one of the most horrible moments in Hans' life because he expected to be killed at any moment. Luckily for him that didn't happen.

Now he was left to face the music, Hans was not going to be blamed for this. He was only following orders. And now because of the Benefactor's foolishness of not just killing this woman, she destroyed the lab and all of the research. Luckily for them Hans was able to back everything up. All of their experiments and methods were recorded. And could be easily reproduced.

But of course, that took time and that was lost. The start of the Benefactor's plan was to replace the President with the Clone that was almost done. With the head of state replaced, he was going to then replace others as time went on. Until the Benefactor was able to assume power himself. It was an overall complicated plan, and even Hans didn't know the full details. But he knew there was more to it than he was told.

The Benefactor not only wanted the Cloning process perfected, but also Hans' formula. The one used to create D-1. His greatest creation, destroyed. It was just as well; D-1 would have been disposed of at some point anyway. Through the various specimens from the hospital Hans was able to perfect his formula. And now it was ready to be used on someone he deemed worthy. It was just finding someone, that was the task in that of itself. He sighed, clenching his jaw.

"Yes. I've already contacted them. They should be here soon. As soon as they arrive I shall let you know. Yes, I'll see to it." Just as the call ended, it was right on cue that a black Sprinter, came into view shutting its lights. Hans stuffed the phone into his jacket pocket and picked up the suitcase. He didn't step forward as the black Sprinter came to a slow halt. It took a few moments before the duo finally emerged from within. From the drivers side was a woman, of Spanish descent, who was very pretty with flowing thick black hair. She wore black boots to her knee, with black tights and a white T-shirt. The passenger was Spanish as well; handsome, thin and well dressed.

Trish and Omar cautiously approached Hans. They weren't carrying any firearms Hans could see but, knowing their reputation he knew they weren't just going to come out in the open with no way to defend themselves if this was indeed a trap.

"Welcome…" It wasn't every day Hans fraternized with known killers. The German licked his lower lip, he'd be lying if he said he wasn't nervous. These two would just as well kill him for the fun of it. Only the reputation of the Benefactor kept them in check. The duo didn't answer as they looked beyond Hans and at the complex now totally engulfed in flames.

"Nice bond fire." Omar said, placing a cigarette on his thin lips. Trish allowed herself to chuckle despite herself. She wasn't exactly keen on meeting out in the middle of nowhere. But being it was the same guy that recruited them the last time. They figured it was a legit meeting.

"The person that did this, are they long gone?" Trish asked, getting deadly serious. It didn't take a detective to figure out how things went down out here. Hans nodded.

"Yes, but not unfindable." He approached them and made his way to the hood of their Sprinter placing the suitcase upon the hood.

"Here," He opened it and handed them a folder and a tracking device. "The folder has her photograph, and this is a tracker. We bugged her car, a few days ago, and it's still active." Neither one made to grab it from him. So Hans just placed it on the hood, closed the suitcase and stepped back.

"Once the job is completed and proof is shown you shall retain payment the usual way. This is per 'His' instructions." Omar went and grabbed the folder and tracker from the hood. He did a little nod. "Oh yes, and one more thing." Hans reached into his other pocket and produced a cell phone. It was Priscilla's. "This was hers, we tried to hack it, but was unsuccessful. Your Employer wishes for you to hack the phone and send all the information on it to him. Of course, use whatever you find on the phone for your purposes as well." Hans smiled, as he stretched out his arm and handed it to Omar, who took it and slipped it in his pocket.

"Pleasure doing business with you." He was the first to get in, followed by Trish. Hans watched them turn around and drive off down the path. Luckily for Hans he had a car of his own to use and didn't have to rely on asking them for a lift. Not that he would anyway. Just being within their presence gave him goose pimples. And besides, he highly doubted they would be obliged to take him anywhere but to a grave.

Once he was totally alone Hans took out his cell phone and looked at it like it was something alien to him. He looked ahead again and then back to the phone and just let it go. The screen cracked as it hit the ground. Hans then smashed it with the heel of his foot. He wasn't going to call the Benefactor again. This was his chance to disappear. He got what he wanted. His Super Human formula was completed.

Hans was no ones fool. He knew the Benefactor wanted the formula for himself. And at some point, Hans was going to keep his word and provide it to him. But now after all of this, there was no guarantee he would be allowed to live once the Benefactor got what he wanted.

Nothing in life was guaranteed. Self-preservation was key, and Hans would reemerge in a far stronger position ready to take on not only his enemies but the world.

Chapter 19
Survival

After finally collecting herself Priscilla put as much distance as she could between her and the Cloning complex. Along the way she found a local Walmart, grabbing some necessary things. One of which was a burner phone. She had to call Derlin, she'd been off the grid for two days.

Two days she thought, felt like a fucking month. Luckily, there was a company debit card nicely concealed in the middle console; all company vehicles had them for emergencies such as these.

There was a five hundred dollar limit per day on them. She was afraid that the car wouldn't have it, being it was a proto-type. It would've been highly ill advisable, to go back to her hotel or even any hotel. So as soon as she purchased her stuff she ran into the women's room. This was a 24-hour Walmart in the middle of rural Pennsylvania. There was hardly a soul in there aside from the overnight workers and they didn't give her a second glance as they went about and worked with their loud music playing over the PA system.

Before she changed into her new clothes, which were jeans, T-shirt and a new pair of sneakers. Priscilla took a sink shower. It was the next best thing to a shower at the moment. As she did that she observed her face. She looked like a train wreck. Black eye, bruised cheekbone that not only looked horrible, but hurt like a son of a bitch. There wasn't much she could do for that aside from taking a few Excedrin's. For the cuts, she applied Neosporin, and that was pretty much it. Thankfully, aside from the pain she had, she was lucky with no broken bones. The only thing that was broken was how she viewed the world. She still couldn't believe anything she'd seen. Cloning, the experimentations, the crazy giant, and….Priscilla looked at herself in the mirror. She couldn't even bring herself to say it, let alone think it.

"Invisible...he was invisible." She said it out loud. She had to; saying it to herself, didn't make it real enough. She was frightened to her very core, that there was something out there like that.

Where someone could be standing right next to you and you wouldn't even know it. Even now she was having a hard time not thinking about it and expecting something to happen to her. And his strength! It was unlike anything from a normal man. Which she assumed he was, she didn't know who the invisible man was, but she figured that he was just like her. Aside from being invisible.

And that thing, D-1. That was a whole other issue right there. But at least she could wrap her head around that. She knew about experiments like that. In fact, her own government was doing things just like that. Trying to create the perfect soldier. That was something every world power from the beginning of time tried at least once. And then there was Derlin, what the hell was she going to say to him? He was going to think her crazy. And she couldn't blame him, she saw it herself and she still doubted what she saw.

The prepaid phone was sitting on the sink still in the packaging as she thought about this. Priscilla took a deep breath and looked herself over one more time. She sighed, turning away, she grabbed her soiled clothes and stuffed them into a plastic bag and left.

She parked the Charger right in front of the store just off to the side of the entrance. She didn't want to take a chance and park to far away. She popped the trunk, throwing her soiled clothes inside. She then took out an emergency lock box that had an extra gun. It was a smaller 9mm, but anything was better than nothing at this point. If she didn't have this, she'd have to go back into Walmart and steal one of the rifles and that was something she didn't want to do. With that done, she scrambled into the car and locked the doors. She shivered in fright, sitting still for a moment. The silence was eerie. Priscilla then, leaned over and banged on the seat, she did the same to the back seats. She was safe. This was the only safe place, her car. She chuckled at that one. She even double-checked the doors. They were locked. She then took a deep breath and opened her pre paid phone, set it up and called Derlin.

It took a few rings to get through by the time the call was bypassed and rerouted to Derlin's cell phone. When he picked up she could tell he was sleep from his groggily voice. Once she started to speak, Derlin woke up quickly rubbing the sleep out of his eye as he got up from bed. He was still in the clothes from today. He at times fell asleep in his clothes, it was an occupational hazard. While she spoke, he listened and never interrupted her. He was in his living room, going for the laptop.

"I feared the worst when I didn't hear back from you, Jesus Christ Priscilla. The main thing…is that you're all right. Now lets see, I have a visual of the satellite reconnaissance taken. Son of a bitch."

"What is it John?" She asked, looking around. The parking lot was more or less the same. There were a few people that came and went in the middle of the night.

"Just yesterday, there was nothing…now from a pass just a few hours ago there's what seems to be a giant fire raging. I'll try to see what that's about."

"Gotta be the complex. I trashed it before getting outta there. They are probably covering their tracks." John nodded.

"Looks that way. Stand by for a moment." John left the line; she heard him talking to someone, but couldn't hear the conversation clearly, and honestly wasn't trying to. She was too focused on who was coming and going. She found herself looking, for anything that didn't belong, such as an extra shadow, or movements.

"Priscilla, I'm sending the Philadelphia branch of the NSA, they should be there by the morning. I gave them a full account of what to expect." John sighed; he leaned back on his couch.

"I left the invisibility detail out, for obvious reasons. Priscilla, I really need you to think. You've been drugged and beaten. Is it possible that maybe-"

"John as sure as I'm sitting here telling you this, there's someone out there, invisible to the naked eye. And I have no doubt he'll be looking for me. I'm not stepping foot anywhere near my home, the office, anywhere until I know for sure he's dead!"

She tried her best to keep calm, it was hard. Here was John, doubting her on something she knew as the truth. With someone out there like that, she'd never go home again. She couldn't, too much was at stake. John sighed again.

"Very well, so now where will you go?" That was indeed a good question. Where was she going to go? First and foremost, if she wanted to lure someone out of hiding, she'd have to use herself as bait. Judging from what she knew of this 'Invisible man' he'd seek revenge on her. At least that's what her initial read on his behavior told her. But where? There was one full-grown clone of the President. But that was destroyed. Could there be more than one? Not likely, but very highly probable. Nothing could be assumed or taken off the table.

"Washington." Derlin didn't like that at all. It was too risky being so close to the spotlight. Truth be told, John didn't believe her. How could he? There has been no evidence nor rumblings from Intel about someone creating or even trying to create an invincibility potion. But then again, they'd never have known about the cloning if it weren't for them using the vast shipping network, a drug lord had at his disposal. John sighed again.

"Okay, I'll call ahead. I'll contact Lens. You're familiar with him, correct?"

"Yeah…we've worked together before." Lens was part of the super secret Watchmen. Their job was to observe, and report back. They were deep cover Ops, on missions that had no time limit. They could be on one for weeks, months or years.

"Head over to D.C. I'll send you the contact information. And Priscilla? Please just relax ok?"

At that moment it felt as though she stopped breathing. As she repeated the way he said that. He thought she was on edge. She had to admit she felt and sounded like it. But she wasn't, she was never sharper. She was focused, and determined.

"Yeah…of course. John, just make sure you tell Lens everything, even the invincibility part please."

"Of course. You be careful, I'll be in touch." And the call ended. Priscilla closed the phone and tossed it to the side. She leaned her forehead on her fist. She wanted to punch something right now. John thought she was crazy. And more than likely would tell Lens to try to bring her in. Hence the reason he's allowing her to go down to D.C.

Lens, whom Priscilla knew well enough was for the most part a level headed guy, but could he be trusted? She wasn't sure. She didn't even know what he looked like. She sighed again, sitting up, she started the Charger and peeled out of the parking lot.

Chapter 20
Concerns

John Derlin leaned back on his couch, the leather creaking with the slightest movement. He hated this couch. If it were up to him, he'd have bought the fabric couch. Less noisy and it didn't stick to your skin in the summer time. He sighed again, playing back the entire conversation with Priscilla.

He was legitimately concerned about her. She was tough, strong and a very capable Op. But even the best can crack under pressure. She was tortured, and drugged and more than likely dehydrated. That could play a heavy toll on one's mind. John sighed again, getting up from his couch. He made his way into the kitchen and retrieved his pipe and tobacco. He needed a smoke after that conversation. As he made his way outside, he packed his pipe and lit it, his wife hated it when he smoked in the house.

Under the night sky, it was cool out. Taking deep puffs he opened his phone and scrolled to the name listed as Lens. It only rang twice before he picked up. Derlin then proceeded to explain the situation. Derlin looked at his watch as he spoke. It was just after 01:00 more than enough time to get to D.C. before Priscilla.

“Of course, she's under extreme duress. Look at what she's been through. But John, what if she is right? We should prepare just in case. I'll coordinate efforts in D.C, and once I meet up with Agent Roletti, I'll evaluate her.

I'll keep you in the loop John, don't worry.” And the call ended, it was all that could really be done at the moment. Lens was reliable, Derlin trusted his judgment. Derlin sighed again, and then took one last puff from his pipe. He knew sleep was going to elude him, so he may as well get a start on the day. He'd shower and maybe even get to the office early. Sometimes being behind the desk was the worst. You were helpless to do anything and had to wait for others. Something Derlin wasn't used to. He was a hands on man, but old age said something different. The Spy Master sighed again, as he emptied his pipe into the bushes and went back inside.

Chapter 21
Trish and Omar

"So, did you hack it?" Trish was driving the windowless Sprinter following the tracker still attached to the Charger. Their mark was on Highway 30 heading for the I-95. Omar was sitting next to her, punching away at the keys. Priscilla's phone was connected to his laptop.

"Not yet Trish for the tenth time." Omar shook his head, never taking his eyes off the screen as he moved his fingers across the touch pad. Putting a curser where it needed to be and then started to type again. "This phone is pretty solid. Good software, so it's giving me a hard time. But luckily for us, with a little Patience." He made sure he telegraphed the last word, so she knew it was meant for her. "We should be able to get in there. It's a good thing, we got this new software. Otherwise, I wouldn't be able to hack this phone...ah bingo!" The phone was now unlocked, and as he opened said phone and scrolled through last calls and messages he was also downloading a copy for their Employer.

"The old man should have a field day with this. What do you think he's gonna do?" Trish just shrugged her shoulders as she drove and watched the screen with the map and blinking blue dot.

"Fuck do you care? Just as long as the checks are signed. Crazy son of a bitch can have whatever he wants. Just send it to him already! She's about a mile ahead." Omar nodded, creating a folder and dropped it into the file sharing service they used with the Benefactor.

Omar waited until the download was completed and then sent an email to give 'Him' a heads up. Once that was done, he closed the laptop and placed it to the side.

"Done." He slid Priscilla's phone in his pocket. Trish then put the pedal to the metal. Unlike Priscilla's Charger the Sprinter didn't have as many modifications. There weren't hidden missiles behind the headlights. But it did have bulletproof windows and tires and the most important thing was a speed boost. The engine was heavily modified so it was able to keep up with a car like the Charger.

"Get ready! We'll be coming up fast!" Omar nodded, jumping up and going to the back. He threw off his suit jacket and rolled up his white sleeves. Secured in the middle of the van was a black Multistrada 1200 Enduro. On the wall were assorted hand weapons one of which was a GLM grenade launcher with a six round drum more than enough to take care of the Charger. He grabbed it.

"No fucking around Omar! You blow her to fucking hell!" Trish called back. Omar didn't need to be told that. He vividly remembered their defeat at her hands. They had waited a long time to get back at her. They even at one point looked for her, with no luck.

So, when they found out, this hit was on the very same woman from the last time. They'd have done it for free, but of course, they never told that to the Benefactor. The old man wanted to pay, then let him pay.

Just before she came around the bend, Trish shut the front headlights off. The road they were on had no street lamps. Which made it perfect to ambush her. The red taillights shined brightly in the darkness like a beacon. Trish smiled. This was it… finally! While Trish's thoughts were already handing them victory.

Omar was in the back strapping a harness around his shoulders. On the ceiling were latches that he secured himself with. Once he was secured he slid the side door open. The frosty night breeze hit him in the face. Omar then reached over and grabbed the grenade launcher. He leaned half of his body out of the Sprinter as he propped the weapon against his shoulder. Licking his lips with anticipation, he lined up the cross hairs and counted to three before pulling the trigger three times in quick succession. His face lit up like a mad man revealing the blood lust in his eyes as the grenades slammed into the back of the Charger.

Chapter 22
The chase is on

Priscilla was barreling down Highway 30 taking the narrow two-way road with little care. At this hour there was no one on the road. She checked the GPS. She should be coming to the I-95 in about ten minutes. As she was on a straight piece of road she just happened to look up in her rearview when suddenly she was slammed from behind. The explosion propelled the Charger forward. If she didn't have her seat belt on she'd have went flying into the windshield.

"Son of a bitch!" The back of the Charger was engulfed in flames. They found her, how the hell they did that, was beyond her comprehension at the moment. She'd worry about that later. Right now, she had to deal with whoever this was and fast.

She activated her rear defenses, the tail lights flipped up; she was getting ready to fire a mini-missile. But her assailant fired off another grenade. The impact threw off Priscilla's aim. The missile went wide, and into the forest exploding. Trees fell onto the road blocking it, as fire lit the night sky.

The unknown vehicle caught up to her now; neck and neck they drove in a race to the death. The black Sprinter, slammed into the Charger. They were trying to force her off the road. If the Charger were stuck in a ditch it wouldn't matter how in impenetrable the car was. Whoever this was, would somehow force her out. But that wasn't going to happen. As the road warriors fought for supremacy neither one of them took notice of the semi coming straight for them. The trucker was blowing his air horn and yet neither Trish nor Priscilla took notice until he nearly obliterated them.

They threw their wheels in opposite directions at the last possible second, allowing the semi to pass between them. Trish recovered quick enough to avoid the side. But Priscilla almost smashed into a tree before recovering. Side by side again, they rammed each other, it was a stalemate. Priscilla was about to kick the Charger into gear and blow them out. When the Sprinter suddenly rocketed past her and out of sight.

"This is getting us nowhere! That damn car is like a tank!" He said, after he came back in and slid the door closed, throwing the grenade launcher to the floor. Trish just nodded as she got up right along side the Charger and was trying to slam her off the road.

"Let's see if that car can survive a direct hit into a tree!" She tried to ram her again, off the road. Trish wasn't watching, but Omar was and he saw dead ahead a semi blowing his air horn.

"Trish! Back down! Look!" He yelled, pointing. But Trish was in a blood lust. She wanted this bitch so bad she could taste it. If it wasn't for Omar reaching over and grabbing the wheel they'd have been killed. Omar gave her the dirtiest look he ever gave her as he sat back down. But Trish was too focused on the task. She then glanced at the GPS and according to that there was a bridge up ahead.

"I got an idea! Get on the bike! Keep her busy!" Omar jumped up and ran to the bike. The jet-black matching helmet was perched on the handlebars. He slipped it on as he straddled the beast of a bike. He radio checked the two-way receiver inside the helmet.

"Trish you online?" Trish fitted an earpiece in her ear.

"Check."

Omar kick started the bike to life; the revving of it was like a woman purring. In between the handlebars were some controls. There were two green buttons. The first one he pressed opened the back doors. The chilly wind blew around anything that was not tied down. Trish's hair was doing a dance of its own. She tried to clear the strands away from her eyes but failed miserably. The other button Omar pressed, released the two steel claw grapplers that held the bike in place. Omar revved it hard spinning the back tire and then shot out the back. Picking up speed he U-turned gaining on the Charger. Just as he turned around Trish was already long gone.

Now, unlike the Sprinter, the bike had an arsenal. It had extra armor plates covering the fuel tank, and concealed behind the headlight was a machine gun with armor piercing rounds. The down side of course, was that there was no protection for the rider, but for a psychotic like him, only the kill mattered and tonight they were getting the kill one way or the other!

Priscilla sped up trying to distance herself from them. According to the GPS, I-95 wasn't far from her current position. She glanced at her side view mirror, and then looking to the right, she saw a single headlight. The van sped in front of her and disappeared into the night. But the motorcycle lagged behind. Priscilla was trying to get a 'target lock' on the weaving motorcycle. Rapid gunfire pelted the back of the car, managing to crack her rear windshield. She licked her lips, as she poured on more speed, the bridge was just a mile and a half away.

Trish, getting in the lead of her prey, tapped a red button on the dashboard, giving the Sprinter a little extra kick of nitrous boost. She reached the bridge with at least a minute and a half to spare. She turned the Sprinter violently, blocking the entrance and jumped out, grabbing from the back, a long, rectangular-shaped box with four holes on both sides. It was a M202A1 multi-shot disposable rocket launcher. If grenades couldn't crack open that car this would! She thought as she mounted the weapon on her shoulder, aimed and fired a single rocket into the bridge.

Trish was engulfed in smoke from the discharge of the rocket. She waved a hand in front of her face, looking at her handiwork. She destroyed a good portion of the bridge. They effectively boxed her in.

Trish raced to the other side of the Sprinter, facing the now distant headlights of the Charger coming towards her. She could see Omar was falling back a bit waiting for the Charger to stop, but they were both mistaken. They were about to find out she was just as crazy as they were.

The bridge was coming up. While occupied by Omar, who was relentlessly firing his machine gun, Priscilla didn't hear the drowned out distant explosion. Her eyes were on the view screen lining up a shot when her attention shifted ahead. The Sprinter was blocking the way onto the bridge. Priscilla turned her attention to this new threat; her front headlights were already slid back. The green cross hair appeared on her windshield, she was toggling for a target lock. She increased her speed and was just about ready to fire.

Trish held the rocket launcher firmly. Taking aim, the Charger was clearly not going to stop, she fired. Trish watched on waiting for the inevitable impact, but the Charger swerved at the last possible second.

"Shit!" The assassin exclaimed aiming carefully again.

Priscilla saw the incoming projectile. She wasn't going to put her trust into the car's better armor. She tightened her grip on the wheel, bracing herself. At the last possible second, she jerked the wheel to the right narrowly avoiding impact. She glanced in her rearview as the projectile shot past her and into the forest. The explosion would've been seen miles away.

Trish could not believe what just happened, that bitch is way too lucky for her own good! She had one last rocket left; she was about to take aim when she saw two projectiles heading her way fast. She had no idea what the hell they were; Trish dove off to the side of the road into a ditch. Not a moment later the Sprinter was destroyed, clearing the way for the Charger.

Priscilla wasn't waiting a moment longer, she fired two missiles at the Sprinter blocking her way. The impact cleared the way, but there were large chunks of wreckage that could still impede her. On the floor-mounted gearshift, there was a hidden button. She pressed it and held on tight. The rear license plate folded down, revealing a mini rocket booster. In a delayed action, it activated. Priscilla felt her body press against the seat as the car picked up speed.

She cleared the wreckage at maximum velocity, sending whatever was in her way flying in all directions. Being the Sprinter had blocked her view of the bridge; she didn't know a good portion was taken out until it was too late. At first she thought she wasn't going to make it and would free-fall to a fiery death. But she cleared the chasm, the hard landing made her lose control of the car, but she regained control before she drove into a tree head on. She side swiped another tree bouncing off that like a pinball doing a little fishtailing as she sped off into the night, never looking back.

Chapter 23
Defeated

"FUCK!!!" The words echoed like the roar of a wild beast. Trish glared at the speeding off Charger. She then turned her eyes to what remained of their Sprinter. Large pieces were scattered all over the place. A few trees were ablaze. Omar came up behind his sister. He was always the cool headed one. His stone face gave no sign of emotion. He took out one of his thin cigars, lit it and took a deep drag, letting it out slowly. Trish walked closer to the wreckage and eyed the area, seeing if there was anything worth salvaging. But everything was destroyed.

"Sis, relax."

"Oh Yeah!?" Throwing down the rocket launcher. "Well, now we have to fucking double back! You familiar with the area Omar, because I'm fucking not!" She was beyond angry; if there were any one else here she'd kill them. Omar shrugged his shoulders.

"Don't worry about all that. I got an idea. One that will bring her right to us. Come on." She turned and glared at him with eyes of hate. He walked away, going to the idling bike that was on the side of the road.

"Let's go!" He yelled over the engine, not sure if she heard him. She stood there for a moment longer, then turned around and walked towards her brother. She climbed on and wrapped her arms around his thin waist. Revving the bike, they bolted off, leaving a tire mark in their wake.

Along the way, they spoke on their two-way receivers. Omar filled her in on his plan. And for the most part, it seemed probable, if not foolhardy. But if planned right, they could escape and fight another day once they had accomplished their task and that was putting to rest the blonde bitch once and for all!

Chapter 24
Down time

Priscilla had finally made it to the I-95. All the while, she couldn't help herself; she kept her eyes darting everywhere for some kind of attack. It was like that other mission from hell. Where she was eluding assassins from all angles. Thankfully the fire, on her rear end was out. That was the last thing she needed was a car on fire. There was no way she was getting out to put it out. Not with those new players, and for the moment she wondered just who they were. They were on the scene pretty quickly and found her just as fast. Which led her to think now there must be some tracking device on her car.

"Fuck." She muttered under her breath. Now she'd have to look for that, at some point before this was over.

As the adrenaline rush wore off, Priscilla found herself beyond exhaustion. Remembering what Pete told her about the new advanced CPU, she figured why not give it a try. She sat back, tapping the touchscreen, bringing up the 'auto drive program.' She tapped in her destination. Hopefully this thing would do just as Peter said it would. The program took a moment to respond, but then a green icon popped up informing her the car was now on autopilot. She was hesitant to let go of the wheel, but did so.

The Charger was still on course. She was amazed, and relieved. She sat back and closed her eyes. Looking out the window, the sky looked so peaceful. It was clear and the stars were out as bright as could be. A thought came to mind about the time she bought her son a telescope. She smiled at the thought and remembered he was so excited that he dragged her to the roof of their house. They sat there and looked at the stars for hours. He showed her where all the planets were. They saw the rings of Saturn and one of Jupiter's moons, it was a wonderful time. She never had an interest in it, but for him, he had her undivided attention. With those happy thoughts, she closed her eyes and was soon dreaming of the stars.

Chapter 25
Back to the mall

It took them some time, but Trish and Omar finally managed to get to I-95. The good thing about that was they managed to get ahead of Priscilla. It gave them time to plan and decide where they were going to go.

Murray City was as good a place as any. It was about fifteen miles north of D.C. it was a typical suburban community that was like any other across the country. It had fairly good schools and a low crime rate. It basically wasn't gonna know what the fuck hit them. A small, close knit town like that, was cut off from the world. All they knew of the outside was what they saw on CNN. It was one of the newer more up to date cities. There were plenty of stores, supermarkets and a mall.

The Bay Berry Mall was perfect for what they had in mind. It was a large mall by today's standards, but at this hour it would be easy enough to take over. At 07:00 they arrived, parking their bike in the underground garage and made their way. They at first were going to stop at a hardware store. But thankfully there were stores within the mall that had everything they'd need. They just needed to round up whoever was here, which they were doing now.

The many stores inside were closed, but the mall itself was open for the early morning walkers who enjoyed strolling through it for their daily exercise. First, they took out the Mickey Mouse security detail. They split up; they didn't have all damn day for this. Luckily for them, the day and night shift guards were in between the shift changes. Which made taking them out quick. They didn't know what hit them when they were gunned down, in their locker rooms, half naked talking about irrelevant bullshit. The last three were in the security office with its wall of screens. They weren't even on the clock yet when Omar burst in and took them out with nothing more than a blade. With the keys to the castle, they then seized the few people doing their morning walk and locked them up, behind one of the many-gated stores. With time now running short, the next phase was to create homemade bombs. That was easy enough all of the necessary ingredients and components needed were easily found in the yet unopened Sears. Any over night workers or staff coming in were taken as well and locked up. Making homemade bombs was something of a second nature for the duo.

Once that was done, they booby-trapped each of the entrances. They were planning on the police to show up, and would be ready for any idiotic attempts on their part to storm the mall. They left only two doors unsecured one of which was the main entrance and the underground parking lot where the bike was parked. When people trickled in to start their workday, they were taken. Stripped of their cell phones and locked up with the rest.

There was one that thought he was a hero and was met with a blade to the throat for his efforts. Once they had enough hostages, Trish ran outside and fired off a few rounds at incoming workers. That would be good enough to keep anyone else at bay. Even when the cops showed up it wouldn't be a problem. Between the hostages and the booby-trapped entrances they wouldn't know what hit them.

With all the preparations done it was time to lure in the prey. Trish and Omar sat on a marble bench near the front entrance.

"Ok, should I make the call, or you?" She asked her brother, smirking like a devil.

"Why of course you may have the honor to do so, dear sister." Omar handed her Priscilla's hacked phone. They may not have her number, but they had the next best thing. The last person to call her was someone named John. They were sure he would get the message to her.

Chapter 26
An unwanted phone call

John Derlin hurriedly made his way to his office. And didn't even get a chance to sit down yet, or even turn his computer on when his phone started to ring. He missed the call, and then not even five seconds later it rang again. This time he managed to pull it from his pocket and see who it was. When he saw it was Priscilla he was relieved, he had programmed her burner phone into his for the time being.

"Pris-"

"No mother fucker, it ain't her." When he heard Trish's voice Derlin's heart skipped a beat. His forehead broke out into a cold sweat. He couldn't believe it.

"How did you get-"

"Listen up mother fucker! We took a mall, we got hostages and we'll kill them all. All we want is the bitch, the one named Priscilla. You know her and she works for you. Fuck around and it's a wrap!" And the call ended. It happened so fast Derlin couldn't even register it. He fumbled for the remote and turned on the flat screen and immediately turned to CNN and sure enough there it was. He turned it up.

"Mary...all we know now is that the mall is totally taken. The captors inside have not said anything to authorities just yet. Swat and FBI are en route." Derlin muted it again, calling Priscilla with a trembling hand.

Chapter 27
Knowingly walking into a trap

Priscilla awoke to the sound of her phone going off on her lap. She was so wiped it took her a while to stir and answer. She didn't even look at who was calling as she rubbed the sleep from her eyes. Derlin was the only one with the number. She sat up, as the Charger went on its way. It was so surreal to her. A self-driving car, the future is truly now. The bright rays of the warm sun that was starting the new day, felt good on her sore face. She finally answered the phone with a stifled yawn.

"Yeah?"

"Priscilla…listen." He took a breath. The tone in his voice was enough to pull Priscilla out of her sleepy state. A sudden sense of dread filled her stomach. "We have a situation." He went on and told her.

"Son of a bitch!" She punched the steering wheel in a fit of rage. She totally forgot about those two. Never thinking she'd cross paths with them again, or at least not like this. But now thinking, it made further sense. They were hired by this mysterious behind the scenes player along with the other bounty hunters to hunt her and Carmine down.

She nibbled at her lower lip. She didn't want to go there, she knew this was a lure to bring her in. Also, she didn't wanna deviate from her present course. She sighed, she had to do what needed to be done, regardless of the obvious and her personal vendetta against the faceless man she was after.

There were innocent lives at stake, those animals wouldn't think twice about killing them all.

"I'm on my way John." Derlin sighed, he didn't wanna throw her into the wolfs den. But he had no choice, Priscilla was one of the best, if anyone could come out from this alive it would be her.

"Very well…I'll make the call, telling the locals you're on your way. Just Priscilla please…play it smart. You know this is a trap so be prepared for anything."

"Always." And the call ended.

Priscilla checked the GPS. She just passed that area about a half an hour ago. Putting the Charger back into manual drive. She turned forcefully around, cutting across the other side of the highway into the oncoming traffic. She barely missed an oncoming pickup truck as it swerved out of her way, blowing its horn. She paid the incident no mind, putting the pedal to the floor.

Chapter 28
The locals

The sheriff, wearing a cowboy hat and dark sunglasses, stood leaning against the driver's side door of his cruiser. He took the last drag of his cigarette, before dropping it to the ground. He had his cell phone pressed hard against his ear listening intently to the person on the other end. His deputy walked over to him with his M-16 slung over his shoulder, waiting for his boss to finish the call.

"Ok. I understand. I'll give her all the cooperation I can." He folded the phone and tossed it on the front seat. He looked over at his deputy.

"Damn fucking bastards!" He spat out.

"What's wrong, sheriff?"

"We have to wait and do nothing. That was some government official saying someone is on the way and when they arrive, they are to handle the situation."

"Oh, that's a bunch of bullshit! Damn Feds always thinking they can just come fly in and take over!" The young deputy spat out brown gunk after he said the words.

The entire perimeter was barricaded with numerous police vehicles. State and local police departments from the surrounding counties joined in helping to contain and, hopefully, put an end to the terror that was going on inside. Medics were on the scene, ready to treat the wounded. The media, as always, were there too. Their vans littered the area.

There was at least ten or more of them with their satellite dishes rising from the roofs to report what was going on to the world. Reporters standing almost side-by-side to each other were giving information of what they knew and what they think might be happening inside the mall.

When Priscilla arrived, she parked the Charger out of sight. She sat there and watched the scene for a moment, taking it all in. She checked her 9mm before getting out; she chambered a round and took the safety off. She took a deep breath, she was as ready as she'll ever be. She slowly got out of the car and approached the crowd. No one really glanced at her. They probably thought she was one of the many spectators trying to get a better view of what was happening in their quiet town.

She pushed through the mass of people, not even saying excuse me or pardon me. She made her way to a cop standing behind some yellow tape that was blocking the path. She was lifting it up to enter, when the cop came over.

"Excuse me, ma'am. You're not permitted to enter here for your own safety." He said, trying his best to be friendly.

"I'm Priscilla Roletti, whoever is in charge here is expecting me."

The wind blew some of her hair in front of her eyes after she said that. She moved it out of the way and gave the man a hard look. He cleared his throat, looking at her face and probably wondered what the hell happened to her.

"Sorry ma'am, right this way." He said as he ushered her to the front. As they got closer the cop walked ahead of her approaching a man in a cowboy hat who was talking to a couple of other officers.

"Sheriff? Excuse me, Sheriff." He turned around looking at the cop, and then to Priscilla, then back to the cop. "This is agent Roletti, the person we got the call about." He said this quickly and walked away before the sheriff could further question him. He was only a patrol officer after all. The sheriff looked at Priscilla, eyeing her up and down.

Two other officers were standing by his side eyeballing her as well. She hated when the local law enforcement got involved in matters. Many of them hated the feds and for good reason. She would hate it too, if some hot shot fed came in and took over making you feel worthless and incompetent. But, there were some who were all too glad to give you the reins. She was hoping the sheriff was the latter. She didn't have the time or the patience to get into a debate.

"Sheriff, come with me please," she said as she walked past him to the front of his car.

"I take it you were told that I'm in charge now, right?" She asked, as he stood in front of her crossing his arms over his chest.

"Yes, I was, miss. But I'm gonna be honest with ya. I don't like it at all, you feds think you can come in and take over anytime you want." She could already see where this was going, and had no time for it. She had to make her point perfectly clear.

"Listen, I'm not here to get into a pissing contest with you. I'm sure you and your men are very good at what you do, but this is something that is totally out of your league, believe me." He rolled his eyes behind his sunglasses and waved a hand in dismissal.

"Come on. There's a couple of hotheads in there. Nothing more, Swat could take'em down hard." He gestured at the mall as he said this walking away from her, with his hands on his hips. Priscilla followed him, wishing it was that easy. With Trish and Omar, anything was possible. Standing by his side, she gestured to the mall.

"Inside that mall, are two of the world's most lethal assassins. They've left a trail of bodies larger than your department. They are wanted for crimes you couldn't possibly imagine. They could kill everyone in that mall and leave without you even knowing. I'm willing to bet your Swat wouldn't even make it through the front door. The place is probably booby trapped." She waited a moment, giving him a cold, heartless stare. She wanted it all to sink in before she continued.

"I'm the one they want anyway. I'm in the middle of a mission where national security hangs in the balance. They are involved and this is their way of getting me to come to them. Now, I don't give a fuck about glory, you and your men can have it. I have a fucking job to do. And, when it's over, say whatever you like and take all the credit for all I care. As a matter of fact, I'd prefer it that way." He took off his glasses, revealing brown eyes of intensity.

"I'm sorry, ma'am. Didn't mean to come off that way, just hate it having my toes stepped on."

"I understand I'm not here to do that. I just want to do my job, and then I'll be on my way. Now listen, if anyone asks, tell them I'm a negotiator, have your SWAT team in place and ready when you get the signal."

"And that'll be what exactly?"

“You’ll know it when you see it. Once I take them out, have your men go in, shoot a couple of rounds and make some noise. I’m sure you get the drift.”

“Yes, yes I do.”

“Good…don’t do anything, unless you hear from me, are we clear?”

“Yes.”

Priscilla was going to walk to the mall, but the sheriff offered to give her a lift. As they slowly approached the mall, Priscilla couldn’t help but feel déjà vu as she looked at it. She swallowed on a dry throat, wondering just what was waiting for her inside. The sheriff pulled as close as he could to the main entrance. Priscilla, didn’t hesitate a moment, she opened the door and stepped out of the car.

“Be careful.” He said in a low voice, before she closed the passenger door. She glanced at him and nodded.

“Just be ready.” He nodded and drove off. Priscilla didn’t watch him go. She turned and faced the mall. With no more delays she slowly walked into the mall of horrors.

Chapter 29
A three-way dance of death

As she approached the glass doors Priscilla, tried to look in before just walking in blindly. It was hard to see anything, and she wasn't going to stand out here all damn day. She walked right in, half expecting to get blown to hell. But nothing happened as she slipped inside the mall. She just stood there, among the shuttered storefronts. Gamestop, Burger King and Bose. It was eerie to see a mall this quiet.

There was a smell in the air, and a vibe that made her flesh crawl. There was no reason to sneak around, they knew she was here. They wanted her and that's what they were going to get. Priscilla took a deep breath and walked on ahead, slowly and out in the open. But keeping her eyes and ears sharp. They were near; she could feel their eyes on her. Their intentions for her were felt in the pit of her stomach. The anticipation of an attack was high. Her hands were sweaty, as she pressed on through the darkened corridor devoid of anything. There was lighting just up ahead most likely from the windowed ceiling.

As she made her way deeper into the mall, it curved into the main courtyard. She stopped and analyzed the area closely. In the middle of the large open space was a fountain/wishing well. She could hear the relaxing flow of water. She stepped closer looking up to the skylight. She was as far as she could go without being picked off from the upper levels. She eyeballed the area.

"Son of a bitch, where are they?" And just as she was about to walk forward her question was answered. Omar came out of nowhere, on her right. Had it not been for the light above reflecting off his blade coming for her throat she'd have been dead. Priscilla's eyes widened as she clumsily stumbled back out of the way.

The blade was so close she felt the air it cut. Before she could even recover, she was kicked in her ribs. She stumbled back again. Trish joined the fray.

"Hey cunt! Time to pay!" Trish kicked her in the solar plexus. Priscilla hit the floor, dropping her gun in the process. In as much pain as she was in, she sprung to her feet, turned and squared off. The duo gave her no time to amount an offensive. Omar was already coming for her, spinning a knife in the palm of his hand. He cut the air in rapid succession.

Priscilla was bobbing and weaving, trying to get in closer. But Trish kept up her attack, trying to distract her so her brother could get the killing blow. These two could have easily killed Priscilla, they had guns. But they needed to do it this way. To not only prove to her, she wasn't shit, but to themselves. Here was a woman that made fools of them not only once but twice. No one had ever done that and lived long enough to gloat about it. She needed to be taught a lesson, the bitch needed to know before she died who her betters were.

Omar was a master knife fighter, his movements were graceful and unwasted. To win this, she needed to take him out first. Trish was the easier of the two. She was tough, but had no real skill, she was just raw power and rage unchecked. Omar came in for a slash; he was so fast he almost cut her shirt. Priscilla dodged and spun, the momentum took him forward and out of her way for precious seconds as Priscilla met Trish head on with a solid right to her jaw, she was stunned and stumbled back. Using that, Priscilla stepped on her foot and shoved her; Trish went flying onto the tiled floor.

With Trish out of the picture for now, she spun around and not a moment too soon. A slash aimed for her throat came within a hair's breath, she ducked under another strike. Omar was getting frustrated; Priscilla used that to her advantage. She batted away another slash and countered with a punch to the jaw, he dropped the knife but quickly recovered, backhanding her. She grabbed him by his shirt before he got out of reach and head-butted him square on the bridge of his nose, breaking it.

She tripped him off his feet and stood over him. He was dazed with blood pouring from his nostrils onto his designer suit. She raised her foot and crushed his skull into the tiled floor.

"NO!" Trish screamed, seeing her brother die before her eyes. That's what Priscilla wanted; Trish unhinged. Trish reached behind her back for a gun. By the time she cleared it, Priscilla darted forward and weaved just in case Trish managed to get off a shot.

Priscilla rocked her with a hard right and left that sent her reeling. Trish dropped the gun, and before she could even defend herself Priscilla was on her giving Trish no room to breathe. Victory was within reach, Priscilla felt it, and saw it, as she put an end to this.

Trish threw a wild punch that Priscilla easily sidestepped. She kicked her knee out from under her breaking it. The sound of bone and sinew cracking echoed throughout, just before Trish fell Priscilla placed her in a tight, behind the back chokehold. To her credit Trish put up a fight, but she only helped in her own demise as she lost air and consciousness. Priscilla ended it breaking her neck, and shoved the corpse of the devil to the floor. Coming down from her adrenaline rush, she hunched over and leaned her palms on her knees.

Priscilla was breathing heavily, but there was never rest for the weary. The screams of the hostages caught her ears. Not giving either of the dead bodies a glance she turned and jogged away.

"Here! Over here! Help us!" Voices rang out as she approached hands poking out of the gates. Priscilla ran towards them and found them all huddled in a clothing store. She let out a sigh of relief.

"Everyone! I need you to be quiet!" She clapped her hands getting their attention. "I need you all to understand, I'm going to release you, and then you are going out the main entrance does everyone understand! Come on people nod, do you understand!" They did. Once released they all did as instructed and walked calmly out. Priscilla followed behind them, and once they were out the door. She leaned against the wall, bracing her head against it. She needed this, just a moment alone. Because this wasn't done yet. There was a man out there, an invisible man. And she had to find him and stop him, at any cost. She pushed off the wall and made for the exit, there was no time to waste.

Chapter 30
And now on to the next

Priscilla finally arrived in Washington, D.C. She drove past the White House going five blocks down, then came back around and parked down a side street. She grabbed a light coat from the backseat. She was about to get out when she glanced at herself in the rearview mirror. She looked terrible, how she was going to explain this to the kids was beyond her, she thought.

She chuckled under her breath, as she got out of the car and started to walk. When it came to explaining stuff to her children that she couldn't hide, she sometimes felt like the child, and they the adults. It wasn't just her; every parent feels the same way with certain things regarding their mentally overdeveloped kids.

After making a fast detour, Priscilla waited at the corner to cross. As soon as she had the right of way, she walked to the other side of the street, heading back to the White House. As she walked, Priscilla looked for anything unusual, extra shadows was the first thing that came to mind. Without infrared, how else would you spot an invisible man?

She crossed the street; on the next block at the corner there was a bus stop. She walked towards the bench and sat down. A man was sitting there wearing a baseball cap, sunglasses and a light windbreaker. He was fishing in his jacket for something. Seeing the movement, Priscilla placed her hand over her gun. The man found what he was looking for; it was a pack of cigarettes.

"Excuse me, miss?" He asked, turning to her.

"Yes?"

"You wouldn't happen to have a match, would you?" The man said, with a smile. His facial features were indistinguishable.

"Yeah, I think I do." She dug in her pocket and grabbed a lighter. "How about a trade, a light for a smoke?" He handed her the pack of cigarettes, as she handed him the lighter. Once the stranger lit his cigarette, he handed her back the lighter. Even though Priscilla wasn't a smoker, she had to admit though, inhaling that lethal smoke felt really good. She let it out slowly, it soothed her a bit.

"Don't worry, no one is around. We can talk openly," the man said to her, but not looking at her. Priscilla was skeptical about that, knowing an invisible man could be sitting right in between them.

"Oh yeah? How do you know?"

"Just within the gate is a Secret Service agent, watching through infrared goggles. I'm connected with him via Bluetooth. Then just on your right in the newspaper stand is another Watchman. He's wearing sunglasses which are infrared capable. You will receive a pair as well once we conclude this meeting, for if anything, your peace of mind." She lowered her head.

"Peace of mind…" She repeated finding humor in that. As Lens told her this he never looked or gestured in any of the directions. "And last but not least, there's a sniper just above us." Priscilla didn't try to look for any of this. She just nodded, as she admired the man next to her. Lens was thorough she had to say that.

Lens was part of a special unit within Shadow Ops called Watchmen. It was a very small unit, of highly intelligent agents that specialized in deep long term cover. The average Watchmen knew almost every language and culture, and if they didn't know, they learned it. Their only job was surveillance, nothing more. Watchmen would only act if absolutely necessary. They were also the masters of disguise. Their identities were so secret, only Derlin knew.

"So, what's the status?"

"Nothing, I've sat out here all day. In four different disguises and not a damn thing. I don't think your boy is going to show." She thought about that, maybe he was right. She had to admit this was a long shot. She really didn't have hard facts about what they really had planned. She was going on what she saw. Priscilla leaned forward, taking a drag of the cigarette.

"Yeah…I know." She admitted dejectedly. "But it was all I got. We have to assume he was here already, I mean, how else did he get the President's DNA? This whole goddamn mission is fucked." She ran fingers through her hair. It was obvious she was in a very stressed mental state. Her body language said that. Aside from the way she looked, which was like shit. And that business with Trish and Omar just now didn't help matters either. "Priscilla listen..." Lens called her by her first name. That was a sign he was more worried about her than he let on.

He had to handle this carefully. Not that he thought she would behave like this. But anyone with PTSD could act out in any type of way. "Maybe you should go in. Take a long drive back to New York yeah? No one will look at you in any way." The spy sat back on the bench and looked straight ahead. "I'll admit to you, Derlin is for a lack of a better word skeptical. And who could blame him. I on the other hand, will believe in anything until shown otherwise. I have two more men inside; they have been briefed on the situation.

The President has been on lock down. Confined to the Oval Office. There are Secret Service, with infrared sunglasses stationed in four points. The place is covered. Now please, if not for yourself, then for your children. Go home." Priscilla took a deep breath. She hadn't felt this way before, but now at the end, she was beyond exhausted. She was shaken, and her mind just couldn't focus. She knew Lens was right.

Maybe she needed to pack this in. Maybe her mad dash here was nothing more than the traumatic stress she was given. Even now, sitting here and having a moment to really think about it. Lens may be right. At least one good thing came from this; she'd be given a pair of those infrared glasses. She wouldn't feel as defenseless. As far as going home, she wasn't going to do that. She'd wait that one out a few days. She'd go back to Long Island, rent a hotel for a week and see. Pretend to have a false sense of security. Put herself out there and hope that this 'Invisible' man was looking for her, make herself easy to find and put an end to him. Priscilla finally nodded.

"Okay…you're right." Lens shook his head.

"It's not about who's right, it's about common sense. You've been stretched to your limits. Let me take it from here, and if or when something should go down it will be handled. Trust me, I've dealt with far worse things than Invisible men." Priscilla chuckled, giving him an amused look. She wanted to blurt out who are you? But then decided not to.

He wouldn't tell her anyway. But knowing what little she did about him, she had to believe him. There were plenty of rumors about Lens, and usually rumors were a form of the truth. Priscilla then got up and glanced around. It was going to be a nice day. The drive back should be nice.

"Do you have another cigarette?" Lens nodded, reaching into his pocket for the pack. She took two, one for now and one for later. "Thanks." She lit it, taking in a deep drag.

"Just go buy a newspaper, and then walk right back to your car. You'll be watched the entire time." Priscilla smiled, nodding and walked away.

Lens watched her satisfied. He liked Priscilla and most of all respected her. The last thing he wanted was to forcefully send her home. He breathed a sigh of relief and then took out his cell phone. He placed an earpiece into his ear and dialed Derlin. Just as his boss answered Lens finally got up and walked along the south side of the White House.

"She's inbound. Will she report in right away? Doubtful. She's still worried; she'll probably play it safe for a few days. Go to a hotel or something." Derlin nodded as he took this in. Once Priscilla did come back he'd put her on a leave of absence just so she could collect herself.

"Very good Lens. Now that you've seen her, do you believe her? About this so called Invisible man?"

"Hard to say. She was tortured, and drugged. Anything is possible. She certainly believes it. The world is changing John. How can we not? With what you and I know? Roswell? Area 51?" Derlin nodded, he understood well enough. And it wasn't that he didn't believe Priscilla it was just she was put under high duress. They'll just have to wait until she has a few weeks to gather herself.

"Thanks. Keep me posted on your end." And the call ended. Derlin was in his office, with a packed pipe, he leaned in his chair staring at the muted TV.

The media were still covering the mall incident. Derlin should be relieved, but in truth he wasn't, he just couldn't shake the feelings he was having. This was far from over. They had nothing, aside from a burned out complex and Hospital staff that knew of nothing of what was going on under their noses. He knew people lied. There were hidden threats and money exchanged to keep people that knew quiet. Would it ever come to light? It was hard to know, but they would sure as hell keep trying to pry the truth and kick down the doors to these nests of rats hiding from the light of Justice. He sighed again, lighting his pipe and taking a deep pull. It may be frustrating now, but Justice always prevails.

Chapter 31
Happy Trails

Priscilla did exactly as Lens instructed. She walked over to said newspaper stand, and bought a paper. The man, in the cap and sunglasses, handed her the folded newspaper of her choice and then went on to the next customer. She then hurried off, making sure the infrared glasses were inside. She could feel the bulge. Even with being watched as she made her way back to the car, Priscilla couldn't shake off the fact that she was so exposed. She couldn't wait to get back in the confines of her car, and get the hell outta here. She was no fool; she knew exactly what was going on here. Derlin thinks she's losing it. The way Lens was behaving, he was analyzing her. More than likely he was already on the phone with Derlin.

She sighed, just great, she thought. Everyone thought she was nuts. More than likely once she did report in and debrief, she'd be sent to be evaluated. She bit her lower lip, as she crossed over, not even waiting for the light.

Once she saw the Charger she jogged to it, casting her eyes all around. She slammed her hand on the window. The all to slow green line analyzed her hand and finally unlocked the doors. She tossed her rolled up newspaper on the seat and slammed the door shut locking herself in. She allowed herself to relax taking her gun and putting it in the middle console for easy reach. The starting of the engine was the best thing she could hear now as she threw it in gear and slowly eased out onto the main road.

Her windows were fogged up; she hadn't realized it until she got in the car. The extreme tint of the windows made it hard to notice from the outside. Once she wiped her side clear she peeled out and made for the expressway.

Once on the wide-open expressway, she put the pedal to the metal. Wanting to put as much distance as she could between herself and this fucked mission. The only good out of it was she met some nice people, it was a shame she couldn't reach out to them. Life will take over and they'd soon forget about her.

She sighed again, pressing the pedal harder. The sun was bright today. Even with the visor, the sun was hurting her eyes. It usually doesn't, but her eyes have been kinda sensitive the last day from lack of sleep. With nothing else to use aside from the infrared glasses she reached over and grabbed them. She was familiar with these.

There was a button on the right arm that activated and deactivated the infrared option. She flipped the arms up and slipped them on, and happened to glance in the rearview mirror, as she was about to turn off the infrared when her eyes widened in horror. She was in such a state she jerked the car to the left and nearly sideswiped the car passing her.

She had all to do, not to gasp and scream. It was him! Sitting in the back to her right. Her entire body broke out into a sweat just then, her throat was closing. Her hands grew clammy and sweaty. There was a part of her that wanted to cry like a little girl hiding under the bed from the monster of her imagination. But this was no trick of her mind, this was real. The nameless man, who was invisible, was sitting in her back seat. How? Was beyond her.

That either would be answered later or never. The priority was, he was here. And as scared as she was, she had to take him out. With the infrared you couldn't see clear facial features, on the heat signature of the person. So she hoped she didn't alert him to her knowing he was here. Hopefully he just thought she was being careless.

Priscilla kept her eyes straight on the road, gripping the steering wheel at 10 and 2. Her knuckles were tight; she didn't have to see them. She felt them. With only her eyes, she looked down and spotted her gun just inches from her. If she could grab it, all it would take is one clean shot. He wouldn't expect her to be going for that. She licked her lower lip; the anticipation was growing in the pit of her stomach. But the question was how to move her hand closer to the gun without raising his suspicions. She had it, the cigarette. She took it from behind her ear, and then cracked her window open.

The cigarette lighter was mere centimeters from the gun. She pressed the knob in; waiting for it to pop out, it took forever. Once it did, she reached for it and then with the reflexes of a pro, she grabbed the gun and managed to point it. But he proved to be even faster, he snarled and grabbed it from her hand breaking her wrist in the process. Priscilla screamed out, as the car swerved, people beeped at her giving her the finger.

Claude then smacked her glasses to the floor. With her left hand now, she held the car steady. She was hunched over in pain.

"Son of a bitch!" She spat, glancing at the empty space. He laughed at her.

"Thought you were safe didn't you?" The feral yet intelligent English voice said. "That is but a small taste of what is to come. You ruined everything for me. I was promised…to become whole again and now nothing. But I may yet get what I want. Through you." Priscilla's wrist was hurting, her arm was going stiff. And of course, it had to be her right hand too.

"I'll get what I want. Once I show 'Him' what I've done."

"Fuck off scumbag!" He laughed at her.

"We'll see how well your mouth works when I break it and then before I kill you, I want you to know I shall take everything you hold dear. Your kids, if you have any, and then only after you watch me strangle them before your very eyes, I shall do the same to you. And you will be powerless to stop me. It's the reward I owe myself for the restraint.

I had to suffer with the indignity of riding with those savages until you destroyed their van. Then I had to steal a car. Once I finally managed to catch up to you at the mall. I could have killed you anytime I wished. I watched you fight 'them', watched you release the hostages and all the while the urge to kill you was intense. But no…it wasn't time. When you took your little breather, I snuck off to your precious car and waited for you, using this."

Floating in the air was her car key. She wasn't surprised. "Tracking you was easy enough with the tracker we placed on your car. And the German thought I was beyond mad Ha! Once I have my way with you, I shall deal with him as well." There was silence, for the moment. Priscilla turned cold; her heart was beating a mile a minute. She thought it was going to burst.

"And now…you shall drive." She heard him sit back. Priscilla was beyond scared right now, but even scared she wasn't going to allow this crazy bastard near her kids. He was really crazy if he thought she was gonna drive him the entire way home. There was no chance in hell. This was it, she thought, her life was going to come to an end. She was prepared for it. The main thing was her kids. They would be well taken care of. There would be enough insurance money and people to care for them.

She took a deep breath; the only question was how to do it. He had her dead to rights. Her wrist was broken, and she couldn't see him. Priscilla sat up a bit straighter, trying to block out the pain. She was in the middle lane, and then just as hopelessness was about to engulf her, she saw her window.

They were coming up on a bridge, which crossed over D.C River. Priscilla had never heard of it and didn't care. All she saw was, an opportunity to take him out. And to make it even better, he wasn't wearing his seatbelt. But she was. She kept glancing at the back; it was a natural thing to do when someone was sitting behind you. Only thing was she didn't see anyone.

They hit the bridge, and she increased her speed. Her knuckles were tight. She was mentally ready. She said a silent prayer, for not only her kids and friends. But for herself. She has a lot of sins on her soul. Once they were in the center of the bridge Priscilla turned hard to the right, sideswiping a car right out of the way. That caused a chain reaction of other cars slamming into each other.

Claude growled as he thrust forward and attacked Priscilla. The Charger spun three times in the middle of the bridge, smashing into other cars. She could feel the invisible hands around her throat. Already the breath was being taken from her. She struggled as best she could with one good hand. She choked out a scream when her broken wrist hit the middle console.

They struggled as the car slowly came to a stop right in the middle of the bridge. Priscilla with her free hand tried to rake his eyes out. If she was going to die she'd leave him something to remember her by. Her helpless right hand slammed into the middle console again, she screamed out, lurching up and as she did so her elbow smashed into the self-destruct button. She had twenty seconds, just as she slammed into the door it was thrown open by a driver.

If he had not grabbed her, she'd have smashed her head on the pavement. Claude was in such a rage, he growled like a beast clawing for her.

"NO!" He yelled not only scaring her, but the man standing over her, not sure if he even heard what he did. She kicked the door closed on his invisible arm. The cry of pain was unlike anything anyone heard. By now there was a crowd. She was helped to her feet.

"Fucking move! Hurry!" She yelled as she ran, looking back the car exploded. Some unfortunate drivers were close enough to be propelled back and some even had their clothes on fire. While others ran away, putting their hands to their faces to protect them from the heat and flames. Priscilla stood there, watching and waiting, for that door to fly open but it never did. She knew he was in there, finally dead, in hell where he deserved to be. With it finally over, she fell to her knees, cradling her broken wrist and cried under the blue sky and the smell of burning flesh.

Epilogue
Sidelined

Two days later.

"So now do you believe me? Still think I'm crazy?" Her tone towards Derlin, wasn't something she was doing on purpose, but it was justified and couldn't be helped. Derlin sat behind his desk, smoking his pipe. He finally took one last puff and then faced her. He held her gaze and then finally nodded.

"Yes…and It's not that I didn't believe you before. It was just under the circumstances that was all." Priscilla just held his gaze. She was satisfied enough that her credibility was restored. With the recovered body, and the eyewitness accounts, it was obvious someone was in the car with her.

Unfortunately, the body of her would be killer was burned beyond recognition. Not even dental records were helpful. Another dead end, in this tangled web involving this faceless manipulator.

Priscilla sighed, at least this was over. And now, she could finally go home. She hadn't gone home yet. Once she was picked up, she came right to HQ. Her wrist was set and placed in a cast, her wounds cleaned and covered. She looked like a train wreck. Her main reason, she stayed at HQ, was because she didn't need to hear it from the kids. How many times can she tell them she was in a car accident, even though it wasn't far from the truth.

"If that'll be all, sir, I'd like to take my leave." Derlin nodded.

"Yes of course. But one more thing before you go." She was starting to get up, but stayed put waiting for what he was going to say. He sighed, giving her a sympathetic look.

"Effective immediately, you're confined to clerical duty-"

"What!?" Derlin gave her that stern look, and she stopped and allowed him to finish.

"This is in no way a demotion. Once I feel you're ready for fieldwork again, even after your wrist is mended, I'll reactivate you. This is not a debate, and this is my final decision. So, before you open your mouth, think before you speak. Now go."

He gave her the floor. But all she did was just stare at him not believing it. She didn't care what he said; in her eyes it was a demotion, no matter how he sugarcoated it. She just sighed and nodded. Once he had made up his mind, there was no changing it. Priscilla then got up, not hiding the disdain she has for this entire debacle.

"Will that be all, sir?" If she hadn't respected John as much as she did, she'd have cursed his ass out.

"No. And Priscilla? Take a week off. Catch up, relax, okay?" She just stood there and looked at him. She had nothing to say, she just wanted to put this behind her and go home.

"Thanks." And without a word more she left. She ignored everyone she passed, even the ones that said hi and especially the ones that stared. She was so deep in thought right now. Being marked on the inactive list may have stung. But that was the least of her problems.

This matter was far from over. She knew that for sure, she felt it in her gut. And knew for a fact that this was the start of something much bigger to come. She sighed, and kept walking, all she could do was be ready for it.

Vol. 4 Revelations

Chapter 1
Justice is served

New York City, NY

The windowless secured room located in the federal courthouse was hot and musty; perhaps it was due to the fact that seven people were in close confines talking. The six sitting closely together looked like they didn't shower in a month and smelled like it too. As they watched intently, the woman sitting across from them. She was going over their defense. The red headed woman tried her best to keep herself composed because the stench was that bad. The men across from her were going to be her possible clients; something that didn't bode well with her, she was just doing her job. She was a public defender. These so-called men were the only ones charged in the September 11th attacks.

For years they sat in cells, while the "powers that be" bickered on the best way to dispense justice for their heinous act. The Attorney General and a few other politicians, decided they should be tried in a US court and in New York City of all places. What were they thinking? She'll never know. In her honest opinion, they deserved nothing but a trial by a firing squad. Unfortunately, it was not her place to question, but to do what she was told. As she read off the documents, she blindly reached into her bag and retrieved a can of Diet Coke. She opened it and took a sip. It felt refreshing going down her dry throat.

"Now, gentlemen, as stated, I will represent you, but I will not have this trial become a platform for you to spew your rhetoric," she said, placing the legal documents back into her folder then closing it. The man in the middle who was known as the mastermind of the 9-11 attacks spoke up.

"We do not care what you think or have to say woman, you are to do as you are told. We tell you what we want, not the other way around." He said, pointing a stern finger at her. Her face flushed, she felt enraged that he talked to her like that. They weren't back in their countries where women had no rights. And since they felt that way, she couldn't ethically defend them just on that way of thinking alone, let alone for the crimes they committed. Leaning back, she took a rather large gulp of soda, and then leaned forward.

"I'm very sorry you feel that way, and I've come to my decision, I will not represent you. I mean, come on, you've admitted to causing over 3,000 deaths-" One man on the right who she couldn't pronounce his name, slammed his fist down so hard the table shook. The move neither startled or scared her. She stopped talking, taking yet another gulp of her soda. As she twirled the last of the fluid around in the can, they spoke in Arabic. The leader raised his hand quieting them, and then he sternly looked at the woman.

"Then Miss, we have nothing further to discuss, please." He said gesturing to the door. She nodded, finishing the last of her soda. She stood shouldering her leather bag, and tossed the empty soda can into the trash. She didn't look back at the six pairs of eyes, no doubt cutting through her flesh. She knocked three times, as per instructions on the reinforced steel door. The pair of US Marshals on the other side opened up and allowed her to walk out.

"Everything ok ma'am?" The brown eyed young U.S. Marshal asked her. Both Marshals were dressed in civilian clothes but were wearing a green tactical vest and heavily armed with a carbine and sidearm. He sounded like he was from the south. She nodded, never looking directly into their faces.

"Yes, pretty much a dead issue. Enjoy them, they're great company!" She said, dripping with sarcasm with a wide eyed look, that indicated she couldn't wait to leave them.

"Very good, ma'am." The Marshal smiled a little bit, and then gestured down the hall. "You know the way back?"

"Oh yes I do and thank you boys." Both Marshals nodded at her as she made her way. She didn't even get five feet when she turned on her heel, and threw two small plastic darts that found their way into their necks.

The men fell instantly from the tranquilizer injected from the projectiles. Moving quickly, the red-haired woman grabbed the first Marshal and pulled him around the corner by his ankles.

Opening a janitor closet, she stuffed him in, then the second. It wasn't easy, by the time she was done, she was breathing heavily. Before she shut the door, she used a screwdriver, she found on the cleaning cart and took off the doorknob on the inside. There were only two screws to take out, so it was done quickly. She then quietly shut the door. As she made her way back around the corner, she reached into her pocket, pulling out a pack of gum. By the time she made it back to the room that held the terrorists, she had it unwrapped. Spitting on it, it softened enough where she stuck it into the keyhole on the door. The saliva activated an acid that melted the lock and the insides, making it literally impossible to open.

Wasting not a second more, she walked very briskly as if late for a meeting. She touched her forehead, feeling for sweat, it was lightly covered. The heat in the basement was brutal. She checked her watch, three minutes left..... She picked up the pace; and bypassed the elevator and the two military guards. At this point she didn't care about what they suspected.

As she made her way to the stairwell door and opened it, both guards watched her. In the reflection of the glass on the door, she saw one of the guards leave, walking the way she just came.

Once she was out of sight she bolted up the stairs, taking two at a time, the main floor was one flight up, not at all far. Right when she came to the door leading back to the main lobby, she took a moment to fix herself, but didn't go crazy with it either. Chances were likely she'd have to fight her way out, since one of the guards walked to where she had sealed the door.

It would only be a matter of time before the place was locked down. Opening the door slowly she walked out. Right across from the stairwell door were three police officers, they didn't pay any attention to her. Looking to her right and left, she made her way towards the main entranceway. It was ripe with activity, just as before reporters were doing live newscasts, and going over the rhetorical questions of 'what if' and 'what could.' They're gonna find out in less than a minute and a half of what 'will.' Glancing at her watch, the time was ticking; she had just under a minute now.

She could see the street, once she got out there, she'd disappear. Trying to get through the sea of reporters and other people was a challenge. There were lines of people trying to get into the courthouse, and the process of checking people through metal detectors was slow. But a little shoulder blocking moved them out of the way pretty quickly. She was so close now that being inconspicuous didn't matter anymore as she pushed more people catching the suspicious looks of a few court officers, who just thought of her as being rude. Just as she pushed the door open someone yelled out, pointing in her direction.

"The woman, the redhead!, Red hair, and black skirt! Stop her!" By the time anyone looked toward the direction he was pointing to, she was already out on the street, and the explosion that rocked the courthouse to its very core distracted them away. It was safe to say that no one was going to come after her now. Once past the doors, she picked up her pace, tearing away her skirt, beige slacks slid down her firm legs, then came off the matching jacket.

As she walked, she threw them into the garbage can, along with the red wig she wore. Blonde hair flowed in the wind, as Priscilla Roletti walked across the street, hailing a cab and quickly got in. She told the driver where to go and just like that she was gone.

As they drove off, she looked back to the building that was now swarmed by police and federal agents. The block was just starting to be cordoned off. She turned back around taking a deep breath. If only every assassination job was as easy as this one. In her opinion, it was unnecessary, the so-called 'powers that be' should have never attempted to do something like this. At least the President knew to do the right thing, unofficially of course. He also pushed to have these creeps tried, but behind the scenes he gave the direct order to John Derlin, Chief Executive of Shadow Ops to take them out before that would happen.

Hopefully the spin that's told will simmer down the news reports and the analyzing and put it to a rest. Being ever so alert, Priscilla still kept a sharp eye out for the police just in case she happened to be followed. She didn't think so, but in this game, it was always smart to think otherwise.

She didn't last this long by not being the best at what she did. Ten minutes later the cab pulled up to the corner she specified.

Before getting out, she paid the man the fare along with a hefty tip and a few choice words.

"And you never saw me got it?" The cabby nodded, knowing the deal, he was an old timer, he more than likely heard those words a few times before, she watched him speed off. She then walked the one block to the Shadow Ops HQ with her mission accomplished.

Chapter 2
Is Derlin ok?

As she walked towards HQ, she glanced at her watch. She may just make the basketball game her daughter was playing in. It was one of the last games of the season. Priscilla tried her hardest to make them when she could, but that was impossible at times. Going down an alleyway, she came to an inconspicuous part of the building. To her left was a steel drum; in her pocket was a keycard. When she slid the keycard just above the surface of the drum, the wall on the opposite side of the alley slid up.

Walking in, the secret door closed and she descended down. She was safe in the confines of the black skyscraper that to anyone was a building that housed various businesses, but in truth was the main HQ to one of the government's secret intelligence operations known as Shadow Ops, which was founded and put into effect by President Reagan.

The elevator brought her to the basement, which housed the R&D department. Once the doors slid open she walked down a darkened gray hall with minimal lighting from above and into a brightly lit work area. She passed techs that paid her hardly any mind at all. These geeks, as they were known to be called, wouldn't even stop what they were doing if a stripper came walking in.

She made her way to a vast expanse where company cars were worked on, heading to the main elevator when she was suddenly stopped by Peter Held, head of the tech department. He grabbed her arm as she walked by. She didn't even see him, he was hiding behind a Dodge Charger he was working on. Priscilla looked at the hand holding her by the arm and noticed it had grease on it, she pulled away making a face checking her sleeve for grease.

"What did I tell you about touching me, let alone with greasy hands?" She said, trying to wipe away the small smudge. Peter stood up, grabbed a rag from a worktable nearby and wiped his hands on it. It didn't make much of a difference being the rag was already covered with grease.

"Right...right, I just wanted to ask how everything went this morning." He said, throwing the rag to the side, "Besides, I was worried about you, I missed you…can I have a kiss?" He made a kissy face, as he approached her.

"Uh, no dick, if you happened to do more than watch porno's all day, maybe you'd have heard for yourself." Peter was taken aback by that comment.

"I don't watch porn all day only half the day, get it right." She chuckled. In truth, he was an alright guy, he was a harmless nut who loved getting a rise out of anyone he came across, for some reason he loved her, she didn't know why.

"Everything went well, that soda bomb was a nice trick." Peter stuck out his chest, proud of himself with a smug smile.

"Those are new." The soda bomb, as it was called, was a simple device. Inside the inconspicuous can was a flat metal top, that once magnetized to the bottom of the can, it charged and activated the explosive. It was perfect, because no one suspected anything even when it was scanned with a metal detector at the courthouse. She chuckled at his cockiness, which he was never at a loss for.

"Since you're so interested in your handy work, why didn't you watch it on TV?" She said as she turned and walked to her intended destination.

"Well, I'm very busy down here you know." He said, trying to keep too her pace, as they made their way through another gray painted hallway. She didn't have all day to chit chat with him.

She continued on and he followed her all the way to the elevator. Fortunately, she didn't have to wait long for one. Just as she walked in and pressed her desired floor, Peter hit the call button and stopped the door from closing. Priscilla was just about ready to threaten him.

"Before you go babe, I gotta ask, you still with the whop?" She felt her face flush. She was surprised he hadn't brought this up sooner. Priscilla against her better judgment decided to go with her feelings and see Pietro on a regular basis. Even though he had a checkered past, he was a wonderful human being. He just kind of got caught up in things. She could relate to that, it happened to her. She crossed her arms over her chest, cocking her eyebrow.

"Yeah, I am as a matter of fact, is that a problem?" Peter hit the call button again when the doors tried to close.

"Well, people have been talking, that's all. I made a wager with someone that you'd still be with the gangster…oh wait, reformed and retired gangster, right?" He said, doing quotation gestures with his fingers. That was another thing, she didn't know how, but since dating Pietro she had become a hot topic. It did not bode well with her in the least.

But what was she gonna do about it? She couldn't stop people from talking. She came to the conclusion that if they needed to waste their time talking about her, then she felt sorry for them that their lives were so meaningless. Priscilla looked past Peter, and waved.

"Hey Ben!" Ben was a Shadow Op's computer expert. Peter turned around and looked, finding no one there; with that opportunity the elevator doors finally closed. She could hear the muffled curses and banging as she made her way to the top floor. In less than a minute she was there, and as always the place was ripe with activity. White collared workers went about their various tasks, as she walked down the carpeted walkway. One was not paying attention and almost rammed into her, he was on his phone.

He said sorry, and moved on never taking his eyes off the phone. Priscilla shook her head and moved on stopping just short of John Derlin's office, Jenny his Secretary looked up, when Priscilla approached.

"Hey Priscilla! I'm glad to see your okay!" Jenny leaned in closer, her smile fading as she glanced around before talking making sure no one was around.

"Did you hear? Another Op died this morning, that's five now in the last month." Priscilla looked right at her, trying to keep her face neutral, but it was hard. Jenny knew her all too well and her eyes gave her away, shock and dismay were apparent.

"Damn, what the hell is going on out there?" Jenny nodded with a somber look. In the last few months, Op deaths, nearly doubled. Yes, it was part of the job and there was always the possibility you were not coming back, but it was like agents were being picked off left and right. It was something that put a lot of people on edge, wondering who'd be next.

"Who was it?"

"Mosses... heard they found him executed, shot right in the face. Can't even do an open casket Priscilla. It's fucking crazy out there. It's like whoever is doing this, they are sending a message you know?" Priscilla nodded. They were sending messages. No one was untouchable. "You better be careful...we all have to start watching our backs now."

"You always gotta watch your back, Jenny. You carrying?" She nodded.

"Yeah, since last week. I'm afraid for my kids." Priscilla placed a hand on her shoulder to try and comfort her. Jenny was a noncombatant. She was a pencil pusher who had limited access to Top Secret information and wasn't a threat.

"These are pros, Jenny. They aren't looking for you." She nodded, clearly not convinced. And neither was Priscilla, thinking about it. "But regardless, be careful."

"Yeah, you too." Jenny's eyes filled with tears, but to her credit, she held back from crying. "I gotta go to the ladies room, Priscilla I'll talk to you." And she was off, never looking back.

Priscilla stood there for a little while longer, and then looked at the closed door leading into John's office. Yet another problem that's been brewing for a while and ready to pop. With the recent Agent murders happening, Derlin was not himself either. He'd been distant with not only colleagues, but with Priscilla as well.

Also not helping was his personal life. It was in disarray. His wife, finally followed through with the threat of divorcing him. She was hammering him with alimony. Plus, she took the kids away from him, citing he's an absentee father. Even with all the clout John had in the government it didn't help with family court it seemed. And now she had to go see him before heading home. She sighed, not in the mood for that. Nowadays you didn't know which Derlin you'd get. He could be depressed, snippy, short or just plain monotone. And being a friend for so long Priscilla wanted to help but every time she built up the courage to say something it was zapped from her by something he said or how his behavior was at the time. She set her jaw nibbling at her lower lip. Maybe this time....with the internal debating and over analyzing put to rest she made for the door dreading it with each step.

She knocked twice before Derlin said ‘enter’. She walked in, closing the door gently, behind her and then sat in one of the two chairs. John was in the middle of signing off on some paperwork. He finished up, giving her his undivided attention. He leaned back, in his chair.

“Well, it’s safe to say everything went well from what I’ve seen.” He gestured at the flat screen on the wall it was on but muted. It was of the scene at the Courthouse. “Very good Priscilla.” She nodded.

“Thank you, John.” In the past, sitting in Derlin’s office was a comfort zone of sorts. Now every time she came in, she felt uneasy, like right now. Priscilla knew Derlin better than anyone, and during the last few months the changes he’s gone through were the more obvious. Even the way he looked at her sometimes, made her feel uneasy. It was as though he felt great disdain for her in some way, but again, when under the pressure he was, you saw a different side to someone. It was just bad timing that she was the unfortunate one that was in the cross-hairs of his bad moods. She tried to push those thoughts from her mind.

As she was searching for something to break the uneasy silence, she noticed John was wearing his wedding ring. She could have sworn he had taken it off some time ago. Following Priscilla’s gaze, he looked down, rubbing the gold band, he looked back to her with a thin smile.

“Old habits die hard I’m afraid.” She smiled, nodding.

“Yeah, I get it...how are you doing with that?” The look John gave her after she said that, Priscilla immediately regretted asking him, she felt her face flushing.

“I’ve been better Agent Roletti, now if you’ll excuse me. We’ve both taken up enough of each other’s time. I trust you’ll file your report and have it emailed to me first thing in the morning?” Her face flushed and she knew it was visibly obvious. She cleared her throat.

“Yes, John...first thing.” He nodded.

“Good.” And that was it. There was nothing else to say, and she left feeling foolish, angry and hurt.

Chapter 3
Basketball night

Once that uncomfortable situation was behind her, she was homeward bound. She was racing the clock as usual, she had just enough time to get home shower and change and just make it before tip off with a few minutes to spare. Now all she had to do was find parking. The school was packed with cars for the game. If she didn't make it at least Pietro was there with her son and his kids Anthony and Isabella to cheer her on until she got there.

It was a slow process, but they were one big happy family. As Peter mocked before, Pietro did give up the life he led. He had sold the clubs and invested the money in some stocks and was partners in a commercial cleaning business. For the last year and a half she was actually happy being with him.

The more she got to know him, the more she fell in love with the man. He was great with her kids, very kind and caring. They took to him rather fast, which was something of a surprise, but a good one. She had heard about horror stories with kids not liking the boyfriend/girlfriend and she dreaded that.

Thankfully, it was an issue that never came up with both sides. When it was time for her to meet his kids, she was a nervous wreck. She kept her fingers crossed that not only would his kids like her, but everyone would get along. If they didn't, that would put a real damper on everything. And if that did happen, then no way was she going to continue something in a situation like that. But thankfully her kids took to him fast, he stepped up as she knew he would and his kids got along great with hers. His kids took a little time to get used to their daddy's new girlfriend.

Which of course was understandable, and as time passed Priscilla grew on them, unlike her kids who didn't know their father. Pietro's kids knew their mother and probably felt guilty to embrace someone else in the role that should still be hers. She respected that.

With game time almost on, she found a spot further away than she liked, parked and ran in.

Being the last game of the season the gym was packed she had to squeeze in. There were so many people, she looked to the court, spotting her daughter Patricia walking out onto it. Priscilla waved hoping she'd see her, she did, her daughter's face lit up seeing her mom.

It warmed Priscilla's heart that she could make such a big impact with something that was in her eyes so small, coming to a game. She was so proud of her little girl, an honor student, now on her way to the playoffs, she never pushed Patricia to play any sports. She came to her asking if she could try out for the girls' basketball team. Priscilla had no problem with that at all, but made it very clear that her studies came first. She tried to hammer that home with both kids.

Priscilla turned away, looking to the bleachers, it took her a minute, but she found Pietro, her son Jonathon and Pietro's two kids. They spotted each other at the same time; Pietro had a seat saved for her. Even after all this time of being together, he still gave her butterflies when he smiled at her. Climbing the bleachers as quickly as she could, she sat down, kissing his kids hello, her son hugged her tightly. She then looked to Pietro and kissed him, realizing how much she missed him for the short time she was away from him. Even though it wasn't new it was something she still couldn't believe had happened, she found love. This cold blooded killer was a happy woman, with a family. She never thought this day would come, and with each day she spent with them, she was most grateful, perhaps someone up there felt it was time to give her a break. She finally took her eyes off him to watch the game that just started.

It was a total blow out, in favor of Patricia's team. The opposing team's coaches face got so red she thought he was gonna explode. She found it quite amusing. The hot as dragon's breath gym was starting to clear out slowly. Priscilla touched her forehead, which was laced with sweat. She felt so disgusting, as though she didn't shower in more than a day. They waited for Patricia near the girl's locker room. Thank goodness she didn't take forever to change. She came out pretty quick, and ran to her mother. It felt so good to hug her tight.

"Great job honey! You scored a lot of points." Priscilla said, beaming, Patricia blushed.

"Yeah, great job kid." Pietro said coming up from the side, kissing her on the cheek.

"How about we go grab a bite and celebrate?" They didn't need to be asked twice. They drove back to Howard Beach, Queens, going to an Italian restaurant called "The Villa," a place where they frequently ate. If anyone else tried to get in, looking the way they did, which was very casual, they would be turned away, but with Pietro leading them, the owner would come out and seat them himself.

The first few times coming here embarrassed Priscilla, the kids loved the attention. But she didn't like to be treated like she was any better than anyone else, but with everything else, she got used to it rather quickly. They always sat at the same table towards the back of the large restaurant; it was as though they never used it for anyone else but them. After the hearty meal they went to Pietro's house.

Nowadays she split her time between her house and his. When she first came here she was floored, he called it a house, but if you asked her it was a mansion. Once things started to get serious Pietro set up her kids with rooms of their own, decked out with all they could ever ask for, video games, DVD's, you name it. When she wasn't around, he had taken her kids on a shopping spree telling them "Anything you want for your rooms, get it."

At first, she wasn't pleased with this. The last thing she wanted was for her kids to be spoiled brats even though she had a good amount of money saved on her own and could buy her kids anything they wanted. She held back just for that reason alone. But in the long run, as long as her kids appreciated it and were thankful and they were happy, then that was all she could ask for. Once back at the house the kids scattered about showering and unwinding. The kids were older now, they didn't need to be tucked in bed anymore. That was something she missed. She loved tucking her kids into bed, maybe reading them a quick story, now it was a quick kiss and a hug good night, time flew by too damn fast she thought. But at least she had the memories to hang on to.

Chapter 4
Loving life

Lying in Pietro's arms after making love was intoxicating, staring at the white ceiling in his massive bedroom, the lights were dimmed. She had a hard time keeping her eyes open as he gently stroked her hair. The silence was great. She wished every day could end like this.

"So how was work?" He asked, breaking that long cherished silence, that woke her up a bit, she moved out from under his arm and propped her head on her hand.

"Work was work. I was mostly fielding calls. Boring shit." He nodded, she never got into her job. It just wasn't something she wanted to talk about. It was a different world. He couldn't relate to that. And besides, when home, work was the last thing she wanted to think about let alone talk about especially with everything going on there now.

"You heard about that shit downtown?" He was referring to the courthouse bombing. She nodded.

"Yeah, crazy. I heard some people at the office talking about it. There's supposedly evidence, linking it to the far-right movement." It was very easy for her to lie, and even easier to lie about her job. It wasn't something you just told. 'Yeah, that was me, I blew the hell outta that place'.

So, this part of the relationship was hard at times. She had to walk a thin line between truth and lies. Even though it wasn't something she enjoyed doing, it was necessary. Because a few times Pietro would hint at her possibly calling it quits. And yes, that notion had come up in her own mind. But she just wasn't ready for that yet. And besides, if they kept her in the office like they have been, then why retire?

Ever since the Pennsylvania incident John had kept her close to home doing actual office work. She was only assigned the assassination job because she was the only readily available Op. It was her first field assignment in a year and a half.

"Far right nuts..." Pietro repeated, shaking his head, reaching to his side, grabbing the cigarettes and ashtray. He placed one in his mouth and offered her one which she took. He lit it for her and handed it off.

"Thanks. The far right have been very active." She took a drag, blowing out the smoke as she continued. "It was only a matter of time before they did something like this." He nodded flicking an ash in the ashtray in between them.

"And you? How was your day, sir?" He shrugged his shoulders.

"Just as boring as yours. Took the kids to school, then had to visit a few perspective clients for the cleaning business. A doctor, hairdresser and another doctor. Shit is really booming too. I'm gonna have to hire another guy."

"That's awesome babe." She took a long drag and finally snuffed out the cigarette. She had, had enough of that. "Now how about we make our night a little more interesting?" She winked at him, and he didn't need further prodding than that. He hastily took a drag and snuffed out his butt, killing the light.

Chapter 5
Great Adventure

Saturday came and it was supposed to be gorgeous, so they planned a trip to Great Adventure. It was a great move, it was spontaneous, the kids were excited about going and, everyone had a great time. Priscilla, believe it or not, was not a ride person. She'd do the water rides or the kiddie rides when her kids were younger. But now they were into bigger and better things like roller coasters that flipped, spun, and God knows what else. And she hated those, just like boats, it would get her sick to her stomach.

Pietro was more than happy to jump on every single ride with the kids, while she sat, watched and took pictures. The fun filled day flew by, exhausted, they left by five and were home a little after eight. Pietro and the kids rehashed the day's events, over Chinese Takeout while Priscilla took it all in, glad they had a good time.

Once dinner was done, and the clean up finished, everyone pretty much did their own thing. Jonathon was playing games with Anthony. Patricia and Isabella were watching a movie with Pietro. Priscilla was tired and sat out of the night's activities, opting to shower and lay down. And just when she entered the bedroom and went to the dresser draw she heard a texting notification. And it wasn't from her personal phone.

She nibbled at her lower lip, not thinking much of it. It could have been one of those group texts about an office function or even a change in her schedule. She was going to ignore it, but her curiosity told her to check it. And she did as she made her way to the bathroom, she grabbed the phone and looked. Her eyes widened, rereading it twice.

Agent Roletti, you are to report at 09:00, tomorrow. URGENT. Confirm.

A sense of dread shot up through her spine, and back down to her feet. All tiredness gone. She hadn't received a message like this in a long time. So whatever it was, it must've been important. What could it be? She was going to be freaking out all night. These weren't normal times, not with Agents being targeted. Derlin suddenly popped in her head, she hoped he was ok. Being the Chief officer of Shadow Ops he was a prime target. He knew more of the nation's secrets than even the President.

She stood there for a few moments longer, clutching the cell phone tightly in her hand. There was no sense in thinking about it anymore. She didn't want the kids or Pietro seeing her upset. The last thing she needed was to be third degreed about what was wrong. She'd get undressed, shower and go to bed, she was tired enough from the day. She shouldn't have a problem falling asleep at least she hoped so. But she knew she wouldn't. It'll be a long night, and something told her from here on out the days would be even longer.

Chapter 6
A blast from the past

She wasted no time getting to the office. She left before anyone got up, the kids stayed in bed late. They probably went to bed just as the sun was coming up with their video game playing and who knows what else. When the weekend came, she didn't care when they went to bed. Pietro was knocked out on the couch, so she didn't worry about waking him either. It was just as well anyway, she didn't need the hassle this morning.

As she arrived at the office, her uneasiness only grew worse. By the time she approached John's office, she felt sick to her stomach. It didn't help that she was going on hardly any sleep. She could feel it in her eyes. They were heavy, she was so tired that if she closed her eyes for a second she'd fall out. And the coffee, she got only made it worse, it didn't do anything to keep her awake and it upset her stomach.

Thankfully, the office wasn't busy as she made her way down the walkway and towards Johns office. As she approached, she could hear John's voice from behind the closed door. That eased her anxiety a little. At least he was okay. She hesitated just as she was about to knock, and prayed that whatever was so goddamn important wasn't as bad as her gut feeling kept telling her. She knocked twice, and then heard the muffled 'Enter'. She opened the door, slipped in and closed it slowly, sitting down. He didn't even acknowledge she had just entered the room. He was looking at something on his computer screen. She eyed him closely while he pretended, she wasn't there, trying to read his thoughts. But John was never easy to read. Traits of the Master Spy.

Almost two minutes later, he finally turned to face her. That was another thing, every time she spoke to him, it was as though he looked at her in such a way she could not place a finger on it.

"Good morning, Priscilla, I hope after that little assignment yesterday, you're ready to get back in the field again." That wasn't at all surprising, she already assumed as much.

"Of course John." John nodded, as he reached into his desk draw and took out a black folder. He placed it before Priscilla.

"Good, because, your next mission is in that folder." Priscilla eyed that black forbidding folder as though it contained a rattlesnake ready to strike at her once she opened it.

She hesitated, she didn't know why, but she finally grabbed it and slowly opened it. She took in a sharp breath as her eyes widened as she peered at the black and white picture. She looked back to John then the photo showing it to him as though he hadn't seen it before.

"That's Hans!" She exclaimed, pointing a finger, she felt a flush of anger engulf her. It may have been almost two years, but she never forgot about what he put her through. She wished she had the chance to kill him, and it looked like she was being given that opportunity.

"How did you get this!? Where is he?" John sat back in his chair, clasping both his hands on his chest.

"That was taken not more than three days ago in Venezuela." She soundlessly worded the name, Venezuela. As though reading her mind John sat forward again.

"For the last couple of days every despot dictator or their representatives have been congregating there, it's only because we tried to figure out why, is how we found him. We suspected this was Hans from the physical description you gave." She nodded, looking back at the picture again.

"But why is he there?" She asked in a frustrated tone. Derlin shrugged his shoulders to the query.

"Intel is sketchy at best, but from the looks of it, he's the one who called them there, you think he's trying to sell the invisibility formula?" Just the mere mention of the word sent shivers up her spine. It took her quite some time to get over the fact that someone out there discovered that, and the possibility of someone else standing next to you, without you even knowing freaked her out to no end.

"With Hans we have to assume everything. There's no telling what he's capable of."

"Agreed. That's why you're leaving first thing in the morning." Priscilla nodded, she wouldn't say it out loud, but she was scared.

There was no telling what she might find this time. But she wouldn't allow her fears to get the better of her. She'd finally be able to put to rest some of her ghosts from the past. She'd been itching to get this opportunity again, she just never thought she would, for all they knew Hans went underground. They weren't the only people looking for him, she knew that the operation was funded by an unknown sponsor, who wanted whatever research he had.

"This will be a joint effort, you'll be going in with support on this one, you know agent Colbert, Roger Colbert?"

She didn't know him personally, mostly just from what she'd heard, she's seen him once in a while, it was more quick hello's. But from what she did hear of him, he was a good Op, but had his flaws. He thought he was some kind of playboy, who had a way with women, and a great casino player, which spelled trouble for her.

Just great, she mused, that's all she needed now was someone with a big ego, both in and out of the bedroom. But before she jumped to conclusions she'd wait to see for herself, with any luck maybe the gossip was wrong.

"You're in charge of the operation, but it would look better if you were there with your husband; he should be there now, he's posing as a rich, real-estate tycoon looking to maybe invest in the clubs there, and you're his wife, who will be meeting him down there." Again, she nodded, she didn't object to any of this. There weren't many times where Ops partnered up, but for something like this, the more eyes the better, especially with Hans involved he was very formidable.

"And my objectives?" She asked.

"Your primary is to ascertain any and all data regarding what he's up to, if you can retrieve live samples, even better, and your second, you are to eliminate Hans." She leaned back, feeling uneasy. Killing Hans was something she'd love to do, but getting samples? That didn't bode well with her at all.

"Samples, sir?" John glanced at her nodding.

"Yes, the more information the better, who knows, perhaps we could use whatever he has for ourselves, is that a problem agent Roletti?" The way he said that sent a chill up her spine. "Because if it is, I can find someone else to handle this if you like?" She shook her head.

"No, it's not a problem sir, not at all." She got up, John nodded,

"Good, tomorrow morning you'll retrieve your passport and necessary documents. Get some sleep Priscilla from the looks of it you need it." Again, she nodded,

"Yes, John…and thank you." No more words were said as she left and walked the longest walk she ever took. Hans…that son of a bitch, coming right back into her life again. She balled a fist so tight her knuckles whitened. Thinking about him flooded her with emotions of anger and fear. The torture he inflicted on her, and not to mention an Invisible Man. She had all but forgotten about him. The nameless man that, beat her to an inch of her life and she was helpless to do anything about it.

After that mission, it really played a toll on her. That was why John took her off 'active status'. The emotional scarring took a while to leave her, even with the help of a therapist. Maybe with this mission, she could put those demons to rest once and for all. She could only hope as she tightened her fist even more wishing Hans was right in front of her. Damn Derlin for throwing this on her, she was grateful to be the one to take care of him yes.

But in less than ten minutes he unraveled hours of therapy sessions. She clenched her jaw, so tight her teeth hurt. She needed to push this aside for right now and deal with the here and now. Because when Pietro and the kids find out she was leaving tomorrow morning that would add even more stress onto an already stressful situation something she didn't need. She laughed to herself. She was right, her days were about to get a lot longer and worse. She only hoped she was ready for it.

Chapter 7
Bursting her bubble

"Are you nuts?!, You're really gonna go down there? How could you after the first time?" That was her first mistake to give him the brief history, that only added more fuel to the fire. He had been nagging her for the past hour about this, and it was starting to slowly get under her skin.

"I'm a big girl, babe, I know what I'm doing." He made a face at the comment.

"Yeah, like the last time? Why couldn't he choose someone else? Why you?"

Pietro didn't understand she was the only one that knew what he looked like, how he thought and operated, she really was the only one suited for this. And regardless, if she hadn't been picked for this she'd have been pissed. She wanted another shot at Hans, she owed him big time.

"Listen, I'm not in the mood to be lectured by anyone, least of all you." She told him with her back towards him as she packed her bag, taking the essential items.

"What's that supposed to mean? You throwing shit up in my face?" She stopped packing for a moment, closing her eyes. This was gonna get ugly, she knew it already. She turned to him folding her arms over her chest.

"No, I'm not, but let's not make believe you were ever perfect either, I'm not looking to fight with you on this, you're only making it worse." She turned back to what she was doing, but he kept going on.

"Oh yeah, I know, and I've done just that, I've changed my life. What about you?"

"I never promised anything! I'm not doing anything illegal, remember that sweetheart, you knew this from the get-go." He threw a hand up in disgust. And all of a sudden she felt like she was in John Derlin's shoes. This must've been and every day or night thing with him. No wonder why he was stressed and snappy at times.

"I knew you were fucked up, but I never knew the extent of it though. You truly ask for everything you get, you know that?" She felt her face get flushed, her anger started to boil now.

"What the fuck did you say?!" Pietro abruptly stopped when he saw her approach him, his face dropped. He knew he'd pressed the wrong buttons, "I ask for everything I get!? So, I guess being raped as a kid, was something I asked for?! You son of a bitch!" She spat out as she flung the remote at him, it shattered against the wall. He looked back to the wall, then to her. Priscilla's hands were clutched into fists. Pietro knew better than to come over and soothe her. She went back to packing her bag, throwing things in.

"Priscilla, I'm sorry babe, really I am." She ignored him as she made for the door. "Don't leave like this hon, please." She stopped just at the threshold.

"It's ok, don't worry about it, I'm sorry too, but I need some time alone to think, when I get back, we'll talk ok?" She didn't even look back when she told him this, he nodded to her back as he watched her walk out the bedroom. During the argument, Priscilla's kids were already packed and ready to go. She had them get ready the moment she got back. They were going to stay at Patrick's while she was away. So that this way their routine wouldn't be disrupted. They still had school. He of course said his goodbyes to the kids, they were unfortunately in the middle of this. As they pulled away Pietro, stood by the front door and watched them leave, wondering if this was the last time, he'd see her, he hoped it wasn't.

Chapter 8
Why Her?

Once Priscilla dropped off the kids at Patrick's and gave him the short version of everything, she wasted no time in getting home and throwing herself into the bed. She was crying. She couldn't remember the last time she cried. The last few years for her have been strange to say the least. The involvement with Pietro didn't make this easier. Everything was so new to her, it was strange and pathetic all at the same time. She was over forty for Christ's sake. She was going through what women went through in their twenties, and strange because she never loved anyone or cared for anyone like that.

She should have just stayed alone, it was simpler. She didn't need someone to watch out for her. She's been doing just fine all along. Maybe she was going through her 'change of life' as they call it, who the hell knew she mused. She really didn't care, wiping tears from her eyes, she got up, made tea and sat at the kitchen table, she never made it a habit of smoking in the house but she did so tonight.

The kids wouldn't smell the lingering smoke by the time they came back home. By the time she turned in, it was late, after three a.m. She smoked more than she wanted to and her mind felt like jelly with everything on her plate. She fell out on the couch. She didn't want to get too comfortable, she had to get up in a few hours and make her flight.

The few hours of sleep, she managed to get were enough for her to get through the morning. Once she arrived Priscilla didn't even bother to see John one last time before leaving. She was at ease with herself. She needed to stay focused for what may lie ahead. She parked her minivan in the underground parking lot, and made her way to the R&D department, to get what she needed from Pete, who was waiting for her in his overstuffed office of photos of cars, and various models he built. Upon seeing her he drank the last of his V-8 and tossed it blindly at the garbage can and missed, the empty container joined the others on the floor.

"Oh god!" He feinted being scared, cringing away from her. "Who did you and ran? Frankenstein?" She gave him the finger, she knew she looked terrible. Pete chuckled. "Here's your shit." He slid the paperwork towards her, picking it up, she looked at her passport.

"Tanya Stykes?" She said with disdain as Peter got up from his chair and walked past her. She followed him looking over the passport, "You guys outdid yourselves with the Photoshop this time." Peter looked back to her, nodding.

"What can I tell you, I teach them well…" He walked to a workbench and picked up something flat that was covered in a cloth, he gestured the covered item towards her.

"Ok now listen up, there's a little change in your method of disguise this time."

"Oh no, we're not going back to the latex, again are we?" She didn't mean for that to come out as a child whining, but she hated them.

When having to change their facial appearances dramatically, the company used to use latex-like masks, it was good yes and it got the job done, but if you were allergic to latex you were screwed, and aside from that, if someone with a keen eye noticed that you weren't sweating when everyone else was. Well, you were doubly screwed.

A few agents met their doom from this oversight. That's when the holographic disguise collar came up. It was slightly larger than a stamp and could be programmed with up to ten disguises so it was great if you were being chased down and needed to blend in with a short amount of time to do so. It also detected when the user exerted themselves, so if you sweat, your holo-face would also. They weren't used all the time, only when necessary. They were very expensive to produce.

"Shut up! And no, we're not. But we've been having trouble with the collars lately, two Op's I sent them out with, shorted out and at the most inconvenient time too. The units were not retrieved, but I can only come up with two factors. One, they were faulty, but I doubt that, and two, perhaps some type of interference disrupted them. Either way, I can't send you out there with them and risk something happening." She smiled, he looked a little uncomfortable at the way she looked at him.

"Aww, you do care, don't you? And after all these years I thought you just looked at me as a piece of ass."

"I do, and I meant I can't send Ops out there ok? Not you personally, Ops as in plural, so don't get a fucking swelled head." She loved getting a rise outta him. Even in the worst of moods, as she was in, he was able to lift her spirits even if he annoyed her to no end doing it.

"Ok, now check this sucker out." He lifted the cloth, and revealed what looked like flesh perfectly stripped from someone's face.

"This is called syn-skin, short for synthetic skin. It's not rubber, think of it as living tissue. It adheres to the wearer flawlessly. See, we needed something that can be used long term, the holo-collars need to be charged." She reached out and touched it, it felt uncannily real too. The look on her face pleased Peter, he chuckled.

"You want me to wear that? That's fucking gross man." He rolled his eyes.

"This is cutting edge stupid! This mask is yours, it was made from the mold of your face. Why the hell do you think I asked you to take another mold for, moron? Anyway, you can shower with it, the whole spiel." She shrugged her shoulders still unsure,

"Yeah, well it sounds kinda claustrophobic to me." Peter made a face, gesturing the lifelike mask to her. She hesitated at first, but then took it, pressing it to her face firmly. It felt as though the mask was spreading on its own to the contours of her face. She reached up feeling the edges, they were smooth and she could hardly feel them. Peter gave her a mirror and looking back in the mirror was someone that looked European. She was more than impressed by this, she couldn't believe her eyes. It felt so natural, she tried to scrutinize it and find some type of flaw, but could not, she looked at Peter who looked all too pleased with himself.

"See, what'd I tell you? Fits like a glove, your skin can breathe, and the syn-skin will mimic your true skin's status like sweat and the like. The only thing you gotta do is change your hair and eye color if you want to, and then you're all set." She smiled at him. He gestured her to come with him.

They walked out into the main bay area, in that short time, some of his staff had already arrived to work going about their duties. She caught up to him. Side by side now they walked to the back exit, where she'd catch her cab to the airport.

"Have you spoken to Derlin today?" She asked, he looked down at his feet as he walked, then looked up shaking his head.

"Nah, lately I've been avoiding him, I don't know what the hell is going on up there, I've known that man for over twenty years, and when I talk to him it's like I'm talking to someone totally different, fucking weird man, that bitch of a wife totally fucked him up man." Priscilla nodded.

"Pete, people get affected differently. I mean I know it's hard to believe that a guy like Derlin, would let something like this affect him so much, but we gotta be there for him when the time comes." He nodded.

"Yeah, you're right, but between you and me." He leaned in close to her ear, "His judgment is off, he should've stayed away, when he took that two week leave of absence, till his shit was taken care of, you know? With the influx of Ops killed, what's he doing? Seems to me he's got his finger up his ass.

John needs to take some more time for himself, or maybe it's time to call it quits, you didn't hear any of this from me by the way." She agreed, maybe it was time for Derlin to retire. But nevertheless, this would need her attention when she got back, there was nothing she could do about it now. She was about to step out the door, when Peter grabbed her by the arm.

"Be careful out there Priscilla, huh? No bullshit, I have a bad feeling about things." She smiled, she didn't tell him, but she felt the same way, she felt the overwhelming desire to hug Peter, but thought better of it. As she walked outside and made her way to Lexington Ave, Peter yelled back to her one last time.

"Oh, by the way, don't bend over in front of Roger ok? He'll dick ya in the ass before you say ouch!" He winked at her after he told her this, laughing his ass off and walked back inside. She shook her head, just great, like she needed to hear that.

She put aside what Peter just said, replaying the more important parts of the conversation. If things worried Peter like the way they did, then there was truly cause to worry, nothing ever seemed to bother him. This mission didn't sit right with her, but then again when did any? Knowing you may never return wouldn't sit well with anyone.

As she made her way to the corner, she didn't have to wait long for a cab. She jumped in and sunk down in the seat, closing her eyes. The last few days were a bit hectic and she knew that from here on out, when she returned things were going to be different. It was like the calm before the storm. That feeling of dread, was only getting worse. She took a deep breath, thankful the cabbie wasn't talkative. With the traffic, it gave her time to close her eyes she needed it. As the cab pulled away with a skid, another car double parked down a side street pulled away, slowly following.

Chapter 9
Venezuelan hospitality

She touched down in Venezuela by the midafternoon, as she traversed through the airport, she kept her wits about her. She was in no man's land now, being an American here didn't bode so well with the locals. Unlike the airport back home, she couldn't just grab her luggage and flash her ID, over here she needed to go through the checkpoints, she did so without incident. She hailed a taxi, telling him where to go in Spanish, the cabbie gave her a sly grin.

"Ok lady." He said. As they drove, he tried to make small talk, Priscilla was hardly interested, but talked enough so she wouldn't come off as rude to the man. Within the hour he pulled up to the gate that encircled the large resort. The pictures she saw from the brief didn't do it any justice, it was a resort/hotel skyscraper. It dwarfed the entire city that surrounded it. All along the property were bars, clubs and various other casinos, it was like a mini city.

As they drove along the path she saw all manner of people from various different countries, even some Americans. From what she could see, they looked to be having a grand ol' time, in their bathing suits and robes as they drank and gambled their lives away. Priscilla didn't think very highly of this lifestyle. She was not a drinker in the first place, she saw it as a waste of money, just pissed away, literally. And gambling, that was an even bigger waste. How could people sit at a table for hours on end, lose and still hope to hit it big was beyond her comprehension. Before you even walked to the table, the odds were stacked against you. She had no doubt this place was rigged too. If Hans was involved, then that would be almost guaranteed.

The cabbie let her out right in front of the main doors, she tipped him well. He was more than happy with that. Wishing her luck, he drove off. Just as Priscilla was about to grab her bag a bellhop appeared and grabbed her bag for her. She thanked him as he led her to the front desk. The attendant was well dressed in a sharp suit, new haircut and smiling brightly as she approached. He had a shiny gold name badge on his lapel, his name was Juan.

"Afternoon, how are you?"

"I'm wonderful and welcome to the Venezuelan Palace. Do you have reservations with us already?" She nodded, handing the polite young man her passport and reservation paperwork. It didn't take Juan long to look her up and find her.

"Welcome Mrs. Stykes excellent! You're all checked in. I just saw Mr. Stykes only a few moments ago. He was heading to the pool I believe, shall I page him for you?" He went to pick up the phone and do so.

"No that won't be necessary, I'll just take a key and head up. It was a long flight I'd like to freshen up."

"Of course! I understand!" Juan then grabbed a card from beneath the counter and slipped it into a reader and in seconds her card was programmed and ready.

"Here you are Mrs. Stykes, I hope you enjoy your stay with us! Shall I have someone help you with your luggage?"

"No, thank you. I think I can manage." But he rang the bell anyway.

"Please Mrs. Stykes, no one who just came in from a long flight, shall be allowed to carry their bag." And then Juan gestured at the bellhop in crisp shorts with an even crisper polo. She reluctantly nodded and before she could say her thanks Juan was off to a task down the counter helping a young lady who was having an issue with the computer.

The bellhop then stepped forward,

"Ma'am?" Priscilla smiled.

"Okay, there it is." She gestured at the bag. The young man, picked it up and asked her to follow him.

As they walked, she took in her surroundings. There were a few private guards here, which was expected. They wore just as equally sharp looking suits as the front desk attendant with the clear ear pieces as they nonchalantly made their rounds. She didn't doubt there were some plain-clothes guards roaming about also. She couldn't help but notice that no expense was spared.

The large circular lobby had all white marble floors, and leather couches that were spread throughout. Waiters were readily standing by as vacationers came in from the hot day to cool off, to get them whatever they wanted. Hanging above them was the largest chandelier she ever saw, all glass and shining brightly. She had to say she was impressed so far, as she started to make her way to one of six elevators. They were all decked out in gold, with red carpeting and a couch. The bellhop passed them, and gestured for her to enter the last one.

"This elevator is reserved for new guests. We like to have them settled in immediately after a long trip." She nodded, of course you do she thought. The faster you rest, the faster you spend your money.

"Thanks." She smiled as she walked in first. Within seconds they were up on the fourteenth floor.

The room, like the rest of the place was immaculate. There was a seventy-inch TV on the wall, the carpeting looked as smooth as silk, there was a full kitchen and bar, she even had a balcony. Just as she was about to turn to the bellhop, she was startled by none other than her "husband."

"Hello darling! I'm so happy to see you. I'm glad it didn't take you long, love." Priscilla and the bellhop turned their heads at the same time, and immediately saw Roger coming from the bedroom in a white bathrobe, holding a glass of wine, as he strode towards them smiling.

"Really?" She said, grimacing, in a low tone and yet was still heard by the sharp eared bellhop.

"Excuse me, ma'am?" She turned to the young man, visibly embarrassed, clearing her throat.

"Nothing… sorry." She tried to block out the scene she was just forced to witness. She was getting ready to take care of the bellhop. When Roger strode closer, putting down the glass on a table as he passed. By the time she could even react, he grabbed her and planted his lips firmly on hers.

She fell into the kiss just for the sake of keeping the cover in front of the bellhop. She tried her hardest to pretend she was enjoying it, as his tongue danced in her mouth; he even grabbed her ass, and lifted her off the floor. Seeing this the bellhop put his gloved fist to his mouth and cleared his throat clearly indicating that he wanted to be tipped before things got too out of hand.

Roger, caught the hint, releasing Priscilla. Then reached into his robe pocket and took out a twenty. The bellhop smiled and ran off closing the door. Now alone, Priscilla gave Roger a look of disdain that could kill as she wiped her lips with her sleeve.

"Do that again, and I'll kill you." She said clearly pissed. Roger smiled.

"Blondie, don't you know that the key to a successful cover is keeping said persona both publicly and privately, as though it were second nature." She agreed whole heartily.

"Yeah, but let me say it one more time, do that again and I'll kill you." Roger chuckled, putting both hands in his robe pockets as he walked over to the couch and sat down. Not even five minutes with him and she wanted to hang him off the balcony. She did have to admit he was a handsome man. He had thick brown-combed back hair, a square jaw, and was clean shaven, she could see why he had that much arrogance. But still, if he thinks for one minute that he was gonna have a chance with her, he had another thing coming.

She threw her bag on the glass table, taking out her company cell phone. Opening it, there was a keyboard. She input a few commands, the screen changed to a radar read out. Aside from being a company phone, it was her all in one device, she could drive her car with it, activate explosives, and even detect any emitting radio waves no matter how weak. If the room was bugged for sound or video she'd know in an instant. Roger looked upon her with keen interest.

"I've already scanned the place for any type of surveillance , there's nothing here, Blondie. I've checked every time I come back as well." She didn't acknowledge him. She wanted to be sure for herself, she wasn't gonna take some wanna-be playboy's word for it. Perhaps after he showed her some professionalism, then maybe. She walked the entire room, doing a sweeping back and forth motion, she headed to the bedroom which was pretty big, and nice. It was a simple set up-one large bed, two dressers, each with a mirror, and a bathroom with a hot tub. She could get used to this, half of her wished she came here with Pietro, he'd have loved this.

She was saddened for a moment, thinking about him. She didn't like the fact that she left on bad terms, but there was nothing that could be done about it now. Yet another problem, she didn't need right now on top of everything else, she needed to deal with that once she got back to the States. She pushed all those thoughts away, she had a job to do and as much as she wished otherwise she wasn't here on vacation.

The room was clear just as Roger had said. That was a surprise, but perhaps her room wasn't bugged, perhaps only VIP rooms were. She didn't really care just as long as her area was clear, that's all that mattered. She walked back into the living room to find Roger still sitting on the couch, finishing his wine. He smiled at her, as she came into view, placing the empty wine glass on the table.

"Priscilla Roletti, it's such a pleasure to be working with you, although I'm not too sure of the European/Russian vibe I'm getting." He said, referring to her Syn-skin, he leaned forward, clasping his hands together. "You're one of the few old timers left. I've been an Op for almost five years, I first heard about you when I was in training. You remember Conner? He says you're one of the best he trained." She crossed her arms over her chest, hearing Conner's name brought back a few memories, she hadn't thought about him in a long time. He was the lead instructor at the academy. She wasn't surprised he was still there, tormenting the newbies.

Although she felt flattered that she was looked up to in such high regard, she didn't wanna be. She was hardly the role model. And she didn't take kindly to his brown nosing.

"Thank you, Roger that's very kind of you, I've heard some things about you also, but let's hope they aren't all true hmm." She flashed him a quick smile, it was a little dig and he caught the meaning of it.

"Touché."

"So what's the status?" Upon her direct question Roger got up. That goofy smile faded and he turned all business, running his hand through his hair.

"Nothing that I can see. I've tried to spend as much time as I can out there. So far this place runs like a casino resort." He said as they walked towards the balcony.

"I've seen your boy once since being here too, he met some Iranians in the main lobby just last night. They shook hands, embraced quickly, and went to the top floor." She nodded.

"You think Hans is quartered there?" Roger shrugged his shoulders.

"More than likely." As they walked outside, the cool breeze felt good going through her hair. She peered down observing all the vacationers. They looked like mere specks from way up here. Surrounding the city and resort, was a vast jungle. She had a lot of ground to cover if she couldn't find anything on the property, but her instincts told her that whatever she was looking for would be on the property.

The forest in Pennsylvania isn't anything like the jungles here. It would take far too many resources to set up something like a lab. If anything, the lab or research area would be fairly small. She had no doubt that Hans was more than well on his way to completing whatever he sought out to accomplish in Pennsylvania. He had more than enough time to do so. Roger touched her on her shoulder, breaking her out of her thoughts.

"Listen, Blondie, I know you have it in for this guy, but be careful, Hans has three personal body guards. Three women, and one looks like she'll tear anyone apart if you so much as look at him the wrong way. She's friggin' huge." Her mind flashed back to the single photo of Hans. It was a zoomed in shot, so you couldn't tell if anyone was near him or not.

"Well, that's why you're here Roger." She tapped him on the shoulder. "You're gonna charm the pants off them." She winked at him. He laughed slightly, then started to walk back in the room as he talked to her.

"Get some rest, Priscilla, we'll hit the casinos tonight." She nodded, as he disappeared inside. Looking out over the balcony, she closed her eyes.

She took a deep breath and exhaled it slowly trying to release some of the frustration. Priscilla had her work cut out for her, she knew that much.

An untold amount of time passed before she went back inside, she didn't see Roger. She looked towards the bedroom doors, they were closed. She grabbed the remote control for the TV and plopped down on the couch. There wasn't much of anything on, she just wanted something in the background while she closed her eyes and cleared her mind and readied herself for what was to come.

Chapter 10
Rolling the Dice

Priscilla was awakened from her light sleep by a gentle nudge from Roger, who was standing over her.

"Priscilla, wake up." He took a step back as she stirred, stretching out her arms, she tried to stifle a yawn. She couldn't believe she fell asleep like that, she was more tired than she thought. She looked up to Roger, who had obviously showered and dressed for their night out.

"Oh shit." She muttered as she got up from the couch. "What time is it?" She asked as she grabbed her bag and went to the bathroom.

"It's time to gamble and drink the night away, darling." Roger said with his arms out, smiling devilishly. She wasn't amused, and the face she gave him said so. She walked into the bathroom and closed the door, locking it.

"You know what Blondie, by the time this is over you're gonna have a sense of humor yet, I swear." He said to the closed door, she didn't answer. She rolled her eyes silently mimicking him as she undressed and prepared to shower. The shower felt refreshing. She felt so sticky from traveling. Once done, she checked herself out in the mirror, the Syn-skin was still holding up, she was impressed. She grabbed a small pouch that was on the counter. Opening it, she took out a spray bottle, with instant hair dye, this one was brown, the user could quickly spray the dye on without fear of it staining the skin.

There was a special chemical that only turned hair the desired color, and it easily washed out with soap and water. Completing the look, she used brown contact lenses. Looking as good as she'll ever look she robed herself going outside. Roger was on the couch channel surfing. He hadn't noticed she came out. She quickly ran into the bedroom, locking the doors, and dressed. She wore formal dress slacks with special high-heeled boots that she could run in without a problem, with a red form-fitting top, that exposed one shoulder. She looked very casual but elegant. Roger was at the door by the time she came back out. To say he was impressed was an understatement. He gave her a wolfish smile.

"Well Mrs. Stykes, you look beautiful. Shall we go, my love?" He said, gesturing her first. She had to admit he was too charming for his own damn good.

When they finally made their way, it was half past eight that evening…. After all the elbow rubbing with numerous people and countless sitting at various gambling tables, it was close to two in the morning. They stayed together the whole time for the most part. While Roger played the role of a high roller, she played the role of a sometimes-bored wife just staying with him because she had nothing else to do. She observed that Roger was indeed a good card player, and was surprised to see he wasn't as arrogant as she thought he was, careful not to win too much or too overly lose either.

The place was watched by not only pit bosses and undercover security, but the unblinking eyes in the sky were upon them as well. She paid no heed to them her main focus was to see if anybody of interest was here. She looked at her watch, she was growing weary. She had enough for one night. She was satisfied with the little recon she did, and she came to terms that it was gonna be a lot more difficult than she first surmised. She'd be doing a lot of late night wandering. She turned to Roger, giving him a little nudge.

"Darling sweetie, can we go upstairs now?" She said as she rubbed the back of his head. Roger was too transfixed, to pay attention now. He was in a heated game of blackjack with six other players. It came down to the last hit when Roger decided to wager.

Priscilla turned away from these card-playing fools, and looked around a bit. And that's when her eyes widened, her body tensed, she felt that chill sensation rocketing up her spine. Hans Goring finally made his appearance. The entourage of ten people, he was with looked to be very important.

One of the men was getting his ear chewed off from Hans. They were walking too briskly for Priscilla to read their lips, aside from the fact people kept getting in her line of sight. Not far from Hans was a blonde woman, who had to have been over six feet tall.

She wore a women's dress suit, that looked about ready to pop from the muscle mass beneath. Roger was right, she was big.

She eyed anyone that came within arms reach of them. Priscilla tried not to make it obvious that she was looking right at them, and turned away quickly when the Amazon looked her way for a moment. She didn't so much as notice Priscilla was watching them. They were heading to the elevator, as she got up out of the chair, she tapped Roger on his shoulder.

"Spotted and marked." She whispered in his ear, he heard her and nodded. He didn't get up, he knew better. They didn't want to make it too suspicious looking. Priscilla slowly walked through the crowd trying not to look in any kind of a rush, as a matter of fact, she wasn't. She had no intention of doing anything now. She just wanted to confirm something, she cleared the lobby to the elevators. Just as Hans' elevator door closed, she hit the call button on one of the other adjacent elevators, to look as though she was waiting for her own. She was really watching the numbers to Hans' climb, it went straight up to the top floor, number forty.

"Bingo." She said loud enough, where only she could hear, at least the night wasn't a total loss. She was just about to go and fetch Roger when he came striding along, wrapping his arm around her waist, he gently kissed her cheek, and spoke in her ear.

"You saw our man, huh, good eyes." She pulled away, nodding, their elevator arrived and they hastily moved inside heading for their room, for an even longer night ahead of them.

Chapter 11
After Party

Roger and Priscilla quickly made their way back to the room, and prepared for the task at hand. Priscilla had a feeling Hans would be at the top floor and her original plan was to make her way up there, but now knowing that he was indeed up there and conducting business, all the better.

At least she knew for sure she wasn't gonna waste her time tonight. As she got undressed, Roger prepared also. Priscilla took off her Syn-skin mask, just on the outside chance she didn't get through the night unmolested. She went to her suitcase, opening it she fondled for the hidden compartment that held her gun, with extra clips, and her pen sized laser torch. She grabbed only the laser torch pen along with a black skin tight one piece sneaking suit.

By the time she donned it, Roger had out his laptop, and was going over the layout of the entire property, which was pretty vast. Aside from the various casinos and small resorts there was also an airfield north of the main complex. When she sat next to him, he zoomed in on the top floor, in a three-dimensional layout of what was up there. It consisted of the offices, conference room and a very large suite.

"It's very likely that, he's got an encrypted PC, so take the auto decrypter." She already had it. Her point of entry was going to be the roof, she'd climb it and cut her way in from a vent, it should be pretty simple enough. As Roger showed her, she had a black camouflage stick that she applied all around her eyes down her nose and almost her entire forehead. Then very carefully, she put on a matching skintight mask that had a wide slit across her eyes. Roger pointed out some exposed skin, that she touched up quickly. Roger handed her the black Velcro utility belt, with all the essential items she'll be using. She grabbed her laser torch, auto-decrypter, slipping them into an empty slot on her belt. She didn't need her gun on this one.

As they walked to the balcony, Roger handed her a small pouch, it was something he had in his bag. He looked at his watch.

"Ok, we'll keep in touch via earpiece." She nodded, as he handed her a pair of goggles and the small ear sized communicator. "Good luck up there." He added as she made her way outside. Roger closed the door, and prepared himself, inserting his earpiece. Priscilla's earpiece also had a tracer in it so Roger could track her progress and relay instructions of where she was, in case she needed him to. Out on the balcony, Priscilla put on her black goggles. Once on, she tapped a button, she had a heads-up display with a three-dimensional map for her to follow as well. Unzipping the pouch Roger gave her, she took out the grappling gun, that was the size of a Walther PPK. Priscilla hoisted herself up on the railing as carefully as she could, the last thing she wanted was to go splat down below. Blinking her right eye fast three times, the goggles magnified the roof, she aimed her grapple gun and fired. The soundless titanium arrow speared into the concrete. She pulled on it twice, it felt secure enough. Pressing the trigger twice she was pulled up at a slow pace. When she fired the hook, she took extra care to make sure that when she was ascending the building not to go past any windows or balcony's, and even if someone was out on a balcony, unless she was right on top of them, they wouldn't see her. The night was dark and cool, perfect for this little recon.

Once she got to the ledge Priscilla found her footing and hoisted herself up onto the roof. She placed the grappling gun down carefully, that was her ticket back. Once she was on the roof, she quickly ran for the shadows to a large air conditioning unit, putting her hand to her ear, she spoke.

"I'm on the roof." She said in a tiny whisper.

"Acknowledged, you're coming in loud and clear, head to the north part of the roof. The rooftop unit should be about 20 feet from where you are."

"Confirmed, heading there now." She crept where he had indicated, he marked the point of entry on his map and she saw the same layout as he did. Her goggles were linked to his PC.

Once there, she noticed a grated cover over the square opening. Before doing anything, she looked it over. There were no booby traps that she saw. Not wanting to leave any signs that someone was up here, she tried to lift the grate off first, instead of just cutting her way in. As she surmised, it was secured in place with simple latches. Once unsecured, she pulled and lifted the grate off and placed it on the side, she climbed in.

"Ok, you're in, you're on your own now, Blondie. I'll relay anything if something comes up."

She didn't reply, as she traversed her way deeper into the air duct, she stopped every so often. It was slow going as she crawled her way, but she made it to the first grated opening. Reaching into her waist, she grabbed an optic worm, which she plugged into her goggles, enabling her to see what she needed to. She slipped the tiny camera through, bending the wire slightly, for better viewing angles.

She was right above the main corridor by the elevators. There were two hallways, going away from the elevators. She reeled back her optic, but before continuing, she reached into her belt again and took out a quarter sized magnetic camera, that was linked to her goggles. Once she angled it at the best point of view, she moved on, for an untold amount of time she crawled till she heard distant conversation up ahead.

As Priscilla got closer to the source, she could distinctively hear it was Hans. She picked up her pace, trying not to make any sound. It wasn't until she was right near the grate, looking down, when she could finally make out some of the conversation.

She listened very closely, daring not to breathe more than what she was now.

"So, gentlemen, I hope the food and drinks were good, now...."

Hans said as he walked around to his desk. Priscilla couldn't see the office all that good, but it looked big. She was annoyed about her viewing angle. She really didn't have a great view, she only saw the heads of three men, she couldn't see Hans at all. She would bet her life that his bodyguard was there, she was tempted to slip the optic worm through the grate, but knowing her luck Hans would spot that, she wasn't putting anything past him.

"When is the demonstration Hans?" One of the men asked, not sounding very friendly.

"The demo will take place tomorrow night gentlemen. At which time you will have one day to agree to my terms, and payment must be up front before you receive anything." There was audible unhappy grumbling, from what Hans said.

"Before you get ahead of yourself, let's wait until your demo is concluded. This had better be worth the haste of this little get together." This was from someone that sounded Middle Eastern.

Once again silence ensued.

"I assure you it will be well worth your wait, now please, it is rather late. I have some other details to see to, but in the meantime, eat, drink and gamble to your heart's desires, all on me." Again silence, then some of the men murmured. Chairs were moved and they were making their way out the door.

As the light went out, she relaxed her body. She looked at her map. This was the location of Hans' office. Blinking her left eye three times, she saw the group at the elevator. There were three men, Hans and the Amazon bodyguard. She watched them go in and head down. She took a deep breath as she looked at her watch. She'd stay put for half an hour and wait. The last thing she wanted was someone coming back for anything.

She let forty-five minutes pass by; she stretched out her body as much as she could. It was terribly stiff from not moving all that time. As with the other grate, this wasn't fastened with screws either. She manipulated the cover off, slowly bringing it in the vent, and out of her way.

As she prepared to go down, she watched the video feed by the elevators. So far so good she thought. As she clamped her hands tight on the edges of the opening, she slid out headfirst. Once her feet cleared the opening, she flipped right side up. She took one hand away and reached into her pouch, feeling for a magnetic grappler. The magnet was super strong, able to carry weight of up to 300 pounds. She eyeballed the opening she just came from and threw it up. With a light clang, it stuck to the vent. Attached at the end was a rope-like piano line.

She slowly let herself down to the carpeted floor. She didn't make a sound. She spotted the computer right away and went to work. Hans had logged off, the decrypter should take care of all that. Not only does it bypass a password locked computer, but it also downloads every file it has.

The whole process took three minutes. Within that time, Priscilla took a quick glance at the spacious office. There really wasn't anything that stood out. Once the download was completed, she took the device and traversed back up the vent and without incident made it back to her room.

Roger was waiting by the balcony, and helped her in. She was stiff as hell, but hopefully it would be well worth it. As she changed and cleaned up, Roger went right to work on the data she had ascertained.

By the time Priscilla cleaned herself up, Roger was still sitting on the couch. A look of deep concentration was affixed upon his brow, she sat down next to him, watching the screen. There were a few programs running in the background, she wasn't gonna disturb him, but he started to talk to her.

"These files are encrypted in a way I've never seen." He shook his head in disgust. Priscilla bit the bottom of her lip, a little annoyed at this.

"I hope we didn't just waste the night away, only to hit a dead end." He nodded, as he tried to stifle a yawn, it was almost five in the morning. Finally giving up, he placed the laptop on the table.

"I'll let the programs run for a few hours, but in the meantime, I gotta get some rest. Tomorrow is the investors' meeting and Hans will be there, to give his spiel, hoping to lure them." She didn't answer him, as he got up and made his way to the bedroom, she turned around in the sofa talking to him as he walked.

"You want me to tag along?"

"No, there's no point, it's supposed to be about an hour or so. I'm not the only one attending, once I'm done, I'll hook up with you. Good night Blondie." He said as he walked into the bedroom and closed the doors. She was left alone with her thoughts and was far from tired. All that time wasted for nothing. She punched the couch as she got up and went to her purse for a cigarette, inhaling the deadly smoke calmed her a bit. They didn't have all goddamn week to find this lab, and now from what she heard, there was some type of demonstration, of what, she could hardly guess.

With Hans she was only limited to her imagination and that was very scary, being in this profession for so long, you saw too much for your own good at times. She took a deep frustrated breath as she snuffed out her smoke, walking towards the couch, she rubbed her eyes.

"Crap." She muttered as she fell back onto the comfy couch and closed her eyes, allowing sleep to take her.

Chapter 12
The meeting

She didn't sleep much, only a few hours and it felt like it. Her eyes stung, and were hard to open. She stretched out her arms, yawning and slowly sat up on the couch looking and feeling like she had the biggest hangover in the casino.

"Ah, good, you saved me the trouble of waking you up." Roger walked over, dressed in a polo and slacks. "The meeting starts in twenty-minutes. I'm gonna head up there now. Probably won't yield much. But I figure what the hell." She nodded, moving like an old woman.

"Knock yourself out."

"You gonna be here when I get back?" She shrugged her shoulders,

"Maybe, depends on how long you take, and if I can get off this couch, I may take a walk. Your decrypter is still trying to hack those files." She gestured at the laptop. Roger followed her gaze, looking annoyed, it was taking this long.

"Okay, if you're not here I'll text you." She gave him a thumbs up as he turned and strode for the door.

"You got it." She replied as he opened and closed the door. "Ah, Christ." She muttered disgusted, as she finally peeled herself off the couch and prepared for the day.

The investors' meeting was a total drag, doing keynotes weren't Hans' forte, at least not on this subject. And from the looks of other investors, he clearly wasn't the only one thinking this. But nevertheless everyone listened intently, there weren't many Americans here, mostly Middle Eastern and Europeans.

When the conference finally wrapped up, it was almost two hours. Hans' three associates or rather bodyguards, because they all looked like a force to be reckoned with, stood up at the podium with him, clearly not interested either and eyeing everyone closely. Out of the three, the tall blonde was clearly the leader of the pack. Roger couldn't help but be intrigued by her, she wasn't like one of them female bodybuilders that looked more manly. This blonde clearly didn't lose the beauty, as well as the other two, who were much smaller muscular wise.

One had short burgundy colored hair that covered one side of her face and the other had long black hair. Roger couldn't help but think how Hans handled them, if he was sleeping with either one of them.

"Now before any of you depart, ladies and gentlemen, my associates Zora, Velvet and Hunter, will hand out pamphlets, for your viewing convenience. It pretty much reiterates what we went over this morning, danka." He concluded with a small head bow. Everyone in the room wasted no time in gathering their belongings. There weren't many investors here, only about fifteen in all.

As Roger picked up his suitcase and walked down the narrow aisle to the door, his name was called out.

"Is there a Mr. Roger Colbert in attendance?" Judging from the look on Hans' face he didn't know what Roger looked like. Roger stopped and turned around, walking back the way he came. Roger wondered what this was about. He knew he didn't do anything to warrant Hans' attention, so he'd humor this and see where it goes.

"Mr. Goring, a pleasure to meet you, sir." Roger said as he approached, extending his hand, which Hans took, shaking it firmly.

"Likewise, Mr. Colbert." He said, with a friendly smile.

"I wasn't sure if I'd have a chance to tell you this, but this place is amazing. There's not a place in the States that matches this." Hans smiled.

"Thank you, I can't take all the credit though, I had some very good people to work with, I only put up the money."

"Well money does help sir."

"Indeed it does." Hans replied.

"So, what can I do for you?" Roger asked, wanting to get right to the point, without looking too eager to leave. With a guy like Hans, one had to play his cards close to the vest.

"Well from what I hear, you have quite a lot of property in the States correct? This is a family business, yes?" Hans asked as he placed a gentle but firm hand on the back of his shoulder, leading them out of the conference room. Roger looked forward and saw two of the women walking ahead, while the blonde who was named Zora walked with them.

"Yes, it is, my father started it, he retired, we have property in Las Vegas, New Jersey, New York, before coming here I bought a huge piece of land in Japan."

Hans nodded, looking very impressed.

"This is good, because I want your opinion on a property I'm looking at in the States, if you wouldn't mind coming to my office?" Roger didn't break stride as they walked, he didn't want to go there, this didn't seem right, but what was he gonna do? He couldn't try to skate out of it, that would look too suspicious.

Roger tried to move his head without looking too worried. He was looking for where the woman was, she was too far behind them. Roger was sure that whatever happened, he could handle it, he may be just jumping the gun.

"I'll be more than happy to look at it." Hans smiled.

"Splendid."

The office was on the other side from where the conference room was, this was the same area Priscilla passed last night. They turned the bend and entered his lavish office, with various pieces of art and artifacts. He had bookcases stocked, with volumes about art, history and culture. Hans walked him to one of the three seats in front of his large brown desk, Hans walked behind his desk and sat down.

"Would you like something to drink Mr. Colbert?"

"Roger please,… um yeah maybe a Vodka martini with a lemon twist?" Hans smiled.

"Excellent choice, I think I'll have the same. Zora please my dear." Roger didn't turn around, but he heard the woman walk over to where the liquor was kept and prepare the drinks as Hans put on his reading glasses and looked to his computer monitor.

"Just give me a moment Roger, while I find this file. I tend to misplace them at times in a rush saving them." He said, forcing a laugh. Roger just smiled back, eyeing the office. Coming up to his left was Zora, who handed Roger his drink, he thanked the woman, she didn't reply.

As a matter of fact, she didn't even look at Roger. She then walked to Hans' desk, placing his drink down, he took a quick sip from the straw.

"Zora, my dear, thank you." Roger took a sip from his, aside from being a little too strong for his taste, it felt good going down.

"Ah yes, here we are." Hans said, as he turned the flat screen monitor around. Roger leaned closer, the screen was blank, then Hans tapped a key and a video played, it was in infrared. It was a quick video, of someone in front of a computer screen, Roger's eyes suddenly widened. He was looking at Priscilla! Hans watched him closely.

"Well, Roger, it would seem that from the look on your face, how do you Americans say it, the jig is up." Roger let the drink fall from his hand, as he got up, his chair fell back and at the same time he reached into his waist in one quick fluid motion.

Hans did nothing, the look he wore implied over confidence. Before Roger could even bring his small gun to bear, Zora in blinding speed stepped in front of him and hoisted Roger up by his neck. Fully extending her arm, her clamp like grip immediately cut off his air. He dropped his weapon, clawing with both his hands at hers in a vain attempt to release himself.

Hans got up from his seat and slowly walked over to Zora's side looking up at the helpless Roger with distain, shaking his head as though disappointed. Hans gestured to Zora as he walked away. With the slightest movement of her wrist, she broke his neck, dropping him. Hans then turned back around to Zora.

"It would seem the tip was correct." He said gently, rubbing his chin thinking. Yesterday at some point in the early evening, via email from an unknown source, he was told that there would be a married couple by the names of Roger Colbert and Tanya Stykes coming to steal his research. It seemed the anonymous emailer was right, but the thing that plagued him was, who sent it? And why? Was this meant to be a distraction? Not one to turn a blind eye, he set up that hidden camera. He looked up to Zora.

"Zora, go fetch this woman and bring her here." She nodded, stalking off. Hans turned around and spoke to her again before she left. "Alive my dear, if you can," she nodded and continued on her way.

Chapter 13
A knock at the door

It took Priscilla almost an hour and a half to get ready. She took her time, hoping that Roger came back already, she didn't want to go roaming around without him. They needed some type of plan, to find what they were looking for and maybe figure out a way to find out what the big demo was tonight. Hopefully with any luck, the data will be decrypted and then if it was detailed enough, she'd forgo finding any lab, or demo and just take Hans out, simple and to the point. Even though Derlin said to bring back samples if she could, she wasn't going out of her way to do so. She sat back down on the couch, picking up the laptop.

Whatever program Roger was running it was still trying to crack open the files. She sighed replacing the laptop, got up and reapplied her syn-skin. Just as she finished, there was a faint knock at the door. At first she wasn't going to answer it, perhaps it was someone knocking at the wrong door, but the knocking persisted. A gut wrenching sensation overtook her. She went to her bag and grabbed her gun. She cocked the hammer back as she approached, the shaking door. Priscilla was inches from the door, when it suddenly flew open, slamming into the wall. It missed Priscilla by mere inches. She looked up and saw Zora standing in the doorway, who tilted her head sideways and smirked.

"Ah, Christ!" Priscilla said, as she took aim, Zora dashed forward, side stepping her and grabbed her wrist, twisting it to the point of almost breaking it. Priscilla cried out, dropping the gun, then pulled her hand away. Zora reached out and tried to grab her. As she did this, Priscilla jumped back, but wasn't quick enough. Zora ripped off her 'Tanya Stykes' syn-skin. Zora looked at it clearly disgusted and then threw it down.

"Cute." The Amazon said, as she stalked towards Priscilla, who was peeling off the rest of the syn-skin. There was no where to go, it was fight or die. Priscilla squared off, as Zora walked towards her without a purpose. Once the Amazon got within arm's reach; Priscilla unleashed her attack, which was defended effortlessly by the woman.

Zora even let Priscilla get a shot in. It felt like she just punched solid steel. She yelled out, holding her hand, Zora smirked again, backhanding Priscilla so hard, she was sent flying across the room. She almost blacked out as the Amazon reached down and scooped her up to her feet and pulled her along by the arm, digging her nails into her skin.

Chapter 14
Who says blondes have all the fun?

If the Amazon didn't viciously pick her up and pull her along, Priscilla would have blacked out. It felt as though she was hit with a brick. As Zora pulled her along, she was starting to slowly regain her bearings. They passed some guests who stared at them, trying to hug the walls in fear of Zora. The Amazon looked like she was a security officer, who was just escorting an 'unruly guest' to the door and no one wanted any part of that.

In the elevator alone, Zora used a silver key and turned the elevator to private taking it to the top floor with no stops. With just the two of them, nothing was said. Priscilla dared to glance at her, standing this close to Zora, her size was obvious. Priscilla had never seen someone like her before. She dared to think she was perfect. By the time they arrived, Priscilla was out of her daze and ready for round two with this Amazon. As Zora pushed her out of the elevator, she grabbed Priscilla's arm again, cutting off the circulation. She didn't take kindly to this and her anger was gonna get the best of her again. The digging of the nails in her arm was the breaking point.

"Get your fucking hands off me!" She yelled at the muscled woman, growing tired of being manhandled. She pulled her arm from her iron grip as they made their way to the large oak double doors. Zora was caught off guard by this and grabbed Priscilla again forcefully digging her nails into her arm. She swung Priscilla around and backhanded her so hard that Priscilla's head snapped to the side like a spring-loaded crossbow.

If she was hit any harder, she would have snapped her neck. The blow dazed her again, but the taste of blood brought her back to her senses quickly. She tried her best to keep her anger in check, she knew losing her head, would mean certain death. There was no doubt they were going to kill her, but they haven't yet. Hans obviously wanted her alive, and she'd do her best to stall her untimely demise further.

The Amazon shoved her along, opening the doors to the large, lavish office, with wall to wall brown carpet, white walls, with finely painted pictures, simple furniture, and a wall mounted TV. Ahead of her was a large brown desk. Upon her arrival, the large black chair swung around revealing the occupant. Hans Goring stared at her over his clasped hands. As they made their way closer, he got a better look, cocking a single eyebrow, he let out a snicker.

"Murphy? Diane Murphy?" He said with a sneer spitting out the name like poison. But then his sneer turned into the ugliest smile she'd ever seen, as he leaned forward. "Or should I say, Priscilla Roletti, of the United States government." A sudden sensation of vertigo hit her; the entire room spun.

Did she hear him right? Did he just say her name? Hans saw the turmoil all over her face taking great pleasure in that. From the shock of her identity being compromised, she stumbled, but caught herself. She was on the verge of a panic attack.

"Why Ms. Roletti you don't look very well. Perhaps you should sit." He said with false sincerity. She refused of course, standing straighter. Her resolve only hardened once the initial shock wore off. She was compromised, and there was nothing to do about that now. She just needed to play along and stay alive now more than ever, for the sake of her kids. She doubted they were in any danger… as of yet. Hans would no doubt have thrown that in her face.

"I'm perfectly fine, thank you. Just...recovering from your girls' company." Priscilla gestured toward Zora who was just within arms reach of Priscilla. Hans smiled, as he slowly stood and stepped around the desk.

"Yes, Zora does have a way with people at times. Now, tell me Ms. Roletti or whoever you may be, what do I owe the pleasure of this visit hmm?" Priscilla licked her lower lip. Being so close to him since the incident in Pennsylvania, a jolt of rage crept up on her. She wanted to dart to that desk and smash his face, but seeing the Amazon Zora, watching her like a hawk, she thought better of it. Plus more importantly, now than ever, she needed to live through this.

Priscilla glanced to her sides, and then at Zora before regarding Hans again.

"Let's not play games Hans. You know who I am, which means you know who I work for and you know why I'm here." She was trying to bait him.

Among many things, she needed to find out who compromised her. Hans raised an eyebrow and then nodded.

"Very well, Ms. Roletti." He perched atop the corner of the desk analyzing her. He crossed his arms over his chest. "If it was your intention to bait me into telling you who compromised you, you'll be disappointed in knowing that even I don't know.

In fact, it was an anonymous email sent to me. It had your fake ID, all of your information as well as your charming friends." Hans then tilted a bit and gestured. The other two Amazon women walked in dressed in women's suits. One had close cropped hair, tan skin, the other with long hair, and both were as chiseled as Zora. But she was bigger than the two that just walked in.

Priscilla turned to see the newcomers, the one named Velvet, carried the corpse of Roger, by the back of his neck. Priscilla didn't so much as react to that. She wasn't surprised under the circumstances and she didn't want to give them the reaction they were looking for. It was bad enough she allowed herself to look weak already. Good-bye Roger, your death will be avenged she thought to herself as she turned back to Hans, who was grinning at the sight. He then looked back to Priscilla.

"It is safe to assume someone in your Organization or someone who has ties to your Organization wants you dead." That much was obvious. And now she understood why so many agents were being picked off.

Hans continued, allowing her to digest all of this.

"As you can see Fräulein, all hope is lost for you this time. What you set out to do will not happen, as a matter of fact." He said, raising a finger. "You will be my guest for the next couple of hours, under constant supervision of course."

"Of course." Priscilla repeated snidely catching an evil look from Zora. "And as your 'guest' am I lucky enough to attend this 'demo' you have planned?" Hans gave her a scathing look, and then nodded.

"Why of course! Ms. Roletti. You of all people deserve to see the fruits of my labor." He said in a sarcastic tone, then turning serious he continued. "After all, you have some right to know since you are partially responsible for my fortune." He leaned over reaching for a cigarette from a small brown box on the desk lighting it.

"You remember D-1 I'm sure?" He said, blowing smoke into the air. She nodded, how could she not, that freak almost killed her. Hans and The Invisible Man, were doing all kinds of freaky stuff at the lab in Pennsylvania, including cloning, which they planned to use to switch prominent members of the government with, including the president. She barely stopped them.

"I figured you would, you see…the cloning was one of many operations. I only agreed to participate if I could further my own research. I had no interest in what they were doing. Our Benefactor was more than pleased to allow this since it would benefit his own ends as well. We all had our own goals to meet. Claude Griffin had more to lose than anyone."

Before he continued, he took notice of Priscilla's puzzled look. He laughed a bit, rolling his eyes, putting a hand to his forehead feigning embarrassment.

"Forgive me, I'm getting ahead of myself. You fondly remember him as The Invisible Man." He said with a grin. "Claude Griffin was a foremost scientist in the field of human genetics. His research covered such things as limb replacement, invisibility and of course, cloning. But due to unfortunate events and a foolish impulse, he ruined a promising career.

He could have been bigger than Einstein. You see, when he discovered the formula to make a human being invisible, he tested it on himself with no regard of the consequences. The fool, he succeeded, of course, but he overlooked two very important things. One, was how to revert back to visibility and the last, but the most important thing, was what kind of side effects would take place not only on the physical standpoint but on a psychological one as well. As for the physical effects, they were the obvious, he was invisible. The only other unknown side effect was enhanced strength. But with these godlike powers, there's always a flaw and that was the longer you stayed invisible, the more it ate at your mind.

It made him mad, he'd have fits of rage out of nowhere. He'd knock your brains out for something as trivial as mixing the wrong chemicals." Hans took a deep breath, seeming annoyed to rehash these events, but continued on.

"It was primarily because of you, that we failed. After your escape, he went mad. You see, my dear, Claude was promised the formula to gain back his true self, whether or not he was being led on I'll never know and do not care. Now if the operation went as planned, he'd handle the cloning aspects while I created the supreme being and together infuse that in one.

The cloning of the President was merely the tip of the iceberg. We were going to start off small, clone a senator and move from there. In time, the government would be in our control. Let it be known once again, I cared not for their goals, trust me, all that mattered to me was advancement in my work, and money was the main motivator.

But thanks to you my dear, the data I compounded proved useful. After the incident, I took all my research and disappeared. The great President of this country was all the more happy to provide me with not only a safe haven, but anything I needed when I showed him what I had to offer in return. It was mere luck that he was in the process of constructing this place as I arrived. I agreed to run its day to day operations, in return, he funded the rest of my work, and he would get first crack at the finished product." He got up, taking one last puff of the cigarette and snuffed it out before walking towards her. His hands were behind his back.

"Your being here, now compromises a host of many things. One being that the Benefactor knows where I am. I have no doubt he was behind this. Setting you up, having me dispose of you. He wants to distract me, he wants my work. But I am no fool. I will not be distracted by the likes of him or you."

He walked past her towards the doors, and turned abruptly. "The world as you know it will be in complete anarchy. Times will be changing, trust me. The Benefactor is out there." It was always believed that someone was pulling the strings, but they never had proof. This was as close to it as they had. Hans gestured them towards the door, Zora pushed her forward. Priscilla stood there defiantly a few seconds longer with the urge to spin around and take a swing at this bitch. She kept that urge in check for now. The time will come soon enough.

"Do you know who this Benefactor is?" She asked as they approached the doors.

"I wish I knew for sure, but I have my suspicions. I'll tell you this, he's very powerful and fully committed to his mad task." He looked at his watch. "Now if you'll excuse me, Velvet and Hunter will escort you, to your new room. Rest and refresh yourself. The demo will start this evening and then dinner right after." He then looked at Hunter and Velvet.

"Please make sure Ms. Roletti is kept out of trouble. She has a habit of making plenty of it." They both nodded and walked her out of the open door. Hans closed it and then looked at Zora. Zora never held back on how she felt. And Hans didn't have to be a mind reader to see, she wasn't happy about his handling of this.

"Zora dear, you don't approve of me keeping her around?" She nodded.

"No, I don't." He looked to the floor, contemplating what she said then walked to her and gently stroked her face with two fingers, she closed her eyes like a cat would, all that was missing was her purring.

"And I agree with you. But there's another angle at play here. Is Ms. Roletti meant to be a distraction or is someone else manipulating things so that I may do their dirty work? Or is it both? Nevertheless, my dear, I want to show her the future. She thought she won the last time. I want to show her how gravely wrong, she is."

Zora would never say this to Hans but one day his ego and pride would get the best of him, she only hoped if and when that day came she was there to protect him. "As soon as the presentation is over and we finalize our contracts, you can have the pleasure of killing her." She nodded again. "But in the mean time my dear, you best be ready, it all rests on your shoulders." She nodded.

"I will never let you down." Hans smiled.

"Of course you wouldn't, I would never think of it." His smile slowly faded as he looked deep into her eyes. "And Zora, be alert.

This woman was only a distraction. The real threat is yet to come." She nodded again.

"Let them come, nothing will ever happen to you." Hans smiled,

"Go, my dear." And without a word further she ran off while Hans remained there with his hands clasped behind his back in deep thought. Zora was the key, only she would be able to keep The Benefactor at bay. The man had unlimited resources at his disposal, yes but up against Zora none of that mattered

Once these deals were done, they were leaving. And as long as he had Zora by his side, he was invincible. His enemies will know, pain and suffering. And that example will be made with the death of Priscilla Roletti.

Chapter 15
Helpless

Priscilla was brought to a room just one floor below. It was very small, with only a bed and a small bathroom, Velvet stayed behind while Hunter left them alone. Velvet didn't so much as say a word to Priscilla, she stood by the door, leaning against the wall staring at nothing in particular. Priscilla walked towards the bed and plopped down.

She frustratingly sighed, her emotions were in a tangle. She wanted to cry so hard right now. If there was a god, she prayed that her kids were alright. Not knowing was the worse thing. But she kept telling herself, the kids were safe. That's all she had at the moment was hope. And with hope came a chance of her living through this. It was going to be hard, but she needed to put everything behind her now.

Roger's death, her being compromised, her kids. Right now, it was all about her, and getting the hell out of here. So that she could do something about these revelations dropped at her feet. This is what they trained you for, to handle situations like these. And the only way to do that was too rest, because without rest she was useless to everyone.

She glanced at Velvet, who was now facing her. Priscilla just gave her a little nod, and then slowly laid down, turning her back to the woman. She took a deep breath and tried to relax, it helped somewhat as her eyes grew heavy. And before she could think anymore thoughts of helplessness and despair, she was off to dreamland.

Chapter 16
The Women of Tomorrow

Priscilla was shoved awake so hard she almost fell off the bed. "Wake up!" Velvet spat out, Priscilla was awake enough that her feet hit the floor. She sprang up. Hunter had returned. Velvet walked to the open door and was waiting for Priscilla. She followed her captor while Hunter brought up the rear. They took the elevator back to the top floor. Upon exiting, Priscilla felt déjà vu hitting her. She saw way too much of this lobby as she was led to the conference room.

It was a simple set up of about a hundred chairs and a stage with a podium, and a rather large barbell set in the middle. Military guards flanked all the exits, there were two at each doorway. As Priscilla was rushed along closely shadowed by her escorts who didn't say much of anything to her, but tell her where to go, she took notice to some big time heads of state here.

She managed to spot the Iranian president with his own band of security. The Libyan president was in attendance dressed in his outlandish robes, along with a host of many others she recognized and many she did not. She was led to the front row, Hunter and Velvet sat her down and walked backstage. Velvet, the one with the short cropped hair, gave her a stiff warning.

"Move and I'll break your face." Priscilla didn't even acknowledge her, she continued to look around while the rest of the invited audience made their way in. Once the last of the stragglers sat down, everyone's eyes were on the stage. The military guards stationed at the entrances, closed and locked them. In no time Hans, came striding out with his hands behind his back. Going over to the podium, he waited for the murmuring to quiet down before he cleared his throat and positioned the mic. Priscilla watched him closely. She could tell he loved every second of being in the spotlight.

"I want to thank all the esteemed guests that were able to make it here on such short notice with little information on what you were being called for. I apologize for that, but as you know, nowadays secrecy must be the first and foremost thing heeded.

I hope you all think the time you've spent here will be well worth it." He fixed the pair of glasses he wore, then spoke again. "Now what I have to offer you is simple, what I want to present to you is something more important than any weapon you could possibly develop in your wildest dreams. As history states, the best weapon is the one who wields it."

He looked to his left, then looked back to his audience as Zora walked onto the stage clad in a sports bra, tight black shorts with her hair pulled back. The Amazon walked towards the barbell and stopped inches from it. There were gasps from some in attendance. The sheer perfection of Zora was truly something to behold, even Priscilla was impressed. Every muscle looked as though it was sculpted from the finest artist, in the simplest term, she was raw power.

"Now bear in mind, gentlemen, individual results may vary. Aside from super strength, stamina and agility, your subject will be nothing without the proper training, and intelligence." With those words Hans stepped towards the barbell with two thick weights on either end. He raised his voice a bit more since he was away from the podium.

"Now, gentlemen, the barbell you see at my feet, weighs over 2,000 pounds, that's 1 ton." He said, gesturing with one finger in the air while looking at everyone, some of the faces in attendance were skeptical to say the least, which was something he expected to see. "If there's anyone here that wants to try to lift this, then you're more than welcome to do so, as many as you want."

Some in attendance looked at each other, whispering. Some even challenged their rivals to do so, but no one, took up the challenge. A small smirk crept upon Hans' face. He then turned to Zora.

"My dear, would you please?" Zora stepped forward and squatted. Grabbing the bar, veins popped from her forearms as she prepped to lift what many thought was impossible. Priscilla found herself intrigued also. Then, before their eyes, with not even a show of exertion, she lifted the one-ton bar over her head. Some of the attendees got up from their seats, gaping and walked closer.

She took one hand away, holding the incredible weight effortlessly. Some clapped, muffled conversation could be heard throughout. Hans stepped forward with his palms out to quiet the small crowd. Some saw this and told the ones closest to sit.

"Now, as you can see, what I have to offer you is not of fantasy or fiction. What you see before you is the world's first super human. Five of these super soldiers could replace a small army." He turned to Zora nodding. Before she placed the barbell back down on the stage, she curled it with one arm and then slowly placed the barbell back to the floor with little more than a sound and stepped away.

Hans gestured to his left and walking out on the stage were Velvet and Hunter in the same clothing. They stood next to Zora.

"These two received a lesser dose of the serum, Zora is the finished product. But make no mistake my friends, these two are just as deadly." He stepped back to the podium. Before he could talk someone yelled out.

"And the side effects? Surely there must be!" Hans squinted to see who it was, it was the representative of Cuba, the German smiled. Directing his next comments to him.

"As I stated, there are none of what you are referring to, such as psychological, as I stated before. That is on you to choose the right subjects. As far as side effects on a physical level, the only side effect of the transformation is the muscles must be worked out daily a minimum of two-hours a day to be exact. If not, the tissue will decrease and grow soft. That is a side effect that I'm currently working to eliminate. But if you're putting them to use, which I'm sure you will, then you'd have no worry about that.

Now, since this information is a need to know, only people that are interested will be shown further results. I have extensive video documentation and for those more skeptical, a live demonstration could be arranged. But only once, when payment is delivered, then will you be able to view this. For security concerns of course, you understand, but for now I will show you another demo. Observe the screen behind me. Please." At his word the curtains parted, revealing a large screen. A video immediately came on, and it was of Zora standing next to a standard issue army Humvee. She nodded to the camera and then proceeded to destroy the hummer with her bare hands. Within seconds, the pristine vehicle was turned into a pile of scrap. She capped off the demo by catapulting the Hummer far off the screen. It was quick, but it left an impression on them all, including Priscilla who felt her throat dry.

How the hell was she gonna stand up to that. She looked around seeing everyone else's reactions; they were all in a frenzy. Zora smiled, proud of herself, Hans quickly took the stage again.

"Now, gentlemen." He said over the mic, they quickly quieted down. "Please take some time on this, I'm sure some of you must make phone calls back home, and consult with the powers that be. But by tomorrow at midday you must tell me yes or no. Now for your enjoyment, a banquet will be served downstairs, thank you for your time." In a very quick manner they started to leave. As Hans watched them go, he turned to Priscilla.

"So, my dear, your thoughts?" She didn't have any. She was speechless that this could even happen. If any one of these rogue nations got their hands on this information, the endless chaos that would ensue, would be too much for words. He walked down off the stage towards her.

"I'll take your loss of words as a comforting thought then, come, we are going to have a more private dinner just the four of us. I have more to tell you and I'd like to know a thing or two also." He walked off. Hunter and Velvet followed him while Zora stayed and waited for Priscilla.

Even though she was shocked by what she saw, she wasn't going to show she was intimidated or afraid of her. Priscilla got up and walked while Zora followed her never taking her eyes off her, all the while hoping that this woman gave her a reason to tear her apart.

Chapter 17
Dinner is served

They sat in silence at a long table draped with a white tablecloth, as they waited for the meals to come. The other two Amazons didn't so much as give Priscilla a second glance, but all the while Zora kept a close eye on her, it was obvious she had a deep hatred for her. It was something Priscilla was really tired of and she said so.

"Hey Hans?" She said, breaking the silence. He looked up. "Let me ask you, did you use dykes? Because your girl here can't take her eyes off me." The table shook as Zora got up, Hans placed a firm hand on her, as if that would stop her from jumping the table and bashing her head in. But she was amazed by the control he had over them, especially Zora, as she sat down.

"Words Zora, only words my dear, you must refrain yourself. There will always be a time." Hans said, as he gently rubbed her shoulder, he then looked to Priscilla and smiled.

"I'd be careful with your taunts Priscilla, the next time Zora may not be so easily controllable." He failed to intimidate her and he knew it. He quickly changed the subject.

"Now my dear, I had forgotten to thank you..."

"For what?" Priscilla asked. Hans smiled.

"For ridding the world of those animals Trish and Omar, they were a wretched pair to say the least, The Benefactor employed them to tie up loose ends, Claude and I hated dealing with them." She cocked her eyebrow, images of Trish and Omar flashed in her mind. She was glad they were gone too.

"Yeah, too bad I didn't send someone else with them." Zora gave her a sharp look while the other two talked amongst themselves, not even paying any attention to the verbal fencing. She noticed they were a little closer than normal. Hans smiled, leaning in closer.

"Now let me explain to you, in better detail on how you served my work for the better." He took out a cigarette, he offered her one, at first she wasn't going to take one, but the more she stalled the better, she really needed to think of something for when the time came to escape. She reached over to the open pack grabbing one, he then stretched out his other arm with a lighter. The urge to grab it and break it, was intense. Leaning back in her chair she took a long drag.

"Now one of the main reasons a hospital was chosen was because it was the perfect cover for what we were doing. Aside from that, there were plenty of test subjects. Unwilling ones of course, but I needed to see what would work and what wouldn't. I had no choice but to manipulate the mind, being that they were involuntary.

Lobotomizing, I soon realized was one mistake. With all the power they were given, it was useless. They needed to have their hand held the whole time. But at the same time, I was worried that if I granted this power to someone willingly then what's to say they won't turn on me. That was something I didn't want.

So, in my travels, Zora was the first one I found, she was young, naive, with no family, no future, and she was dying. She was suffering from multiple sclerosis; it was in the advanced stages. Before me, no one showed her a single act of kindness and through that I earned her undying love and loyalty. She looked to me as a father figure. Not only did I make her a supreme being, I cured her.

One of the many effects of the serum is that, it's capable of curing diseases in a way no one can imagine. I've cured AIDS, Cancer, it can even make the crippled walk again. That is why I stressed the choosing process must be flawless, because the power can go to one's head. You give it to someone arrogant, then you'll pay for that in the long run. You give it to someone like Zora, who was at death's door, then you have a loyal person that will do anything for you." He said gesturing to Zora, Hans then looked past Priscilla, and smiled.

"Ah dinner's served." As the words came out, four waiters came up and passed out four plates covered with a steel cover, removing them at the same time, the steam billowed up. Priscilla took in a deep breath, hunger overtook her aside from the circumstances. The food looked tasty and it was.

She wasted no time digging in. If and when the time came to make a move, she doubted she'd get another chance to eat like this for a while. Better to take advantage of it now. As she ate, Hans thought to make more small talk with her.

"Ms. Roletti, there's a question I've been wanting to have answered." She looked up chewing, with a curious look.

"Back in Pennsylvania, we checked you for any weapons, but how on earth did you manage to cut open the vent cover in your holding cell?" She was sipping on her water when he finished, she'd never tell him the truth that all Ops had those laser torch pens, concealed in certain parts of their clothes. Hers was concealed in her shoe, a minor oversight on their part which cost them, she thought of a better explanation to give him.

"That's simple I used my go-go gadget laser, here I'll show you." She gave him the middle finger. He furrowed his brow.

"Charming, you Americans..." He said, chuckling, going back to his food, Priscilla had some questions of her own.

"Hans, if this serum is everything you say it is, and you've found a way to cure diseases, why not share it with the world? I mean, if you're looking to profit, you would from that alone, and it would fill your ego to boot. You'd be the savior to millions." Hans sat back in his chair, studying her.

"I've thought of this, I really have, but you and I know that if I came forward with this, governments starting with yours would try to bog me down.

You'd have drug companies from all over the world trying to disavow me. The last thing they want is someone to cure anything with a single needle, you know this is true, don't deny it." He said with a sly smile. She was the last person to agree with him, but he had a point. Even though she worked for the Government, she'd be the first one to tell you it was corrupted to the core. She's had to silence a few officials in her time, and drug companies weren't any better. If you looked at the world under a microscope you'd see one big contradiction, wrapped in a bow that said, "Fuck you."

Hans swallowed his food and was about to add something more to this topic when the doors to the small dining area were flung open, and a uniformed man rushed over to Hans, whispering in his ear. Priscilla tried to strain her ear to listen. Zora listened in; the other two Amazons stopped their private little chat then and waited for Hans' reaction. The look on Hans' face said the message wasn't a good one, in fact, he turned and looked right at Priscilla with a deep scorn, Hans nodded to the man.

"Tell them I'm on my way." With that, the man was off as quickly as he came. Hans pushed his food from him, wiping at the corner of his mouth as he looked right at Priscilla.

"It seems someone else is out and about tonight." With those words, he rose from his chair.

"Zora, Velvet come with me. Hunter, take Ms. Roletti to her room and stay with her, until you hear from me." Zora got up protesting.

"Hans, let me go with her." He raised a finger silencing her.

"No, my dear, there may be more dangerous people lurking about. That's why I need you by my side." He then looked at Priscilla. "Looks like, you've been bought some extra time, Ms. Roletti." He gestured for Zora and Velvet to follow him.

Priscilla watched him go wondering what was going on, whatever it was, it wasn't going to bode well for her. Which made it all the more imperative for Priscilla to make an escape now that she was alone with only one Amazon. Priscilla then looked up at Hunter, she was the smallest of the three. Could Priscilla handle her? She hoped so.

"Let's go." The woman said, standing back, as she kept a close eye on her. Priscilla nodded and got up, as they made their way back to her room.

Priscilla couldn't shake this new sense of dread that things were about to get more fucked than they are now.

Chapter 18
A thief in the night

It didn't take long for Hans and his bodyguards to get to the lab. It was located right on the grounds, on the east end of the compound. The entrance was a large oak tree, only those with a magnetic card reader could open the secret entrance that led down.

It was a high end lab, consisting of an operating room, freezer and an observation wing. The staff was small too, aside from Hans there were two other scientists here. As he entered the main lab, Hans saw the direness of the situation. The lab was in shambles, computers were purged of their hard-drives and destroyed.

As Hans took all this in, his mind was racing now. His heart skipped a beat, fear gripped him. From the corner of his eye, he saw one of his frantic scientists run towards him with his hand on his head. He was still in his work clothes from the day, he looked tired.

"Hans! Thank God, there's been a murder! They killed Edwin! And…and the serum we had on hand was destroyed. There's not a single vial left!" Hans quickly raised a hand, silencing the rambling man. He then placed two fingers to his temple, trying to rub out the headache sure to come. Zora and Velvet stood by his side unmoving.

"Unfortunately, there's nothing we can do at the moment, did the surveillance cameras get anything?" The pudgy man shook his head, Hans wanted to grit his teeth.

"Whoever it was disrupted the feed."

"And the body, it was vandalized? Where is it?" The man gestured over to the door that led to the cold storage room. Hans walked inside to find a gurney in the middle of the room. He ripped off the white sheet and gasped at what he saw. Zora gave a fast squint at the sight unmoved. The scientist had a single bullet to the head. But that wasn't what shocked them, what put them ill at ease was his face, it was bleached whiter than a bone.

Chapter 19
A Blast from the past part 2

The elevator ride down was short, giving Priscilla little time to think of a plan for her escape. She may have been bought more time by whatever happened that took Hans away, but it won't be for long. The next time she saw Hans or Zora, she was dead.

So, she needed to think of something and fast. They had just exited the elevator and turned down the hall. They were almost to the room, it was within sight.

Hunter, had Priscilla walk in front of her, keeping a good five feet from her. So, trying anything now wouldn't be advisable with her great strength, Priscilla's only chance would be a confined fight. She just needed to strike fast and hard, because she wouldn't get a second chance at it. Perhaps, there might be something in the shower, she could use. A bar of soap, wrapped in a towel? Maybe rip off the mirror to the medicine cabinet, smash her head with that.

They were all desperate ideas that had little chance of working. Something would come to mind, a solution would present itself, they always did. One just needed to see it. Once she calmed and gathered herself, she'd be able to think clearly. There was still too much going on in her mind.

Just as they got to the door, Hunter stopped her, by grabbing her shoulder and moved her to the side.

"Stay right there." She said, giving Priscilla a stern look. Priscilla didn't say anything at all. While Hunter unlocked the door, that dreadful feeling she couldn't shake off was screaming at her. Her stomach was in knots, making her want to go to the bathroom. She was antsy, glancing back and forth. What the heck was wrong with her? This impending sensation of dread, was driving her crazy. Hunter, slipped the card into the slot unlocking the door, and pushed it open, stepping aside. "Let's go." Priscilla wasn't looking in her direction she was looking down the hall, which was eerily quiet.

She's never seen anyone else but them, which led Priscilla to believe this was a private floor of some kind.

"Hello!" Hunter snapped her fingers, which caught Priscilla's attention. Priscilla embarrassingly smiled.

"Right." Stepping forward, she pushed the door open all the way, and was looking down as she entered, still with that sense of dread nipping at her side. Priscilla glanced behind her, as Hunter followed her in, then turned and locked the door.

Priscilla turned back around and looked straight ahead, and couldn't believe who she was seeing right now. Her eyes widened,

"Shit!" She ducked at the sight of the silver revolver being pointed right at her. Hunter didn't even have a chance to know what the hell was going on when a single round nailed her in the forehead as she turned around splattering her brains on the door.

Priscilla held her gaze on the corpse for a moment. She was breathing hard, the sense of dread turned up now by 9,000 points. She then looked the other way and stood. Straightening to her full height, she never took her eyes off the man sitting in the chair. She was literally speechless.

The Albino, who by rights should be dead was in this very room. She should know, she shot him in the head at the diner at point blank range no less.

"Well, from the look on your face little lady I'd say you're quite shocked to see me now." He smiled at her, his golden eyes were just as frightful as ever.

"You're supposed to be dead…" She replied dryly. He nodded, his smile gone. With his free hand, he tapped the back of his skull; it thudded.

"Metal plate. The next time you shoot someone, make sure they're dead."

"Yeah…well...I was kinda in a rush at the time." He laughed slightly.

"Yeah, you were, weren't you. You caused me a lot of trouble after that being brought to the hospital, then having to break out. I had to kill a lot of people because of you, and I hate killin' people I don't have to. Brings too much of the spotlight onto you, you know what I mean?" She didn't respond, she was still too shocked seeing him here. If she wasn't fucked before she certainly was now. How the hell was she going to handle this, this guy is no joke. He leaned in closer to her.

"Now let's go. We're leaving." She looked at him dumbfounded.

"You're joking, right? In case you didn't realize, I'm not here on a fucking holiday."

"I'm well aware of that, but you are coming with me, one way or the other." She nervously licked her lower lip, this guy was whacked himself. If he thought they were just going to walk up out of here with no one noticing, he had another thing coming.

She looked at him, then into the barrel of the gun, frowning. The only thing that could have riled Hans enough to make him leave so abruptly, was something happened to the lab, and she had a good idea who was responsible now.

"You were why Hans was called away?" He nodded. "So, were you sent here to get the serum and kill Hans? If that's the case, then let's team up together, you and I have the same purpose." She said gesturing to herself then to him. "Then you and I can settle our thing." In truth, the last thing she wanted was to team up with this guy, but being so far away, she couldn't lunge for him, she'd never make it in time. She'd be dead the moment she even made a move like that, she had to buy herself some time.

"Well, that's where you're wrong little lady, I'm not here to kill Hans or his freaks, I've completed one part of my job, and I offered you a partnership way back when, but that was before you shot me from behind. So, you'll excuse me if I don't believe you now." He stood up. "Besides, Miss Roletti, the second part of my obligation, is you. I was paid a lot of money to make sure you never return alive, and I always follow through with a contract. I'm not going to lie though; you have been on my mind since that time. I was even thinking of trying to track you down myself, but then got involved in my own matters.

But when someone came a calling and gave me the chance to settle this and get paid, I was all the more pleased to accept." Her face dropped, he knew her name as well. If this had been any other time she'd have been shocked as before. But now she was more annoyed than anything else. Hans was right, the Benefactor was behind it all.

"Not surprised I know who you are, little lady?" She shook her head,

"Not on a day, like today I'm not." The Albino chuckled,

"Better get used to'em." The deadly smile faded just then. "Ok Priscilla, it's time to move, before you die someone wants to have a word with you." He said her name in a taunting way, "Let's go."

No doubt this Benefactor. But why? She wasn't going to find out, the time for stalling and playing hostage was over.

She spun on her heel facing the door. She could feel the gun being pointed to her back even though he was a good five feet behind her. As they approached the door, he ordered her to stop.

"Stop, move the body." She set her jaw tight. But nevertheless did as she was told. She didn't have to move it far, only a few inches so they could open the door. And thank god, Hunter was freaking heavy as she pulled her by the ankles.

"That's enough, now open the door slowly." She stood in the doorframe of the now opened door. "Make sure no one's out there." He said from behind. She was gritting her teeth so hard in anger, that they hurt.

She looked to the right and left quickly turning back, giving the thumbs up. He nodded to her and gestured her to walk. She did so. She walked out into the hallway, going right. The Albino was right behind her stepping over the body of Hunter.

He came right up behind her, the elevator was to their left side, the stairway was further down the hallway. She could see it from where she was. She licked her lips with anticipation, her eyes darted around looking for anything that could be used against him. She needed to distract him, throw him off guard, then take him.

But there was nothing until she spotted a fire extinguisher. It was on the wall coming ever so closer on her left. She bit her lip as they made their way, this was it.

She only had one chance at this, she had to make it count. She was mere inches from it, sweat beaded her forehead. In less than a blink of an eye, she threw out her left hand, grabbing the extinguisher then spun around with all her might and threw it straight at him.

The Albino was fast, damn his quickness. He fired his weapon bursting the metal canister, creating a wall of foam, temporally impeding his line of fire. Foam also splattered all over the walls and red carpet. She bolted for the stairway, she was only a few feet from the door now, when a gunshot rang out missing her then another hitting the wall in front of her. Just as she flung the door open, a sharp stinging pain surged through her shoulder, blood splattered the door. She kicked it shut. Her right arm was starting to go numb, if not for the adrenaline rush, she'd be screaming her head off in pain. She looked to her wound, it was bleeding pretty badly, the bullet was in-lodged.

That was the least of her worries right now. He'll be through that door any second she thought as she looked around the cramped spiraling staircase, she was on the 39th floor. She leaned over the metal rail, she then looked up, she was fucked royally. She bolted down the stairs, skipping steps as she could. She tripped a few times, she felt herself losing her balance from the loss of blood.

She didn't even glance back.

She ran down two more floors coming to the 36th floor, she didn't even bother to worry about being seen at this point. Bursting into the hallway, she was about to make for the elevator when she saw another fire extinguisher. Grabbing it, she went back to the stairwell door, and slammed the doorknob off on the stairwell side and slammed it closed. That would give her some time, but not much. She ran to the elevator, hitting the button.

The seconds felt like hours as she watched the numbers tick up and down, there were three elevators. She held her shoulder, squeezing it. She blocked out the pain, as best she could as blood was dripping from her fingertips like a leaky faucet. Keeping a sharp eye on all the hallways, Priscilla looked back and forth eagerly waiting when finally, the bell chimed. The heavy doors slid open, and waiting for her inside was the Albino. He stepped back into firing position, she lunged right in, grabbing his wrist. Just as he fired his weapon, the bullet harmlessly hit the wall as the doors closed.

They were entangled in a fierce close quarters battle. The Albino didn't have any skill whatsoever. Even with her wound, Priscilla took charge of the situation, pummeling him. The first thing she did was disarm him, without his weapon he was nothing. The pain surging from her shoulder to the tips of her fingers was intense. Every movement hurt, but she didn't let up for a second. The Albino tried to defend himself, he didn't even get a chance to strike back. The rage that was going through her was like none other, her blood was going all over the place.

The Albino's face was smeared with it looking like war paint he applied. She repeatedly slammed him against the steel walls of the elevator shaking it back and forth. She applied a choke hold from behind and it was locked in tight. He struggled, slamming her against the wall that only increased her resolve. Her hold only became tighter, within seconds his arms were going limp, his struggles decreased. She watched closely as the last embers of life faded away.

She thought she had him, that was until she felt a splash of liquid touch her hairline which started to trickle down towards her eye, almost instantaneously it burned like acid. She released him, he fell limp. She frantically clawed at her face, the elevator was starting to fill with smoke. Using her shirt to wipe away whatever he just threw at her, she looked around, with one eye closed to the floor.

She spotted what caused this in his hand was a silver flask with the cap off. It had screaming skulls carved into it. She then spotted his revolver. Picking it up, she cocked the hammer. She'd end this one way or another, but at that second the elevator stopped and the doors slid open and waiting for them were two security guards who were no doubt alerted by someone. She didn't waste a single second. She turned and opened fire, killing them.

Chaos erupted from the gunfire, tourists ran in all directions. Priscilla stuffed the silver revolver in her pants, then reached down to the closest guard taking his gun as well. She ran into the mass of people fleeing outside. She fell right into place and was propelled outside into the evening sun. It was hot, she took a deep cleansing breath, then ran as fast as she could. She never looked back.

More security flooded the lobby, with guns drawn it was completely empty. They came to the opened elevator, seeing their fallen comrades, they took a closer look inside finding no one else.

Unclear of who else may be involved, they were unaware that the Albino had slipped away in the confusion.

Chapter 20
Medical assistance needed

It had been hours since the commotion at the casino resort. Priscilla was exhausted and ready to pass out. She had no resources of any kind to fall back on so she did what she had to do to survive.

Priscilla was walking down one of the many busy streets where hundreds of vendors were hawking their goods. The crowds were big that evening, mostly of tourists from all corners of the world, hardly paying any notice to their surroundings as they shopped, ate and took pictures.

Being it was well after sunset, the bloodstains were hard to see in the twilight. She passed a rack of summer shirts. Some so tacky, she couldn't imagine ever wearing one. But tonight, she'd make the exception.

As she walked, she grabbed the first button down, she could, and very quickly put it on, before the vendor even took notice. She grew cold, even though it was in the high eighty's. She lost too much blood and needed to tend to her wound, which was throbbing badly. She thought it might be too late to do anything at this point. But she quickly pushed those thoughts aside.

As she carried on and after some time she spotted a pharmacy. She walked passed the glass front. It was a small privately owned place. Which was good for her. She'd be able to get in, subdue whoever was in there and get out. Priscilla then walked back to the front door and quickly entered, slipping down one of the aisles. As she heard people pass her by in the other aisles, she walked towards the back. As luck would have it, the pharmacy was closing. She wasn't surprised, small places like this always closed early.

As the pudgy man, in his worn white pharmacist coat made his way up to the front she followed him. Once she heard the door close, and the blinds being drawn, she made her move. She came out of hiding. By the time he turned around, she was right next to him pushing her hand to his mouth before the man could yell out. His eyes were darting back and forth, most likely searching for a gun. Once his fear was abetted, he calmed down a little.

Priscilla spoke to him in Spanish. She was slurring her words pretty badly now, she removed her hand from his mouth, and he backed away. Priscilla hoped she did the right thing. She didn't want to pummel some innocent guy, but if she needed to, she'd find the strength to do so. But seeing the shape she was in; the man walked to her and slowly opened her shirt. He was frantic, asking too many questions. He was going to call the cops, she waved that suggestion away, telling the man that she was shot and couldn't go to a hospital.

The pudgy, balding man threw his arms up and slapped his hands on top of his head, frustrated with the look of 'why me?' Priscilla stepped towards him, only to lose her balance and fall into a shelf throwing various items to the floor. The man ran over to help her, placing her arm around his neck. With enormous effort he slogged her towards the back where his office was. By the time he dumped her on a couch, she was already passed out and at death's door.

Chapter 21
The Lens of Truth

She awoke gasping for breath. She felt as though someone had just pulled her head from a bucket of cold water after holding it there longer than she could hold her breath. She sat up a bit, but the room was spinning. She fell back closing her eyes, putting a shaky hand to her head. She was soaked with sweat. She tried to get up again, but she felt sick to her stomach. Her thoughts were as twisted as a dead tree branch, she couldn't remember anything.

Then out of nowhere she heard a voice that quickly made her come to her senses, and ignore how she was feeling. She threw her feet to the floor sitting up now, unsteadily. It was very dark in the room she was in, and as weak as she was, she readied herself for anything, but felt the overwhelming urge to throw-up and lay down.

"Who the hell is here!?" She called out not sounding very threatening. The man cleared his voice.

"Maybe you can understand me without a mouth full of food. I said, don't try to get up, you're very weak. I removed the bullet from your wound and stitched you up. You almost died." The voice sounded American, and very familiar.

"Oh yeah?" She said, taking the advice, and laying back down again. She came to the conclusion if they were going to kill her they'd have done it already, and not bother to patch her up.

"And who might my savior be then? Can you tell me that?" There was no answer; as a small night-light was turned on. She tried to get up, but was pushed back down by a firm hand. From the quick glimpse, she was in a furnished room. There was a couch and an old TV. The man squatted next to her, she squinted to make out who it was, but the man's face was concealed. He wore a tacky yellow shirt with palm trees and jean shorts.

"Why agent Blondie, I'm hurt, you don't recognize my voice." Hearing her code name, her eyes snapped wide open.

"Lens?!" He nodded, getting up and grabbing a chair, he sat next to her, as he told her what happened.

"I've been tailing you since you left the country. I couldn't rescue you from the casino and for this you have my apologies, and the loss of Roger, even more upsetting. But I couldn't break my cover and risk being compromised, I hope you understand.

When the commotion was going on, I tried to intercept you. From what I had found out, you were shot. I figured you'd seek some type of medical attention. I knew a hospital was out of the question and there weren't many pharmacies. The man you passed out on, had left you in the shop. He was frantic looking for the police, but I reasoned with him. He was well paid for the supplies and his silence. It's great that in this country people can still be bribed." He chuckled at that last part, while Priscilla tried to crane her head towards him as he talked.

"But why are you here?" Since her identity was compromised, she had to suspect anyone as an enemy. And as much as she appreciated him being here and saving her. She had to be sure.

"I'm here with an urgent warning for you." He looked at his watch. "Rest, I'll give you something for the nausea, and then I'll prepare you something to eat. I don't have much time." Before she could even ask a question, he got up and walked to the kitchen.

As it turned out, Lens was great at whipping up some food from nothing more than a few canned goods. She stuffed her face, sitting on the couch now in just a sports bra, and boxer shorts. Her shoulder was stiff and sore, she tried rotating it every now and then.

Lens sat in the chair to her left, she felt like a pig eating the way she was in front of him. But being as starved as she was, she didn't care for long. She finished her bowl of food, throwing the fork inside and placing both to the side. She sat back, tilting her head and closed her eyes, taking a deep breath.

"Satisfied?" He asked from his chair, aside from the kitchen light the only other light on was a lamp, and even with that on, she couldn't see him clearly. The lamp was positioned so that she couldn't see his face, not that it would matter, he'd be disguised somehow. She looked at him with heavy eyes. With her belly full, she got a little tired. She nodded.

"More than satisfied ...you saved my life, thank you." He waved his hand at the comment. Reaching into his breast pocket, he grabbed a pack of cigarettes, taking one out he slid the pack to her. She was more than inclined; she needed a smoke right about now. Lighting his first, he slid her the lighter. She lit hers taking a long drag, letting the smoke out slowly savoring it.

"I've always liked you Blondie, I don't care for or like many people. In my line of work, everyone is a potential enemy." She nodded at that analogy, and believed that more than ever now. Trust moving forward wasn't going to come easy.

"So why are you here?" She knew it sounded too harsh, and felt kinda bad. But Lens was a pro and she knew he wouldn't take it personally. He leaned forward, taking a drag of his cigarette.

"You know, I've been around a long time. I know many things, been to Area 51, I know the truth of the J.F.K. assassination, the Roswell crash site. If I were ever caught, the secrets I have in my head could topple the government." He pointed to his skull to emphasize the point. "But in all my years, I never came across something that I had a hard time believing." Priscilla hated it when he talked this cryptic crap, it drove her nuts.

"Lens, just for once, can you stop talking in riddles and just say what's on your mind! What does all this have to do with me?" She said, running her fingers through her hair. Just doing that, her shoulder throbbed.

"I can't tell you much right now...only for the fact that I'm still weeding through it all myself, and trust me, I don't believe it, but the truth is right there." She was about to speak again when he cut her off. "Don't talk! Let me finish, please. Now, from what I understand, Derlin asked you to bring back any and all data pertaining to the serum, correct?" She nodded. "And did you?"

"No, I wasn't going to." Lens nodded.

"Good, he only wanted to bog you down, keep you busy. Second, when you get back, under any circumstances do not go see Derlin, do you understand?" She nodded even though she didn't know what to make of this.

"Events are taking a turn for the worse now, with your identity compromised, and the deaths of agents. By now I'm sure you realize this conspiracy goes very deep, beyond a simple double agent in our midst's." She nodded; a blind person could see it.

"Upon your arrival back to the States, lay low and wait to hear from me." He took a drag from his cigarette and snuffed it out, leaning back. Priscilla was at a loss for words, she didn't know what to say.

"Lens, what the hell are you getting at?"

"Again, Blondie, the less you know for now the better. You need to concentrate on your survival.
If-"

"No! God dammit, you fucking tell me now, what's going on! Or I'll beat it outta you if I have to!" She yelled as she sprang up from the couch. She was furious at herself, with the mission, the situation, and now with Lens. She started to get dizzy from the outburst, but ignored it.

Lens didn't even budge from his chair. He only sighed, as Priscilla sat back down. There was silence between them. Her outburst made her shaky, and her breathing rapid. Her mind raced with so many scenarios and they all pointed to one conclusion. She wanted to ask the question that may shatter the world she thought she knew. She didn't want to ask it, she really didn't, but she had to know.

"Derlin's the double agent isn't he?" Silence ensued after she asked that, his reply was world shattering.

"Yes." From that single answer she was light headed, she buried her face in her hands in total disbelief. It can't be, it just couldn't be. Lens had to be wrong.

"Priscilla, I know it's hard to believe, but it is Derlin." She turned to Lens with tear filled red eyes.

"Is there anything else you're keeping from me Lens?" She asked, ignoring him. Lens sat back, as though contemplating the question. It took him too long for her liking to answer.

"No."

She nodded, knowing he was lying, he knew far more. She took a deep breath, the unbelievable happened. Derlin a double agent, a traitor to everyone that trusted him, cared for him, and loved him. Lens went on.

"When you return to the States, the tides are gonna change very fast and you're gonna be in the center of the storm. From here on out I wouldn't expect it to get easier for you. But I leave you this one last thought and don't forget it. The person you may think is your enemy, will turn out to be your greatest ally." She nodded, she wasn't going to ask what the hell that meant. She was sure to find out one way or another. With all that said, he rose up from the chair, Priscilla got up also. But Lens gestured her to stay. He pointed towards another chair in the room.

"In that bag is everything you need for right now. A change of clothes, a gun, a pen laser torch, and some cash." He went into his pocket, taking out a small key. He tossed it to her. On the key were three numbers indicating the locker it would open up. "That key is for a locker at the closest airport. You'll find a passport, clothes, and a disguise. There's more cash to work with as well. I wish I could do more, but I can't." He turned to leave.

"Wait! Lens what are you saying? That I abort the mission? Just up and leave?" Lens stopped, and turned half way, never facing her directly as he spoke.

"You do what you gotta do Blondie. I've given you, your way out. Personally, I'd take it and go. You've been compromised, your children could be in danger. Although I can't verify that for sure. Scuttle the mission. It's over." That was easier for him to say. She was the one with her ass on the line. The thought of allowing Hans to escape made her sick.

"Good luck, Blondie. Remember what I told you. Keep your wits about you." And just like that, he turned and left. She didn't even have a chance to say thank you again. He was out the door before she could even blink. Alone now, she threw her face into her hands, rubbing her cheeks then her eyes. She was tired. She took a deep breath, she spread out on the couch playing back everything she was just told. She didn't know what to think at this stage.

The aspect of Derlin a traitor freaked her out, he was everything to her. One of the few people she could trust with her life, the first person. She mentally shook her head NO! It's not him! It can't be, not John. It's gotta be someone in the office or an agent. She cursed Lens for planting these seeds of uncertainty. She hoped against hope he was wrong or misinformed, but she knew in her heart, that Lens was right.

Once she got back, she was going to see John herself. And get to the bottom of this. She knew John well, if he was lying she'd know. But then again would she? She had to admit Derlin wasn't acting himself. But that also didn't mean he was playing both sides.

"Fuck!" She sighed, there was nothing to do about that now. She was here. She then cast her eyes on the key and bag. Her ticket outta here. Lens was right. She should clean up, get dressed and get the hell out of here. Put this mission as far behind her as she can. But she couldn't. It would be a loose end, that she knew would come back to bite her in the ass later. Hans, the Albino and now Zora, would only pop back up again. Here and now, one way or the other. She was going to end this.

Chapter 22
The beginning of the end

With little time left, Priscilla did what she had to do, she washed up quickly and for the first time, she saw her face after her encounter with the Albino. The extent of the damage from that acid he threw in her face wasn't as bad as she thought. There was skin irritation, and some hair was bleached white.

Thank God she didn't lose her sight. Before getting dressed in a T-shirt and pants with sneakers. She injected some antibiotics that Lens had given her along with some pain reliever. It helped a bit, but the pain was still nagging her. Before leaving, she double-checked, making sure she left nothing behind.

It was just after seven in the morning as she finally made her way, walking the strip, she kept her head down, not wanting to attract any unwanted attention.

As quickly as she could, she walked down the crowded streets coming to an internet café. She stopped there for a quick moment, stepping aside so no one walked into her. She thought about contacting Patrick. But then thought better of it.

This was after all Venezuela, run by a strongman dictator. Who kept the country in his iron grip. There was no doubt, that every known source of communication was listened in on. No, her situation was bad enough. Patrick was smart, he knew what to do. As soon as she made it back, she'd call him. And so, without further debate, she moved on, before she changed her mind. As she made her way back to the casino, she stopped in a café ordering a tea. She then quickly made a beeline to the bathroom, which was a single occupancy.

Locking the door, Priscilla prepared herself. She unloaded the bag she carried. Shoving the pen torch in her pocket, and the locker key in her sock. She chambered a round, sticking the gun in her waist. She was as ready as she'd ever be at this point. It was a little bit after nine in the morning, hopefully she still had time, before Hans was gone.

Chapter 23
Shattered Dreams

Hans Goring sat in his high backed chair with his hands clasped, resting them on his lips. He stared out into the space around him as he played back the events that had transpired. He had managed to seal deals with five countries in the sum of 5 billion dollars, enough to set himself up for life.

But the last 24 hours have put a major snag in his plans. And it all started with the arrival of Priscilla Roletti. He gritted his teeth just thinking that name. He had never grown to hate someone more than her. Once again, he made the mistake of leaving her alive and now she had escaped and in the process killed one of his prized possessions, Hunter.

He underestimated her, Hunter had nowhere near the endurance of Zora or Velvet. Fool! He lambasted himself. That was just one major issue he was having now. The other, because of the incident from the day before. His prospective buyers, got scared and backed out. He couldn't blame them in a way. He'd have been wary too after what had happened. Also to add more misery was the fact that there was another assassin running around who was most likely responsible for the purging of his lab.

He had no doubt that the Benefactor was behind that. He had to be. And that made him worry even more. He was glad to be departing soon. He took a deep breath; trying to calm himself. He was frustrated and scared. He looked at his watch. It was half past nine. He had sent Zora down below to double check the lab, he wanted to be sure there wasn't anything left behind. He was wondering what was taking Zora so long to come back, his patience was starting to wear thin.

Just as he got up to go downstairs to see what the hold up was, Zora burst into the office, startling the already on edge Hans. It didn't help that the look on her face implied something was terribly wrong. Before he could ask, she spoke.

"Velvet's dead!" She sounded a bit distraught when she said it. Hans was going to ask her to repeat what she just said again. He thought he was hearing things. He fell back down into his chair, putting his face in his hands.

The Benefactor had found him, that was definite now. To kill Velvet would have taken more than one man. It was only a matter of time before this place was seized, even with the added soldiers. The Venezuelan President upon hearing about what transpired insisted on locking down the casino, that was another reason to leave. The wrath of the government would no doubt be turned on him for this.

"Hans! What are we gonna do?" Zora's words echoed through his mind. She walked to his side and placed her powerful hand on his shoulder, it was amazing how gentle she could be. He looked up to her with a thin smile. He took a deep breath, collecting himself from his near breakdown. He got up again, gently stroking her cheek.

"To answer your question my dear, is simple, you were the first and the best. I did things to you that weren't done to the others. You'll find out soon enough the extent of your true power." He took a deep breath; she looked into his eyes, understanding his words. "We will handle this, my dear. We are not walking away empty handed. I have funds already transferred, enough to see us through for some time." She nodded, knowing Hans would protect her as she would him. It was always them to the end.

"Zora," She looked up, stepping closer, ready to do whatever he asked her to do. "We must hurry, go down to the airstrip and prep the jet, we must leave within the hour!" She hesitated at first, then spoke up.

"Hans, why leave now, let's rebuild!" Hans gave her a thin smile. She was so loyal and naïve. He walked to her, placing his hands on her shoulders.

"My dear, we must leave, we'll never be safe here, we'll start over in a different place."

"But why leave? I'll protect you. No one will touch you; I swear!" Again, he smiled.

"You continue to amaze me, Zora, but in the end you'll see it was best to leave, trust in that, now go." It looked as though she was going to protest again but decided not to. She knew he was right. Hans was the smartest man she'd ever met. She raced off to do as he asked.

With her gone, his features took a wearier look; he didn't want to worry her. But in truth the Benefactor scared him to no end, and he even doubted leaving would free them of his shadow.

Chapter 24
Closed for business

Priscilla walked her way back to the casino all the while thinking of how she was going to get back in unseen. That was going to be tough. Then, as she was walking, she spotted a couple of vendors on the street selling used clothes and hats. She quickly went over, buying a sunbather's hat and sunglasses, then continued on her way. As she got closer, she saw the gates were closed.

She wasn't surprised by this, who'd keep a casino open after what happened yesterday. No one would want to come here for a while fearing for their lives. She stood by the front gate, peering in; she noticed an increased guard presence, she was expecting that too. She quickly looked around; no one nearby paid any attention to her. She climbed the gate, she was up and over in no time, even with her shoulder that was throbbing.

She stood still for a moment, it was way too quiet. Near the center by the main complex, she saw a jeep, with three soldiers. It took her some time, but she managed to sneak her way to the complex, making her way inside. There may have been a slight increase in the security, but the hotel staff weren't around. Which made it easier for her. She waited for two soldiers to walk past her as she hid behind one of the couches. Once the coast was clear she ran past the front desk. She bit her lower lip, in frustration, as she called the elevator, to the final showdown.

Chapter 25
The Showdown

Zora returned to Hans' office in a hurried manner. He at first thought something was wrong, he was startled as he was double checking his computer. He didn't want to leave any information behind that could be used against him. He was on edge now; he couldn't wait to leave.

"The jet is fueled and ready Hans." Hans nodded calming down a little. Zora had that effect on him, with her around, he feared nothing.

"Do you have an idea of where we're going?" Hans shrugged his shoulders.

"Anywhere but here, my dear. I think we'll have more to worry about than the woman, just wait for it." As though timed with his reply, Hans heard a loud explosion. It sounded like it was on the east end of the property. He punched up the security screen on his computer; figures decked out in a wide array of gear, were running through the newly made hole in the gate. The small Venezuelan forces on the grounds would be overtaken in no time. And it wouldn't be long before they headed this way.

"Zora, come! Time to leave now!" Just as Zora was about to come around to the other side of the desk, the double doors to his office were flung open. They both turned around at the same time to see none other than Priscilla, standing there with her gun drawn.

"Don't move Hans! It's over! The grounds are being overrun, you're done!" Upon those words, Priscilla walked closer to them. She was ready to fire when Zora's visage turned deadly, as she blocked her line of fire at Hans.

"Back off! He's not worth your life, you've been lied to and manipulated. Go and start a new life, I'm giving you a way out!" Priscilla hoped she sounded better than she felt, for, truth be told, she didn't want a confrontation with Zora, not here and not now anyway.

Then Hans and Zora's line of sight looked past Priscilla. She didn't notice that until she heard the ever-familiar grainy southern voice she detested more than anything.

"I'd release that trigger very slowly now little lady, and drop the piece." She bit her lip; she could feel the cold hard steel of his gun pressing very lightly against the back of her ear. She slowly dropped her hand, throwing her gun to the side.

"Step over there for me now why don't cha." He said to Priscilla, she complied, she backed up enough where she could watch all three of them. Hans stood behind his desk, looking slightly amused. Zora looked ready to rip both their heads off.

"You! I'm…I'm gonna rip your fucking heart out!" Zora stepped forward, the Albino quickly aimed his weapon at her.

"Stay where you are freak, otherwise, let's see if you can dodge a bullet." The threat had little effect on her, it looked as though it only pissed her off more.

"Well, it would seem, we have a peculiar situation here." Hans said with both hands before him. "Stealing my serum wasn't enough, I see." The Albino tipped his black cowboy hat up.

"I do the job I'm paid for, I gotta score to settle with your friend here." The Albino was clearly referring to Priscilla, "And now you're added to my list. The Boss man didn't think it was wise to let you walk outta here." Hans furrowed his brow. The Albino then gave his next instructions. "Ok Blondie let's go." Priscilla ignored the command standing where she was, Zora on the other hand, took two steps forward.

"Not you, muscle head." The Albino then took aim. He fired at Hans. Zora, in a blinding display of speed, intercepted the bullet, she fell to the floor. The Albino smirked, seeing the dead Amazon.

"I guess that serum isn't all that it's cracked up to be, huh?" He said, cocking the hammer back and taking aim at the now, unguarded Hans. The German only stood defiantly smirking.

"Oh really?" Was all Hans said as the Albino fired again. The Albino's aim was dead on, Hans would have been hit square in the chest but he wasn't. Zora, who should have been dead, jumped up and caught the round in her bare hand, crushing it. The bullet wound she had in her chest, had healed.

"As you can see, it'll take more than you have to stop her." He said, smiling, then his features turned deadly as he looked to Zora.

"Zora, my dear, now you'll see the full extent of the powers I've given you. Destroy them, destroy everything and anyone in your path, make it known that anyone who stands in our way will meet the same fate. Then meet me at the rendezvous."

She didn't acknowledge Hans, she heard him and would obey. Priscilla and the Albino in turn looked at each other quickly. Hans tapped a button on his keyboard and slowly started to descend, disappearing through an emergency exit. Priscilla only glimpsed in that direction. She had a bigger problem to deal with now. As she spread out, the Albino did the same while Zora walked closer, flexing her hands in anticipation.

"Looks like you'll have to take that offer now Goldie."

"Still doesn't change a thing, Blondie."

"I didn't think it would." She said sarcastically readying herself for the final encounter with not only Zora but the Albino. For if she could take him out now too, she would. No doubt he was thinking the same thing, but the real question was how the hell were they going to kill Zora? Priscilla just witnessed her get back up from being shot. She doubted the both of them would even get a chance to finish their little spat. And on top of everything the place was under siege, The Benefactor was really tying up loose ends now she thought.

She heard boots pounding the floor, getting ever so close. She turned in the direction just for a moment, trying to strain her ears. Zora was gonna make her move just then too, when the doors to the office exploded. Priscilla dove to the floor, avoiding the javelin pieces of wood coming her way, the Albino also. Zora just stood there as though it had no effect on her, as debris bounced off her. Before the dust settled, three men stormed in wearing full tactical body armor with helmets, armed with sub- machine guns ready to open fire. Sweeping the room, their weapons fell upon Zora, who was already on the move, moving faster than a human was supposed to.

She pummeled the three men as though they were mere toys, ripping the arms off one, throwing the other across the office and the third man was thrown clear through the wall falling 40 floors. More mercenaries showed up opening fire on her. The adrenaline was pumping so much through her that some of the bullets merely bounced off her.

Some did penetrate into her skin, but Zora didn't even acknowledge them as the wounds healed just as fast. She screamed out in a bloody rage as she started to jog down the hall, picking up speed like a juggernaut. In her wake there was nothing but sheer carnage. More bodies were mangled, ripped apart, and broken. Nothing was going to stop her. Before any more mercs came upstairs, Zora ran past the elevator. She had a faster way down.

She ran to the stairwell, plowing through the door and without even a second thought, she jumped over the railing and plummeted straight down like a rocket. She landed in a crouch, her impact cratered the spot. She slowly walked forward to the exit and continued her onslaught.

Mercenaries tried to stop her, but when they soon realized that nothing was having an effect on her, they ran at the sight of her. Zora wasn't going out of her way to track down the intruders, but anyone stupid enough to challenge her would be killed. Zora was blinded by the adrenaline coursing through her veins. She had never fully realized the extent of her power until now, she knew that nothing would stop her and she'd use this power to protect the man she grew to love and care for as a father.

She'd kill in his name. She wanted people to fear him and to know that if anyone was to try to harm him, it would be the last thing they ever tried.

Chapter 26
Shock and Awe

While screams of agony rang out mixed with sporadic gunfire, Priscilla slowly got up, brushing off dust and debris. She stumbled over debris, making her way out into the hallway. Slightly disoriented, she took in the utter destruction. Priscilla wouldn't have believed someone was capable of this if she didn't see it for herself.

It looked like she even plowed through a wall in her escape. She quickly put aside her awe, going to one of the fallen mercenaries. She stripped him of his sidearm and submachine gun. Just as she was about to follow in the wake of Zora, Priscilla almost forgot about the Albino, who must've been buried in the debris. Half of her wanted to rummage through it and confirm he was dead or kill him if he wasn't.

But the more time she wasted in even deciding, the more Hans slipped through her fingers. She didn't like the circumstances, she had to choose. If the Albino survived, she knew this wouldn't be the last time she encountered him.

"Ah fuck it." She said under her breath, as she bolted down the hallway jumping over debris and bodies. Now Priscilla had the unfortunate task of stopping the human juggernaut. How the hell she was going to accomplish that feat was beyond her. If she even caught up to the Amazon, Zora had a good head start. But she'd at least be easy to track.

She took the elevator down, preparing herself. She cursed the slowness if it. She finally hit the ground floor, as the door opened, she was met with destruction everywhere. The whole lobby was in shambles, mercenaries' were all over the place, like discarded dolls. The chandelier was on the floor, blocking half the lobby. She sprinted straight for the doors.

Priscilla was hoping she wouldn't come across hostiles, until she almost plowed into one of the mercs, who quickly leveled his gun. Priscilla was faster and took him out before he even got a shot off. She continued on her way mostly unhindered. By now soldiers were fighting the mercenaries, which helped her. As she managed to avoid some of the commandos, she didn't have time to gun battle anyone. Just as she reached the airfield north of the complex, a dirt bike riding merc suddenly came out of nowhere. Almost running her down, she dove out of the way. The merc spun around and came to a stop reaching behind his back for the shouldered automatic.

Priscilla was on her feet and before the soldier of fortune could bring his weapon to bear, she opened fire killing him. She ran to the fallen bike and hoisted it up by the handlebars, and hopped on. She spun the back wheel as she took off, hoping she could still catch up to Hans.

Chapter 27
Almost Free

Hans grew increasingly worried, his window of escape was slowly closing. It would only be a matter of time before the opposition came this way and Zora wasn't here yet. What was keeping her!? He thought, as he looked out the cockpit window, surely she should have been here by now. There was nothing that could impede her unless he gave her too much credit.

She was one of a kind, his finest work. Thinking that something could stop her was madness. But truth be told, he had to go soon. The last thing he wanted to do was leave her. Hans wasn't loyal to many, but to Zora he was. If only for the simple reasons that she was his protector and the last thing he wanted was her thinking he betrayed her and turn her wrath on him. With those thoughts racing through his head, he glanced to his left.

Zora was coming, and it was a sight to behold. He smiled despite himself. It was amazing watching her, she was perfect. The first true superhuman. Every move she made, every muscle used screamed power and perfection. As she got closer, judging from the way she looked, it wasn't easy. Some of her skin was blackened, her clothes had specks of blood, her hair was a mess. But yet here she was, unscathed by anything that was thrown at her. Zora leapt into the jet, putting her hands out to stop her momentum.

Then, without further delay, Hans quickly throttled the jet forward, picking up speed. Zora spun around to close the door, she just entered, when out of nowhere she was hit. Thrown off balance, she fell in the middle of the six seat aisle. Picking her head up, she saw none other than Priscilla, closing the door and sealing it. She then squared off to meet the Amazon head on.

Chapter 28
Flying the friendly skies

Priscilla was just in time. As she came within view of the airfield, she saw Zora running towards the jet, leaping into the aft door in a single unbelievable bound. She was expecting it to be sealed any second. Priscilla shifted the dirt bike to its max speed, pushing it to its limit. The jet started to move; she may just make it. She licked her lips as she got closer.

She was almost there, revving the dirt bike one last time she prepared herself to jump. While holding onto the handlebars, she hopped up onto the seat and crouched tensing herself to jump. Zora had just appeared getting ready to close the door. She never noticed Priscilla until she jumped colliding into her. It felt like slamming into a brick wall. Shaking it off, Priscilla jumped to her feet and sealed the door.

Turning to meet Zora, the Amazon was caught by surprise. The look on her face implied nothing but loathing, as she got to her feet, while the jet took off ascending for the sky.

"Zora! Rid me of this woman!" Hans yelled out. Priscilla may have bitten off more than she could chew this time. There was no possible way she could win outright. Her only saving grace was the small confines of the jet and the fact that Zora couldn't unleash herself for fear of punching a hole through the plane. At this height, a sudden loss of cabin pressure would suck them into the void.

Zora came at her so fast, Priscilla barely dodged the punches. One wild punch obliterated a headrest. Priscilla tried to skirt around her, and beeline it for the cockpit, but was grabbed and pushed to the floor. Just as the Amazon was about to come at her, Priscilla thrust her foot forward slamming it into her knee. That seemed to throw her off for a second while she scampered back, getting to her feet and going for Hans.

He wasn't watching the ensuing fight, so when Priscilla came up alongside him and gave him a rushed glancing blow to the head.

He lost control of the plane trying to protect himself, she managed to get in a few good shots with one hand while she tried to bring the jet down. But Zora grabbed Priscilla by the back of the neck, and threw her into the last row of seats. Dazed, she sat up. There was no place for her to go, no place to hide. Zora was on her in an instant, her arms were raised over her head, ready to smash Priscilla into oblivion.

And that's when a wild idea came to mind. Priscilla reached into her pocket as she rolled to the left falling to the floor. Just when Zora was about to destroy her, Priscilla brought to bear her pen torch twisting it. She unleashed the full power of the laser, cutting a hole right through her chest. Zora screamed out, the force of the blast sent her into the wall, tilting the jet from the impact. Priscilla jumped to her feet wide eyed in astonishment by the sight before her.

Even with a smoking gaping hole through her, the Amazon was still alive and obviously not finished with her. Zora looked down at her wound and then up at Priscilla. The Amazon took an unbalanced step towards her. Without even thinking of the consequences of her next action. Priscilla wrapped the unused seat belt around her left wrist, while gripping the pen torch with her teeth, she twisted it with her free hand. The concentrated beam ripped right through the aft door. With the sudden cabin pressure loss, it created a vacuum, sucking the breathable air and anything not bolted down right out of the plane.

Alarms blared as the jet went into a free fall from the sudden loss of cabin pressure. Caught by surprise Zora was pulled and sucked towards the open door. She screamed, trying to hold on.

“NO!” Just as she was sucked into the threshold, she caught onto the doorway. Her strength was on full display as she dug her hands into the steel. Priscilla holding her breath, and held in place by the seat belt took aim. With her now numb frosty hand, she fired. The yellow beam severed Zora’s arm and gravity took her into the heavens.

With the plane slowly coming back under control, and leveling out, the air was more breathable. The fear of being sucked out less likely. She untwisted her wrist, and fell to her knees, crawling into the aisle. She was out of breath and dizzy, but taking in large gulps of air helped her regain her focus. With Zora out of the way, meeting her just deserved fate, it was time to end this once and for all. She was about to get up when she was viciously kicked in her ribs three times. Sprawled on her back, she looked through half opened eyes, and saw Hans.

As Hans was trying to regain control of the jet, he reached down on the side of his seat for the emergency oxygen mask. While taking the jet down, to a safe level, something caught his eye. Hans gasped as he saw Zora falling. He put his face against the glass.

"Zora." He whispered, he would have wept just then. But he had more pressing matters, with the jet level and at a safe altitude he took off his breathing mask. Unbuckling himself, he proceeded to smash the controls. The jet would crash and burn now. He got up and walked to the first row. Reaching down into the floor, he opened a small compartment; there were two parachutes inside. He quickly put one on and buckled all the straps.

As he made his way to the door, he saw Priscilla on her knees, trying to catch her breath. This was an opportunity he wasn't gonna pass up. He tossed the extra parachute out the door. He only wished he had more time to really make her pay for all the trouble she had caused him. Before she even saw him, Hans kicked her as hard as he could. He wished he broke a rib, so it would puncture her heart. He kicked her two more times.

He had almost lost himself in the pleasure of her suffering. He needed to escape now. He affixed goggles to his eyes and looked back at Priscilla. She was on one knee, looking up at him, clutching her mid-section.

He gave her a two-fingered salute and his last words to her.

"Auf wiedersehen." And he jumped out of the jet.

Priscilla climbed unsteadily to her feet using the back of a seat to brace herself. She held on as she looked out the door, watching Hans fall to freedom. She then looked to the cockpit clearly seeing the controls were destroyed. She had a look of worry, mixed with despair, as she looked back into the blue sky. She came to a conclusion, there was only one thing to do, and that was to go after

Hans. Which would most likely result in her death. But if she was gonna die, then she damn well would try to take him with her.

Her features turned to a steely resolve as she stepped out into the blue. Gravity took hold of her as she tried to gain control of her body. But her velocity made it difficult to do so. Thanks to her skill and stubbornness of not giving up, she managed to straighten out. Pressing her arms and legs together as tightly as she could, she picked up speed like a falling javelin.

The wind pelted her, stinging her eyes. It was hard to see where to guide herself, but the thought of hitting the earth made her deal with the pain. She kept Hans in her sight. She hoped to reach him before he pulled the chute. As she got closer, she stretched out her arms. Getting ready, she braced herself for the impact as she slammed into him, obviously he never expected it.

He cursed in German as they interlocked in a struggle, tumbling end over end, rolling and flipping. Priscilla punched and kicked him as she attempted to unlock the buckles on his chute. Hans was too much in a panic and made it difficult, he was just trying to shove her off him and pull the chute. Her grip was too strong as she struggled to hold on and unlatch each buckle, which wasn't going so well.

Priscilla knew impact would be in mere minutes, if not seconds. She had no way of gauging the time without knowing the height they were at to begin with. Forgoing her first approach of wrestling the chute from him. Priscilla reached out with both hands and choked the life out of Hans. Her grip was firm, her nails were marking his throat, blood was running down his collar.

One of his lashing hands pulled the ripcord by accident. With the momentum of the sudden uplift, she broke his neck, her legs were wrapped tightly around him. She held his lifeless body close to her. She thought this was ironic, her tormenter was now her savior.

Trying to steer with a corpse and hanging on for dear life wasn't easy. She tried to head for the outskirts of the jungle as best she could. She didn't want to end up lost after all this. Within minutes, she slammed into a sea of trees. She used Hans' body as protection as best she could, breaking branches and coming to a sudden wrenching stop.

The chute ripped, they were suspended mere inches from the ground, swinging back and forth. She let go of Hans and fell to her feet. She hunched over with her hands on her knees breathing hard. Exhausted she flopped on her butt, taking in this short time of quietness. It was only her, the sounds of the jungle and the swinging body of Hans. The perfect way to end the day.

Chapter 29
Looking into the eye of a stranger

Her trip back to the States took her longer than she'd have liked. Trekking from the jungle to the airport was impeded by bad weather, a lot of walking and hitchhiking. But thanks to Lens, she made it with the money, passport, and disguise. It was free and clear. Now standing before the main lobby doors of Shadow Ops H.Q. she tried to gather herself as best she could before going upstairs. This was going to be the hardest moment in her life.

Lens' warning about coming here rang loudly in her ears. But she was going to disregard that, no matter how foolish it might be. She had too, even knowing that Lens could very well be the double agent, and was playing some complicated mind trick on her. She highly doubted that, but it was still there in the back of her mind.

Regardless of all that, she needed to confront John and ask him herself. No more bullshit, no double talking. If Derlin was indeed the double agent, she was going to take him down. And if not, then they would work together to take down whoever it was. Priscilla silently prayed it was the latter.

With a deep breath, she walked inside. She couldn't put it off any longer. Making her way along with other white collared workers, to the black marbled lobby. She was greeted by the security guard sitting at his desk with a fast 'hello' and moved on to the elevator.

Within minutes she was at the top floor, it was quieter than usual. There was a somber like atmosphere. She walked straight ahead towards Derlin's office. She passed his secretary's desk, but Jenny wasn't there. She knocked once and entered just as Derlin told her to enter.

"Right, right....I have someone here. We can discuss this later." He hung up, she already closed the door and was making her way to one of the two vacant seats. He didn't even smile at her. She felt like more than ever she was unwanted. As she slowly sat down, she tried to read what was going on in his mind but he was totally unreadable. He finally broke the uncomfortable silence.

"Well....Priscilla I'm so glad to see you've made it back in one piece. And although I'm relieved by that, I cannot say the same for that new look you're doing now." She looked at him for a second not understanding where that came from. But then remembered the long thick streak of white hair. It was something she was not yet used to. She fondled the front a bit, hoping to hide it from view, but the streak was too big for that.

"Yeah, a permanent reminder of what's to come." And then silence. She didn't know what to say or how to say it. How do you ask someone, without sounding accusing if they are a double agent? There wasn't. The only way she was used to, was with the barrel of a gun doing the talking or her elbow jammed into their neck making them admit to it. But she couldn't do that, not here and not to Derlin. Priscilla leaned forward, resting her elbows on her knees and crossed her fingers.

"John…" She started to say, trying her hardest to pick the right words. "John…" She repeated again, reminding herself of a repeated verse to a song. She chuckled, leaning her head on her crossed hands, glancing away for a moment. "There's really no easy way to say this…I'm-" and just as she was about to accuse him, and detain him. The door to his office flew open, slamming into the wall. The blinds rattled so bad she thought they were going to fall off.

She jumped, jerking for her concealed weapon at her waist. John didn't even so much as flinch. He looked in the direction as though he was expecting this to happen. In the doorway was a man in a dark blue suit, a velvet tie, with short brown receding hair. Priscilla watched as he stepped forward, not knowing what to make of this. The stern looking man looked at Priscilla then to John.

"John Derlin, you're under arrest." He said with authority. Priscilla wasn't sure she heard him right, the man looked at her ready for her challenge.

"What?! Who are you?" She demanded, he grinned, reaching into his suit, producing his identification.

"Jonas Ferrer, N.S.A. Ms. Roletti is it?" She nodded, "Pleasure to meet you, I've heard a lot about you." Jonas replaced his credentials and then gave Derlin his full attention. "John Derlin, you are under arrest for the crimes of high treason, murder, and tampering with evidence. And that's just to start." Derlin slowly stood, with no hint of objecting to this in the least. "Let's go John, you and I have a long talk ahead of us." Derlin slipped into his suit jacket, and then made his way around the desk. Priscilla grabbed his arm out of reflex as he walked by her wanting to protect her mentor. Yes, she was going to arrest him as well, detain him. But not like this. She wasn't going to put on a show for everyone to see. Derlin deserved better than this.

He stopped at her touch and looked at her with a cold, vacant stare that went right through her. His face was like stone. He grabbed her hand, with a grip she had not thought Derlin was capable of, and released her hand from his forearm and walked off.

Ferrer stepped aside. Behind him were three burly looking N.S.A. agents who stepped apart as John walked out. They then quickly handcuffed him and led him off. Priscilla watched the whole scene speechless. She felt like she was in the twilight zone.

As Derlin was led to the elevator, Jonas waited until the doors were closed. He then turned to everyone in the office who had stopped what they were doing. They were all frozen and in shock by what they witnessed.

"Listen up people!" He yelled out, then clapped his hands loud and hard. "I want all of you to stop what you are doing, grab your belongings and go home. The party's over. All personnel ordered by me are not to leave the state. This is not a vacation people. In the next couple of days, you will be questioned and debriefed." No one moved after the speech. They were dumbfounded and looked every bit of it as well. Jonas stepped forward.

"What? Am I talking in a different fucking language? Leave! Go home!" Then, almost at the same time everyone did as they were told, hurrying about, putting things back in order. Ferrer then turned to Priscilla, who was staring at the floor in utter shock. He came within inches of her and leaned into her ear.

"As for you, Ms. Roletti, I'm taking a special interest in you, don't wander off too far. You, like everyone in here, are under my supervision, by order of the President of the United States. I'm in command of Shadow Ops effective immediately." He smirked at her, she never looked at him.

"See 'ya around" He said as he walked off, and for the first time since she was a kid, Priscilla was left in the unknown and didn't know what to do.

Epilogue
The Coming Storm

The Albino stood by the rail of the slow moving boat. He was taking in the clear night sky, bright moon and calm sea. He was hatless, for fear of the wind taking his beloved cowboy hat into the sea. Aside from his battered ego, he hadn't suffered any real injuries, just a tender cheek bone. He gently touched it, only to jerk his gloved hand away. It was sore to the touch. And then just as he was about to turn and head inside, his phone buzzed. He grabbed it out of his black pants and placed it to his ear.

"I got it." He said in his grainy sandpaper voice, as he looked down at the steel suitcase leaning against the walled rail. The coveted serum was inside. The Albino listened closely to the man on the other end. His face was blank as he was spoken to.

"No, she got away, even with the boys you sent in. I told ya it wasn't gonna be that easy." Still no reaction as the other party laced into him for his failure.

"She won't get away again, I've already made the arrangements." The Albino picked up the suitcase and went inside his quarters of the smuggler's vessel.

"You want me to stick around and oversee this through, my fee again only doubled. I don't care a lick for your cause, old man." The old man didn't bat an eye, he agreed to the Albino's terms.

The Albino ended the call slipping the cell phone in his vest pocket. He sat down on the stiff bunk keeping the suitcase close to him. He smiled, thinking what was coming for her. He kinda felt sorry for her, the life she had was gonna be turned upside down. And before she died, whether it was by his hand or someone else, everything she held dear was gonna be stripped from her. He closed his golden eyes as he laid down, relishing in the thought of the death of Priscilla Roletti.

Vol. 5 Retribution

Prologue
The Proposition

The following events take place the morning of Priscilla Roletti's return from Venezuela.

Long Island, New York

He stood among the relics of a time long past. A time he secretly wished he could jump back to at any moment. But he knew he couldn't do such a thing, for that was only the stuff of science fiction books and movies. So he had the next best thing, the relics of his youth. The musty smells of these time capsules stored in the basement of his childhood home, couldn't be diminished even after all these years.

Bill Bobcatz, was in his mid-fifties, but looked more like he was in his late forties. He was in better shape than most his age or even younger. With his round youthful face, thick mustache and neatly combed hair with a straight side part. You'd never think anything of this mild mannered man in very casual clothes. Which were brown slacks and a white polo.

He stood with his head lowered, hands in his pockets as he allowed his mind to wander. He smiled, lifting his head, as he cast his eyes on a stack of boxes containing photographs. They were labeled and organized from year to year. His father was a very organized man, and instilled that onto Bill.

Old clothes, in see through plastic bags belonging to his mother. She passed away about a year ago, and it was hard to relinquish himself of those just yet. Soon, he mused.

He then cast his eyes over to the wall. Various hand tools were neatly hung with white outlines of said tool, so you wouldn't forget where it belonged. His Dad loved his tools. What Dad didn't? They were trophies, only instead of given, they were bought from

Sears. The Singer sewing machine, which his mother used almost every day. And she took such great care of it; it looked as new as the day she bought it.

Every now and then Bill would come down here and reminisce. It wasn't as often as he liked, of course, between working and his other curricular activities, time was scarce. He sighed, taking in a long, deep breath. He then glanced at his watch.

"Time to wrap this up." He said in a low tone, as he turned around from the shadows of the past to return his attention to the present. Just as he was about to hit the light switch off, the doorbell rang.

He looked at his wrist watch again. Who would call on him at this hour? It was half past nine on a Sunday morning. Just as he thought that, the bell rang again. Bill took a deep frustrated breath. He hated unannounced company. Before going upstairs, Bill went into the top drawer of the work table and grabbed a gun. Chambering a round as he walked up the stairs tucking it in his pants, better to be safe than sorry, he always thought.

The doorbell was still ringing as he called out in a calm lisping voice.

"Just a minute, please." He opened the door, and standing on his porch was someone he never expected, and someone that no one would expect a man such as himself to associate with. She was thin with curves, tattoos covered most of her body. She even had some on the side of her face, in a strange way it enhanced her erotic beauty ten fold. Her hair was jet black with red streaks, she wore heavy make-up, but again, it added to her looks instead of detracting from it. She smiled, flashing her pearly whites as she laid her eyes on him.

"Bill Bobcatz, I hope I didn't bother you on a Sunday morning, it's been all too long sweetie." Bill wasn't affected by her aura.

"If you consider a long time a little over a year ago, then yes. What can I do for you Luna?" Even though the tone was cold, it didn't affect her one bit as she stepped forward into the house without even being asked to come in. Closing the door, he gave her a curious look while Luna took in her surroundings. She was impressed by this quaint little home he had here. It was both modern and old school. Like the living room, which had a couch that looked thirty years old, but was well preserved and a 50' HDTV.

"You sure made yourself some little life here Billy, now I see why you don't stay in the game anymore." Bill walked past her and into the kitchen; opening the refrigerator he grabbed an orange juice carton shaking it. And then went into the cabinet to grab a glass. Luna followed him.

"Luna you always seem to pop up at the wrong times, I'm presently busy at the moment." She looked at him smiling, and then placed a finger in her mouth and gently stroked it. Most men would have stopped what they were doing to watch her, slack jawed wishing she was doing that to their dicks. But not Bill, oh, he enjoyed such pleasures. But not with Luna, not anymore.

"Busy? With what baby? Stroking your cock hmm?" Bill rolled his eyes.

"Hardly." He poured himself some juice. "I take it you'd like a beer?" Luna enthusiastically nodded.

"You know it baby. I'll meet you in the living room." Bill nodded, as she turned and strutted away. He was both annoyed by her being here and intrigued. It was obvious this was no social call.

The last he heard she was on the West Coast free lancing. He'd at least humor her for now.

Just a few seconds later, Bill entered the living room with his glass of orange juice and a bottle of beer with an overturned glass on top. He handed it to Luna, who didn't even bother using the glass; she drank it straight from the bottle as she put her booted feet up on his pristine wooden table.

Luna enjoyed making him cringe, she knew he hated that. She then got serious, telling him the reason for her unannounced visit. As she spoke, Luna handed him a single piece of paper. He didn't seem to be intrigued by what he was looking at.

"And this is why you came across the country, to recruit me? I'm not interested. I've made a nice life for myself here." He said, handing the paper back to her, she ripped it from his hand, and then folded it back up.

"Shut the fuck up! Why'd you come on the Hamas job last year?"

"Because the Hamas job was personal. They're responsible for many deaths in Israel." He said, with conviction. "And this job you're trying to sell me is too close to home for my liking."

"Bullshit, you miss it." She said winking at him. "And me." She added.

"I do miss it. You on the other hand I don't. But just out of curiosity, why come to me? Why not the others?"

"I did, it's me and Emil. I tried to track the others down, but only found two, and they turned me down. Their loss man." Bill considered her story. "But fuck them, Emil and I have been making some good bucks. I was in the area and thought you wanted in on the action." Luna threw her feet to the floor, leaning closer to Bill, the look on her face turned deadly serious.

"When I first heard who 'He' was, I was like no fucking way. But then when I met him. I was bugged out, pretty freaky shit, huh?" Bill nodded, as he placed his glass of juice down on the table.

"Luna, it all sounds too good to be true and usually it is. But the risk may be great, especially for the price that's on this woman's head." At his words she sprung up from the couch, slamming her bottle down. As she slowly made her way towards him, she stuffed the paper in her back pocket.

She wrapped her arms around him, rubbing his back; she looked him dead in his eyes as she talked.

"Yeah, it may be but I'll need you, do it for me. $500,000,000 split three ways you know what that can do? We'll retire together on some island alone." Bill looked deeply into her eyes seeing nothing but lies. At one point, he'd have said yes. But Bill wasn't a man to be fooled again. As hard as it may have been, he removed her hands from his body and stepped away. Luna looked slightly hurt.

Bill shook his head, putting both hands in his pockets.

"I'm sorry Luna, but I cannot for the moral reasons alone. I can't believe you took this job from a man, a man… that did unspeakable things to my countrymen. I can't accept that. Hunting 'Them' down was the reason I got involved in intelligence and information gathering in the first place." Luna placed both hands on her hips.

“Oh, fuck you man! Give me a break, huh, you're such a hypocrite, like you’re any better! Intelligence and information gathering, you mean torture!”

“True, but I didn’t do anything to those who didn’t ask for it.” He gave her a sympathetic look. “You on the other hand, are not of Jewish descent like me. Yes, I trained you along with the others… but you’ll never understand.” Luna looked red faced now, walking to the door and swinging it open.

“Yeah, whatever Billy, enjoy your life, huh, I’ll be sure to send you a postcard, you fucking faggit!”

She stalked off never looking back. Bill watched her go and waited until she got in her car and sped off, before closing the door. Although Luna was gone, Bill stayed where he was thinking about what just transpired. He knew her visit was going to start a chain reaction that would lead to his eventual involvement. He sighed; he was prepared for whatever may come his way. And when or if it did, he would deal with it then. He sighed, turning from the door to finally start his day.

Chapter 1
Death waits for no one

Priscilla Roletti didn't know it yet, but her life from here on out was about to be turned upside down and inside out in ways she never thought possible. She was still in Derlin's office, coming to terms with what just happened. The whole incident vividly replayed in her mind like an endless loop.

Derlin arrested! Priscilla still couldn't believe that Derlin was the traitor, and had set her up. That part alone, she was having trouble digesting. Derlin had a lot of enemies, in and out of the government.

He had to have been set-up, just as she was set-up and perhaps information was given to make her and others believe that he did it. The real question was, if it wasn't Derlin then how did she get compromised and who was behind it?

That golden-eyed son of a bitch, the Albino knew who she was, and now her kids may be in danger. One of the first things she needed to do was get in touch with Pat and give him instructions on what to do and what to expect. He was the last person she wanted to drag into all this. She could already feel the noose tightening. And to add grief to an already complicated situation was this guy Jonas Ferrer. Someone that she knew was going to be a thorn in her side from here on out.

She cleared her throat as she turned in her seat. The door was still ajar; from her vantage point she could see some of the office workers going about their new orders. It was sad to see things coming to an end the way they were.

"Ah fuck." She said, with a sigh.

She reached into her pocketbook, she needed a smoke, after some rifling she found them. There were only two left. She lit it, taking in a long drag, it soothed her somewhat. As she searched for her cigarettes, she took out the burner phone, she bought once she arrived back in the States. She'd use that to check her voice mails. Hopefully, there wouldn't be any more surprises today. As soon as she logged into her account her eyes widened. She had 20 voice mails. That uneasy sensation just shot up through her spine, as she listened to the first voice mail. It was her sister Lorraine. She almost dropped her phone from shock.

Her mother died.

Priscilla's mouth went dry, and her throat felt like there was something wedged inside all of a sudden. She got up from the chair a little too fast, her legs felt wobbly, she listened to five more voice mails by the time she got into the elevator. One was from her daughter crying about grandma dying.

At least the kids were safe. The other two were from her sister Terri, wondering where the hell she was and Pietro. She didn't even bother to listen to the rest. First, she thought, Derlin getting arrested was unbelievable now her mom died! In a way she couldn't believe that. It was a running joke that she'd outlive everyone.

It was one of those things that you knew would come, but just never thought it would. She always wondered how she'd feel when this day came, she didn't know whether she'd cry or not. So far, she didn't have the overbearing desire to do so.

Priscilla, over the years, had become very unemotional to things. There were a few times she had to force herself to show emotion, just to appease people. Her kids were the only things that could evoke her true emotions. Maybe the flood gates will open once she sees her mom, laid out. But then again, who knows? Even though her mother changed for the better as she got older and treated her kids very well as a way to make up for her wrong doings to Priscilla. She still had a huge grudge against her. I mean, how can one forgive their mother for beating you, and throwing you out into the street?

Once the elevator doors opened to the basement, she was taken from her thoughts from the flutter of activity going on. Techs were busy hurrying about, she wondered what was going to happen to them. The office workers were one thing, they were expendable, they had nothing to offer. But the techs on the other hand, they were an asset. She doubted that they'd be out of work long, if at all.

Priscilla squeezed her way past some techs with boxes and managed to make her way to the garage area. She hoped to find Peter; he had the keys to her minivan. It took her some time, but she finally found the trickster Pete and for once in her life she saw him acting serious for a change. As she walked up from behind he turned spotting her. He gestured her over, even though she was clearly walking towards him.

"Put those boxes in the truck by dock one, hurry up asshole!" He yelled out to a passing tech who didn't pay any mind to the insult. If you worked with Peter, you got use to being called something other than your name, he glanced at Priscilla. "Hey, give me a second I gotta talk to you." She was almost taken aback by his tone, she was always used to him insulting her or pretending to hit on her.

She saw a side of him she didn't think ever existed; she's been seeing that in a lot of people lately. After a few minutes, he grabbed a tech standing nearby, and shoved a clipboard in his hands.

"Do something useful instead of standing there with your thumb up your ass."

"But I was doing something, you just made me drop that folder with paperwork."

"Well...this is more important!" He walked toward Priscilla, before the tech could protest further.

"I guess you're being moved huh? You know where yet?" Peter nodded.

"Yeah, some place out on Long Island, all the way the fuck out in the boonies." Priscilla nodded.

"Listen, I know you're busy, but can you get my key, or just tell me where you put it." He shook his finger.

"Forget the van, I'm gonna use it. I wanna pack it up with my personal shit. Come with me, that's what I wanted to talk to you about." She followed him to his all glass windowed office. He entered first, she followed.

"Close the door." She did so, as he grabbed a set of keys and tossed them to her. She caught them noticing instantly they were for a Charger. She furrowed her brow at this.

"Take it, I fully stocked it with everything I thought you'd need, disguises, a syn-skin, a few extra weapons, the works." She raised an eyebrow spinning the keys around her finger twice.

"What did you hear." It wasn't a question; she knew he knew something because once she said that he looked very uncomfortable. He started to nibble at his thumbnail.

"Listen, Priscilla you know, aside from all the kidding around and insults I love ya. I really do, and I'd do anything I could to help you and that's what I'm doing. But outside of being asked to do this, I know nothing. I swear I really don't-"

"Who asked you?" She said, cutting him off. She didn't want to be too forceful with him; she loved him too and would do anything in her power to help him. But the fact that people knew stuff pertaining to her and kept her in the dark about it was starting to piss her off.

"Lens." He said in a low tone, she muttered a curse under her breath at hearing his name. Goddamn him she thought.

"What did he tell you? This is important Pete; he came to see me when I was in Venezuela. He told me something was gonna happen when I came back and that I was gonna be in the middle of it, and you know what? I think he may be right. I was compromised, and now with Derlin getting arrested, so please Pete if you know anything tell me!" She felt her face flush; she played back what she just said in her head. She sounded like she was begging, she hated sounding like that, Peter threw up his hands.

"I didn't even see him. He called just an hour before Derlin got locked up, warning me too, of something going down. I asked, but he didn't say. You know Lens, he doesn't say shit, the last thing he told me was to prep you, give you a car and fully stock it. That's it, I didn't ask or debate it, you don't need to be a rocket scientist to figure out that something's going down, that's it. I swear Priscilla, I'm sorry I wish I could tell you more." She nodded, believing him, if there were anyone she could trust now it was Pete.

"Thanks." He smiled, she returned the smile before turning to leave.

"Wait! I have one more thing." He reached into his pocket and tossed her something. She caught it, it was a pocket sized solid steel tube with a small lens.

"It's a holo-projector, one of a kind. It'll last about five minutes, so make it count, you see the sliding button?" She looked finding it. "Not only will that project what you're doing up to fifty feet. It'll project you standing up even if you're crouched down, the only movements, it'll follow will be from the waist up, just make it look like you're standing and no one will even tell the difference. It may come in handy." She smiled at him as she placed it in her pocket.

"Thanks."

"Good luck kid, I hope to see you soon." She, smiled.

"You will…. who else would you antagonize?" She said with a wink, and left.

Chapter 2
The Black Hand

In the company Dodge Charger, she was finally heading home. Priscilla used the drive to try to sort out what was going on. Derlin arrested for treason and perhaps the one responsible for setting her up. Shadow Ops disbanded, her mom dying and to make matters worse, this all started with Lens and again he pops up requesting Peter to prep her, prep her for what? She thought. She was beginning to think that maybe Lens was the traitor, but then if that was the case why not end it in Venezuela. He had her, but he brought her back from the brink for God's sake, he'd have to be an overconfident, sick bastard to arrange all this.

There were too many questions, she rubbed the side of her head, all this needed to wait, for now anyway. She needed to find out what was going on with her mother; she called her sister Terri. Once she got through to her sister, Terri was pissed and chewed her out for not getting in touch sooner.

They were about to file a missing persons report with the police. Priscilla was in no mood for a lecture, least of all from her. She should talk, going away for months at a time to Hawaii during the holidays just because she was trying to escape the redundant life she hated so much. But being that Priscilla had too much on her plate as it was she didn't need to start an argument now at this time.

Her sister told her that their mother died peacefully in her sleep and the wake was at a funeral home on Cross Bay Blvd, Howard Beach, Queens.

Priscilla knew the place, and it was tonight of all nights, too. Her mother had died three days ago, they waited as long as they could for Priscilla to get back, and they couldn't wait any longer to lay her out.

Speeding more than she needed to, Priscilla thought about her mother, she was torn by the fact that she wasn't there, didn't get to see her or talk to her before she died. But on the other hand, after all she put her through when she was a kid, she asked herself, why? Why would you even care about a woman that treated you like a dog? She took a deep breath, trying to clear her mind. More importantly than her torn feelings, she needed to call Pat, and think of what to do with her kids.

As soon as she got home, she'd call him. As much as she wanted to see her kids, she didn't think that was a good idea now.

Finally pulling up to her home, she backed up the driveway. Getting out, she looked about quickly. It was very quiet, too quiet for her. It was like the calm before the storm, she hated that feeling, she knew it all too well.

As she stepped into her home, she took a deep breath. Her safe haven from the outside world, a place that once she entered, nothing else mattered.

All she wanted to know was her bed right now. A shower to wash away the filth and grab a few hours of sleep. With a refreshed mind, she'd be able to deal with all of these new developments.

She closed and locked the door, throwing her bag on the kitchen table. The house was dark except for a little night-light in the kitchen that's on a timer. Turning on the kitchen light she went to the cabinet and grabbed her cup, filling it with water and placed it in the microwave. A good cup of tea always calmed her. Although she'd prefer to boil the water, she didn't feel like waiting. She always thought it tasted different for some reason.

Now if she had a smoke, that would be even better. She put it in the back of her mind to pick up a pack, something she'd be doing more often with the way things were going. It still hadn't totally set in, her mom died; everything else on top of that didn't help either. The timer on the microwave expired beeping, she popped open the door and grabbed her cup. She placed it on the counter and while dunking her tea bag, she caught sight of the coffee pot that was off. But had left over coffee inside.

The hand that held the tea bag was still, as she stared at the pot. With her other hand, she slowly reached out and touched it. It was warm! Someone was here! Just as those words flashed in her mind, someone spoke.

"Your milk is out of date." Hearing a strange voice in her home startled her. But she managed to keep her features unreadable, and herself calm, as she went into the refrigerator and grabbed the milk, poured some in her tea and put it back. Taking a deep comforting breath, she slowly turned towards where the voice came from, which was inside her living room.

She saw the silhouette of a man sitting in her chair. He reached over and turned the light on, the man sitting there had a gun on his lap. In his hands was a saucer with a cup. Picking up the cup and gesturing to her, he drank, never taking his eyes off her. Taking the liquid down in one gulp, he put the saucer and cup to the side and smiled.

"But it was still good for my coffee thanks." He said,

"Don't mention it, friend." Priscilla, stiffly replied, as she walked a little towards him. "Obviously you know who I am but I don't know you, you gonna give me the pleasure of knowing who my company is?"

She asked before taking a sip of her tea, trying to keep this as casual as possible. She needed time to think, who the hell was this guy and what did he want? He leaned closer towards her, where she got an even better look at him, he looked tall but she couldn't be sure while he was sitting. He had a gaunt face with pock marks and olive skin. He was bald with a hairline of spiked hair, it looked weird.

"Call me the Black Hand."

"Black Hand huh? And why is that?" She asked, walking even closer while she sipped her tea. He didn't even move while she advanced, he was dressed in a white suit with a black tie. He raised his left hand, pulling off the leather glove with great care. The hand concealed in the glove was as black as night, it looked horribly burned, she nodded, all the while lambasting herself for letting her guard down like this.

He was watching her the whole time, he could have killed her. She was such a fool; she knew then that she was losing it, allowing this to happen. If she hoped to survive this, she better snap out of it and wake up. He looked over picking up a picture of her kids.

"You have beautiful children, it's a shame they weren't here. I'd have liked to meet them…it's gonna be even more a shame to make them orphans too…no kid should lose their momma." She totally disregarded that last comment. If anyone was gonna die it'll be him.

"Now why would you want to do that? I don't know you friend…. At least tell me what I did, that's the least you can do, yes?"

He flashed her a quick smile,

"Come on over here, have a seat." He motioned her over to the couch; she hesitated, then grabbed a chair from the kitchen and sat down in the living room placing it up against the wall.

"I've never laid eyes on you till just yesterday," he lifted his butt off the seat just enough where he could reach into his back pocket. He pulled out a folded piece of paper. He unfolded and looked at it, then looked at her as though comparing something. Then gestured for her to take the paper, she got up, walked two steps taking it.

She didn't convey her emotions, but she was shocked. On the paper was a picture of her, with a small bio, her address, her kids' names and other known facts. At the bottom in bold letters it stated.

"Amount will be the same, dead or alive, but alive preferable. Once the job is completed and verified, the amount will be forwarded to any account specified."

There was no price. She nodded her head a few times; finding twisted humor in this, then put the paper to the side. She gazed at the Black Hand, who was watching her closely.

"Nice to be wanted, huh?" He nodded, leaning back.

"If you're wondering how much the price is, it's $500,000,000." Priscilla's left eye twitched, the same one that the Albino's acid touched. "Make no mistake, there are others out there looking for you. Not the so called hitmen, that get nailed on stakeouts, accepting money from housewives that want to off their husbands for insurance money.

I'm talking heavy-duty players; the art of the assassin is a dying breed. I'm just glad I got to you first." Now she was really floored, a bounty on her?! From who? Only two people came to mind instantly. The Albino and the Benefactor, that Hans spoke about. But with the amount being offered, she didn't think it could be the Albino, no way he had that kind of money. But she could bet her life that he was involved somehow. The Black Hand went on.

"Now, I gotta ask you a question. I've never seen a bounty that high. I've killed people far more important than you before."

Priscilla wanted to laugh out loud at the assuredness of himself, of assuming that he 'killed' her. "What makes you so threatening?"

He looked quite relaxed in her home, she thought, with bloody thoughts of ripping him apart flashing through her mind.

"From what I've seen, you're just a single mom who takes really good care of her kids, it's a sin that I gotta take you from them." He said shrugging his shoulders, she nodded.

"Yeah, it is." She retorted, he nodded to that comment, gripping his gun.

"I know how it is to lose a momma, it's tough, but kids are resilient. They'll get over it." He raised his gun in a flash, Priscilla was faster, throwing her cup at him. That gave her seconds to act, sliding off the side of the chair at the same time she elbowed a certain part of the wall as hard as she could.

The section gave way and a sawed-off shotgun took its place. On her backside, she fired, Black Hand was just as fast kicking off the floor, and falling backwards in the chair, she missed him by inches. She fired again, blasting apart the bottom of the chair, quickly regaining her footing; she approached the chair as she cocked another round into the chamber blowing the lounge chair apart.

"Take me from my kids, huh!? Come on out you fuck!" She yelled, a rage was surfacing in her like no other; she needed to keep it in check, before it got the best of her. She caught movement, Black Hand stood up from behind the couch and fired, Priscilla dove out of the way returning fire, she recovered rolling over, and fired again blowing sheet rock fragments all over as the assassin ran to the back of her house. She was back on her feet, and stood still, listening intently for any movement, while making her way towards the direction he ran in. She walked slowly. The life she led has finally caught up to her. This was the last thing she wanted to happen.

She stopped just short of the small hall that split two-ways. To her left was the bedroom; to her right was her office and the bathroom. From her vantage point she didn't have a great view, she licked her lips, her throat was dry. Where did he run to? She only had one chance at this, she slowly peeked into her bedroom, then started to walk to her office, when she caught movement in the corner of her left eye. She turned blindly pulling the trigger on an empty shotgun. In her blood lust she didn't keep count of her ammo, there were however, six more slugs taped to the side of the shoulder stock. She stepped back from the gunfire aimed at her face and slipped on the wet floor from her smashed teacup, slamming hard on her backside.

She recovered quickly but struggled trying to chamber a slug. Her fingers were sweaty, in mere seconds she'd be dead if she couldn't slide it in. The Black Hand came around the corner ready to end her life, but was met with a slug to the face, he fell back headless.

It took some time for quietness to reclaim the house. On her back, she let out a deep sigh of relief, allowing herself a quick moment to gain her thoughts, that was too close, way too close. Once she calmed herself Lens came to mind, when he first warned her of things going south she didn't really believe it. Now she tried to remember every single thing he said the other day. She slowly got back to her feet, quickly going about the house and checking for any other surprises that might lie in wait, once the house was cleared she preceded to lock all the windows and doors.

Once done, she stood over the headless body of the Black Hand, what the hell am I gonna do with this body? She thought she needed to act fast. Staying here was totally out of the question now. She came up with a solution that may buy her some time.

Priscilla moved quickly, there was too much information here that could be linked to her, the kids, and her friends. She didn't want anyone else to be in danger because of her. In her office was a safe with spare cash. She then took out her hard drives to the PC and other notes and books that she kept over the years, along with a few other important documents stuffing them inside a large leather tote bag. Throwing that on the kitchen table, she grabbed the gun from her purse, stuffing it into her pants. She went out the side door to the garage. Grabbing a can of gasoline, she proceeded to douse each and every room, doing this to the kids' rooms hurt the most.

Once done, she grabbed whatever bottles of liquor she could, using ripped sheets as a wick. Just before she lit the cloth, she stared at her kids' rooms. She stood there for a moment with a lighter in one hand and her 'cocktail' in the other.

Never in her life she thought she'd need to do this to her own home. Everything she worked for, everything she wanted in life was in this house and now it was going to be burned to the ground. She felt sick in the pit of her stomach. Lighting the cocktail she threw it, the flames engulfed everything in its path, then she threw another one in her daughter's room, running downstairs, she threw another one in her office, she had one more left, she lit it throwing it blindly, as she walked outside.

She never looked back; it would hurt to do so. Hopefully whoever else came looking for her will think she's dead with no way of identifying the charred body right away. The sacrificing of her home will give her time.

Once this was over, she'd build a better home, make new and better memories. Getting in the Charger she pulled away. Stealing a glance in the rearview mirror, she saw flames jumping from the windows, by the time the fire department came her house would be but a faint memory. In the reflection of her door window, if you looked closely, you'd see a single tear running down her cheek.

Chapter 3
Facing reality

Priscilla took her time getting to the funeral home, she was gripped in paranoia, doing everything she could to make sure she wasn't being followed. Taking detours when she could, going in circles, down side streets, on and off parkways. By the time she did all this it was the late afternoon. She needed to grab a bite to eat and get a fresh change of clothes for the wake.

She went to Queens Blvd; there were plenty of places to shop. First, she went to Macy's and grabbed a simple black women's suit. Then she went to one of the small diners. Once she was done, she made her way to Ozone Park. On Cross-bay Blvd there was a hotel. She needed a place to just chill for a while.

After a long hot shower, she felt a little at ease. She was so wound up. She needed the time to calm down; she needed to think with a clear head. And most importantly, finally call Pat. She gave him the heads up, and he reassured her the kids would be safe. Even though under the current climate of things, she didn't think any place would be safe. But what other choice did she have? Nothing, at least Pat could be trusted where anyone else couldn't be.

She couldn't wait to get this over with, she really couldn't. She didn't even know why she was here. Under the circumstances, she should be laying low and trying to sort her other problems out. But she felt compelled.

The wake had started by the time she checked out and drove across the street. She was glad; she didn't want to be the first one there. Pulling into the lot, she sat in the car for a moment gathering herself. She took a deep breath; she couldn't put it off any longer. The faster this was done, the faster she could move on in so many ways. She took another deep breath, got out of the car, and went inside.

Chapter 4
Saying goodbye

Seeing her mother in the coffin was bizarre. She couldn't believe it, she couldn't think why though, everyone dies. That was the way it was but for some reason seeing her lifeless body, it was as though it was not possible. She never thought this day would come, as silly as that sounds, but here she was. Priscilla was numb, but never shed a tear. Maybe it was because she still had hard feelings for the way her mother treated her. But then again Priscilla had more pressing matters to deal with once this was behind her. She looked around at everyone that was here, there weren't many people. Her brothers and sisters, and their kids and a handful of people she'd either not seen in over twenty years or never saw at all.

They stood and sat around talking and laughing as though this was some reunion, as though there was not a dead body in the same room with them. That was another thing she never understood. Some people she never even knew came up to her trying to chitchat, she thought the look on her face clearly indicated she wasn't in a chatting mood. Just say, 'sorry for your loss' and be on your way, she wanted to say to anyone that tried to talk to her. But Priscilla was as nice as she could be under the circumstances. She looked at her watch, she was getting anxious. She told Pietro about what happened and he said he was going to come.

She just hoped soon. As though Pietro read her thoughts, her phone rang, it was him.

She quickly walked outside to greet him. The parked Lincoln's door swung open, Pietro got out slipping into his coat, Priscilla met him half way, and they embraced. It felt good holding him, she hadn't seen him since she left and they had a fight too. She could care less about that now. She was just glad he was here with her.

"The kids are ok?" He asked as they separated and walked up the three stone steps. She nodded.

"Yes, they are fine. They are in good hands."

"You know that if you need anything I'm there."

"Yes, I know. But I don't think you or anyone else can help. The only thing that matters is the kids are safe. I don't want them to be used against me or anyone else that I care about for that matter." She said as she looked at him. They stood now, by the door. She gave him a long kiss before they entered. She needed to feel him. She took a deep breath as he opened the door, letting her in first. She stopped and waited for him.

"Now don't mind anything that goes on, my family can be crazy and a fight can break out at a moment's notice." She tried to make light of the situation, but it was true. They walked past two rooms with other wakes going on. Theirs was the last door. She walked in first, an almost in unison, all eyes suddenly fell on them.

Priscilla's face flushed, and her ears got hot all of a sudden. She flashed a quick smile. Everyone then went back to their conversations. Pietro took off his jacket and placed it on one of the seats as he made his way to the coffin. Along the way she introduced him to people that mattered like Lorraine. When she did, Priscilla's sister's eyes lit up like a Christmas tree. Pietro had that effect on women.

As they walked on, Lorraine whispered in Priscilla's ear, asking if he had a brother. Priscilla couldn't help but chuckle and shake her head no. As they made their way to the coffin Priscilla got queasy, she didn't go up there yet. She was going to ask Lorraine to go with her, but didn't want to look weak or something.

So, she figured to wait for Pietro, she felt comfortable to go with him, and besides, she didn't have to ask him, it was a natural thing to do when you go to a wake, you head to the coffin and pay your respects as soon as you arrive. She even kept her apprehension from him, not that she didn't feel comfortable to let Pietro into her thoughts, but she hated looking weak in front of anyone.

Pietro kneeled, making the sign of the cross and bowed his head. Priscilla stood there like an idiot staring at her mother. An overwhelming impulse was to touch her; as if this was the first dead person she'd ever laid eyes on. In the snap of a finger a lifetime of memories flooded her. She was engulfed. Jesus, focus!

She yelled in her mind. She couldn't have a breakdown, not now of all times. For the first time in her life she just wished she could break down and cry her eyes out.

But she couldn't. She peered behind her; no one was paying any attention to her. Pietro had just finished his silent prayer when he looked up at her.

"You ok?" He leaned over whispering. His words snapped her out of her transfixed state, she stepped forward and kneeled. She crossed her fingers, leaning her forehead on them. She closed her eyes, saying an 'Our father.' She then picked up her head and stared at her mother. Pietro didn't move, but he was watching her.

Impulsively, she reached out and touched her mother's hands. The ice-cold flesh sent a chill up her spine. Again she didn't know why, she'd seen a thousand times worse and it was done by her hands. Pietro got to his feet and waited for Priscilla to do the same. A few seconds later she slowly got up, turned to walk, but quickly turned around, stepped forward, leaned in and kissed her mother on the forehead. Pietro grabbed her by the hand and led her away. Pietro thought she was going to cry, and he even asked that very question but she waved him off.

"No… no…. I'm fine, can't I show a little emotion?" She asked, trying to make light of what just happened. He led her to the back of the parlor. They stood there for a few moments, until Priscilla saw her brothers talking not far from them. Bobby was a little worse for wear, after all, he lived with their mother all his life.

They all knew he'd be lost without her. Even though Priscilla and him never got along, she felt bad for him. She knew that at some point either her or one of her sisters would have to step up and take care of him. Yet another thing she'd have to worry about. Fuck me, she thought. As she continued to stare she was reading their lips. Her brother John or 'Junior' as their mother liked to refer to him as, was deep in Bobby's ear. She wasn't going to get involved with what they were talking about, not until she caught a few choice words,

"Apartment and money." She stormed off in their direction. Pietro did a double take, chasing after her.

"What's the matter?" He whispered. She merely threw her hand up to silence him. He made a face and followed her to the two men talking.

"What are you two talking about?" She asked suddenly, startling both men. Bobby didn't say anything; he just stared at the floor. John 'Junior' tightened his tie, and then spoke.

"We…we were discussing the apartment. That once all of this was behind us, that he could either give me money for the place, or move out so I can get my money back. After all, I bought the place for mommy." Priscilla was at a loss for words. She crossed her arms over her chest.

"Are you kidding me, you can't do that, besides Bobby's name is on the lease so technically it's his place now." Junior shrugged his shoulders, flashing that arrogant smile with his overly large teeth, she wanted to knock out right now.

"Yes, I can, I bought it for mom not him. He's a big boy, I think it's time for him to get out into the world a little."

"I don't give a fuck what you think, he's not leaving and you're not gonna do a goddamn thing about it!" A few people looked in their direction as she raised her voice. Junior looked a little uncomfortable just then, Pietro, gently touched Priscilla's arm, but she jerked it away.

"Ok… ok fine… but he has to pay me back. I bought it for mom not him." Priscilla felt so enraged now, she wanted to scream. How the hell can this prick be so heartless? Her brother Bob couldn't go anywhere else, everyone was close by for him. He didn't make a lot of money; the apartment was fixed rent so he could afford that. As the two of them had their standoff, Bobby walked away and sat in a chair in the last row crestfallen.

"I can't believe you're doing this at mom's wake, John."

"Doing what? I'm just talking, besides, since when do you care so much about mom?" That comment stung her, she may have hated her mother at one point, but time heals all wounds and she more than made up for her sins through her kids.

"Ok, whatever, but this is not the time or place to bully our brother. You better not try anything or so help me Junior..." She stepped closer, but was grabbed by Pietro, she looked at him, then back to her brother, taking a deep breath.

This was something she didn't need right now. Bobby wasn't a favorite of hers, but she certainly wasn't going to let someone throw him in the street. And with things uncertain for her, she may not live long enough to help him. So, she took care of it now. She glanced behind her, giving Pietro a little nod.

"I'm fine Pietro, really." At first, he wasn't sure, but then slowly let go. He was ready to restrain her in case she had other ideas. Priscilla took a deep breath, as she gathered her thoughts looking her brother Junior in his eyes.

"Ok…. how much did you pay for the apartment?"

"$10,000 why?" He asked in a skeptical tone not really knowing where this was going.

"$10,000 huh? Ok Mr. Big shot, with all the money you say you have. Yet you're bitching about a measly sum for a man of your stature." She reached into her purse and fished out her checkbook, quickly writing, she had the overwhelming desire to shove it down his throat.

"Here…here's your fucking money, choke on it, and if you bother Bobby again, I'll break your face, got it?" And walked away before she did just that. Before she walked outside, she went to her brother Bob.

"Don't worry, you're taken care of, ok?" Bobby looked up at her with teary eyes and smiled. She returned the gesture, rubbing his shoulder and then made her way outside Pietro was right behind her.

She leaned on the metal railing, the wind felt good hitting her. Pietro, just stepped outside, he offered her a smoke which she took, he looked at her with concerned eyes,

"You ok?" She nodded.

"Yeah, great, that's been a long time coming." She said as she took a long drag. Pietro was searching for something else to say as they smoked their cigarettes.

"After this, I'm done…" she suddenly said breaking the silence. She was looking into the street as she said that. "I want a normal life…" She looked at him with sad eyes. He nodded.

"I can do normal." She smiled.

"Listen…meet me at the diner on Cross Bay Blvd, in one hour. I'll fill you in on everything then." Pietro nodded.

"Ok, let me grab my coat." Pietro walked back inside and came back out not even a minute later. Priscilla kissed him on the cheek. She watched him walk to his car as she finished her cigarette. Once he was gone, she took one last drag and flicked the butt to the street and went back inside.

Chapter 5
Cutting ties

It took her a little longer than an hour, but Priscilla finally showed up at the agreed upon diner. She hurriedly walked in and saw Pietro at a booth in the back. Sitting down, Priscilla wasted no time; she told him everything that had transpired since she went to Venezuela. Not once did he interrupt her as she tried to recall every last bit of information that would make the story easier for him to understand.

Once she had finished, he had a look on his face, she very seldom saw. It was like almost in a flash, dark circles crept around his eyes. Just as he was about to speak a waiter came along to refill their cups with more coffee.

"So, what's gonna happen now?" She shrugged her shoulders,

"I don't know, I really don't know at this point. But I need to get on the offensive. I just gotta figure out where to start." She took a sip of coffee continuing "All I know is this, I have a death mark on me. I have an idea from whom, that Albino is the key, if I can track him down I'll get the answers." Priscilla was frustrated beyond anything; Pietro grabbed her hand, trying to do his best to console her.

"Relax…" she nodded,

"I'm fine, really, I just needed to vent to someone…. thank you." She said with sad eyes and a small smile. She rubbed his hand, it felt so warm. She then looked at her watch.

"I gotta get a move on, and you gotta get outta here. I'm like the plague, the last thing I need is someone getting hurt because of me." Pietro shrugged that off, as they got up, paid the bill and left. Outside, they stood for a moment, Pietro took out his cigarettes. Priscilla asked for one, he gave her the pack, he had another one in his car. She was grateful too, she still hadn't stopped to buy a pack of her own. As they enjoyed the quiet moment, Priscilla realized something.

"With all I've told you, I'm surprised you haven't tried to stop me from going out there." Pietro shrugged his shoulders, as he put the cigarette to his mouth.

"Would it have worked?" Priscilla turned her head left and right. "I didn't think it would." He said, blowing out smoke. "Besides, you're right, you gotta do something. You can't just let this go, running forever is not a way to live." She nodded, he was right. Priscilla would rather die fighting than running. He turned to her as he spoke again, flicking his cigarette into the street.

"Just be careful, that's all. You got kids waiting for you, and me too." She smiled. He was stepping towards her, but she stepped away. She didn't want to drag this out. It was gonna be a long night and she wanted him away from her.

"Go…don't make this any more harder than it is now. Go home, I'll be in touch when I can." He nodded; he didn't take it personally, she was right. And besides Priscilla needed to have her head in the game. She needed to be focused with no distractions, no emotions… nothing.

She needed to revert back to the Priscilla, who had nothing to lose. She watched Pietro walk to his car, before opening the door, he took one last look at her, got in and drove off. Watching the car fade away, she took a deep breath. With all these distractions put to rest she thought of her next move. The only thing she could come up with was sneak back to Shadow Ops HQ, access the mainframe and try to find this NSA guy Jonas Ferrer.

Maybe he knew a few things, he had to have, or perhaps he was the one behind all of this. She wouldn't be surprised. Once she tracked him down, she'd ask in her own subtle way. Checking her watch again, twenty minutes flew by since Pietro left, holy shit, she thought.

The cool night air felt good as she walked to her car and got in, she waited another five minutes before she pulled out of the lot, and headed north on Cross Bay Blvd.

Priscilla didn't get far, she got caught at a red light, she cursed under her breath. As she waited, a car suddenly appeared behind her. She paid it no mind. The light turned green, she was about to press the accelerator when out of nowhere a car from the other side of the boulevard crossed over and blocked her path, she looked in her rearview and saw the car behind her didn't move, she was boxed in. She immediately brought her weapon systems online. Her car could withstand the damage she was about to invoke on these two cars. Her front and back headlights slid open and mini-missiles were ready to fire. Her finger was seconds from pressing the button when there was a knock on her window. It startled her, she wasn't expecting that. She reached for her gun, two men in suits stood there with no weapons on them that she could see and other than boxing her in they didn't show any hostility towards her.

"Ms. Roletti, if you could come with us, please." The man said calmly. Pricilla had her window closed and she wasn't opening it either. She was in one of the most vulnerable positions. She wondered what this was about, with few options to go with, she had nothing to lose at this point.

"Lead the way." She said with a raised voice behind the window. Both men walked off to their cars. Priscilla settled back in her seat, taking a deep breath. She'd humor this for now. She had a feeling she knew what this was about, but would hold her conclusions until she was sure though. The lead car sped off and she followed.

Chapter 6
The final mission

Within a half an hour they arrived, pulling down a darkened side street in Astoria Queens. All three cars pulled up to a small building, from the looks of it, it was abandoned. The two men quickly got out and walked toward their destination. Priscilla never hesitated, she got out of her car and walked towards them. She had her gun in her hand close to her thigh. If they noticed it, they didn't make it obvious. One of the men moved aside, he was standing in front of an alleyway.

"There's metal stairs on the left, take them up." One of them said. She nodded, looking at both of the guys for a moment and then walked down the dark alley. She had her gun at the ready, her senses were sharp. She stole a fast glance behind her; the two men were still there with their backs towards her. As she made her way she relaxed more, taking the steps one at a time. She made her way up; at the top was a metal door. It was unlocked, she entered.

Priscilla walked into an open area that looked a little like a kitchen. There was an L shaped counter with a sink. She looked up, seeing a large skylight.

The single source of light came from the ceiling right above the countertop and sink. Just in front of her was a chair that someone was sitting in. She couldn't make out who it was. They sat in the darkened part of the room. Priscilla placed her gun down on the counter in a gesture of good faith and walked forward. She slit her eyes, trying to get a better look at the occupant.

"So, we gonna talk or are we gonna play games all night?" She said, clearly losing some patience. The man chuckled and then got up and revealed himself. Priscilla wasn't surprised.

"Son of a bitch, Jonas Ferrer. I knew it!" Ferrer smiled as he walked towards her, he looked relaxed and arrogant.

"I told you, you'd be seeing a lot of me."

"Yeah, lucky me." She replied, in the most sarcastic tone she could. "What do you want from me?" Priscilla got right into it.

Ferrer walked to the counter top, sitting on a stool that was on the other side. He leaned over, grabbing something from below, it was a manila folder, he plopped it in front of her. She didn't make a move to grab it; she just stood there with her arms folded across her chest.

"Ok Roletti, I'm gonna give you a crash course in history. As you know, when the Nazis were defeated, many fled, under disguise, with the help from various countries and organizations including the Catholic Church. Now, many were caught by the Nazi Hunters in the sixties and seventies, brought to trial and hanged." As he talked, she grabbed a cigarette from her coat lighting it, she didn't ask if she could and she didn't care if he liked the smoke or not. Ferrer wasn't exactly her favorite person right about now.

"There was one very high profile Nazi that eluded justice. His name is Josef Mengele, otherwise known as the Angel of Death. Now there were reports that he died a few years ago and the Nazi Hunters went to Argentina to confirm this but could not, the grave they dug up was empty." She took a drag flicking the ashes on the floor, Ferrer saw that but didn't say anything.

"And what does this have to do with me?" Ferrer stiffened frowning.

"Are you dense? The mysterious person who funded the research in Pennsylvania, the man that Hans was hiding from and now who is making your life a living hell is Dr. Josef Mengele, the Angel of Death. The main architect of the Final Solution as the Nazis called it or in better terms. The extermination of six million people. Men, women, children, Jews, and anyone else that didn't adhere to the Master Race. You've heard of him haven't you?" She wasn't at all interested in any of this. But once he started to make references to The Benefactor, she gave Ferrer a sharp look.

"You're not saying? Come on, the guy has to be over a hundred years old." Priscilla couldn't believe her ears. "Are you sure your intel is right?" Ferrer nodded.

"Absolutely, I've been tracking the leads down since you uncovered everything." Priscilla waved him off still not believing him, but Ferrer held his ground.

"It all fits, Dr. Mengele performed all types of experiments on the prisoners in various concentration camps. His main focus was human experimentation striving for human perfection. The Supreme Being. Super human if you will. I have an eyewitness account of Mengele alive, not all that well, but alive nonetheless.

As you stated he's old. Part of the reasoning for his research was to find the key to immortality hence the cloning. He dreams of leading a new age Fourth Reich, finishing what the Nazi's started." Priscilla still couldn't believe all of this, but he did have a point, she always wondered if the cloning was for a motive other than taking over the government.

"With a new body and perhaps even adding Hans' formula into the mix, it could be disastrous. He must be stopped and that's where you come in." That possibility scared her, she'd seen first hand what Hans' formula can do, and she wasn't eager to face that again. The last words he said sunk in, she shook her head frowning.

"Where I come in? Listen Ferrer, if you think for one second you're gonna put me through the ringer, you have another thing coming. I got major problems of my own to deal with, on top of that my mom just died. You seem to have a good handle on things."

"I'm deeply sorry for the loss of your mother, my condolences." Ferrer shot back, obviously disregarding what she said. "But now is not the time to mourn. There are more dire matters that need your attention right now." She didn't like the cold comment and was about to say so, but he kept going.

"The mission, which you have no choice but to accept..." Priscilla, gave him a wide-eyed look, shaking her head.

"Whoa, whoa, wait! I ain't accepting anything. Besides, you disbanded Shadow Ops, remember?" She said poking her finger on the counter. "Go get someone else, I'm done." Ferrer smirked.

"The assassin at your house, you think they are going to stop just like that? You think Mengele will just say she's dead? No. He's not a fool; Mengele has vast resources as you already know. Anyone can be on his payroll. You want this to stop you take out Mengele, and in the process you take out this mysterious Albino. Until this guy is dead, it's only you and me." He said, pointing a finger at both of them.

"I'm on your side, if I wanted to kill you, I could've already." Priscilla looked away, then looked down at the floor and then gave him a sideways look as she slowly nodded. She knew he was right. She was just tired. She never thought she'd feel this way, but she was done. She wanted out. She had enough. She was worn both physically and mentally. She took a deep breath.

"Fine." She said, defeated. Ferrer nodded, he didn't wear a smug look. He just got right down to business.

"Ok, in the manila folder are some of the people that may be coming after you. We have a location on one of them, so start there." She picked up the folder and looked at the pictures of six people.

"That's the A-6. They are a group of highly trained assassins; they are more or less freelancers now. They were trained by a Bill Bobcatz, who was part of the Israeli Secret Service. Now I'm not sure if all of them are coming for you, the last job they did was about a year ago, and they have since disbanded. Even though Bill has been retired for years now and resides right on Long Island in Great Neck. He participated with them on that particular job. The other five are AWOL." Priscilla, looked up when he said that.

"So, you're saying a Jewish hit team is in league with a former high ranking Nazi? Come on Ferrer." She said, not believing this at all, and it was clearly evident in her voice. Ferrer shook his head.

"No, no, Bill is the only one that's Jewish, the other five are not. See they were trained to take out high value Hezbollah targets. Bill trained them and led them, so he may know where they are or at least know some way of getting in touch with them. So start with him first, he may not be so accommodating to give information out on former comrades so be careful. The Israeli's provided us with this information." She nodded, not looking all that happy about this.

"So, this is a ghost hunt?" She let out a frustrated breath, Ferrer shrugged his shoulders.

"Possibly, but at least it's a lead, now if it turns out to be good, once you ascertain the whereabouts of Mengele, kill him with extreme prejudice, and anyone involved. I don't care who it is. I'm sure your buddy the Albino won't be far from him, so keep that in mind." She nodded, she didn't need Ferrer to tell her that. She wasn't leaving any loose ends, anyone she comes across even remotely involved will be killed. Something just occurred to her, and she felt like a fool for not even thinking about this before, she swallowed before she asked on a dry throat.

"What's going to happen with Derlin?" Her friend and mentor was taken away in handcuffs from the very man now giving her a new mission. He looked away from her when she asked that. He grunted.

"Never mind Derlin, keep yourself focused on the matter at hand." She nodded, she didn't want to argue. Ferrer reached into his pocket and slid a Visa debit card towards her.

"There's ten-thousand available now. And if you dip below five-thousand you'll be given another five and so on. The code to take out cash is 0978." She nodded, taking the card and slipped it in her pocket. The conversation was evidently over. She took her gun, which was still on the counter.

"You have a number I can reach you at?" She asked before leaving.

"I'll call you, just remember no matter where you are, I'll be watching." She nodded again and turned to leave when he called out to her.

"Good luck Priscilla." She stopped in mid-stride, she was going to say something snide, but decided not to. She wasn't really in the greatest of all moods right now. She left, not looking back; ready to begin her final mission.

Chapter 7
Bill Bobcatz

Priscilla took her time making her way to Great Neck. Taking a long detour, she couldn't take any chances of being followed. She finally got off the Long Island Expressway and took the narrow two-way road, heading north. She kept to the speed limit; she didn't want to draw unwanted attention to herself. In this town, the cops looked for anything to pull you over. And at this hour, it was dead, Great Neck was like a ghost town.

Hopefully this Bill Bobcatz should be well into his seventh dream by the time she was going to pay him a visit. Retirement softens people up. It doesn't take long for you to forget where you came from, even though you may have retired and called it quits, your enemies have not. Living in a town that radiates money will certainly make you soft; this place was really a total false sense of security. Priscilla took a few side streets until she finally parked two houses away.

She had a view of the house. With her windows tinted, she was perfectly hidden from all eyes. Even the light from the onboard touchscreen computer installed in the dashboard, couldn't be seen from the outside. Before she parked, Priscilla did a drive by of the house twice, but from the looks of it no one was home. She wondered where he was, she hoped he wasn't out looking for her, but then again she doubted it. This whole story, with a Nazi who should be long dead, didn't sit right with her. Although she shouldn't be doubting anything after what she encountered. But still, it was hard to swallow. An ex-Israeli spy in league with a Nazi? She'd believe in the fountain of youth before that one. She scrolled through the data Ferrer showed her before; he said he'd upload the files in case she wanted to look at them more.

It wasn't anything she hadn't encountered before. The A-6 were typical Black Ops assassins. They knew all of the cloak and dagger stuff, just like her. If push comes to shove, she knew she could handle them one at a time, but all at once, that was another story. She hoped that this Bill would be level headed enough and help her. He certainly has to know or at least have some idea what his former team members must be doing and who they may be working for.

If a confrontation ensued that's the card she'd play on him, but again she hoped it didn't have to come to that. She just wanted to get in and get the hell out. She had so much work ahead of her. She sat in the car stewing the entire night, at one point she grew tired and dozed off. Unless someone used a missile this was the safest place to rest. She didn't sleep long. She kept a close eye on the house. She looked at her watch. It was a little after four in the morning. If this guy was coming back then he would have already, something was up.

Priscilla wasn't going to waste any more time sitting here. She already wasted enough. She grabbed her gun, got out of the car and manually locked it. She didn't want it to beep at this hour.

She slowly looked around as she walked to the supposed empty house. She wasn't worried about an ambush. Three cars came down this block the whole time she was sitting there. Crossing the street, and on the sidewalk, she picked up her pace, she held her gun tight in her hand keeping it snug to her thigh.

Walking on Bill's front lawn, she made her way to the front door. She skipped one of the three steps getting on the porch. Stuffing the gun in her waist, she cuffed her hands over her eyes, as she looked in the window. It was too dark to see anything. Priscilla stepped back admiring the house, it was a simple two-family home. It was very modest for someone like him. One would have thought an old couple or a married young couple with kids lived here.

She walked off the porch, walking around the house. She was looking for any type of alarm system. She didn't find anything. Going back to the front door, she reached into her jacket pocket and took out a lock-pick. Upon further observation Bill's front door locks were nothing to worry about. She had the door unlocked in a matter of a minute.

She stepped in and very slowly closed the door, locking it again. She stood right where she was, holding her breath. Reaching into her coat again, she took out a miniature flashlight and shed light on her surroundings. To her left was the kitchen, where she was, was the living room with a couch and a coffee table to her right. Shining the light ahead, she walked slowly. To her left was a small hallway, with a closed door and a bathroom further down. From where she stood, she could see a little bit of the bedroom. She continued to walk on. She entered a study room. It was mostly unassuming. It was neatly kept, with various keepsakes and pictures. When she looked closer at some of the pictures on the wall she gasped. She didn't know why she was surprised; many in her profession had other jobs.

Even teachers, which Bill was, but what surprised her was he taught right here on Long Island in Franklin Circle. It really was too much of a small world. Along his walls were diplomas from colleges he graduated from. On a bookshelf were yearbooks dating back over ten years ago. She took the latest one off the shelf and fingered through it, as she held the light between her teeth. She flipped right to the staff pages and found her man.

"Bob Bogatz." She said in a low tone. Not very original, she thought as she studied the picture, he hardly looked like a former Israeli Black Ops. She replaced the yearbook, and then went to his desk. All in all she didn't find anything that could help her. If she didn't know any better, she'd have thought of him as a sheltered man. Who had inept social skills. He probably portrayed himself really well at the school.

Priscilla took a deep breath, she was done here. The only thing she could do was wait a little while longer, but in her car. The last thing she wanted was getting caught snooping. She killed the light and turned around to leave, when the ceiling light was suddenly turned on and standing in the doorway was Bill Bobcatz.

"Oh fuck." She didn't dare to make a sudden move. Her eyes dropped to the Walther PPK that was firmly pointed at her chest.

"Please." Was all he said in a lispy voice, as he gestured her out of the office. He walked backwards, never taking his eyes or gun off her. He blindly turned on the hall light. And then again without taking his eyes or gun off her, reached into the hallway, and opened the closed door Priscilla passed by earlier. She had no choice but to follow him. He was too far for her to make a move, and she didn't want to. She wasn't here to fight, and in a way she couldn't blame him for acting like this. She'd have done the same thing too. She had to go with the flow; he seemed like a reasonable man.

"Listen, guy. I'm sorry for breaking into your home. Trust me, it's not what you think it is. I just wanna talk…my…" He shushed her, as he gestured her down the stairs.

"We can talk downstairs please, you've seen enough of my home." She nodded, biting her lower lip. She didn't want to go down there. She turned and looked over her shoulder. There was a light on. She then looked back to Bill.

"I can assure you, if I wanted to kill you, I'd have done so up here." She didn't answer. She turned around and walked to the stairs. She was about to take the first step down, when Bill came right behind her, and felt her waist area. He found and took her weapon. He was good; she'd give him that. Even if she wanted to resist and fight back, all he'd have to do was push her down the stairs.

"You won't be needing this. You may go now." He said in his educated lisp voice. As they descended the hard creaky wooden steps, Bill kept his pace with hers. Priscilla didn't look behind her; at the base of the stairs was a small doorway on the right. Without him having to tell her she walked in. It was dark, but the place must've had motion sensors because the overhead lights came on almost immediately. She stood there for a moment, gazing at what was here; she knew this wasn't going to be easy from here on out. Off to the left was a big old oak table. She saw the workbench, with various tools. On her right was one of those old cast iron tubs. The mustiness of the place, clogged her sinuses.

If she didn't do something this was going to be the last place she was going to see.

"Don't be afraid. Go right inside." His voice broke her out of her thoughts and she did as he said. She walked to the far side of the room, passing an old chair, and then turned around. In the bright lights, she got a better look at Bill, he was dressed in casual pants and a polo shirt with neatly combed hair and a thick brown-mustache. He was studying her as well.

He smiled in a way that would put anyone at ease before he killed them. It didn't work on her, though. He held his gun on her, in his other hand was her gun, he looked at it and then placed it casually on the worktable. She took a deep breath through flaring nostrils, inhaling more dust that clogged her sinuses even more.

"Well.... You hardly look like the stereotypical, burglar fumbling about in the dark." He said as he walked a little closer. He gestured to the oversized wooden chair with his other hand. She made her way towards it and just stood.

"So that would lead me to my next questions, who are you and why are you here?" Priscilla tensed a bit as she held her eyes on Bill. Then finally spoke, slowly.

"I was looking for someone." She simply said. Bill flashed a quick smile, amused by the way she said that.

"And you found them, although probably not in the way you wanted. So, what was next hmm, you break into my home in the wee hours of the morning and...." She took a deep breath, before answering, trying to stall just to gather her thoughts.

"Well, it's a bit of a long story, and I'm pressed for time."

"Time is all you have, and it may be shortened if you don't continue." She nodded she had to choose her words carefully. If this guy wasn't the enemy, and was willing to help her, then she better try to rectify her big mistake.

"I was informed that, you may be able to help me. I'm looking for some people. When I first drove by your house and saw you weren't home, I decided to wait for you. And call for you in the morning. But when I saw you hadn't returned yet, I thought maybe something was wrong. I'm not here to harm you in any way. All I need is information. And that's the truth, no bullshit." Bill didn't relax any more after she told him this. He had a quizzical look on his face.

"I see, and how did you come about this information?" Priscilla wasn't going to lie or play games.

"I wasn't told this first hand, but it was someone from the Israeli government, they told my superior and then relayed it to me." Bill still didn't relax himself. But she could tell he was mulling all of this over.

"Ok, so lets say for the sake of the argument, you're telling the truth. What can I do for you then?" Priscilla felt half relieved, although she wasn't out of the woods yet.

"I'm looking for what's left of your former crew, the A-6. A woman named Luna leads them now, right? I was told they went rogue."

Bill scratched the corner of his eyebrow, after she said this. He wore a smirk. He knew this was going to happen. Goddamn Luna.

"As a matter of fact she was here, just yesterday morning." She wasn't totally shocked by this, but the luck of missing her by a day was better than Priscilla thought.

"Can you tell me where she is?" Priscilla asked eagerly, she wanted to get the hell outta here already. Bill snorted a laugh.

"No, because I don't know where she is. We didn't exactly leave on good terms." Priscilla nodded, relaxing a bit. A goddamn dead end she thought, she knew it from the get-go.

"I'm sorry to have bothered you then. My apologies. I'll just take my leave then." She said the words fast, as she made her way to the backdoor. The cocking of the hammer stopped her in her tracks. She looked in his direction. He was gesturing her to go right back where she was. She did so. That relaxed feeling evaporated. She tried to remain as calm as she could.

"Listen guy, I don't want any trouble, ok, I just wanna go about my business. I'm sorry that I broke into your home. Just let me pass through, please." Bill gave her a piercing look, and then he suddenly snapped his fingers.

"I just realized something." He said totally ignoring what she just said, as he pointed at her. "You're the one they are after." He embarrassingly chuckled, at the sudden oversight on his part. "The whole time I'm standing here, I kept saying to myself, you look oddly familiar, and then it dawned on me Luna showed me your picture." He chuckled again. "I don't know whether to call this good fortune or rotten luck, and as much as I would love to let you leave, I'm afraid I can't now more than ever." Priscilla figured as much. He continued.

"Look at it from my end, you break into my home." He gestured around. "Then I have Luna and her crew to deal with if they get wind that you came here looking for them, and then found out that I let you just walk out of here." He shook his head, pursing his lips. "I certainly don't need that headache. If you knew her you'd know that wouldn't go over well. And the last reason… I don't trust you; you saw everything pertaining to my life. The last thing I need is you trying to use me as leverage."

"I don't give a fuck about you."

"You say that now. But who knows in the future, if you even have a future. You know who's after you, I presume?" She nodded; Bill pretty much confirmed what Ferrer told her.

"Good. And that is the number one reason you cannot leave here alive. I will not participate in dealing with or helping in any way a Nazi criminal. I shall deny him the opportunity to take out whatever sick, twisted agenda, he has in store for you. Killing you is the only way to see to that. Plus preventing anyone from knowing you were here, and in so putting me in harm's way.

It's nothing personal, it's strictly for the sake of self-preservation. But I'm sure you're familiar with that already. I promise it'll be quick and painless." Priscilla couldn't believe her ears. She licked her lower lip. She was ready for the fight to come. Bill stepped away from the table.

"Take off your coat if you like. Then turn around, and go on your knees. I promise it'll be quick." He added, as though being polite about killing her would make her feel better. "Again, this is nothing personal." Priscilla didn't even acknowledge the remarks.

Priscilla took a deep breath. She lifted her head; she was staring at the floor. She looked right at Bill, who was waiting by the end of the table. She quickly glimpsed at her gun, it was still where Bill placed it. Obviously he failed to notice it still there. She slipped off her coat, she wasn't gonna need it, she didn't need to be impaired by its bulk. She needed to strike fast and hard.

She took two steps, faced the table and was about to turn, when she lunged for the weapon. Bill saw this, moving quicker, but Priscilla feinted the move and now that he was within arm's reach, she grabbed him by the wrist, and slammed his hand on the table knuckles down, a wild shot went off. She slammed his hand again, even harder, he cried out, releasing the gun, which she quickly batted away onto the floor. She then, with her free hand, went for her own gun, but Bill was way ahead of her and batted that away as well, for his efforts, she head butted him, he fell back into the wall hard enough that various items dropped on and around him from the shelves overhead and one was a Taser gun.

He lunged for it, grabbing it with two hands and aimed it at Priscilla, who grabbed her jacket and threw it at him just as he fired the pointed electrodes that would have incapacitated her. Bill scampered away, throwing the Taser at her. By the time she closed the gap, Bill was already on his feet and met her head on. A fast and furious exchange of fisticuffs ensued; it was quite evident from the onset that Bill wasn't a good fighter.

He was skilled, yes, but not refined, a lot of his moves were clumsy. He was more the brain, and that gave Priscilla the edge. She was hungry and fierce. The fight didn't last very long, it became clear right away Bill wanted no part of her in this way, anything he could throw at her was grabbed, aerosol cans, knives, and a hammer. He was trying to stop the momentum of her attack, throw her off balance. It was frustrating her to no end. Priscilla unleashed a roundhouse kick, which he barely dodged. She went in for a follow up, but by the time she came back around, Bill slipped out the doorway and a solid metal shutter shot down. She had so much force behind the attack; she just stopped inches from punching the metal shutter. She stepped back and thrust kicked it twice. She then turned to the back door, and saw metal shutters snap down over the door and the only window that she couldn't even slip out of anyway, it was so small.

She could hear his feet pounding the stairs on the way up, she cursed herself for realizing too late it wasn't her commanding the pace it was him. She wasted no time sprinting to the back door that led outside; she grabbed her fallen gun on the way stuffing it in her waist. She reached into her pocket, taking out her pen-laser torch.

It would make fast work of the shutters. But then just as she was about to turn the cap and cut the gate. She was suddenly overcome with the smell of gas. She looked up to the ceiling, squinting. She saw and now heard where the gas was coming, and could now hear a hissing sound, over the fast beat of her heart.

"Fuck!" She looked around, she was gonna fry down here. Her eyes then fell to the cast iron tub, she ran to it. She dragged it to the oak table, with all she was worth. Straining her back and legs, she tilted it so it leaned against the table as she skittered underneath, and not a second sooner as she let the tub fall around her, the place suddenly exploded into a fiery deathtrap.

Chapter 8
Close call

Bill couldn't believe he almost lost back there; he really underestimated her, a small oversight on his part, he thought as he removed a panel off the stairway wall and flicked three buttons. But nevertheless she wasn't going to leave. She should have chosen the quick and easy death. But now she'll be burnt alive. Bill took a deep breath. He was annoyed though that his basement would be totally destroyed. His entire life was down there. Memories of his family, now burned to a cinder.

A small price to pay, in spiting the Nazi. His family would understand.

He raced up the stairs and quickly grabbed his car keys off the kitchen counter. Before leaving, he looked back at his home, memorizing where everything was. He always did that before he left. Today was Monday, and he had work today. He didn't see any reason to deviate from the norm. His intruder was dead now. He had no worry about the house burning down. The basement was insulated where the fire would be contained and expire on its own.

The clean-up could wait until tonight. He'd make sure he'd leave as soon as his last class was over. No putzing around with paperwork or grading test papers. He could do all of that once this was taken care of.

In a tight fetal position that strained her stomach, Priscilla had her arms over her head tucked deep into her chest. Her knuckles touched the tubs side; burning them, but she didn't move at all from the pain. Just moving an inch could move the tub and allow the flames to spew in. She concentrated her ears to listen for the flames to die down. She mentally counted in her head, and waited three minutes.

Everything was quiet. She wasn't going to sit here all goddamn day either; she lifted the tub and saw indeed it was safe. Getting to her feet, the place was burned out to hell, the smoke was suffocating her. She didn't waste a second longer. She ran for the back door, with the pen torch in hand, she cut the metal shutter, kicking it down. She unlocked the door and bolted up the concrete steps two at a time, she stood at the top, taking in large gulps of fresh air. It was close to dawn, as Priscilla ran to the front of the house through the little walkway. Bill was gone, but she may be able to catch up.

Priscilla remote started the car before she even got in. From a logical standpoint, going after him didn't help her in any way. He didn't have anything to do with her problems at all. But she wasn't leaving loose ends with this one. Anyone, that hindered her had to die. She was leaving nothing to chance. Aside from that, his death will play with the heads of his comrades, sometimes that's just as effective as smashing someone's head into a wall. At the corner leading to the main road, she looked both left and right. To her left led more to the north shore, which didn't have any outlets. But to the right was the Long Island Expressway, perfect for losing anyone. Being it was so early in the morning there was hardly a car on the road. She only passed two and knew they weren't Bill's because they didn't try to evade her and plus when she drove past them she looked at the drivers. She was doing close to 70mph on a straight run, and within no time she caught up to a car that suddenly picked up speed.

She pressed the pedal down harder, closing the gap further. She wasn't worried about him seeing her; he couldn't outrun her in his car. She slid back, the top cover on her middle console, revealing the on-board weapons system controls; the HUD (Heads up display) appeared on the windshield, the ominous green cross hairs lined up her target. She already slid back the front headlights; two mini-missiles were armed and ready. She just needed to make sure her aim was dead on. There was the potential of collateral damage if she missed. She gritted her teeth, he was weaving back and forth, making it hard for her to get a lock-on.

Slippery little bastard, she thought. The sound of a train horn bellowing pulled her from her thoughts; she looked ahead and saw they were coming up to a railroad crossing. The red lights and the warning bell were flashing and sounding off, the long red and white striped arms descended. She pressed harder on the pedal, she watched Bill, perhaps this was to her benefit. He'd have no choice but to stop and try to turn around, but it quickly became evident he wasn't gonna stop.

He was going to try to beat the train. She was so close now, she was almost locked-on, Bill gunned it, going up the slight incline. From the speed and momentum the car lifted off the ground and slammed on the other side sending sparks flying. Priscilla cursed aloud, seeing this. He was not getting away! Pushing the Charger to the max, she looked towards the train, she may make it too. Launching off the slight incline she soon realized that her timing was off, just as she crossed over, the train clipped the back of the car sending her spinning twice. Her hand slipped and sent off a single missile into one of the storefronts blowing it to atoms. She landed with a hard bounce on the pavement, spinning once more before coming to a stop.

Bill really underestimated this woman. She survived! Unbelievable. Who was she? He may just have to call Luna after all. Someone like this woman will chase you to the depths of hell. He looked in his rearview mirror, shaken a bit by his narrow escape. He was cutting it pretty close by beating that train; he kept his eyes on the mirror watching his pursuer. She followed, but was clipped by the train and at the same time something was fired from the car, which blew out a storefront lighting up the predawn sky. With that type of gear, she must've been backed by the government, only governments had tech like that, he thought. He cursed Luna, for bringing this to his doorstep.

But then again, the one that did was whoever told this woman about him to begin with. He'd have to call one of his many contacts in Israel and find out who indeed did tell this woman about him. Thinking about Luna again, he grabbed the cell phone on the passenger seat. She was on speed dial, but her phone was shut off, it went right to voice mail. Damn her! He thought. He looked at his watch, it was after six-in the morning. He didn't want to chance going anywhere and running into the woman again.

So, the only place that was safe for now was work, the school. He'd be safe. He didn't care who this woman was, or how dangerous she may be, no one would be brazen or stupid enough to come to a school with kids and start anything, not many professionals would do such a thing. That brought way too much attention and plus, if she was in fact government-backed which she must've been, then she surely wouldn't. Governments don't want the spotlight shined onto their murky endeavors.

Priscilla swung the door open and stumbled out, her head was spinning. She looked in the direction of the speeding car that eluded her. She was helpless stopping him, she looked at the burning storefront that she destroyed, thank God there wasn't anyone in there, she thought.

The train that clipped her stopped at the station, most likely the operator didn't even know he hit her it wasn't a hard impact. Feeling the effects of the dizziness subside, she got back in her car and left the scene before the cops showed up. She thought her options through and there was only one that came to mind. Bill was going to the school and that's where she was going to finish him. It was perfect, and unexpected. Yes, he'd still keep his guard up, but he'd fall into a false sense of security as the day progressed.

It was a long shot, of course he may just go into hiding, but no it was perfect, it was a safe haven. And she had all day to plan. She'd look up the schedule for the day. She knew Bill's alter ego's name. It would be simple. The only thing nagging her was the fact that she would gun down a man, a man that many of these students looked up to as a role model, no doubt.

If it could be helped she never wanted to put anyone's life in danger, let alone kids. She was a mother herself. But unfortunately, this was the only way. Bill was too much of a loose end to let go. And if she waited to catch him alone, that would give him time to plan and maybe contact Luna. The children will get over it. Kids today are strong and resilient. The facts will come out and it will prove to be a valuable lesson in life for them. With it firmly decided, she pushed the pedal closer to the floor making for the Expressway.

Chapter 9
Back to school

By the time Bill made it to the high school he was calm or as calm as he could be. He kept a sharp eye out for this woman that would no doubt turn up again. He was under no delusions about that, some of his fellow teachers walked by waving at him as they walked on to the school. Bill gave them the smile of his alter ego, Mr. Bob Bogatz, or as his students affectionately called him, Mr. B.

His colleagues looked at him as the guy who never got married, never had kids, perhaps even a momma's boy. He purposely portrayed himself in such a manner. The harmless humble man. He had everyone fooled. When no one was around, he reached under his seat and pulled out an extra gun he kept stashed there. It was another Walther PPK, he loaded a round in the chamber, for the moment he wished he had a bigger weapon. The Walther only held seven rounds, he took a deep breath, nothing he could do now.

As he got out of the car, he stuffed the gun in the small of his back. He then reached in the back of the car, grabbing his suitcase, then closed and locked the door and walked to the school. Once he crossed the threshold, he immediately felt the relief of sanctuary, kids from all grades knew Mr. B and they loved him, they looked at him as one of their own.

He was old, quirky and sometimes corny but cool. He was stopped a few times by students who talked to him about sports. Bill also announced sporting events from time to time, he stopped one kid, and gave him a high five for a great game he had the other day. He walked into his class that was adorned with various topics related to history. He made his way to his desk and sat down.

Once settling in, he took out his cell phone, the kids wouldn't be in here for another five minutes yet. He called Luna again and again she didn't pick up. Curse her, he thought, he left her a message, stating the utter importance of her returning his call. He took out his gun and placed it in the middle desk drawer. He got up and peered out the window, where he had a good view of the parking lot. He didn't want to make it a habit of watching it all day.

Whoever this woman is, the last thing she would do is come here, that's what he kept telling himself every five minutes, but sometimes he wasn't so sure.

He needed to have a plan made up, before he walked out of this building. Because even if she didn't come into the school, he knew for a fact that once he walked out of this building she would be waiting for him. With time for now on his side, he put aside those thoughts.

Bill wasn't some rookie, this is and was his life and he would deal with it. He turned away from the window and went back to his desk to make the necessary preparations for the first class. He took out the lessons for the day and started to write some notes on the chalkboard, as his students shuffled in.

Priscilla waited down a side street near the school. She had a perfect view of the place. It was half past ten, the third period just started. She wasn't waiting here any longer, she needed to end this. She looked at herself in the mirror, in between the time she got here she made a fast pit-stop. She went to a diner grabbing a bite to eat, then went to the bathroom and took out a small bottle of instant brown hair dye, something the company uses-it came in an array of colors. You rub it in, and wash it out, and it absorbed every piece of hair, Priscilla Roletti was now a brunette. The dye could be washed out just as fast, once it dried. The last part she added, was brown contacts.

It altered her appearance, enough for what she needed to do. She reached for her gun, unscrewing the silencer. There was no need for quiet, the more confusion the better. She got out and walked briskly to the front of the building. She tucked her weapon in her waist and threw her sweater over it. She also wore a light tan colored trench coat to further the illusion of her being a cop.

When she walked into the building, a group of kids walked by giving her a fast look but moved on about their business. Her eyes fell to a hall monitor that was right near the main office; she walked over to him flashing a smile.

"Hey, good morning, the main office is that way?" She pointed in the direction, pretending not to know. She studied the layout of the building, in her down time. She wanted to make sure she had all the bases covered. The hall monitor simply turned and pointed, then went back to his book. It was so lax here, middle class Long Island she thought, no other place like it.

Once she walked into the main office, all three secretary's looked up at her, only two went back to their duties, while the one closest to her kept her eyes on Priscilla. She didn't even smile as Priscilla approached her.

"May I help you, Miss?" She said in a mundane tone. Priscilla smiled at her, reaching into her jacket pocket, and flashed her fabricated police badge.

"I'm detective Manheim, is there a Bob Bogatz here today?" The other secretaries, stopped what they were doing and looked at Priscilla dumbfounded.

"Bob?" She said, with some surprise. "Yes, he's here, is there a problem officer?" Priscilla waved a hand of dismissal at those words.

"No, ma'am, there was a gas leak in his house. There was a mild explosion this morning, and his house suffered some damage. I just need to inform him and ask a few questions, it won't take long, it's just procedure." The woman nodded

"Ok, I'll call him down, give me one moment." Just as she picked up the phone Priscilla stopped her with a harmless gesture.

"I'd appreciate it if you didn't make a commotion about it. I don't want to wait, his house wasn't the only one damaged, I have two more stops after this." The secretary nodded, a badge backed up anything, even bull shit. She moved her hand from the phone.

"Well, let me show you…"

"I know where it is, ma'am." Priscilla said quickly but not with any type of impatience. "My cousin's kid comes here, his name's Darren Long. He plays basketball, he always talks highly of Mr. B." Upon saying that name the secretary smiled.

"He's a good kid, great ball player too." She added, Priscilla nodded; the kid's name she used was from the yearbook, she fingered through at Bill's house. The name had just stuck out, it was easy to memorize, plus looking the kid up on Facebook helped her in knowing he played sports.

"Thank you for your time Miss." Priscilla said as she made her way to the door, just as she was about to open it, the secretary called out.

"Um, Miss. Manheim" Priscilla turned around; the secretary came around her desk and approached Priscilla, handing her a school ID sticker badge.

"Just show the hall monitors this." She said with a smile, Priscilla took a very small unnoticeable deep breath, for a second she thought the lady had second thoughts about her roaming the halls alone.

Priscilla was glad she didn't. The last thing she needed was someone in the way. Once out of eye shot from the office Priscilla picked up her pace, walking down the hall, there was another hall monitor who she flashed the ID sticker too.

He hardly acknowledged it as he waved her by. Bill's classroom was going to be to her right, she picked up her pace even quicker now and passed it by, through her peripheral vision she saw him at the chalkboard giving a lesson. She stopped, turned on her heel, reaching for her gun, as she slowly walked back to the door. It was a shame that the man these kids knew and respected was going to be shown in a different light before the day was out. She flattened her back against the smooth brick wall, with her left hand, she gripped the doorknob, her gun was gripped in her right hand, and in one smooth motion she swung the door open.

Bill was giving his lesson on the founding of the United States when he saw someone pass by the room. The day wasn't even half over yet and he was still jumpy. He lost his train of thought for the second, but recovered before any of his students noticed. Two o'clock couldn't get here fast enough, he thought. Just as he was about to turn and write something on the board, he heard his cell phone vibrate on his desk.

He stole a look and saw the name he was waiting for. It was Luna, finally! He normally wouldn't answer the phone during a class, but this wasn't a normal circumstance.

"Just give me one second guys, I need to take this call. Just look ahead to the next lesson." He told his students in a more exaggerated lisp as he picked up the phone off his desk and flipped it open, and just as he did so, the door to his room burst open and standing in the doorway was the woman.

Bill's features were neutral, a few students looked in the direction of the newcomer, wondering who she was and what she wanted. Bill knew this was it; he could hear the faint voice of Luna yelling his name. He pursed and licked his lips and as quickly as he could, he pulled open the desk drawer and cleared the gun almost aiming. When a single shot rang out, the kids in the classroom screamed, ducking almost at once, some ran to the back of the room. Bill stumbled back from the gunshot wound in his chest. He almost fell, but managed to lean on the desk to support himself.

Priscilla walked into the classroom and blindly closed the door with her foot. She walked over to Bill and shot him twice more. Kids screamed out in terror. She did her best not to look at them and block out the screams. After this, she definitely earned her one-way ticket to hell, too little too late to worry about that.

Priscilla stood over the dead Bill Bobcatz. She shot him one more time in the head. No student cried out then, thank God, she thought. She then turned her gun to the classroom window and shot that out sending glass flying outside. Before she made her mad dash, she spotted the cell phone that he dropped, she grabbed it. She then looked at the children finally, and held their sympathetic frightened eyes. She wordlessly said sorry and bolted out the window, running as fast as she could. She triggered the remote control of the Charger, so by the time she made it to the car, it was ready to go.

As she sped down the street, Priscilla stole a glance behind her. No cops, good. By the time they pieced anything together, she'd be long gone. She then turned her attention to the opened cell phone, Bill was about to answer. She looked at the screen and saw the name Luna, the call was still connected. Priscilla put it to her ear, she knew Luna was there listening.

"Hey, Luna. Bill is dead, and so are you, if you think about following through on anything got it!?" Before the woman even answered, Priscilla closed the phone and threw it out the window. She knew the threat wouldn't work. She just wanted them off balanced and put on notice that their bounty was coming for them.

Chapter 10
An old friend

Much later, just inside Westchester County, well past nine o'clock at night. Priscilla sat in the back of a diner with a good view of who was coming and going. It was a smaller than normal diner. She chose it because of that. After the school incident, she laid low. It didn't take long for that to hit the airwaves. All day and night was talk about the killer who gunned down the favorite teacher in cold blood in front of students. Also coming to light was the fact that said favorite teacher led a double life as a Black Ops assassin, with the media assuming it was a retaliation hit.

In truth, no one knew what the hell they were talking about. It was always the back and forth blah blah, bullshit. Little did they know, the information fed to them was intentional to keep the local authorities off her trail. And she had Jonas Ferrer to thank for that.

Who she was talking with right now on a Bluetooth earpiece. She expected him to find out, what surprised her was it took this long to hear from him.

"And that's it Ferrer. Your hot lead turned out to be shit." She added at the end, just to zing him. While telling him the real facts of what happened. There was silence on the other end, as he took in what she told him.

"It seems that way," he finally added. "So what's your next move?" That was a good question, she mused to herself. She did think about that.

"The only thing I can think of, is maybe try to track down the Albino. A guy looking like that can't be too hard to find. I may know someone who can point me in the right direction." Ferrer grunted.

"Ok. Just keep me in the loop."

"You got it." She wondered what this guy's deal was. One thing was for sure, he knew more than he was telling her. And that pissed her off to no end. When she saw him again, she'd make sure she'd get it out of him one way or the other. But regardless, at least he was on her side, for now anyway. She wasn't going to fully trust him.

"Oh, and, just try to keep a low profile. No more school shootings, you like going two for two." He ended the call, before she could even reply. She'd take responsibility for one mall incident, not two.

"Fucking jerk." If he's gonna take a jab at least get his facts straight. She took a deep breath, as she finished writing out an email on her phone. She was writing to Arthur Zipp, Derlin's army buddy.

Zipp was forced by the kidnapping of his daughter to kill various heads of state, of a foreign country he helped liberate from a despot dictator.

Derlin sent her to stop him. In the process, Priscilla rescued his daughter from the kidnappers. Zipp, being that he used to be a former assassin bounty hunter, might know of the Albino or point her in the direction of someone who does. With the email sent, all she could do was wait. Zipp lived in Westchester, so in the meantime she'd go to one of the local hotels, take a hot shower and get a good night's rest.

She got up, settled her bill, taking the leftover food with her.

Not far from the diner was a small rinky-dink hotel. All she cared about was that it was clean and it had hot water. She rented a room that had the best vantage point of all vehicles coming into the place. By the time she settled in, showered and relaxed, Zipp had gotten back to her with his contact info. She spoke to him briefly, just to discuss a meeting place.

With that finally taken care of, she got dressed and rested fully clothed, falling in and out of sleep for most of the night. She was already prepared for many more nights like this. If she could snap her fingers and resolve this she would. She should be used to these dire life and death situations. But unlike the others, she faced, this was personal and people that were close to her heart were libel to be exploited by her enemies. And that was the last thing she wanted, her kids, Pat, Pietro, and even her family. If it took her last breath so that they could be forever safe, then so be it. Priscilla wasn't afraid to die, she was just afraid to die before she completed her tasks.

In the early morning hours Priscilla looked at the clock, the meeting time was fast approaching. She gave up on trying to sleep and made her way there before the sun rose. It was just as well, she needed to detour and make sure she wasn't being followed. The last thing she wanted to do was jeopardize Zipp or his daughter in any way, the man suffered enough. He wasn't stupid, he knew she was in some type of trouble; he could have just ignored her. So, she owed him that much.

She arrived at the meeting place, three hours before Zipp, at the agreed Starbucks. Priscilla grabbed the best table, where she had both entrances covered; there were two, a front and rear. She bought a coffee and set herself up, she brought in her laptop trying to fit in with everyone else that brought in their laptops.

But all the while, she kept a close watch on every single person who came in, sizing them up. She was pretty much web browsing. She tried to keep her thoughts straight. With everything going on with her, she kinda forgot about Derlin, in a way she felt ashamed that she wasn't thinking about him as much as she should. But what the hell was she gonna do? Ferrer locked him up for treason.

The only thing she could do was find the facts to prove otherwise. She knew the Benefactor had a hand in this as well. But then again, was he really innocent? Just before he was led off, she felt threatened by him, that's something she can't push aside, no matter how many excuses she tries to come up for him.

With her thoughts and feelings on the verge of spiraling out of control, she checked her watch; it was exactly the time Zipp agreed to meet her. She needed to keep her mind on the here and now. Derlin wasn't going anywhere. Her palms sweated, she hoped no one followed her; she took great pains in making sure of that.

Her worries started to subside when she finally saw the old man, Arthur Zipp, walking with the aid of a cane. She watched him from the window. She smiled to herself, he looked great, but seeing him also made her feel awful. It was because of her, he walked with a limp. She took a moment to think about that, it was a simpler time, she wished it was the same now.

As soon as he walked in he spotted her through his thick coke bottle glasses, he flashed a quick stiff smile. As he walked over Priscilla got up and hugged him tight, giving him a little rub on the back.

"Arthur, you look great, I'm so glad you came on such short notice and under the unfortunate circumstances." She added with a fading smile.

"No worries, anything I can do to help," He said in a low, clenched jaw reply, as he sat down and settled in. Priscilla asked him what he wanted; she went to the counter and got him a black coffee, while getting her third cup. Once she sat back down, Priscilla wasted no time getting right into the whole situation.

Zipp watched her intently, hardly blinking his beady eyes as he sipped his coffee. She didn't get into anything about Derlin. It was too much of a long story and she didn't want Zipp to know any more than he needed to know for his own safety. Derlin was a problem she needed to handle alone. When she finally wrapped up her story, he straightened up in his chair, putting his fist to his mouth as he cleared his throat.

"Oh man, Priscilla, I…don't know what to say, you're in some tough bind." She nodded.

"Yeah, tell me about it." She said stiffly, she didn't need the obvious pointed out. But she didn't tell him that. She didn't want to be rude, it wasn't her style to take out her problems on others.

"I wish I could be out there with you," she smiled, gently touching his hand, she thought it was touching that the old man still had some fight left in him. "Now this guy your talkin' about, this Albino, I never heard of him." Priscilla had the feeling that would be the case. This son of a bitch was like a ghost. Zipp snapped his finger as though he had an afterthought.

"But there may be someone that does, it's a long shot, but it's better than what you got now." Priscilla was all ears.

"You've heard of assemblers right?" Priscilla nodded, of course she did. Assemblers acted as the middleman for big time contracts. So that employer and employee didn't have any knowledge of the other. And the Assemblers reaped from both, taking a big cut from both sides. Aside from brokering the deals, they set up the contracts, and made sure the word was out. They used anything and everything from Facebook, Craigslist, MySpace or even simple ads in papers.

Some of it was plainly written out and a lot of it was coded. They ran the assassins for hire network. The majority of them were spineless trolls, who'd sell out their mother if they could. They had no shame, and no code of honor. Zipp nodded, leaning in closer.

"There's one in the South Bronx. I've never been there, but I know where he is. He runs it out of a pawn shop called Pugg's Pawn." He gulped down the rest of his coffee and then continued. "Another thing Priscilla, this guy is big time, no one messes with him. So be careful, if anyone knows about this Albino fella it'll be him. That's all I have, I wish I could be of more help to you." She smiled, grabbing his hand.

"Zipp you've done more than enough and I thank you, I've already asked to much of you. Just sitting here with me can get you killed, even your kid." Priscilla swallowed hard, just remembering Sammy, the bright young girl who she rescued from the kidnappers, she smiled, figuring a change of conversation for the moment would be good and besides she was curious about the kid.

"How is Sammy? She's out of high school now, yes?" Zipp nodded, with a wide smile stretching his leathery skin.

"She's great, she's about to start her first year of college. She's gonna study veterinary medicine."

"That's great, really great Arthur. I'm so happy, please give her my regards, if she remembers me that is." He gave her a wide-eyed look.

"You kidding?! She'd never forget you, from time to time she's asked about you. I just never had anything to tell her. But I'll be sure to tell her now." Priscilla smiled, as she glanced at the clock on the wall behind the counter. They had been here for a few hours. Longer than it felt and longer than she wanted to be here. She needed to take her leave. They sat in silence for a few seconds, Priscilla searched for the words to say, while the random chit chat of others could be heard. He nodded to her as he started to get up. He knew it was time to leave as well.

"Let me walk you out." He said, standing with a little effort. Priscilla helped him, seeing he was struggling. He tried to wave her away.

"Zipp you go on ahead, I don't want to be seen with you, I'll keep watch from here." He nodded, and then hugged her tight. As they pulled away she gave him a kiss on the cheek. He turned a bit redder than he already was. She thought it was cute; he tipped his cap to her and limped out.

Priscilla watched him make his way slowly to his car and pull out. She then threw the empty coffee cups in the trashcan. Gathering up her stuff, Priscilla waited another half an hour before she left for her next stop, which was Pugg's Pawn.

Chapter 11
Luna's fury

"I don't give a fuck! I want her dead! I want everything about her dead! She took out Bill for no reason!" Luna was screaming into her cell phone. Her face was red and contorted with anger. A single vein appeared in her temple, she was so out of control. She was alone in the hotel room, that she trashed.

The TV was busted up; the bathroom mirror was smashed, the bed thrown off the box spring. The manager called her about complaints, but he quickly decided that the people complaining should mind their own business after she threatened to cut his balls off and shove them in his mouth.

Luna had the phone pressed to her ear, listening to her employer who was indeed the Benefactor. Luna was just yessing him to death. She wasn't taking this bitch alive! This was war! Yeah, he may get pissed, but he knew the deal. Luna or anyone else wasn't going to try to take someone alive when it proved fatal to your health. This bitch was too damn good. Dead was the only way.

"Fine! I'll be here." She ended the call and threw the phone off to the side. She stared at the broken mirror in the bathroom; she felt her face getting hot again. Her temper was flaring. She thought about her other comrades. Aside from one, the rest turned her down. She was pissed beyond belief that they did, Luna thought about calling them again, but she didn't want to look weak or desperate. She wasn't at all, she could handle this herself. She didn't need anybody, fuck'em all!

She wished she could leave right now. She hated this old fucking bitch, Priscilla Roletti. They all think she's some bad ass. Ha! Maybe in her heyday, and that was a big maybe.

Luna stalked into the bathroom and came right back out. It was too early to make her move, she wanted to wait until she was sure her intended target would be home. The more she thought about Bill's fate the more insulting it was that some upstart dared to come after her own, the balls on them to even want to fight back. That was Luna's way of thinking.

They had no right, but the right to die. And this Priscilla was no different; she should have just accepted her fate. But now she took to the offensive, and killed Bill, fucking Bill, her mentor, friend, comrade and lover.

Bill refused to even take the job on and yet she killed him. Luna wondered how that entire confrontation went down and ended up at the school. What was done was done….. Now it was time to play for keeps. It was time to hit the bitch where it really hurt. She opened Pandora's box now. Luna wasn't going to go down this route, but now all bets were off. She wasn't going to play this cat and mouse game, no way. By the time this was over, Priscilla Roletti was going to wish she was never born!

Chapter 12
Pugg's Pawn

Priscilla found the place with no problems. By the time she arrived it was well after dinner time. She drove by twice. It looked unassuming, just a run of the mill pawn, 'Pugg's Pawn.' She smiled, cute name just another meaning for life taker and heart breaker. In that place there must be plenty of the belongings of the murdered, conned and countless other victims. She curled the upper part of her lip.

She was no angel, but she never thought of robbing and stealing the personal possessions of the dead for the sake of financial gain. Sure, she skimmed some money she came across, but that was different. Money wasn't as personal as a ring, a watch or even a necklace. She thought it was not only bad karma but tacky. There were some professionals that stooped that low, she had no doubt about that.

Priscilla expected to be marked as soon as she walked in the door. The price on her head was so big, just that alone would make you remember someone. The Pugg's eyes must've bulged from his sockets when he saw the numbers. He probably wished he could grab the bounty for himself. Not many could turn their heads from that price, no matter what the risk involved. She hoped Robbie the Pugg would just answer a few questions so she could be on her way, otherwise he was going to find out, what it was like to feel the fear others felt looking into the eyes of their murderer.

Priscilla parked five blocks away; she didn't want to arouse the suspicions of anyone. The walk was good; she used it to clear her head. Priscilla walked as though she owned the streets, in parts like this you had to. Thugs were like dogs, they smelled fear a mile away and it only enticed them more.

Beneath her coat she carried double Beretta's locked and loaded with two extra clips in her jacket pockets. If anyone challenged her, they were either going to get their face bashed in or filled with holes.

No one was getting in her way. Everyone was the enemy, and she wasn't leaving loose ends. That's the phrase she kept saying to herself since she killed Bill.

'No loose ends.' She wondered how much blood was going to be on her hands after this was over. At this point she didn't care, just as long as it came to an end. As she came upon the shop, she slowed her pace. Everyday people walked by her, some glanced at her while others didn't even pay her any notice.

She continued onward, passing a mother and her children. The little boy caught her eye, he was looking at her, she gave him a smile, and he returned the gesture walking on. Priscilla glanced up and saw the flashing red, yellow, and black sign.

Pugg's Pawn. As she walked into the place, the corner of the door, tapped the bell chimes alerting the owner someone was paying him a visit. Priscilla ignored it and went to look at the first cruddy glass showcase. She leaned in a bit, looking at all the jewelry and keepsakes neatly placed and some just thrown in on top of one another. Thin gold chains were knotted, gold rings, and wedding bands and other types were neatly lined up, ready to be used again. Everything she saw screamed of the lost soul they were taken from.

Of course she gave this guy a little benefit of the doubt, everything in here can't be from victims. There were some desperate people out there and they'd sell their soul if they could. It didn't take long for someone to come out from the back. The hanging beads in the doorway alerted her to that. She kept her head straight though; she didn't want to seem too eager either.

No doubt too, he was watching her on a hidden camera or two from where he came from in this shit-hole. In her peripheral vision, she saw him leaning on the counter; it looked like he was writing something down. Priscilla then straightened up and looked in his direction as she walked to a showcase closer to him. She could see why he was called a Pugg, he looked shorter than the average man, she could tell even though the floor behind the counter was elevated, almost all of them were.

He was balding with almost gray-slicked hair, in a stupid ponytail. She hated that look in men, like they were trying to hold onto a piece of their long-gone youth. Only rock stars can pull that off, and he wasn't one.

He finally glanced at her, his face was red and chunky with pockmarks, he had a larger than life nose. Years of hitting the bottle did that to you. He then looked back down at the paper on his clipboard.

"Get off on the wrong track Blondie?" He growled in a deep voice, he didn't look up as he said that. Priscilla turned in his direction.

"I don't think so, why are blondes not wanted in these parts?" The Pugg chuckled.

"Nah not at all. But I can just tell you ain't from around here, that's all." Priscilla nodded, and then walked closer towards the man. "What can I do you for?" He asked as he shuffled the paperwork together and placed it to the side. He took out a cigarette from the breast pocket of his checkered flannel shirt which looked wrinkled and faded.

"I'm looking for work." The Pugg raised his eyes at her, as he took a drag and let the smoke out slowly.

"Work, huh?" She nodded. "Well I ain't got work. As you can see, I own a small shop." He gestured with his hand. Priscilla did a fake chuckle, and then got serious.

"Not shopkeeper work, bub. I'm looking for some freelance stuff. I'm new in town. Heard you could lead me in the right direction." Robby frowned, giving her a suspicious look, she expected that.

"Oh yeah, and who might've said that, Blondie?" He asked, leaning closer to her. She smiled.

"An Albino, with gold eyes." The corner of his lip involuntarily twitched ever so slightly. Bingo, she thought to herself. He then leaned away from her, really sizing her up. The red in his face dulled a bit. He regained his composure as he picked up his papers, throwing them into a filing bin.

"How is Moe doing? Word was that he got capped, but survived." Moe! She got a name. Well, that was a start, finally a lead on this ghost face killer. Priscilla, made a mock gesture of concern.

"Don't know I heard the same thing too. Haven't run into him in years, last time I saw him was in Pennsylvania. We were competing for the same job. We wound up teaming up, when we split he told me about you. I heard only a few days ago that he was backing a large contract, I didn't believe it though. But regardless I want a piece of that."

Robby shrugged his shoulders, as he went over to a part of the counter that was blocked off from her vision. She could see him, but from the middle of his arms and up. He was evidently doing something. Priscilla, wasn't worried just yet, but was ready nevertheless.

"Yeah, I heard about that too, he resurfaced in Vegas. That's Moe's stomping grounds. He runs or used to run a casino." Priscilla nodded. She wouldn't have ever thought to look there. The saying what happens in Vegas stays in Vegas must be true after all.

"This job he's backing is big. Although, I don't think he's fronting the money. That's just my two-cents." The Pugg said as he walked back in front of Priscilla and placed down a single piece of paper in front of her. It was the same wanted poster the Black Hand had. Without moving her head, she glanced at Robby. She was marked; she knew that was going to be the case. Robby thought he was fast, but Priscilla was faster. He swung at her head with a hand sized Blackjack club. He missed smashing the glass on the showcase. With a bleeding hand he swung again, Priscilla caught his wrist and twisted it. The bone snapping sounded loud in the small store, Robby cried out in utter agony. She grabbed him by his collar, as she walked around to the other side of the counter, glaring at him. He was sweaty; he was scared out of his wits. She pulled him closer.

"You're too fucking stupid to have any sense!" She said through a clenched jaw and gritted teeth.

Fifteen minutes later.... Priscilla walked out of the darkened shop. The storefront sign was shut off before she walked out the door with her hands in her pockets and her coat collar up. She calmly walked, passing a few other people going about their business. She gripped both her guns tightly; she wasn't out of the woods yet.

This neighborhood can get a little rough, and anyone that stepped to her was getting killed plain and simple. Before she strangled the life out of Robby, he squealed like a pig and told her everything she wanted to know.

Then, like anyone else, he became a loose end, there was no way she could allow him to live. She had no doubt that at some point he'd get in contact with someone and get the word out. And she couldn't allow that. Robby gave her the name of the casino the Albino worked in. She smiled to herself. Thinking about it now, the Albino was perfect for a job like that. Just the mere sight of him would scare all the wannabe tough guys half to death.

With her car in sight, she reached up and touched the corner of her eye that was splashed with that bleaching concoction. It didn't hurt her, or impair her vision at all but it was a constant reminder of that bastard every time she looked in the mirror at her half white eye. Finally in the car, Priscilla wasn't wasting any time, she was heading to Vegas.

She was torn as to whether she should drive there or just leave the car here all together and fly. But not knowing what may lie ahead for her, she convinced herself that taking the car was better. She had all her gear, plus there wasn't any rush, the people gunning for her weren't going anywhere.

An idea popped in her head. She called Pietro; she didn't get too much into it. She asked him if he could pull in some favors with some of his old mob buddies who run truckers' unions, she needed to transport the Charger, no questions asked and that all expenses to and from would be taken care of plus it was worth $10,000 cash. She knew it wouldn't be that hard to find someone willing to stick their neck out for that kind of money. By midnight, she rendezvoused with a trucker in New Jersey, and was off.

With the Charger safely stowed in the enclosed trailer, she could finally rest. The last thing she wanted to do was take public transportation. The trucker with her seemed like a tough enough guy. Without getting too much into it, she only told him that if trouble came to keep his head down. With both of them taking turns driving, they made the drive in two and a half days. Priscilla had the guy drop her off just on the outskirts of Sin City. She could drive the rest of the way. It was still early, she had enough time to get a room, clean up, and then check out said casino.

Chapter 13
A night out in Vegas

Priscilla checked into the Trump Tower. She took the cheapest room and settled in for the remainder of the day. She wasn't in any rush. She lost herself in the large round bathtub. It felt so good, to be clean. On her cross-country trek she insisted on only stopping as they needed. When they did stop it was a relief to stretch out, grab a bite and use the bathroom.

She was used to not showering for extended periods of time, but she didn't like it. In the plush soft-white bathrobe she sat on the large comfy bed studying maps of the area. The casino she needed to go to was about a fifteen-minute drive from here. It was called the Treasure Trove. But instead of driving, she'd walk to the casino. Parking in Vegas was just as bad as New York City. The walk would clear her head, and would make her more familiar with Sin City.

Once she arrived at the Treasure Trove, she decided to wait across the street at an outdoor café. It was perfect to watch who was coming and going.

She waited there for some time well into the evening. No one in the café cared how long she sat; it was more or less a high-end Starbucks. She kept the coffee coming plus had a bite to eat. To anyone that walked by and glanced at her, they'd think it was just some woman enjoying her time reading the paper. But that was far from the truth. The look in her eyes spelled chaos. Formalities, donning disguises and sneaking around were over. There wasn't a goddamn thing in this fucking city that was going to stop her from dragging that white devil outta there.

She was going to take great pleasure in busting his face all over this strip. She wondered what a guy like the Albino or Moe was doing running a place like this. She wouldn't have thought him the type. But then again, she didn't know him from a hole in the wall either. It made sense, though thinking further on it.

The Albino was a scary looking dude, just seeing a guy like that would deter the scammers and hustlers trying to beat the casinos at what they do best….beating the gambler. But in the long run she really didn't care, it was only idle thoughts because she was sitting here anxious as anything else, and tired, that was an understatement. She had never been tested like this before.

She was scared because this was when anyone, no matter how good they are, can make that single mistake that could lead to your untimely demise. She couldn't wait for all of this to be put to rest… one way or another. But then even after tying up all of these loose ends she had Derlin to think about.

That was a whole other story. What the hell was she going to do? She needed to do something, but what? Ferrer had him locked down somewhere. Priscilla knew Derlin wasn't a traitor…it was impossible, she didn't care what the evidence said. Derlin was set up period. But then her mind goes to how he was acting…the only angle here is that something must've happened to his family, that's the only sure fire reason. Derlin's family must have somehow been caught in the middle.

She took a mental note to suggest that to Ferrer, and if it fell on deaf ears, then she'd check into it herself. Regardless of the outcome or what she found out she had to do this… for all the years of him helping her and being there for her it was a matter of obligation. She took a deep breath, then sipped some more of her tea, she was getting tired of the coffee. She pushed those thoughts aside.

She needed to focus on the here and now. She looked to her cell phone; it was half past nine and not a sign of the Albino. She wondered if he used the back entrance, or maybe a secret one, she was going to get up and check the back out.

But she quickly dismissed that; the Albino wasn't someone that took the back door. It was too dark to read the paper even with all of the lights around her; she was just tired of reading anyway. If this guy didn't show up by ten, she was going to take a walk around inside and check it out for herself. But then as she thought this, she saw a blue Toyota pickup truck slowly pull up to the casino.

Something odd struck her about it. The truck was out of place as the valet hustled to the driver's door, opening it. Priscilla leaned off her chair even from across the street, she spotted her man. How could you not, his white skin was like a beacon in the dark. She tossed aside the newspapers, got up and left a generous tip.

She wasn't waiting, she walked across the street, her pace picked up with each step, her gaze was right on him as he slowly walked up the three carpeted steps. Priscilla was so focused on him that she walked in the middle of the strip, with no concern for her safety as cars swerved to avoid hitting her.

But all of that didn't matter to her nothing was going to stop her. She watched him go through a set of glass doors held open for him. For the first time he wore something different. He wore a burgundy suit with a black collared shirt and black tie. His trademark black cowboy hat was missing. His white hair was combed back, and held in place with hairspray. He was already inside when Priscilla stepped onto the sidewalk; she took the three steps and entered.

The doors were held open for her as well as for other people entering behind her and next to her. She stopped just for a moment and took in the surroundings. The place was pretty big. The carpeting was red with gold designs. Cheers and jeers could be heard throughout as fortunes were made and lost. Priscilla walked on, the dress code here was lax, some people were dressed in suits and ties and dresses. While some tourists wore T-shirts and flip-flops. It was a good thing; Priscilla was dressed in her simple black slacks and white collared shirt. Once again, she repeated to herself. 'No loose ends.' Nothing was going to impede her tonight.

Walking past a group of people, Priscilla spotted her target; he was with three other men. All in suits with earpieces. They weren't going to be a problem; she touched her gun at her waist feeling the cold steel. She wasn't taking any prisoners tonight. She was gaining on the Albino. They walked by rows upon rows of slot machines. She was so focused, not even the sound effects could break her concentration. They passed the poker tables that were seeing a lot of action. Priscilla was now mere feet from him…when he suddenly stopped and looked over his shoulder. Their eyes locked just then.

They held their gaze for what seemed like forever. Priscilla was never intimidated by this man, even from the first time she saw him. His main weapon, fear, was totally ineffective on her. She knew what he was really made of. You take away his ability of fear, and he was nothing, she proved that already and she'd prove it again right here, right now.

Now in the middle of the casino the Albino fully faced her, the three other men with him faced her as well. The Albino crossed his arms over his chest, and smiled shaking his head.

"I knew you'd be comin' little lady. When I heard what you did to Pugg, I knew you showing up here wasn't far behind." Priscilla nodded, even while keeping her eyes on him she was alert to her surroundings. If she had to, not even bystanders were going to stop her; this guy was going down tonight.

"Oh yeah cowboy so you know what's in store for you." The Albino smirked.

"I don't think so Roletti. I don't think you got the guts to start something in here." Before Priscilla could reply he continued. "But then again, maybe you do... your eyes give away your intentions. If I gave you a reason to draw, you wouldn't think twice, if you want me so bad go for the kill, you got me dead to rights!"

Priscilla felt a tingle run up her spine. She was so tempted to take him out right now and it wasn't because of the people, she needed answers. She needed to find the guy he was working for. The Albino was the answer. The three thugs standing with him didn't know what to do; their looks of uncertainty said that. Priscilla's hand inched closer. She was having second thoughts, maybe just taking this guy out was the best thing. Her mind was almost made up when he spoke again.

"But if you kill me right here...you'll never know where I got your boy." He caught her attention now.

"Boy?" Her first thought was her son.

"Derlin, your boy." She smiled, relaxing a bit.

"Now you're reaching, Derlin was arrested a few days ago. Stalling for time to save your ass?"

"Not likely. I'm no more afraid of you than you are of me." She knew that, but still, what was his angle with this?

"Ok… so if Derlin wasn't arrested then where is he?" She walked closer to her enemy. She was relaxed; this was the closest she ever stood next to him without choking him. He had a peculiar smell of cologne; she couldn't place a name with.

"He's in the back office just across here, see it?" He pointed, Priscilla followed his white finger. She looked back at him, staring for the first time in his golden eyes mere feet apart.

"But he was arrested." The Albino smirked.

"You already know who I work for. Who do you think owns this place?" Priscilla pursed her lips. She was stuck, her gut feeling screamed this was not good. But what else did she have to lose at this point? What if he was telling the truth? Ferrer hasn't been in contact with her and even if Derlin was taken from wherever he was, Ferrer didn't tell her and he was hardly to be trusted even though he was a supposed ally.

"Bring him here…I ain't going anywhere with you or your thugs." The Albino smirked, reaching into his jacket pocket, he produced a cell phone, which he tapped twice and then placed to his ear. He turned away from her as he spoke.

Priscilla watched him closely and then glanced at the three men standing close by. The Albino then turned and faced her.

"Look at the door, little lady." Priscilla was hesitant to do so. But then did as he said. Not five seconds later the office door opened and standing in the doorway was none other than Derlin. She couldn't believe her eyes. She glanced at the Albino who wore a smug smirk. Priscilla kept her face as unreadable as she could.

"Lead the way." The Albino was two steps away as Priscilla followed, he never looked back. The three suited men spread out, they didn't get behind her. Priscilla walked by more unsuspecting gamblers as they approached the doorway. As people from all walks of life celebrated their shallow victories, they failed to see anything around them like this confrontation going on right in front of their faces. I mean, how the hell can no one, not notice this? She felt pity for them, how can people walk through life blind? Perhaps it was just her that looked at it like this. Maybe if she was normal, she too would have been blind to many things. She doubted it though, being observant wasn't something you taught someone.

The Albino entered, first, followed by the three suited men who stood close to the wall on the other side of the office. Priscilla glanced around before she entered. She stood right in the doorway. She was mindful to leave the door open. No way was she going to be stuck in here alone. The office only consisted of a desk, and behind the desk was a wall of CCTV's. Priscilla glanced at all the small color screens, as her eyes fell on Derlin standing right beside the desk. He was staring coldly at her. Priscilla gasped as she took in a sharp breath.

"No....no..." she said, even though she saw him from a distance she never really believed it was him. The Albino smiled as he looked back and forth to them both. Derlin didn't look at the Albino; he just kept his cold gaze on Priscilla's confused face.

Priscilla didn't know what to do. So, he was a traitor! She was betrayed by Derlin! Now her whole world shattered, there wasn't a shadow of doubt now.

"Agent Blondie.... So nice to see you once again." Derlin then looked to the Albino. "Looks like I lost Moe, I should have assumed she'd stumble along sooner than later. Oh well." The Albino nodded, looking from Derlin to Priscilla with his evil grin. Priscilla was too shocked to respond, the words replayed in her mind over and over. Focus goddamn it! Then it dawned on her, the shock was slowly going away. The look of confusion was replaced by a cold stare of her own as she clenched her jaw.

When Derlin spoke it didn't sound like Derlin at all. He had an accent of some kind. She straightened up.

"You're not Derlin." She said in a low, matter of fact tone. It sounded as though she was more convincing herself than anyone else. Derlin mockingly clapped and then removed the eye patch, throwing it at her. She followed it to the floor and then looked back to the man who was pretending to be Derlin. Seeing the imposter Derlin with two eyes, she immediately noticed that the eyes were two different colors one brown the other which was covered was green. Priscilla, took a step forward now.

"Who are you?"

"One of six."

"The A-6." She said dripping with contempt. He nodded.

"Emil. And I'm very pleased to meet you. I've heard so much about you. Luna is dying to meet you too, especially after what you did to Bill."

"Fuck with the bull, you get the horns." Emil shrugged; he didn't really care about the vendetta.

"Yes, it seems so." She took a deep breath analyzing the scenario. It was five against one, not very good odds. There were no options other than fighting her way out. She couldn't believe she walked right into this. She really should have known better, if she was killed she deserved it. Priscilla calmed herself. She relaxed her body and her arms. She looked at each and every one of them before her eyes returned to Emil.

"So…what now? Seems we're in a stalemate." Emil shook his head, taking a step closer.

"Not at all. I would love to kill you now and be done with this. But due to the fact that money is involved I cannot." Priscilla looked confused. "Mengele, as I'm sure you've already figured out, is the one after you. He did want you dead. But plans have changed."

"Ok…where is he?" Emil smiled, stepping closer again. This close, Priscilla got a really good look. The guy looked just like Derlin, right down to the wrinkle. She would be amazed, but the question that really came to mind now was… where was the real Derlin?

"Oh no my dear, Mr. Mengele is not ready to meet with you yet. But trust me, it will be soon. But in the meantime, you can't be allowed to run amok either."

Emil then walked past Priscilla and outside the office. He turned around and gestured her to come forward. She was hesitant, but she walked out and stepped to the right of the doorway. Emil stepped back in front of the doorway with his hands behind his back. Priscilla faced him.

"I'm not leaving, not until you tell me what happened to Derlin!" It took all of Priscilla's willpower not to draw and fire even with all of these people here.

"I think, in the next two minutes, you're going to have more to worry about than Derlin." And with those words, Emil, took one arm from behind his back and fired off rounds in the distance, gamblers dived, ducked and ran. Emil fired five rounds into the closest tables sending chips and cards flying. By the time Priscilla reached for her gun, Emil jumped back into the office throwing his gun at her.

She instinctively caught it and fired three rounds into the now closed door. She ran and pounded the door. Priscilla then glanced at the gun it was a Beretta like hers. She dropped it and calmly made for the exit, when Las Vegas cops suddenly appeared with their guns drawn. Priscilla stopped in her tracks. Two more came running towards her from another direction, she was totally covered.

Priscilla glanced around, this was a no win for her. There weren't any options, but surrender. She went to her knees and placed her hands on her head.

Chapter 14
A friend in high places

The fat, overweight detective certainly wasn't changing Priscilla's opinion about cops anytime soon as he interrogated her, using every trick in the book cops were known to use. Scare tactics, head games, word trips, intimidation or outright threats. But Priscilla said the same thing over and over again. Which was her name and a number to call. She wasn't even sure if that number worked, being that Shadow Ops was now disbanded.

It was protocol if detained or arrested in the U.S. to give that to the authorities. From there either someone would fetch you, or the police would release you.

It took all of her willpower not to taunt this prick. He even threatened to throw her in general population. In the mood she was in, she'd embrace that. If she could now, she'd break this guy's face open. But that wasn't going to get her anywhere.

So she continued to sit and wait for what? She had no idea. She couldn't get in touch with Ferrer; the prick wouldn't give her a number. And speaking of, she couldn't wait to get a hold of him. What the hell happened at that casino? An imposter Derlin was there! What the hell was going on? She was going to get answers from Ferrer one way or another. The fat cop was in a white striped collared shirt with sweat circles under his armpits, he walked and stood next to his buddy, a skinny cop who was sitting.

They were in the middle of the bad cop, good cop routine. She'd seen it before and it was always funny. One played the prick, while the other played the voice of reason trying to help you, when in reality they were both looking to screw you and trip you up to confess to something. These cops didn't even play by the rules either, she asked for a lawyer just to stall and they kept jerking her around with bullshit excuses.

"Ok, so lets take this from the top once again." The portly cop said, snuffing out his cigarette. "Eyewitnesses fingered you as the shooter." The cop threw down the paperwork in front of her and approached her. "I mean, what kind of sick animal shoots up a casino? I mean you could have killed someone. You're lucky you didn't, one guy said the bullets came so close he felt it whiz by his head, those were some pretty lucky shots, right Charlie?" The fat cop said, looking back to the skinny one who nodded.

"Some lucky shooting, is right Frank." He said scratching his head. The fat cop named Frank nodded, as he got closer to Priscilla.

"Oh yeah baby, you're going away for a long time, six-counts of attempted murder, criminal intent, weapons possession. And that's not even the half of it." He said as he leaned on his hands, for the first time sitting here she looked up at the guy with the dirtiest look she could give him. Her hands were cuffed in front of her. The sudden urge to sweep his arms out from under him was intense. Watching him slam his fat head on the table would be somewhat entertaining.

She averted her eyes back to the wall and said nothing which pissed him off more than anything she could say. He ran his fingers through his sweaty hair, walking back to the other side of the room and grabbing another cigarette.

"Goddamn you! You're gonna talk to us before the night is out or so help me-" He never got a chance to finish the empty threat. The two cops looked past her to the door. There was conversation going on, on the other side of the closed door. Priscilla didn't turn around, but she did try to listen. The door suddenly opened. The two cops looked wide-eyed, at the new entry.

"Who the hell are you!?" Frank demanded, pointing.

"Jonas Ferrer, NSA." Hearing Ferrer's voice Priscilla was shocked as well, not believing it. When Ferrer walked to her left, she glanced at him. He didn't look at her; his gaze was on the men as he held out his ID. He then slipped it, back into his suit jacket.

"This woman, is now in my custody. Any objections will be met with harsh action. Here is the paperwork indicating such. Your supervisors have a copy as well." Ferrer said with no room to argue the matter further. He reached into his jacket pocket and threw down the rolled up paperwork. Neither cop picked it up, as they looked from Roletti to Ferrer.

"Let's go Roletti, get up." Ferrer said as he stepped away. She didn't need to be asked twice. As she got up Ferrer grabbed her under her arm. Frank clearly wasn't going to let this go without a fight.

"Hey, wait a minute, goddamn it! This woman just shot up a casino! Who the hell do you think you are? You can't come in here like this and take her!" Ferrer smiled.

"Yes, I can, the paperwork clearly states that. This woman is a wanted federal fugitive. For what, is a need to know. Now if you'll excuse me." Ferrer started to walk forward when the portly cop stepped in front of them.

"Now wait one minute-"

"No, you wait! One more damn word out of your mouth and so help me, you'll be policing crosswalks in Alaska." Frank didn't like the sound of that and suddenly stopped, backing off. He then looked at Priscilla, pointing a chubby finger in her face.

"I hope you fry girl. I hope they string you up!" Priscilla smiled, and kneed him in the groin. The fat man's face turned purple as he fell to the floor.

Charlie rushed to the fat cops aide as Ferrer led Priscilla out, trying to contain a smile.

"Jesus Christ! I told you to track down Mengele, what the hell are you doing out here, shooting up casinos?" Ferrer yelled at Priscilla once they were outside in the warm night air. A few cops entering the precinct looked their way, but paid them no mind after a few seconds.

"I fucking was! I got a tip on the Albino." She shot back; she wasn't going to be lectured from him. Ferrer nodded, glancing at her as they approached his car. He opened the door for her, she got in, and he followed. The driver took off as soon as he was told to do so.

"Yeah, I heard, some lead. You killed him too. What if he was gaming you?" He said, reaching into his pocket. "Give me your hands." Ferrer unlocked her cuffs throwing them on the floor. Priscilla rubbed her wrists.

"Fuck some goddamn low life. You better start playing straight with me! And let's start with Derlin! Because I just ran into someone that looked a lot like him!" She yelled pointing her finger inches from his cheek. Ferrer, looked at her taking a deep breath. The angry look slowly softened, turning to sadness.

"You want the truth? Derlin is dead."

Chapter 15
The horrible truth

"For an untold amount of time, Derlin was secretly under surveillance. How he was marked is still unknown at this time. But the surveillance covered everything. His work habits, his home life, you name it. Mengele wanted to use the resources at the disposal of Derlin to track down Hans, killing you was a bonus." Ferrer took a deep breath and then continued. "The person who took over as John is Emil, part of the A-6 gang. Mengele wanted the best, he got it. Emil is a master of disguise. He copied Derlin right down to his retina test." Priscilla looked ahead, thinking about that. She wanted to cry, but she made a tight fist whitening her knuckles. She didn't even want to think about what they did to her friend. She took a deep breath, putting a hand to her forehead.

"Why didn't you tell me this? Why keep me in the dark, Ferrer? I thought we were on the same team!" She raised her voice, but quickly controlled herself.

"Believe me, I wanted to, I didn't want you distracted. I know how much Derlin means to you, I didn't want anything to cloud your judgment." She nodded; Ferrer did have a point in a way because she was totally pissed now. She could live with the fact that Derlin was framed. Which she kinda thought even though he was acting very strange just before they arrested him.

"How did you figure this out?" Ferrer, raised his eyebrow, facing her.

"Lens." She averted her gaze, for a moment she was back in Venezuela, replaying his warnings. It was hard to believe him then. But the encounter in Derlin's office almost cemented her belief in Lens' words. Now in a way she was relieved in a weird sense, that Derlin wasn't a traitor or tried to set her up.

But it still didn't change the fact that he was gone… taken from her. She caught herself as she was about to grind her teeth.

"Who by the way, we are still trying to locate. He went AWOL. We don't believe he's involved with Derlin's death. But we have reason to believe he has more intel that may be valuable."

Priscilla laughed to herself, good luck with that one, she wanted to say out loud. She really didn't know a thing about Lens, but she could say this, the man was a pro.

He could be anyone, do anything, he could very well be your next store neighbor. "Lens provided us with the information. I've known Derlin for a long time; I had a hard time believing it. We investigated it as best we could, but there weren't any leads. The arrest was the only way to be sure." Priscilla didn't understand that last comment. Ferrer reached into his pocket and took out a ring.

"Here, take a close look." She took it, carefully scrutinizing it. She saw what he was referring to, at the bottom of the ring was a very small needle.

"When Derlin was cuffed, a sample of his blood was taken with this. It was en-route to lock up, when he killed my men, he had help too. At least we knew without a doubt it wasn't Derlin. Those bastards covered their tracks right down to removing Derlin's eye and surgically implanting it in the imposter." Ferrer shook his head. Priscilla turned back around. She was totally nauseated envisioning Derlin being subjected to torture and who knew what the hell else as they tried to get information from him.

"Priscilla, now is not the time to dwell on this. Derlin is dead and he's not coming back. If you want to right the wrongs, take out the one responsible." Priscilla nodded; she didn't even look at Ferrer. She knew he was right. Every goddamn person responsible will be held accountable. They are all going to die.

They didn't speak anymore on the matter. Priscilla leaned her elbow on the armrest as she looked out the window. She couldn't help but think about Derlin, she felt guilty, sad and like a fool. Guilty and foolish because she was so quick to assume Derlin did indeed set her up. She should have known better. But then again, she didn't have time to think anything through. Before long they pulled up in front of Trump Tower. Priscilla was about to get out when Ferrer grabbed her by the arm.

"Be careful Priscilla, I'll be in touch if I hear of anything else." She nodded, got out and watched the car speed off. As she watched the car fade into the night a thought came to her. How the hell did Ferrer know about her arrest? Maybe he was really watching her. She looked back in the direction of where the car drove off. If it wasn't harming her then whatever, let him watch her all night long for all she cared. She took the marble steps one at a time with her head held low.

The doorman opened the doors for her and watched her walk past. He greeted her, but she didn't reply, this was one of the few times in her life Priscilla craved a drink. She knew drinking should be the last thing she did. But she needed to have a little bit of a distraction, and mourn the loss of her friend.

Chapter 16
Going for the Heart

Long Island, NY Before the casino set up.

On the other side of the country, it was the same old usual day in the Pat household. Priscilla's kids were in school as well as Pat's kids. Kathleen, his wife, was working and his elderly mother, Louise was in her room sitting in her chair resting. Patrick was retired, and took care of his ailing ninety-three year old mother. Who had slowed down quite a bit.

Her age had taken a toll on her mind; she couldn't be left alone anymore. She was in a sad state, she was fully mobile, ate well and was spry but was a shadow of her former self mentally.

Priscilla always lent a helping hand when she could; it broke her heart that this woman she knew for so many years hardly remembered her. And like every other day, at this hour, Pat was sitting in his chair waiting for the kids to come home while he watched Fox News. Every now and then he would talk to the TV when a topic came up, he didn't agree with making a noise of disgust as he sipped his warm coffee.

Shuffling feet caught his ear, he didn't pay it any mind, it was his mother coming out of her room for the fiftieth time in the last half an hour. It was what she did all day was aimlessly wander back and forth.

"Pat?... Pat?" She said, sounding a little agitated.

"Yeah, ma? What's the matter?" Patrick replied. Louise made her way to the front window and peered out, she walked right in front of the TV.

"Ma, what are you doing?" Pat tried to contain the annoyance in his tone. She didn't know any better.

"Pat, a car just pulled up, I saw someone walking up the driveway." Pat waved a hand, dismissing her.

"Ma, it's the people upstairs, the tenants remember? Someone must be coming home."

"No Pat I swear to Jesus Christ on the cross, someone is coming up the driveway. Now why would I lie about that, you should be ashamed of yourself for thinking that!" She scolded her son, who got up and went to her.

"Ma, come on now, stop looking out your window. You're getting yourself all nerved up." Pat's mother was always a nervous person. She kinda slowed down in that aspect, but there were times like now she worked herself up over nothing. Pat was used to this.

"Ma relax, the kids will be home soon, and then we'll have a little food okay?"

"Oh, go fuck yourself, you son of a bitch bastard!" It was hard not to laugh when she went off like that, Pat did. Then, as he brought her in the room, the door chime rang out.

"See? There it is! That's the one, I told you!" Pat rolled his eyes. Usually when the tenants get company, their guests make the mistake of ringing the doorbell because there was only one. The one for the upstairs broke some time ago and Pat had yet to replace it.

"Just sit down, Ma. I'll be right back?"

"Ok." The old lady replied, as she sat fiddling with her hands and turned to the television. Pat then walked to the alcove, and opened the door.

Standing there was a woman with jet black hair and dark red streaks. She was covered in tattoos. She wore tight leather pants with knee high boots and a tight sleeveless top showing a little too much cleavage than she needed. She wore purple circled sunglasses, that she slid to the tip of her nose as she smiled at Patrick. Pat's throat was dry for the moment as he gazed upon the sultry woman.

"The doorbell is busted, I'll go upstairs and see if anyone is home." Pat was about to turn away, when the tattooed woman stepped closer, placing a hand on the storm door handle, she tried it very slowly.

"No, fat man, I'm not here to see anyone upstairs. I'm here to see you." Pat stared at her dumbfounded, as fear gripped his heart. He stepped back and slammed the door in her face, shaking the very foundation of the house. "You're only making it worse for yourself fat man!" Luna yelled through the closed door. Pat rushed through the living room passed his mother.

"Ma go in your room!" He yelled as he ran through the kitchen and into the back room. He had a small handgun tucked away behind the bookcase. He grabbed it, taking it from the holster. He switched the safety off.

Just as he was about to run back inside Luna came out of nowhere, grabbing him by the back of the neck and punched him so hard he fell back into the door leading into the basement. The gun dropped from his grip. Luna took two steps forward, with a devilish smile. She saw the gun and picked it up. She admired it, even though it was too small for her taste.

"Nice piece. She give it to you?" Pat didn't respond, he was frozen in fear. His head was wet in sweat. "I just want you to know, this is personal!" Luna aimed and fired. One shot was all she needed to kill him. A single round through the forehead.

"Pat! Pat! Where are you?" Luna, lowered her gun and walked forward towards the kitchen to greet Louise. "Oh! Hello!" The old lady warmly smiled, happy to see Luna. Pat's sprawled out body was out of eyesight. Not that she'd notice it anyway.

"Do I know you? I think I do… my mother and your mother used to be friends from the old neighborhood, and we used to play and go shopping, we had so much fun…oh my God." The old lady approached Luna with those made up happy thoughts. Luna couldn't help but chuckle. The senile's were always amusing. "How is your mother by the way?" Louise asked, walking closer to the assassin.

"You're a talkative old broad aren't ya?" Louise chuckled. "Time to put you out of your misery." The old lady didn't even realize her life came to an end as Luna grabbed her and broke her neck. The assassin stood over mother and son. They lived and died together. "Rest well, lady. You'll be having company soon enough." Just as she was about to turn and make her way downstairs, she heard voices coming from the front of the house.

"Uncle Pat? Uncle Pat we're home!" Luna snapped her head in the direction the voice came from and walking through the living room, were three kids with bulging backpacks strapped to their backs.

Patricia was the first to spot Luna, she gasped, reaching for her brother who looked just as stupefied as Pat's son.

"Oh my stars and garters, look what just walked in the door." Luna couldn't contain herself, as she slowly turned an stalked towards the trio of kids.

The kids were frozen, they couldn't even run if they wanted to.

"You!" Luna pointed at Pat's kid. "Get the fuck outta here!" The boy stood stock still, his jaw slacked. The assassin's patience was at an end. She raised her arm and pointed the gun she used to kill his father with and fired a single shot. It missed him by mere inches scaring the kids.

"Go!" Patricia yelled with tears brimming her eyes. Luna cocked the hammer back again, only this time the boy bolted out. Alone now with this maniac both brother and sister clutched each other for safety. Luna, stalked them like a tiger. She leaned forward and caressed little Jonathan's cheek, wiping away the tears.

"Don't fret yet, pray your cunt mother plays by the rules. If not you'll be cut up an spread across the desert for the vultures to feed on. Now fucking move!" The kids were pushed forward. With no understanding of what was going on, or how their mother even fit into this. All they had now was each other, because no one was going to save them.

Chapter 17
A rude awaking

The day after…

Priscilla shouldn't have drank as much as she had. The blaring phone pulled her from her hung over sleep, with the headache that was slowly coming on. As she stirred, she couldn't even remember how the hell she got in the bed. If she couldn't remember that, then she must've been drunk off her ass.

She was still in her clothes. She ran her hand through oily hair. She needed a goddamn shower in the worst way. Cooling your feet in police station's grimed you up. The phone stopped ringing, and then started up again. It was constant.

At first she thought it was the Hotel phone on the night stand. She picked it up and answered, but it wasn't that phone it was her cell phone. Her personal cell phone. As she slowly erected herself, she felt a tinge of nausea creep up on her. The room spun behind her closed eyelids. She moaned as she slogged to her purse, the phone stopped just then.

She just missed the call, she squinted to see who it was, but the number was blocked. She had no idea what time it was, and when she saw it was just after 11:00. That spurred her to get the day started. Just before she took one step, the phone rang again. Priscilla picked it up on the first ring.

"Hel…hello?" She replayed what she just said in her mind, she sounded like crap her voice was grainy, her throat felt raw, she rubbed it while waiting for the caller to answer her.

"Hello Bitch!" Pricilla's red eyes widened, her heart started to race, the nausea, and tiredness suddenly vanished in the blink of an eye.

"Luna." Priscilla said through gritted teeth, before she could even ask the question of how she got this number, Luna spoke.

"Don't run your mouth, just listen closely." Before Priscilla could even say something, Luna handed the phone off.

"Mommy? Mom? Help us…she killed uncle Pat-" Patricia couldn't even finish her sentence, emotions overtook her as she started to cry. The phone was taken from her.

"Bitch, you there?" Luna was back on the line, Priscilla almost gagged hearing her kid's voice on the other end of the phone. She had all to do to contain her emotions.

"You better not have hurt them! They have nothing to do with this leave them out of it!" Her voice rose with each word. She needed to get a grip on herself and fast, the last thing now was for her to fall apart.

"Yeah, neither did Bill but you took him out!" Luna shot back.

"He tried to kill me!" Priscilla was filled with a whole slew of emotions. Pat her friend, father figure dead, Louise. All because of her, and now her kids, her worst nightmare realized, caught in the middle, being used against her. Priscilla needed to focus, she needed to shake off this hangover and get back on the clock.

"Yeah, whatever. So now you know I ain't fuckin' around. You wanna see your kids alive? Meet me in one hour at Tony's Steakhouse, look it up! Don't be fucking late either, otherwise I'll scatter these little fuckers all over the desert!"

Before Priscilla could reply, the connection went dead. She dropped the phone and ran into the bathroom, splashing ice-cold water on her face. She needed to wake the fuck up. She opened the medicine chest and found a vast assortment of pain relievers and other over the counter medicines for the gamblers or binge drinkers that stayed here. The casino wanted you back on your feet so you can throw more money away.

Using a plastic cup she gulped down three Advil's. Then drank three more cups of water, hoping to lessen the hangover she had. Closing the cabinet, she noticed herself in the mirror. She rubbed a finger under her eye, she had dark circles beneath. She looked so tired, and beat to hell. Under the circumstances she could've looked worse. She whirled grabbing what she needed and left praying she didn't cause the death of her children.

Chapter 18
The Death's Head's

While there were many motorcycle clubs in the United States, the real badass outlaw clubs were nothing but a mere shadow of the past. Nowadays, clubs were more or less founded for the purpose of that extended family, in a sense you belonged to something and stood for something.

Even the Hells Angels, and other outlaw clubs, cleaned themselves up. While their exploits of being outlaws were legendary. They were now a commercialized fundraising club. But there were a few clubs that refused to follow this path and tried to go against the times.

The Death Heads motorcycle gang was one of those clubs. Word was the FBI was cracking down, and the Death Heads were in the crosshairs. Their ranks were dwindling, but that didn't make them any less dangerous to the community. They terrorized the west coast from Nevada all the way to California. At one point they were brazen enough to try to muscle in on Vegas. And that was when the hammer was brought down on them hard. The politicians out here were just as vicious as the mob who built and once owned, and if you asked around still owned Vegas.

Now the outlaw motorcycle gang were riding around in a sky blue cargo van. Penniless, four of the Death Heads gang were living day by day, in the small confines of the van.

"This shit sucks mate, riding around in a goddamn van. We should be out there taking what's ours!" The man in the passenger seat yelled out to his three partners. It was evident he was the wannabe leader of the group. The driver and the other two in the back sitting on the wheel wells listened to him. But this was a rant they heard before.

If they wanted to stay alive and/or out of jail, they needed to find some other way. The driver named Dalton, nodded to his passenger, Mick, who sat back around in his seat disgusted. Dalton agreed, but the other two didn't.

"I'm telling you, mate, we need to find us a score. I'm tired of living like this. We need to get back on top. This whole fucking city here is ripe for the taking, everyone has grown soft." Mick gestured with his arms, referring to Las Vegas. Dalton, nodded, the other two in the back, snickered.

"Yeah, right, and have the faggot Feds after us? You best just shut the fuck up, man." That came from Billy sitting on the driver's side wheel well. Mick didn't respond as he reached down at his feet grabbing something.

"I know, but we need coin. We should pull off a job or...or maybe a kidnapping!"

"You're outta your mind! And who would you want to kidnap, Mick?" That came from the same biker. Mick then turned around and showed him the paper he was holding. Billy got up and walked on his knees, taking the paper from Mick.

He read it as Mick watched him closely. He sucked his teeth clearly not impressed.

"You're outta your mind. And even if we went off on this wild goose chase, she ain't anywhere near here, it says New York. See it?" Billy pointed to the word, but Mick, tore it from his hands, looking back at the wanted poster of Priscilla Roletti.

"Fucking asshole! We should sure as shit try! Instead of driving around wasting what little money we have on gas." Dalton glanced at the wanted poster of Roletti.

"Mick, you gotta ask yourself somthin', though. What the hell did this chick do? I mean you see the amount of that bounty?" Mick looked at the poster again, his eyes going immediately to the amount with a whole lotta zero's.

"Yeah, I thought of it mate, but come on now. It's only a woman, have you ever ran into a bitch you couldn't beat down! The day I get my ass kicked by a woman, shit, shoot me right then and there cause I don't deserve to be walking with real men." Dalton, didn't reply as they came to a red light. Mick sat back, peering at the wanted poster.

His thoughts were wild with money and power. With that kind of haul they could restart again. Recruit and hit the road hard, take no fucking prisoners. They'd be able to get bikes again. Mick gave Dalton a sideways glance. He took a deep breath. Maybe he was right though. Where the hell were they going to find this chick? It was just by mere chance Mick found it on the internet a few days ago on one of those black-market websites where people like him look for work or jobs that need filling.

He crumpled the paper up and almost threw it out of his open window when he saw something. Or better yet, someone. Mick's eyes widened as he uncrumpled the paper, looking at it again. His eyes were going back and forth. He elbowed Dalton, who was lighting up a cigarette, he gave Mick an annoyed look.

"Fuck man… you almost made me burn myself."

"Look at this here mate, hurry!" Mick clearly ignoring Dalton as he pushed the paper in his hands.

"Surely my eyes ain't playin' tricks on me?" Dalton looked back from the poster to the blonde woman that was walking on the sidewalk. Dalton almost choked on his cigarette.

"No way…" Dalton took one big drag before throwing his smoke out the window. The light just turned green. Someone from behind beeped at them. Dalton quickly put on his hazard lights and double-parked.

Mick and Dalton watched the woman, she was in a hurry. They both looked at each other. The other two in the back came up alongside them wondering what the hell was going on.

"Yo, what the hell are you two doing?" This came from Timmy kneeling behind Mick.

"Shut up fool!" Mick yelled, shushing him. He then pointed to the woman showing the two men in the back the wanted poster. They looked at it, and then looked at the blonde woman. They didn't see her face only her backside. But it was enough to grab their attention.

"Why, I'll be goddamned I don't believe it." Billy said behind Dalton, keeping his eyes on her fast shaking butt. Dalton nodded, licking his upper lip. Mick, looked away, and turned to the three men.

"Listen up! You two will grab her. Dalton, let's go, she's in an awful hurry. We can grab her before anyone even knows what's what." Mick said, hitting him on his shoulder as he turned back around in his seat. Dalton, sat up straighter, signaled he was merging and slowly drove off. The two men in the back got ready, Mick glanced at them.

"Get ready mates!" Dalton came to the next intersection, just as the blonde did, he made the right turn purposely as she started to walk. She was about to walk around the van when it came to a sudden stop. The side door was thrown open, and before she could even react Billy and Timmy grabbed her. As Billy put her in a bear hug, Timmy threw a dirty bag over her head. The woman tried to struggle but was overpowered.

"Hurry it up you bums!" Mick yelled out as they threw her in the van and slid the door shut. The sky blue van sped off as onlookers who saw the broad daylight abduction pointed and dialed 911 on their cell phones.

Chapter 19
A slight detour

"Take off the hood! I wanna make sure we got the right bitch!" When the hood was removed it took a few seconds for Priscilla's eyes to focus upon the face scrutinizing her. He was squatting in front of her holding up her wanted poster; he was a rather ugly looking white guy with scars on his face.

He looked at it, then back to her, a smile crept up, as he folded the piece of paper and handed it to the guy in the passenger seat. It didn't take long for Priscilla to get back on the clock, as she took in her surroundings. There were a total of four men, two in the front, the one squatting in front of her and the last one trying to bind her hands; she wasn't making it easy for him. The man in the front passenger seat turned around.

"Well lookie what we got here, payday mates! Yeehaw!" They all laughed,

"Do you know who we are?" The man asked from the passenger seat, he was another ugly looking guy with orange hair and a beard to match. Priscilla couldn't care less who they were. She wasn't stroking any more men's egos. She was more focused on trying to prevent her hands from being tied up.

"We're the Death Heads." The biker squatting in front of her said proudly, at the mention of the name she knew then, they were an outlaw biker gang, the last of a dying breed.

"You know, it's a shame, I'd love to have a couple of hours with her before we make delivery." The man squatting in front of her said, while gently stroking her cheek with his finger. The man in the driver's seat nodded.

"Yeah bro, but the amount that's on her head, outweighs the thought of having that pussy, you know what I'm sayin'?" That coming from the man in the passenger's seat.

"Yo, Billy, what the fuck are you doing? Why are you having such a hard time with her hands?" Timmy asked both amused and annoyed.

"This bitch keeps pulling away, she's stronger than she looks! If she'd stop fidgeting." He said, sounding very frustrated. To help his friend, Timmy punched her in the cheek; she was expecting that and braced herself for the attack. She snapped her head back and looked at the man with defiant eyes, her cheek was bruised already.

"The contract never said anything about bruises, right?" He said, turning and looking at Mick with a give a fuck attitude. Priscilla didn't pay any attention to the response, the man finally succeeded in tying her hands with the plastic binds, her muscles tensed, she broke out in a sweat.

The van was awfully hot, her eyes were darting everywhere. She analyzed the situation, the man behind her was close enough to take out, she could feel his hot breath on her neck. The guy in front of her would be easy as well. The guy at the wheel, would be too busy driving to pose a threat. The only one she was worried about was the guy in the passenger seat. She readied herself, her adrenaline was pumping, if she was going to die, she'd be dammed to die at the hands of these white trash.

"Put her out man." The orange bearded man told the guy in front of her. He grabbed a white rag that looked wet, and leaned in closer to her.

"Now, pretty lady, let me have a few words with you." Before the rag even came close to her face, Priscilla went into action with as much force as she could muster. She slammed the back of her head into the man's face behind her. It was a perfect hit, she felt his nose break against the back of her skull.

Before the man in front of her could react, she propelled her head forward and smashed him in the face with her forehead, breaking his nose. By the time Mick reacted, Priscilla already slipped her bound hands from behind her, and with her arms extended she lunged forward. Mick was already in motion brandishing a large knife. The deadly blade was swung at her, but Priscilla feinted, ducked and elbowed the man in the face.

She grabbed the hand with the knife and broke his thumb. The bearded man cried out dropping it. She elbowed him again, and put his head through the window.

As this was going on, the driver was trying to grab at her, as he tried to control the speeding van, she turned around and slid her bound arms over his head, and pressed tightly against her chest. She was trying to break his neck. As they struggled, they were hit. The van rolled over twice and was back on its wheels, rocking back and forth. The engine was smoking, just after the van settled, the side door slowly opened and a dizzy Priscilla stumbled out.

She had a cut on her forehead; she leaned against the doors, trying to shake off the dizziness. She needed to get going, her kids' lives were at stake. She felt like throwing up. Priscilla erected herself a little bit more. She glanced at the inside of the van, finding the knife the bearded man brandished against her, she used that to cut her bound hands free. She then turned and noticed bystanders coming her way. Just as she was about to walk off, she caught movement in the corner of her eye, one of the bikers was stirring, she heard a moan. Her eyes fell to a Snub-nosed.38 revolver just lying on the carpeted floor. She grabbed it and emptied the gun, putting a bullet into each of the bikers, she dried fired it once and then tossed it back in and casually walked away.

Bystanders ran at the sound of the shots, others watched on, some were taking pictures with their cell phones. Priscilla ignored them all. She obstructed her face with her hand as she walked on past them and lost herself in a crowd of people on the next block.

Chapter 20
Table for two please

As she continued on her way, Priscilla tried to gather her thoughts. She was looking all over the place, making sure no one was following her, or worse yet, the cops. The accident wasn't far from the restaurant she was headed to. She took a few side streets and finally hailed a cab. The detour gave her time to gather herself. By the time she was in the cab her thoughts were more focused, she was angry at herself for getting caught just then, it was a rookie mistake that almost cost her. But how could she remain calm and focused? Her kids were taken because of her and now were being used as a pawn in all of this. The deaths of her friends hadn't fully sunk in, but when it did, it would hit her hard. Damn this fucking life, she thought. But there wasn't anything she could do. She had to focus, find her center and move on.

The cab pulled right up to the swanky restaurant, Priscilla checked her watch just to double-check, she was right on time.

Her forehead was peppered with sweat; irritating the cut just above her eye. She wiped her brow, as she walked through the double glass doors. She scanned the high-end clientele, looking for Luna, a few people that walked by gave her quick concerned glances. Aside from not being properly dressed to be here, she looked a mess too. Within seconds of her walking in, the Maître d' approached her, giving Priscilla a 'look', but nonetheless he smiled.

She smiled back, but it was a forced smile, she was totally on edge now, with all the near misses she's been having. Priscilla needed to get her head clear; she closed her eyes and took a deep breath, that helped somewhat.

"Um, excuse me, madam, are you looking for someone?" He asked, he must've asked her more than once because he sounded snotty. She looked at him, nodding.

"Yes… yes I am...someone told me to meet them here for lunch."

"And the name, madam?" He asked as he checked a small sheet.

"Luna." Upon hearing the name, he curled his lip into a sneer, and slumped his shoulders, gesturing her to follow him. As they walked, she kept an eye out for anyone that may be watching her, Luna said she'd be here alone but Priscilla wasn't a fool. She'd bet her life that Luna would have back up with the time she had to prepare for this meeting.

As the Maître d' led the way Priscilla tried to pick out Luna. And it wasn't hard to spot her in a crowd. If she thought she was outta place here, then Luna was from another world. She was dressed like a Goth just coming back from a heavy metal concert, with a loose fitting top cut at the shoulder where it sagged a bit, her long jet black hair had red highlights. She was pale and had a little too much make-up on; Priscilla could see she was tatted to the max. They were everywhere, even on her face. The look Luna gave her, as she approached, was death itself. If someone wasn't pulling the reins on her, Luna most likely would have attacked her on sight. The Maître d' pulled the chair out for Priscilla, she sat down, quickly glimpsing back at him all the while keeping her eyes on Luna who was sitting with one leg under her.

The Maître d' handed menus to the both of them, he flashed a quick smile and said a waiter will be with them shortly.

Priscilla acknowledged him while Luna didn't say a word, she was sizing Priscilla up, who now stared back at Luna. She looked so uncouth as she sat there, breaking off a piece of bread in the basket on the table which Priscilla failed to take notice of.

Luna looked young if Priscilla had to guess no more than twenty-five at best. She eased herself a bit, ready for the inevitable sparring of words.

"So, you got me here, where are my children?" Luna didn't answer right away as she took a gulp from one of the two glasses of water on the table and slammed it down hard to catch the attention of a couple at a nearby table, Pricilla flashed them a sheepish smile. Then turned back to Luna.

"Don't think your gonna come here and boss me around and ask the questions lady, I'm in charge here. You do as I say, got it?!" She said, pointing a butter knife at her; Priscilla cocked her eyebrow at the way this young woman talked to her. She could see this wasn't going to be easy at all.

"Now, as for your brats, they're safe, for now anyway. If I had my way, I'd have gutted them." Priscilla felt a chill speed up her spine at the mere mention of her kids, the emotions of thinking about them were overtaking her train of thought. She needed to focus on the matter at hand, which was this crazy assassin.

"Oh yeah?" Priscilla said, leaning in closer, Luna did the same, her eyes grew a little wider with mayhem shining in them. "Let me tell you something girl, if you did something as stupid as that we wouldn't be talking right now, you'd be dead." Luna let loose a loud open mouth laugh, showing Priscilla the unchewed bread in her mouth, the young assassin sat up straighter moving some hair from her face.

"Anytime you're ready, lady. I owe you. You took out Bill, he was good people." Priscilla disregarded that.

"Then he shouldn't have tried to kill me. It cost him his life, and perhaps yours as well if you don't stop this." Again, Luna chuckled, she was about to say something when the waiter finally came over, easing the high tension. They both looked at the menu quickly, and ordered, the little interruption calmed the girl down a bit. Priscilla looked at her with forgiving eyes.

"You're so young, how old are you? Stop this now, it's not worth your life, you can get outta this, trust me. I wish I could and look where it led me. You should go home to your family, just knowing who is putting you up to this, tells me you're naive." Luna didn't flinch at the lecture; she shrugged her shoulders, leaning in closer now.

"Don't fucking tell me to go home, I have no home, this is what I was born to do."

"No one is born to do this, we're made to be this way, and we can change if we want to…." Priscilla's words resonated, as her life flashed before her eyes. "If you don't want to change, then change your employer. Don't you even care who's behind all this? I mean, for Christ's sake, the innocent lives he snuffed out. What do you think he'll do with a loose cannon like you once he succeeds, hmm? You're not looking at the bigger picture, personal gain and anger are clouding your judgment." Luna dismissed Priscilla's words of wisdom with a wave of her hand.

"I don't give a fuck about any of that, I'm gonna be part of the new world order lady." Luna pointed her thumb at her chest as she told her this, she sounded proud. Priscilla sat back; she realized talking to her wasn't going to work. This kid wasn't gonna back down, she had something to prove, she could relate to that. Was she this bad when she was that young? Looking at her, Priscilla saw a much more darker, twisted version of herself.

The only thing that separated them was that Priscilla had morals in a strange sense of the word. This kid was beyond her help; it was a vain attempt on her part. Priscilla was done trying to convince her to see things her way.

"Ok then…so what do you want? I'm here." Luna nodded.

"I don't want shit lady, 'He' does, your kids are being held at his place. The old man wants to talk to you, in person, that's the only reason why you're not dead, after your last meal, we're gonna go there together." Priscilla nodded, that wasn't happening.

She wasn't going anywhere with this nut, if the old Nazi wanted to finally meet she'd oblige him, but she wasn't going with this kid. Luna shook her head in contempt throwing down an unfinished piece of bread.

"Make no mistake about it cunt, when this is over, and the old man gets whatever it is he wants from you…. you're dead, and your fucking kids, I'll sell them to a slave trade." Priscilla cocked her eyebrow to the threat. "Look at you, you look so worn, haggard," Luna continued dripping with over confidence. "To think you'd even have a chance against me? Forget the fact that you're what, almost fifty, maybe older? Even if you were younger, you wouldn't stand a chance." She said poking her finger at her chest, the look of disdain Priscilla had couldn't be hidden; this tattooed assassin was naive, arrogant and needed to be put down quickly.

"Anyone at any age and at any given time, can be beaten, best remember that youngin." Priscilla said, mocking her. Luna made a face in obvious disregard of the veiled warning. As Luna started to talk again, Priscilla listened deeply, but paid more attention to her surroundings.

The worry of Luna having back up was gone, this kid thought she was the best and couldn't be taken down. Priscilla's back grew stiff, she was ready to pounce, Luna was right, she was younger and perhaps even stronger than her. But Priscilla made up for that with experience. She licked her lips; their waiter just arrived with their order, momentarily distracting Luna. He gingerly placed each plate before them, and smiled at them both. Just as the waiter was about to turn away, Priscilla's hand flashed out, grabbing the steak knife on Luna's plate and impaled it in her hand. She screamed out from the unexpected attack, Priscilla didn't let go of the knife as she jumped up from her seat, and stepped to her side, Luna clawed at her hand, with her free hand.

"How's that for an old woman! Where are my fucking kids!?" She yelled in her ear, getting ready to break her neck, when Luna, with her free hand struck out at Priscilla, punching her in the stomach twice. Hunched over from the blows, Luna grabbed her by the hair and head-butted Priscilla, who stumbled back.

By the time Priscilla recovered, Luna already freed her impaled hand, and with precision aim threw the knife at Priscilla. She barely dodged it, as it bounced harmlessly off the wall and onto the floor. Priscilla stood where she was and squared off as Luna, in a screaming rage, threw the table aside with all the contents onto people close by as they tried to flee the chaos that was unfolding before them.

Luna was on top of Priscilla in a heartbeat, throwing a fast combination of punches, which Priscilla dodged and batted away, while sneaking in two quick jabs to break her out of her deadly rhythm. That only fed into the young assassin's rage, another quick punch to the face rocked Luna, who recovered in zero time, it was as though she felt nothing, each blow fed more into her offense.

Priscilla had to end this fight quick, forget the fact that too many people were around trying to get out of their way, but for the fact that she was at her end, she was on overdrive now. She was tired and worn, mentally and physically. Luna looked as though she could keep this up all day, the longer this lasted the more in favor it went to her, getting old sucked.

Priscilla side stepped a thrust kick, which she caught in midair, and with as much force as she could get behind it, threw the raging woman onto a table flipping it over on top of her, with food and all.

Priscilla didn't let up; she shoved the upended table to the side and grabbed Luna by her rat's nest of hair, propelling her up. Luna thrust her head forward, smashing it into Priscilla's, breaking her grip, then followed it up with two quick punches that sent her stumbling back, into a vacant table.

Luna turned and grabbed a steak knife, lunging for her. Priscilla blindly found a steak knife too, and met her head on, with a new burst of energy, they sparred. The amount of skill displayed by both was something remarkable to those not daring to take their eyes off this battle that they'd soon never forget.

Neither one gave any leeway, every counter was countered, it was a stalemate. The look of arrogance on Luna's face quickly turned to worry tinged with frustration that she finally had met her match. In all her life leading up to this, she'd never been challenged like she was now.

She was even starting to respect the old bitch, but not much though. She was gonna die, here and now. Fuck what the old man wanted, Priscilla broke through Luna's defense, giving her a vicious cut on her forearm, she dropped the blade, screeching. Unarmed now she jumped back and did a quick flip, making for the door. Luna underestimated her, and it proved to be an almost fatal mistake.

Priscilla saw Luna making her escape, that wasn't gonna happen. She wasn't going to chase her down, it was gonna end here, she was too far away to stop her, she'd be out the door and on the street and gone by the time she closed the gap. Priscilla launched the knife with the aim of a marksman, and missed the assassin!

She was way off, she'd have killed the waiter if not for the fact he jerked his silver tray up in time deflecting her wild throw. She bit her lip, she wanted to scream out, but that wouldn't help her now, she needed to move her ass.

The cops would be here any moment and the last thing she needed was another run in with Las Vegas PD. She bolted out the back of the restaurant, taking the alleyway, escaping just in time as police pulled up.

Chapter 21
Aftermath

Priscilla sat at the edge of the bed crying into her hands. She trashed the room, turning over the loveseat, shattering the bathroom mirror and throwing bottles of liquor across the room. The events of today were finally setting in and because of her rash way of thinking her kids may already be dead, joining her friends whose blood was on her hands.

Priscilla trembled, trying to imagine how it all played out at the house. How can that bitch kill a helpless old lady! She was going to pay as god as her witness; she was going to hunt down these motherfuckers! She shuddered to think what was going on at the house now after Pat's wife came home.

"Goddamn it!" She yelled, as she got up from the bed, walking to the bathroom. She turned on the water, and splashed her sticky face, rubbing her eyes. The cold water felt refreshing.

Now she was totally out of options with no leads. Either she waited for Ferrer to get in touch with her or take a flight back to New York. What other options were there? The running water was loud, at first she thought she was hearing things, but her cell phone was ringing. Priscilla dashed out of the bathroom and grabbed it. The caller didn't block their number this time. It could be only two people.

"Yeah?" She said as soon as she put it to her ear. There was silence for a moment.

"Yeah bitch… thought you were slick today huh? Fucking cunt… you're so dead."

"Come on! Let's go! Where are you?!" Priscilla yelled back pacing. The voice that responded wasn't Luna's it was Patricia's.

"Mom…?" The child sounded tired, Priscilla suddenly stopped yelling.

"Patricia baby! Are you okay?!" Before the child could answer, the phone was ripped from her ear, Luna was back.

"She's fine, so is the boy, for how long is up to you. The Man wants to see you." Priscilla nodded.

"When and where?"

"You hear of Port Angeles? It's in Washington State. It's a small fishing town. On the main strip is a small diner called Sunny Side. I'll text you the address GPS it. Text me when you arrive, and I'll meet you there." Priscilla nibbled her lower lip as she listened to all of this.

"You pull another stunt like today and I don't care what the old man says, I'll kill them, when you see him you better thank him. He's the only thing that stopped me from killing them after the restaurant thing, see 'ya!" And the call ended. Priscilla stood there replaying the entire conversation in her mind. Not even a minute later a text message came in with the name of the place and the address to said place.

Priscilla closed her phone. Standing there, she knew this was it. She closed her eyes. She needed to focus right now. She was so tired…. She had never felt like this. She was at the edge. She didn't know how the hell she was still standing, but she thanked the powers that be for giving her this stamina. She ran a hand through her sweaty oily hair. It was too late to drive now. Tomorrow morning she'd head out. She needed a good night's rest, to be useful to anyone. But she doubted rest would come so easily.

She started to cry again, her poor kids. She had to push all of that out of her mind and focus, she had to treat this like any other mission before. Because right now, if she faulted, then her kids were as sure as dead.

Chapter 22
Rendezvous

Priscilla arrived at Port Angeles, WA in two days. As she drove, she couldn't help being overcome by the serenity this town possessed. It was so small and quiet. When she arrived it was close to dinnertime. She didn't waste a single moment. She headed to the diner Luna told her to meet at. She parked in the graveled parking lot just next to the quaint old diner and walked in.

The air here was cold and moist, mixed with the smell of the sea. When she entered, the place wasn't very full. No one really looked her way as she went to the counter and sat. She ordered a coffee from the very prompt waitress. Priscilla added milk, stirred and slowly sipped. The coffee was fresh. She needed this. As she sat Priscilla stared into the void, wondering what was going through the minds of her children. She hoped that after all of this they didn't wind up hating her, and if they did she wouldn't blame them. She lied to them about everything, it would only be right; karma always comes full swing good or bad.

The waitress came back over noticing Priscilla had finished her coffee, and gave her a refill. Priscilla thanked her, and just put the cup to her lips when someone walked into the diner. The door needed to be oiled. Priscilla didn't look behind her. She knew this was Luna. She got that sensation coursing through her spine when she felt danger near. And sure enough, taking a seat on the stool just to her right was Luna. She gave Priscilla a hard stare. Priscilla glanced her way, noticing her bandaged hand. The waitress came over and asked Luna if she'd like to order something, but Luna told her to go away.

When someone that looks like Luna tells you that, you listen and don't make a big deal about it. Priscilla could still feel the young girl's eyes on her. She finally turned and looked the tattooed assassin in the face. Their eyes locked, the waitress couldn't help but look on, while pretending to work. Priscilla looked down at her hand, then back to Luna.

"How's the hand?" She asked, sipping her coffee. She could tell Luna wanted to take the bait. But she didn't fall into that. Luna now respected Priscilla more than the last time. The look in her eyes was evident of that. She laughed under her breath as she looked at her hand.

"You wanna, do round 2 or do you want your kids to die?" She said, in an even tone. Priscilla placed her cup on the saucer. She reached into her pocket, leaving a few dollars on the counter. It was more than enough for the coffee.

"Lead the way youngin." Priscilla said, gesturing for the door. Luna hesitated at first, but then got up and walked to the door. Priscilla looked at the waitress, nodded and thanked her. Outside now, the wind picked up, she looked to the west, a storm was rolling in. She could hear the distant thunder. She followed Luna to her car, which was a burgundy Maserati, it was parked right next to Priscilla's Charger.

They drove north for about fifteen minutes, coming to a densely wooded area. Luna took a left down a hidden graveled driveway. The driveway was long and winding. They finally came to an opening. Luna drove to the left, Priscilla took the right. The expanse was large, aside from Priscilla's and Luna's cars, there was one other vehicle, a Mercedes Sprinter with handicap plates.

Priscilla looked ahead at the house before her. It was a simple looking home. But you could tell it was well taken care of and very expensive. She parked off to the right, before getting out she activated the self-destruct system. Even if you had the keys and the alarm remote, it would still go off, unless you knew the correct button sequence on the alarm remote to deactivate it.

With that done, she got out and locked the car. She had her gun in her waist. She didn't bother to take extra clips. She knew it would be taken from her once she set foot in the place. Luna waited for her on the large porch. She stood in front of the frosted glass double doors. As Priscilla approached, Luna opened them and stepped aside. Priscilla didn't hesitate, she climbed the four steps.

"Stop." Luna said, holding her good hand out. "I know you're packing. Hand it over." Priscilla reached behind her back and placed it in her hand without a word and walked on.

It was obvious this place, cost a pretty penny. She was in a marbled hallway, with old works of art on the walls. She walked over to one, and read the artist's name. He was Jewish. Don't hate them enough to hang their art, huh?

She thought as she walked on. There was a staircase that led up, and just past the stairs was a small elevator. To her left was another hallway that was darkened. She stopped walking and turned around to Luna, who was following her.

"Where am I going?" Luna pointed ahead.

"Through those doors." Priscilla turned back around and walked to the double white doors. She opened them both without knocking and found herself in a very large office with two couches on the right side of the room in an L shape and a glass coffee table in the middle of them. She looked ahead and was greeted with a window that spanned the entire wall. She walked deeper into the dark gray carpeted office, approaching the giant window.

The house sat just on the edge of a cliff overlooking the ocean. On a nicer day, the view from here must've been breathtaking at sunset, while listening to the waves crash against the jagged shoreline below. There weren't any lights on, you didn't need any. Even with the darkened sky, there was plenty of illumination. It was nice to have money she thought. Maybe she'll buy a house with a view like this. She turned around and saw Luna coming up behind her. Priscilla turned back around to the view, stormy weather or not, it was amazing.

"Don't go anywhere. I'll be back." Priscilla didn't acknowledge her as she looked on. She then turned to her left and saw a large dark oak desk and installed in the wall behind it was a large water filled tank. As she approached the tank, she saw something floating about, which to her surprise were two jellyfish.

A species she'd never seen before. The sky-blue transparent creatures with a bright orange polyp core came close to the tank. Its wiggly tentacles reached out and touched the glass. Priscilla was about to press her hand to the tank when she heard someone approach her from behind. She turned around and was finally face to face with, Josef Mengele, otherwise known as the Angel of Death.

Chapter 23
The Angel of Death

"Beautiful aren't they?" The old Nazi, said softly. As he wheeled towards her in his electric wheelchair. He wore loose black sweat pants with a gray sweatshirt. Priscilla almost sneered at him. Not in contempt, but in how grotesque he looked. His skin looked rubbery, age spots marked his bald head and face. You could tell his breathing was labored, his chest looked heavy. The sweat suit made him look far more bulkier than he was beneath it.

The only thing that looked alive on this man were his eyes. He gave her a weak smile. Priscilla looked away from him and saw Luna right behind him with Emil, who looked less like Derlin with a close-cropped haircut and a clean-shaven face.

Seeing the man who was impersonating Derlin, made her blood boil. She resisted the urge to ball her hands into fists. She didn't want to show any act of aggression just yet. Mengele pointed his wrinkled, twisted branch looking finger at the giant walled fish tank.

"That is the, Turritopsis Nutricula, otherwise known as the immortal jellyfish. Constantly turning back time by cycling its polyp from a mature to immature state." She looked at the tank, then back to the old man. His features turned soft as he admired them, like a father would his children. Mengele then blinked his eyes rapidly coming out of his trance and regarded Priscilla. He gestured her to follow him as he turned his wheelchair around and started to ride to the other side of the giant office.

"I shall show you, the fruit of my labor for almost seventy-years." With no choice Priscilla followed, as Emil and Luna let her pass. While Emil stayed, Luna followed her. On the far side of the office was an elevator door. Mengele slowly punched in a code on the side and then the doors split open. He rolled in first and then spun around.

When Priscilla took a step forward, Luna grabbed her by the shoulder. The urge to turn around and clock her was almost overwhelming. But for now this was perfect. Let the old man talk. She needed to buy time; she still didn't know where her kids were.

"Do you think this is smart? At least let me cuff her hands." Luna said, looking from Priscilla then to Mengele. He did a throaty mucus laced chuckle.

"There is no need, my dear, you will be with us. Plus, I think Miss Roletti will behave herself, we hold her precious bastard children." Mengele looked right at Priscilla when he said this. She fought back what she wanted to say, and walked into the elevator. Luna followed, and once inside, the door closed.

"This property was bought forty-years ago, under an assumed name of course. As this house was built, a section beneath was hollowed out. I didn't need to worry about attracting attention at the time, there was hardly anyone here. It was and still is a perfect place for privacy and a easy escape if I was ever found." Priscilla didn't reply, as the elevator came to a stop and the doors split open again.

The expanse was dark, but from the sterile smell that engulfed her senses, she knew what this was. When Mengele wheeled out, the lights came on. Priscilla walked out looking around. It was a domed shaped lab. It was pristine with various machines, and equipment. In the center was a large machine that connected two metal tables. One empty and one covered with a large white sheet. Mengele wheeled on going towards the covered table. Priscilla followed, keeping his pace because, between his German accent and weak sounding voice it was hard to hear him.

"You see Ms. Roletti, the Turritopsis Nutricula, with its constant cycling life span, holds the key to immortality, and I succeeded twenty-years ago in isolating the cells after working on it for almost twenty years prior." The old Nazi spun around suddenly, and faced both Priscilla and Luna but he looked at Priscilla. Luna walked towards the covered table. "By the time I achieved this great miracle in science, I was at death's door. I had no choice, I tested it on myself. Almost immediately the serum took hold of my body. Long dead cells rejuvenated, I felt my body strong again. My heart, lungs, legs, everything was getting stronger and younger!" The old man's eyes sparkled to life. But then grew sad. He looked away from her and stared at Luna, then to the floor and back to Priscilla.

"Because of my desire to live! I never tested it, the thought of side effects didn't occur to me. In the back of my mind, I knew there had to be some, but nothing I couldn't fix later. I was wrong. The serum worked yes, but at the same time as it cycled my cells, it was also damaging them. Human cells aren't made to cycle backwards. With each treatment I had to increase the dosage. It got to the point where, my body couldn't take it any longer.

In other words, my body was embracing and rejecting the serum at the same time. I needed to alter my body somehow. While I searched for ways to do so, I had to use other means to prolong my life." He gave her a sharp look and then continued.

"With the advancement of cloning and genetic engineering, a new hope surfaced. With the help of a young but brash scientist by the name of Claude Griffin, I was able to alter my DNA. It was a temporary solution though, until the permanent one was achieved. Claude secretly helped me fulfill this at the lab in Pennsylvania unbeknownst to that double crossing Hans Goring."

When he said Hans' name, Mengele almost spit it out, like a bad taste.

"I'm ashamed to say he was my country man. My ultimate goal Ms. Roletti, is to successfully transfer my neural patterns into the Supreme Being, and tonight the dawn of a new era shall be born!"

Mengele gestured at Luna, who then uncovered the table. Priscilla couldn't help but be repulsed and amazed at the same time. Laying dormant was a giant of a man with a square jaw, and a chiseled physique. From head to toe it was perfection. An unstoppable killing machine.

"Cloning was the missing link, I needed to alter the body from creation. I cloned my new body around the Turritopsis Nutricula serum. All that was needed was Hans' super-human serum, which I acquired. And by the way, I found the solution to the flaw in his serum where the muscle tissue grows soft when not in constant movement. All that is left, is the transfer." Mengele gestured again, and Luna covered the soulless clone. Mengele then wheeled past Priscilla, who was still staring at the covered clone. She finally pulled her eyes away, looking at the Nazi. Luna stayed behind with Priscilla.

"You're out of your mind, old man." She said as she followed him back to the elevator. He didn't reply. The doors split open, he entered, Priscilla and Luna followed. "If you're so sure of this, why didn't you do it already?" Priscilla asked. Mengele grunted.

"I had more pressing matters to tend to, such as you. I am not sure how long it will take me to get used to my new body, disorientation could last days or months." Priscilla nodded, not that she cared at all. She just needed to drag this out longer.

"And bringing me here, what do you want?" Mengele looked up at her, just as the elevator stopped. The doors split open and Emil was still there, but this time with her kids.

Priscilla felt her heart flutter at the sight of them. They looked disheveled, frightened, and, confused. She wanted to run to them, embrace them, kiss them and tell them that everything will be all right. But she couldn't…not yet.

Her thoughts and feelings, were well hidden, she didn't give them so much as a second glance, as if they were irrelevant. She couldn't for the sake of holding it together and to keep them as calm as possible. Mengele wheeled to the wall of windowed glass. Priscilla followed and looked out upon the horizon. The seas were starting to get rough. The storm was here; the dark gray clouds were testament to that as the rain started to fall. The view grew blurry with rain.

Mengele then spun and wheeled away from the window, towards his desk, he spun around and faced Priscilla. Emil stood close to the kids while Luna stood near the windows crossing her arms over her chest. Priscilla stepped closer to the middle.

"And now to answer your question. There are various other officials I have yet to influence or touch. I know there are people looking for me. It could be a year before I am able to take full command of everything." He looked to Luna, who tossed Priscilla a cell phone. She glanced at it, and then looked at Mengele.

"In the mean time, you will inform your superiors, that you have in fact killed me as ordered. You will give the detailed description I present to you. Once they are pacified, of course, they will want a more detailed debrief. En route you shall be the victim of a horrible accident. An ironic twist of luck, you survived some of the world's most ruthless assassins and yet you fall victim to an airline accident. Most unfortunate indeed." Priscilla glanced at the phone in her hand, she even turned it over to look at the back and then to the front again.

She couldn't help but chuckle and smirk. He had it all planned out nicely. When she returned her attention to the Nazi, her smirk faded.

"Agreed. But you release my kids, put them on a plane home, and when they are safe I'll do as you ask." Mengele laughed deeply in his throat.

"My dear woman, you're in no position to negotiate anything. You will do as I say and perhaps hope I spare their lives!" The old man raised his voice. She was getting to him, she smirked again.

"I don't think so, they have nothing to do with this. If that option is off the table, then no. And if you try to use them as leverage against me, I'll just remove them from the equation…myself." Mengele, stiffened, Emil and Luna stood where they were.

"Brave words, my dear… but we both know you'd never do such a thing." Priscilla shook her head disagreeing with that comment.

"There's not a fucking thing you can do to keep me from killing you. Anyone, and I mean anyone…" Priscilla looked at Emil, Luna and finally her kids. Seeing their mother behave like this frightened them. Her son started to cry; Patricia stayed strong for both of them as she pulled him closer to her. "You throw in front of me will not stop me, retribution has waited long enough."

"This is getting us nowhere." Mengele wheeled backwards out of the way. And just as he did so, everything moved so fast then.

Luna was making her move on Priscilla's right. While Emil suddenly had a switchblade in his hand and was pressing it to Patricia's neck. Reacting the fastest she ever did, she threw the cell phone at Emil nailing him right in the eyebrow. She had less than a few seconds before he recovered. She ducked and leg swept Luna just as she fired her gun. The bullet hit the wall, as she fell back on her rear-end.

Priscilla then sprang up and tackled Emil, wrestling the blade from his hand. She elbowed him twice in the chest, before he managed to get out from under her. Priscilla was on her feet.

“Move! Stay out of sight!” She yelled at her kids, who were reeling in terror of how close their lives came to an end. Her voice snapped them back to the here and now. Patricia threw her arm around Jonathan, as they ran off obeying their mother’s plea.

By then Luna and Emil were already on their feet, coming at her. It was two on one. Against regular people the odds were in Priscilla’s favor, but against these two, she had all to do to survive this.

She needed to separate them long enough that she could just incapacitate one of them at least just to give her breathing room. But that wasn’t happening, they fought like a well-oiled machine, totally in sync with one another.

Priscilla was outmatched and was already winded. Time was not on her side. If anything, she was controlling where the fight was, she managed to get them in the middle of the large office.

Priscilla flipped out of the way of an attack from Emil, only to be nailed by Luna, the kick to the side of her body knocked the wind out of her. Priscilla jumped back to her feet, going after Luna, but then was grabbed from behind by Emil.

He whacked her in the back of the head, and applied a full nelson. Priscilla struggled to break free, Emil had her locked in. Luna smashed the glass coffee table and picked up a piece of glass and approached Priscilla. Gripping her jaw, Luna tilted Priscilla’s head back, she was mere inches before the jagged glass slit Priscilla’s throat when a single gunshot rang out. Priscilla jumped from the unexpected gunfire. But quickly snapped out of it when the pressure suddenly loosened.

She didn’t have time to ponder it. Luna was looking in the direction of where the shot came from. Priscilla shook off the obviously dead Emil and didn’t waste a single second, she punched Luna in the jaw with everything she had, breaking it.

Priscilla pummeled the young assassin, giving her a beating she’ll never forget. Grabbing her by her long hair, Priscilla threw her against the wall of glass windows cracking a section from the impact.

Luna didn’t even get up, she was alive but defeated. Priscilla, went to one knee and with a single punch she crushed her windpipe.

She stood back on her feet, out of breath, and spent. She leaned on the sofa close by. She then finally looked in the direction of her savior.

"Lens!" There was no mistaking her shadowy, elusive friend who wore the same clothes from Venezuela, the tacky yellow shirt with palm trees and jean shorts. He stood in the doorway holding a gun at his side. He wore a brimmed hat, obscuring his face.

"Agent Roletti, we seem to be meeting like this all too often." Priscilla couldn't help but smile. He was a sight for sore eyes.

"And once again your timing couldn't be any better." Finally, this was over. She started to walk around the couch when gunfire erupted, Priscilla was powerless to help Lens as he fell forward.

Chapter 24
The duel

"NO!" Priscilla yelled, reaching out in vain, she then instinctively ducked behind the couch ready for more gunfire. It was eerily quiet, her ears were throbbing. She didn't dare look up.

"Little lady, I know you're behind that couch. You can stand up." The Albino's voice echoed in her ears. Goddamn it! She cursed herself. How the hell could she have overlooked him? Priscilla hesitated at first, all she had to do was poke her head up and bang!

"If you don't stand up, a couch is hardly protection from gunfire." He was right. She licked her lower lip, spotting Luna's gun just inches from her; she grabbed it making sure the weapon was loaded and stuck it in her waist. She closed her eyes, cleared her thoughts, and slowly stood.

Seeing her, Moe the albino smiled and nodded at her. Priscilla glanced at his gloved hands; his revolver was stuffed in his pants.

"I finally got ya where I want you. I could just shoot you now, you know. Be done with all of this and put you on the pedestal as one of my greatest adversaries to be remembered till the day I die.

But no, that would be too easy. And one question would linger. Who truly is the better person here in this room? Forget about the time you got the drop on me at the diner, that was my fault I deserved that. I'm talking about from Venezuela when you escaped from my grasp not once but twice. Then you somehow made it back to the States and then for all this time you managed to not only elude every hunter out there but you killed anyone in your way.

You didn't run and hide, you hunted the ones hunting you. You came at them hard, man if that ain't balls, then I don't know what is. That's something even I gotta respect. You truly are a breed in that of your own lady. And I'm gonna be the one to put you down."

"Moe! What are you waiting for, shoot her!" Mengele yelled, in his feeble voice. The Albino slowly turned his head, in the direction of the old Nazi.

"Shut up old man! Your only job is to sign my check, not tell me how to kill someone! We do this my way!" He then looked back to Priscilla, who was almost taken back by the way he snapped at Mengele. The Albino never lost his cool; she felt satisfaction, that she was the cause of that.

"Ok lady, it's time to see, who's the best. No sneak attacks, no more interference, just you and me, mano-a-mano." Priscilla licked her lips, throwing her eyes about. They fell on the old Nazi who looked on with wide eyed worry, his face was contorted, he threw on his breathing mask, the panic going through his frail body was too much to handle. Her blue eyes locked with the Albino's golden ones, a smile crept up, he straightened.

"You got your pistola?" He pointed a gloved finger at her waist, she nodded.

"Yeah, I got it." He smiled, nodding back.

"Good, you're all locked and loaded?" Again she nodded. "We're about even then, mine's right here." He pointed to his silver revolver.

"Whenever you're ready." He said as he stepped back two steps his features were that of steel, those yellow eyes pierced right through her.

This was it.... she didn't so much as move a muscle. All she needed to do was breathe wrong and he'd draw, time seemed to freeze as she looked around from Josef Mengele, who was wrought with anticipation as his old eyes darted back and forth between the combatants. Priscilla then looked to the still figure of Lens who was shot in the back by this bastard.

Then to Emil, who had half of his face blown off and then to Luna. She finally looked back to the Albino biting her lower lip. This was it, she thought, the final obstacle. She knew in her heart of hearts that she wasn't gonna walk away from this. This was his element. She tensed her body and mentally prepared herself. Everything was on the line, the fate of the future, her kids, everything.

She took a silent breath, her right hand inched ever so closer, so did the Albino's it was a matter of seconds before one or the other drew, sweat peppered her forehead. She felt a tingly sensation all over her body, her mouth was dry.

The next ten seconds were the slowest she'd ever experienced. She wasn't sure who made the move first, but she was already in motion going for her gun, she didn't even aim it when the Albino already had his gun in hand and fired, emptying the five remaining shots of his revolver. The muzzle flash was blinding in the room. He grinned in devilish accomplishment as he finally killed his adversary!

But he made two fateful mistakes. The first was, he emptied his weapon, leaving himself defenseless and two, as he fired, his eyes blinked with every shot which pretty much blinded him. He didn't have time to savor the victory, he thought he had. Once his eyes adjusted to the lighting of the room again, his golden eyes widened.

He looked at his revolver in horrible disbelief, then back to Priscilla, who was still standing unharmed from the deadly barrage of bullets that went through her body, impacting the thick windows behind her.

"Fool! You killed us, with pride and theatrics!" The old Nazi yelled out. The image of Priscilla flickered out and faded as she sprung out from behind the couch. Her arm was already extending into firing position with a clenched jaw and gritted teeth, she fired just as the Albino reached behind his back for his extra gun. She nailed him in the collarbone. He staggered back, still trying to bring his gun to bear, she fired again, ripping into his chest.

Then another, until he finally fell back. Priscilla stood there for a moment, savoring the victory as she reached into her pocket. The mini-hologram projector Peter had given her saved her ass. She closed her hand tightly around ιhe device, good ol' Peter; she could never thank him enough. Priscilla then looked at Josef, her tormentor for far too long. She took two steps toward him when she caught movement in the corner of her eye from where the Albino lay. She broke out into a run getting to him and not a second too soon, he was trying to get up.

He had his back-up weapon gripped in his gloved hand. As Priscilla stood over him, he tried to point it in her direction, for his effort she stomped his wrist as hard as she could. He grunted and in a vain attempt tried to free his hand, the gun slipped from his loosened grip.

She didn't even say anything to him, but she wanted to get one last look in his eyes. Those eyes that haunted her, and would still haunt her until the day she died. Even at her mercy he glared back never once looking away, he was defiant to the end, she expected no less from him. She emptied her weapon into his face, eleven bullets in all.

She never felt such exhilaration over killing someone; she was always indifferent about it, it was second nature to her, like what breathing is to others, unthinking, natural. But this time she enjoyed it and didn't even think there was anything wrong with it either.

She kept the gun pointed at what was left of his face. She held her gaze for a few seconds longer just to make sure he was really dead this time. Satisfied, she dropped the empty gun, and turned away from the specter of her past.

She had one more loose end. Just as she brought her attention back to Josef, he was reaching on the side of his wheelchair. Priscilla closed the gap fast, as he struggled to pull out a Luger. She slammed his frail wrist down so hard she felt the bones break against the armrest of the wheelchair. A wild shot went off before the gun fell from his limp hand. The old man whimpered in pain clawing at Priscilla's hand.

"You think after all this, you of all people are gonna get the drop on me?" She released her grip from his wrist, picked up his gun, and then spun him and pushed him to one of the nearest windows. She then turned him around to face her, he looked up at her holding his wrist, he was breathing heavily, his watered eyes looked no less hateful as he glared at her.

"It's over…." She told him. This man would be the second person that she'd get enjoyment from killing. He almost took everything from her. Her life was in shambles, her friend's dead. She walked behind him for a moment.

"Please, what are you doing? I implore you to help me! Let us make a new world from the ashes." He pleaded, he couldn't turn around. Priscilla ripped out the cord to the control panel for the wheelchair. "I will give you anything! Right now! I offer you immortality!" Priscilla then stood back in front of the pitiful old man.

A man that crushed the hopes and dreams of millions, now looking to her for the same mercy that others no doubt pleaded to him for. She thought of it as poetic justice. She held the Luger pistol at her side.

"You have nothing I want." She said with no emotion, the sad face he wore now turned vile.

"Heil Hitler! I curse you to a thousand painful deaths! You bitch! Whore! Cunt! You'll burn in hell!" Bile flew from his lips; there was a fire in his eyes. She smiled, and then fired off a few shots behind him. He jerked up and ducked his head. The large glass window shattered, rain and wind billowed in. She then spun him around, grabbed the handles, and with all she was worth she shoved him through the opening to meet the jagged rocks below. She watched him plummet to his death.

He screamed the entire time, until he smashed into the rocks below. She stood there for a moment, the twisted body of Josef Mengele, tormenter and murderer of millions, finally received justice over sixty years in the making.

Chapter 25
Finally over

Priscilla tore her eyes away and looked out upon the sea. The rain felt good hitting her face, it cleansed her of the clamminess.

"Mom!"

"Mommy!" Priscilla whirled around at the calling of her name and ran to her kids, her eyes were filled with tears, as she dropped to one knee, spreading her arms, she hugged them tight against her.

"I'm sorry… I'm so sorry…." She repeated, letting her emotions out. Priscilla didn't want to let them go, not ever. She was so close to losing them. She pulled away looking at them, cupping their faces in her shaking hands. She couldn't help but be joyous seeing them smiling back "You know that I'd never let anyone hurt you."

They didn't answer her, and she wasn't expecting them to. The looks in their eyes were the only answer she needed. They knew. She then pulled away and ran to Lens, who was laying on his back. Priscilla on her knees, picked up his head, cradling it. She removed his hat, and was looking down at the smiling face of Lens, or better yet Jonas Ferrer.

"Why am I not surprised." She said as she returned the smile. Ferrer let out a chuckle, but paid for it. It was painful to laugh.

Priscilla took a good look at his gunshot wound. It wasn't serious thank god. The bullet missed his spinal cord. Patricia and Jonathan approached with worried looks

"Mom, is he okay?" Patricia asked, Priscilla turned to her nodding.

"Yes, just help me get him on the couch." Priscilla grabbed one arm while the kids grabbed the other, once on his feet, she led him to the couch laying him on it. Sweat broke out on Ferrer's forehead. It was hot in this room, she realized just now even with a smashed window. She gently wiped his forehead down with the palm of her hand. He then looked at her and smiled.

"The roles are reversed." She nodded.

"Yes." She replied.

"Blondie, I'm sorry for keeping you in the dark. It wasn't that I didn't trust you. I just didn't want to burden you all at once. Maybe I should have done it differently." Priscilla shushed him.

"Never mind that, Ferrer. Let's just get the hell outta here." She turned her head, looking behind her, and then looked back to Ferrer.

"The kids will keep you company, I'll look for a first-aide kit patch you up and then I'll tie up some loose ends. I'm not leaving anything behind for anyone." Ferrer didn't protest. He knew it had to be done. She gently kissed his forehead. She then turned to her kids who were standing at her side watching on.

It pained Priscilla that her children had to witness not only these acts of violence, but also their mother taking part in them as well. She watched them go to Ferrer's side, they were such great kids, they didn't deserve this. She swore to god she'd make it up to them by being the mother they deserved and needed. After finally pulling herself away she went and did what needed to be done to finally put this behind her for good.

Chapter 26
Debriefed

Five days later. Washington, DC

Priscilla was never in the Oval Office before, she's seen it many times in movies and television.

The office of one of the most powerful men in the world was pretty basic. Sitting at the old oak desk that countless other Presidents used before him, was the current President.

He was the first black one. She never really thought much of that, and didn't make a big deal of it. Priscilla never looked at a person's skin color. In fact, she didn't see color. It was who you were, on the inside that mattered most.

She was here for most of the afternoon with the leader of the free world, and was thankful he was so easy going. He was charming, funny, articulate and an all around cool guy.

Also in the office was the old grizzled Senator from Arizona who was part of the oversight committee Derlin mentioned to her a few times. Along with these two was another Senator from Ohio. She was getting debriefed; there was a recorder on the President's desk.

"And so after I got my kids to safety, I proceeded to destroy the home. It toppled into the sea. All of the research and data was destroyed as well sir. I left nothing to chance." She said, leaving out the role Ferrer played at the house.

Ferrer told Priscilla that no one is to know he and Lens are the same. The President nodded, as he leaned back in his chair. He then looked over at the two Senators, they both nodded. The President then leaned forward again and stopped the recording.

"On a personal note and I'm sure I speak for the two Senators, I can't thank you enough for the service you've given to your country. You are the example of above and beyond the call of duty." The President looked past her. The Senator from Ohio nodded and so did the Arizona Senator.

"Now, unless there's anything else, I think we can finally wrap this up." The President got up, and came around to the front of the desk, extending his hand towards Priscilla. She got up and gripped it. "And let me say again, I'm truly sorry for the loss of John. He'll be missed." Priscilla nodded, looking away from him. She was sorry too. She still hadn't come to terms with Derlin's death, it was one of the things that made this victory bitter sweet. She didn't even get a chance to say good-bye. The two Senators got up as well and shook Priscilla's hand, as the President guided her out.

"You'll hear from someone, if there's any follow up questions regarding this debrief." Priscilla nodded. The President opened the door; she started to walk out when she saw, sitting in a chair just outside, Jonas Ferrer. Priscilla held her smile. She looked back to the President.

"Thank you, sir." He nodded and disappeared back inside his office. Priscilla walked over to the smiling Ferrer, whose arm was in a sling. He got up as she approached, but had a bit of trouble. She put her suitcase down and helped him. He put his hand out to stop her, but she still helped anyway. They quietly spoke as they walked down the long hallway.

"I take it everything went well." Priscilla turned her head at him and nodded.

"Yes, I'm done. I'm out. That's pretty damn good to me." She said smiling. Ferrer nodded.

"What if Shadow Ops is reinstated down the road, would you come back?" Priscilla was caught off guard by that. She never thought of that.

"I don't know, I doubt it. My field Op days are over, that much is certain." Again he nodded.

"I was just wondering what you'd say. And besides, if it was reinstated, you'd be asked to train the new Ops or maybe even take up Derlin's position. I couldn't think of someone better." Again, she was caught off guard. The training she could do.

But taking Derlin's job, that would need some serious thought if that was presented to her. It was always in the back of her mind that when the day came and Derlin retired, she always had a feeling he'd ask her to take up his post. If he was still alive, and he asked her to do that then she'd have done so without question and hope she could do half as good a job as he did.

But now…. who knows being it was only talk, she didn't want to think about that. She just wanted to go home and hug her children and start their lives over. Ferrer left Priscilla to her thoughts as they made their way to the awaiting car. Priscilla wasn't sure when she'd come back to Washington, so she wanted to stop at Arlington National Cemetery and pay her respects to Derlin.

They didn't stay long; Priscilla wanted to say goodbye to her mentor one last time. The tombstone was beautiful. Thinking about the circumstances a tear fell from her eye. They never found Derlin's body, that enraged her to no end, knowing that he was disrespected like that. Ferrer stood close to her, his face was unreadable. He then nudged her, she looked at him.

"I've been waiting for the right moment to give this to you. I think now is the best time." Tucked under his arm was a small brown paper wrapped item.

Priscilla took it. It felt like a frame, she ripped off the paper and gasped, putting her hand to her mouth. She wanted to cry, but held back. It was a personal keepsake, inside was Derlin's pipe, eye-patch and a picture of her and him. It was an older picture. She couldn't remember when it was taken. She looked at Ferrer, holding the frame tight he put a comforting hand on her shoulder, as she laid her head on his.

"I found those things in his apartment. I knew you'd want something." She pulled away.

"Thanks," Jonas Ferrer AKA Lens, was truly a friend. Before finally turning away, she touched the tombstone one last time.

They hardly talked as they drove to the airport, Priscilla couldn't help admiring the contents the frame held. She thought it was the best thing anyone could have given her. Once they pulled up, the driver got out and grabbed Priscilla's single bag. Alone she was speechless, she didn't know what to say to Ferrer.

"Well Roletti, this is it. Maybe we'll see each other soon." She nodded.

"I'm no good with these drawn out goodbyes Jonas."

"Yeah, me either." She was about to get out, when he grabbed her by the arm. "Oh wait!" She closed the door, wondering what was the matter.

"I almost forgot something, I didn't have a chance to do this before." He reached into his jacket pocket and produced a small jet injector. "Remember when you asked me if I was following you? In Venezuela when I brought you back from the brink of death, I injected you with a nanobot. It was programmed as a homing device. This injection, will neutralize it." Priscilla smiled as she held out her arm, she wasn't surprised. The injection didn't have to be anywhere in particular. He placed it on her wrist.

"It was the only sure fire way to keep tabs on you, without anyone knowing in case you were caught." He looked away from her, searching for the right words.

"I lost one friend... I didn't want to lose another." He said and quickly got out. Priscilla followed. The driver got back in the car. Lens walked around to her side to see her off, and was about to get in when Priscilla grabbed him and held him tight. She fought back tears. She pulled away, picking up her bag and frame.

"If you ever need me, my friend, you know where to find me." He nodded.

"And the same for you." He replied. And then he stepped back and watched her walk inside the airport wishing her all the luck for a bright and happy future.

Epilogue
So, it wasn't all for nothing

Two months later.

In a local hospital on Long Island, the nurse on duty was making her nightly rounds. It was around 3 a.m. she was stationed in the Terminal wing for children. There were about twenty children here waiting to die. They had no hope of surviving their incurable ailments; it was a sin that lives so young were going to be snuffed out.

They didn't even get the chance to try to make their dreams come true. But tonight, that was going to change. The nurse went to each and every one of the dying children and with a single syringe administered via their peripheral IV line the Super-Human serum.

Priscilla Roletti, didn't tell the entire truth when she was debriefed. It was true that she did in fact destroy the lab below the house. But what she kept to herself was the fact that she stumbled upon Hans' serum. And in a mindless impulse, she took some.

At first, she wondered why she did that. What would she do with it? She certainly didn't want it for herself. She made her choices good or bad, she lived her life, saw the world, she had no regrets. Doing this was one last act of spite against the people who ruined the lives of so many others.

She wanted all the lives lost and uprooted not to have been in vain, and she couldn't think of a better way than this. And here she was, injecting the last of the Super-Human Serum into the final child.

Now it was time to go home. By the time the doctors came in and their parents came back, these children would be healed. Doing this, it was the greatest thing she could ever do. She stuffed the syringe in a paper bag she brought with her. She'd dispose of it at home.

This was something she wanted to do much sooner. But there were things close to home that needed her full attention. Her children first and foremost. There was going to be bumps in the road from here on out. Patricia was starting to feel resentment against her, because of everything that had happened. Plus, she felt betrayed that her mother had lied to them all this time.

Priscilla knew that as time passed, she would hopefully understand. She was a young girl, who only understood at the moment that her mother lied to them. The therapy sessions they went to seemed to help with some of that resentment. Her son was too young to care. He was just glad mommy was home all the time now.

The funeral for Pat and his mother was the real heartbreaker. And what made it even worse was that she couldn't even stay the entire time nor attend the church service because his wife held her solely responsible. And she was right. In hindsight Priscilla shouldn't have asked him to care for her kids. And that was something she'd have to live with for the rest of her life.

As far as Pietro, she was taking her time getting back into that. She just wanted time to herself and with her kids. And then once she was settled, she'd get back into the relationship. Things will never be the same, but they couldn't get any worse, or at least she hoped they couldn't. Nevertheless, the future never looked brighter and she was never happier. Time will heal all wounds, it always does, she was confident of that. She just needed to be loving, nurturing and patient.

She walked past the nurse's station; the two nurses doing paperwork didn't give Priscilla a second glance. A young couple walked passed her. Priscilla nodded, the young man returned her greeting in kind, but his wife did not. She was clearly distraught. It was one of the terminal kids' parents. Priscilla stopped at the doorway leading out of this wing. She watched as the young couple made there way, she wished she could be there when they found out their child would live. Just as she was about to turn and leave, she heard gasps, and a commotion.

"Nurse! Oh my god!! Nurse!" The exclaiming young mother burst from the wing with her half dead child now walking on his own. The Nurses at the very station Priscilla passed were torn away from their logs and notes and were awestruck as more children made there way from their rooms.

Priscilla smiled; all of the sacrifices weren't for nothing. She took in the scene for a moment longer and then finally turned and left. The closing of the automated door was in essence the closing of this chapter of her life. And now it was time to start a brand new one with a future as bright as she wanted to make it.

Mike DeClemente

The Priscilla Roletti stories

The old neighborhood

How neighborhoods change, it was really unbelievable, Priscilla thought as she drove down Pennsylvania Ave heading North from the Belt Park Way. She hadn't been this way since she was a kid. And that was twenty something years ago. The only reason she even ventured this way was because the damn Belt was at a standstill as always. And not wanting to deal with that, she figured street driving would get her home faster. So far not likely with her slowing down to take in this once great part of Brooklyn.

The innocence of the 60's and 70's were replaced by the congested streets of double-parked cars, and more MTA buses than the roads could handle. The Projects, that were promised to offer a better life for many were nothing more than thug filled dens where in some cases dealers used some of the apartments for their business. The law abiding were afraid to even come out in the middle of the day without being harassed by out of work wannabe toughs that did nothing but smoke weed, drink and play loud music.

Even FedEx, UPS, and Postal workers couldn't do their job without being harassed in some way. Stalked as they left packages at people's doors only to be snatched once the deliverer was out of sight, or even worse, they would get beaten up or even conned out of said parcels. Yeah, the neighborhood certainly changed. But even so, there were at least some landmarks she recognized as she went.

The YMCA was there, on her left. Even though it was in need of a long overdue renovation, it looked just as busy today as it was when she was a kid. She passed the parks with the laceless basketball hoops, happy to see there were kids playing basketball, like she did on those very same courts with her siblings and friends.

Someone honked her, as the light turned green, she glanced at the rearview annoyed and then moved forward. She was a believer that everything comes full circle so she knew one day the old neighborhood would turn around. The only question was when.

If it happened in Dumbo and Williamsburg two places that were once the biggest shit holes in Brooklyn then it could happen here. She just may never see it in her lifetime.

As she drove along, she felt like a little kid again. Memories of her walking down this very street with her mother and siblings hit her hard. She did love this place. The summers were the best, they'd play stick ball and basketball until it got too dark to see the balls or the hoops. And then rushing home, they would stop at the corner store for some sort of tooth rotting sweets that filled them up where they couldn't eat their dinner.

Priscilla's eyes widened, the old corner store!

"Holy shit!" She exclaimed, was the place even still there? And the old man was he even alive still? "Damn, what was his name?" She asked to no one but herself. She was, after all, in her caravan. No kids, she was just coming back from the city, she had to do some clerical work at the office. Mandatory training, John told her.

"Harry! Old Harry!" She slammed her hand on the wheel. The memories of her, her siblings, and friends spending their big bucks on gum and chocolates made her smile, but with those happy thoughts there was one memory, that started her down the life she was on now.

Old Harry also showed her an act of kindness not many would. The day her mother threw her out into the street like some discarded dog. He showed her kindness that could never be repaid. He gave her food and money, and most of all a warm smile that assured her everything will be alright. She was never resentful that he didn't take her in, or offered to do so. As a matter of fact, she was grateful, she would never want to relive her life again. Her kids, Patrick, John, Peter, even as bad as it was, they are the most cherished part of it. And for that alone it was worth all the heartache and pain.

Since she was already driving through she had to go and see him to at least say hello and again thank you.

It didn't take long for her to find it, it was like she never left and before she knew it she was there. She parked just at the corner. It was a no parking area, but whatever. She'd pay for the damn ticket. She wasn't in the mood to go searching for a spot. She took a minute to gather herself, her heart was racing and a little burst of sweat formed on her palms. She was a little nervous, walking through that store may emotionally hit her and could cause her to cry like a kid again. That was part of the reason of her hesitation. She didn't wanna start getting emotional, but now that she was here, she had to do this. With a sigh, she ran her fingers through her hair and got out.

As she approached the store, she cast her eyes up, and smiled. The original sign was there. It had a yellow background with the words 'Jelly Bean' in a comic like font with multi colored jelly beans bouncing around the letters. But as she grew closer her smile faded, the door leading inside was hanging off, the window cracked. Priscilla rushed towards the doorway, her hand instinctively went for her gun. And as she looked inside instead of being greeted with the all too familiar memories of how she knew the store used to be. With its creaking wooden floor, the aroma of candy, sugar, cardboard and other smells she couldn't even identify. The magazine rack that used to be stacked with the latest comics or the four planks of wood that stretched across just under the counter holding open boxes of more candy than a kid could wish for.

Instead of all those wonderful things, she was shown a trashed store. The magazine rack was torn down, all the latest issues trampled and torn. The planks that held the candy were thrown to the floor along with the candy and empty boxes. She was almost brought to tears as she stepped inside.

"Excuse me miss, can I help you?" Priscilla jerked her head up, at the voice. She was in such a state of shock, she hardly noticed the man, who if she had to guess was maybe in his early to late fifties with a broom clenched in his hands. She nodded, trying to find her voice and the words to go along with it.

"Yeah...Hi...sorry." She gestured around the place with a sad look, and finally she looked right at him.

"Are you a Detective?" He asked before she could even get her words out. She shook her head.

"No, no I'm not. But I grew up out here. I was driving through and remembered this place. Wanted to say hello to the old man." The man nodded, "If you don't mind me asking what happened?" With a sigh, he leaned the broom against the wall.

"The gangs happened. They came in here a few nights ago and robbed the place. He's in Brookdale all banged up." If there was ever a time she felt nauseated and angered this was it. How could anyone do this? He was a harmless old man!

"Shit… I'm...I'm so sorry." He shook his head.

"You have nothing to be sorry for. It's the goddamn police, it's like they gave up on the neighborhood." He sighed and shook his head again. "I told pop to give it up, sell the place, goodness knows he had a few offers, but the stubborn old fool wouldn't do it. I kept telling him to close up." He sighed again, looking at Priscilla. "Bad enough they beat him, and trashed his store. But to add insult to injury, they stole a gold cross my dad always wore. He had my mother's wedding ring attached to it after she died. Goddamn son of a bitch no one has any… oh forget it." He sighed again, clearing his throat and then tried his best to smile and change the subject.

"How do you know him? He never mentioned you before."

"And he shouldn't. He only knew me as a kid. This store was the hottest spot in Brooklyn." She laughed a little. "I grew up down the block from here. My sisters and brothers were always in here." Priscilla then extended her hand.

"I'm Priscilla."

"Chris." They shook hands, he was surprised by her grip.

"Can I help out with anything?" He shook his head.

"No, but thanks. I was about to leave anyway. I gotta go back to the hospital, just wanted to clean up a bit because when he's on the mend. I don't care what he says, he's selling this place and that's it." As sad as that sounded, she understood. Harry was an old man after all, and good or bad everything comes to an end.

“Now if you’ll excuse me, It was nice meeting you, Priscilla. When I see dad later, I’ll be sure to tell him you were looking for him.” She nodded. The conversation was clearly over. And she didn’t hold it against him at all. She understood grief can be a bitch in that of itself.

She took her leave, once she was back in her van Priscilla drove up the block and double parked. She sat in the running caravan for a while replaying the entire conversation, imagining the entire incident play out over and over again. And it only made her madder by the minute. So mad in fact her face was getting flushed and her heart was racing. She glanced at her watch, it was already dinner time. She was surprised the kids didn't call her to find out where she was. And just as she thought that her cell phone started to ring. Even though she knew it was them, she glanced at it and yes, sure enough it was them. She sighed, letting it go to voice mail.

“Fuck.” She said, sighing and threw the van into gear pulling off. She had better get going before it got any later. But all the while, she couldn’t take her mind off this or Harry, and would be thinking about it all the way home.

The kids were fast asleep, but unfortunately for Priscilla, she was not. She’d been tossing and turning all night until finally she just gave up and sat in the kitchen with a piping hot cup of green tea. It was hard to play mom tonight, while trying to get homework done, and keep up with her daughters gossip, she couldn’t stop thinking about Harry. She kept telling herself not to get involved, this was not her problem, let the police handle it. But then on the other side of that argument she was having with herself, she thought ‘well the police weren’t doing anything.’ The police moved three times backwards. They were bogged down with other stuff. And how would this be different from anything else she’d been involved in? She’s helped people before, but then again that was while on missions.

She wasn't in the middle of a mission, she was on standby. And besides, if Derlin found out he wouldn't be too happy. Derlin expressly forbid agents to work outside the office on personal missions. That turned you into a freelancer, and freelancers weren't looked upon with that much respect. They were a level above mercenaries, their skills up for sale to the highest bidder no matter how unscrupulous they may be.

Priscilla was biting her lower lip, as she had this internal back and forth debate. But she wasn't getting paid and this was kinda personal. A one-shot deal.

“Fuck...” She got up and put her cup in the sink and then flung open the kitchen cabinet where the vitamins were. She chuckled, what a contradiction this was she was worried about keeping herself healthy and yet trying to fish out her smokes she hid from the kids. After moving a few bottles, she found them. They were stale, but they would do.

She lit it, by the time the kids woke up the smell would be gone. As she puffed away, her mind was spinning. She could do this, and no one would be the wiser. She’d find these gang bangers, send a message to not only the streets but to the police. Hopefully, whatever she does will spur some kind of reaction. It was her hope anyway. She sighed again, with that settled, she grabbed her phone.

She had some personal time coming to her, so a simple lie about going away will be good enough. All she needed was a week to handle this, maybe a few days, and things would be set right and debts repaid.

“Fuck it...” She said as she placed the call to the office, she left a message on Jenny’s voice mail. She’d let Derlin know and that would be it. With that done, Priscilla made another cup of tea as she went about and started to think about how indeed she was going to do this.

As she surmised it only took her a week to get all the fine details down, and most of it was just all PC work. First, she remotely hacked the Police precinct’s computers and downloaded the entire case file for Harry and the known gangs in the area. The program used was a simple one, developed for someone like herself that wasn't computer savvy with coding. Once that was done, she skimmed through it, the police suspected it was a gang called the Kings of the East, meaning East New York. There had been an increase in gang related violence with new gangs coming in. The Kings were trying to consolidate their turf. Harry's store was in between their turf and another rival gangs. The detectives working the case assumed the hit on the store was simply a protection racket, also stated in the report was Harry's store wasn't the only one hit and people that weren't left unconscious at the scene said the same thing. Thugs coming in, looking for protection money.

She sighed, while sitting in a darkened alleyway across the street from a pool hall. It was the known hangout for the Kings of the East. This was their spot, from the low level to the higher ups. She'd been watching the place for the last two days with high powered binoculars. Every one of them were packing. The lookouts, were brandishing their guns like they were in the wild west. She sighed again, it was a damn shame. They were kids, maybe the youngest fourteen. She hated violence against kids, no matter what they were involved in. But this wasn't a perfect world, and if a kid is man enough to be robbing, beating up, or worse killing people. Then he/she had to be held accountable for their actions and whatever payback was coming their way… as the old sayings go 'everything comes full circle' and 'Karma can be a Bitch.' And that Bitch tonight was Priscilla, and she wasn't going to be pleasant. She not only needed to hold the ones responsible for Harry and the others, but she also needed to put a stop to this, and send a message to anyone else that wants to fuck around.

She glanced at her watch, it was just after nine, it was just about time. Dressed in all black she slowly got out of her rented car. She couldn't use a company car, no one was allowed to take them home unless on official duty. And she wasn't going to be using her personal one, so a rental would have to do. If something happened to it, then she would trash it and report it stolen.

In the trunk was her bag of goodies. Night vision goggles with a breath mask attachment, two silenced Beretta's one with live ammo and one with rubber bullets and a smoke grenade. These punks have no idea, what's in store for them. Aside from her investigating and supply gathering she managed to come here during the day and rigged the power box that supplied this place with electricity with a small plastic charge.
Nothing more than the force of a few firecrackers just enough to overload the box and put the entire place in darkness.

She wasn't concerned with the front and back doors being unsecured. She wanted some to run for their lives, word would spread quickly.

With both Beretta's strapped to her hips and the goggles perched on her head Priscilla closed the trunk and walked towards the place. She threw on a long ragged looking cloth, and made sure her face looked dirty even in this neighborhood the streets were lively. She didn't want anyone to see her packing and her strange attire.

Once she was close enough, she reached into her pocket and produced a small black remote with one button on it. She paused where she was, just across the street. A few people walked by her giving her strange looks. They probably thought of her as homeless, which was the look she was going for. In the aftermath, people will say they saw a homeless person loitering about. No one capable of doing what she was about to do.

Once a couple with a child passed, she placed her thumb on the white button and counted to three. Once she pressed it in a delayed reaction a small pop could be heard, unless you were standing next to the box you'd see it explode, but the people just walking by, didn't notice a damn thing except for the thugs that were outside who suddenly exclaimed in surprise when their hang out just went pitch black. Just as the gang bangers ran inside to the commotion Priscilla ran across the street and as soon as she stepped foot on the sidewalk, she threw off the cloth blanket, slipped the goggles on her eyes and ran in with the smoke grenade in hand and tossed it. The sudden explosion confused them even more as she unholstered her guns and laid down true street justice, one these thugs and this town will never forget.

Even with the high-powered flashlight unable to light the entire expanse the sight of blood was unmistakable, as tangled silhouettes of gang bangers lay where they were shot. The pool tables were soaked in crimson, pool sticks were thrown about and balls were left as they were with the exception of a few that were tossed at her in a blind attempt to hit her. Some would say this was overstepping the line between good and bad, that by doing what she did, she was no better than them. Plus, they were young adults. And she would agree to some extent, but in her belief of how the world works is, if you wanna fuck around, then be prepared to get fucked around as well. Even for herself, she was always expecting for the inevitable time to maybe run into someone from her past.

Some hell bent crazy looking for revenge against her. And she could accept that, it came with the job. And young adults or not, these were heartless gangbangers, that have murdered, robbed, raped and beat innocent people. Maybe because someone was just in the wrong place, wrong time, maybe someone turned down their recruitment attempts. The bottom line is this, the life they chose is simply only the strongest survive and they were not the strongest tonight. Priscilla knew this, she was from the streets of East New York and they should know it as well. This is the way of the streets.

But even in the middle of her bloodshed, she spared the ones that ran away, and the ones that were obviously very young and hiding for their lives. She saved the rubber bullets for them. It was the ones that tried to shoot at her and attack her that lay dead.

Now with the commotion done, it was just Priscilla and one lone gang banger that tried to attack her, but a well-placed bullet in the knee stopped that. It was done intentionally; she needed an answer to just one very simple question.

"So, let me ask you again, one of your boys sold the cross, a gold cross with a soldered gold wedding band in the middle right?" The thug had to have been maybe in his early twenties shook his head. He was leaning against the wall, his fingers tight against his bloody knee while the high-powered flashlight was right on him. She did this intentionally so that he could see the bodies of his friends and plus make him sweat a little. Between the pain, and the blood loss, he wasn't doing well right about now.

"I told… you lady…. It's there. Gem Pawn. On the… corner of Fleming Ave." Priscilla nodded, she was sitting on a folding chair away from the light and in the darkness just in case anyone tried to come back and take a shot at her. She knew that wasn't going to happen. And the cops were not inbound yet. She would make sure they would get the phone call once she left.

"I know you did, I just wanted to make sure I heard you right that's all." She smiled toying with him. Priscilla glanced at her watch, twenty minutes had passed. She far outstayed her welcome. She then got up, the sudden noise of her moving the chair and getting up startled the young man. She smiled again noticing this.

"Relax tough guy." She looked down on him, as the smile faded. "How does it feel, hmm? Being helpless? Not good, yeah?" The thug squeezed his eyes shut, and he was crying. He felt his end was near, there was no way she would leave him alive. "Open your fucking eyes!" She yelled, the young man jumped and did so as best he could with the bright light hurting them. "Take a good look at what happened here tonight. This is the real world; these are the consequences of what it means to be a bad ass. You never know who you might be fucking with, that goes for everyone, you, your friends, even for myself. The only difference between you and me, I don't fuck with people that don't deserve it. And if someone is dumb enough to fuck with me, it'll be the last fucking thing they do." She allowed the veiled threat to sink in. "Now… I'm gonna let you live. But I want you to remember this. Remember what happened here. Spread the word, that a bad ass bitch was here, and she ain't fuckn' around. If I catch wind of any kind of revenge, I hear even so much there's a spot of graffiti on a bathroom stall. I'll be back, and I know where you live. I have your name, and address memorized. You have a chance to start over, don't fuck it up." And with no more words to be said she grabbed the light shutting it off. The room was cast back into darkness and the young man was left alone, crying his eyes out as Priscilla left not even looking back as she made for the door.

By the time she was all done, she was at the hospital, it was just after six in the morning.

Once she left the pool hall, she quickly went over to that pawn shop. She made fast work of the alarm system and managed to find the gold cross, to cover her tracks she stole some other pieces of jewelry and broke open the safe. The said jewelry she'll leave somewhere so it can be found by whoever and the cash, she'll keep it and write a check out to the church in her neighborhood. It was tainted money, let it do some good. She wished she could go back there, and explain in her own 'subtle' way that it isn't wise to buy more than likely stolen goods from thugs. But she made enough waves tonight, as she watched on the TV about her handy work.

As soon as she was in the rental she called the cops and it didn't take them long to get there. And now every major news network was covering the 'Pool hall massacre' She was standing in Harry's room, watching the coverage for the last two minutes. She was glad that nowadays in hospitals they didn't care if family members came and went all night long. It saved the nurses and other staff the hassle of tending to the needs of the patients when their loved ones can do it for them.

A sudden yawn caught her by surprise, she tried her best to stifle it but failed miserably. She was tired, and wanted to head home. She tore her eyes away from the TV and saw Harry. The kind-hearted old man from her youth. He looked so peaceful sleeping there, she then reached into her pocket and produced the gold cross and chain. It looked nice and shiny even in the dimness of the room. She approached the old man, as she unclasped the chain and gently slipped it around his neck. She wished she had time to have it blessed. But if Harry wanted to do that then she'd let him do so. The cold blooded killer, fixed the cross so it was in full view and took a few steps back.

She smiled at the sight, just as the old mans eyes fluttered, she was about to leave before he could see her but she wanted to stay. She wanted to see him smile, and most of all she wanted to thank him for what he had done for her so many years ago.

Seeing that the old man was trying to sit up, she placed a firm but gentle hand on his chest, she startled him a bit, he looked up at her groggy.

"Stay still my friend." He squinted at her, he tried to speak, but his throat was dry, the words came out raspy.

"Water..." was all he said, on the rolling table was an empty plastic pitcher. She quickly filled it and poured some into a cup, putting it to his mouth.

As he sipped from the cup, his eyes slowly focused upon her. He was coming about slowly, Priscilla was smiling to herself. She took the cup from him, and pushed him gently back down.

"Who...who are you?" He asked as he strained to sit up again. Priscilla helped him get comfortable. His hand then fell to his chest, feeling the cold metal his eyes widened, he knew what that was; he studied the cross before looking back to the woman.

"I… the last thing I remember before blacking out was those kids pulling this off me, I thought it was lost forever." He said weakly. "Did you get this back for me?" There was no point in hiding or lying about it. She nodded, as he tried to hold back the tears threatening to come.

"Thank you, I'm indebted to you." Priscilla shook her head.

"No, you're not, I came to thank you for the kindness you showed me so many years ago. It's me that needs to thank you." Whether or not he understood she didn't know, she kissed his forehead.

"Take care of yourself Harry." She said, and then turned to leave. Just when she was about to walk out the door, Harry called out to her.

"You're the little girl that…. that was kicked outta the house weren't ya?" She stopped and turned around nodding and smiled, he returned it. And with no more words that needed to be spoken, she left wishing him well for the remainder of his days.

A (Normal) day in the life of Priscilla Roletti

She fell asleep in her clothes from the night before. She got in very late, it was around 5 a.m. or close to that. She was totally out of it, tired as hell, in her half-asleep stupor she could hear the distant calling.

"YO!!! Wake up!" She stirred a bit, moaning. She finally recognized the voice and was not happy about it. She cracked a stinging eye open, it was half past nine in the morning. She threw her face into the pillow, which wasn't a good idea, the surge of pain jostled her awake. She delicately placed two fingers to her swollen eye, she had forgotten about the fight she had a day ago that resulted in the black eye. Getting up slowly she stretched out. Priscilla felt her back crack, her mouth was as dry as a desert. Slowly getting to her feet, she slogged towards the kitchen and found her dear friend Patrick sitting at her kitchen table eating a donut, his third to be exact. Priscilla, shuffled over to the table and opened the box of donuts and took one.

"Well, you look great this morning." Pat said with a mouth full of donut, handing her a large coffee. She gave him a look, as she took the cup taking a sip. Pat was watching her kids while she was away. He also had keys to her house, which right about now she regretted giving him. She sat down, a little hunched over. Pat looked at her.

"Nice shiner, I'd love to see how you're gonna explain that to the kids." He said, she shrugged her shoulders.

"I'll think of something by the time I see them."

"Yeah, and to the teachers also." She cocked her eyebrow, not knowing what he meant, but then she smacked her forehead.

"Damn, tonight's Back to School Night isn't it?" Pat nodded. "Christ, the last thing I need, of all the days."

"You want me to go?" She shook her head.

"No, No...I'll go. I'll just deal with it." She should let him go, but Pat does enough for her and the kids. She could handle a few nosy looks.

Even though the coffee was piping hot, she gulped it down, in the hope it would hasten her alertness. As she bit into her donut, she caught Pat glancing at her.

"What?" She said defensively.

"That's some shiner boy, you gonna tell me how you got it?" She took a deep breath and sat back with her coffee.

"Oh… shit went down, and a brawl broke out. I got sucker punched, is it that bad?" She asked gently touching it, it was sore as hell. And from the way it felt, she couldn't put cover up on it, the skin felt scaly putting that crap on it would only irritate it or worse she'd get an infection. Pat started to laugh.

"Shut up." She said, trying to suppress a smile. Pat chuckled.

"What's going on at home? Where's Kath?"

"She's home, I told her I was coming here to check in on you after I dropped all the kids off at school. She asked me to ask you if you wanted to go out for lunch, Gran was asking about you too." Pat's wife and mother were awesome people, his mother cracked her up with the stuff she'd say. She'd curse every other word.

"Did you ever tell them what I really do? Kath never asked?" She waited a moment for him to respond as he stuffed the last of his fourth donut in his mouth.

"Yeah, I kept it simple I told her you work for the FBI, a counter terrorism unit." He said with his mouth stuffed with the last remaining donut as he swallowed.

"That's cool. Hey, can we make it a late lunch? I wanna hit the gym for a bit, work out the kinks, I haven't been there in a while anyway, I think I need a good workout."

"Ok, no problem, I'll get cold cuts and we can have sandwiches at the house."

"Fair enough, let me treat this time." Pat got up from the chair getting ready to leave, putting out his hand, stopping her from going to her room.

"No… no, get outta here."

"Come on tub, you're always treating the kids, you never take my money." She said as she walked in her room and came back with a fifty. He didn't take it, so she shoved it in his pocket. He threw his hands up with a smile, knowing the argument was closed. She kissed him on the cheek goodbye and walked him to the door. Once he pulled out of the driveway, she jumped in the shower, the steaming hot water felt so damn good she wished she could stay in there all morning.

She tried to wash out her eye as best she could, but it was so raw she just left it alone. Once out of the shower, she looked at herself in the mirror. It wasn't the worst thing that had happened to her in her career as a Shadow Ops agent, but it sure as hell was bad. It was swollen and black and blue, with nothing other than dealing with it, she combed her hair, threw on her form fitting sweats and sports bra, and stuffed a bag with an extra set of clothes to change into after her workout.

Hitting the gym hard was something she loved doing, it relieved a lot of stress, pumping iron. She was going on two hours and wasn't even ready to stop. Between her job and taking care of her kids it was sometimes hard to hit the gym at all and being in her line of work she needed to be in the best shape she could be in. When she did manage to work out it was at home in the basement, doing pull-ups and pushups and free weights but there was nothing like a real gym.

Priscilla, at a quick glance, didn't look like anything but a woman that took care of herself, but she was rock solid.

She was bench-pressing now, and on her last set, on the last rep, she strained to get the bar up onto the rungs, but managed. The more the strain the more the muscle worked. She sat up, wiping sweat off her brow when Rocco suddenly sat on the bench just next to her, smiling. She rolled her eyes at him, he was the last person she wanted to see today.

Rocco was one of those gym rats that came to the gym to bullshit instead of working out, but she did have to admit he did have a well sculpted body and he flaunted it, wearing muscle shirts and flexing in front of the mirror at every chance he could get, all the while trying to pick up his next conquest. When Priscilla went to the gym it was only to work out, and she didn't want to make friends, and the people she did see often it was 'Hi, how are you?' 'Great' You too' and 'bye'.

But this guy Rocco, failed time and time again to get the hint. She was always nice because she didn't want to stir up trouble, this place was close to her house, it was convenient. But today was not a good day, and she knew already he was gonna push her buttons.

"Hey Priscilla, what's happening? I haven't seen you in a long time." She took a deep breath.

"Not a whole hell of a lot. And yourself?" She got up, before he could even answer her and walked to the free weights picking up two dumbbells. As she was banging out her reps, he came over and stood right next to her, checking her out in the most uncomfortable way.

"You know something Blondie, you're stronger than you look, I watch you when you work out, I wouldn't mind giving you some private training though." The thought of him 'watching' her work out sent a shiver down her spine. It just sounded so damn creepy.

"Please, don't call me Blondie." She said in a very cold tone, giving him a piercing look, which didn't hit home. But of course he finally noticed the black eye.

"Oh man, what happened to your eye?" Picking up another set of heavier weights she started a new set of reps, up until now she was very cordial, but one of her pet peeves is that she hated being questioned by anyone, especially someone like him.

"None of your fucking business." She said between breaths as she tried not to lose her count.

"Ouch! Is that any way to talk? You know, I'm sick of your attitude, you walk around here thinking you're a bad ass. Maybe that's why you have no one in the first place, because you've never been shown how to respect people. Yeah, that's gotta be it, you walk around here with a chip on your shoulder, you might be one of them broads who thinks who the fuck they are, thinking they have a golden pussy or somethin'." He was raising his voice and now a few people were looking on, there were even some snickers from some of his muscle headed friends. Priscilla said nothing, she simply clenched her jaw and pumped harder. "Isn't that right,

Blondie?" He said, 'Blondie' in a very exaggerated way. Now her face was getting flushed, her initial reaction right now was knock him the fuck out. But she couldn't, it was too close to home, and she was in full view of everyone. What if a parent from her kids' school saw her? Then that would be the gossip of the month, with these bored and lonely divorcees and housewives. Let them continue to talk about who's fucking who in the neighborhood instead of her.

She took a deep breath, trying her best to keep her composure.

"That's why you got a black eye bitch. You run your mouth, serves you right." He snickered and walked away, the show was over. He had his time in the limelight, got his ego on and the laughs from not only his friends but from a few people watching on.

A man and woman working out next to Priscilla had stopped because of the scene. Once Rocco was out of earshot they both approached her.

"Hey miss you okay?" The middle-aged man asked, as he looked in the direction of where Rocco walked off too. Priscilla, knew these two from seeing them around the gym, they were nice enough, she didn't know their names and didn't ask. Now she was done with her workout and wiping herself down.

"Yeah I'm fine." She said not at all fazed by what just happened at least not on the outside. It took all her will power, but she was proud of herself.

"You should report him. If you need us to come with you, we got your back." The woman added stealing a look at Rocco, before bringing her attention back to Priscilla.

"Nah, why give him the satisfaction, that I'm still standing here talking and thinking about him." She took a gulp of water from her bottle, turning to face the concerned duo. "But I appreciate both of you wanting to support me. But a scumbag like that will get his day, and sooner than you'd expect, karma is a bitch." She smiled and winked at them. "I gotta get goin' I'll see you guys around." Both the man and woman looked on after Priscilla.

"Damn shame, she must be abused so much that it doesn't even faze her." The lady said. The man shrugged his shoulders

"Or too scared to say anything. She might think she'll be the one to get in trouble. You can't help someone like her. They gotta help themselves." The lady nodded, still not feeling good about it, but her friend was right. You can't help someone that doesn't want it.

Rocco was in the locker, with nothing but a towel on, he had just come out of the sauna, it was empty for a change which was good. He hated being cooped up in there with a bunch of swinging dicks. He didn't even like bullshitting in the locker room with other men, while their cocks just swayed back and forth. And it was always the mother fuckers that should keep their clothes on, the ones with the giant belly's and sagging skin that just pranced around like they were an Adonis. Now it was time to shower, he was meeting a few of the boys later, hopefully it'll be a good night to score some chocha.

Rocco with his rubber crocs made his way into the shower, taking the last stall in the back. The back was always less used, once inside, he threw the plastic mildew ended curtain across and finally removed his towel. He didn't even get the chance to regulate the water, before he was viciously ripped from the stall.

"What the fuck!" By the time, he realized it was Priscilla, she was already on him. To his credit though he did try to fight back, but Priscilla not only being the better fighter was also fueled by her rage. That this piece of shit embarrassed and humiliated her. She quickly overpowered his bulk, strength and ego.

She learned a long time ago, that you truly found out who a real man is, when you caught them alone, and not with his boys, or an audience to feed on. Rocco was one of those men, in public he talked a good game around his boys, he put on the show. Now alone, he was nothing.

She landed a crushing right to his jaw, breaking it, then a left to the temple which brought him to his knees. She grabbed a hand full of hair and brought her knee to his face twice breaking his nose and knocking out his teeth. She turned and walked away before he even fell on his side. By now, some heard the commotion and came to see what was going on. Their looks said it all, shock and awe.

"Fuck you looking at?! You want some of this too?!" She yelled to the first guy she thought was gonna try to be the big man. She shoved him so hard, he skidded back. Needless to say, he quickly got out of her way as she walked passed. Priscilla then stopped and without even looking back gave a stern warning.

"If I hear anyone talking about this, if the cops show up at my door. I'm gonna fuck everyone up in here got it!?" She didn't wait for a reply, she knew they heard her loud and clear and that not a single person in there was gonna say a word.

Because of that unfortunate bullshit, Priscilla ran home to change, her clothes were wet and there was blood on them. So by the time she made it to Pat's they had an early dinner, pasta and sauce.

When the kids finally saw their mother, the reaction that ensued was to be expected. It wasn't the first time they saw her battered or bruised and it was getting harder to come up with new reasons of why she looked like she went 10 rounds in the ring. Most of the time she said it was a car accident, just for the fact that it left little room to question further. But that was getting old fast, so she needed to come up with new reasons for her beaten up looks. As soon as she walked in the door, her daughter with the eyes of a hawk, spotted the black eye. She immediately ran to her repeatedly asking what happened almost on the verge of tears.

Priscilla told her, she was hit in the face accidentally by a patient at the hospital she was working in. Her son being so young, he'd believe anything you told him. They all ate like a family, which was great, even with the various noises coming from Pat as he took in shovelfuls of food, and the kids acting like clowns.

Later that evening....She arrived at Back-to-School night. It started at seven and was supposed to run until ten. Just like their children, the parents had to endure nine periods, which were only fifteen minutes each. During that time, the parents were lectured as to what their children were learning. Priscilla knew all about this already. She kept a close eye on Patricia's studies. Any parents that had questions about their children, were told to hold all their questions until after the class. Once again Priscilla didn't need to know how her kid was doing, she made sure she knew. There was not a trick that went by that she didn't know about. With her daughter, she tried to not only be her mother, but her confidant and friend, a very fine line to walk, but she felt she was doing a pretty good job at it.

Surprisingly, the night went quickly, and thankfully no one noticed and gawked at her black eye, or at least Priscilla didn't see anyone gawking or noticing it. Which was good because the last thing she wanted was to ask someone 'What the fuck are you looking at?' It was bad enough she did what she did earlier today. Not that she had regrets about that, she didn't, she just didn't want to embarrass her kids.

Now at her last 'class' she was sitting in the back, in a cramped desk ready to bolt out of there as soon as the bell rang. And not soon enough, as she got up and started for the door, she heard her name being called.

"Ms. Roletti?" Priscilla turned around, the fairly young science teacher smiled at her, trying not to look annoyed Priscilla walked over throwing her hand out.

"Hi, how are you?" The young teacher shook her hand, smiling.

"I'm so glad to have finally met you, your daughter is one of my best students, you should be proud of her." Priscilla smiled, she sure was.

"Thank you, Mrs. Mason." They made their way to the door.

"Um, Ms. Roletti if I may ask you...what happened to your eye? It looks like you were punched. Is everything ok at home?" Priscilla felt her face flush, she spoke too soon and jinxed herself. Why is it that if a woman has a black eye everyone has to assume she's abused? Now stuck in this very uncomfortable situation she regretted not letting Pat come after all. She gritted her teeth before she answered the concerned teacher. Priscilla didn't want to be nasty, Mrs. Mason was only asking out of concern for the children.

"No, no Mrs. Mason, it's not like that at all, I'm not married…"

"Then your boyfriend?" She quickly added, Priscilla shook her head.

"No, Mrs. Mason, I don't date I don't have the time, my full attention is on my children between them and work trust me, my plate is full." She should only know, Priscilla thought.

"What do you do for work? If you don't mind me asking." Priscilla stared at the inquisitive teacher, trying to figure out where this was going.

"Mrs. Mason, do you always interrogate your students' parents?" The young teacher laughed that off.

"No, no I'm sorry, forgive me, it's just that, aside from teaching, I also volunteer, I counsel battered women. It pains me to see them when they feel they have no place to go or no one to talk to, you must understand it's a very embarrassing thing to talk about. You just happen to show signs of that, you're fielding my questions, denial, and hostility to those that can see the truth and want to help. I just get the feeling your hiding more." From the look on Priscilla's face, the teacher quickly back peddled.

"Well, I mean, maybe I'm wrong, but in any event, I just felt I needed to make sure everything is ok at home, that's all." Priscilla was really touched by this, but at the same time a little offended that this teacher had the balls to come at her like that. That almost left her speechless. In a way she wished people were like her growing up. When Priscilla was being abused, anyone that knew turned the other way not wanting to get involved. Mrs. Mason should only know the truth, Priscilla, for a second, thought about telling the nosy teacher, what she "really" did, she'd love to see the look on her face when she told her in detail of all the things she'd done and the people she'd killed. But she couldn't and wouldn't, this teacher would then call child protective services on her, and that wasn't something she wanted to deal with.

"Mrs. Mason, I'm very flattered and happy that you're concerned, but I assure you everything at home couldn't be better. Now, it is getting late and I have to pick up my kids. It was a real pleasure meeting you." The young woman nodded, grabbing her hand tightly.

"No, Ms. Roletti the pleasure was mine, you're doing a great job, but if you ever need someone to talk to, here's my card." She handed it to Priscilla, who glanced at it.

"Uh, right… thanks." Priscilla said, flipping it back and forth before stuffing it in her purse. She then left, taking a deep calming breath as she walked down the hall.

By the time she got to Patrick's house her son was fast asleep and Patricia wasn't far behind him, Pat carried him to the minivan while Patricia walked in a half-asleep stupor.

She was finally home after the long, tiring, and weird day, with the kids finally in bed, Priscilla washed up, got undressed, and put on sweats and a T-shirt. She couldn't wait to say hello to her pillow and put this day behind her. It didn't take her long to fall asleep.

Floyd

Montana, not far from the Canadian border.

Priscilla Roletti thought this was the end. She was paralyzed from the bitter cold; the jaws of death were finally closing in on her. Laying in the frozen snow, she waited for death to take her. Even though mentally she tried to tell her body to get up, it wasn't happening. At least she could die knowing the fact that she succeeded in her mission before the eternal darkness took her. But, she would never be able to kiss her kids goodbye, and tell them one more time how much she loved them.

While in deep reflecting, she could have sworn she heard movement not far from where she was, Jesus Christ she thought. Now was a good enough time to die, before being eaten by a pack of wolves. She only hoped that the shadows of the forest concealed her well enough, but no matter how well she was hidden her sent would lead whatever it was out there to her.

The sloshing through the snow came closer until whatever it was, was right on top of her. She tried to move but her body was frozen. The last thing she felt before succumbing to the calling of death was her body being dragged through the snow and into the den of some beast to be devoured. She hoped by the time that happened, she'd be dead. She at least deserved to die before being eaten right? She was a good enough person to be granted a painless death, or at least she hoped so. Her eyes grew heavy and any fears of being eaten alive were gone as she fell into the eternal darkness of unconsciousness.

Her dreams were wild, with images only the dark reaches of one's imagination could conjure, disturbing and psychedelic. She saw images of death… every inch of her body twitched from fear and cold. A cold sweat broke out all over her body. A crashing sound threw her eyes wide open; she bolted up, but only a few inches. She was tied down and wrapped up to her neck. Laying her head back down on the soft surface, she calmed her breathing.

Every time she took in large gasps of air her chest burned. She tried to stifle a cough that felt like a knife going through her chest.

The overwhelming sensation took her; she felt a shadow loom over her. Then a gentle hand raised her head, propping it up better, allowing her to cough without choking herself. Once she was done with her coughing fit, piping hot thick liquid was put to her lips. She drank, almost choking again.

The server saw this and allowed her to swallow what she had in her mouth before giving her more. Almost immediately she stopped coughing. The itch in her throat subsided. She tried to look into the face of the one helping her, but the light from behind him darkened his features to her. She couldn't even hold her head up. She tried to talk, but her throat was raw, as her eyes rolled over white. The last thing Priscilla felt before she sank back into the darkness was a warm, damp cloth gently dabbed across her forehead.

She screamed out, jerking up this time. She was able to erect herself upon the bed. She put a shaky hand to her forehead. It was sweaty, she felt dizzy. If she were standing she'd collapse. Priscilla looked around quickly before she was overcome by exhaustion and had to lay her head back down. A rather large man walked over, pressing her down slowly.

"Rest.... Rest, don't get up." He said, in a grainy deep voice. She swallowed on a dry throat as she looked up into the worn face of a man. He gently ran his fingers through her hair with a caring smile.

"Water, can I have some water?" Priscilla asked weakly. The man, without a word of acknowledgment, walked off and returned with a piping hot drink. She got up as best she could. While he held the cup, she took a mouth full of a tangy liquid, and then laid back down.

"Thanks." She said just barely audible. He nodded, placing the cup off to the side.

"Do you think you have the strength to sit up, I prepared a chair for you." She wasn't sure. Priscilla didn't even know how long she was out for, let alone if she could stand. She tried to move her legs, they were stiff. She looked back to the man, nodding.

"I'm not sure, but… but… let me try. I don't want to lay here any longer." He smiled through a thick gray beard, then stepped back, taking off his very heavy fur coat that was tied around him with a rope. Underneath he wore winter pants with heavy-duty boots. She took notice that the man was missing an arm and was about to tell him she could do it herself. But before she could get the words out, he was already helping her. It took the use of a walking stick and the help of her savior, but with effort she managed to get to the chair made of fur and pillows that was near the fireplace.

He helped her get comfortable wrapping another fur around her. Even though it was hot where she was, she couldn't get rid of the chill in her body. When the man was satisfied that she was comfortable he walked to a table. With his back to her, Priscilla eyed her environment. It was a cabin, but a very well-built cabin. Outside, she could hear the wind howling and not a single draft seeped through. All along the wall were furs of various animals. A moose head was adorned above the fireplace. Her eyes then fell on the man who saved her, he was definitely, a peculiar looking fellow. He looked like a lumberjack.

As though feeling her eyes on him, he turned around. They met eye to eye. He smiled, and then continued doing what was keeping his attention.

She was about to blurt out 'who are you?' But the thought of talking made her head spin at that moment. She closed her eyes, rubbing her forehead, trying to focus. He turned around with two plates full of food gently cupped over each other. She took the top plate with shaking hands. Breathing in the aroma, immediately made her stomach hurt of hunger. She didn't know what he served her and she didn't even care. She had no idea when the last time she had eaten. She dug right in; she didn't even wait for the utensils he was going to give her. He looked at her smiling.

"You have an appetite, this is good!" He said, tearing into his own food. The only sounds that followed were from their chewing, Priscilla didn't care about manners, she ate like a pig. Once contented she slumped back, handing off the empty plate to her new friend.

"Thank you." She said softly. He nodded, taking the plate onto his empty one and putting it off to the side. He then reached into his clothing and pulled out a pipe. He gestured her with the pipe, she nodded.

"So, my friend, you care to tell me your name? I'm Floyd." He extended his hand, Priscilla took it, firmly shaking it.

"Priscilla, thank you." Floyd waved his only hand, dismissing her thanks.

"Thank God, not me, I just happened to be traveling when I saw you, you almost died."

"Story of my life." She said, giving him a faint smile. He didn't get it. He furrowed his brow to the dry humor. "It was a joke." He smiled a few seconds later, after running the words through his head again.

"What were you doing out there?" She asked, wondering. He gave a cocked eye of amusement.

"I should ask you the same thing young lady, yes?" Priscilla chuckled, lowering her head and running her fingers through her greasy hair. He had her there, here she was the one found almost dead in the middle of a forest and yet she wanted to know what he was doing out there. Evidently, he was faring better than her. Floyd took a large pull of his pipe, letting the smoke out slowly, before he spoke.

"But since you asked first young lady, I'll oblige ya. I was coming back from hunting." She nodded, she'd never been hunting before and didn't imagine it to be all that wonderful and exciting as a lot of men think it to be. Priscilla only killed to survive. Floyd then gestured to her indicating it was her turn to talk now.

She thought about this for a few seconds on whether or not to tell the truth. But this man was no dummy. She knew he could tell she was as much from around here as he was a New Yorker.

"I work for the Government. I stopped a huge arms deal between some anti Government groups, and while on the run got lost. I vaguely remember anything." He chuckled, repacking his pipe.

"Working for the Government yeah? Like James Bond?" Priscilla always chuckled when people said that.

"Yeah, Something like that." She said with a smile.

"You're lucky to be alive, you had Pneumonia, frostbite, you were hardly breathing." Priscilla stared at him for a moment all humor gone from her features. She was afraid to ask the next question, but she had to know.

"How long have I been here?"

"One week and a day, and tomorrow is Thanksgiving." Her eyes widened in disbelief, he nodded, lighting the pipe again, then handed it to her. She took one long drag. She couldn't help but think about the kids, they must be going crazy Pat too. Weakened state or not she had to get out of here and call home.

"What's the closest city from here?" She asked as smoke exited her mouth.

"You mean town," he corrected her. "Foster, it's about 10 miles south of here."

"Is there a way to get there? I really appreciate all you've done, but I can't stay here, I have to get back… I have a family… kids who are no doubt going crazy wondering where I am." She tried to get up and got as far as standing almost straight when dizziness took her. She was very unsteady. She quickly sat back down. Floyd laughed, slapping his leg.

"Even if you were up to it, you'd freeze to death."

"You have a truck?" He shook his head,

"Yes, but I'm not giving it to you, it's the only one I own." She slumped back down defeated, but then she tried a different approach.

"Can you drive me back to town?" The old man chuckled a bit.

"Listen Priscilla, I would but you're not well enough to go anywhere, and besides, we're caught in the middle of a storm. You hear the wind out there?" He gestured to the door with his thumb. "As soon as the storm passes and you're well enough, I'll be more than obliged to take you to town." She nodded, then suddenly remembered something.

"Was there anything on me?" Floyd nodded, getting up, he walked to the back of the small cabin and returned with a leather satchel. Handing it to her, she quickly rummaged through it; frustrated with not finding what she hoped she didn't lose. She emptied it out on her lap, the old man watched with a slight curiosity. "Where is it? Yes! Got it!" She found her cell phone, it was off, she turned it on.

"I wouldn't get too excited, reception up here is zilch." And just as he said those words she saw it for herself. The rage filling 'No Service' in the upper right corner made her want to crush the phone in her hand or better yet, throw it against the wall taking full pleasure in seeing it shatter into a million pieces. But all she did was sigh and let it fall in her lap. Floyd smiled.

"I told ya. That's God tellin' ya to stay here rest and when the storm passes and you're at your full strength you can go home." Priscilla made a face, and then flashed a phony smile. He certainly had a way about himself. He was right, even though she was being petty about it and wouldn't tell him he was right. She then looked around the place, there was no electricity, phone, baseboard heating or a TV. Who the hell would want to live out here, and alone for that matter. And being Priscilla, she couldn't help her verbal thoughts coming from her mouth.

"Why do you stay here? I mean, you could have a better life somewhere else, no?"

"Perhaps. Or perhaps I had a life already. And isn't it rude to ask personal questions young lady, especially since you're a guest in my home, hmm?" Her face flushed with embarrassment, in a way he was right. It's one thing to wonder what the hell he was doing out there when he found her. But his personal life, is his personal life. He proved no threat to her, so he was entitled to it. She nodded.

"I'm just frustrated, that's all. I'm sorry." Floyd nodded, looking away from her as he relit his pipe.

"Apology accepted." There was an uncomfortable silence between the two for some time as Floyd rocked along in his chair. The rhythmic rocking back and forth with the cracking of wood in the fire were the only sounds. Priscilla cast her eyes around the place and took in more of the details. This was the most well-built home, she'd ever seen. There was so much stuff in here you could spend days looking at everything. He had various books, rifles, both old and new hanging on the walls. There was even a black powder musket that looked very old.

Floyd then suddenly rose to his feet, and walked over to the coat rack taking his heavy fur coat off and slipping it on.

"I'm gonna go out to the shed. There's food I'm preparing for Thanksgiving. You stay here and rest. Later, if you're feeling up to it, maybe come out. There are some clothes for you over there, along with the ones I found you in." She followed his finger to where he was indicating to. She looked back to him.

"You didn't have to go through all the trouble."

"There is no trouble I was making the food anyway. I have more than enough. I may live alone, but I still celebrate the holidays. When someone stops doing that, then they are truly dead." Priscilla nodded, it was an interesting point of view.

"See ya in a few." And with that he threw up his hood, and flung open the door. A gust of wind blew in sending snow inside. Priscilla was chilled to the bone again by the suddenness of it. She cursed out loud, because she was just starting to feel warm with no more chills.

Once Floyd was gone, she leaned back in her chair, wrapping her arms around herself and covering her body with the fur blanket. With her head leaned back, she tried to concentrate on keeping her body warm, while she was doing that, she couldn't help but think of her strange friend. There was definitely something off with his guy, he certainly had his secrets. And in the grand scheme of things, so did she. Her entire life was practically one giant lie. So, let Floyd keep his secrets, just as long as he posed no threat to her, they'd be fine.

With the warmth returning to her body, Priscilla felt her eyes go heavy, as she stared up at the ceiling. She wasn't going to fight it, she needed the sleep, she just hoped that her dreams were filled with joy instead of death.

An untold amount of time passed by when Priscilla awoke. She looked around the cabin and saw no sign of Floyd. Taking a deep breath, she told herself it was time to get up dizzy or not. She wasn't going to sit here another minute. As she got up, she was unsteady, but quickly regained her balance. Her joints cracked with the movement, and protested in pain. She was as stiff as a board, but managed to get dressed, but she exhausted herself from doing that. As she wrapped herself in a fur she broke out into an uncontrollable coughing fit. Her throat was raw. She cursed aloud, slamming her fist hard against the wall in frustration.

"Damn fucking cough." She said a little too loud irritating her throat more, as she made her way to the door and prepared to meet the harsh weather. When she opened the door a blast of cold hit her in the face. The air was so sharp she started to cough again, but she managed to stifle it, and covered her mouth. As ready as she'll ever be Priscilla stepped outside.

She trudged through the almost ankle-deep snow. She was pushing herself so much it was hard to breathe with her mouth and nose covered. She had to remove the fur, so she could breathe better, but doing that allowed the sharp cold wind to make her cough again. She was damned either way, it was either faint from lack of oxygen or cough from too much of it.

Thankfully the shed was closer than she thought, but took longer to get to because of the snow and her current condition. She squeezed through the double doors, and was engulfed in warmth. The snow in her hair started to melt. She immediately saw Floyd by a furnace. He had a bloodstained apron on, and turned around as soon as she came in.

"Oh, look who's up and about. I'll give ya credit young lady. You have more balls than most men." Priscilla shook off the snow, as she cracked a smile. She wasn't sure if that was a straight up complement or a backhanded one. Nevertheless, she nodded.

"Thanks." She said dryly as she hung her coat and hat. Floyd laughed as he turned back to what he was doing.

"Don't push yourself too hard now." He said, with his back to her, shaking his head. Priscilla walked deeper inside, and took notice to his pickup. It was an older model Chevy 4x4 but it looked like it was well taken care of. It was red with white trim. She walked alongside the pickup, admiring it when she spotted the side mirror. She hadn't seen what the hell she looked like in over a week.

"I look like shit." She said in a low tone, as she scrutinized every inch of her face. She had dark circles under her eyes, her hair was matted and greasy looking and she lost weight because her face looked thinner than normal. She made a face of disgust, and gave the image a dismissive wave as she turned away from the mirror.

"You need a hand with anything? I don't wanna feel totally useless." The old man shrugged his shoulders never looking at her.

"There isn't much help needed." Priscilla curious walked over and saw he was cutting up meat. She watched him, marveled at the sight, that this man was able to do so much missing an arm. The knife he used was so sharp that cutting the meat one handed looked easy. There was a clamp attached to the table, with dried blood most likely used when he needed the added support.

"Should I be afraid to ask what's for dinner?"

"Of course not, and the best damn Moose, Deer and Turkey you'll ever have I guarantee that." He said as he pointed the tip of the bloodied knife at each section of meat cut up. And just in front of him hanging was a plucked, gutted and headless turkey.

"Can't wait."

"Is that sarcasm, young lady?" He asked, slicing up a steak.

"Not at all...In fact, I find it pretty awesome. Truly fresh meat, being seasoned and cooked. I wish Thanksgiving was today." Floyd smiled.

"That's nice to hear. Tonight's dinner is beef stew." She didn't say anything as she watched him work for a few moments and then looked at him again. It hit her hard that if it wasn't for this man, this stranger, she wouldn't be here today. She'd be frozen out there, chewed and shitted out by some wolf or bear.

"Thanks, really for everything." She placed a hand on his shoulder. Floyd turned his head slightly nodded and smiled. The moment came and went, Priscilla then removed her hand. With nothing to help the old man with, she figured she may as well try to work out some of the stiffness in her body.

She found a corner away from Floyd, she stretched out her arms, legs, back and neck. She started with some shadow boxing, which between the heat and her pushing herself, she built up quite a sweat. She did that for almost ten minutes straight and then went and did push-ups and pull-ups. There was a beam just above her head, it wasn't perfect, but it did the job.

While she was doing that, she caught the attention of Floyd, he was impressed with her recovery and her physique. It may be male chauvinistic to think this way, but he'd never think of a woman to be able to do the same things as a man. But watching the skill she possessed, he'd hate to be on the receiving end of those punches.

A half an hour passed by the time Floyd wrapped everything up.

"There that'll do it. Everything is seasoned and ready to go." Priscilla just stopped her last set of pushups. Her arms were throbbing, but it felt good to be active.

"The food won't spoil?" She asked, coming up alongside him.

"Nope, this shed isn't insulated. Once the fire is out, it gets extremely cold overnight." Priscilla nodded, feeling like she should have known that. Floyd then removed his apron and put out the wood-burning stove.

Once they made their way back, the rest of the evening was filled with eating, and idle conversation. Priscilla made sure she steered clear of personal topics because it was evident he wanted to keep certain parts of his life private. That was fine with her, she just wanted this storm to pass so she could be on her way.

"Gin! Ha-ha! I got ya again!" Floyd, aside from being a good cook and a survivalist was a good card player too, even while drinking. And god can he drink, he was two sheets to the wind on 'Some pretty good stuff I made.' And boy if you loved strong alcohol, then you'd love this.

Priscilla was inclined and had a shot with him, she regretted it ever since, mind you Priscilla wasn't a drinker, but has tasted her fair share of liquor. Jack Daniels, Absolute, Hennessy and a host of others. But none of those compared to his 'Pretty good stuff.' It burned as soon as she swung it back, she couldn't even spit it out, before her throat involuntarily swallowed it. She thought she was gonna throw up right there, but thank god she didn't because she was already entertaining Floyd enough with the scene.

But old Floyd, he killed the bottle, and was well into the second one.

"You...shuffle." He belched, pouring himself another glass, he gulped it down and then got up.

"Where you off to?" She asked, shuffling.

"Well Ma, I'm goin' outside to smoke and have some fresh air and to take a piss. That okay?" He said, trying his best to sound like a little boy and then belched again, smiling that missing tooth smile she was getting used to.

"Smart ass, so I care. Now I hope a bear eats you, how about that?" Floyd laughed, slapping his leg.

"That's a good one, but they'll have a damn hard time with this up their ass!" He reached behind his back producing a 357. It was polished so nicely it shined in the dimness of the room.

"Nice piece, just be careful anyway." Floyd slipped on his coat, once it was buttoned he slipped the revolver in the outer pocket and then gave her a mock two fingered salute. She returned the gesture with a smile.

"And don't ya be tryin' to cheat!" He said with a chuckle as he opened the door and left. The short amount of time the door was open sent a chill through her, enough that she shivered and got up to get closer to the fire. Priscilla's been to a lot of cold places, but this was by far the coldest she'd ever been too. It had to have been more for the fact her body was in a weakened state.

As she rubbed her hands in front of the fire Priscilla lifted her head, and glanced around on the ledge of the fireplace and found something peculiar. She cocked her eyebrow.

"What's this…" She said in a low tone. Before she reached out, she glanced at her sides and then back at the door. She didn't want Floyd to see her snooping, not that she was per se, she just happened to notice something out in the open on the ledge, which was kinda hidden.

It was a photo of a much younger and happier Floyd, with a woman and a child. The kid had to have been about ten years old at the time. She flipped it over and read the names.

"Dawn and Jett." Just below was the year the photo was taken. She flipped it around, it was a nice photo too. Priscilla bit her lower lip, trying to piece this together, and it didn't take much to figure out. It was obvious they died, she just had that feeling, plus Floyd's self-imposed isolation. He felt responsible… she lifted her head and stared straight ahead. A sudden sadness crept up on her. She knew something was off, and she'll bet anything the missing arm was part of it too.

The banging of feet, caught her by surprise Floyd had returned. She quickly replaced the photo and leaned over towards the fire again. And just as the old man came in, Priscilla was making her way back to the table.

"Fuck, I just got warm." She said, trying to be funny now going back to the fire.

"I'll be right there with ya. It's colder than a witches tit out there."

"Nice." She laughed, shaking her head, not only a drunk but a dirty old drunk. Floyd shook off the coat and hung it up, placing the now ice cold 357. on the table. She moved over, so he had room to warm himself.

"You ready for another round Missy?" Priscilla nodded.

"Yes, I am." Floyd nodded, looking straight ahead, he tilted his head back.

"Oh...you found Dawn." He reached up and found the photo Priscilla was just looking at. She watched him do this feeling her face flush.

"Sorry, I...I wasn't snooping...I just happened to look up and saw it." Floyd nodded.

"It's alright Missy. To tell ya the truth, I was looking for this. I probably was drunk the last time I looked at it." Priscilla nodded, swallowing on a sudden dry throat.

"You wanna talk about it?" She offered, even though she had already pieced it together.

"I'd rather not..." he said through half open eyes that reflected the flames of the fire. "Although you probably figured it out by now haven't you? You're a smart cookie." Priscilla laughed at that part even though she didn't mean to. It just caught her as funny, he called her a 'smart cookie'.

"It didn't take a rocket scientist to figure it out. But sometimes talking helps yes? I've always found it easier to talk to a complete stranger. Nobody cares what a stranger thinks, plus you'll never see them again. And once I'm well enough, I'm gone. You won't see me again." Floyd glanced at her nodding.

"Yeah..." He flashed a fake smile, lowering his head, he looked into the fire. "I can still remember that day as if it happened yesterday." He shrugged his shoulders, clenching his jaw. "It was a night just like this, cold and stormy, up here a storm can hit anytime." He snapped his fingers to hammer home the point. "We were coming home from her mothers, when that bitch of a storm hit. Damn semi ran the light, was going too fast. He came out of nowhere, I couldn't even move." He sniffled and then continued.

"Once everything was done with the courts and such I packed up and came here, this here cabin and land was from my great great granddaddy. He built this place and we all kept it up." Floyd sighed, "And that's the story of old Floyd."

"And you sit out here waiting to die." Priscilla added, Floyd nodded.

"Somthin' like that." He said, repeating the same reply she gave him to the 'James Bond' comment.

"And do you think Dawn would have wanted that? Dying alone?"

"Of course not. If she was still here, she'd have broken her foot in my ass for sulking like this. I do this because, I'm not man enough to end it myself. So I let...God decide and pray every day it happens." Priscilla just looked at him, she had nothing to say. The man wanted to die, she could understand that, there were plenty of times she wanted to die.

"Come on." She gently laid her arm across his shoulders, and took the photo from his hand, and placed it back on the ledge so that it was in full view.

"Where are we goin'?"

"We aren't going anywhere aside from bed. It's late. I'm tired and you need to sleep it off, because I'm not gonna be stuck eating all that food by myself." Floyd chuckled as she led him away and walked him towards the bedroom in the back of the cabin. His room like the rest of the cabin was small but neatly arranged. Priscilla lit two candles that were on the nightstand, and then finally lowered the inebriated Floyd into the bed. She wasn't going to undress him, but at least unlaced and took off his boots. Before she could even turn around and say good night the old man was snoring. She smiled at the scene he looked so peaceful there, she could have sworn there was even a smile.

"Sleep well, my friend." She blew out the candles and quietly left.

Sleep eluded her, she was tired when she was getting Floyd into the bed, but then for some reason as she laid down and tried to go to sleep it didn't happen. It pissed her off to no end when this happened to her. With nothing to do in the cabin, Priscilla got dressed and walked out onto the porch. She grabbed the 357. Floyd left on the counter, she highly doubted she'd need it but out here, she wasn't messing around coming out unarmed.

It wasn't because she was fearful of anyone looking for her, no she just didn't want some wolf or bear making a meal out of her.

She cleaned off an old rocking chair of snow and sat. She always found rocking therapeutic, she even took Floyd's pipe. She wasn't much of a pipe smoker, but would make the exception, there was nothing else here. She could see why John enjoyed the pipe. The smoke was not only sweet smelling but smooth, and refreshing unlike cigarette smoke, which was dense and foul smelling. She thought about John, wondering what he was doing and if he sent anyone to find her. By now news of her mission reached him, she after all, created quite the show.

The storm was abetting too, which was good. She needed to get into town and get word to HQ that all was well, and call her kids. She sighed, every now and then she felt anxious if she could reach out and touch them she would. She sighed again, trying to push those thoughts aside, she then cast her eyes up as she took a long pull, and noticed how clear the sky was, she'd never seen the stars this clearly before and it was amazing. As the night drew on a chilly wind was starting to really pick up and even in a heavy fur she felt a chill, and besides, she felt herself finally getting tired hopefully now she'll fall out. And she did, once she locked down the cabin, put out the candles and stoked the fire, she laid down and within seconds was fast asleep.

Thanksgiving.

Priscilla was the first to rise and being Floyd was still asleep, she started to cook and prepare for tonight's dinner. Most of the cooking was done in the shack, on the giant wood burning stove and in the fire pit just next to the shack. With all of the food seasoned and prepared all she had to do was throw it on the fire and watch it. Simple enough. By the time Floyd stirred it was almost noon, when he stumbled out of bed, he was jolted awake, not finding his house guest, he at first thought the worst. She probably took off and stole his truck to boot. But those fears subsided when he smelled the fire and the unmistakable smell of turkey.

"Well, I'll be a son of a gun." He quickly dressed and threw the door open. As soon as he turned, he spotted her watching over the meat. It was a blue sky, sunny day. Although the snow wouldn't be melting anytime soon, it was nice the sun was finally out.

"Hey!" Priscilla heard old Floyd approach and turned waving. "Happy Thanksgiving!" She walked over and gave him a strong hug, one that he wouldn't have expected from her.

"Same to you Missy!" He smiled and returned the hug. "Wow, who'da thought, not only like James Bond, but a chef too!" She smiled, as they separated from their embrace, and waved his flattery off.

"All I'm doing is watching the food, making sure it's not burning. You did the hard part." Priscilla then, reached into her waist, and gave him his 357. "Here, just in case you were looking for it." Floyd smiled, looking at the polished handgun, he took it and stuffed it in his waist.

"Looks good." He breathed deeply, and then glanced around. "I think tomorrow morning, we'll go to town, roads should be clear by then." Priscilla nodded, she didn't want to show too much enthusiasm for leaving for fear of hurting the old man's feelings. But she couldn't wait to get outta here. John must be freaking out, Patrick and the kids, no doubt were worried. Before she called them, she was going to have to think of a story to tell the kids. She was tired of saying a car accident, they must think she's the worst driver in the world, a lost cell phone or perhaps she got food poisoning. That may work, she'll definitely think hard about it.

"Yeah, my family and no doubt my boss are freaking out." She said as she was flipping the steaks over. Once that was done, she regarded Floyd, she was not going to bring up last night or about what was said, out of respect for the old man. But then to her surprise, he did.

"Hey Missy, thank you for last night. It's been a long time since I spoke about Dawn and Jett. And you're right, they wouldn't want me to die alone. Thinking about it now, maybe they sent ya to me, to maybe give me hope...I don't know." He glanced at her, he was embarrassed. “If you even believe in that sort of thing.” She smiled and placed a hand on his broad shoulder.

“I believe no matter what your faith is, everything happens for a reason, good or bad, big or small. We may never know why it happened either, but it does and there’s a reason. And with ‘us’… I do believe.” Floyd nodded.

“Yes ma’am, right you are.” She nodded and then brought her attention back to the meat.

“Everything is almost done, except the turkey. How about we pick up another game of Gin? I wanna at least even the score.” That perked him up a bit.

“Oh, you’re on Missy!” So, with the blue sky, and snow covered land, they sat on the porch and played cards. Floyd smoked and drank coffee, Priscilla did as well, but not the smoking. She had her fair share of that for one day.

By five o’clock the rest of the food was done. While Floyd prepared the food, Priscilla set the table.

Floyd’s handmade table was large enough for two people, but with the smorgasbord he cooked, there was hardly room for their plates and utensils.

“Are you a god-fearing gal?” He asked as he finally sat. She nodded, although she wasn’t a holy roller she did believe.

“Yes. Why?”

“Would you like to say grace then?”

“I would love to.” She made the sign of the cross and interlaced her fingers, as she lowered her head. Floyd made the sign of the cross as well and lowered his head.

“Lord, I thank you for this meal, and for my life. You’ve given me the chance to not only see my children again, but you’ve honored me with the friendship of a kind and selfless man. Please grant him peace, happiness and good health. Would you like to add anything?” She suddenly asked, catching him off guard. Floyd was at a loss of words for the moment. But then he nodded and cleared his throat.

"Lord, allow me to thank you, for the company you've given me on this fine day. I couldn't have asked for more. Please watch over her and her family and I hope they are safe and sound. And Dawn and Jett, I hope you've forgiven me, and I pray you are okay, and I love you both." Priscilla nodded at the old man when he raised his head. His eyes were a little watery, but to his credit, he held it together. He nodded back, affirming he was done.

"Amen."

"Amen" Floyd repeated, and they dug right in. Their meal was quiet and peaceful, once done, they cleaned up and had more coffee, there were no pastries which was fine by her, she didn't need to tack on the pounds from her lack of activity.

The rest of the evening consisted of more gin rummy, surprisingly Floyd did not drink, which she was glad about. It wasn't until after midnight they called it quits and hit the sheets.

By the time 10AM rolled around they were in town, sitting at a diner. The town was something time had forgotten in Priscilla's eyes. People still smoked inside, it seemed as if everyone had an older model pickup and everyone knew one another.

Once they had sat down, Priscilla immediately called Derlin, who then made phone calls to see to her evac. When she called Patrick and the kids, she couldn't even get a word in between all three of them. The story she told the kids was simple enough, she came down with a very bad stomach bug, for children who were 10 and 7 the bullshit story was perfectly fine. Patrick on the other hand had to play along, once she was home, she'd fill him in on the details.

And now after the hearty breakfast they sat, knowing their time together was almost up. She could tell Floyd was upset, but to his credit, he was putting on a happy face.

"I'm glad to see your goin' home Missy. Old Floyd will miss ya." Priscilla just looked at him, she didn't know what to say.

"It's gonna be fine Floyd. You're more than welcome to come back with me. Leave the quiet life, you think you can handle the big city?" Floyd smiled, shaking his head.

“Hell no. But you can come visit anytime you like Missy.” She smiled.

“I will, and I’ll bring the kids too. They’ll love all the snow.” Floyd nodded again, but his smile faded.

“Floyd, come on, it’s gonna be okay.” The old man nodded, looking away from her, fearful of tears bursting forth from his already watery eyes.

“I know…” He then snapped out of it, smiled and looked at the clock on the wall knowing their time was ticking away.

“You gonna be alright?” Priscilla asked, concerned. Floyd smiled as he nodded.

“I think I’ll manage…” And just as he said that two State Troopers came rolling up with their lights flashing.

“Come on you wanna walk me out?” Floyd nodded. He settled up the bill, and now standing outside with her, he stood by while Priscilla threw her stuff in the back seat of one of the cruisers. Among her things was a large plate of food Floyd had given her. She couldn’t wait to have that later.

“Give me a minute boys.” She said to one of the troopers who was standing outside. He nodded and then got back in his car. Priscilla then turned to Floyd.

She admired this lonely man; her heart went out to him. This was one of the few times, she wished she could do more, but without him wanting to be helped she couldn’t do anything.

“I’ll be in touch, I’ll write you to let you know I got home ok.” Floyd smiled.

“You better.” And before Priscilla could make the first move, the old man grabbed her and hugged her so tightly it felt as if he had his missing arm back. They held their embrace for a few moments. When they finally broke away, Priscilla leaned in close and kissed him on the cheek.

“Thank you… for everything.” Floyd smiled.

“You be safe, young lady.” He stepped away, they held each other’s gaze for a moment longer before Priscilla got in and sat in the front seat of the cruiser.

As they pulled away, she looked back once to see a crestfallen lonely man, she waved, and he returned the gesture as Priscilla sped off.

One month later.

Floyd hardly got company up here if ever. And that was only during hunting season when hunters wanted to hunt on his land, he would of course allow them to for a fee, plus some meat. So, when he was on his porch smoking and rocking, he was flabbergasted when he saw some custom FedEx pickup truck coming up towards his house. He had a P.O. box in town so no mail ever came here. The FedEx man, killed the engine and got out. He was a young man, in his mid-twenties.

"Good morning, sir!" The young man said, spotting Floyd, who was now standing, and making his way towards the FedEx man.

"Mornin' son." Floyd said, scratching his head.

"This is some piece of property sir. It took me a damn while to find it, but I did. World on time right!" The FedEx man chuckled, but then stopped when Floyd didn't get the meaning of the joke. The FedEx man, was referring to the FedEx slogan. He then cleared his throat. "Are you Floyd?" Floyd nodded.

"The one and only son." The FedEx man nodded, clearly happy.

"Great. I have a delivery for you, sir." Floyd was really at a loss for words. Who the hell was sending him a FedEx package? He knew FedEx wasn't cheap. Floyd followed the young man to the back and once he opened the back gate he gasped. There were two crates with holes all over them. It was obviously for something to breathe inside, and by the noises they were pups. They were barking and whimpering seeing the new face.

The young man took out his scanner and scanned the barcodes on the shipping crates.

"Please sign here, sir?" Floyd did so, it was more a scribble than a signature.

"Great, let me take these off for you sir. The porch is fine?"

"Yes, yes of course." The FedEx man took each crate off and gently placed them on the porch.

"Who in the hell sent these?" The FedEx man shrugged his shoulders.

"No idea sir, my job is only to deliver and that's done. Check the shipping label, there's also some kind of invoice taped to the top of one of the crates. Have a great day sir." The FedEx man, didn't wait for a reply as Floyd slowly walked towards his porch. He never paid any more attention to the FedEx man who had already started his pickup and was turning around to make his way down the mountain path.

He sat down and slid both crates to face him, and then opened them and popping out was a German Shepard and a Siberian Husky. As soon as they saw the old man, they attacked him with wet tongues as both were vying for his attention. Once he settled them down, he tore off the folded invoice and gasped. It wasn't an invoice it was a letter from Priscilla. He was almost brought to tears as he read it.

Floyd,

Since you wanna stay up on that mountain, there's no reason to be up there alone. It's not something I want to see, and I have no doubt Dawn wants that either.

Enjoy your new companions. And again, thank you.

Priscilla.

Floyd smiled and reread that letter a few times, until finally putting it down. These boys were no doubt hungry, and there was plenty of food to be had.

"Come on boys, I know you're hungry, you had yourselves a damn long trip, come on." He sprang up and the dogs followed him, yelping and barking. And for the first time in a long while Floyd had a reason to live. Now all he had to do was name these little guys. He had time to figure that out, Floyd had all the time in the world.

ABOUT THE AUTHOR

Mike DeClemente is the author of Rosecroft Chronicles, and the Priscilla Roletti series. He is also an amateur photographer who loves to capture the intimate details of life. He is always around and up for conversation on tech, comics and video games.

Made in the USA
Middletown, DE
12 September 2021